The Mammoth

BEST BRITISH MYSTERIES

The Mammoth Book of

BEST BRITISH MYSTERIES

EDITED BY MAXIM JAKUBOWSKI

Running Press
PHILADELPHIA · LONDON

Running Press Book Publishers
2300 Chestnut Street
Philadelphia, PA 19103-4371

Visit us on the web!
www.runningpress.com

CONTENTS

COPYRIGHT AND ACKNOWLEDGMENTS

INTRODUCTION

Welcome to a new beginning, or should that be a new life of crime?

Six years ago, slightly peeved that various best of the year anthologies published in America deliberately restricted themselves to publishing only stories by US authors, I made a proposal to a London publishing house for a similar series but this time exclusively devoted to British crime and mystery authors. Not only did I believe there was enough good material out there in magazine, anthology, radio and Internet territories to fill a respectable annual volume, but was also aware that many of these stories were, for market reasons, only available in the USA and thus unknown to a specifically British readership. Talk about not being a prophet in your own country!

The initial volume, titled BEST BRITISH MYSTERIES, was a runaway success and was even advertised on TV come that Christmas and earned deserved plaudits for both the book's concept and many of its illustrious contributors. The series has gone from strength to strength since then, adding first the number of the year from which the stories came from and, later, just a series number to distinguish the respective volumes. Rewardingly, many of the stories, albeit by British authors, had only appeared previously in the USA and thus became eligible for the Crime Writers' Association best short story Dagger award, and have since dominated a large proportion of the annual shortlist.

The principle is the same every year: read virtually all the crime and mystery stories published in a variety of sources, some predictable, others much less so, and I select the best. You will find, in these gripping pages, hardboiled tales, grisly murders, ingenious puzzles, cosy traditional tales of sleuthing and derring-do, memorable characters, heroes and dastardly villains, psychological landscapes of evil, thrills and spills and even laughs, etc . . . The idea is to present the whole breadth of what is being written in the mystery field today and a large field it is indeed, which continues to surprise and delight me on a daily basis.

Some authors are indeed big names and familiar to many readers, while others are talented newcomers I expect you to hear more about as their next books confirm their undoubted talent, but first and foremost it is the intrinsic quality of their storytelling that caught my attention, and will I hope please you. Shock you maybe, surprise you even, but principally entertain you. The settings of the stories range far and wide both geographically and historically and demonstrate how far ranging the crime and mystery field can be in the hands of its superior craftsmen and craftswomen.

Colin Dexter returns to the familiar and popular world of Inspectors Morse and Lewis, while Len Deighton – in his first short story in almost 20 years – welcomes back the familiar figure of Sherlock Holmes. Bill James ventures out again with those devious cops Harpur and Iles and many other favourite authors trip the murderous light fantastic with glee and dark resolve. There is so much talent in British crime writing these days and I would encourage you to pursue some of these authors well beyond this book and explore full-length books by them, should their respective story catch your eye (or your gut . . .).

Help British writers make crime pay and have a ball in the process. What a noble mission!

Maxim Jakubowski

THE .50 SOLUTION

Lee Child

Most times I assess the client and then the target and only afterward do I set the price. It's about common sense and variables. If the client is rich, I ask for more. If the target is tough, I ask for more. If there are major expenses involved, I ask for more. So if I'm working overseas on behalf of a billionaire against a guy in a remote hideout with a competent protection team on his side, I'm going to ask for maybe a hundred times what I would want from some local chick looking to solve her marital problems in a quick and messy manner. Variables, and common sense.

But this time the negotiation started differently.

The guy who came to see me was rich. That was clear. His wealth was pore-deep. Not just his clothes. Not just his car. This was a guy who had been rich forever. Maybe for generations. He was tall and grey and silvery and self-assured. He was a patrician. It was all right there in the way he held himself, the way he spoke, the way he took charge.

First thing he talked about was the choice of weapon.

He said, "I hear you've used a Barrett Model Ninety on more than one occasion."

I said, "You hear right."

"You like that piece?"

"It's a fine rifle."

"So you'll use it for me."

"I choose the weapon," I said.

"Based on what?"

"Need."

"You'll need it."

I asked, "Why? Long range?"

"Maybe two hundred yards."

"I don't need a Barrett Ninety for two hundred yards."

"It's what I want."

"Will the target be wearing body armor?"

"No."

"Inside a vehicle?"

"Open air."

"Then I'll use a three-oh-eight. Or something European."

"I want that fifty-caliber shell."

"A three-oh-eight or a NATO round will get him just as dead from two hundred yards."

"Maybe not."

Looking at him I was pretty sure this was a guy who had never fired a .50 Barrett in his life. Or a .308 Remington. Or an M16, or an FN, or an H&K. Or any kind of a rifle. He had probably never fired anything at all, except maybe a BB gun as a kid and workers as a adult.

I said, "The Barrett is an awkward weapon. It's four feet long and it doesn't break down. It weighs twenty-two pounds. It's got bipod legs, for Christ's sake. It's like an artillery piece. Hard to conceal. And it's very loud. Maybe the loudest rifle in the history of the world."

He said, "I like that fifty-caliber shell."

"I'll give you one," I said. "You can plate it with gold and put it on a chain and wear it around your neck."

"I want you to use it."

Then I started thinking maybe this guy was some kind of a sadist. A caliber of .50 is a decimal fraction, just another way of saying half an inch. A lead bullet a half inch across is a big thing. It weighs about two ounces, and any kind of a decent load fires it close to two thousand miles an hour. It could catch a supersonic jet fighter and bring it down. Against a person two hundred yards away, it's going to cut him in two. Like making the guy swallow a bomb, and then setting it off.

I said, "You want a spectacle, I could do it close with a knife. You know, if you want to send a message."

He said, "That's not the issue. This is not about a message. This is about the result."

"Can't be," I said. "From two hundred yards I can get a result with anything. Something short with a folding stock, I can walk away afterward with it under my coat. Or I could throw a rock."

"I want you to use the Barrett."

"Expensive," I said. "I'd have to leave it behind. Which means paying through the nose to make it untraceable. It'll cost more than a foreign car for the ordnance alone. Before we even talk about my fee."

"Okay," he said, no hesitation.

I said, "It's ridiculous."

He said nothing. I thought: *Two hundred yards, no body armor, in the open air. Makes no sense.* So I asked.

I said, "Who's the target?"

He said, "A horse."

I was quiet for a long moment. "What kind of a horse?"

"A thoroughbred racehorse."

I asked, "You own racehorses?"

He said, "Dozens of them."

"Good ones?"

"Some of the very best."

"So the target is what, a rival?"

"A thorn in my side."

After that, it made a lot more sense. The guy said, "I'm not an idiot. I've thought about it very carefully. It's got to look accidental. We can't just shoot the horse in the head. That's too obvious. It's got to look like the real target was the owner, but your aim was off and the horse is collateral damage. So the shot can't look placed. It's got to look random. Neck, shoulder, whatever. But I need death or permanent disability."

I said, "Which explains your preference for the Barrett."

He nodded. I nodded back. A thoroughbred racehorse weighs about half a ton. A .308 or a NATO round fired randomly into its center mass might not do the job. Not in terms of death or permanent disability. But a big .50 shell almost certainly would. Even if you weigh half a ton, it's pretty hard to struggle along

with a hole the size of a garbage can blown through any part of
you.

I asked, "Who's the owner? Is he a plausible target in
himself?"

The guy told me who the owner was, and we agreed he was a
plausible target. Rumors, shady connections.

Then I said, "What about you? Are you two enemies,
personally?"

"You mean, will I be suspected of ordering the hit that misses?"

"Exactly."

"Not a chance," my guy said. "We don't know each other."

"Except as rival owners."

"There are hundreds of rival owners."

"Is a horse of yours going to win if this guy's doesn't?"

"I certainly hope so."

"So they'll look at you."

"Not if it looks like the man was the target, instead of the
horse."

I asked, "When?"

He told me anytime within the next four days.

I asked, "Where?"

He told me the horse was in a facility some ways south. Horse
country, obviously, grand fields, lush grass, white fences, rolling hills. He told me about long routes through the countryside,
called gallops, where the horses worked out just after dawn. He
told me about the silence and the early mists. He told me how in
the week before a big race the owner would be there every
morning to assess his horse's form, to revel in its power and
speed and grace and appetite. He told me about the stands of
trees that were everywhere and would provide excellent cover.

Then he stopped talking. I felt a little foolish, but I asked him
anyway: "Do you have a photograph? Of the target?"

He took an envelope from his inside jacket pocket. Gave it to
me. In it was a glossy color picture of a horse. It looked posed,
like a promotional item. Like an actor or an actress has head-
shots made, for publicity. This particular horse was a magnificent animal. Tall, shiny, muscular, almost jet-black, with a
white blaze on its face. Quite beautiful.

"Okay," I said.

Then my guy asked me his own question.

He asked me, "How much?"

It was an interesting issue. Technically we were only conspiring to shoot a horse. In most states that's a property crime. A long way from homicide. And I already had an untraceable Barrett Ninety. As a matter of fact, I had three. Their serial numbers stopped dead with the Israeli army. One of them was well used. It was about ready for a new barrel anyway. It would make a fine throw-down gun. Firing cold through a worn barrel wasn't something I would risk against a human, but against something the size of a horse from two hundred yards it wouldn't be a problem. If I aimed at the fattest part of the animal I could afford to miss by up to a foot.

I didn't tell the guy any of that, of course. Instead I banged on for a while about the price of the rifle and the premium I would have to pay for dead-ended paperwork. Then I talked about risk, and waited to see if he stopped me. But he didn't. I could tell he was obsessed. He had a goal. He wanted his own horse to win, and that fact was blinding him to reality just the same way some people get all wound up about betrayal and adultery and business partnerships.

I looked at the photograph again.

"One hundred thousand dollars," I said.

He said nothing.

"In cash," I said.

He said nothing.

"Up front," I said.

He nodded.

"One condition," he said. "I want to be there. I want to see it happen."

I looked at him and I looked at the photograph and I thought about a hundred grand in cash.

"Okay," I said. "You can be there."

He opened the briefcase he had down by his leg and took out a brick of money. It looked okay, smelled okay, and felt okay. There was probably more in the case, but I didn't care. A hundred grand was enough, in the circumstances.

"Day after tomorrow," I said.

We agreed on a place to meet, down south, down in horse country, and he left.

*   *   *

I hid the money where I always do, which is in a metal trunk in my storage unit. Inside the trunk the first thing you see is a human skull inside a Hefty One Zip bag. On the white panel where you're supposed to write what you're freezing is lettered: *This Man Tried to Rip Me Off*. It isn't true, of course. The skull came from an antique shop. Probably an old medical school specimen from the Indian subcontinent.

Next to the money trunk was the gun trunk. I took out the worn Barrett and checked it over. Disassembled it, cleaned it, oiled it, wiped it clean, and then put it back together wearing latex gloves. I loaded a fresh magazine, still with the gloves on. Then I loaded the magazine into the rifle and slid the rifle end-on into an old shoulder-borne golf bag. Then I put the golf bag into the trunk of my car and left it there.

In my house I propped the racehorse photograph on my mantel. I spent a lot of time staring at it.

I met the guy at the time and place we had agreed. It was a lonely crossroad, close to a cross-country track that led to a distant stand of trees, an hour before dawn. The weather was cold. My guy had a coat and gloves on, and binoculars around his neck. I had gloves on too. Latex. But no binoculars. I had a Leupold & Stevens scope on the Barrett, in the golf bag.

I was relaxed, feeling what I always feel when I'm about to kill something, which is to say nothing very much at all. But my client was unrelaxed. He was shivering with an anticipation that was almost pornographic in its intensity. Like a paedophile on a plane to Thailand. I didn't like it much.

We walked side by side through the dew. The ground was hard and pocked by footprints. Lots of them, coming and going.

"Who's been here?" I asked.

"Racetrack touts," my guy said. "Sports journalists, gamblers looking for inside dope."

"Looks like Times Square," I said. "I don't like it."

"It'll be okay today. Nobody scouts here anymore. They all know this horse. They all know it can win in its sleep."

We walked on in silence. Reached the stand of trees. It was oval-shaped, thin at the northern end. We stepped back and forth until we had a clear line of sight through the trunks. Dawn light was in the sky. Two hundred yards away and slightly downhill was a broad grass clearing with plenty of tire tracks showing. A thin grey mist hung in the air.

"This is it?" I said.

My guy nodded. "The horses come in from the south. The cars come in from the west. They meet right there."

"Why?"

"No real reason. Ritual, mostly. Backslapping and bullshitting. The pride of ownership."

I took the Barrett out of the golf bag. I had already decided how I was going to set up the shot. No bipod. I wanted the gun low and free. I knelt on one knee and rested the muzzle in the crook of a branch. Sighted through the scope. Racked the bolt and felt the first mighty .50 shell smack home into the chamber.

"Now we wait," my guy said. He stood at my shoulder, maybe a yard to my right and a yard behind me.

The cars arrived first. They were SUVs, really. Working machines, old and muddy and dented. A Jeep, and two Land Rovers. Five guys climbed out. Four looked poor and one looked rich.

"Trainer and stable lads and the owner," my guy said. "The owner is the one in the long coat."

The five of them stamped and shuffled and their breath pooled around their heads.

"Listen," my guy said.

I heard something way off to my left. To the south. A low drumming, and a sound like giant bellows coughing and pumping. Hooves, and huge equine lungs cycling gallons of sweet fresh morning air.

I rocked backward until I was sitting right down on the ground.

"Get ready," my guy said, from above and behind me.

There were altogether ten horses. They came up in a ragged arrowhead formation, slowing, drifting off-line, tossing their heads, their hard breathing blowing violent yard-long trumpet-shaped plumes of steam ahead of them.

"What is this?" I asked. "The whole roster?"

"String," my guy said. "That's what we call it. This is his whole first string."

In the grey dawn light and under the steam all the horses looked exactly the same to me.

But that didn't matter.

"Ready?" my guy said. "They won't be here long."

"Open your mouth," I said.

"What?"

"Open your mouth, real wide. Like you're yawning."

"Why?"

"To equalize the pressure. Like on a plane. I told you, this is a loud gun. It's going to blow your eardrums otherwise. You'll be deaf for a month."

I glanced around and checked. He had opened his mouth, but halfheartedly, like a guy waiting for the dentist to get back from looking at a chart.

"No, like this," I said. I showed him. I opened my mouth as wide as it would go and pulled my chin back into my neck until the tendons hurt in the hinge of my jaw.

He did the same thing.

I whipped the Barrett's barrel way up and around, fast and smooth, like a duck hunter tracking a flushed bird. Then I pulled the trigger. Shot my guy through the roof of his mouth. The giant rifle boomed and kicked and the top of my guy's head came off like a hard-boiled egg. His body came down in a heap and sprawled. I dropped the rifle on top of him and pulled his right shoe off. Tossed it on the ground. Then I ran. Two minutes later I was back in my car. Four minutes later I was a mile away.

I was up an easy hundred grand, but the world was down an industrialist, a philanthropist, and a racehorse owner. That's what the Sunday papers said. He had committed suicide. The way the cops had pieced it together, he had tormented himself over the fact that his best horse always came in second. He had spied on his rival's workout, maybe hoping for some sign of fallibility. None had been forthcoming. So he had somehow obtained a sniper rifle, last legally owned by the Israel Defense Force. Maybe he had planned to shoot the rival horse, but at the last minute he hadn't been able to go through with it. So, depressed and tormented, he had reversed the rifle, put the muzzle in his mouth, kicked off his shoe, and used his toe on the trigger. A police officer of roughly the same height had taken part in a simulation to prove that such a thing was physically possible, even with a gun as long as the Barrett.

Near the back of the paper were the racing results. The big black horse had won by seven lengths. My guy's runner had been scratched.

I kept the photograph on my mantel for a long time afterward. A girl I met much later noticed that it was the only picture I had in the house. She asked me if I liked animals better than people. I told her that I did, mostly. She liked me for it. But not enough to stick around.

THE DEBT

Simon Kernick

Now I've got a cousin called Kevin. Just like in that song by the Undertones. Unlike in the song, though, the Kevin I know isn't going anywhere near heaven. In fact, the no-good cheating dog's far more likely to be disappearing through a trapdoor into the fiery underworld, and deservedly so too. In fact, if I could get hold of him now, I'd gladly give a helping hand sending him there. Only problem is, there's a queue of people wanting to do just that, and I'm sitting opposite one of them now. None other than Jim "The Crim" Sneddon: gangland legend and all-round wicked hombre, renowned for his extreme cruelty to his fellow human beings, although they do say he loves animals.

The Crim leans forward in his immense leather armchair and points a stubby, sausage-like finger in my direction. I'm sitting on his "guest" sofa, a flashy leather number that's currently covered in tarpaulin, presumably in case things turn nasty, and as you can imagine, not being either cute or furry, I'm feeling less than comfortable. The Crim's thin, hooded eyes are a cold onyx, and when he speaks, the words come out in a low nicotine growl that sound like a cheap, badly damaged car turning over.

"A debt is a debt is a debt," he rumbles, speaking in the manner of a Buddhist monk imparting some great metaphysical wisdom.

"I'm aware of that," I say, holding his gaze, not showing any fear, because if you let them see your weaknesses, then you may as well throw in the towel, "but the debt in question is between you and Kevin."

"No no no no," chuckles The Crim, shaking his huge leonine head. "It don't work like that. Do it, boys?"

There are two men in charcoal black suits flanking the sofa on either side, and they both voice their agreement.

To my left, blocking out much of the room's ambient light, is one Glenroy Frankham, better known as "Ten Man Gang", a six feet six, twenty-five stone hulk of a human being, with a head so small it looks like it's been professionally shrunk, and hands that can, and probably do, crush babies. Such is his strength, he's reputed to be the only man in British penal history to tear his way out of a straitjacket, although I'm surprised they found one that fit him in the first place. His belly looks like a storage room for cannonballs.

To my right stands Johann "Fingers The Knife" Bennett, so-called because of his propensity for slicing off the digits of uncooperative debtors while The Gang holds them in place. The going rate's a finger a day until the money's been paid in full. As you can imagine, The Knife's somewhat "hands on" approach has an enviable success rate, and only once has a debt not been cleared within twenty-four hours of him being called in. On that occasion, the debtor was so broke they had to start on his toes before he finally came up with the money. The guy was a degenerate gambler and I still see him limping around sometimes, although he plays a lot less poker these days.

It's poker that's been Kevin's downfall. That, and the fact that he chose to play his games against Jim the Crim, a man whose standards of fair play leave, it has to be said, a great deal to be desired. You don't rise to multi-millionaire status in the arms and loansharking industries by adhering to the rules of the level playing field, or by being compassionate.

"It ain't my fault, is it?" continues The Crim now, "that your cousin decides to take off into the wild blue yonder without paying me the thirty-four grand he owes."

"You told me it was thirty-three."

"That was Monday, Billy. Today's Wednesday. I've got the interest to think about. It's a lot of money we're looking at here."

"And I still don't know why it's suddenly mine and my family's responsibility," I say, thinking it's time to get assertive.

The Crim bares his teeth in what I think must be a smile, it's not too easy to tell. "It's the etiquette of the matter," he says, clearing his throat, then spitting something thick and nasty into a plate-sized ashtray balanced on one of the chair's arms. "I can't be seen to be letting off a debt this size. It would do my reputation no good at all. And since there's about as much chance of your cousin reappearing as The Gang here taking up hang-gliding, someone's got to pay. And that someone's his mother."

And this, my friends, is why I'm here voluntarily. Because it is my aunt Lena – my dead mother's only sister, and the woman who brought me up from the tender age of thirteen – who is the person currently being treated as The Crim's debtor, and this is a situation that, as an honourable man, I can't allow to continue. She's prepared to pay up too by selling her house, in order to protect her only son from the consequences of his rank stupidity, but I've told her to leave it and let me see what can be done to alleviate the situation, although I'm beginning to think that it's not a lot.

"I understand your position, Jim," I say, trying to sound reasonable, "but my aunt hasn't got the money to pay you, it's as simple as that. However," I add, wanting to avoid a confrontation I know I can't win, "I haven't come here empty-handed. I've got five grand in my pocket. Consider it a deposit on what's owed. Then, when I track down Kevin, which I promise I'm going to do, I'll make sure I get you the other twenty-eight. You've got my word on that."

"Twenty-nine, you mean, and I want the lot now."

The trick in circumstances like these is always to have some room for manoeuvre. "I can get you ten by the end of tonight," I tell him, hoping this'll act as a sweetener.

It doesn't.

"I don't think you're hearing me right, Billy," he growls. "I told you what I want. Now, if you ain't got it, we'll have to see if we have better luck extracting it from your auntie."

"He came in a nice car, Mr Sneddon," says The Knife, his voice a reedy whisper, like wind through a graveyard. "It looks like one of those new BMW 7 Series."

Uh-oh, I think. Not my pride and joy. But, oh dear, The Crim's craggy, reddened face is already brightening. It is a most unpleasant sight. "Now that's what I like to hear," he says.

"And it'll cover the cost of your cousin's misdemeanours, no problem."

I shake my head, knowing I'm going to have to nip this one in the bud pretty sharpish. "That car belongs to me, Jim, and it's not for sale. I bought it with the proceeds of my last fight."

"I remember that last fight. Against Trevor 'The Gibbon' Hutton. I had a bet on it. Cost me five grand when you knocked him down in the eighth." His expression suddenly darkens at the memory, as if this is somehow my fault.

"Well, you know how hard I had to work for it then, don't you?" I tell him, making a final stand. "I'm not giving it up, no way."

The Crim nods once to The Knife and I feel the touch of cold metal in the curve of skin behind my ear.

My heart sinks, especially as I still owe fifteen grand to the finance company. I love that car.

Although I feel like bursting into tears, I keep my cool. "You've changed your weapon, Johann," I say calmly, inclining my head a little in his direction.

"A gun's less messy," The Crim replies, answering for him. He puts out a hand. "Now, unless you want The Knife here to be clearing the contents of your head off the tarpaulin, you'd better give me the keys."

So, pride and joy or not, I have no choice but to hand them over.

The Crim thinks he's doing me a favour by driving me home. Instead, it is akin to twisting the knife in a dying man.

"This really is a sweet piece of machinery," he tells me as we sail smoothly through the wet night streets of the city, the tyres easily holding the slick surface of the tarmac. As if I don't already know this. "Ah, this is what it's all about," he adds, sliding his filthy paws all over the steering wheel, and reclining in the Nasca leather seat. And he's right, too. There's nothing like the freedom of the open road, coupled with all the comforts the 21st Century has to offer; it's like driving in your own front room. The problem is it's now The Crim's front room. And it's his music too: a Back to the Seventies CD he picked up from his office, which is blaring out track after track of retro rubbish.

As we drive, a Range Rover containing The Knife and The Gang inside brings up the rear. The Crim tells me he never likes travelling in the same car as his two bodyguards. He strokes the car's panel and tells me that they're Neanderthals who don't appreciate the finer things in life, although quite how *Tiger Feet* by Mud fits into this category is beyond me. He tells me all this, even though I am hugely uninterested, and when he drops me off, he even gives me a pat on the shoulder and requests that I punch Kevin for him, next time I see the treacherous bastard.

I tell him that I will, meaning it, and clamber lonely and humiliated from the car as the Range Rover pulls up behind us. The Knife is driving and he gives me a triumphant little smirk. The Gang just stares with bored contempt, like he's viewing a side order of green vegetables. Then both cars pull away, and I'm left alone.

I used to be a handy middleweight boxer. I never troubled the top division but in a career spanning nine years and twenty-seven professional fights (seventeen wins, two draws and eight losses, before you ask), I managed to save up enough money to invest in property. I own a flat in Hackney outright, and I put down fifty percent on a house in Putney last year, which I've been doing up ever since.

But my main job these days is as a doorman. I don't need the cash particularly, but it's easy work. The place is called Stallions, not that there's much of the stallion about any of the clientèle. They're mainly middle-aged men with plenty of money. It's billed as a gentleman's establishment but, to be honest, it's more of a high-class brothel with a bit of card-playing and drinking thrown in.

Two hours after being dropped off by Jim The Crim, I arrive at the door of the club in Piccadilly, freshly showered and dressed in a dickie bow and suit, having had to get a taxi all the way down here. Needless to say, I'm not in a good mood, but I'm on floor-duty tonight, which is some compensation.

The club itself is a lavish split-level room with cavernous ceilings, and was obviously kitted out by someone who liked the colour burgundy. It's busy tonight, with all the tables taken, and the girls outnumbering the clients by less than two to one, which is rare. How it works is this: you pay an annual fee of several grand to be a member, but you don't have to sleep with any of the women. You can just come and drink and play cards if you want to, but most people indulge in the more carnal pursuits. There are private rooms upstairs to which you take your chosen girl. You pay her cash, usually along the lines of £200 an hour, and then pay a separate room fee to the management which equates to the same amount. It's pricey, but these are men without money worries and ladies with very generous looks.

As I pass the small, central dance-floor, I'm greeted by several of the girls. They wink and blow me kisses, and one – Chanya from Thailand – brushes against me like a cat as I pass, her expression inviting. But I know it's only a bit of fun. She doesn't want me. Like all the girls here, she's after a ticket out, and someone of my standing simply hasn't got the resources to provide that.

Still, the attention puts me in a better mood, and this lasts as long as it takes to round the dance-floor and take the three steps to the upper level. Because it's then I spot the man who is my current nemesis, none other than The Crim himself.

This is a surprise. I've not seen The Crim in here before. He's sitting at a corner booth talking animatedly to one of our regulars, the right honourable Stephen Humphrey MP, a former junior defence minister, who always seems to have plenty of money. There's some skulduggery afoot, I've no doubt about that, and I wonder what it might be.

I watch them from a distance for a full minute as they hatch whatever evil plot they're hatching, and I think they make a right pair. The Crim is a big lumpy ox of a man with looks to match, while the MP is tall and dapper, with every pore of his Savile Row besuited form oozing expensive education. He sports a quite magnificent head of richly curled, silver-white hair that makes him look like Julius Caesar on steroids. To be honest, I've heard it's a very expensive rug, but then you hear a lot of intimate details in a place like this, not all of them pleasant, or true.

I'm not so bothered about all that at the moment, though. What I am bothered about is getting my BMW back, since it was taken from me under duress, as I think you'll agree. Clearly, if The Crim's here then so is the car. And what's more I've got my spare keys on me. I'm taking a risk by repossessing it, of course, because The Crim is definitely not a man to cross, but I can't bring myself to do nothing when I know that it's probably in the underground car park, only yards away.

I take a look round for The Gang and The Knife, but they're nowhere to be seen.

However, when I look back at the Crim's booth, I see that one of the girls, Vanya, a tall, statuesque blonde from Slovakia with an icy smile and a model's poise, has approached the table, and is leaning over talking to Humphrey. The Crim meanwhile is surreptitiously peeking down the top of her cleavage, and trying without success to be all nonchalant about it.

As I watch, The Crim reaches into his pocket and pulls out what look suspiciously like my car keys. With a reluctant expression, he hands them over, not to Humphrey, but to Vanya, and she gives the big ox an enthusiastic peck on the cheek. What the hell's going on here, I wonder, as the politician gets up and the two men shake hands?

A second later, Humphrey and Vanya turn and walk hand in hand across the length of the club and disappear out the exit.

Not for the first time in my life, I'm confused. What's he done with my car now?

It's one of the club's rules that senior members (i.e. those the management want to keep on good terms with) can take selected girls off the premises and back to their own places, by prior agreement. Stephen Humphrey is one such member, but since he's married with a sizeable brood of kids, I doubt he's taking her back to his place for a bit of slap and tickle.

Which means they could be going anywhere.

So, what do I do now?

For the next half hour or so, I don't do a lot, just keep walking the floor of the club, making sure that everyone, clients and girls alike, feels happy and secure. But all the time I'm thinking about my car and the heinous way it's been taken from me. And, of course, what I need to do to be reunited with it.

Finally, I can take no more. I've got to have it back. It's just turned midnight when I head outside and make a call to the firm who monitor the tracking device that's installed in it. I tell the man on the other end of the phone that a friend of mine's driven off in my car for a prank. I don't want to involve the police but I do want the car back, so can he please activate the tracker and let me know where it is? He doesn't like the idea, and to be fair, it's a bit of an unusual request, but eventually, having ascertained that I am who I say I am, he does the honours and informs me that my car is currently outside Number 21 Bowbury Gardens in Hampstead.

Ah, the wonders of technology. Now all I need to do is get there.

As I turn round, putting the phone back in my pocket, I see The Crim hurrying down the steps with The Knife and The Gang in tow. They don't see me, but keep on going round to the entrance of the underground car park. Something's up, I think, but I'm no longer so worried about them. The important thing is to get my rear across to 21 Bowbury Gardens before anyone else does. So, after a quick few words with my fellow doorman, Harry "The Wolverine" Carruthers (so-called because of the thick black mat of hair that covers his body from neck to toe), he agrees to lend me his car. He's not too happy about it, obviously, since number one he's going to have to cover for me and number two, when finishing time comes round at the unearthly hour of 4 a.m., he's going to have some trouble getting home.

I tell him not to worry about this since I'll have it back well before then, and anyway, he owes me one. The Wolverine's not happy, there's no doubting that, but eventually he parts with the keys, and I drive off towards Hampstead in the hunt for truth and justice.

It's just turned quarter to one and raining when I pull into Bowbury Gardens, a quiet residential road of rundown three-storey townhouses, and I'm immediately confronted by an alarming sight. The front door of one of the houses about halfway down is open and I can see Vanya, the girl who left the club in my car, being manhandled by a number of men who all have their back to me.

Hearing my car approach, one of them turns round and I see that it's Jim The Crim. He immediately turns back and grabs Vanya by the arm, pushing her back into the house. I carry on driving, looking straight ahead, hoping they won't recognize me, and as I pass I see that they've all now disappeared inside. I also see my motor – sleek and metallic-black, like a crouching panther – parked at the side of the road.

I find a space nearby and pull in. The spare keys are in my pocket. Now is the time to pretend I never saw Vanya being accosted by The Crim and his boys, grab my car and drive off, end of story. Obviously, I'm going to have to get out of London for a while, in order to escape The Crim's wrath, but I was planning a holiday anyway, and Stallions isn't exactly a job I'll miss.

But the problem is that I'm an honourable man, as I've told you before. I can't just walk away from a damsel in distress; it's not right.

However, there's another problem. I am outnumbered, and if I remember rightly (which I do), the Knife is carrying a gun. Since I know that The Wolverine is a man who sometimes strays on the wrong side of the law, I check in his glove compartment for any useful accessories and, lo and behold, I find a can of pepper spray. It's not a lot but it'll have to do.

Putting it in my pocket, I get out of the car and jog through the rain past my car, resisting the urge to kiss the paintwork, and carry on to the door where I saw the altercation. I try the handle and it's locked. There's a buzzer lit up on the wall beside it and I see that the house is split into three flats. Taking a step back I note that the third floor's the only one with lights on, so figure that this one's Vanya's place. I come forward again and launch a flying karate kick at the lock on the door. It looks pretty old and it gives easily, flying open with an angry crack.

Surprise has never been my strong point and I wonder again why I'm helping Vanya. She's never been particularly friendly to me. In fact, I've always thought her aloof and cold. I think maybe I'm simply a sucker for punishment.

I shut the door behind me and move forward in the darkness, listening. I can't hear any sounds from above so I head over to the stairwell opposite and take the steps upwards, my shoes tap-tap-tapping on the cheap linoleum floor. It smells of damp in here and I suddenly feel sorry for Vanya, coming thousands of miles to work in a brothel servicing middle-aged men, and living in a dump like this.

There's a scream. It's short and faint, but it's definitely coming from the top floor. Before my fights, I used to get so nervous and pumped-up that I'd be bouncing off the walls, counting down the seconds to the action. I get that feeling again now. I can sense impending violence and it's weird, but I'm actually looking forward to it. It's like I'm living again for the first time in months, years even.

And now, of course, I know why I've come here, and why I'm defying Jim The Crim Sneddon himself. I crave the excitement. It's like a drug.

The pepper spray's in my left hand as I mount the last step, see a door in front of me, all plywood and chipped paint, and do a Jackie Chan on this one as well. It flies open as well and this time I'm confronted by a sight that's alternately hilarious and shocking.

First, the shocking part: Vanya, dressed in civvies, is sitting rigid on her threadbare living room sofa, her pale blue eyes as wide as saucers. Above her, with one foot on said sofa, stands The Knife, the tip of his trademark stiletto touching the little fold of skin just below her left eye. In his free hand, he holds a thick lock of blonde hair that he's clearly just lopped off, and it looks like he's about to embark on some more physical damage. The expression on his face is one of cold pleasure.

Now for the hilarious part, and believe it or not, there is one. Wailing like an angry baby in the middle of the room, is the right honourable Stephen Humphrey MP. Except his resplendent silver mane is no longer attached to his head, but is actually bunched up in Vanya's hand, like a sleeping Jack Russell, where she's obviously removed it with some force. So, the rumours are true. Humphrey really is as bald as a coot, and I think it must have been his screams I heard, because his shiny dome is red and raw, and laced with the remnants of torn adhesive.

The Crim is the only other person in the room, and he's having a bit of a laugh at Humphrey's plight. At least he is until he sees me bursting in like some avenging angel. The MP is the nearest to me, but I don't bother with him. As Defence Minister, he had a reputation as a tough guy in parliament. But it's one thing making the brave decisions that send other men to their deaths, and another getting in the firing line yourself. He makes his intentions admirably plain by jumping out the way very fast, and burying his newly naked head in his hands.

I identify the priority target as The Knife, since he's the one with the weapons, and as he turns my way, I let him have it with a liberal burst of the spray. He tries to cover his face but he's not fast enough, and as he chokes and splutters against the fumes, at the same time bringing his knife round in my direction, I knock him down with a swift left hook. He hits the sofa, out for the count.

But The Crim's a bit quicker, having had that much more time to react, and he yanks his head away as I fire off another burst of the spray. He's exposed in this position, and I come forward and punch him in the kidneys, twice in quick succession. He stumbles and loses his footing, and I grab him by his coat and pull him close, shoving the canister against his nose and spraying off the last of its contents straight up his nostrils.

He starts gasping for air and twisting round uncontrollably, smashing into the stereo unit, part of which falls on his head with a loud clunk. I let go of him and turn round to look for Vanya, who's giving the prone, mewing Humphrey a bit of a working over. I pull her off him and, at that moment hear the sound of a toilet flushing round the corner, just out of sight.

Oh no! The Gang! In all the excitement, I've forgotten about him, and now I'm out of spray. A second later, he comes into the room – twenty-five stone of muscle and jelly. The guy's amazingly fast for one so immense, I have to give him that.

"Run!" shouts Vanya rather unnecessarily, but he's almost upon me, leering like a demented clown and, worse still, The Knife is starting to get to his feet, obviously not quite as knocked out as I'd thought.

I strike The Gang with a three-punch combination, every blow slamming into his tiny, childlike face, but they might as well be kisses for all the damage they're doing, and he keeps coming forward, wrapping great arms round my torso, and dragging me into a vice-like bearhug that quite literally takes my breath away. I try to say something but no sound comes out. I feel my ribs giving way. I have never been in such pain in my life, and I think that if I die like this, it will be a truly terrible way to go. And it's all because of that arsehole, Kevin.

In the background, I can see The Knife rubbing his eyes. He hisses to his colleague not to kill me. He wants to end my life himself. It almost seems preferable to what I'm going through now.

But then The Gang's grip loosens, and he suddenly goes bosseyed. I get my right arm free and deliver an uppercut that catches him under the chin. The grip loosens still more and I struggle free, bumping into Vanya, whose hand is thrust between The Gang's legs, twisting savagely. As the Americans would say, this girl has spunk.

We turn together, just in time to see The Knife slashing his weapon in a throat-high arc, and it takes all my old reactions to fend off the blow, using my right arm to block his, and my left to deliver two vicious little jabs – bang bang – right into his pockmarked mug.

He actually says "Ouch!", then goes straight over backwards, landing on the carpet, only to be trampled on by The Crim, who is still blundering around the room like a drunk gatecrashing a ballet performance.

And then we're out the door and down the stairs, taking them two and three at a time, and I can hear The Gang lumbering behind us. Vanya stumbles and I grab her arm and pull her upright. We hit the street at a mad dash, veering right in the direction of the BMW. She starts fiddling in the pocket of her jeans for the keys, thinking that's she's going to be the one driving, but there's no way that's going to happen.

"This is my car, darling!" I shout, pulling out the spares and flicking off the central locking.

Reluctantly, she jumps in the passenger side, while I leap in the driver's seat and switch on the ignition. The engine purrs into life, and I pull out into the road. I can see The Gang in the rear view mirror, coming down the road after us. He's gaining but there's not a lot he can do now and I accelerate away, feeling pleasantly satisfied, at least until Vanya tells me that the Bowbury Gardens is actually a dead end road, and I'm going in the wrong direction.

I do a quick three-point turn in the middle of the road, and swing the car back round, accelerating. Twenty yards away, The Gang is in the middle of the road, looming up like an immovable stone monolith, but this is a strong car, and a good deal more substantial than the man currently standing in front of me.

I think The Gang must belatedly realize this because at the last second, he leaps to one side, belly-flopping onto the bonnet of some poor sod's Renault Megane with a huge crash. It takes me a moment to realize that it is in fact The Wolverine's car and that now he's definitely going to be walking home tonight.

I keep driving, gliding round the bend and onto the main road. Mission almost accomplished.

"Thanks for that," says Vanya, leaning over and putting a hand on my arm. She smells nice, and I think there might be passion in her pale eyes, although to be fair, I've been wrong about this sort of thing before.

"What the hell was that all about?" I ask her, and she tells me.

Apparently, Stephen Humphrey is providing lucrative defence contracts to one of The Crim's front companies in return for cash. A very big contract is coming up and, on hearing that The Crim is driving one of the new BMWs, Humphrey wants to take possession of the car in lieu of his usual payment. The Crim reluctantly agrees and Humphrey and Vanya go for a spin. Vanya, however, has been tiring of Humphrey of late, and they end up having a violent argument. In the ensuing mêlée, Vanya physically removes the MP from the car, damaging his toupee in the process, and then drives off home, concluding that actually London life isn't for her. She decides to take the 7-Series and drive it, and her meagre possessions, back to Slovakia.

But just as she's leaving, The Crim and his boys turn up, along with a crooked-haired Humphrey thirsting for revenge. Which is where I came in.

I ask her if she's going to take the plane home now.

She looks disappointed. "Is this really your car?" she asks.

"I'm afraid it is," I tell her.

"So," she says, looking at me with an interest she's never shown before, "what are you going to do? The men you attacked are going to be pretty upset and I understand that Mr Sneddon is a very powerful man."

It's a good question, and one I haven't really given a lot of thought to. "We'll have to see," I say enigmatically.

By this time, we've pulled up outside Aunt Lena's house. I know that whatever happens, I've got to keep her out of the way of The Crim, who's going to be looking to settle scores in any way he can.

But there's something odd here. In Aunt Lena's one-car carport sits another 7-Series, brand new like mine. I park up behind it and, taking the spare keys from Vanya, just in case she decides to do another runner, tell her to wait for me.

As I reach the front door, it opens and who should I see standing there but the fugitive himself, cousin Kevin? He immediately opens fire with a barrage of excuses for his absence, as well as heartfelt apologies and gestures of thanks. The whole tirade's a pile of bullshit, of course, but you have to give him ten out of ten for effort.

"Where's your mum?" I ask him, and then remember that I actually told her to stay round her friend Marjorie's house on the next street until all this boiled over.

"Have you got The Crim's money?" I demand. "He reckons it's thirty-four grand."

"Thirty-four thousand?" he pipes up. "That's ruinous. Tell you the truth," he adds, which is usually the prelude to a lie, "I've been down in Monaco. Made some money on the tables. Had everything ready for The Crim, but then I saw this motor in the showroom near the casino . . ." He motions towards the car, "and I just had to have it. It's beautiful, Billy," he says. "Supreme engineering."

"I know," I answer, "I've got one. So, I'm taking it you haven't got the money."

He gives me a rueful expression. "Supreme engineering doesn't come cheap."

"No, it doesn't," I say, pondering the evening I've had, then clap him on the shoulder. "Look, stay here tonight, Kevin, and we'll straighten out The Crim in the morning. I'm just popping off back home."

We say our goodbyes and I get back in the car, and put a call into The Crim on my mobile as we drive away. Not surprisingly, he's none too pleased to hear from me and is full of curses and bluster until I tell him that Kevin's waiting for him at Aunt Lena's house with a present that I guarantee will make him happy, and which will simultaneously clear the debt.

I also add that it would be a lot better for everyone if my family stayed in one piece and no one got to hear about The Crim's crooked relationship with Mr Hairpiece himself, Stephen Humphrey MP.

Before he can say anything else, I end the call, settle back and turn to Vanya.

"So," I ask, as we reach the bottom of the road. "Which way to Slovakia?"

THE CASE OF THE CURIOUS QUORUM

Colin Dexter

Triply marked had been the white envelope, Personal Private Confidential; and after reading its contents, Inspector Lewis's forehead registered considerable puzzlement. Furthermore, after re-reading the two-page letter, such puzzlement appeared compounded with each succeeding paragraph.

> 53 Cumberland Place
> London W2 5AS
> 0207 3736642
> 10 April 2006

Dear Inspector,

My only connection with you is via the late Chief Inspector Morse, who once came to talk at the Detection Club's annual jamboree at The Ritz. We had known of him because one of our number had written accounts of some of his high-profile investigations, particularly into murder, a crime ever nourishing the life-blood of our distinguished membership. Morse spoke rather stiffly, we thought, although after his speech he was somewhat more relaxed with his plentiful supply of single-malt Scotch.

It was at that point he came to speak of you, and in a most complimentary fashion. Clearly you formed an illustrious partnership and I know you will have learnt a great deal from

*him about the solving of crime. Indeed, one of our cruciverb-
alist members wrote an anagrammatic clue about his rank and
name: "Person with crimes to resolve (9, 5)". And it is in
order to resolve a crime that I write to you now. Please,
Inspector, consider the following facts.*

*I was myself, until a few years ago, the President of the
Detection Club, during which time I naturally held an open
cheque book on the Club's account. I attended a committee
meeting two weeks ago in the hotel lounge at Paddington
Railway Station, taking with me the cheque book and intending (belatedly) to surrender it to the current President.
There were five of us there, all male: our President, myself,
and three other senior members. The business was conducted
expeditiously; and before repairing to the bar with my
colleagues, I collected up my own material, consisting of a
few personal letters, the minutes of the last meeting, the
morning's agenda, my notes, etc, and stuffed them into my
briefcase.*

*On returning home and taking out these papers, I found
that the cheque book was missing, although I clearly remember that I had forgotten (yet again) to hand it over. Was my
memory playing cruel tricks on me? I am certain this was not
the case. My brain cells have not let me down for many a
decade, to be frank – eight of them almost! I did not allow this
matter to disturb me unduly, but it should have done. Why?
Because two days ago I learnt that a considerable amount had
been withdrawn from the Club's account on a cheque from
that very book, a cheque ostensibly signed by me.*

*My mind has been going round whirlygigwise this last
forty-eight hours, since I am certain that it was one of us
at the committee meeting who was responsible for the theft, as
well as for the criminal usage made of it thereafter. One of
those men is a complete monster – bit of one, anyway! One of
them is a d— arrant robber! One of them ought to be roasted
under a grill – he deserves it! Do I sound a little incoherent?
So be it.*

*Where does this leave my reputation? I used to be called the
Crime King – Father of Detection! And now I am left in
much anger and despair as I see myself the victim of a person
who is that most despicable thing – faker of cheques! He*

would need a cheque, of course, as well as a copy of my signature, which he could (did) practise. It may therefore be of some help to you to have a list of those members to whom, reasonably recently, I wrote and signed semi-official letters: Len Deighton, Anthony Lejeune, Simon Brett, Lionel Davidson, Peter Lovesey, James Melville, Reginald Hill, Robert Barnard, Jonathan Gash, John Malcolm, Ian Rankin, John Harvey, and Robert Goddard. All men. But it was a man. And the only reason I am not listing the names of those members attending the committee meeting must be fairly obvious. I find myself unwilling to point a finger at any specific person.

Now that Morse is no longer with us, I am looking to you, Inspector, feeling confident that after working for so many years with that remarkable man, some of his skills will have rubbed off on you. Yes, I am certain you can help me, if you will. Alas, the resolution of this sorry affair is urgent and imperative. We need no private eye on the assignment: let's have it under your eye — let's prove, between us, who this villain is!

> *Yours truly,*
> *HRF Keating*

PS On looking through what I have written, I notice that the phrase "I am certain" is used three times. Please know that what I tell you three times is true.

Later that morning, rather more quickly than Lewis, it had been Detective Sergeant Hathaway who read the letter.

"Puzzling, don't you think?" queried Lewis.

"Well, yes. I don't suppose everybody knows what a cruciver—"

"*I* know," interrupted Lewis sharply. "I worked with a chronic cruciverbalist for twenty years."

"Sorry, sir."

Lewis pointed to the letter. "Don't you find it all a bit of a mystery?"

Hathaway hesitated. "To be truthful, sir, I don't, no. It seems pretty clear that either it's all a joke or else this fellow's more than halfway round the twist."

"Really? Doesn't read much like a joke to me. And I don't reckon the fellow's lost his marbles, either. I remember Morse talking about this Keating chap. Said he'd got one of the shrewdest brains in the business."

"But no one could expect us to take this sort of stuff seriously. He's told us next to nothing—"

"Except his home address and his telephone number."

"So?"

"So ring him up."

"And say what?"

"You think of something. You're a university graduate, remember."

Lewis pushed the telephone across the desk; and a few moments later both men could hear the words: "This number is not receiving incoming calls. I repeat, this . . ."

"Never mind," said Lewis. "The President – ring him."

"How do we know—?"

"The Club'll be on Google, man."

Hathaway looked up from the screen a minute later. "Fellow called Simon Brett. There's a telephone number, too."

But again both men were shortly to hear an automated voice. "The person you require is not available. Please try again later".

Lewis grinned wryly. "They all seem to be telling us next to nothing, just like you said."

But his eyes remained steadfastly on the letter as he wondered what Morse would have thought in the same situation . . .

He was still wondering a few minutes later when Hathaway interrupted whatever might have been going through the inspector's mind.

"You remember we're due out at ten o'clock, sir?"

"Yep. But just you get a copy of that letter and take it home with you tonight. You see, I'm beginning to think we may be wrong about it not telling us anything. If I'd said that to Morse, do you know what he would have said?"

Hathaway shook his head indifferently.

"He'd have said that fellow's probably told us *everything*."

"Not told us how the guilty party sorted out the transfer of the money; not told us which bank it was or how much dosh was taken out . . . Ridiculous, really, that letter!"

Lewis made no reply, and Hathaway continued:

"Tell you something else, sir. My old tutor once told me that if I kept on using as many exclamation marks in my essays as this fellow's done, he'd refuse to read 'em. And any writer who kept on using those long dashes all the time hadn't much idea on how to write the Queen's English."

Again Lewis made no reply, but something – some small, vague idea – was struggling into birth in the depths of his brain as Hathaway spoke again.

"I wonder whether Morse would think he was much of a writer, our man here. Things like 'arrant monster'—"

"Arrant *robber*," corrected Lewis.

"Ugh! Would your old boss have written that?"

"Dunno. He never wrote much. And if he had to *read* a lot of bumph, it was always the commas he was most particular about."

"Wish I'd known him, sir," said Hathaway with gentle irony as he closed the door behind him.

"A lot of people would!" said Lewis quietly to himself in the empty room.

Hathaway had finished his supper, and was looking through the evening's fare in the *TV Times* when his mind drifted back to the Keating letter. He'd won himself no Brownie points when he'd misquoted "arrant robber" from the letter. "Robber" . . . not all that different from "Robert", was it? And Lewis's Christian name must surely be Robert, with his senior colleagues always calling him "Robbie" . . . He took out the letter from his jacket-pocket: yes, there it was, "arrant robber". What *was* this stupid bloody letter all about?

But suddenly something clicked in his mind and his eyes were gleaming as he wrote out the letters of "arrant robber" and crossed them off one by one against a name on the members' list. One letter short, agreed. But there it was, immediately before those two words: the letter "d—", which he'd assumed to have been the way some people who'd never sworn in their lives expressed "damned".

"Wow!"

It was 8.45 pm and he rang Lewis immediately. Almost. But if one of the four names was hidden there in the text, in "anagrammatic" form (the very word Keating had used), yes! If one of the names was nestling there, what about the other three?

Lewis was watching the 10 o'clock news on BBC1 when Hathaway rang.

"I went through that letter line by line, sir, letter by letter, and I've found them, found all of them. All four: 'd—arrant robber' is an anagram of Robert Barnard. Next one: 'monster – bit' is an anagram of Simon Brett, our honourable President. Then we've got 'grill – he', not quite so clear, but it must be Reg Hill. The last, near the end, is 'eye – let's prove', which works out as Peter Lovesey. I checked all the other names on the list, but there's no one *else* lurking there. No one!"

After finally replacing the receiver, Hathaway felt an inner glow of forgivable pride. Yet he realised that four names didn't help all that much when the problem was deciding on just *one* name. But the other four would go down to three if the President (surely) could be shunted along with Caesar's wife into the above-suspicion bracker. Which left him with Barnard, Hill, Lovesey . . .

When Hathaway had rung, Lewis had only just got back from hearing Papadopoulos conducting the Oxford Philomusica at the Sheldonian. He felt pleasingly tired, and would have welcomed an earlyish night. But he knew he would have little chance of sleep with Hathaway's clever findings topmost in his mind, and with the idea that had begun to dawn on him that morning still undeveloped and unexamined. Unusually for him, he was aware of a strongly competitive urge to come up with something that could complement his sergeant's discovery. But who *was* that one crook on the committee? One of the four – or perhaps one of the three – for he (like Hathaway) felt prepared to pass over the President.

Think, Lewis! Think!

How would Morse have looked at the letter? Probably looked at it the wrong way round, say? How do you do that, though? Read it back to front? Ridiculous. Read the PS before the salutation? But where had he read the PS's "what I tell you three times is true" before? From Lewis Carroll, wasn't it? He located the words immediately in *The Oxford Book of Quotations*, from "The Hunting of the Snark". So what? What had *that* got to do with anything? Just a minute. Three suspects . . . but Keating hadn't mentioned any single one of the suspects three times. He hadn't mentioned *anything* three times.

Or had he?

Well, even if he had, it was past midnight, and he was walking up the stairs when he remembered what Hathaway had said about punctuation. Morse had once told him that Oscar Wilde had spent two hours one morning looking through one of his poems before removing a comma; and then spent a further two hours the same afternoon before deciding to re-instate the said comma. And after standing motionless on the third step from the top of the staircase, Lewis finally retraced his steps downstairs and looked at the letter for the umpteenth time, now paying no attention whatsoever to what things were being said, but *how* they were being said.

And suddenly, in a flash, eureka.

Thank you, Hathaway! Thank you, Morse!

Lewis took a can of beer from the fridge and drank it before finally completing his ascent of the staircase. Hathaway may have fallen asleep that night with a look of deep satisfaction on his face, but with Lewis it was one bordering on the beatific.

It was three days after the aforementioned events that Mr HRF Keating received a letter at his London address with the envelope marked "Thames Valley Police HQ, Kidlington, Oxon".

13 April 2006

Dear Mr Keating,

I write to thank you for your letter of 10 April 2006. You asked for my help.

Between us, my sergeant and I finally fathomed the anagrammatized names of the committee quorum; and leaving aside yourself, and giving the benefit of the doubt to your successor as President, we were left with three names from the list you gave us: Messrs Barnard, Hill, Lovesey. The clues were there and we spotted them. But this didn't get us very far. Which of the three men was it?

It was more difficult for us to spot the vital clue, but in reality you had made it quite complex. The three names we had, as well as the President's, were each signposted by two items of punctuation: the long em dash and the exclamation mark. It was cleverly done. But we were a bit slow to notice the full implication of this. These two punctuation marks were each used, always closely together, not four times, but seven times, and used nowhere else in your letter. Why had our suspect-list suddenly grown so much longer? The reason eventually became clear. The name of the perpetrator of the "crime" was not included in the list of club-members. But there he was, three times: "frank—eight"; "King—Father"; "thing—faker", and each of the three is a perfect anagram of the man responsible for the alleged theft of the chequebook: a man, as I say, who was not listed among the suspects. A man named HRF Keating. You, sir!

Only one problem remains, a more difficult one than that posed by your letter. Why on earth did you go in for all that rigmarole? What was the point of it? If, as we suspect, it was for sheer amusement, please remember that irresponsible wasting of police time is liable to be interpreted as a crime, and as such be liable for prosecution.

Please satisfy our curiosity about your motive, although we trust that your reply can be rather shorter than your original communication.

Yours sincerely,
R Lewis (Detective Inspector)

16 April 2006

Dear Inspector Lewis,
Thank you so much for your letter, and heartiest congratulations on your cleverness.

An American philanthropist was one of our guests when Morse spoke to us, and the two of them got on finely. This same person revisited us a month ago, and was naturally saddened to hear of Morse's death. He remembered Morse mentioning to him the work of the Police Service of Northern Ireland Benevolent Fund, and expressed the wish to make some donation to this fund. But on one specific condition. Together we amused ourselves by jointly composing the letter

I originally sent to you. The agreed condition was that the police should prove themselves still able to exhibit the high degree of mental acumen and flexibility that Morse himself had shown with crossword puzzles, and with criminal cases.

It was also agreed that I should write to you to explain the whole thing should you have shown no interest, or have been utterly flummoxed by our letter. Had such been the case, we had decided to consider the merits of the next two charities on my friend's giftlist: the Salvation Army, and the Donkey Sanctuary. I rang him immediately on receipt of your wonderfully welcome letter, and a cheque is now on its transatlantic flight to the police charity: a cheque for $25,000. This I hope should compensate in some degree for the time you and your colleague spent on the puzzle, and perhaps you can now cross my own name off the list of those potentially liable for prosecution. It remains for me only to subscribe this letter, which I now do.

A right nerk?—Ay!

PS Please note the punctuation.

THE BOOKBINDER'S APPRENTICE

Martin Edwards

As Joly closed his book, he was conscious of someone watching him. A feeling he relished, warm as the sun burning high above Campo Santi Apostoli. Leaning back, he stretched his arms, a languorous movement that allowed his eyes to roam behind dark wrap-around Gucci glasses.

A tall, stooped man in a straw hat and white suit was limping towards the row of red benches, tapping a long wooden walking stick against the paving slabs, somehow avoiding a collision with the small, whooping children on scooters and tricycles. Joly sighed. He wasn't unaccustomed to the attentions of older men, but soon they became tedious. Yet the impeccable manners instilled at one of England's minor public schools never deserted him; and besides, he was thirsty; a drink would be nice, provided someone else was paying. The benches were crowded with mothers talking while their offspring scrambled and shouted over the covered well and a group of sweaty tourists listening to their guide's machine-gun description of the frescoes within the church. As the man drew near, Joly squeezed up on the bench to make a small place beside him.

"Why, thank you." American accent, a courtly drawl. "It is good to rest one's feet in the middle of the day."

Joly guessed the man had been studying him from the small bridge over the canal, in front of the row of shops. He smiled, didn't not speak. In a casual encounter, his rule was not to give anything away too soon.

The man considered the book on Joly's lap. "*Death in Venice.* Fascinating."

"He writes well," Joly allowed.

"I meant the volume itself, not the words within it." The man waved towards the green kiosk in front of them. Jostling in the window with the magazines and panoramic views of the Canal Grande were the gaudy covers of translated Georgette Heyer and Conan the Barbarian. "Though your taste in reading matter is plainly more sophisticated than the common herd's. But it is the book as *objet d'art* that fascinates me most these days, I must confess. May I take a closer look?"

Without awaiting a reply, he picked up the novel, weighing it in his hand with the fond assurance of a Manhattan jeweller caressing a heavy diamond. The book was bound in green cloth, with faded gilt lettering on the grubby spine. Someone had spilled ink on the front cover and an insect had nibbled at the early pages.

"Ah, the first English edition by Secker. I cannot help but he impressed by your discernment. Most young fellows wishing to read Thomas Mann would content themselves with a cheap paperback."

"It is a little out of the ordinary, that accounts for its appeal. I like unusual things, certainly." Joly let the words hang in the air for several seconds. "As for cost, I fear I don't have deep pockets. I picked the copy up from a second hand dealer's stall on the Embankment for rather less than I would have paid in a paperback shop. It's worth rather more than the few pence I spent, but it's hardly valuable, I'm afraid. The condition is poor, as you can see. All the same, I'd rather own a first edition than a modern reprint without a trace of character."

The man proffered a thin, weathered hand. "You are a fellow after my own heart, then! A love of rare books, it represents a bond between us. My name is Sanborn, by the way, Darius Sanborn."

"Joly Maddox."

"Joly? Not short for Jolyon, by any chance?"

"You guessed it. My mother loved *The Forsyte Saga.*"

"Ah, so the fondness for good books is inherited. Joly, it is splendid to make your acquaintance."

Joly ventured an apologetic cough and made a show of consulting his fake Rolex as the church bell chimed the hour. "Well, I suppose I'd better be running along."

Sanborn murmured, "Oh, but do you have to go so soon? It is a hot day, would you care to have a drink with me?"

A pantomime of hesitation. "Well, I'm tempted. I'm not due to meet up with my girlfriend till she finishes work in another hour . . ."

A tactical move, to mention Lucia. Get the message over to Sanborn, just so there was no misunderstanding. The American did not seem in the least put out, as his leathery face creased into a broad smile. Joly thought he was like one of the pigeons in the square, swooping the moment it glimpsed the tiniest crumb.

"Then you have time aplenty. Come with me, I know a little spot a few metres away where the wine is as fine as the skin of a priceless first edition."

There was no harm in it. Adjusting his pace to the old man's halting gait, he followed him over the bridge, past the shop with all the cacti outside. Their weird shapes always amused him. Sanborn noticed his sideways glance. He was sharp, Joly thought, he wasn't a fool.

"As you say, the unusual intrigues you."

Joly nodded. He wouldn't have been startled if the old man had suggested going to a hotel instead of for a drink, but thankfully the dilemma of how to respond to a proposition never arose. After half a dozen twists and turns through a maze of alleyways, they reached an ill-lit bar and stepped inside. After the noise and bustle of the *campo*, the place was as quiet as a church in the Ghetto. No one stood behind the counter and, straining his eyes to adjust from the glare outside, Joly spied only a single customer. In a corner at the back, where no beam from the sun could reach, a small wizened man in a corduroy jacket sat at a table, a half-empty wine glass in front of him. Sanborn limped up to the man and indicated his guest with a wave of the stick.

"Zuichini, meet Joly Maddox. A fellow connoisseur of the unusual. Including rare books."

The man at the table had a hooked nose and small dark cruel eyes. His face resembled a carnival mask, with a plague doctor's beak, long enough to keep disease at bay. He extended his hand. It was more like a claw, Joly thought. And it was trembling, although not from nerves – for his toothless smile conveyed a strange, almost malevolent glee. Zuichini must suffer from some form of palsy, perhaps Parkinson's disease. Joly, young and fit, knew little of sickness.

"You wonder why I make specific mention of books, Joly?" Sanborn asked with a rhetorical flourish. "It is because my good friend here is the finest bookbinder in Italy. Zuichini is not a household name, not even here in Venice, but his mastery of his craft, I assure you, is second to none. As a collector of unique treasures, few appreciate his talents more than I."

A simian waiter shuffled out from a doorway, bearing wine and three large glasses. He did not utter a word, but plainly Sanborn and Zuichini were familiar customers. Sanborn did not spare the man's retreating back a glance as he poured.

"You will taste nothing finer in Italy, I assure you. Liquid silk."

Joly took a sip and savoured the bouquet. Sanborn was right about the wine, but what did he want? Everyone wanted something.

"You are here as a tourist?" the American asked. "Who knows, you might follow my example. I first came to this city for a week. That was nineteen years ago and now I could not tear myself away if my life depended on it."

Joly explained that he'd arrived in Venice a month earlier. He had no money, but he knew how to blag. For a few days he'd dressed himself up as Charlie Chaplin and become a living statue, miming for tourists in the vicinity of San Zaccaria and earning enough from the coins they threw into his tin to keep himself fed and watered. But he'd hated standing still and after a few hours even the narcissistic pleasure of posing for photographs began to pall. One afternoon, taking a break in a cheap pizzeria, he'd fallen into conversation with Lucia when she served him with a capuccino. She was a stranger in the city as well; she'd left her native Taormina after the death of her parents and drifted around the country ever since. What they had in common was that neither of them could settle to anything. That night she'd taken him to her room in Dorsoduro and he'd stayed with her ever since.

"Excellent!" Sanborn applauded as he refilled his new young friend's glass. "What is your profession?"

Joly said he was still searching for something to which he would care to devote himself, body and soul. After uni, he'd drifted around. His degree was in English, but a career in teaching or the civil service struck him as akin to living death. He liked to think of himself as a free spirit, but he enjoyed working with his hands and for six months he'd amused himself as a puppeteer, performing for children's parties and at municipal fun days. When that became wearisome, he'd drifted across the Channel. He'd spent three months in France, twice as long in Spain, soon he planned to try his luck in Rome.

"I wondered about learning a trade as a boat-builder, I spent a day in the *squero* talking to a man who builds gondolas." He risked a cheeky glance at Zuichini's profile. "I even thought about making masks . . ."

"An over-subscribed profession in this city," Sanborn interrupted. "I understand why you didn't pursue it."

"Well, who knows? One of these days, I may come back here to try my luck."

"You have family?"

"My parents are dead, my sister emigrated to Australia where she married some layabout who looked like a surf god. So I have no ties, I can please myself."

"And your girlfriend?" Sanborn asked. "Any chance of wedding bells?"

Joly couldn't help laughing. Not the effect of the wine, heady though it was, but the very idea that he and Lucia might have a future together. She was a pretty *prima donna*, only good for one thing, and although he didn't say it, the contemplative look in Sanborn's pale grey eyes made it clear that he'd got the message.

"You and she must join us for dinner, be my guests, it would be a pleasure."

"Oh, no, really, we couldn't impose . . ."

Sanborn dismissed the protestations with a flick of his hand. He was old and deliberate and yet Joly recognized this was a man accustomed to getting his own way. "Please. I insist. I know a little seafood restaurant, they serve food so wonderful you will never forget it. Am I right, Zuichini?"

The wizened man cackled and nodded. A wicked gleam lit his small eyes.

"Well, I'm not sure . . ."

But within a couple of minutes it was agreed and Joly stumbled out into the glare of the sun with the American's good wishes ringing in his ears. Zuichini's small, plague-mask head merely nodded farewell; he'd uttered no more than two dozen words in the space of half an hour. Joly blinked, unaccustomed to wine that hit so hard; but the pleasure was worth the pain.

When he met up with Lucia, she made a fuss about the dinner. It was in her nature to complain; she regarded it as a duty not to agree to anything he suggested without making him struggle.

"With two old men? Why would we wish to do this? After tomorrow we will be apart, perhaps for ever. Are you tired with me already?"

Exaggeration was her stock-in-trade, but he supposed she was right and that they would not see each other again after he left the city. The plan was for him to travel to Rome and for her to join him there in a fortnight's time when she'd received her month's pay from the restaurant. He'd arranged it like that so there was an opportunity for their relationship to die a natural death. He hated break-up scenes. It would be so easy for them not to get together again in the Eternal City. If he wanted to return to Venice, he would rather do so free from encumbrances; there were plenty more fish in the sea. As for their argument, in truth she found the prospect of a slap-up meal at a rich man's expense as appealing as he did and after twenty minutes she stopped grumbling and started to deliberate about what she might wear.

They went back to her place and made love and by the time she'd dressed up for the evening, he could tell she was relishing the prospect of meeting someone new. Even if the men were old, she would love parading before them; admiration turned her on more than anything exotic he tried with her in bed. At first he'd found her delightful, he'd even managed to persuade himself that she might have hidden depths. But in truth Lucia was as shallow as the meanest canal in the city.

Against his expectations, the dinner was a success, early awkwardness and stilted conversation soon smoothed by a rich, full-blooded and frighteningly expensive red wine. Sanborn, in a fresh white suit, did most of the talking. Zuichini remained content to let his patron speak for him, occupying himself with a lascivious scrutiny of the ample stretches of flesh displayed by Lucia's little black dress. Her ankle tattoo, a small blue heart, had caught the American's eye.

"In honour of young Joly?" he asked, with an ostentatious twinkle.

Lucia tossed her head. "I had it done in Sicily, the day of my sixteenth birthday. The first time I fell in love."

"It is as elegant and charming as the lady whom it adorns." Sanborn had a habit of giving a little bow whenever he paid a compliment. "Take a look, Zuichini, do you not agree?"

The wizened man leaned over to study the tattoo. His beak twitched in approval; the gleam in his dark eyes was positively sly. Even Lucia blushed under his scrutiny.

Sanborn said smoothly, "I have long admired the tattooist's art and your heart is a fine example."

Lucia smiled prettily. "Thank you, Mr Sanborn."

"Darius, please. I like to think we are friends."

"Darius, of course."

She basked in the glow of his genial scrutiny. Joly broke off a piece of bread and chewed hard. He was revising his opinion about their host's sexual orientation. Perhaps the old goat fancied trying his luck once Joly had left town. Fair enough, he was welcome to her.

"Do you know, Zuichini, I rather think that young Lucia's heart is as elegant as Sophia's dove. What do you say?"

The bookbinder paused in the act of picking something from his teeth and treated Lucia to a satyr's grin. "Uh-huh, I guess."

He didn't speak much English and his accent was a weird pastiche American. Perhaps he'd picked it up from watching old movies. His idea of a matinee idol was probably Peter Lorre. Why did Sanborn spend so much time with him, if they were not lovers, past or present? Joly asked if Sophia was Sanborn's daughter.

"Good heavens, no. Alas, like you, I have no family. Sophia was a young lady whom Zuichini and I came to know – what? – two or three years ago. She worked behind a bar down the Via Garibaldi. We were both very fond of her. And she had this rather lovely neck tattoo, in the shape of a flying dove with broad, outstretched wings. As with Lucia's lovely heart, I have no doubt that it was carved by a gifted artist."

"You admire well-made creations?" Lucia asked, preening.

Sanborn patted her lightly on the hand. "Indeed I do, my dear. My tastes are not confined to fine books, although my collection is the most precious thing I possess."

"Tell us more," Joly said, as the food arrived.

Over the meal, Sanborn told them a little about his life. He'd inherited money – his grandfather had been president of an oil company – and he'd devoted years to travelling the world and indulging his taste for curios. Although he had never visited Venice until he was fifty years old, as he sailed into the lagoon and drank in the sights from the Bacino di San Marco, he resolved to make the city his home. By the sound of it, he lived in some grand *palazzo* overlooking the Canal Grande, and kept his income topped up with the rent from apartments that he'd been wise enough to buy up as the years passed. For all the talk of flooding, you could make good money on property in the city. Demand would always exceed supply.

"I always had a love of books, though it was not until I met Zuichini here that I started to collect in earnest. Are you a reader, Lucia, my dear?"

She shook her head. "No, I am too young. I tell this to Joly. He is of an age where there should be no time to read. He should live a bit."

"Well, books are not simply a delight for desiccated old rascals like me or Zuichini here You must not be hard on your young man. Seems to me he does pretty well for himself, living the *dolce vita* on a budget while indulging in old books when-ever he finds a moment to spare."

Joly caught Zuichini peering down the front of Lucia's dress. Their eyes met briefly and the little man gave his toothless smile. Perhaps even he would find time to break off from binding books if only he could spend a night with Lucia. It wouldn't happen, though, unless Sanborn was in a mood to share. Joly savoured his swordfish. He didn't care. The Amer-ican was welcome to her. If he showered her with money and presents, there was little doubt that Lucia would be content to do his bidding until she got bored. She'd confided in Joly that

she'd worked in a lap dancing club in Milan and finished up
living with the man who owned the joint. He was something
high up in the Mafia, but after a few weeks he'd tired of her
complaining and she'd managed to escape him without a
scratch. Joly reckoned there wasn't much she wasn't willing
to do, provided the price was right.

He felt his eyelids drooping before Sanborn snapped knob-
bly, arthritic fingers and asked the waiter to bring coffee. Before
he knew what was happening, Lucia had accepted Sanborn's
offer that they dine together again as his guests the following
night. He didn't object – it was a free meal, and who cared if
Sanborn was a dirty old man with an ulterior motive? Already
he had spent enough time in the American's company to know
that he was both persuasive and determined. If he wanted to
spend his money, if Lucia wanted to sell her favours, who was
Joly to stand in their way?

Sanborn insisted on paying a gondolier to take them back to a
landing stage not far from Lucia's apartment. On the way home,
she prattled about how wonderful the American was. Joly knew
it was unwise to argue, but in the end he couldn't resist pointing
out that she was the one who had been unwilling to waste her
evening in the company of two old men. Now she had committed them to a repeat, on his very last night in the city, when
he would have preferred them to be alone.

"And you would have been able to match Darius's hospitality? I do not think so, Joly."

The next day was even hotter. Lucia went out to work early
on and was intent on shopping during the afternoon. After
lunching on a ham sandwich – no point in spoiling his appetite
for the evening's feast – Joly embarked on a last stroll around
the gardens of Castello. Finding a seat beneath a leafy tree, he
finished *Death in Venice*, then ambled back through the alleyways, absorbing the smells of the fish-sellers' stalls and the
chocolate shops, wondering how long it would be before he
returned to La Serenissima. He understood what had kept
Sanborn here. Once you became intoxicated with the beauties
of Venice, the rest of the world must seem drab by comparison.
But he was keen to sample Rome and after the previous night,
he was more than ever convinced that this was the right time to
make a break with Lucia. Sanborn was welcome to her.

When he arrived back at the flat, Lucia was short-tempered in the way that he now associated with her rare attacks of nervousness. She was bent upon impressing Sanborn, and she'd bought a slinky new red dress with a neckline so daring it bordered on indecent. It must have cost her a month's wages. A carefully targeted investment – assuming she had footed the bill, that was. Joly wondered if she'd met up with Sanborn during the day and managed to charm the cash out of him. He wouldn't put it past either of them. So what? It was none of his business; soon he would be out of here.

The American and his sidekick were waiting for them at the appointed time, sitting at a table inside a restaurant close to Rialto. Sanborn's suit tonight was a shade of pale cream. Zuichini was scruffy by comparison, his face more reminiscent of a scary carnival mask than ever.

"Lucia, you look dazzling!"

Sanborn kissed her on both cheeks and Zuichini did likewise. Joly had never seen the bookbinder show such animation. The little dark eyes seemed to be measuring Lucia's tanned flesh, no doubt wondering what she might look like when wearing no clothes. His attention pleased her. Perhaps she was hoping the two old men would fight over her. Even the waiter who took their order allowed his gaze to linger on her half-exposed breasts for longer than was seemly. The restaurant specialized in finest beef steak and Sanborn ordered four bottles of Bollinger.

"Tonight we celebrate!" he announced. "Over the past twenty four hours, we have become firm friends. And although Joly is to move on tomorrow, with the lovely Lucia to follow, it is my firm conviction that all four of us will be reunited before too long."

As their glasses clinked, Lucia's eyes were glowing. While they ate, the conversation turned to Joly's plans. He made it clear that they remained fluid. It was his style, he said, to trust to luck. Sanborn challenged this, arguing that even a young man needed roots.

"Learn from my mistake, Joly. Until I discovered the wonders of this marvellous city, my life lacked direction. You need something to anchor your existence. A place, firm friends, perhaps a trade."

Zuichini nodded with unaccustomed animation. "Right. That is right."

"Listen to this good man. He knows the joys of a craft, the unique pleasure that comes with creation. This is where you can steal a march on me, Joly. I am proud of my collection of books, undeniably, but I have never experienced the delight of creating a masterpiece of my own. I cannot paint, or compose, or write to any level of acceptable competence. I lack skills of a practical nature. But you, my young friend, are different. If you were to put your talents to good purpose . . ."

"I have an idea!" Lucia clapped her hands. Champagne went to her head. After a single glass, already she was raising her voice and her skin was flushed. "Once you have seen Rome, you could come back here and train as Zuichini's apprentice!"

The plague doctor's face split in a horrid smile, while Sanborn exclaimed with delight. "Perfect! There, Joly, you have your answer. How clever you are, Lucia. That way two birds could be killed with one stone. Joly would learn from a master at the height of his powers, and Zuichini would have a good man to whom he could pass on the tricks of his trade before it is too late." Sanborn lowered his voice. "And there is something else that I have omitted to mention. Zuichini, may I? You see, Joly. This good fellow here, as you may have notice, is afflicted by a dreadful malady. Parkinson's attacks the nervous system and he has been suffering stoically for some time. But it becomes increasingly difficult for him to work. An utter tragedy, sometimes I despair. Not only because Zuichini's disability saddens me, but also from a selfish motive. For who will succeed him in business, who will practise his very special skills, so as to keep me supplied in fine books? In you, perhaps I have found the answer to my prayers."

"I don't think so," Joly said slowly.

"Oh, but you must!" Lucia exclaimed. "Such an opportunity, to learn from a genius!"

Sanborn must have primed her with this idea and asked her to offer support. They'd met during the day, not only so that Sanborn could pay for the new dress. The American was, Joly thought, like the most demanding parent. He wanted to have the young folk beholden to him, at his beck and call and used his control of the purse strings to make sure they did not escape.

"I suppose I can mull it over, when I am in Rome."

He'd expected Sanborn to suggest that he abandoned his trip, but the old man surprised him, giving a broad smile and murmuring that he could not say fairer than that. Zuichini went so far as to give him a playful punch on the shoulder.

"Good apprentice, yes?"

While Joly tucked into the succulent beef, Sanborn talked about the art of binding books. He spoke of the pouch binding of Japanese books and the unique technique of *nakatoji*, of Jean Groller's leather-bound tomes covered with intricate geometric paterns, inlaid with coloured enamels and books bound in the flayed skin of murderers and highwaymen. He told them about cheverell, a goatskin parchment transformed into a binding both supple and strong with a bold, grainy pattern, popular in Italy during the fourteenth century, he described methods of fatliquoring leather, he explained . . .

"Joly, wake up!"

He became aware of Lucia's sharp elbow, digging into his side. Sanborn was beaming at him like a benevolent uncle, surveying a favourite nephew who has overdone the Christmas pudding. Zuichini was savouring his wine, still casting the occasional frank glance at Lucia's ample cleavage.

"Sorry, must have dropped off."

"Please do not apologize, I beg you," Sanborn said. "Put your sleepiness down to a combination of the wine and the weather. Perhaps accompanied by a tinge of *tristesse* – am I right, young man? This is your last night in La Serenissima for a little while and who could fail to experience a *frisson* of regret at departing from here?" He refilled their glasses, taking no notice when Joly shook his head. "So let us drink to our good friend Joly, and express the sincere hope that soon he will be back here for good!"

He reached out and patted Joly's arm. Blearily, Joly tried to focus on how to interpret the old man's behaviour. His hand did not linger. Had it been unfair to impute to him some sexual motive for such generosity? Perhaps in truth Sanborn's generosity did not amount to anything out of the ordinary. For a rich man, the cost of a couple of meals and a few bottles of fine wine was small change. Was it possible that Sanborn was no more than he seemed, a lonely old millionaire, keen to share the company of the young and beautiful, as well as that of his ailing friend, and that he had no ulterior motive at all?

Sanborn made some remark and Lucia laughed long and loud, a noise that reminded Joly of a workman drilling in the road. She had a good head for drink, Joly knew that from experience, but even she was beginning to lose control. He remembered her telling him about her last night with the Mafia boss. She'd plucked up the courage to put a small knife in her bag. If he'd attacked her, she'd steeled herself to fight for her life. Joly did not doubt the strength of her survival instinct. If she thought herself threatened, she would lash out without a moment's hesitation. What would happen if Zuichini made her afraid with the clumsiness of his overtures?

He yawned. His head was spinning and he couldn't keep worrying about what might happen between consenting adults. *Que sera, sera.*

Next thing he knew, someone was tapping him on the arm. Through the fog of a hangover, he heard Sanborn's gentle voice.

"Joly, my boy. Are you all right?"

Even the act of opening his eyes made him want to cry out, it hurt so much. Christ, how much had he drunk? He had no head for champagne, but he'd never felt this bad before. He blinked hard and tried to take in his surroundings. He was lying on a hard bed in a small, musty room. The sun was shining in through a small high window but he had no idea where he might be. Sanborn was standing beside the bed, arms folded, studying him. Suddenly, he felt afraid.

"Where am I?"

"Listen, my friend, you have nothing to fear. You just had rather too much to drink, that's all."

"The drinks were spiked." Nothing else could explain how he had come to black out; this had never happened to him before.

"No, no, no." Sanborn had a first-class bedside manner, though Joly was sure he was lying. "You overdid it, simple as that. And you threw up all over Lucia, which frankly wasn't such a good idea."

"Lucia?" He gazed at the peeling wallpaper, the unfamiliar cupboard and door. "Where have you brought me?"

"Listen, it's all right. Lucia was upset, that's all. Zuichini took care of her, no need to worry. As she wouldn't entertain you in her bed last night, I volunteered to bring you here. Now, you need to get up and dressed. I think you said you plan to take the one o'clock coach from Piazzale Roma?"

A wave of panic engulfed him. Effectively, he was the old man's prisoner.

"You haven't told me where you've brought me."

"There's no secret, Joly, keep your hair on, my dear fellow. This is an apartment I bought six months ago. Hardly the lap of luxury, but it's only a stone's throw from the restaurant. It seemed like the best solution. We could hardly leave you to your own devices, the state you were in, and Lucia was in no mood to take you back with her."

Joly coughed. "Then – I'm free to go?"

Sanborn's parchment features conveyed benign bewilderment. "I don't understand. Why should you not be? I was only striving to do you a good turn."

I've been a fool, Joly thought, this isn't a man to fear. The question is – what happened between Lucia and Zuichini? Did he try it on, did she let him get away with it?

"Sorry, Darius. I'm not myself."

"Not to worry, these things happen. There's a bathroom next door. No gold taps, I'm afraid, but you'll find the basic necessities. I'll leave you to it, if I may. Your bag's over by the door, incidentally. I went over to Lucia's this morning to pick it up."

"Thanks," Joly whispered.

"Here's the key to the front door. Would you be kind enough to lock up for me? I have a little business to attend to, but I'll be there at the coach station to see you off. It's the least I can do."

Joly stared at the old man's genial expression. Hoarsely, he said, "Thanks."

"Think nothing of it. That's what friends are for, don't you agree?"

Two hours later, Joly arrived at the Piazzale Roma, bag in hand. Within moments he caught sight of Sanborn by an advertisement hoarding and the American lifted his stick in greeting before limping to greet him. He had a black velvet bag slung over his shoulder.

"You're looking much better. Remarkable what wonders can be worked by a simple wash and brush up."

"I'm very grateful to you," Joly said humbly, handing over the key to the apartment.

"Think nothing of it." Sanborn cleared his throat. "Actually, I talked to Lucia before I made my way over here. There isn't an easy way to put this, Joly, but I don't believe she has any intention of joining you in Rome. I'm sorry."

Joly took a breath. "Maybe things had run their course."

Sanborn bowed his head. "That was rather the impression that I had gained. Well, I don't care for prolonged farewells. I hope you will reflect on our conversation last night and that soon we shall see you again in La Serenissima."

Forcing a smile, Joly said, "Who knows, I might take Zuichini up on his kind offer. There are worse ways of making a living than binding fine books, I guess."

A light flared in Sanborn's old eyes. Voice trembling, he said, "Joly, the moment I first saw you, I knew you were made of the right stuff. In fact, I'll let you into a secret. I'd seen you a couple of times at the Campo Santi Apostoli before I made so bold as to introduce myself."

"Is that so?" Joly didn't know whether to be puzzled or flattered. "So did you see Lucia as well?"

"As a matter of fact, I did. Such a pretty creature, with that gorgeous dark hair and honey skin. Oh, well, there are many more lovely girls in Venice. Despite my age, I can guess how sad you must feel. I felt the same about my friend Sophia, after I'd talked to her for the last time. But she and I were not lovers; the physical loss makes it doubly hard for you."

"These things happen."

"Yes, life goes on. And you will never forget Lucia, of that I am sure. But your life will be so much richer if you take up Zuichini's offer. Truly, his craftsmanship is unique. Think of it! You could follow in his footsteps. Make a name for yourself and earn a not inconsiderable fortune."

"Is Zuichini rich?"

"My dear fellow, do not be deceived by appearances. If – no, *when* you return, you will have a chance to visit his splendid home near the Rialto. Even though he and I are close associates, he never fails to drive a hard bargain. But I, and others like me, are willing to pay for the best. For something unique."

They shook hands and Sanborn pulled out of his shoulder bag a parcel wrapped in gift paper. He thrust it at Joly.

"I want you to have this. A token of our friendship. And a reminder of the esoteric pleasures that lie in store, should you accept Zuichini's offer to help you learn his trade."

"Thanks." Joly's cheeks were burning. He'd harboured so many false suspicions and now he couldn't help feeling a mite embarrassed. "I'm not sure that bookbinding is . . ."

"Think about it. That's all I ask." Sanborn smiled. "I have seen enough of you in a short space of time to be confident that you would relish the chance to become a craftsman in your own right. As you told me, you have a taste for the unusual. And with your love of books . . ah well, you must be going. Goodbye, my friend. Or as I should say, *arrivederci*."

Joly found himself waving at the old man's back as he limped away. At the notice board, just before he moved out of sight, Sanborn raised his stick in salute, but he did not turn his head. The bus was waiting and Joly found himself a seat by the window. As the driver got into gear, Joly tore the wrapping paper from his present. He stared at it for a long time.

The present was a book, carefully protected by bubble wrap and old newspapers and that came as no surprise. The title was *A Short Treatise on the Finer Points of Bookbinding*. But it was not the text that seized Joly's attention, though deep down he knew already that, one day, this would become his Bible.

The front cover was tanned and polished to a smooth golden brown. He'd never come across anything quite like it. To the touch, it had slight bumps, like a soft sandpaper. The spine and back cover felt more like suede. But what entranced him was not the texture of the binding.

At first sight, he thought the cover bore a logo. But with a second glance, he realized his mistake. In the bottom corner was a design in blue-black. A picture of a flying dove, with broad outstretched wings.

He held his breath as he recalled kissing Lucia's toes. Recalled the delicate heart shape traced in ink upon her ankle. Recalled, with a shiver of fear and excitement, Zuichini's admiration of the tattooist's work, the way those dark and deadly little eyes kept being drawn to Lucia's tender, honey-coloured skin.

He settled back on the hard seat. The countryside was passing by outside, but he paid it no heed. Sanborn understood him better than he understood himself. After searching for so long, he'd finally found what he was looking for. Soon he would return to La Serenissima. And there Zuichini would share with him the darkest secrets of the bookbinder's craft. He would teach him how to make the book that Sanborn craved, a book for all three of them to remember Lucia by.

TROUBLE IS A LONESOME TOWN

Cathi Unsworth

Dougie arrived at the concourse opposite the station just half an hour after it had all gone off. He'd had the cab driver drop him down the end of Gray's Inn Road, outside a pub on the corner there, where he'd made a quick dive into the gents to remove the red hood he'd been wearing over the black one, pulled on a Burberry cap he'd had in his bag so that the visor was down over his eyes. That done, he'd worked his way through the mass of drinkers, ducked out of another door and walked the rest of the way to King's Cross.

The Adidas bag he gripped in his right hand held at least twenty grand in cash. Dougie kind of wished it was handcuffed to him; so paranoid was he about letting go of it even for a second that he'd had trouble just putting it on the floor of the taxi between his feet. He'd wanted it to be on his knee, in his arms, more precious than a baby. But Dougie knew that above all else, now, he had to look calm, unperturbed. Not like a man who'd just ripped off a clip joint and left a man for dead on a Soho pavement.

That's why he'd had the idea of making the rendezvous at the Scottish Restaurant across the road from the station. He'd just blend in with the other travellers waiting for their train back up North, toting their heavy bags, staring at the TV with blank, gormless expressions as they pushed stringy fries smothered in luminous ketchup into their constantly moving mouths. The way he was dressed now, like some hood rat, council estate born and bred, he'd have no trouble passing amongst them.

He ordered his quarterpounder and large fries, with a super-size chocolate lard shake to wash it all down, eyes wandering around the harshly lit room as he waited for it all to land on his red plastic tray. All the stereotypes were present and correct. The fat family (minus dad, natch) sitting by the window, mother and two daughters virtually indistinguishable under the layers of flab and identical black-and-white hairstyles by Chavettes of Tyneside to match the colours of their footie team. The solitary male, a lad of maybe ten years and fifteen stone, staring sullenly out of the window through pinhole eyes, suck-ing on the straw of a soft drink that was only giving him back rattling ice cubes. On the back of his shirt read his dreams: 9 SHEARER. But he was already closer to football than foot-baller.

Then there was the pimp and his crack whore; a thin black man sat opposite an even thinner white woman with bruises on her legs and worn-down heels on her boots. Her head bowed like she was on the nod, while he, all angles and elbows and knees protruding from his slack jeans and oversize Chicago Bulls shirt, kept up a steady monologue of abuse directed at her curly head. The man's eyes were as rheumy as a 70-year-old's, and he sprayed fragments of his masticated fries out as he kept on his litany of insults. Sadly for Iceberg Slim, it looked like the motherfuckingbitchhocuntcocksucker he was railing at had already given up the ghost.

Oblivious to the psychodrama, the Toon Army had half of the room to themselves, singing and punching the air, reliving moment-by-moment the two goals they'd scored over Spurs – well, thank fuck they had, wouldn't like to see this lot disap-pointed. They were vile enough in victory, hugging and clasping at each other with tears in their eyes, stupid joker's hats askew over their gleaming red faces; they might as well have been bumming each other, which was obviously what they all wanted.

Yeah, Dougie liked to get down among the filth every now and again, have a good wallow. In picking over the faults of others he could forget about the million and one he had of his own.

Handing over a fiver to the ashen bloke behind the counter, who had come over here thinking nothing could be worse than Romania, Dougie collected his change and parked himself inconspicuously in the corner. Someone had left a copy of *The Scum* on his table. It was a bit grubby and he really would have preferred to use surgical gloves to touch it, but it went so perfectly with his disguise and the general ambience of the joint that he forced himself. Not before he had the bag firmly wedged between his feet, however, one of the handles round his ankle so if anyone even dared to try . . .

Dougie shook his head and busied himself instead by arranging the food on his plastic tray in a manner he found pleasing: the fries tipped out of their cardboard wallet into the half of the Styrofoam container that didn't have his burger in. He opened the ketchup so that he could dip them in two at a time, between mouthfuls of burger and sips of chocolate shake. He liked to do everything methodically.

Under the headline STITCHED UP, the front page of *The Scum* was tirelessly defending the good character of the latest batch of rapist footballers who'd all fucked one girl between the entire team and any of their mates who fancied it. Just so as they could all check out each other's dicks while they did it, Dougie reckoned. That sort of shit turned his stomach almost as much as the paper it was printed on, so he quickly flipped the linen over, turned to the racing pages at the back. That would keep his mind from wandering, reading all those odds, totting them all up in his head, remembering what names went with what weights and whose colours. All he had to do now was sit tight and wait. Wait for Lola.

Lola.

Just thinking about her name got his fingertips moist, got little beads of sweat breaking out on the back of his neck. Got a stirring in his baggy sweat pants so that he had to look up sharply and fill his eyes with a fat daughter chewing fries with her mouth open and to get it back down again.

Women didn't often have this effect on Dougie. Only two, so far, in his life. And he'd gone further down the road with this one than anyone else before.

He could still remember the shock he felt when he first saw her, when she sat herself down next to him at the bar with a tired sigh and asked for a whisky and soda. He caught the slight inflection in her accent, as if English wasn't her first language, but her face was turned away from him. A mass of golden brown curls bobbed on top of her shoulders, she had on a cropped leopardskin jacket and hipster jeans, a pair of pointy heels protruding from the bottom, wound around the stem of the barstool. The skin on her feet was golden brown too; mixed race she must have been and, for a minute, Dougie thought he knew what she would look like before she turned her head, somewhere between Scary Spice and that bird off *Holby City*. An open face, pretty and a bit petulant. Maybe some freckles over the bridge of her nose.

But when she did turn to him, cigarette dangling between her lips and long fingers wound around the short, thick glass of amber liquid, she looked nothing so trite as "pretty".

Emerald green eyes fixed him from under deep lids, fringed with the longest dark lashes he had ever seen. Her skin was flawless, the colour of the whisky in her glass, radiating that same intoxicating glow.

For a second he was taken back to a room in Edinburgh a long time ago. An art student's room, full of draped scarves and fake Tiffany lamps and a picture on the wall of Marlene Dietrich in *Blue Angel*. This woman looked strangely like Marlene. Marlene with an afro. *Black Angel*.

She took the cigarette from between her red lips and asked: "Could you give me a light?" Her glittering eyes held his brown ones in a steady gaze, a smile flickered over her perfect lips.

Dougie fumbled in the sleeve of his jacket for his Zippo and fired it up with shaking fingers. Black Angel inhaled deeply, closing her bronze-coloured eyelids as she sucked that good smoke down, blowing it out again in a steady stream.

Her long lashes raised and she lifted her glass to him simultaneously. "Cheers!" she said and he caught that heavy inflection again. Was he going mad, or did she even sound like Marlene too? "Ach," she tossed back her mane of curls, "it's so good to be off vork!"

"I'll drink to that," Dougie said, feeling like his tongue was too big for his head, his fingers were too big for his hands, that he was entirely too big and clumsy. He slugged down half his pint of Becks to try and get some kind of equilibrium, stop this weird, teenage feeling that threatened to paralyze him under the spell of those green eyes.

She looked amused.

"What kind of work do you do?" she asked.

Dougie gave his standard reply. "Och, you know. This an' that."

It pleased her, this answer, so she continued to talk. Told him in that smoky, laconic drawl all about the place she worked. One of the clip joints off Old Compton Street, the ones specifically geared up to rip off the day trippers.

"It izz called Venus in Furs," she told him. "Is fucking tacky shit, yeah?"

He started to wonder if she was Croatian, or Serbian. Most of the girls pouring into Soho now were supposed to be ones kidnapped from the former Yugoslavia. "Slavic" was a word that suited the contours of her cheeks, the curve of her green eyes. But how could that be? Dougie didn't think there was much of a black population in Eastern Europe. And he couldn't imagine anyone having the balls to kidnap this one. Maybe she was here for a different reason.

Images raced through his mind. Spy films, Checkpoint Charlie, the Cold War. High on her accent, he didn't really take the actual words in.

Until at some point close to dawn, she lifted a finger and delicately traced the outline of his jaw. "I like you Dougie," she smiled. "I vill see you here again, yes?"

Dougie wasn't really a one for hanging out in drinking clubs. He had only been in this one because earlier that evening he'd had to have a meet in Soho and he couldn't stand any of the pubs round there. Too full, too noisy, too obvious. This was one of the better places. Discreet, old fashioned, not really the sort of place your younger generation would go for, it was mainly populated by decaying actors skulking in a dimly lit world of memory. It was an old luvvie who'd first shown him the place. An old luvvie friend of a friend who'd been ripped off for all his Queen Anne silver and a collection of Penny Blacks by the mercenary young man he'd been silly enough to invite back for a nightcap. Dougie had at least got the silver back, while the guy was sleeping off what he'd spent the proceeds of the stamps on. He really didn't come here often, but as he watched the woman slip off her stool and shrug on her furry jacket he felt a sudden pang and asked: "Wait a minute – what's your name?"

She smiled and said: "It's Lola. See you again, honey." And then she was gone.

Dougie found himself drifting back to the club the next evening. It was weird, because he'd kept himself to himself for so long he'd felt like his heart was a hard, cold stone that no one could melt. It was best, he had long ago told himself, not to form attachments in his line of work. Attachments could trip you up. Attachments could bring you down. It was better that no one knew him outside his small circle of professional contacts and the clients they brought. Safer that way. He'd done six months time as a teenager, when he was stupid and reckless and had vowed he'd never be caught that way again.

He was mulling over all these facts as he found himself sat at the bar. He didn't quite know what he thought he was doing there, just that he felt his heart go each time the buzzer went and a new group of people clattered down the steps. Lola had come into the place alone. He supposed he could ask the Guv'nor what he knew about her, but that didn't seem very gentlemanly. After all, he wasn't a regular himself. Who knew how long she'd been making her way down here after the grind of an evening "huzzling the schmucks" under Venus' neon underskirts?

At half past one she had wound her way down the stairs towards him. A smile already twitching at the corners of her mouth, she was pleased to see him. One look up her long, bare, perfect legs to her leather miniskirt and that same leopard jacket and he felt the same.

"He-*looo*, Dougie," she said.

Dougie felt drunk, as he had ever since.

Gradually, over whisky and sodas with the ice crinkling in the glass, she'd told him her story. It was all very intriguing. Her father was Russian, she said, ex-KGB, who since the fall of Communism had managed to create an empire for himself in electronic goods. He was a thug, but a charming one – he had named her after a character in a Raymond Chandler book that he'd read, contraband, as a teenager. They had a lot of money, but he was very strict. Made her study hard and never go out. There was not a lot of emotion between him and her mother.

Her mother was an oddity, a Somalian. Lola didn't know how they met, but she suspected. Back in the old days, it was quite possible her father had bought her out of semi-slavery in a Moscow brothel. Her mother always claimed she was a princess, but she was also a drunk, so what was Lola to believe? She was beautiful, that was for sure. Beautiful and superstitious, always playing with a deck of strange cards and consulting patterns in tea leaves. She might have mastered dark arts, but never managed to speak Russian – probably she never wanted to. So Lola grew up speaking two languages, in one big, empty apartment in Moscow.

Right now, she was supposed to be in Switzerland. She looked embarrassed when she told Dougie this. "At finishing school. Can you believe? Vot a cliché." Lola had done a bunk six months ago. She'd crossed Europe, taking cash-in-hand work as she did, determined to get to London. She wanted to escape while she was in the "free West" rather than go back to what she knew would be expected of her in Russia. Marriage to some thick, bastard son of one of her father's ex-comrades. A life of looking nice and shutting up, just like her mother.

But she feared her father's arm was long. There were too many Russians in London already. Someone was bound to rat her out before long, the reward money would be considerable. So she had to get together a "travelling fund" and find some-where else to go. Somewhere safe.

"Vere are you from, Dougie?" she purred. "Not from round here, eh?"

"What do you reckon?" he said archly. "Where d'you think I got a name like Dougie from, heh?"

Lola laughed, put her finger on the end of his nose.

"You are from Scotland, yes?"

"Aye," nodded Dougie.

"Where in Scotland?"

"Edinburgh."

"Vot's it like in Edinburgh?"

A warning voice in Dougie's head told him not to even give her that much. This story she had spun for him, it sounded too much like a fairytale. She was probably some down-on-her-luck

Balkans hooker looking for a sugar daddy. No one could have had the lifestyle she described. It was too far-fetched, too mental.

The touch of her finger stayed on the end of his nose. Her green eyes glittered under the optics. Before Dougie knew what he was doing, words were coming out of his mouth.

She had given him the germ of an idea. The rest he filled in for himself.

The Venus In Furs was not run by an established firm, even by Soho standards. Its ostensible owners were a bunch of chancy Jamaican wide boys whose speciality was taking over moody drinking dens by scaring the incumbents into thinking that they were Yardies. Dougie doubted that that was the case. They could have been minor players, vaguely connected somehow, but Yardie lands were South of the river. Triads and Micks ran Soho. He doubted these fellas would last long in the scheme of things anyway, so he decided to help Lola out and give fate a hand.

Trying to help her, or trying to impress her?

It helped that her shifts were regular. Six nights a week, six till twelve. Plenty of time to observe who came and went on a routine basis. Maybe her old man really was KGB 'cos she'd already worked out the day that the Suit came in would be the significant one.

There was this office, behind the bar, where they did all their business. Three guys worked the club in a rota, always two of them there at the same time. Lynton, Neville and Little Stevie. They had a fondness for Lola, her being blood, so it was usually her they asked to bring drinks through when they had someone to impress in there. She said the room had been painted out with palm trees and a sunset, like one big Hawaiian scene.

Like everyone, Dougie thought, *playing at gangsters – they were playing* Scarface.

Once a week, a bald white guy in a dowdy brown suit came in with an attaché case. Whichever of the Brothers Grim were in at the time would make themselves scarce while he busied himself in the office for half an hour. One of them would hang at the bar, the other find himself a dark corner with one of the girls. Then the bald man would come out, speak to no one and make his own way out of the club.

Every Thursday, 8 p.m., punctual as clockwork he came.

That proved it to Dougie. The lairy Jamaicans were a front to terrify the public. The bald man collected the money for their unseen, offshore master. With his crappy suit and unassuming exterior, he was deliberately done up like a mark to blend in with the rest of the clientele.

Dougie had a couple of guys that owed him favours. They weren't known faces, and it would be difficult to trace them back to him, their paths crossed infrequently and they moved in different worlds. On two successive Thursdays, he gave them some folding and sent them in as marks. Both confirmed Lola's story, and gave him more interesting back-up on the Brothers Grim. Both weeks, it was the same pair, Little Stevie and Neville, little and large. Large Neville, a tall skinny guy with swinging dreads and shades who was always chewing on a toothpick, sat behind the bar when the bald man showed up. He practised dealing cards, played patience, drank beer and feigned indifference to the world around him, nodding all the while as if a different, slow skanking soundtrack was playing in his head to the cheesy Europop that was on the club's PA.

Little Stevie, by comparison, always grabbed himself a girl and a bottle and made his way over to the corner booth. While Neville looked like a classic stoner, Little Stevie was mean. He wore a black suit and a white shirt with thick gold chains around his bulldog neck. A pork pie hat and thick black shades totally obscured his eyes. Ocassionally, like when the girl slipped underneath the table, he would grin a dazzling display of gold and diamond dental work. Stevie always drank proper Champagne – not the pear fizz served to the punters as such – and both Dougie's contacts copped the telltale bulge in his pocket.

Stevie's booth was the one from which the whole room could be surveyed and, even while receiving special favours, he never took his eye off the game. The minute the office door clicked open and the bald man slipped away he would knee his girl off him, adjust his balls and whatever else was down there, and swagger his way back over to the office all puffed up and bristling, Neville following at his heels.

Yeah, Stevie, they all agreed, was the one to watch.

While they were in there playing punters, Dougie was watching the door.

The Venus was based in a handy spot, in a dingy alley between Rupert Street and Wardour Street. There was a market in Rupert Street and all he had to do was pretend to be examining the tourist tat on the corner stall. The bald man went the other way. Straight to a waiting cab on Wardour Street. Each time the same.

On the night it all happened, Dougie felt a rush in his blood that he hadn't felt since Edinburgh, like every platelet was singing to him the old songs, high and wild as the wind.

God, he used to love that feeling, used to let it guide him in the days when he was Dougie the Cat, the greatest burglar in that magical city of turrets and towers.

But now he was Dougie Mackingtosh Investigates, the Private Eye for the sort of people who couldn't go to the police. He had changed sides on purpose after that first prison jolt, never wanting to be in close proximity to such fucking filth ever again. If you couldn't be a gentleman thief these days, he reckoned, then why not be a Bad Guy's PI? His methods may have differed from those used by the Old Bill, but Dougie had kept his nose clean for eighteen years, built up his reputation by word of mouth and made a good living from sorting out shit without causing any fuss. Filled a proper gap in the market, he had.

His blood had never sung to him in all that time. He supposed it must have awakened in him that first night he met Lola, grown strong that night she'd finally allowed him back to her dingy flat above a bookie's in Balham, where she had so studiously drawn out the map of the Venus' interior before unzipping his trousers and taking him to a place that seemed very close to Heaven.

Bless her, he didn't need her map. He didn't even need to know what Neville and Stevie got up to, only that they were good little gangsters and stayed where they were, in that little palace of their imagination where they could be Tony Montana every day.

He wasn't going to take them on.

All he needed was the thirty seconds between the Venus' door and Wardour Street. And the curve in the alley that meant the taxi driver wouldn't be able to see. All he needed was the strength of his arm and the fleetness of his feet and the confusion of bodies packed into a Soho night.

At the end of the alley he slipped a balaclava over his head, put the blue hood over the top of that and began to run.

He was at full sprint as the bald man came out of the door, fast enough to send him flying when he bowled into his shoulder. The man's arms spread out and he dropped his precious cargo to the floor. Dougie was just quick enough to catch the look of astonishment in the pale, watery eyes, before he coshed him hard on the top of his head and they rolled up into whites. He had another second to stoop and retrieve the case before he was off again, out of the alley, across Wardour Street, where the taxi was waiting, its engine running, the driver staring straight ahead.

Dougie was already in the downstairs bogs of the Spice of Life before the cabbie was checking his watch to make sure he hadn't turned up early. Had pulled out his sports bag from the cistern where he'd stashed it and bust the lock on the attaché case by the time the cabbie turned the engine off and stepped out of the car to take a look around. Dougie's deftness of touch was undiminished by his years on the other side. He counted the bundles of cash roughly as he transferred them into his sports bag, eyebrows raising as he did. It was quite a haul for a weekly skim off a clip joint. He briefly wondered what else they had going on down there, then chased the thought away as excess trouble he didn't need to know.

By the time the cabbie was standing over the crumpled heap in the alleyway, he had put the attaché case in the cistern and taken off the blue hood, rolling it into a ball as he nipped out of the side door of the pub. He junked it in a bin as he came out onto Charing Cross Road and hailed himself a ride up to King's Cross.

Dougie looked up from his racing pages. As if struck by electrodes, he knew Lola was in the room. She walked towards him, green eyes dancing, clocking amusedly his stupid cap and the bag that lay between his feet. Sat down in front of him and breathed: "Is it enough?"

"Aye," nodded Dougie. "It's enough."

He hadn't wanted there to be any way in which Lola could be implicated in all this. He'd had her phone in sick for two days running, told her just to spend her time packing only the essentials she needed and gave her the money for two singles up to Edinburgh.

The night train back to the magic city, not even the Toon
Army could ruin that pleasure for him.

"You ready?" he asked her.

Her grin stretched languidly across her perfect face.

"Yes," she purred. "I'm ready."

Dougie gripped the Adidas bag, left his floppy fries where
they lay. As they stepped out onto the road, St Pancras was lit
up like a fairytale castle in front of them. "See that," he nudged
her shoulder, "that's bollocks compared to where we're going."

His heart and his soul sung along with his blood. He was
leaving the Big Smoke, leaving his life of shadows, stepping into
a better world with the woman he loved by his side. He took her
hand and strode towards the crossing, towards the mouth of
Kings Cross Station.

Then Lola said: "Oooh, hang on a minute. I have to get my
bag."

"You what?" Dougie was confused. "Don't you have it with
you?"

She laughed, a low, tinkling sound. "No honey, I left it just
around the corner. My friend, you know, she runs a bar there
and I didn't want to lug it around with me all day. She's kept it
safe for me, behind the bar. Don't vorry, it von't take a minute."

Dougie was puzzled. He hadn't heard about this friend or this
bar before. But, in his limited experience of women, this was
typical. Just when you thought you had a plan, they'd make
some little amendment. He guessed that was just the way their
minds worked. She leaned to kiss his cheek and whispered in his
ear: "Ve still have half an hour before the train goes."

The pub was, literally, round the corner. One of those
horrible, bland chain brewery joints heaving with overweight
office workers trying to get lucky with their sniggering secre-
taries in the last, desperate minutes before Closing Time.

He lingered by the door as Lola hailed a bored-looking
blonde behind the bar. Watched her take a small blue suitcase
from behind the bar, kiss the barmaid on each cheek and come
smilingly back towards him.

A few seconds before she reached him, her smile turned to a
mask of fear.

"Oh, shit," she said, grabbing hold of his arm and dragging
him away from the doorway. "It's fucking Steve."

"What?"

"This vay," she had his arm firmly in her grasp now, was propelling him through to the other side of the bar, towards the door marked TOILETS, cursing and talking a million miles an hour under her breath.

"Steve was standing right outside the door. I svear to God it was him. I told you, he is bad luck that one, he's voodoo, got a sixth sense – my Mama told me about *sheüt* like him. We can't let him see us! I'm supposed to be off sick the night he gets ripped off – he's gonna know! He's gonna kill me if he sees me."

"Hen, you're seeing things," Dougie tried to protest as she pushed him through the door, down some steps into a dingy basement which smelt of piss and stale vomit.

"I'm not, it vos him, it vos him!" she looked like she was about to turn hysterical, her eyes were flashing wildly and her nails were digging into his flesh. He tried to use his free hand to extricate himself from her iron grip, but that only served to make her cling on harder.

"Hen, calm down, you're hurting me . . ." Dougie began.

"There's someone coming!" she screamed and suddenly began to kiss him passionately, smothering him in her arms, grinding her teeth against his lips so that he tasted blood.

And then he heard a noise right behind him.

And the room went black.

"Fucking Hell," Lola looked down on Dougie's prone body. "That took long enough."

"I told you he was good," her companion pouted, brushing his hands on his trousers. "But I thought you'd enjoy using all your skills on him."

"Hmm," Lola bent down and prised Dougie's fingers away from the Adidas bag. "I knew this would be the hardest part. Getting money out of a tight fucking Jock."

That slinky Russian accent had disappeared like a puff of smoke. She sounded more like the petulant queen she was now.

"Come on." She stepped over her would-be Romeo and the pile of shattered ashtray glass he lay in. "Let's get out of here."

The car was parked nearby. As Lola got into the passenger seat, she pulled the honey-gold Afro wig off her head and ran her fingers through the short black fuzz underneath.

"I am *soooo* tired of that bitch," she said, tossing it into the backseat.

Her companion started the car with a chuckle.

"He fucking believed everything, didn't he?" he shook his head as he pulled out.

"Yeah . . . and you said he was a private detective. Well, let me tell you honey, you wouldn't believe what I suckered that dick with. My dad was a Russian gangster. My mother was a Somalian princess. I was on the run from Swiss finishing school. Can you believe it?"

Lola hooted with derision. "Almost like the fairytales I used to make up for myself," she added. "You know, I thought he might fucking twig when I told him I was named after a character in Raymond Chandler. But I couldn't resist it."

"Well," her companion smiled at her fondly. "You certainly made up for the loss of that Queen Anne silver. We've got enough to keep us going for months now. So where do you fancy?"

"Not back to Soho," Lola sniffed, as the car pulled into the slipstream of Marylebone Road. "I've fucking had it with those posing thugs. I know. I fancy some sea air. How does Brighton sound to you?"

"The perfect place," her companion agreed, "for a couple of actors."

Dougie came around with his face stuck to a cold stone floor with his own blood. Shards of glass covered him. He could smell the acrid stench of piss in his nostrils, and from the pub above, he could hear a tune, sounding like it was coming from out of a long tunnel of memory. He could just make out the lyrics: "*I met her in a club down in old Soho/Where you drink Champagne and it tastes like cherry cola . . .*"

In loving memory of Lee Hazlewood 1929–2007, who had all the best stories and all the best songs.

GREEN TARTS

Deryn Lake

God grant me grace, but I am getting on in years. I looked in the mirror this very morning and an old man stared back at me. I gazed at him in horror, hardly believing that I had come to this. But sooner or later we all have intimations of mortality. Thus I will do as my conscience dictates and set down a record of those times, so long ago, when a man met his death in the Tower and the part that I played in it all. As far as I can recall, if memory serves correctly, it all started with a bed.

It arrived in pieces, as was customary, and was carried up to the master bedroom by a team of servants, then handed over to the craftsmen to assemble. Watching them work, its new owner thought it a beautiful thing that grew beneath their hands; richly carved and sumptuously adorned. In fact he could hardly wait for them to finish that he might stretch out on it and measure his length on the silk cover, letting his eyes take in the marquetry panels on the headboard, created by German craftsmen, a number of whom now lived in Southwark. His gaze wandered over the elaborate carvings, one of which was a grinning satyr to represent fertility. It seemed to smile at him in a devilish manner. All in all, he thought to himself, this new bed summed up his status, his standing, his enviable position as the best-loved favourite of that most malleable of monarchs, James I.

Robert Carr, Viscount Rochford, took a step forward and touched the gorgeous draperies, presently being hung beneath the intricately carved oak tester. The workman responsible looked up.

"All right, my lord?"

"Splendid. I think this bed is going to be quite wonderful."

"It will indeed, my lord."

And tonight, thought Robert, I shall show it, totally complete, to my closest friend, Thomas Overbury. He gave a quiet sigh, thinking of the pleasures ahead, and turning, left the room.

As he went downstairs, Robert glanced admiringly at himself in a mirror. He was a handsome man, some twenty-four years of age, with long straight limbs and broad shoulders. He had a head of thick fair hair which he wore tightly frizzed as fashion dictated, meanwhile dressing himself to the inch in fine clothes and jewels, including a sparkling earring worn in his left ear. Unfortunately all this frippery made him appear effeminate, a feature which, no doubt, pleased his royal master enormously. For there could be no doubt that the King worshipped Robert – leaning on his arm, pinching his cheek, kissing him quite openly in full public gaze – a fact which the self-seeking young man positively encouraged, responding with melting looks and suggestive gestures. Yet, despite the love of King James, Robert had formed another liaison with Thomas Overbury, a bright young Englishman with literary pretensions. In fact the couple were devoted and it was Thomas who was to visit this very night.

In order to pass the time, Robert decided to have a bath, thus causing an army of servants to plod up and down stairs with pails of boiling water. After being towelled dry, he oiled himself then dressed in stockings and doublet, executed in silks and gold and silver thread. On his feet he put on a pair of low-heeled shoes, decorated with an enormous frill of black and yellow. Then, having shaved closely, a feature much admired by the King, he awaited Thomas's arrival. Quarter of an hour later, a thunderous knock announced his presence. Robert immediately assumed a negligent pose, his fingers idly toying with a book, the other hand supporting his chin. He looked up as his friend was announced.

"My dear Overbury," he said.

But once the bowing servant was out of the way, Robert hurried over and embraced the newcomer warmly, kissing him on both cheeks, then on the mouth.

Thomas disentangled himself. "You're pleased to see me, I take it."

"I always am. You know that."

His friend allowed a small smile to light his features, a fact which made him appear more attractive. Older than Carr, he was not so blatantly good looking yet it was a more intelligent face, though spoiled by an expression of arrogance. Now, though, he was anxious to please.

"Have you persuaded the King to like me any better?" he asked eagerly.

Robert pulled down his mouth. "No, I'm afraid not."

"You know why it is, don't you?"

"I think I can hazard a guess."

"Because he's jealous of me. He knows damn well that you love me better than him – and that is something the lecherous old beast cannot stomach."

Robert simpered and for a moment looked utterly feminine. "I think what you say is true. He cannot take his eyes off me, even at court."

Thomas Overbury scowled. "Besotted old fool."

"Shush. Someone might hear you."

"Let them." He turned to Robert. "Now, what is this surprise you have to show me?"

"Come upstairs. Come and see my new toy."

Somewhat mystified, Thomas followed him up the staircase to the master bedroom, Robert firmly closing the door behind him. A few minutes later came the sound of muted laughter as the two men sampled the new bed's delights.

"I am in despair," said Frances, Countess of Essex, bursting into a spectacular torrent of tears. "Oh, my dear, what am I to do?"

The dear in question was a small, comely widow with a pleasing face and hair like golden thread. But at present her expression was one of deep sympathy which did not totally become her.

"Think of it," Frances continued, not waiting for a reply. "Think of being wedded to a lanky brute who at first would not consummate the marriage and now expects me to lie with him, which I do not wish to do. And, sweet Anne, just at this stage I have received a love letter from another man."

Anne's expression changed rapidly to one of acute attention. "Really, my pet? Who?"

"You'll not believe it – the King's favourite! Robert Carr himself."

"Robert Carr? But surely he has other interests."

"So I always thought, but the letter was most ardent."

"What did it say?"

"How much he admires me and how much he would like to converse with me."

Anne shook her head. "I am surprised indeed."

Frances, who was one of the most beautiful women at court, looked very slightly annoyed. "Oh?"

"I'm just surprised that he had the courage to write," Anne answered swiftly.

"I see," answered the Countess, slightly mollified.

"I hold your heart close to mine as I hope you do to me," said Sir Thomas Overbury, dictating.

"Is that grammatically correct?" asked Robert Carr, pausing in his writing.

"Oh, to hell with grammar. It will certainly attract the attention of the silly bitch."

Robert laughed carelessly. "I don't know why I'm bothering with this."

"Oh, yes, you do. It's because you can't resist a challenge and the fact that the lady is in a loveless marriage appeals to you."

"What shall I do if she says yes?"

Overbury gave a careless shrug. "That, my dear, will be entirely up to you."

At that moment both men looked up as there was a noise in the corridor outside. They were in the royal palace at Greenwich, in Carr's apartments, but this did not guarantee them privacy.

"Hide the letter," hissed Overbury and Robert thrust it beneath a book as the door opened without ceremony and they saw, standing in the entrance, his royal majesty James.

He glanced at Thomas unsmilingly. Ever since the affair last year when both he and Carr had been caught laughing at the

Queen, any affection the King might have felt for Robert's friend had been totally banished. However, his feelings for Carr remained undiminished.

Now he said, "There you are, my lad. I would ask you to walk with me a little."

Straightening himself from his reverential bow, Carr smiled flirtatiously. "Of course, your Majesty."

Advancing on him, James lolled an arm round his favourite's neck and kissed him on the lips. Carr turned towards him as sweetly as any woman. "If I can do anything to please your Majesty."

The King's rheumy eyes had an inner fire. "We'll walk a little way first, eh, Carr?"

"As your Majesty pleases."

Ignoring Overbury the pair left the room, weak-legged James hanging round Robert's neck as though his very life depended on it. Thomas could not help but notice that the fingers of the King's other hand were fiddling round his codpiece as he shuffled out.

They met privately and for the first time in Carr's apartments in Hampton Court, he full of charm and prattling nonsense, she virtually tongue-tied. Looking at her, intending to use her as a plaything and then discard her, Robert was struck by how very good-looking she was at close quarters. Her hair, reddish-gold in colour, was frizzed out in the latest fashion with an aquamarine and pearl headdress, while her eyes – matching the stone – flashed shy but definite messages in his direction. As for her figure, he could see from her exceedingly low-cut gown that her breasts were truly beautiful. It was rumoured throughout the court that she was a virgin, a fact which stimulated Robert's wicked side with thoughts of deflowering her.

"Well, Lady Frances, how good of you to come."

"I come in response to your letters, Sir."

He had not written one of them; Thomas Overbury was responsible for them all. Thinking of the ribaldry as they had been composed, Robert felt himself flush and turned away.

"Would my Lady like some wine?"

"Yes, please, I would."

Carr poured two glasses and having handed her one, sat down in a chair opposite hers.

"You truly are bewitching," he said, speaking his thoughts aloud.

Frances pulled a face. "Much good it has done me."

"You are not happy?" asked Robert, hoping that this would start off the story of her marriage.

"No, Sir, I am not."

And that indeed released the floodgates. She spoke of her wedding to the Earl of Essex when she had been fifteen and he a few months younger, how her father had at first kept them apart but, following that, when her husband had returned from his trip abroad, he had failed dismally in the bed chamber. So much so that after a year of trying he had given up completely.

"And now?" Carr enquired.

"Now I would hate sexual connection. I dislike the Earl, may God forgive me."

"Why Madam?"

"Because he is not pleasing to look at, he cannot talk to me, and he is only happy in the company of other men." Tears filled the lovely bright eyes. "All in all, he is not a pretty fellow."

There was silence in the room and then Robert put down his glass and held out his hand. After a moment's hesitation, the Countess of Essex slowly put out hers and twined her fingers round his. They said nothing but sat quietly, simply looking at one another.

That evening Overbury, calling on his friend as usual, found him strangely withdrawn.

"Well, Robert, how did it go? Did you woo the hussy?"

"Don't call her that, I beg you."

Thomas was so shaken that he sat down abruptly. "God's life! Do I hear aright? Don't tell me that you have fallen under her spell."

Robert, looking at Thomas Overbury, noticed for the first time that the man had a spot with a head forming on his right cheek.

"Of course not," he said abruptly.

Thomas raised an eyebrow. "If I didn't know you a great deal better I would say that you are extremely interested in the girl. Well, don't be so I beg of you. The Howards are a poisonous bunch and you know perfectly well that her father loathes you."

"That is hardly her fault."

"Agreed. But I assure you that you will place yourself in great danger if you pursue this."

"Perhaps," Robert answered. He changed the subject. "Now, dear friend, would you care for some wine?"

"I'll have some Alicante."

"A favourite of his Majesty."

"Yes," said Thomas with much meaning. "Let us hope that he does not lose interest in it."

After he had gone, rather abruptly Robert thought – though he had been thankful, for once, to see the back of him – Carr lay on his bed. Over and over in his mind came the vision of the beautiful Countess, so young and so unhappy. A strange feeling came over him, one that he was quite unaccustomed to, and he wondered what could possibly be causing such an unusual sensation. Yet, despite it, he knew that she was indeed dangerous to him. And he also knew for certain that his original plan to use her as a plaything might well have to be abandoned.

Thomas Overbury was in a state of high alarm. There had been a definite change in his friend's attitude, all stemming from the time he had seen that wretched Howard girl on his own. It was a known fact that Thomas detested all the Howards – nobody, himself included, quite knowing why. Possibly, he often thought, he had been born hating them. But the fact remained, he had an obsessive private malice towards the entire family.

He had helped Robert write those silly letters to the Countess of Essex, born Lady Frances Howard, for one reason and one reason alone; to ruin her reputation and thus bring dishonour to her clan. But now it looked as if the entire scheme had blown up in his face. Could it even be possible that Robert Carr, Viscount Rochford, was falling in love with the woman? Alone in his room, Thomas seethed with silent rage.

Yet his position was assured. Robert, frankly, had neither the brains nor the will to wade through interminable papers, and having been raised to the role of Privy Councillor now sent various secret documents to Overbury for him to look over first. Yet this very power was making Thomas unpopular in certain quarters. And one quarter was extremely dangerous. The King himself had conceived a violent dislike of his favourite's best friend, a dislike which he barely bothered to conceal.

"I am deep in love," said the Countess of Essex, sighing.

"I am sure you are, my dear," replied Mrs Turner, wishing she were being paid a guinea for every time she had heard that remark.

"Yet I fear the situation," Frances continued. "If my husband should discover my association he would wreak havoc."

"But he is not a husband in the true sense of the word. Is he?" she added, a trifle uncertainly.

"Most certainly not," Frances replied roundly. "You know I hate the sight of him. And now I love Robert I could not bear to sleep with another man."

"But surely you and Carr have not . . ."

Anne Turner paused delicately and the Countess blushed. "No, not yet. But I fear – what am I saying? – I mean I hope that it won't be too long. That is why, my dear, I want you to take me to your Cunning Man. He has a fearsome reputation in dealing with matrimonial matters."

Mrs Turner nodded her blonde head. "He certainly has. He also has a reputation for taking his clients to bed." She laughed, a little nervously.

"Well, he won't get anywhere with me," Frances answered with asperity. And in that moment Anne saw her determination, her ruthlessness in achieving what she wanted regardless of the cost.

In this way Frances was introduced to Simon Forman, a man who combined the art of medicine with that of magic. An astrologer, a clairvoyant, and most of all a sympathetic listener, she begged him to make Robert Carr love her passionately and at the same time render her husband totally incapable in the bed-chamber. She also asked, though this in the greatest secrecy, that the Earl of Essex should die, thus leaving her free to marry again should she so desire.

Then, in the following spring, while still married to the lugubrious Earl, she and Robert met in secret at his house in London. She arrived by coach, heavily veiled, and was immediately shown into the salon. Awaiting her, in a frenzy of love, was the young nobleman, gorgeously attired as was customary but today not caring how he looked, determined, as he was, to get her upstairs to see his wonderful bed.

As soon as the servants had left the room he started to kiss her, wildly and voluptuously, knowing that she would weaken under such a barrage.

"Sweetheart," he said, close to her ear. "Oh, my darling, I want you so badly."

"But . . ." Frances protested half-heartedly.

"But what?"

"I am still married."

"To that miserable fool. To hell with him."

Robert was more aroused than he had ever been before. All his life he had found men more attractive than women but now he was in the throes of a desire so strong that it was barely containable. Turning Frances round he headed purposefully for the door.

"Where are you going?" she asked him

"There's only one place for us to go. To the bedroom."

"Oh, Robert, I'm afraid."

"So am I," he answered truthfully, making her laugh.

But once inside his bedchamber, the door locked safely behind them, she stared in wonderment at his beautiful bed.

"Oh, God's truth," she exclaimed. "I have never seen anything so glorious."

"Do you refer to me or my bed?" he asked, half seriously.

She moved round to face him. "Both," she said.

Afterwards, when they lay entwined, naked as on the day of their birth, she shuddered a little.

"What's the matter? Did I hurt you?"

"A bit. But it was worth every second."

"You belong to me now, Frances Essex."

"Don't call me by that name. I hate it. Call me Howard."

"But the Howards hate me," said Robert ruefully.

"One day they won't."

"It will take a magic spell to make them change their minds."

"Well, who knows, that might even happen."

Overbury was beside himself with anger. He was positive that his friend was deeply besotted with the wretched Howard woman, despite all his warnings of dire peril if Robert continued to associate with her.

"Abandon the bitch now," had become his war cry.

But he misinterpreted the situation. Robert had for the first time in his life fallen deeply in love – physically, mentally, and every other way. He now had one goal and that was to marry Frances as soon as she could obtain a divorce.

Things came to a head between the two men in the following March. Returning to his rooms in Whitehall in the small hours, having spent the evening in the embrace of Frances, Robert was horrified to find Overbury pacing up and down in the Privy Gallery through which he had to pass.

"Are you still here?" he asked angrily.

"Am I here? Where have you been?"

Brushing him aside, Carr went on his way only to have Overbury shout at him, "Will you never leave the company of that base woman?"

"I haven't seen her," muttered Robert.

"It is too manifest," Thomas screamed at him.

Carr wheeled about, his face livid, but Overbury was in full spate. "The King has bestowed great honours and gifts upon you and you overthrow yourself and all your fortunes in the company of that base woman. As you clearly intend to ruinate yourself I think it best if I have nothing further to do with you."

"So be it," growled Robert.

But Thomas was not done yet. "If you would kindly pay me the £1,500 you owe me then our obligations to one another are at an end. You must stand as you can, and I shall shift for myself. Good night to you." And he stormed off in a towering rage.

"Prick," yelled Robert at his departing back.

"The man is dangerous," said Frances when told of the incident next day.

"No, darling. Difficult perhaps, but not actually menacing."

"He might try and stop my suit for nullity going through."

"On what grounds?"

"On the grounds that you and I committed adultery, a fact which he knows well."

"It would be his word against ours."

"He would dig up other witnesses from somewhere."

Furthermore, thought Robert, Thomas Overbury has been thwarted in his love for me and will never forgive Frances as long as he lives. While Frances, unaware of what her lover was thinking, considered the fact that Thomas might yet reassert his power over Robert and send her packing.

"It would be better for all of us if the man could be spirited away," said Carr quietly.

"I could try and get someone to murder him," Frances remarked brightly.

Robert Carr, Viscount Rochford, merely laughed, thinking that she spoke in jest. But actually the Countess of Essex was in earnest, even going so far as to approach Sir David Wood – a Scotsman with a grudge against Overbury. Unfortunately he refused point blank, saying, "I might be accounted a great fool, Madam, if upon a woman's word I should go to Tyburn."

In the end it was the King himself who provided the solution. He decided that Overbury was to be offered an ambassadorship abroad, thus removing him and his potential for making trouble, yet at the same time treating him very fairly, for to be created ambassador was considered a good promotion.

Strangely, Overbury decided to be defiant. He believed that if he went overseas he would fade into obscurity. His prospects in England were far better, he argued. In view of the King's dislike of him and the fact that Carr had fallen out with him, this was very odd reasoning, to say the least. Yet Thomas would not budge, probably thinking that Carr was behind it all and wanted him out of the way. The possibility of blackmailing Robert – a difficult thing to do from a distance – had also crossed his mind.

King James was thrown into an almost uncontrollable rage by Thomas Overbury's contemptuous refusal of his offer.

"How dare that arrogant upstart treat me with such derision, Carr? You know I did this for you and I thought it a brave way of saving Overbury's face. And now the poxy pillcock has turned down my offer. I'll have him for this, mark my words."

The spittle was running down from the King's mouth, a sign that he was labouring under some great emotion. Robert, not so keen these days on giving his Majesty whorish looks and flirtatious glances, felt genuinely alarmed. Yet alongside this alarm there rose a ray of hope.

"What do you mean, Sire?"

"I'll call him before the Council and then send him to the Tower. I'll teach him to treat me with disrespect."

Robert was so overcome that he had to sit down suddenly, despite the King being present. So their problem was going to be solved for them. Overbury was to be condemned to imprisonment.

James looked at him from a little eye. "And what do you have to say to that, eh, my Carr?"

"I say good riddance."

"I think it well if you take to your bed for a few days, Robert. And when the news does come to you, plead ignorance."

"I will, Sire, never fear." And Carr kissed the royal hand more fervently that he had done for the last several months.

At long last Frances's marriage was declared null and void. But what a terrible time she had had to endure in order to obtain her objective. The entire Howard clan had been thrown into a panic when the Court of Commissioners had insisted that she be investigated by midwives and ladies of rank to see whether she was "virgo intacta". The fact that she was having an affair with Carr was common knowledge among the family so they had substituted another girl – very young and heavily veiled – to undergo the examination. However the head of the commissioners, Archbishop Abbot, had expressed doubt about the proceedings, but once again the King had intervened. He had issued an order that each commissioner was to vote whether he was for or against the annulment without stating his reasons. Seven to five voted in favour of the Countess's marriage being annulled.

The populace at large were vaguely amused by it all and some wit wrote a ditty which went into common circulation:

This dame was inspected, but fraud interjected,
A maid of more perfection
Whom the midwives did handle, whilst the knight held the
  candle,
O there was a clear inspection.
Now all foreign writers, cry out on those mitres
That allow this for virginity
And talk of ejection and want of erection,
O there is sound divinity!

Seventeen days after Thomas Overbury was admitted to the Tower, the Governor, Sir William Wade, was dismissed and Sir Gervase Elwes was appointed in his place. Behind this extraordinary turn of events lay the hand of the Earl of Northampton, great-uncle to Frances and himself very attracted to Robert Carr. No sooner had this happened than Richard Weston, a shady character who had once worked for Mrs Anne Turner and who had latterly helped Frances and Robert to meet in secret places, was appointed as Thomas's gaoler.

Shortly after this, Mrs Turner sent for Weston to come to Whitehall to meet the Countess of Essex, as she still then was. She asked him to give Overbury "a water", insisting that Weston did not take it himself. He suspected at once it was poison but on his way to administer it he was stopped by Sir Gervase Elwes. Weston was then approached by a strange man called Franklin in the White Lion on Tower Hill, who enquired about Overbury's health. Weston told him that the man was far from well and had to have enemas regularly. Franklin immediately suggested that a strange apothecary would come and give him a poisoned glister, or enema. Weston promptly reported the matter to Sir Gervase.

Right from the start of his imprisonment, Thomas had been writing to Robert in letters that showed he had no conception of how deeply wounded Carr had been by his references to Frances. Instead he spoke blithely of plans to get him out of the Tower, most of them saying how sick he was, indeed fit to expire. In a welter of self-deception, he begged Carr to say that he – Robert – would die of a broken heart if Thomas were not released. In other letters still he tried to manage Carr's affairs, just as he once had long ago. But his greatest mistake was to refer to Frances as a "catopard"; a derogatory term that he had used about her when Robert merely regarded the girl as a plaything.

Meanwhile a steady stream of tarts and jellies had been arriving at the Tower, purporting to come from Robert. But, shortly, other foodstuffs arrived, from the Countess of Essex. Elwes kept these particular tarts, which were a bright green in shade, in the Tower kitchen and noted that after a day or two they had turned black and foul. While the jellies, left standing, grew fur on them. Then came the day when she sent another batch of emerald green tarts, this time accompanied by a letter.

In it she insisted that Sir Gervase should not allow his wife or children to taste the tarts or jelly, and that they were to be given to Thomas Overbury. "Do this at night and all will be well," she concluded.

That evening, lying next to Robert in the great and beautiful bed, she whispered, "Darling, why do you write to Overbury? Surely you must hate him as much as I do."

There was a silence, so profound that she thought her lover must have dropped off to sleep, but eventually he spoke in the darkness.

"No, I don't hate him. I just wish he weren't such an arrogant bullying creature. I truly hoped that being in prison would make him see sense and that he would swear allegiance to your family. But he continues to write in his old vein; ordering me about and . . ."

His voice died away.

"Insulting me?" asked Frances.

Carr propped himself up on one elbow. "I didn't say that."

"No, but you meant it. Oh, sweetheart, I fear that fellow. I fear his influence even from the heart of the Tower."

"What influence, pray?"

"That he will poison you against me. That he will regain his place in your heart."

"Never," answered Robert forcefully. "I swear to you that he shall never do that."

"All the same I wish he were dead and leaving us all in peace."

"Shush. You are not to say such things."

"But I think them."

The final straw in the relationship between the imprisoned Overbury and Robert Carr came in August. Thomas's brother-in-law, Sir John Lidcote wrote to him and told him of a visit he had made to Carr. Having read the letter Overbury, much enfeebled since his commital to the Tower, made a gesture of despair.

"What's the matter with you?" asked Weston, who had just come into the room.

"It's Carr. He's played me false. Listen to this. My brother-in-law told him of my plight in this place and the fellow gave a counterfeit sigh. And then do you know what he did?"

"No."

"He grinned widely in Lidcote's face. Just couldn't help smiling. And to think of my miserable condition and the number of times I have begged him to help free me. Why, I would like to kill the bastard."

"No chance of that," remarked Weston dourly.

"Indeed, indeed," replied Overbury heavily. "But at least I can put pen to paper. That is if I had any."

"I'll get you some," Weston answered, suffering an unusual moment of pity for the shambling wreck that Overbury was fast becoming.

Later he took the letter to be posted without telling Sir Gervase Elwes, little realizing that its contents would finally give Robert Carr a motive for murder, because in it Overbury threatened to expose all the secrets he and Carr had shared over the years, ending with the ominous words, "Thus, if you deal thus wickedly with me, I have provided, whether I die or live, your nature shall never die, nor leave to be the most odious man alive." He also stated that he had made copies of this indictment and sent it out to all his "friends noble".

Knowing that the contents of the letter would send Frances into a frenzy, Robert did not show it to her. But going about the Court as usual he heard nothing to make him believe that Overbury had kept his word and written to various noblemen. On the contrary, everyone was cheerful and nobody mentioned a word about receiving such a libellous document. Carr concluded that Thomas simply had threatened in vain.

But the sands of time were running out for Thomas Overbury; that arrogant bully was now seriously ill. Throughout the month of August, 1613, his condition slowly deteriorated. According to Weston, his gaoler, Thomas had a large sore on his back which he kept covered with a plaster. Apparently the changing of this caused him so much pain that he would shout and swear when Weston did it.

At the end of the month Sir John Lidcote wrote to Robert that it was virtually impossible to contact Overbury and asked if he knew anything about it. Then, almost immediately, Carr was informed that the wretched man's condition was deteriorating fast. He immediately wrote to Dr Mayerne – who was visiting

Bath at the time – and told him of the situation. The physician replied that he was sorry but there was nothing he could do at the moment. Might it not be better perhaps if Overbury wrote to him direct describing his symptoms.

But the time for writing letters was almost over. On the morning of the 14th September, Overbury begged Weston for an enema.

"It might ease me a little."

Weston looked noncommittal, his usual expression. "Aye, it might. Shall I ask Paul de Loubell, Dr Mayerne's apothecary, to make you one up?"

"If you wouldn't mind."

Two hours later an apothecary's boy had come into the room where Overbury lay, looking quite ghastly.

"You're wanting an enema, Sir?"

"Oh, God, yes. I'm in a terrible state and I'm hoping it might afford me some relief."

"Should do, Sir. Now let's to your arse."

"What's your name?" asked Weston as the boy administered the glister.

"William, Sir."

"Do you know what you are doing?"

The boy had given him a look from the eyes of a leopard. "Oh, yes, sir. I know what I am doing very well."

That evening, as Weston lay fitfully slumbering, he heard the most terrible cry from Overbury's room. Going to him he saw that the man had thrown himself half out of bed.

"What's up?" he asked laconically.

But he had to bend over Overbury to hear the reply, which came from a mouth with the lips drawn back and upwards in a kind of terrible snarl.

"I am in agony, man. For the love of Christ, help me."

"Where does it hurt you?"

"Everywhere. I have never known pain like it."

"I can change the plaster on your back if you like."

Overbury nodded. "It might help me. Can you do it beneath the bedclothes?"

"I can try."

Fumbling about beneath the sheets Weston did his best to follow Thomas's instructions as to where the ulcer was, but

when sticking the plaster down he heard Overbury give vent to a
terrible oath as he touched the place where it was situated. He
pulled back.

"That's the best I can do."

There was no answer. Weston looked down and saw that
Thomas had closed his eyes, but not peacefully. Instead there
was an agonized expression on his face.

Throughout that night the gaoler kept close watch, listening
to the screams and groans of the sick man. He even moved him
to another bed to see if this might ease his sufferings. As dawn
broke Overbury spoke to him in a feeble voice.

"Weston, go and buy me some beer, I beg of you. I have such
a thirst that I think it will kill me if I don't drink."

The gaoler, paid creature of Mrs Anne Turner, took another
look at the prisoner, then did what was necessary. After that he
went out of the Tower for fifteen minutes. When he returned he
was greeted by death. For the corpse of Thomas Overbury lay
alone in the chamber to which he had been brought exactly four
months previously. It was finished.

The wedding was one of the most splendid the court could
remember. It took place on 26th December, 1613, exactly three
months after the death in the Tower. Celebrated in the Chapel
Royal at Whitehall – where Frances had married the Earl of
Essex, her first husband – the service was conducted by the
same man, the Bishop of Bath and Wells. Frances played the
part of virgin bride by wearing her hair loose, Robert Carr –
who a month before had been raised to the status of Earl of
Somerset – was dressed resplendently. It was indeed a sight to
behold.

The marriage was followed by extravagant festivities. A
specially written masque was performed, then came dancing
in which both bride and groom took part. The couple finally got
to bed at about three o'clock in the morning, utterly exhausted
and too tired for consummation. Acting on a whim, the new
Earl had had the great bed dismantled and reassembled in his
apartments at Whitehall. So that when Frances finally entered
the room she exclaimed aloud in delighted surprise. And later
when the groom was brought in surrounded by his male
attendants, he found her sitting up in it, smiling at him.

"Oh, sweetheart, you've brought our bed here," she whispered as the last one left the room.

"Yes, goodnight, darling."

And she laughed a little as she saw that he had immediately fallen asleep.

The celebrations went on interminably. At court the entire twelve days of Christmas were taken up with masques and feasting, while poets wrote verses praising the bride's beauty and purity. On New Year's Day a tournament was held in which the teams wore the colours of either bride or bridegroom, while on the 4th January the entire court rode through the streets of London to feast with the Lord Mayor. The bridegroom went on horseback, Frances rode in a brand new coach, richly ornamented, drawn by a team of horses presented to the Earl as an additional wedding present.

It seemed as if nothing could ever go wrong for this glittering couple. Robert had made up his quarrel with Frances's family and still stood high in the King's estimation. He had estates, money, a key position, and, above all, a wife with whom he was deeply in love. Life had never been more worth living. And yet, somewhere, a worm began to turn.

Making his summer progress through the country, the King stayed at Apethorpe in Northamptonshire. And it was there that he first set eyes on George Villiers. It was love at first sight undeniably. James had never seen such a vision. For George's face and hands were effeminate yet handsome, his hair hung in chestnut curls, he was tall and well made. From that moment on the star of Robert Carr, Earl of Somerset, began to go into the descendent.

Robert's many enemies met at Baynard's Castle, four Earls being amongst their number. They determined, almost gleefully, to use Villiers to bring Carr down. They decided to clothe George, giving him spending money. The impecunious young man, owner of one threadbare suit, was now dressed in the very latest fashion. He was young, he was attractive, he was gleaming with self-awareness. At long last the Earl of Somerset had been outshone.

Furiously, Robert did everything to block his rival's rise to power. But to no avail. He had finally met his match.

"But, sweetheart," said Frances, who had been sitting patiently listening to her husband's complaints for a good thirty minutes, "surely you should try and win the King's favour back."

"I do try."

"I beg to differ. You sulk and show him open fury. You will never gain his love again like that."

Much to her surprise, her husband rounded on her. "How dare you? I know the King of old. Leave the way he is handled to me, if you please."

"Certainly," Frances replied, and stalked out of the room.

But walking down the corridor she had a frightening experience. She thought that something moved in the shadows, a dark shapeless thing.

"Overbury!" she exclaimed. And just for a second the thing took form and raised its hand at her before it vanished.

Frances ran to the bedroom and flung herself down on the bed – that wonderful bed that had accompanied her throughout her love affair with Robert Carr. She felt cold and afraid as if something unknown were rising from the grave to come and taunt her. Turning, she looked up at the woodwork but all she could see was the face of a grinning satyr.

By that summer, with George Villiers now knighted and made a Gentleman of the Bedchamber, something else, something far worse, began to worry Robert Carr. A whispering campaign had started about the death of Thomas Overbury. Talk of poison and poisoners was spreading, and all this nearly two years after the event. It occurred to the Earl of Somerset almost at once that his enemies at court had deliberately rekindled the old scandal.

Meanwhile Mrs Anne Turner, Frances's friend and confidante, to say nothing of Frances herself, was growing distinctly worried. It was widely believed that Richard Weston had been working for them and that he had insisted on being paid for his services – namely the demise of the prisoner. Had he anything to do with Overbury's death or was he demanding payment under false pretences? He continued to badger the women who had supplied him with the green tarts until the time when, in order to keep him quiet, they gave him £100 in gold, followed by another four score pounds, also in gold, both sums paid to him by Mrs Turner.

In the spring of 1615 Frances felt certain that she had become pregnant and removed herself to Greys, near Henley. Mrs Turner, who had moved in with the Somersets a short time after their marriage, accompanied her. Walking in the garden, certain that they could not be overheard, they conversed.

"My dear Anne, what are we going to do?"

"I have no idea, my dear Frances. After all, we did send in the green tarts."

"Not to mention the jelly. It was full of poison as you know."

"We must just deny everything and hope that these wretched rumours will stop."

Frances Somerset burst into tears and stamped her foot. "Horrible Thomas Overbury! He will make trouble for us yet, I swear it."

Mrs Turner made no reply but simply pursed her lips and walked steadfastly on.

Robert Carr, Earl of Somerset, had now grown frantic. He had sought from King James a pardon which would absolve him of crimes he had previously committed. But though the King seemed willing enough to sign it, it had come unstuck before the Council when the Lord Chancellor had refused to seal it. The King had become angry and had walked out of the meeting, straight to the Queen, who had, hating Somerset as she did, put the final nail into the coffin and told James not to sign.

Shortly after, His Majesty left on his summer progress. And it was while he was staying at Beaulieu that news reached him of the fact that Sir Gervase Elwes had set down an account of the events leading up to the death of Sir Thomas Overbury. Having thus been informed, it left James no option but to order a full enquiry into the death of the prisoner.

The Lord Chief Justice himself, Sir Edward Coke, who seemed to be everybody's enemy, headed the investigation, driven by his own desire to punish Somerset. He interviewed hundreds of people, everyone from the highest to the lowest – well, almost the lowest – determined to capture the big fish via the little minnows.

In mid-September Richard Weston was arrested and confessed that he had been given a phial of greenish liquid by a Doctor Franklin, a quack that both Frances and Mrs Turner had consulted to aid them with their respective love affairs. That night Franklin was summoned to the Whitehall apartments of the Countess. As he entered the room, Robert Carr, who was present with his wife, gave him a dark look and walked out, leaving him alone with the two women.

"Weston has been taken into custody," said Frances hysterically.

She looked terrible; pale, her hair wild, her body swollen by the child she was carrying.

"How very regrettable," Franklin answered, not knowing quite what else to say.

"Regrettable! It's a tragedy," she answered. "You will be next, Franklin, mark my words, and you must deny everything. If you confess anything you will be hanged. By God, if you confess, you shall be hanged for me, for I will not be hanged."

"No, Madam," said Mrs Turner in a quiet voice, "I will be hanged for you both."

Frances did not reply but left the room. In the silence that followed they could hear her speaking through the wall, and Robert answering her. When she came back again she looked slightly calmer and warned Franklin again about remaining silent when being questioned.

He bowed and left. Two days later both he and Mrs Turner were arrested and questioned.

That night, climbing into their bed, Frances and Robert hugged each other like two children.

"What shall we do?" she asked him in a tiny, frightened voice.

"Deny," he answered. "We must deny everything."

"But Weston will tell them about the green tarts, about the jelly, about the apothecaries . . ."

"Say no more, not even between these walls. All we can do is swear they are liars."

"I'm terrified, Robert."

"We should have thought of that before," he answered bitterly.

Like a rat in a trap, the Earl of Somerset did everything to defend himself; burning letters, writing to Overbury's servant, pleading with the King, objecting to the panel of commissioners investigating the case. But all to no avail. On 17 October an order was made placing him under house arrest in his apartments at Whitehall. Frances – now seven months pregnant – was similarly confined to a room in Greys.

Now, it seemed, that Overbury reached from the grave and claimed his victims. Weston was hanged by the neck until he was dead; Sir Thomas Monson, a shadowy figure who had worked behind the scenes assisting the Countess of Somerset, was arrested pending trial; Sir Gervase Elwes was stripped of office and placed in confinement; Mrs Anne Turner was taken into custody, James Franklin, the quack doctor, likewise. Somerset himself was transferred to the Tower. Because of Frances's pregnancy she was placed under house arrest in the care of Sir William Smithie, a London alderman. She was now completely isolated.

The trial of Mrs Turner proved sensational because various magic dolls were produced, all coming from the time when she and Frances had consulted cunning men about their love affairs. But in the eyes of the public it meant that she was a sorceress, a dabbler in the black arts, and it was hardly surprising when the jury found her guilty. Thomas Overbury had his second victim.

Sir Gervase Elwes was hanged, swiftly, because one of his servants took hold of one foot while the hangman's assistant tugged the other. There was a general feeling that no one thought he deserved the verdict. James Franklin was sent to the gallows and died muttering as the cart was driven away and he was left hanging. Four people had now gone to the grave.

On 9th December Frances gave birth to a baby girl after a normal confinement. The child was christened Anne a few days later. Then, on 4 April, 1616, the Countess and her daughter were parted, for the mother was taken to the Tower pending the court hearing. She lived separately from her husband – who had yet to see his baby – and it was elected that she would be the first to go to trial, to be prosecuted by no less than Sir Francis Bacon. As she entered court every man present drew breath for that day she looked radiantly beautiful. She held up her hand for the reading of the indictment.

"Frances, Countess of Somerset, what sayest thou? Art thou guilty of this felony and murder, or not guilty."

Curtseying to the Lord Chancellor, the Countess uttered a single word in a low voice, wondrous fearful. "Guilty," she said.

That, you may feel, was the end of the story. The Earl and Countess of Somerset were both found guilty and condemned to die, she by the rope and he by the axe. But, strange as it may seem, they received royal pardons and eventually walked free from the Tower.

What does that mean? Had Overbury been murdered or had he died of an illness contracted in the Tower? Had all the so-called evidence been doctored by Coke in his determination to condemn Somerset?

And what of me? You see, I was the smallest player. No one asked me what happened, but I knew all the facts.

Poor little Frances. She supplied green tarts and jellies to the prisoner, but they were intercepted by Elwes and never eaten. They were each and all so convinced of the parts they played that they trapped themselves by their own guilt.

So did anyone kill Thomas Overbury, I hear you ask?

Indeed. I killed him, dead as pork.

I, William Reeve, apprentice to Paul de Loubell, the apothecary who made up prescriptions for Dr Mayerne.

On the way to the Tower to give Sir Thomas an enema, I was approached by a shifty fellow – I have no idea who he was – and given a substance which I was asked to substitute for the one I was carrying. He offered me £20, more money than I could earn in years. So I did. I applied the enema right under the eyes of Weston, who had no idea what was really happening.

Then I fled to Paris and stayed there for several years until the whole affair was over, before returning to London and setting myself up as an apothecary. I heard the whole story from my master, Paul de Loubell, just before he died, and I have set it down for you as he told it to me.

Yet even he did not know the truth about my part in the affair. Now you alone know how I outwitted them all, even the greatest in the land. Will you find it in your heart to forgive me?

DAPHNE McANDREWS
AND THE SMACK-HEAD JUNKIES

Stuart McBride

Half past eight on a cold autumn evening and Sergeant Dumfries had his feet up on the reception desk, a mug of tea in one hand, a copy of the *Oldcastle Advertiser* in the other. Reading about the hunt for little Lucy Milne. The lobby door clattered open, letting in a howling gale, setting the posters flapping on the notice board. He sat upright with a sigh, put the newspaper away and plastered a professional smile on his face. An old lady with a walking stick was wrestling a tartan shopping trolley in through the heavy wooden doors. She had a little Westie terrier on the end of an extendible leash, barking happily as bright orange leaves tumbled in around the old woman's ankles, twirling about the police station lobby like demented Highland dancers.

"Can I help you with that, madam?"

She flashed him a smile. "No, no we'll be fine." There was something familiar about her, but Dumfries couldn't put his finger on it. Five foot two, overweight, grey-brown overcoat, tartan headscarf, granny boots, face like a wrinkled cushion . . . With one last tug she got the trolley inside, letting the lobby door slam shut. For a moment the swirling leaves hung in the air, before slowly drifting to the linoleum floor.

She trundled her shopping trolley up to the reception desk and peeled off her headscarf, revealing a solid mass of grey curls, hairsprayed within an inch of their life. "Dear, oh dear," she said, giving a little shiver. "What a dreadful evening! I was saying to Agnes this morning – we always have tea in the Castlehill Snook: they do a lovely fruit scone – and I was saying how the weather seems so much worse this year. I remember when—"

Dumfries stifled a groan as she wittered on – just his luck to get stuck with an old biddy in for a bit of a chat. "So," he said, making sure his fixed smile hadn't slipped, "what can I do for you, madam?

She stopped talking and studied at him for a moment. "Norman, isn't it? Norman Dumfries?"

"Er . . ." He shifted uncomfortably in his chair. "Yes?"

"Who would have known you'd turn out so tall! You were such a wee lad at Kingsmeath primary – see, I told you eating your greens would do you the world of good."

And that's when it clicked. "Mrs McAndrews, thought I recognized you!" This time Sergeant Dumfries's smile was genuine. "How you been?"

"Not too good, Norman," she said, leaning forward and dropping her voice to a conspiratorial whisper. "There's a naked man in my shed, and I think he's dead."

While most school dinner ladies were waxing lyrical about the exotic delights of custard creams and garibaldi biscuits, Daphne McAndrews had remained steadfast: as far as she was concerned it was homemade shortbread or nothing. Humming happily, she arranged some on the tray, next to a fresh pot of tea and six mugs, and carried it out the back door.

The police had set up a pair of huge spotlights, training them on the shed at the bottom of the garden, making the wasp-chewed wood glow. The rest of the garden was shrouded in darkness, the trees groaning and creaking in the buffeting wind. Daphne tottered carefully down the path, trying to keep the tea things from blowing away.

The shed door was propped open and half a dozen men, dressed in those white plastic over-suit things they wore on telly, were poking about inside. It was a big shed, Bill's pride and joy, but she'd barely touched it since he'd gone, just dusted from time to time. It was comforting to know that there was something of him in here: in a grey urn at the back, next to the little wooden fire engine he was working on before he died.

"Is everyone ready for a nice cup of tea?" she asked, stepping over the threshold and closing the door behind her, shutting out the wind.

Someone spun round and stared at her. "You shouldn't be in here!"

"Oh, wheesht. My Bill used to say that all the time, but a bit of shortbread always made him change his tune."

"No, you don't understand. This is a crime scene." He flapped his hands in the direction of the naked young man, sprawled against the far wall – under the shelf with Bill's urn on it – wearing nothing but a pair of argyle socks.

"It's not a crime scene, it's Bill's shed. Now stop being silly: time for tea." She started pouring. "Beside, it's not like I haven't seen a naked man before. And as a dinner lady, you get used to being around death. One lump or two?"

"Err . . ." He looked around at his companions, but no one came to his rescue. Policemen were just like little boys: you had to be firm, stand your ground, and not let them get away with anything. Cheeky monkeys. He cleared his throat and stared at his shoes for a moment, before saying, "Two please."

The shortbread was going down a treat – she wasn't a leading light of the Women's Rural Institute for nothing – when the shed door banged open again. A small pause and then someone roared, "What the hell's going on in here?" It was a man with a moustache and a thunderous expression. "Sergeant, this is supposed to be a crime scene, not a bloody tea party!" The policeman with two sugars blushed and apologized, the words coming out in a shower of crumbs. The newcomer's head looked like it was about to explode. Shouting and swearing, he dragged the policemen out into the back garden and shouted at them some more. Going on about trace evidence and short-bread crumbs and disciplinary hearings . . . Then he noticed Daphne was still in the shed, sipping her tea.

"YOU!" he said, flinging a finger in her direction. "Get back in that bloody house!"

*   *   *

A nice WPC was sent in to take her statement. "Don't worry about DI Whyte," she said, as Daphne opened a tin of Pedigree Chum Senior. "He's going through a bit of a divorce at the minute."

Daphne gave a haughty sniff and scraped a solid tube of chicken and heart into a clean dish. "If my Bill was alive today . . ." But he wasn't, so there was no point even thinking about it. She put the dish down on the floor, and whistled. "Come on darling, din-dins!" An old, yellow-white Westie dog clattered into the kitchen, little stumpy tail going at twenty to the dozen. He had Mr Bunny, his favourite, tatty old squeaky toy, clamped in his jaws.

"Oh, he's so *sweet!*" The WPC beamed. "What's his name?"

Daphne reached down and ruffled the fur between her boy's ears. "This is Little Douglas. Bill named him after my father, on account of the family resemblance. He's going to be fifteen in February. Aren't you Wee Doug, aren't you? Yes, you are! Yes, you are!" He gave a cheerful bark and stuck his nose in the dog food.

"Can you tell me when you found the dead man in your shed, Mrs McAndrews?"

"Hmm? Oh, it was . . ." Daphne frowned in concentration. "*Coronation Street.* That blonde lassie was having an affair with the Asian chap and I was thinking I could really do with a nice cup of tea. So I waited for the next advert break and went through to make one. Only before I turned on the light I saw this naked woman running climbing over the back fence. And I thought—"

"Wait, you saw a naked woman? Not a naked man?"

"Oh, yes. When you work in a school canteen you get to know the difference. Anyway, she was clambering over the fence, and I got Wee Doug and we went out and he was very brave, weren't you? Mummy's little soldier. He's very protective, you know. Anyway, I saw the shed door was open and I went to close it and there he was. So I got on my overcoat and went to the police station and reported it."

"Why didn't you just dial 999?"

Daphne shook her head sadly. Young people these days. "My dear, reporting a dead body isn't like ordering a pizza. Some things you just have to do in person."

★   ★   ★

The Castlehill Snook was nearly empty at half past ten on a Tuesday morning – just a middle-aged couple in the corner, bickering over a map – so Daphne and her best friend Agnes McWhirter had no trouble getting their usual table by the window overlooking the Castle car park. A large coach from Germany was disgorging tourists in front of the pay and display machine, all of them clutching little Scottish flags and plastic bags from the Woollen Mill. The sky was the colour of warm slate, wind making the tourists' cagoules whip and snap as they tried to get round the Old Castle ruins before the rain came on.

Daphne unclipped Wee Doug's lead and let him snuffle about the tiled floor; by the time the waitress arrived with the cake trolley, he was curled up beneath a chair. Snoring.

Agnes ordered her usual fruit scone, but Daphne shocked everyone, even herself, by asking for a slice of Battenberg instead. "Are you feelin' OK?" asked Agnes, staring aghast at the slice of yellow and pink sponge. Taking a deep breath, Daphne told her about the dead body in her shed, the naked woman clambering over the back fence, and what that nice Sergeant Norman Dumfries had said when she'd called in past the station first thing this morning to see how they were getting on.

"Fancy that!" said Agnes, pouring the tea. "Naked drug addicts in your shed!"

"I know, I'm that mortified." Daphne shuddered, took a bite of her Battenberg and chewed suspiciously. It wasn't like her to entertain baked goods involving marzipan. She fed the rest to Wee Doug.

"They were probably having kinky, drugged-up sex. That's what these people do, you know, get high and indulge in filthy sex games: it was in the *Sunday Post*. Mr McAndrews would *not* have liked that!"

Daphne nodded; her husband had been as conservative in the bedroom as she was in the biscuit department. He would never have asked her for a fig roll when there was perfectly respectable shortbread available.

"Of course, they're all at it." Agnes tapped on the window. On the other side of the castle car park a ragged figure was trying to sell copies of the *Big Issue* magazine to the scurrying German tourists. "Drug addicts the lot of them. 'Junkies' – they're everywhere these days. It was in the *Sunday Post*. I tell you, Oldcastle's getting more like that Los Angeles every day. Next thing you know there'll be drive-by shootings and prostitutes on every street corner!" She nodded sagely and the first drops of rain speckled the teashop window, getting heavier and heavier, sending the tourists scurrying back to their bus. The scruffy figure watched them in silent resignation then tromped away into the downpour.

The shed was filthy by the time the police were finished with it, covered in fingerprint powder, nothing put back in the right place. Dressed in her "Sheep of Scotland" pinny and yellow rubber gloves, Daphne scrubbed and polished and tidied until it was all good as new. She stood back and examined her handiwork with grim satisfaction – there was a lot to be said for a clean shed. She frowned. Bill's urn didn't look right.

It was a medium urn, because her husband had been a medium man. His remains would have looked short-changed in a large urn, and buying a small one would have meant leaving bits of him at the crematorium. And you never knew *which bits* they'd be, would you? The last thing she wanted was to get up to heaven and find that Bill was missing a leg, or a hand. Or his gentleman bits. He wouldn't like that. She picked the urn off the shelf and squirted it with furniture polish, buffing it up with a yellow duster until it . . . the lid was loose. With trembling hands she unscrewed it all the way.

Daphne had never felt more like a drink in her life. Not even when Bill died. Sitting at the kitchen table she poured herself a stiff sweet sherry, threw it back and poured another one. "Oh, Bill!" His urn sat on the tabletop in front of her. A big scoop of his ashes were missing. Someone had stolen bits of her husband . . . Wee Doug padded back and forth under the table, his claws clickity-clacking on the linoleum, whimpering. He knew his mummy was upset.

Biting her bottom lip, Daphne screwed the top back on the bottle. Wallowing in self-pity wasn't going to do Bill any good. If she wanted justice, she was going to have to get off her backside and do something about it. It was what Bill would have wanted.

★   ★   ★

Rain clattered against the cobbled street, shining like beads of amber in the yellow streetlight as Daphne trudged along Shand Street, heading back up Castle Hill to the teashop, pulling her tartan shopping trolley behind her. Wee Doug's nose poked out through a tiny opening in the top, sniffing the cold night air for a moment, before sensibly ducking back down again, out of the rain. The teashop would be closed, just like all the other shops she passed on her way up the hill, their windows glowing, but lifeless. Like the empty streets. "That's because everyone with an ounce of sense is indoors!" she told herself, stopping for a moment to rest. It was hard going and her hip was beginning to complain. Dampness seeped in through the seams of her old raincoat, her left boot squished as she walked, and her glasses were all fogged up. Sighing, she leant on her walking stick and thought about turning round and going—

A noise.

She froze, struggling to locate the sound over the rain drumming off her plastic headscarf. Nothing. She tried all the settings on her hearing aid, but it didn't make any difference. Probably just her imagination playing tricks . . . And then she heard it again, someone singing and swearing softly to themselves.

Slowly Daphne crept up the road, pulling the trolley with her, scanning the empty shop doorways on either side. A wee cobbled close disappeared off between the knitwear place and the kilt shop, the little alleyway roofed off by a hairdresser's on the first floor. It stretched away into the darkness, a link between the towering sandstone buildings on Shand Street and the dour brick of Mercantile Road. Gloomy and forbidding. That was where the noise was coming from.

Plucking up all her courage, Daphne stepped into the alley. It was dark in here, the streetlights on Shand Street barely making a dent in the shadows, but she could just make out a figure, huddled in a doorway, a grubby pink blanket pulled round his shoulders, sitting on a pile of flattened cardboard boxes. The flare of a match and she saw his face as he lit a scrawny, hand-rolled cigarette – bearded, dirty. Not the man who'd been trying to sell the *Big Issue*; but, as Agnes said, they were *all* drug addicts. He was probably doing drugs right now, chasing the rabbit, or whatever it was called. Straightening her shoulders she marched right up and said, "Excuse me?"

The man didn't answer, just kept on swearing away, so she poked him with her walking stick.

"I said, excuse me."

He squealed and scurried backwards into the wall, jittering and twitching, watching her suspiciously. "What you want?" His eyes glittered in the dim light like a snake.

"I'm looking for a woman."

The man leered. "You wanna them big fat lesbians?" She poked him with her stick again. Hard. "Ow! Cut it out!"

"This particular woman was in my shed last night, with a young man. She took someone . . . something of mine and I want it back!"

There was a silence as the man stared at Daphne – probably undressing her with his eyes. These drug addicts were all alike. Sex mad. "So . . ." he said, leaving his doorway, the filthy pink blanket still wrapped around his shoulders, smelling of urine and Marmite. "You gonnae make it worth my while, like?"

Daphne blushed. Sex mad – she knew it. Quickly, she rummaged in the damp pockets of her raincoat and came out with a half-empty bag of mint imperials. "Would you like a sweetie?"

He reached out and snatched the bag. "Got any money?"

"Manners!" Daphne bristled. "What would your mother say if she—?" He shoved her aside and she slipped, clattering down onto the cold, wet cobbles, grunting in pain. Oh, God – what if she'd broken her hip?

"Where's your purse?" He loomed over her, digging through the pockets of her raincoat, sniffing anything he found, before hurling it away into the rain. Handkerchief, lipsalve, hairgrips, the tatty old tennis ball Wee Doug liked to chase in King's Park. Then her house keys. Grinning, he held them up to the light. "Brilliant." He stuffed them in his pocket. "Now where's your bloody purse?"

Daphne raised a shaking hand and pointed at the tartan shopping trolley. The junkie rubbed his hands and unzipped the top compartment. A grumpy growl rumbled out and the filthy smile fell from his face: "What the hell's this?" Swearing, he kicked the trolley's wheels out from under it, sending it flying, spilling Wee Doug out into the gutter. Ignoring the Westie's indignant barks, he rummaged inside the trolley. Mr Bunny was hurled out into the night, closely followed by a plastic bag full of rolled-up plastic bags and a spiral-bound notebook covered in shopping lists. Wee Doug scurried off after his squeaky toy as the man grunted, "Ya beauty . . ." and settled back on his haunches to rifle through her handbag.

Gritting her false teeth, Daphne pulled herself to her knees, laddering her support stockings on the rough alley floor as she struggled upright, trembling with rage. Her walking stick was lying in the gutter; she grabbed it. "Did your parents never teach you any MANNERS?" It was a good sturdy walking stick: a shaft of tempered oak and a thick handle carved from a Stag's antlers. It made a satisfyingly wet thunking sound as she battered it off the man's head.

He yowled and she hit him a second time. Harder. He tried to say something, but she swung the handle into his face – something went crack and teeth flew, so she did it again. His cheekbone cracked. And again: his left eye spurted blood. And again: he got his hands up in time to shield his face and she heard finger bones snap. Again, and again and again . . .

Daphne leant back against the wall, puffing and panting, one hand clutching her aching chest, wondering if she was about to have a heart attack. The man lay on his side, curled into the foetal position, not moving. Wee Doug sniffed the back of the drug addict's head, then cocked his leg and peed on it. When he was all done he picked up Mr Bunny, trotted over and sat in front of Daphne, little tail wagging away sixteen to the dozen, happy as could be.

It took her a while to calm down, but eventually the pain in her chest subsided and her breathing returned to normal. She wasn't going to join Bill just yet.

She jabbed the horrible man with her stick, forcing him over onto his back. His face was all swollen and puffy, misshapen, covered with blood, a flap of skin hanging loose on his forehead. Leaking out onto the cobbles. He gave a little cough and a small plume of red sparkled in the dim light. She prodded him in the chest and he groaned. "I asked you a question, young man: who was the naked woman?"

He said something quite rude and Daphne battered the head of her walking stick off his knee. It wasn't quite a scream, wasn't quite a moan, but it sounded painful. "Who was she?"

He was crying now, tears and snot mixing with the blood and dirt. "I don't . . . I don't know . . ."

"You're lying." She hit him again, right on the ankle joint.

"Oh, God, no! Please! I don't know!" Sobbing, rocking back and forth on the ground, covering his head with his arms. "Please . . ."

Daphne scowled and counted to ten. So much for plan A. "If *you* don't know: who does?"

"I don't . . . Aaagh!" It was the elbow this time "Please! I don't . . ." Ankle again. "Aaagh! Colin! Colin'll know! He sells stuff. He'll know!"

She smiled. "And just how do I find this 'Colin'?"

Daphne had never been in a public bar on her own before – it wasn't the sort of thing a respectable lady did – but she owed it to Bill. Screwing up her courage, she marched through the doors of the Monk and Casket, a seedy-looking place at the bottom of Jamesmuir Road. It was mock Tudor on the outside, but inside it was all flashing gambling machines, vinyl upholstery and sticky floors. It wasn't a busy pub, just a handful of men and women looking somewhat the worse for drink at half eleven on a Wednesday night.

Stiffening her courage she hobbled up to the bar, taking her shopping trolley with her, and ordered a port and lemon. And a medicinal brandy – her hip was still sore and she was soaked through after walking all the way here from Castle View.

The bartender was a big hairy man with earrings and a missing front tooth. He leant forward and whispered, "We've actually called last orders, so I can't legally serve you," then slid her drinks across the bar. "If you'd like to make a donation of two pounds fifty to the lifeboat fund, that would be OK by me." Wink, wink. Blushing, Daphne thanked him and slid the money into the orange plastic lifeboat sitting on the bar.

"I'm looking for a man," she said.

The barman smiled. "Sorry, darling, I'm married."

"No, a man called 'Colin'. Do you know him? Someone told me he'd be here."

Silence from the hairy barman, and then, "Are you *sure* you're looking for Colin? Colin McKeever? Crazy Colin?"

Daphne nodded, looking around the bar, trying to see if anyone looked like a "Crazy Colin". It wasn't a big place: just a handful of tables; some framed photos of the local football team; the pinging, chattering fruit machines; and a single door leading off the room marked TOILETS, TELEPHONE AND FUNCTION SUITE. The customers were as seedy as the pub. A pair of over-made-up women cackled away in the corner with their alcopops, a fat man with a beard hunched over a pint of stout, two suspicious-looking types in black leather by the dartboard . . . "Is he the one in the hat?" She pointed at an unusual, weaselly looking man with long black hair and a baseball cap, sitting on his own.

"No, that's Weird Justin. Crazy Colin's upstairs with Stacy. Now, why don't you finish up your drink and I'll call you a taxi, OK? A nice little old lady like you doesn't want to have anything to do with the likes of Colin McKeever."

A small flutter of excitement – he was upstairs with a woman! Maybe it was the one from the shed? "Of course, of course." She downed her brandy in a single gulp, then did the same with the port and lemon. "I'll just nip off to the loo . . ."

Grabbing the shopping trolley's handle, she pushed through the door and into a stinky corridor. A door on either side said GENTS and LADIES, but right at the far end was a set of stairs with a small plaque hanging over it: TO FUNCTION SUITE. Daphne took a deep breath, and started hauling the shopping trolley up the stairs.

One floor up and the sticky linoleum gave way to sticky carpet, with just enough room at the top of the stairs for Daphne to catch her breath. Unrecognizable "music" thumped through from the other side of a battered wooden door. Why did no one know what a tune was any more? When this was all over, she was going to go home, put on some Barry Manilow and get herself a nice cup of tea.

She fiddled with her hearing aid – trying to tune down the horrible music – and opened the door to the function suite. It was about the same size as the bar downstairs, but more neglected. Ancient chairs lined the walls, fold-away tables piled in one corner, a mirror ball hanging from the ceiling, glittering over the small wooden dance floor in the middle. A man and woman rocked slowly back and forth, shambling round to the "music". She had her arms wrapped around his shoulders, he had his hands on her buttocks. Kneading away as if he was making bread.

The current song bludgeoned its way to a halt and then another one, equally dreadful, started. There was one of those "boom-box" things sitting at the side of the dance floor, so Daphne marched straight over and turned the horrible machine off. Blessed silence. The man stopped rearranging his girl-friend's underwear and scowled. He wasn't the most attractive of men – thin and short, with a scabby little beard thing, spiky hair and glasses. But he looked like a Colin.

"What the hell did you do that for?" He let go of his partner, but she continued to dance, shuffling round and round in the absence of music, on her own.

Daphne squared her shoulders. "I want my Bill!"

"I've not sold you anything."

"Don't you play games with me, young man. Your hussy broke into my shed and she stole my Bill! I want him back."

Crazy Colin looked back over his shoulder at the dancing woman. "You saying Stacy's kidnapped someone?" He laughed as Stacy tripped over her own feet and tumbled to the floor. She made an abortive attempt to get back up then gave up, sprawled on her back in the middle of the dance floor, like a dead starfish. "You've got to be kidding – she couldn't tie her shoelaces unsupervised. You got the wrong girl, Grandma."

"I said I want him back!"

"Nothing to do with me, Grandma. You got a problem with Stacy, you take it up with her . . ." He grinned. "After I've finished, like." He started to take off his shirt. "You wanna watch? No charge."

Oh . . . my . . . God . . . He was getting undressed! She didn't want to see some strange man's private parts! She hadn't even liked looking at her husband's. "I don't want any trouble; I just want my Bill back."

"Bill, Bill, Bill, Bill, Bill." He turned his back on her, unfastening his belt.

Daphne hurried back to her shopping trolley and unzipped the top, lifting out Wee Doug. He yawned and looked around the room, then sat down and had a bit of a scratch. Daphne pulled herself up to her full five foot two inches and pointed an imperious finger at Crazy Colin as he unbuttoned his fly. "Go on, Wee Doug, KILL!"

Wee Doug looked up at her, then at the end of her finger.

Daphne tried again. "Kill!"

Still nothing.

She grabbed Mr Bunny from the shopping trolley and hurled it at the undressing man. The toy rabbit landed right in the crotch of Colin's trousers as he tried to get them down over his shoes. Wee Doug growled, his little feet scrabbling on the wooden floor, not going anywhere fast . . . until suddenly his claws got purchase and he was away, tearing across the dance floor like a dog half his age. Barking.

The man spun round at the noise, eyes wide. He grabbed the waistband of his trousers and hauled them up, which was a mistake as Mr Bunny was still trapped in there – his two ragged ears sticking out of the man's fly at groin level. With a final happy bark Wee Doug leapt and clamped his jaws onto Crazy Colin's crotch. There was a high pitched scream.

Daphne took a firm grip of her walking stick and went to shut him up.

Shaking, Daphne washed the blood off her hands and face with cold water and bitter-smelling hand soap in the ladies' lavatory. Wee Doug was happily sitting up in the shopping trolley – the reclaimed Mr Bunny looking none the worst for his adventure in a strange man's trousers – watching as she stuck the head of her walking stick under the tap, the water turning pink as Crazy Colin McKeever's blood slowly rinsed away.

"No one knows . . ." she told herself. "No one knows . . ." Not even the girl – she was comatose the whole time. Couldn't have seen anything. Couldn't have – A knock on the toilet door and she almost shrieked.

"Hello?" It was the bartender, sounding concerned. "Are you in there?"

Oh, God, he's found the body! "I . . . I . . ."

"You OK? You've been in here for ages."

"I . . . I'm fine." She looked at herself in the mirror. He doesn't know. No one knows. "Just a gyppy tummy."

"That's your taxi."

She nodded at her reflection and plastered on a smile, then opened the bathroom door, taking Wee Doug and the tartan shopping trolley with her. "Thank you," she said, trying to keep the tremble out of her voice as he helped her out through the front door and into the cab.

"You take care now." He stood in the street, waving as they drove away.

It was a rumpled Daphne McAndrews who slouched into the Castlehill Snook at quarter to eleven the next day. She'd slept badly, even with a quarter bottle of sweet sherry inside her, knowing that they'd put her in prison for the rest of her natural life. The police would find Colin McKeever's body and do all that scientific stuff you saw on the telly. And they'd know it was her. Provided the nasty man who'd tried to steal her purse in the alley hadn't already reported her for thrashing him. She couldn't bring herself to use the walking stick today, not now it was a murder weapon, and her hip ached.

Daphne collapsed into the chair opposite Agnes and looked sadly out of the window at the Castle car park. Determined not to cry.

"You feelin' OK, Daphne?"

She just shrugged and ordered a fruit scone and a big mug of coffee. When the waitress was gone, Agnes leaned forward and asked, in her best stage whisper, "Did you hear about the murder?" Daphne blanched, but Agnes didn't seem to notice, "Beaten to death," she said, "a drug-dealer – in a pub! Can you believe it?"

Daphne bit her lip and stared at the liver spots on the back of her hands. "Did . . . Do they know who did it?"

"Probably one of them gangland execution things. If I've said it once, I've said it *a thousand times*: Oldcastle's getting more like that Los Angeles every day. I tell you . . ." She launched in to a long story about someone her Gerald used to go to school with, but Daphne wasn't listening. She was wondering when the police were going to come for her.

The patrol car pulled up outside the house at half past seven. At least they hadn't put the flashing lights and sirens on. She'd have died of embarrassment if the neighbours had seen that. She'd spent the day cleaning the place until it sparkled: no one was going to say she went off to prison and left a dirty house behind. With a sigh Daphne climbed out of Bill's favourite chair and answered the front door. It was Sergeant Norman Dumfries, the little boy who wouldn't eat his greens. She ushered him through to the kitchen and put the kettle on. Just because he was here to arrest her, there was no need to forget her manners.

"Tea?" she asked as he shifted uncomfortably from foot to foot.

"Er . . . Yes, that would be lovely." Adding, "Thank you," as an afterthought.

She made two cups and put them on the kitchen table, along with a plate of shortbread, telling Sergeant Dumfries to help himself. "Er . . ." he said, looking sideways at Bill's urn, still sitting on the tabletop from last night. "I'm afraid I've got something very awkward to tell you—"

Daphne nodded. There was no need to make it hard on the boy, he was doing his best. "I know."

He blushed. "I'm so sorry, Mrs McAndrews."

"You're only doing your job, Norman."

"I know, but . . ." he sighed and reached into his police jacket pocket. This was it, he was going to handcuff her. The neighbours would have a field day.

"It's all right." Trying to sound calm. "I won't put up a fight."

He looked puzzled for a moment, before bringing out what looked like a little plastic freezer bag. It was see-through, and full of grey powder. "We, um . . . the man you found in your shed had . . ." He stopped and tried again. "We did a post mortem on him yesterday. He died because he'd injected himself with . . . Er . . ." He held up the bag. "We had to take a sample to make sure. I'm sorry, Mrs McAndrews." Gently he picked Bill's urn off the table and tipped the contents of the plastic bag inside.

"Oh, God."

"I'm sorry, Mrs McAndrews. We think they were already under the influence of drugs when they broke into your shed to fool around. They discovered Mr McAndrews' remains and . . .

Well, the man had residue in his nasal passages and his lungs, so it looks like they tried snorting the . . . ah . . . deceased. When that didn't work, the man tried injecting. And then he died." It was silent in the kitchen, except for the sound of Wee Doug snoring. "I'm sorry."

She grabbed Bill's urn and peered inside. It was nearly full. "Did they both . . . ? You know?" Sergeant Dumfries nodded and Daphne frowned. She wasn't sure she liked the thought of Bill being inside another woman, and Bill would *certainly* not have been happy about being inside a naked man.

"Anyway," Sergeant Dumfries stood up. "I have to get back to the station." He looked left and right, as if he was making sure they were alone. "Just between you and me," he said in a conspiratorial whisper, "we've got a drugs war on our hands! One bloke got worked over right outside the kilt shop last night – said it was a gang with baseball bats – and the next thing you know some drug dealer gets battered to death! Mind you, at least we've got a witness to that one."

Daphne covered her mouth with a trembling hand, the girl: she was unconscious! She couldn't have seen anything – it wasn't fair!

Norman helped himself to a piece of shortbread. "We found this doped-up woman at the scene," he said, in a little spray of crumbs, "who swears blind some huge hairy bloke with a Rottweiler kicked the door down then bashed the victim's skull in with a pickaxe handle." He shook his head in amazement as Daphne went pale as a haddock. "I know," he said as she spluttered. "*Miami Vice* comes to Oldcastle, how bizarre is that?" Sigh. "Anyway, better make sure you keep your doors and windows locked tight. OK?"

When he was gone, Daphne sat at the kitchen table, trembling. Drug War. She let out a small giggle. The giggle became a snigger, then a laugh, and ended in hysterics. She'd gotten away with it. Wiping her eyes she pulled Bill's urn over and peered inside. There was only about a teaspoon missing. What would that be – an ear, a finger, his gentleman's bits? He'd miss them, even if she wouldn't . . .

With a smile she ripped the edge off a couple of teabags and poured the powdered leaves in. At his age he'd never know the difference.

ONCE UPON A TIME

Peter Turnbull

Tuesday Forenoon

It was, he thought, all too human. He was not a man who was medically qualified, but he had seen bones before, actual human bones, often in shallow graves, and much, much older than this bone, sitting there looking quite content in a curious sort of way, looked all too human. It had aged a little, he thought, it was certainly not as old as the bones he was used to examining but it was not recent either. It had a greyness about it, and had been chewed upon by his "friends." The man pondered what to do. He didn't want to appear alarmist but he also knew the value of over-reacting rather than under-reacting; and, after all, were they not told to report anything suspicious? He took the plastic bag he was carrying and walked further into the wood and emptied the contents well away from the bone. He then left the wood and walked back down the lane to the village, and to the red phone box, of the old-fashioned design because the village of Meltham was designated a conservation area, and dialled the police. Not 999; it was not an emergency, no longer life or limb – if indeed the bone ever did represent a life or limb crisis. His call was answered, eventually, by a recording of a female voice telling him that his call was "placed in a queue" and "would be answered shortly". The recording then reminded him that if his call was an emergency he should phone 999 or 112. He was then treated to a tinny recording of Beethoven's "Eroica" Symphony. Eventually, his call was answered by a stressed out and tired sounding officer who took details and asked him to wait by the phone box. This he did, wrapping his duffel coat around him and stamping his feet against the cold. It was the twelfth month of the year and the Wolds are cold, cold, cold during the winter months. It was a windless day, not a cloud in a blue sky, but cold. Very cold.

"It may be only an animal bone," he said eagerly and apologetically at the same time as the officer opened the door of the police car and stepped out.

"Take your time, sir," the officer said, calmly, but with authority as he reached for his notebook and pen.

"It's in the copse."

"Let me ask the questions, please."

The man fell silent.

"You are . . . ?"

"Coleman." The man was short, bespectacled, a mop of wild grey hair, "Clifford Coleman."

"And your address, Mr Coleman?"

"The Old Rectory, here in Meltham." He pointed. "That's my house, just there . . . well, the roof . . . you can see from here."

"You didn't phone from home, Mr Coleman?"

"I didn't, did I." Clifford Coleman scratched his head. "Now isn't that strange, I could have kept warm and had a cup of tea . . . why didn't I do that? That will puzzle me for some time."

"You found a bone, you say?" The officer interrupted Coleman's musing.

"In the small wood."

"The small wood?"

"Is the name by which it is known round here, to differentiate from another larger wood just beyond it which is known as the 'large wood'. That's the 'small wood'." Coleman turned and pointed down the pasty grey road to a copse approximately quarter of a mile distant.

"Can I ask your age and occupation, sir?"

"Why?"

"Just procedure, sir."

"Fifty-four . . . a teacher . . . at the university . . . history . . . I am a medievalist. I often see human bones in old graves that are being excavated. There is an overlap between history and archaeology, you see, and the bone I saw in the small wood looked to me to be human. There is much medieval in the village . . . the street pattern is medieval . . . though the oldest building dates only from the seventeenth century."

"Yes, yes . . . thank you, sir. Shall we walk to the wood?"

They walked to the wood. The constable taking long, effort-less, energy-preserving strides, Coleman taking short, rapid steps, but of the two it was Coleman who had to keep pace with the constable. In the wood, Coleman led the constable to where the bone lay.

"I think you were correct to call us, Mr Coleman." The constable knelt down and looked closely at the bone. "I am no doctor, but I have attended post-mortems and seen skeletons . . . certainly looks human to me. Not recently buried . . . it seems to be aged. Can I ask what you were doing in the wood? You have no dog that you were exercising, for example?"

"Feeding my friends."

"Your friends?"

"Oh, yes . . . foxes . . . badgers . . . creatures of the night. Animals enjoy foraging for their food and I never throw any-thing meaty away. Bones, fat, bacon rind . . . I bring it all to the wood and scatter it. I come at various times of the day, depending on my timetable. I'm teaching at 4.00 p.m. today and then have an evening class of mature students . . . many older than I am, doing something with their retirement. Good for them, I say . . . better than vegetating in front of day time television, I say, and their brains . . . sharp as tacks . . . get a better class of degree than many twenty-year-olds, and also . . ."

"Yes, sir."

"Well, I'll get back home too late this evening to walk up to the wood, so I came now . . . dropped the bone I had brought well away from the bone I had found . . . then phoned you. Should have phoned from my house, though . . . funny . . ."

"Not noticed it before, sir?"

"No. It has probably worked its way to the surface and one of my friends pulled it into the open. Probably a badger. Foxes are too lazy to do that – they prefer to scavenge . . . but old brock will claw anything up. Well, do you need me any more? I have some preparation to do."

"No, thank you, sir." The constable reached for the radio attached to his lapel and pressed the "send" button.

"Human, male." Louise D'Acre looked at the bone. She was clad in a green coverall, disposable hat . . . latex gloves. "Well, male is an educated guess. If it was female the lady would be very tall indeed. It's a femur, leg bone . . . and the person would be at least six feet tall in life . . . as female femurs go, it's very long."

"A six footer." D.C.I. Hennessey ran his liver-spotted hand through his silver hair.

"At least." Louise D'Acre knelt down and picked up the bone and placed it in a productions bag. "Well, there's more than one bone in the human skeleton," she said. "The rest might be around here somewhere. I'll take this to York City." She smiled a rare smile. She wore her hair short with just a trace of lipstick as her only make-up. Aged mid-forties, she was, thought D.C.I. Hennessey, a lady who knew how to grow old gracefully. "You can bring the rest along if and when you find them."

The "small wood" was, thought D.C.I. Hennessey, about one and a half acres in area of broad leafed woodland. A team of constables began to sweep across the wood, and just ten minutes into the sweep one constable stopped, held up his hand and said "Sergeant." He had found disturbed soil, and what appeared to be a bone protruding. It was about one hundred yards from where Clifford Coleman had found the bone. Hennessey looked at the disturbed soil, at the bone, and said, "Better get Scene of Crime People here . . . photograph it as you dig it up . . . bone by bone."

"Very good, sir."

Friday Afternoon

"Hard to determine age." Dr Louise D'Acre studied the bones which had been laid out in order on the dissecting table of the pathology laboratory of the City of York Hospital. "Not young, not elderly either . . . middle-aged. I'll cut a tooth in cross section and determine the age that way, but at a glance I'd say

that this is the skeleton of a middle-aged person of the male sex
. . . white European . . . there is no obvious cause of death . . .
no trauma . . . almost all the bones are here, just a few very
small bones of the feet are missing, but it has been sawn up . . .
quite neatly."

"They were found neatly too." D.C.I. Hennessey stood at
the edge of the pathology lab, observing for the police. "Stacked
one on top of the other, occupied a very small place about the
dimensions of a cardboard box that one person would take both
arms to lift."

"That's interesting." Louise D'Acre tapped the stainless
steel table with the tip of a long finger. "That means that they
were completely skeletal when they were buried. The corpse
was not merely sawn up, it was filleted as well. All tissue, all
organs were removed. Couldn't stack bones neatly otherwise."

"Or the corpse buried and then dug up some time later when
the flesh had decomposed and the bones reburied?"

"It's possible, but the interval between burial and reburial
would be measured in years. The other thing that occurs to me
is that if a skeleton was dug up it would hardly be to rebury it. I
would be inclined to throw it into the Ouse one dark night, bone
by bone. But it does tell you one thing, though: this is your
territory, not mine."

"Oh, please." Hennessey smiled. "All help gratefully accepted."

"Well, it tells you that the person or persons who did this had
a lot of space . . . some means of filleting a corpse without the
risk of being disturbed . . . can't do that in a little terrace house
. . . some means of disposing of the tissue, such as a bonfire.
Human tissue gives off a very sickly sweet smell when burned.
Anyone who has smelled it will recognize the smell again, and
be suspicious. Or alternatively, the space to bury it."

"A farmer?"

"Farm workers, farm labourers . . . again, the risk of a
witnesses. I would be inclined to think of someone who lives
alone in a large house or a smallholding. Enough space to do this
without the risk of being chanced upon." Louise D'Acre
stretched a tape measure along the spine. "It's been chopped
up, as you see, but in life he would have been about six feet tall
. . . and," she added softly, "he walked with a limp."

"He did?"

"Or he wore shoes, one of which, the left of the pair, was built up. His left femur is shorter than the right."

"That will narrow the field down, a lot."

"This is murder," Dr D'Acre said. "It can only be murder, but it's strange . . . the cause of death must have been quite mild, but the disposal of the corpse, very messy indeed. I have rarely come across anything quite like it"

"Nor I," Hennessey said. "It's usually the other way round."

"Indeed." D'Acre paused. "Well, I'll trawl for poisons, doubt I'll find any cyanide, belonged to the Victorians, and I'll determine his age by tooth extraction."

Wednesday Afternoon and Evening

George Hennessey sat at his desk and glanced out of the window of his office at a group of tourists, well wrapped up, who were walking the ancient walls of the city. That's York, he thought, a booming tourist industry year end to year end; even on cold winter days the walls will have tourists upon them. He felt satisfied. A good morning's work had been done. He had then walked the walls into the city and lunched at a pub with a wood fire and had sat underneath a reprint of an ancient map which showed "The West Ridinge of Yorkshyre, the most famous and Faire Citie Yorke described – 1610". Back at his desk, he read the report submitted by Sergeant Yellich about the man who had walked into Micklegate Bar Police Station the day previous and said to the constable on the enquiry desk, "I'm fed up of waiting to be caught. It was me that did all those burglaries." At first the man was thought to be a candidate for detention under the Mental Health Act, but then began to reveal details only the perpetrator could know. He had reached the end of Yellich's report when his phone rang. He let it ring twice before answering it. "Detective Chief Inspector Hennessey."

"Dr D'Acre, York City Hospital. I have the lab results back."

"So soon?"

"Quiet period. The deceased was fifty-three, or-four, or-five, when he died. And poisoned."

"Poisoned!"

"Self-inflicted. He was an alcoholic. It probably didn't kill him – well it would have done had he lived long enough . . . but it wasn't the murder weapon as such. But he was a very serious alcoholic in life and had been for years. It would take very heavy drinking over a long period to leave traces of alcohol in his long bones, but it's there. It's offered as an aid to identification."

Hennessey and Yellich drove out to Meltham. Neither officer had been to the village before. The turn off to Meltham, they found, could easily be missed; a narrow lane, it drove vertically between thick woodland. Upon arriving at the village they saw it to be small, nestling in a fold in the landscape. Yellich parked the car in the centre of the village, in the square which was more of a triangle in terms of its shape. The square had an ancient and preserved pair of stocks and a memorial to the three sons of the village who had given their lives for King and Country in the 1914–18 war. There was, Hennessey noted with some relief, no mention of any loss of life from the village in the 1939–45 conflict. A woman carrying a shopping bag glared at them as she walked, quite content to let the two officers see her staring at them. A burly, well-set man glanced at them suspiciously.

"This village don't like strangers," Hennessey remarked, as he nodded to the man.

"Don't, do it, boss?" Yellich locked the car.

"Well, where now?" Hennessey asked Yellich. "Where do you think?"

"Me, boss . . . tell you the honest truth, I'd try at the post office. Post mistresses in places like this know everything . . . in fact it was once my experience when I was a lad to knock on the post mistress's door at 8.00 p.m. one evening to tell her someone had died. She wasn't a relation, not even a friend of the family, but I was fourteen and the adults who were running round like headless chickens thought the best way to get the news into the community was to send me running up the lane to tell the post mistress that Mr Battie, my great uncle, had died." Yellich laughed. "Classic . . . classic . . . but it actually happened."

Hennessey laughed. "All right," he said. "Sounds good to me."

The Post Office in Meltham was located next to a small, very small, mini market and a hardware shop. It was quiet inside the shop, which had a sense of timelessness, with old-fashioned posters which had never been taken down and which advertised products priced in Imperial, not decimal currency. A youthful, very youthful, looking post mistress emerged from the gloom of the back of the shop in response to the jangling door bell.

"You'll be the police," she said pleasantly. "We thought you'd come. It'll be about the bones."

"The bones?" Hennessey raised an eyebrow.

"The bones that were found in the small wood yesterday by Mr Coleman. Mrs Innes 'does' for Coleman – he's a bachelor, you see, and Mr Coleman told her what he'd found and she told me. So we thought you'd come."

The woman seemed to be in her mid-twenties and Hennessey thought that, in terms of attitude and temperament, she had the makings of an excellent village post mistress. He asked if she had lived in the village for long.

"All my life," she replied with pride. "My husband didn't want to live here, but if he wanted me, he had to live in Meltham. He's been here nearly five years now and is beginning to get accepted."

"Lucky he."

"Well, it means he gets a game of darts in the Beggar now. For the first few years he had to stand alone at the bar."

"The Beggar?"

"The Fortunate Beggar." The woman smiled. "It's the pub, the only one in Meltham."

"I see. Well, you're right, we are here about the bones. We believe the person who was buried to have been quite tall, probably walked with a limp and had a very bad drink problem. If he was local to this area and not brought here from afar, then someone might recognize him. Our mis per records haven't shown anything."

"Mis per?"

"Missing Persons."

"Oh . . . but yes, I have heard of him. He still gets mentioned from time to time . . . the limping landlord, he disappeared . . . but that was before I was born. I'm twenty-six now."

"No wonder he's not in our records." Hennessey turned to Yellich. "If he had lived, he'd be pushing eighty now."

"He had the Beggar," the post mistress added. "Well, wait till I tell my mum. We took over the post office from her and dad when they retired. She's at the coast now, Bridlington, in a home. Your best bet now would be to try at the Beggar."

"Only by reputation." The landlord appeared to Hennessey and Yellich to be a man close to his retirement and who also subscribed to the Meltham culture of "strangers not welcome". He avoided eye contact with the officers and seemed to begrudge having to give information. "I took over the pub from him when he disappeared. That's thirty years now – thirty years last July, to be exact. He was not a happy man."

"No?"

"His flat above the pub—" the landlord looked up at the low beams above his head "– above the bar here . . . it was like a tramp's doss. The sheets on the bed hadn't been changed for months, newspapers covered the floor, empty bottles everywhere . . . My wife insisted we fumigate it. We threw everything out, stripped it right back to the bare floorboards, then we set up a brazier in the main room."

"Took a risk."

"Not really. We mounted the brazier on a bed of bricks and burned wood and damp vegetation, left all the doors open, but shut all the windows except one. Filled the flat with smoke, and crawling things began to come out of cracks in the wall and from between the floorboards; they found the open window and didn't return. Then we moved in. The lingering smell of wood smoke was better than the lingering smell of Reddick."

"A lonely man, then?"

"Yes . . . Carl Reddick, the limping, lonely landlord. Never did like that name, Carl . . . too close to 'cruel', but in this case it was apt by all accounts. Cruel Carl Reddick, not the right sort of man to be in charge of a pub."

"Irresponsible, you mean? Let youths drink too much?"

"No . . . not from what I heard. He was a soak himself, two bottles a day, and I don't mean beer."

"I get the picture."

"Apparently, so my customers told me, he used to sit on the stool at the end of the bar and be rude to everybody and anybody, customers and staff alike . . . very personally offensive."

"They didn't vote with their feet?"

"The staff did. Nobody stayed very long, but the work round here can be hard to come by, so they were easily replaced. And the customers, where could they go? The next nearest pub is in Ossley St Mary, about two and a half miles away. That could be a pleasant walk on a summer's evening if you are young and fit, but if you're getting on in years, and if it's a cold winter . . . well, it's the Beggar or nothing. So Reddick had a captive audience and he knew it . . . so he was described as spending each evening sitting there and snarling at anything that moved, with a breath so hot it was said it could ignite paper . . . then he disappeared. Here one day, gone the next. Then me and Betty took over, cleaned the place up and it became a village pub again in the truest sense of the word. I like to hear the thud of darts and the rattle of dominoes and folk laughing as they relax at the end of their day."

"Any rumours about his disappearance?"

The landlord smiled. "He got under the skin of a lot of people; a lot of people had cause to do him harm. I bet a lot of people dreamed of doing him in." The landlord broke off the conversation to serve a pint of mild to an elderly man who shuffled up to the bar with an empty glass. The landlord put the man's money in the till and returned to the officers. "So those were his bones they found in the small wood? It was all the talk in here last night."

"We believe they might be. Tell me, did anything happen over and above his abusive nature that might make someone want to murder him?"

"Well . . ." The landlord pondered. "There was the death of the lad Burgess, so I heard tell. It wasn't just that, but the attitude he was said to have taken to the incident . . . but I believe that was some years before he disappeared. Best person to talk to about that is the Reverend Price."

"Where do we find him?"

"The next village, where the nearest pub is, Ossley St Mary. His parish covers three villages, this one, Ossley St Mary and Much Haddle on Ouse. His rectory is at Ossley St Mary, large house next to the church."

"The church moves you onwards and upwards or it leaves you alone, keeps you in one place. Me it kept in one place." The

Reverend Price sipped his tea. Hennessey saw him as being late middle aged, grey hair cut neat and short. A large poster showing York Minster hung on his study wall; outside his window rooks gathered in the leafless branches of an oak tree cawing loudly. "But yes, I remember Carl Reddick's disappearance, remember it well. It was one of the first incidents in the parish of any note since my incumbency began. I've been a minister of this parish for thirty-three years now . . . and yes, I remember the sad death of young David Burgess. Now that was *the* first incident of any note since beginning my incumbency. Bad affair that. I met the Burgess family – good people, gentle-natured people, would have liked to have seen them become parishioners – but . . . well . . ."

"What happened to David Burgess?" Hennessey put his cup of tea down. The tea had been served too cold to drink by the reverend's wife who was carelessly dressed and who muttered to herself as if suffering from the onset of dementia.

"He was knocked off his bike by Reddick, who was driving his car while well under the influence."

"I see."

"Killed outright, poor lad, just fifteen years old . . . his whole life ahead of him. Reddick was fined quite heavily, and banned from driving for life, but he escaped a gaol sentence. Probably fortunate in a way because one of my parishioners is a medical man and he told me that if people have a long term and excessive drink problem, they have to be weaned off the stuff – a sudden and permanent withdrawal can be fatal – and Reddick, when I knew him, would demolish two bottles of scotch a day and would often make a start on a third. Mind you, I imagine the prisons could have given him medication to prevent death."

"They do," said Hennessey. "Massive doses of vitamins and protein given in the form of injections."

"I see."

"But what was unacceptable was Reddick's attitude to the accident. Sitting in the pub in Meltham, 'The Fortunate Beggar' – the name apparently refers to a piece of good fortune which befell a beggar in the middle ages – but he would sit in his pub boasting about how he'd got away with killing young Burgess, gloating at his 'victory' as he saw it."

"Not clever."

"Hardly. David Burgess's parents didn't ever go to the 'Beggar' again, but Meltham is a strange place; in terms of its character, it's quite different from the other two villages in my parish. In effect, it's populated by folk who belong to one of three families, with the odd incomer to make up the numbers. And the families seem to like and understand each other. It isn't a feuding village, by any means. They may not send each other Christmas cards or even say 'hello' when they pass in the street, but they know who each other is and they look after each other. So Reddick's insensitive boasts would have been heard by David Burgess's relatives, his cousins, his aunts and uncles and also other folk who knew the Burgesses but were not related to them. Reddick's trial was in January, almost a year after the accident itself, and he disappeared in the summer after the trial. Six months of drunken gloating and boasting . . . if what happened is as I think you may suspect what happened, then I have to say that it says much for the restraint of the people of Meltham."

"We'll reserve our judgement on that one, Reverend Price. A murder is still a murder. Are David Burgess's parents still alive?"

"I think his mother is still with us. No longer at home, but in the care of the local authority in York."

It was a sudden reminder. On the return drive to York they were overtaken by a motorcyclist who was travelling at speed, angling at 45 degrees as he leaned into the bend which lay ahead of them. As always, Hennessey was then reminded of his elder brother, Graham, who had one such machine and who had driven away on it one evening. Later, his father had woken him up and had told him that Graham had ridden his bike to heaven "to save a place for us". Hennessey had been eight years old at the time and all his life he'd felt a gap where his elder brother should have been. As a reaction to the loss, he never drove unless he had to and was convinced that the motor vehicle was the most dangerous machine ever invented, whether two wheels or four.

Later that day, in the mid-evening, after he had exercised Oscar and had left sufficient food and water to see the brown mongrel comfortably through the night, he drove to Skelton with its quaint eleventh-century church and equally ancient yew tree. He parked his car by the kerb in front of an L-shaped half-timbered house. He walked up to the front door and tapped the brass knocker gently, twice, resisting the pause, then a third tap. That would be the policeman's knock: tap, tap . . . tap. Not appropriate in this case.

"Sorry I'm a little late," he said when the door was opened by a smiling woman.

"No matter." Louise D'Acre hooked a slender finger round the knot of his tie and gently pulled him over the threshold. "The children are in bed. We can go straight up."

Thursday Morning

"I thought you'd come. I heard about the bones, you see." Mrs Burgess was frail, slight. "He'd be nearly fifty years old now, my David, had he lived. Possibly a professional. His father wanted him to be a lawyer – he had that sort of mind, you see – David, I mean. He could build a case for this or for that favour, or treat. So, you'll be wanting to know what happened to Reddick?"

"Yes." Hennessey spoke softly. Yellich remained silent.

"Well, Eddie – that was my husband – said we should move on with our lives and not let the tragedy destroy us, that would give Reddick a second victory . . . but we never went into his pub again."

"So I believe. The Reverend Price told us."

"Nice man. He buried both my son and my husband." Mrs Burgess smiled, briefly. "Nice man." Then she paused. Hennessey thought the heat in the nursing home to be turned up too high to be healthy. "But, you see, that's sometimes the way of it . . . you are often more angry about an injustice done to a loved one than about an injustice done to yourself."

"I have experienced that feeling," Hennessey said, thinking of his dear wife, who had died suddenly when she was just twenty-three years old.

"Well, Reddick's boasts and what he said about my David not being any good anyway . . ."

"He said that?"

"So I was told."

"So what happened?"

"Eddie had two brothers, Ernest and Edwin: They never married. They kept pigs on a small holding, just outside Meltham. They, went to the Beggar one morning, just as Reddick was opening up for the day's trade. They were gentlemen in every sense but they had had enough of Reddick by then, as many folk had. They bundled him into a van and drove him to the small holding. They didn't mean to kill him. They wanted to sober him up – that was their intention, to keep him off the drink so he'd listen when they gave him a piece of their mind."

Hennessey groaned. He knew what was coming.

"He had food and water and it was warm where they kept him, but one morning they found he'd died. Just went in his sleep, it seemed."

"How long was that after they had abducted him?"

"I think it was about three days."

"Do you know how they disposed of the body?"

"I don't. But they butchered their own meat. They would have known how to butcher a human body."

"Are Ernest and Edwin still alive?"

"No . . . both gone before now. They kept what they did from Eddie, then Ernest went. Edwin knew he was dying and so he came to see me and told me what they had done. There's just me left now."

He wasn't angry. Hennessey walked into Easingwold, had a pint of mild at the Dove Inn and walked home. It had all happened thirty years ago, all players, save one, deceased. It was an incident which had happened in a strange, inward looking village once upon a time. And what had happened to Reddick didn't make him angry, unlawful as it may have been. It was a cloudless sky and he glanced up at the Great Bear and followed the pointers to the North Star. Then he noticed for the first time that one of the seven stars of the Great Bear had begun to flicker. It was dying, and he was witness to the ending of a celestial age.

THAT'S THE WAY HE DID IT

Amy Myers

"Why won't you play the Maplechurch pitch, *omi*?" This time Toby Wellaway decided he was going to get an answer out of his father. He had a right – he was as much part of the family Punch and Judy show as his dad, especially since he'd been saddled with the name of the Buffer, the show's traditional Toby dog. If a pitch was going to be rejected, he wanted to know why.

Sam Wellaway sighed. "*Omi*, I've been thinking. It's about time I taught you the squeaker, and handed the show over to you. You've bottled for me long enough and I'm sixty now. The jokes don't come so easy as they used to. Time to step aside, and see the world with her in the kitchen. Your mother could do with a change without old Punch tagging along."

He'd be Professor Toby Wellaway! His son grinned in pleasure. Dad step aside? Dad to teach him that most precious of trade secrets, how to master the swazzle in his mouth to produce Punch's voice? He'd never thought to see the day. "I'll let you bottle for me any time you like, Dad."

"Maybe, but not on the Maplechurch pitch, eh?"

"Because of what happened? That pop star's death?"

"Disappearance," Sam reminded him.

"I wasn't even born then. Sixty-seven, wasn't it? 'Course, she's dead. Fay Darling would never have given up singing, nor her partner neither." Toby pressed his luck. "You were there, *omi*, tell me about it."

Sam reflected. The past was the past, and he was more interested in the present. Old Punch had been his life for over fifty years, man and boy. They'd been good times; they'd used live dogs as the Buffer then, not stuffed ones. That wouldn't pass unchallenged nowadays, but he still remembered his first Toby. How he'd loved that dog. He'd changed the show to keep up to date, but the heart of it still remained: Joey the clown, the Crocodile, the old Mr Punch, his wife Judy, and sometimes still the hangman. He'd introduced new puppets though, TV characters or other famous figures, kept up with the times by using modern catch phrases, gearing the performance according to the pitch. Like Maplechurch. He'd played that for six successive years at the annual charity fête, when the grounds of the Manor were thrown open. He had become quite chummy with the pop singer Fay Darling, who lived there with her husband Peter Browning, a brute of a man, jealous and greedy. Some said he had reason enough. Fay was one half of the famous duo Darling Dan, and it was rumoured she was madly in love with her partner, Dan Smith, who had moved with his wife into a house directly opposite the Manor, across the Thames which flowed between their two gardens.

"Tell me what happened, *omi*," Toby pressed him. "There's no reason I can't play the Maplechurch pitch, is there, even if you don't want to?"

Sam deliberated, then made up his mind. "Mozzy," he called to his wife. Punch language came naturally to him, about to retire or not. "What did you do with the Darling Dan puppets?"

Ada Wellaway placidly strolled in from the kitchen, holding a potato in one hand and a peeler in the other. "Up in the attic where they belong, love, having a barney with all your other has-beens. And if you want them you can get 'em yourself," she added amiably. "Ada may mean the happy one, but don't push it, mate."

"Has-beens? Ma, you can't say that." Toby was appalled at such ignorance. "Their records are still selling in their hundreds of thousands. If you took the slightest interest in the pop scene, you'd know it." His generation had grown up with the music of the singing duo.

His mother snorted and returned to the kitchen.

"Tell you what, son," Sam said. "You go to play Maple-church, and I'll tell you the story on one condition. You find out what really happened. Which of them did it? I'd like to know."

"Did what?"

"Made off with her. Did the husband murder her, or did she run away with Dan? Or did Dan do her in, come to that? And *how* was it done?"

"*Me* find out?" Toby blinked. "Don't be daft. How can I?"

"You'll manage. You can take old Ned with you to bottle for you this time. He was there in '67; maybe he can help. All water under the bridge to me. Now, listen to me, *omi*, and I'll tell you the story. The husband did it, that's what the gossip is. Every-one was sure of it, though they couldn't pin anything on him. Pete Browning was her manager as well as her husband and was greedy and jealous with it. He'd grown accustomed to her money, so he pushed Fay to keep right on singing, and she grew to hate it. There was only one problem for Pete Browning: Fay's fame went hand in hand with Dan Smith, and Pete was convinced that Fay was in love with him. He wanted her to go solo. She refused, said she'd give up altogether if he forced her, and of course that confirmed his suspicions, especially since Dan had just moved in opposite with his wife.

"Anyway, Dan Smith never appeared at the fête that day, and there was a terrible row between Fay and the husband. Every-one could hear it. That had me shivering in my shoes, for when Ned and I got down the evening before to test the pitch's acoustics, I heard Dan and Fay were due to open the festivities, so I planned the whole show round the new puppets, now residing in our loft. Instead, Pete opened the fête, with Fay singing solo. Dan never turned up."

"What was she *really* like, pa?"

"Lovely, just as lovely as her pictures, all delicate and fair, and gentle, not a bit like you imagine a sixties' hippy pop star. With her husky voice, well, she was spell-binding. Since I'd played the pitch ever since they lived there, she'd talk to me sometimes. I reckon she was scared of her husband. She wanted to have kids, but Pete wasn't having any of that. Money, that was all that mattered. I don't know whether she was in love with Dan or not, but I wouldn't have blamed her if so, the life she led. He was a handsome devil, with more than a streak of Romany in him. That's why their signature tune was that pop version of 'The Raggle-Taggle Gypsies oh'. And since she sang it solo that day, just before she disappeared, some folks think she knew she would shortly be 'off with her raggle-taggle gypsy' like the song says. Most think Pete murdered her, though."

"She actually disappeared during the fête, didn't she?"

"That's right, *omi*. The grounds run down to the Thames, and on the far side of the lawns from where I put the booth there is – or was – a boathouse with a longish landing stage running out over the water, and a sort of covered porch and passageway round the building on the far side. Fay and Pete were such having such a humdinger in the boathouse, just before she sang her song, that everyone was listening. It grew very silent because folks had already gathered by the river bank to listen to the formal opening of the fête. Fay's voice being higher, you could hear every word she was saying. 'What have you done?' she kept shouting. I remember that. I was just getting Mr Punch and his chums sorted to be ready for Ned when he began banging the drum after the fête was officially open.

"Fay and Pete both came out onto the landing stage, as though they'd just remembered what they were supposed to be doing. Pete introduced her – he was black in the face with rage – and it got blacker when she sang 'Everything but you' – that's the song jazzing up Glück's 'What is life to me without you' and then the 'Raggle Taggle Gypsies'. She didn't need any accompaniment, not Fay. You could have heard a pin drop. Then Fay went back into the boathouse, while Pete declared the fête open. After that he went in, and a minute later there was a terrible scream that chilled me to the marrow. Inhuman it was. We all, and I mean all, rushed to the boathouse, thinking he was strangling her, but when we got there, we found Pete there alone. 'She's gone,' he blurted out, putting on a good show of amazement. 'Gone back to the house.'

"But she hadn't. She'd have been seen coming out of the boathouse door. Besides, Pete was a tightwad, and he made sure you couldn't get into or out of the fête without passing the cash-points. Even Fay would have had to go through them. No, there was only one place she could have gone, over the side of the far passageway into the river. You couldn't see far because there was a bend in the river, so folks started spreading out along the bank, and another party went to search the fête grounds. I ran through the trees, followed by all the world and his wife, to see if Fay's body had been swept round the bend, for there was a fair old current running. Then I saw her lovely hat, all white and flowers on it, bobbing along the river. A few of the better swimmers plunged into the water, but no trace of her was found. When there was no news by evening, Pete called in the police. The river was dredged eventually, but no body turned up. Only that blessed hat again. Months later a body was dredged up, but it was too far gone to identify, and there weren't no DNA testing in those days. So it was case unproven against Pete."

Sam paused, then continued. "Except in Maplechurch. I stopped in for a drink at the pub that evening."

"And for the gossip, I bet," Toby put in.

"Right, *omi*. That was flowing even faster than the beer. She would never have killed herself. Most reckoned Pete had strangled her and pushed her over the side into the river. Others reckoned she jumped in herself, and swum off to join Dan. He was never heard of again either. Rumour has it they're still busking on a Greek island, singing their hearts out for pennies. Fay had left a will, so it turned out, that in the event of her death – which was presumed in due legal course – all her royalties from her music should go to charity. Dan's went to his wife of course, but Fay wouldn't want Pete to touch a penny of hers. He could have the house, that was all. Fay was mighty scared of Pete. There was no question of divorce, you see, and she knew he'd come after her if she just ran away.

"A few of them thought it was Dan murdered her, however, because she was planning to go solo. He knew that would end his career and preferred to end with a bang, not a whimper. Fay was the leader in the partnership, of course. He was a passionate, headstrong chap, and they too had a stormy relationship, if you believed the tabloids of the day.

"The police questioned Pete endlessly, but in the end there was nothing they could do. There was no body to prove she'd been strangled and if he'd just pushed her into the river in the hope she'd drown, there was no proof of that either."

"So he got away scot free?"

"Oh no, son. Only Mr Punch does that. The whole of Maplechurch had Pete marked down as a murderer, and worse, murderer of both Fay *and* Dan. Where was Dan, they asked, if Fay alone had been killed? Dan's wife hadn't heard a dickey bird from him. He'd just vanished. Pete shut himself up in the house and drank himself to death. The next time I passed that way, five years later, I heard he was dead. Even so I never played the pitch again when the new folk bought the house. It seemed somehow disrespectful to Fay."

"What do you think happened, dad?"

"I'm a *swatchel omi*, son, a Punch and Judy man, not a blooming Sherlock Holmes."

"All right, I'll take you on. I *will* be a Sherlock. I could even do a show based round it." Toby's eyes gleamed. "Think of the publicity for the show, if I sort out what happened."

Sam laughed. "You'll do, *omi*, you'll do. You just come back with the answer. I want to know which of 'em did it."

"This where the booth was, Ned?" Ned was well past seventy now, and ready to throw in his drum and collection hat. He grumbled incessantly, but Toby knew that if his father didn't bottle for him, he'd never have the heart to find someone else, since he had a shrewd idea that talk of retiring was all for show. He'd die in his bottling boots, would Ned.

Ned grunted in his usual fashion, and banged down one of the pegs as answer.

"What do you think happened, Ned?" Toby asked when the booth was up. His first pitch as professor. He'd mastered the swazzle, written his show, and was bursting to get going. At the end of the day he'd have another show to plan: the true story of Fay and Dan. And then he'd be on the map.

"I don't think. I bottles." Ned snorted.

Shortly the gates would be thrown open, and the crowds would throng the grounds. There was no charge now to attend, for the present owners were a benevolent couple in their sixties. There were other changes too, Toby reflected, from the last time his father played here. There was a double-glazing stand here to start with, and what would old Punch make of a bouncy castle? Still, Punch had survived because he kept up with the times, and Toby uneasily wondered whether in the excitement of taking up his father's challenge he had given enough thought to that aspect in his first regular show.

"Point out to me where it happened, Ned, while we can leave the booth."

Ned shot him a look but complied. "Not sure as I know."

"Come on, Ned," Toby said patiently. "You were there."

Grumbling under his breath, and playing up his stiff leg as he hobbled along, Ned took him over to the far side of the lawns.

The boathouse looked derelict, and was roped off, whether to avoid accidents with rotting boards or to prevent morbid curiosity from fans of Fay Darling. Toby looked at the landing stage from where his father had seen it, according to Ned, and then walked past the front of the boathouse to peer at the passageway from which it was presumed Fay had disappeared. His father had been right. If Fay had come through the front entrance to the boathouse, she'd have been seen by at least some of the crowd, and so she must have gone over the side, of her own volition or not. Had she planned her disappearance? The story had all the hallmarks. No identifiable body, singing those particular songs, Dan's disappearance. Fay had had good reason to vanish. She'd probably swum round the bend past the boundary to the gardens, climbed ashore and met her Dan. Romantic, really.

"What was Dan's wife like?" he asked Ned.

Ned shrugged. "Never met her, did I?"

Toby sighed. "I thought Dad said you were to give me all the help I needed. You're sure you were here that day?"

Ned looked pained. "Certainly I was, *omi*. Bottling, weren't I? And now I'm a-helping. Just you follow me. This is the way everyone ran, led by your dad." Making great play of his hobbling, he led the way over the hillock of land around which the river curved. "The 'at your dad saw were over there." He pointed to the middle of the river.

Toby looked at the rows of grand houses opposite, and the reed-fringed edges of the river, trying to imagine the scene thirty-odd years ago. Then he turned his attention to the wooded valley garden bordering the river with its stream trickling down to join it. "I think she just landed there, met Dan and left. No one would have seen her if she kept away from the lawns."

Ned sighed. "Good job you're a Punch professor, not the real kind. You ain't got the brains you was born with, young Toby. They'd still have to get out of the grounds. There was a blooming fifteen-foot fence to keep her little ladyship in when her hubby got mad. And the grounds were searched thoroughly, believe me."

"Then suppose she swam as far as the next property?"

"That's what some said." Ned seemed pleased. "To meet her lover," he added with relish. "Funny thing is that with all the publicity in the papers, no one claimed to have seen them leave the village. You'd have thought *someone* might have noticed. What's more, their cars were still here, and no one came forward to say they'd given a lift to two familiar-looking hitchhikers in disguise. How'd they do it?"

"She swam across the river to Dan's house?"

"Listen, *omi*, if I'd been Fay and there was a wife like Dan's ready to stick a knife in my gullet, I'd have opted for Pete to strangle me and have done with it."

This was getting him nowhere, and the show was about to start. Toby was getting frustrated.

"Who could be here today who would have been present in sixty-seven – at the house, I mean? Not the villagers. They're no more use than—" Toby stopped himself in time from saying "you".

Ned looked pleased. "Now you're talking. There's a gardener I ran into. He was only a lad then, he's head gardener – you can have a talk to him after the show. I'll mind the booth."

The show! Toby had almost forgotten his debut was only minutes away.

"Oh, it was him what did it." Adam Dale took off his sunhat, wiped his brow and sat down in his potting shed. Here, he said mysteriously, they could talk away from the crowds. Talk he could, Toby thought to himself. If Prince Charles was right and growing things responded to being spoken to, Manor Court must have the biggest vegetables and flowers in the country.

"Oh yes," he continued, "that gypsy. Underhand, mean-looking Dan Smith was. The master had a temper, but he loved Mrs Fay. He wouldn't have hurt a hair on her head."

"What about blacking her eyes?" Toby began to recall the footage he'd seen of Fay Darling in huge dark sunglasses on a winter's day.

Adam hardly paused. "They had their differences, but murder – no – not even a *crime passion fruit* or whatever they call it. Mrs Fay – everyone loved her and so did the master. Broke his heart when she disappeared."

"She left her royalties to charity, not him," Toby pointed out. "Doesn't sound like a happy marriage."

"Master told me afterwards that was his idea. He'd plenty to live on, and it would all go in tax anyway. No, it was that Dan was the joker in the pack, believe me."

"You think Fay loved him?"

"Why else would she run off with him?"

"There was no proof she did."

"They both disappear at the same time, to different places? Not on your nelly."

"Would you tell me what you remember, Mr Dale?"

Adam was only too willing, but it matched his dad's account almost exactly. "What you so interested for?" he asked curiously. "Writing a book, are you? We get 'em here quite often. I talk to everyone." Toby could well believe it.

"I want to do a new show with the Darling Dan puppets," he explained. "I need a new angle. An ending. Now everyone is dead—"

"*She* ain't," Adam interrupted.

"Fay? You know that for sure?" Toby stuttered.

"Not Mrs Fay. Dan's missis. Madam bloody Serena Smith. You'll find her out there somewhere hobnobbing with the gentry. Ned'll point her out."

"Ned?"

"She was here that day. Didn't he tell you? I'd have my money on her. Not the late master."

"*Ned*!" Toby roared, as he rushed back to the booth which Ned was minding till the next show. "Why didn't you tell me Dan's wife was here that day?"

Ned paused to disentangle the crocodile's strings. "Didn't think of it, Toby. Anyway, she didn't have anything to do with it. Too busy drinking at the bar. Couldn't be two places at once."

"But she might have seen something. At least it suggests she was expecting to see Dan."

Ned shrugged, and returned his concentration to the crocodile.

It was evening before Toby could talk to Serena Smith. It took some time to track her down, and when he did discover her, at the bar, she refused to speak to him, eyeing him up and down and suggesting he came to the house later.

She couldn't have been more than in her mid-fifties but her face, coarsened with drink, looked much older. As the drink had obviously flowed, so had her figure, though not unattractively so. She probably had Romany blood in her, as Dan had, Toby thought, as the rounded curves bulged in the chair she had dropped into with a heavy sigh. He was a little nervous, knowing what some women could be like, alone in the house with a man, but she didn't appear to have sex on her mind. Or, if she did, it wasn't with him, he realised with relief. He could see she wasn't a woman to be crossed, though.

"'Course it was him did it," she snorted. "That Pete Browning. I'd put my money on his doing in both of them, my Dan too."

"You don't believe the gossip that Dan is still alive, then?"

"Look, Dan was a rover. Of course he was. He'd Romany blood in him. But they always come back sooner or later. Thirty years is *too* late. Besides, he was mad about me, not her. He loved me. No, he's dead, and Pete Browning did it. That's what the row was about. I could hear her yelling from the bar. 'What have you done?' I didn't realize what she meant then."

"Did you know Fay Darling well?" Toby asked cautiously.

"Of course I knew her *well*," she mimicked. "I wasn't taken in by that fragile appearance, either. Tough as nails was that lady. She ruled the roost in the Darling Dan duo. Sure they were a success, but Dan loved me, not her. Miss Fay liked all the attention on her and she went on getting it, even after her death. Her own husband wasn't enough for our little angel. She got what was coming to her, in my humble opinion, when Pete strangled her."

"Where was Dan that day, then, if you were at the fête and he was missing?"

"He'd done it before, I wasn't too worried. Another tiff with Madam Nose in the Air, I thought. He'd been away for a few days

– he did that when he could, to get away from it all. I never knew where he was going, but I always knew he'd be back sometime. I expected him to turn up for the fête though, since he and Fay were opening it. I wasn't too surprised when he didn't, though, for he could be an awkward cuss at times. I asked Pete where he was, but he said he'd no idea. With your missus in the hay, I reckon, I told him. That was before the fête opened, and I was already half-seas over with booze. He might as well know the truth, I reckoned. He went bananas. 'I haven't seen him,' he shouted. 'That clear? And I don't want to.' I suppose," Serena added, as though thinking of it for the first time, "I might have put the idea in his mind to bump them off. First Dan, then her." Then she cheered up. "No, I couldn't have done. Dan was already missing, but I'm still sure Pete did for them both." She looked at her empty glass. "When you ain't got love, money's the next best thing, and I've plenty of that. One of these journalists, are you? How much are you paying me?"

"I'm no journalist." Relaxed after the drink, Toby explained about his new show, the one that would finally reveal the truth, and now he thought he knew it. He didn't tell her what he'd worked out, but she didn't take it well, all the same.

She listened to him in silence and, when he finished, announced pleasantly: "You do that, dear, and you'll land up in the river with them."

"I'm back, *omi*." Toby burst through the front door next day, full of excitement.

Sam put down his newspaper. "How did it go, son?"

"I know how it was done and why."

"Tell me, *omi*."

"I can do better than that. I'll give you my new show. That'll tell you who did it." Toby was highly pleased with his efforts. Not a bad day for his first time with the swazzle. That was a mere rehearsal for the show he'd decided he'd better confine to the limited audience of his parents for the moment. It was going to knock 'em cold.

"Right, son. There's nothing decent on telly. Why not?"

Toby didn't mind being laughed at. He was sure of his ground, if somewhat nervous. He'd decided there was no need for Ned's services with a small cast and no bottling required.

He set up the puppets while Dad went to call Mum to watch. She couldn't miss this one, he heard Sam say to her. Not Toby's first show, and in she came, apron on, and teacloth in hand. Toby nipped round to the front of the booth to give a welcoming roll on the drum, then dived into the back again. He was keyed up, but still remembered to use the indoors swazzle Dad had given him, not yesterday's outdoors caller for Punch's voice. He was so het up he nearly choked on it at first, as he screeched, "Hallo folks" and popped Punch up to join the rest of the cast lined up to greet the audience. Then he came out front again: "Right, *omi*, Mr Punch plays the wicked husband as usual, Judy plays his wife Fay, Scaramouche, Punch's neighbour, is Handsome Dan, and the crocodile is his wife Serena. We've a few other players: Joey of course, the policeman, the ghost, the buffer, the baby – even the publican."

"That's a surprise, son." Sam was impressed. "Haven't heard of a couple of those for years."

"You'll have a few more surprises coming, I reckon," Toby said complacently, and went back inside the booth again.

"Come on then, let's be having you," Sam shouted. "Where's old Judy?"

"Change of routine, Dad," came Toby's muffled voice. "Back to the old Piccini script." In this famous eighteenth-century version, the neighbour had come on first. Sam nodded, surprised, but he couldn't fault that. After a burst of song, "Where are my sausages, Scaramouche?" Punch chased after him, then disappeared while Scaramouche and Judy sang a duet, in Toby's falsetto voice, one of the old Darling Dan hits, their version of "The Gypsy's Warning".

"Do not trust him, gentle maiden . . ." Toby boomed as Judy.

"I'll truss him like a chicken; I'm not scared of him," squealed Scaramouche.

"Oh ho. What's all this? Not content with wanting my sausages, you're after my wife, too. I'll show you." Punch hit Scaramouche with his stick, who promptly lay down and died, then popped up again to berate Judy who was by now nursing the baby. He took it from her and flung it over the edge. "Ha, ha, no babies for you. That's the way to do it."

"Oh, Punch, how can you be so cruel?" sobbed Judy.

"Easy! I'll show you how!" squawked Punch in triumph, turning to whack her. But by now not only Joey the Clown was on the scene, but Jack Ketch the hangman, and Punch hastily changed his mind. "My wife," he squawked. "Isn't she lovely?" As soon as their backs were turned, he swiped at Judy again, but this time Joey the Clown appeared and pulled her away, leaving a string of sausages in her place for Punch to thump. The crocodile swallowed them up, and quickly pretended to be dead when he saw Punch. Jack Ketch appeared to hang Punch, but the publican saved him by handing him a large bottle of whisky, and Jack Ketch joined the row of bodies lying at Punch's feet.

"What's he playing at?" Ada whispered. "I don't understand. It's daft. This isn't a proper Punch and Judy."

"Give the lad time, mozzy," Sam said quietly.

"Let me see now, how many have I killed?" Punch began the body-counting routine, confused this time not only by Joey the clown but by the ghost who kept lying down to complicate matters.

Finally the policeman loomed over him. "Mr Punch, I've a warrant to cart you off for killing your wife."

"But I didn't," squealed Punch. "Honest. She warrant *there*."

"Oh." The policeman threw the warrant away, and just as Punch was chuckling with relief, popped up again: "Never mind. I'll have you anyway."

He called the publican back on – and the curtains closed.

"What did you think of it, Dad?" Toby strolled out.

His father cleared his throat. "Very neat, son. I take it you're saying Mr Punch was innocent of killing Judy, but he killed Scaramouche, but escaped the law, although he got his comeuppance in the end. That right?"

"Yes, *omi*," Toby said. "I think Fay engineered the row beforehand, when she was yelling 'What have you done?' so that everyone would think Pete was mad enough to kill her. By the time he got back in the boathouse, she had already vanished – slipped into the river, round the corner, and landed where she gave out that terrible shriek – which brought Pete into the boathouse right on cue."

"And what *had* he done, *omi*?" Sam asked.

"Murdered Dan. Fay knew it, but didn't know where the body was – so she couldn't prove it. She wanted revenge, and how better to get it than to have people think Pete had murdered her?"

"What did she do after she climbed onto the bank then?" Even his mother was getting interested now. "She still had to escape."

"No Dan to help her, was there?" Sam pointed out. "Scaramouche was dead, and his ghost couldn't help."

"No, but Joey the clown could."

There was a split-second silence, then Toby said quietly to his father: "*That's the way you did it*, omi."

A split second silence, broken by Sam's loud laugh. "How's that, then?"

"I think you helped her, Dad. Fay was friendly with you, and she came to you for help when you arrived the evening before. She told you that she knew Pete had killed Dan, and that she would never be free of him if she tried to get away, so she had to disappear for good. You helped her. You lent her the outdoor swazzle for that scream. When you led the chase over the hillock to look for her body, no one noticed that there was one extra person coming back. Why should they? It was only your bottler. Not Ned, though, he was making himself scarce in the bar. That's what put me on to it. He insisted he'd been at the boathouse with you, but there's no way he could have left you there to go back to the bar, and that's where he met Serena Smith. I think Fay wore a hat and blazer over a pair of her own trousers and a shirt. The hat hid her short hair, and no one's going to look at the face of a bottler; mentally they only see the hat. She stayed dressed like that till you went home."

"And what happened to her then, son?"

"I don't know, but you probably do. Maybe she's still singing her heart out somewhere in the world. After all, it doesn't take much in disguise when folks aren't expecting to see you any longer. Bit of hair-dye, and different hair-do, change of name and no one would recognize her now. *Do* you know, Dad? Have you ever seen her again?"

"Oh yes, son."

"So where is she?"

"Right here, *omi*. She's your ma."

THE LONG BLACK VEIL

Val McDermid

Jess turned fourteen today. With every passing year, she looks more like her mother. And it pierces me to the heart. When I stopped by her room this evening, I asked if her birthday awakened memories of her mother. She shook her head, leaning forward so her long blonde hair curtained her face, cutting us off from each other. "Ruth, you're the one I think of when people say 'mother' to me," she mumbled.

She couldn't have known that her words opened an even deeper wound inside me and I was careful to keep my heart's response hidden from my face. Even after ten years, I've never stopped being careful. "She was a good woman, your mother," I managed to say without my voice shaking.

Jess raised her head to meet my eyes then swiftly dropped it again, taking refuge behind the hair. "She killed my father," she said mutinously. "Where exactly does 'good' come into it?"

I want to tell her the truth. There's part of me thinks she's old enough now to know. But then the sensible part of me kicks in. There are worse things to be in small town America than the daughter of a murderess. So I hold my tongue and settle for silence.

Seems like I've been settling for silence all my adult life.

It's easy to point to where things end but it's a lot harder to be sure where they start. Everybody here in Marriott knows where

and when Kenny Sheldon died, and most of them think they
know why. They reckon they know exactly where his journey to
the grave started.

They're wrong, of course. But I'm not going to be the one to
set them right. As far as Marriott is concerned, Kenny's first
step on the road to hell started when he began dating Billy Jean
Ferguson. Rich boys mixing with poor girls is pretty much a
conventional road to ruin in these parts.

Me and Billy Jean, we were still in high school, but Kenny
had a job. Not just any old job, but one that came slathered with
a certain glamour. Somehow, he'd persuaded the local radio
station to take him on staff. He was only a gofer, but Kenny
being Kenny, he managed to parlay that into being a crucial
element in the station's existence. In his eyes, he was on the fast
track to being a star. But while he was waiting for that big break,
Kenny was content to play the small town big shot.

He'd always had an eye for Billy Jean, but she'd fended him
off in the past. We'd neither of us been that keen on dating.
Other girls in our grade had been hanging out with boyfriends
for a couple of years by then, but to me and Billy Jean it had felt
like a straitjacket. It was one of the things that made it possible
for us to be best friends. We preferred to hang out at Helmer's
drugstore in a group of like-minded teens, among them Billy
Jean's distant cousin Jeff.

Their mothers were cousins, and by some strange quirk of
genetics, they'd turned out looking like two peas in a pod. Hair
the colour of butter, eyes the same shade as the hyacinths our
mothers would force for Christmas. The same small, hawk-
curved nose and cupid's bow lips. You could take their features
one by one and see the correspondence. The funny thing was
that you would never have mistaken Billy Jean for a boy or Jeff
for a girl. Maybe it was nothing more than their haircuts. Billy
Jean's hair was the long blonde swatch that I see now in Jess,
whereas Jeff favoured a crew-cut. Still does, for that matter,
though the blond is starting to silver round the temples now.

Anyhow, as time slipped by, the group we hung with thinned
out into couples and sometimes there were just the three of us
drinking Cokes and picking at cold fries. Kenny, who had taken
to drifting into Helmer's when we were there, picked his
moment and started insinuating himself into our company.

He'd park himself next to Jeff, stretching his legs to stake out the whole side of the table. If either of us girls wanted to go to the bathroom, we had to go through a whole rigmarole of getting Kenny to move his damn boots. He'd lay an arm across the back of the booth proprietorially, a Marlboro dangling from the other hand, and tell us all about his important life at the radio station.

One night, he turned up with free tickets for a Del Shannon concert fifty miles down the interstate. We were impressed. Marriott had never seen live rock and roll, unless you counted the open mike night at the Tavern in the Town. As far as we were concerned, only the truly cool had ever seen live bands. It took no persuading whatsoever for us to accompany Kenny to the show.

What we hadn't really bargained for was Kenny treating it like a double date right from the start when he installed Billy Jean up front next to him in the car and relegated me and Jeff to the back seat. He carried on as he started, draping his arm over her shoulders at every opportunity. But we all were fired up with the excitement of seeing a singer who had actually had a number-one single, so we all went along with it. Truth to tell, it turned out to be just the nudge Jeff and I needed to slip from friendship into courting. We'd been heading that way, but I reckon we'd both been reluctant to take any step that might make Billy Jean feel shut out. If Billy Jean was happy to be seen as Kenny's girlfriend – and at first, it seemed that way, since she showed no sign of objecting to the arm-draping or the subsequent hand-holding – then we were freed up to follow our hearts.

That first double date was a night to remember. The buzz from the audience as we filed into the arena was beyond anything we small-town kids had ever experienced. I felt like a little kid again, but in a good way. I slid my hand into Jeff's for security and we followed Kenny and Billy Jean to our seats right at the front. When the support act took to the stage, I was rapt. Around us, people seemed to be paying no attention to the unknown quartet on the stage, but I was determined to miss nothing.

After Del Shannon's set, my ears were ringing from the music and the applause, my eyes dazzled by the spotlights glinting on the chrome and polish of the instruments. The air was thick with smoke and sweat and stale perfume. I was stunned by it all. I scarcely felt my feet touch the ground as we walked back to Kenny's car, the chorus of "Runaway" ringing inside my head. But I was still alert enough to see that Kenny still had his arm round Billy Jean and she was leaning into him. I wasn't crazy about Kenny, but I was selfish. I wanted to be with Jeff, so I wasn't going to try to talk Billy Jean out of Kenny.

Kenny dropped Jeff and me off outside my house, and as his tail lights disappeared, I said, "You think she'll be OK?"

Jeff grinned. "I've got a feeling Kenny just bit off more than he can chew. Billy Jean will be fine. Now, come here, missy, I've got something for you." Then he pulled me into his arms and kissed me. I didn't give Billy Jean another thought that night.

Next day when we met up, we compared notes. I was still floating from Jeff's kisses and I didn't really grasp that Billy Jean was less enamoured of Kenny's attempts to push her well beyond a goodnight kiss. What I did take in was that she appeared genuinely pleased for Jeff and me. My fears that she'd feel shut out seemed to have been groundless, and she talked cheerfully about more double-dating. I didn't understand that was her way of keeping herself safe from Kenny's advances. I just thought that we were both contentedly coupled up after that one double date.

All that spring, we went out as a foursome. Kenny seemed to be able to get tickets to all sorts of venues and we went to a lot of gigs. Some were good, most were pretty terrible and none matched the excitement of that first live concert. I didn't really care. All that mattered to me was the shift from being Jeff's friend to being his girlfriend. I was in love, no doubting it, and in love as only a teenage girl can be. I walked through the world starry-eyed and oblivious to anything that wasn't directly connected to me and my guy.

That's why I paid no attention to the whispers linking Kenny's name to a couple of other girls. Someone said he'd been seen with Janine, who tended bar at the Tavern in the Town. I dismissed that out of hand. According to local legend, a procession of men had graced Janine's trailer. Why would Kenny lower himself when he had someone as special as Billy

Jean for a girlfriend? Oh yes, I was quite the little innocent back in the day.

Someone else claimed to have seen him with another girl at a blues night in the next county. I pointed out to her that he worked in the music business. It wasn't surprising if he had to meet with colleagues at music events. And that it shouldn't surprise her if some of those colleagues happened to be women. And that it was a sad day when women were so sexist.

I didn't say anything to Billy Jean, even though we were closer than sisters. I'd like to think it was because I didn't want to cause her pain, but the truth is that their stories probably slipped my mind, being much less important than my own emotional life.

By the time spring had slipped into summer, Jeff and I were lovers. I'm bound to say it was something of a disappointment. I suspect it is for a lot of women. Not that Jeff wasn't considerate or generous or gentle. He was all of those and more. But even after we'd been doing it a while and we'd had the chance to get better at it, I still had that Peggy Lee "Is that all there is?" feeling.

I suppose that made it easier for me to support Billy Jean in her continued refusal to let Kenny go all the way. When we were alone together, she was adamant that she didn't care for him nearly enough to let him be the one to take her virginity. For my part, I told her she should hold out for somebody who made her dizzy with desire because frankly that feeling was the only thing that made it all worth it.

The weekend after I said that to her, Billy Jean told Kenny she wasn't in love with him and she didn't want to go out with him any more. Of course, he went around telling anybody who would listen that he was the one to call time on their relationship, but I suspect that most people read that for the bluster it was. "How did he take it?" I asked her at recess on the Monday afterwards. "Was he upset?"

"Upset, like broken-hearted? No way." Billy Jean gave a little "I could give a shit" shrug. "He was really pissed at me," she said. "I got the impression he's the only one who gets to decide when it's over."

"You know, I've been wanting to say this for the longest time, but he really is kind of an asshole," I said.

We both giggled, bumping our shoulders into each other like big kids. "I only started going out with him so you and Jeff would finally get it together," Billy Jean said in between giggles. "I knew as long as I was single you two would be too loyal to do anything about it. Now I can just go back to having you both as my best friends again."

And so it played out over the next few weeks. Billy Jean and I hung out together doing girl things; Billy Jean and Jeff went fishing out on the lake once a week and spent Sunday mornings fixing up the old clunker her dad had bought for her birthday; we'd all go for a pizza together on Friday nights; and the rest of the time she'd leave us to our own devices. It seemed like one chapter had closed and another had opened.

Jess turned fourteen today. Seems like yesterday she came into our home. It wasn't how we expected it to be, me and Ruthie. We thought we'd have a brood of our own, not end up raising my cousin's kid. But some things just aren't meant to be and I'm old enough now to know there are sometimes damn good reasons for that.

I remember the morning after Jess was conceived. When Billy Jean told Ruthie and me what Kenny Sheldon had done, I didn't think it was possible to feel more angry and betrayed. I was wrong about that too, but that's another story.

It happened the night before, when Ruthie and I were parked up by the lake in my car and Billy Jean was on her lonesome, nursing a Coke in one of the booths at Helmer's. According to her, when Kenny walked in, he didn't hesitate. He came straight over to her booth and plonked himself down opposite her. He gave her the full charm offensive, apologizing for being mean to her when she'd thrown him over.

He claimed he'd missed her and he wanted her back but if he couldn't be her boyfriend he wanted to be her friend, like me. He pitched it just right for Billy Jean and she believed he meant what he said. That's the kind of girl she was back then – honest and open and unable to see that other people might not be worthy of her trust. So she didn't think twice when he offered her a ride home.

She called me first thing Sunday morning. We were supposed to be going fishing as usual but she wanted Ruthie to come along too. I could tell from her voice something terrible had happened even though she wouldn't tell me what it was, so I called Ruthie and got her to make some excuse to get out of church.

When we picked her up, she was pale and withdrawn. She wouldn't say a word till we were out at the lake, sitting on the jetty with rods on the water like it was any other Sunday morning. When she did speak, it was right to the point. Billy Jean was never one for beating about the bush, but this was bald, even for her.

"Kenny Sheldon raped me last night," she said. She told us about the meeting at Helmer's and how she'd agreed to let him drive her home. Only, before they got to her house, Kenny had driven down an overgrown track out of sight of the street. Then he'd pinned her down and forced her to have sex with him.

We didn't know what to do. Fourteen years ago, date rape wasn't on the criminal agenda. Not in towns like Marriott. And the Sheldons were a prominent family. Kenny's dad owned the funeral home and had been a councilman. And his mom ran the flower arranging circle at the church. Whereas the Fergusons were barely one step up from white trash. Nobody was going to take the word of Billy Jean Ferguson against Kenny Sheldon.

I wanted to call Kenny Sheldon out and beat him to within an inch of his life. I wanted him to beg for mercy the way I knew Billy Jean had begged him the night before.

But Ruthie and Billy Jean stopped me. "Don't stoop so low," Billy Jean said.

"That's right," Ruthie said. "There's other ways to get back at scum like him."

And by that afternoon, I had started the rumour that Janine from the Tavern in the Town had stopped sleeping with Kenny because she'd found out he had a venereal disease. I don't know how long it took to get back to the shitheel himself, but I do know he'd had quite the struggle to get anyone to sit next to him in Helmer's, never mind hang out at gigs with him. That cheered us up some, and Ruthie said Billy Jean was starting to talk about getting over it. That was so like her – she wasn't the kind to let anybody take her life away from her. She was always determined to control her own destiny.

But all her good intentions went to shit about six weeks after the rape. I'd been helping my dad finish off some work in the top pasture and both girls were sitting on the front porch when I got back to the house. We all piled into my truck and headed out to the lake. We hadn't gone but half a mile when Ruthie blurted out, "She's pregnant. That bastard Kenny got her pregnant."

I only had to glance at Billy Jean to know it was true and the knowledge made me boiling mad. I swung the truck around at the next intersection and headed for the Sheldon house, paying no mind to the girls shouting at me to stop. When we got there, I jumped out and marched straight up to the house. I hammered on the door and Kenny himself opened it.

I know that violence isn't supposed to solve things, but in my experience, it definitely has its plus points. I grabbed Kenny by the shirt front, yanked him out the door and slammed him against the wall. I swear the whole damn house shook. "You bastard," I yelled at him. "First you rape her, then you get her pregnant."

I drew my hand back to smack him in the middle of his dumbfounded face, but Billy Jean caught my arm. She was always strong for a girl and she had me at an awkward angle. "Leave him," she said. "I don't want anything to do with him."

"You say that now, but you're going to need his money," I snarled. "Babies don't come cheap and he has to pay for what he's done."

Before anybody could say anything more, Mrs Sheldon appeared in the doorway. She looked shocked to see her golden boy pinned up against the wall and demanded to know what was going on.

My dander was up, and I wasn't about to back off. "Ma'am," I said, "I'm sorry to cause a scene, but your son here raped my cousin Billy Jean and now she is expecting his baby."

Mrs Sheldon reared back like a horse spooked by a snake. "How dare you," she hissed. "My son is a gentleman, which is more than I can say about you or your kin." She made a kind of snorting noise in the back of her throat. "The very idea of any Ferguson woman being able to name the father of her children with any certainty is absurd. Now get off my property before I call the police. And take your slut of a cousin with you."

It was my turn to grab Billy Jean. I thought she was fixing to rip Mrs Sheldon's face off. "You evil witch," she screamed as I pulled her away.

Ruthie stared Mrs Sheldon down. When she spoke her voice was cold and sharp. I know I hoped she'd never use that tone of voice to me. "You should be ashamed of yourself," she said,

turning on her heel and walking back to the truck, head high. I
never knew to this day whether she meant Kenny or his mother or
both of them.

What happened that evening must have had some effect, though.
A week later, Kenny was gone.

Back in the early Sixties, being an unwed mother was still about
the biggest disgrace around and most girls who got into trouble
ended up disowned and despised. But Billy Jean was lucky in
her parents. The Fergusons never had much money but they
had love aplenty. When she told them she was pregnant and
how it had happened, they'd been shocked, but they hadn't
been angry with her. Her father went round to see old man
Sheldon. He never told anybody what passed between them,
not even Mrs Ferguson, but he came back with a cashier's check
for ten thousand dollars.

Nobody knew where Kenny was. His mother told her church
crowd that he'd landed a big important radio job out on the
coast, but nobody believed her. Truth to tell, I don't think
anybody much cared. We certainly didn't.

Jeff and I were married three months later. I guess we were
both kind of fired up by Billy Jean being pregnant. We wanted
to start a family of our own. We moved into a little house on
Jeff's daddy's farm and Jeff started working as a trainee sales
representative for an agricultural machinery firm.

Half a mile down the track from us there was an old double-
wide trailer that had seen better days. Jeff's dad used to rent it
out to seasonal workers. We persuaded him to let Billy Jean
have it for next to nothing in return for doing it up. We knew
there wasn't enough room in her parents' house for Billy Jean
and a growing kid and I wanted her to be close at hand so we
could bring up our children together.

Jeff and I spent most of our spare time knocking that trailer
into shape. Billy Jean helped as much as she could, and by the
time Jess was born, we'd turned it into a proper little home for
the two of them. They moved in when Jess was six weeks old,
and Billy Jean looked relaxed for the first time since Kenny had
raped her. "I can never thank the two of you enough," she said
so many times I told her she should just make a tape of it and
give us each a copy.

"It was Ruthie's idea," Jeff said, acting like it was nothing to do with him.

"I know," Billy Jean said. "But I also know you did more than your fair share to make it happen."

We settled into a pretty easy routine. I worked mornings on the farm, helping Jeff's mother with the specialty yogurt business she was building up. Afternoons, I'd hang out with Billy Jean and Jess. Then I'd cook dinner for Jeff, we'd either watch some TV or walk down to have a beer and a few hands of cards with Billy Jean. Most people might have thought our lives pretty dull, but it seemed fine enough to us.

There was one thing, I thought, that stopped it being perfect. A year had gone by since Jeff and I had married, but still I wasn't pregnant. It wasn't for want of trying, but I began to wonder whether my lack of enthusiasm for sex was somehow preventing it. I knew this was crazy, but it nagged away at me.

Finally, I managed to talk to Billy Jean about it. It was a hot summer afternoon and Jess was over at her grandma's house. Billy Jean and I were lying on her bed with the only a/c in the trailer cranked up high. "I love him," I said. "But when we make love, it's not like it says in the books and magazines. It doesn't feel like it looks in the movies. I just don't feel that whole swept away thing."

Billy Jean rolled over on to her back and yawned. "I'm not the best person to ask, Ruth. I only ever had sex the once and that sure wasn't what you would call a good experience. I don't guess it's the kind of thing you can talk to Jeff about either."

I made a face. "He'd be mortified. He thinks I think he's the greatest lover on the planet." Billy Jean giggled. "Well, you have to make them feel like that."

Billy Jean yawned again. "I'm sorry, Ruth. I don't mean you to feel like I'm dismissing you, but I am so damn tired. I was up three times with Jess last night. She's teething."

"Why don't you just have a nap?" I said. But she was already drifting away. I made myself more comfortable and before I knew it, I'd nodded off too.

I woke because someone was kissing me. An arm was heavy across my chest and shoulder, a leg was thrown between mine and soft lips were pressing on mine, a tongue flicking between my lips. I opened my eyes and the mouth pulled back from mine. A face that was familiar and yet completely strange hovered above mine. *Jeff with long hair*, I thought stupidly for a moment before the truth dawned.

Billy Jean put a finger to my lips. . . . "Ssh," she said "Let's see if we can figure out what Jeff's doing wrong."

By the end of the afternoon, I understood that it wasn't what Jeff did that was wrong. It was who he was.

Kenny came back a couple of weeks before Jess's fourth birthday. It turned out his mother hadn't been lying to the church group. He had landed a job working for a radio station in Los Angeles. He was doing pretty well. Had his own show and everything. He rolled back into town in a muscle car with a beautiful blonde on his arm. His fiancée, apparently.

All of that would have been just fine if he had left the past alone. But no. He wanted to impress the fiancée with his credentials as a family man. The first thing we knew about it was when Billy Jean got a letter from Kenny's lawyer saying he planned to file suit for shared custody. Kenny wanted Jess for one week a month until she started school, then he wanted her for half the school vacations. If he'd been the standard absent father as opposed to one who had never even seen his kid, it might have sounded reasonable. And we had a sneaking feeling that the court might see things Kenny's way.

Justice in Marriott comes courtesy of His Honour Judge Wellesley Benton. Who is an old buddy of Kenny Sheldon's daddy and a man who's put a fair few of Billy Jean's relatives behind bars. We were, to say the least, apprehensive.

The day after the letter came, Billy Jean happened to be walking down Main Street when Kenny strolled out of the Coffee Bean Scene with the future Mrs. Sheldon. I heard all about it from Mom, who saw it all from the vantage point of the quilting store porch.

Billy Jean just lit into him. Called him all the names under the sun from rapist to deadbeat dad. Kenny looked shocked at first, then when he saw his fiancée wasn't turning a hair, he started to laugh. That just drove Billy Jean even crazier. She was practically hysterical. Mom came over from the quilt shop and grabbed her by the shoulders, trying to get her away. Then Kenny said, "I'll see you in court," and walked his fiancée to the car. Billy Jean was fit to be tied.

Well, everybody thinks they know what happened next. That night, Kenny was due at a dinner in the Town Hall. As he approached, a figure stepped out of the shadows. Long blonde hair, jeans and a Western shirt, just like Billy Jean always liked to wear. And a couple of witnesses who were a ways off but who knew Billy Jean well enough to recognize her when she raised the shotgun and blew Kenny Sheldon into the next world.

That was the end of her as much as it was the end of him.

I knew Billy Jean was innocent. Not out of some crazy misplaced belief, but because at the very moment Kenny Sheldon was meeting his maker, I was in her bed, moaning at her touch. That first afternoon had not been a one-off. It had been an awakening that had led us both into a deeper happiness than we'd ever known before.

If I'd been married to anyone other than Jeff, I'd have left in a New York minute. But I cared about him. More importantly, so did Billy Jean. "You're both my best friend," she said as we lay in a tangle of sheets. "Until this afternoon, I couldn't have put one of you above the other. You gotta stay with him, Ruth. You gotta go on being his wife because I couldn't live with myself if you didn't."

And so I did. It might seem strange to most folks, but in a funny kind of way, it worked out just fine for us. Except of course that I still couldn't get pregnant. I began to think of that as the price I had to pay for my other contentments – Jeff, Billy Jean, Jess.

Then Kenny came back.

They came for Billy Jean soon after midnight. A deputy we'd all been at school with knocked on our door at one in the morning, carrying Jess in a swaddle of bedclothes. He looked mortified as he explained what had happened and asked us to take care of the child till morning when things could be sorted out more formally.

Jess had often stayed with us, so she settled pretty easy. That morning, I drove into town, leaving Jess with her grandma, and demanded to see Billy Jean. She was white and drawn, her eyes heavy and haunted. "They can't prove it," she said. "You have to promise me you will never tell. Don't sacrifice yourself trying to save me. They won't believe you anyway and you'll have shamed yourself in their eyes for nothing. Just have faith. We both know I'm innocent. Judge Benton isn't a fool. He won't let them get away with it."

And so I kept my mouth shut. Partly for Billy Jean and partly for Jess. We'd already made arrangements with Billy Jean and her parents for me and Jeff to take care of Jess till after the court case, and I wasn't about to do anything that would jeopardize that child's future. I sat through that terrible trial day after day. I listened to witnesses swearing they had seen Billy Jean kill Kenny Sheldon and I said not a word.

Nor did Billy Jean. She said she was somewhere else, but refused to say where or with whom. Judge Benton offered her the way out. "Woman, what is your alibi?" he thundered. "If you were somewhere else that night, then you won't have to die. If you're telling the truth, give up your alibi." But she wouldn't budge. And so I couldn't. It nearly killed me.

But I never truly thought he would have her hanged.

I never truly thought he would have her hanged. I thought they'd argue she was temporarily insane because of the threat to her child and that she'd do a few years in jail, nothing more. And I was selfish enough to think of how much my Ruthie would love bringing up Jess for as long as Billy Jean was behind bars.

Sure, I wanted to make her suffer. But I didn't want her to die. She was my best friend, after all. A friend like no other. I swear, I always believed we would lay down our lives for each other if it came to it. And I guess I was right, in a way. She laid down her life rather than destroy my marriage.

When the sentence came down, it hit me like a physical blow. I swear I doubled over in pain as I realized the full horror of what I'd done. But it was too late. The sacrifices were made, the chips down once and for all.

I saw the way she looked at me in court. A mixture of pity and blame. As soon as she heard those witnesses, recognized the conviction in their voices, I think she knew the truth. With a long blonde wig and the right clothes, I could easily be mistaken for her.

There was an excuse for the witnesses. They were a way off from Kenny and his killer. But there's no excuse for Ruthie. She was no distance at all from Billy Jean that afternoon I saw them by the lake shore. She could not have been mistaken.

Why didn't I confront her? Why didn't I walk away? I guess because I loved them both so much. I didn't want to lose the life we had. I just wanted Billy Jean to suffer for a while, that was all. I never truly thought he would have her hanged.

Jess turned fourteen today. She's not old enough for the truth. Maybe she'll never be that old. But there's one thing she is old enough for.

Tonight, there will be two of us standing over Billy Jean's grave, our long black veils drifting in the wind, our tears sparkling like diamonds in the moonlight.

THE CURIOUS CONTENTS OF A COFFIN

Susanna Gregory

London, 1663

Thomas Chaloner, spy for the Lord Chancellor, hated assignments like the one he had been given that morning. He did not mind the physical labour of excavating a tomb in the hour before dawn – although he would have been happier had it not been raining so hard. And he enjoyed the challenge of disguising himself as a gravedigger – donning the filthy clothes of the trade and staining his teeth brown, so that even his own mother would not have recognized him. He did not even mind manhandling corpses. But what Chaloner didn't like was causing distress to the dead woman's son and daughter, who had objected strenuously to their mother's final resting place being disturbed. Nor did he like the possibility that he might be ordered to steal what was in the coffin with her.

"How much longer?" demanded John Pargiter, wealthy goldsmith and husband of the deceased. He was a tall man, with a long nose and a reputation for dishonesty – the Goldsmith's Company had fined him several times for coin-clipping and shoddy workmanship. "My arm aches from holding this lamp and I'm soaking wet."

"This foul weather is a sign of God's displeasure," declared Pargiter's son Francis, hugging his sobbing sister closer to him. "This is an evil deed, and you will pay for it on Judgment Day."

"Please, father," begged the weeping Eleanor. "Stop this. Let our mother rest in peace."

Chaloner waited to see if Pargiter would agree. He was nearing the casket, and knew he would have to be careful not to step through it. The man who usually dug graves for St Martin's Ludgate – currently insensible after the copious quantities of ale with which Chaloner had plied him the previous night in the hope of learning a few useful tips – had confided that there was an art to dealing with rotting coffins, but had then declined to elaborate. Chaloner would have to rely on his own ingenuity to perform the grisly task, and only hoped he would convince Pargiter that he knew what he was doing. The goldsmith had brought two burly henchmen with him, and Chaloner suspected they might turn nasty if he failed to impress.

He exchanged a hopeful glance with the parish priest, Robert Bretton, a short fellow with a mane of long, shiny black curls. Bretton was chaplain to King Charles, as well as Rector of St Martin's, and it was because of him that this particular assignment had been foisted on Chaloner. When he had learned what Pargiter intended to do, Bretton had approached the King in a fury of righteous indignation – the poor woman had been in the ground for more than three years, and it was shameful to disturb her rest. With a shudder of distaste, the King had passed the matter to his Lord Chancellor to sort out.

But the Lord Chancellor said there was nothing he could do to stop the exhumation, because Pargiter had the necessary writs. What he *had* been able to do, however, was lend Bretton one of his men, assuring the agitated chaplain that Thomas Chaloner would not only ensure the exhumation was carried out decently, but could be trusted not to gossip. When Bretton had demurred, the Lord Chancellor had pointed out that he would have an ally at the graveside should he need one, and the family would be suitably grateful to him for "hiring" a man who knew how to be discreet. And, the Lord Chancellor had added slyly, he wanted his spy present anyway, because he was curious to know what Pargiter thought he might find among his wife's rotting bones.

Bretton peered at the goldsmith in the gloom, to see whether he was having second thoughts. He sighed unhappily when he saw he was not, and nodded down at Chaloner, telling him to continue. The spy began to dig again, pretending not to listen to the furious altercation that was taking place above his head. The family had kept their voices low at first, unwilling to let a stranger hear what they were saying – even one vouched for by Rector Bretton. But as time had crept by and Chaloner's spade came ever closer to the coffin, they had grown less cautious, and the foul weather and their increasing agitation encouraged them to forget themselves. In addition, Chaloner had excellent hearing – a valuable asset for a spy – and a decade of eavesdropping in foreign courts meant he was rather good at hearing discussions not intended for his ears.

"This is very wrong," said Pargiter's cousin and business-partner, an overweight man named Thomas Warren, who was the last of the graveside party. His plump face was pale and unhappy, and the hair in his handsome wig had been reduced to a mess of rat-tails in the rain. "Had I known you'd cached our gold in Margaret's grave, I'd *never* have asked for it back. I don't want her defiled."

"You're deep in debt," said Pargiter with a sneer. "You lost a fortune in Barbados sugar, and your creditors snap at your heels. Would you rather go to prison? Besides, Margaret won't be defiled. Once the coffin is reached, I shall jump down and remove the gold myself. I was her husband, so she won't object to me touching her."

Francis snorted his disdain. "She would. She hated you – and with good cause." He added something else in a low, venomous hiss that Chaloner could not quite catch. The spy supposed someone – probably his sister – had warned him to keep his voice down.

"Why are *you* so eager to retrieve the hoard, Father?" asked Eleanor softly, so Chaloner had to strain to hear her. "*You* don't need your share of this gold: you're already rich – certainly wealthy enough to lend Warren what he needs."

"Yes," said Warren, sounding relieved. "That's the best solution. Fill in the hole and I'll have papers—"

"I've lent him too much already," interrupted Pargiter roughly. "No, don't you flap your hand at me to be quiet, Warren! I shall talk as loudly as I please. And, to answer my daughter's question, our cache has been playing on my mind of late. Gold can't earn interest if it's buried, and I want it where it can do me some good."

"Tainted money," said Rector Bretton in disgust. Chaloner had noticed his increasing distress as the exhumation had proceeded, and now he sounded close to tears. "It won't bring you happiness, and I strongly advise you to leave it where it is."

"You did a dreadful thing, burying gold with our mother," said Eleanor in a broken, grief-filled voice that made Chaloner wince at his role in the distasteful business. The gravedigger's disguise had been Bretton's idea, and Chaloner heartily wished the rector had thought of something else.

Francis murmured something Chaloner did not hear, and Pargiter responded with a sharp bark of laughter that had Francis spluttering in impotent rage. The spy glanced up and saw Eleanor rest a calming hand on her furious brother's arm.

"Francis is right, cousin," said Warren in a low voice. "I cannot imagine what you were thinking when you performed an act of such heartless desecration."

"I was desperate," replied Pargiter with an unrepentant shrug. "You and I supported Cromwell, but when the monarchy was restored, Royalists surged into London and started confiscating Roundhead goods. Margaret's death from fever provided me with a perfect opportunity to hide our gold where no one would ever think to look."

"That's certainly true," said Bretton unhappily. "But only a monster would have devised such a plan – and only a devil would consider retrieving the hoard."

"Our mother was right to despise you," said Francis. Chaloner saw Eleanor was hard-pressed to restrain him as he glowered at their father. "And so are we."

Pargiter did not care what his son, daughter, rector and cousin thought, and when Warren took a threatening step towards him the two henchmen blocked his path. But the goldsmith did not so much as glance at his kinsman: his attention was focussed on the grave. Chaloner's spade had made a hollow sound, as metal had connected with wood.

"At last," said Pargiter. "Now, climb out and let me take over."

"You don't want me to open the coffin first?" asked Chaloner.

Pargiter shook his head. "I told you: I don't want anyone to see her. I'm not the heartless fiend everyone imagines and, by retrieving the money myself, I shall spare her the indignity of being gawked at. Then we can cover her up again, and be done with this business. Take my hand."

Scaling the rain-slicked sides was not easy, and Chaloner was muddy from digging. He was not halfway out before his fingers shot out of Pargiter's grasp, and he fell backwards, landing feet-first on the ancient casket. There was a crackle of shattering wood, and the top third of the lid disintegrated. Eleanor cried out in horror, and Bretton began to pray in an unsteady voice.

"Clumsy oaf!" yelled Pargiter, while Chaloner danced around in a desperate attempt to regain his balance without doing any more damage. "You've exposed her for all to see!"

Warren looked as though he might cry. "This has gone far enough, cousin. I don't want the gold any more – I'll find another way to pay my debts."

"I'm not leaving without my money," declared Pargiter, climbing inside the hole himself. He soon discovered it was not easy, and slithered down in a way that broke more of the coffin. One of his men handed him a lamp. "Everyone stay back. I'll finish quicker without an audience."

Sobbing, Eleanor appealed to Chaloner. "Please stop him. You must see this isn't right."

"If you have any compassion, you'll do as my sister asks," added Francis in a heart-broken voice. "I'll pay you – twice what my father offered."

"And I'll pray for you for as long as I live," said Bretton. He sounded distraught. "Poor Margaret doesn't deserve this."

Supposing a real gravedigger would at least consider their offers, Chaloner moved forward. He stopped when he saw the body for the first time. Margaret Pargiter had been buried in a lacy shroud and a veil that covered her hair. Her face was much as he would have expected after three years, but it was the glitter of gold that caught his attention. Coins covered her chest and shoulders – too many to count. Pargiter was busily collecting them. The goldsmith glanced up and saw his order had been ignored: everyone, even his two henchmen, was gazing open-mouthed at the spectacle.

"The bag must have broken," he said in an oddly furtive way that made Chaloner sure he was lying. "I put it under her head."

But Chaloner had spotted something beside the hoard, and he edged around Pargiter to be sure of it. "Gold isn't the only thing to have shared her tomb – there's another body beneath her."

Pandemonium erupted after Chaloner's announcement. Warren accused him of being a liar, although his furious diatribe faltered when Chaloner pointed out the grinning skull under Margaret's shoulder. Francis and Eleanor clamoured for the strange body to be removed and their mother reburied alone. Pargiter wanted his gold out and the two bodies left as they were. But Bretton had the authority of the Church behind him, and once he declared his bishop would want both bodies excavated while an investigation took place, the argument was over.

Knowing the frail coffin would disintegrate if he tried to lift it, Chaloner raised the two bodies separately, using planks of wood, although his task would have been easier if Pargiter had not been in the grave with him, grabbing coins. When he had finished, and the corpses lay in the grass next to the tomb, Chaloner reached for his spade.

"Don't bother to fill it in," ordered Pargiter. "Margaret will be back in it soon. Here's a shilling for your trouble – you're dismissed."

But Chaloner had no idea how much gold Pargiter had retrieved, and the Lord Chancellor would be annoyed if he was not told a precise sum. He thrashed around for an excuse that would allow him to lurk long enough to see the money counted. "For another shilling, I'll find out who was the second corpse," he offered rashly.

Pargiter gazed contemptuously at him. "And how would a gravedigger know how to do that?"

"Fossor used to work for Archbishop Juxon," announced Bretton, before Chaloner could fabricate a story of his own. "And he solved all manner of crimes on His Grace's behalf. Don't let his shabby appearance deceive you. Fossor possesses a very sharp mind."

Warren peered at the spy in the darkness. "You've fallen low, then, if you were in the employ of an archbishop, but now you dig graves for a living."

"He does more than that," said Bretton, before Chaloner could prevent him from inventing anything else. "He hires himself out to many of my clerical colleagues, because we all know him as a man of intelligence and discretion. Why do you think I dispensed with my usual gravedigger and hired him instead? Whatever happened here *must* be investigated and the results reported to the proper authorities – and I would rather Fossor did it than some half-drunk parish constable."

Chaloner wished he would shut up, not liking the increasingly elaborate web of lies or the fictitious name. But Bretton gave him an encouraging nod, and Chaloner supposed he was hoping to curry favour with the Lord Chancellor by supporting his spy's proposal. However, all Chaloner wanted was an excuse to see the money counted, after which he would dispense with his disguise and disappear from the Pargiter family's lives for ever. He had no intention of mounting an investigation – Bretton would have to resort to his "half-drunk parish constable" for that.

"I will discover the truth," he said, hoping he did not sound as unenthusiastic as he felt. "I shall uncover the corpse's identity, and you can make an official report to your bishop."

"Well, *I* don't want to know who it is," said Pargiter firmly. "It is common knowledge that Margaret made a cuckold of me, and one of her lovers must have contrived to be buried with her. And this *is* a man – he's quite tall and look, the fellow was buried wearing spurs."

"Our mother had no lovers!" declared Francis hotly, shooting Chaloner an uncomfortable glance. "How dare you defame her good name in front of strangers!"

Eleanor tried to pull him away, to talk to him privately, but he resisted. "You know she did, Francis. It was her way of defying the husband she didn't love. And I cannot find it in my heart to condemn her for it. And nor should anyone – including strangers who did not know her and so have no right to judge." She gazed coolly at Chaloner, who pretended to be absorbed with the skeletons.

"Nor me," said Warren. His chubby face was wan in the faint gleam of approaching dawn. "Do you mind if we just count this gold and go home? I feel sick."

"We can't," said Bretton angrily. "Something evil happened in poor Margaret's grave, and my bishop will want to know what. We are duty-bound to discover both this man's identity *and* how he came to die."

Eleanor sighed. "Rector Bretton is right. Once he reports the matter to his bishop, it will have to be investigated. He will think we have something to hide if we object."

"How do we know you can be trusted?" demanded Warren of Chaloner. "We have never met you before today."

"*I* trust him," said Bretton, before Chaloner could point out that anyone could be trusted if enough gold changed hands. "And you have known *me* for a long time. That should be enough for you."

Eleanor nodded slowly, staring hard at the spy. "Very well. If there must be an enquiry, then I suppose I would rather this Fossor did it than that horrible Constable Unwin."

"So would I," said Francis, glaring at his father. "Unwin hates us because *someone* made a fool of him over a consignment of clipped coins, and we don't want *him* poking into our affairs. He'll invent something to harm us, and who can blame him?" He turned to Chaloner. "If Bretton says you're all right, then I suppose you'll do. I'll pay you your shilling, if you find out the corpse's name."

"No," countered Warren shakily. "You might not like what he learns. Margaret was a sociable lady, and you should let matters lie while her reputation is still intact."

"It was *not* a lover," snarled Francis, rapidly losing what small control he had. "And I want to know why my mother has spent the last three years with a stranger. Do your work, Fossor."

"Let sleeping dogs lie," argued Pargiter irritably. "Folk will have forgotten her infidelities by now, and I don't want to be labelled a cuckold again, thank you very much."

"You were unfaithful yourself," said Bretton sharply. "And if Fossor needs to ask you questions to solve this wicked business, you *will* answer them. It is your Christian duty."

"You can't order *me* around!" cried Pargiter. "I'm a City goldsmith—"

"Then we shall summon Constable Unwin instead," said Bretton coldly. He nodded his satisfaction when there were resentful glares from Pargiter and his cousin, but no further objections. "Good. Fossor, you may begin."

Chaloner knelt next to the bodies. First, he inspected Margaret, recalling how her graveclothes had been carefully arranged to hide the corpse beneath – someone had been to considerable trouble. Then he turned his attention to the second body. There was nothing left of his face, and the only thing of use was a charm on a chain around his neck.

"Does anyone recognize this?" he asked, removing it. The pendant was made of jet, and was in the shape of a bird. There were shaken heads all around, although a brief glimmer of alarm flashed in Warren's eyes.

Chaloner began the distasteful business of peeling away the decaying clothes, hoping to discover how the stranger had died. Revolted, Bretton invited the others to his house, where they agreed to wait until "Fossor" had finished. From the worn teeth, Chaloner concluded the stranger had been an older man, and his silver spurs suggested he had been wealthy. The only injury was a triangular puncture-wound, clearly visible in the bones of the chest and what little skin still clung to them.

The spy gazed at the bodies and reviewed what he had been told. Margaret had died of a fever three years before, and Pargiter had taken advantage of her burial to keep some of his and Cousin Warren's money from acquisitive Royalists. The grave had been opened because Warren was in debt, although the man had become increasingly unnerved as the exhumation had proceeded. Had Warren's unease derived from the fact that an old crime was about to be exposed? And what about his hesitation when Chaloner had asked about the charm? Finally, it had been Warren who had objected to an enquiry that promised to reveal the dead man's name.

Next, Chaloner turned his thoughts to Pargiter, who did not need more money, but could no longer bear the thought of it lying uselessly underground. From the very start, the goldsmith had made it clear that only *he* was to collect the coins from the coffin, and he had issued all manner of threats to ensure he was obeyed – until Chaloner's fall had inadvertently spoiled his plan. Had he been so determined no one should see the contents of the coffin because he knew what else was in it? He had tried to persuade the others to ignore the grisly discovery, and had joined with Warren in objecting to an investigation. Was it because he had no desire to be ridiculed as a cuckold again, as he had claimed, or did he have a more sinister motive for wanting the matter quietly forgotten?

Then there were Francis and Eleanor, who had loved their mother – or at least, had not wanted her grave disturbed. Were they devoted children, who had taken her side against a hated father? Or had they made use of her death to conceal crimes of their own? But then, surely they would not have asked Chaloner to investigate the stranger? They would have taken the opportunity supplied by their father to have the matter shoved quickly underground again. Or were they afraid that might have looked suspicious?

Finally, there was Bretton, who had also objected to the exhumation. As the family rector, he would have had access to Margaret's coffin three years before. Had he encouraged Chaloner's investigation because to do otherwise would have looked odd – especially in front of the Lord Chancellor's spy? He had always referred to the dead woman as "Margaret", rather than "Mrs Pargiter". The more Chaloner thought about it, the more convinced he became that the rector might have offered her more than spiritual comfort. Did that mean Bretton had dispatched a rival for her affections?

"Anyone could have killed him," said one of Pargiter's henchmen, who had lingered to watch. "Although I suspect *you* think it was Pargiter, because this man was probably one of her paramours."

Chaloner shrugged. "No one likes his wife sleeping with another man, and Pargiter *is* violent – he has been threatening me all night. But I imagine Margaret would have been too ill to entertain lovers immediately before her death."

"She *did* die of fever – I saw her shivering and sweating myself. But I've been thinking. About the time she passed away, there was a fellow who lurked around a lot, talking to Warren. He disappeared after, and I never saw him again."

"Do you know his name, or what he was doing?"

The henchman shook his head. "All I know is that he was tall with a big nose and a stoop."

Chaloner was thoughtful. "There are two peculiar things about Margaret's burial. First, the presence of an additional corpse. And second, the coins were not in a bag, as Pargiter said they would be, but were scattered across her body."

"Worms," said the henchman. "They do odd things underground."

"Not that odd," said Chaloner.

Chaloner did not want to spend too much time with the bodies, in case he missed the counting of the money. He trotted across the sodden churchyard to the Rectory, a grand house boasting ornamental drainpipes of lead – few owners bothered, leaving rainwater to cascade from the roof – and was admitted to a warm, comfortable room with a blazing fire. Piles of gold pieces sat on the table.

"I found these caught in the stranger's clothes," he said, producing two coins he had pocketed earlier, in a sleight of hand no one had noticed. "Are you missing any more?"

Pargiter snatched them from him. "Good. That makes three hundred pounds exactly. It's all there." He had spoken spontaneously and then regretted it in Chaloner's presence. Chaloner wondered how much Pargiter would have left once the find had been reported to the Lord Chancellor – the Court had expensive tastes.

"Tell me about the day Margaret was buried," he said, supposing he had better make a show of investigating the stranger's death, even though he had no intention of furnishing them with answers. His work was done, and he was more than ready to change out of his filthy, wet clothes and move on to the Lord Chancellor's next assignment.

"She died in May, three years ago," replied Bretton with genuine sorrow. "But the churchyard was flooded, and she had to stay in the charnel house for two days until the water had gone down."

"So *anyone* could have shoved that fellow in her coffin," elaborated Warren. "You'll never prove his identity *or* discover what really happened – and if you try, you'll be wasting your time."

Chaloner regarded him thoughtfully. Was it wishful thinking that made him so sure?

"It is a lover," said Pargiter harshly. "Almost certainly."

"No – some felon must have hidden the victim of a robbery," argued Warren, swallowing hard. "And now I must pay my creditors." He took a step towards the door, but stopped uneasily when Francis approached Chaloner and gazed earnestly at him.

"My mother's honour is at stake here, and I want you to prove this was *not* a beau. Perhaps the fellow *was* murdered by felons, as Warren suggests. Go to the local taverns and ask known thieves whether he was one of their victims."

"That will see him killed," said Pargiter scornfully. "Let the matter lie, Fossor. I'll give you *two* shillings, if it's a love of money that makes you persist with this nonsense."

"Margaret's coffin would have been heavy with a second person inside it," said Chaloner, declining to be bribed. "Who were the pallbearers?"

Pargiter sighed irritably when he saw Chaloner was not going to do as he was told. "I was one. My children objected, since Margaret and I were estranged when she died, but I overrode them. The box *was* weighty, now you mention it."

"I was another," said Francis softly. "But I've never carried a casket before, so can't say whether it was abnormally heavy or not."

"We ordered a leaded one," explained Eleanor. Tears began to flow, and Francis put his arm around her. "We wanted her to have the best."

But the one Chaloner had uncovered had been plain wood. Had the killer removed the metal lining, so the extra weight of a second body would go undetected? It seemed likely.

"I understand a tall, stooped man visited you at Mr Pargiter's house around the time of Margaret's death," he said to Warren. "Who was he?"

Warren scowled. "I don't recall. But you're talking about things that happened three years ago, so what do you expect?"

"The visitor was a paramour, I expect," said Pargiter carelessly. "And he was there to see Margaret, not Warren. She often used such devices in an attempt to deceive me."

"That's unfair," said Eleanor, grabbing Francis's sleeve to prevent him from responding with violence. "She was desperately ill, and in no position to entertain anyone. Visit these taverns, Fossor, and talk to robbers. We should at least give this stranger a grave with his own name on it."

Chaloner promised to do his best, and took his leave, knowing there were two reasons why no robber was responsible. First, he would have stolen the gold and the silver spurs at the same time. And second, he would not have gone to the trouble of arranging the two bodies with Margaret on top. The more he thought about it, the more Chaloner became certain that the murder was connected to Margaret's family, and that someone she knew had committed the crime.

It was still raining when Chaloner headed for his home on Fetter Lane. He scrubbed the mud from his face and hands, and shoved his filthy garments in a chest that held the clothes he used for his various disguises. Then he sloshed his way to the palace at White Hall, where he was told the Lord Chancellor was with the Swedish ambassador and would not be able to see him that day. Loath to leave a written message in a place that seethed with intrigue, he decided to return the following morning, and deliver his information in person.

With nothing else to do, he walked to Cripplegate, where his friend Will Leybourn owned an untidy bookshop with cluttered shelves. Leybourn ushered him into his steamy kitchen. He wrinkled his nose in disgust when he heard what Chaloner had been doing, but became thoughtful when he learned one of the bodies had been Margaret Pargiter. As a shopkeeper, Leybourn knew a lot of people and listened to a lot of gossip.

"Margaret's affairs were common knowledge – and so were her husband's."

"Was one of her lovers Rector Bretton?"

Leybourn nodded. "He visited her regularly, long before she became ill of the fever that killed her, although Pargiter didn't know the meetings were far from pastoral. I heard she was faithful to Bretton, though, because he was special to her. So, your stranger may have been a *previous* paramour, but he certainly wouldn't have been a *current* one."

Chaloner rubbed his chin. "Well, that explains why Bretton went to such lengths to prevent her from being excavated. No wonder he was upset – it must have been a grim business for him."

"But you say *he* was the one who urged you to investigate? That should mean you could eliminate him from your list of suspects. He wouldn't demand an enquiry if he had secrets to hide."

"Not so, Will. If he'd agreed to shove both corpses back in the ground with no questions asked, it would have looked suspicious to say the least. He's a priest, supposed to uphold the law, so could hardly turn a blind eye to something so manifestly sinister – especially in front of the Lord Chancellor's spy."

"I suppose not," said Leybourn. "What a pity. I like Bretton – although he does preach the most blustering and wordy of sermons. Never go to St Martin's Ludgate on a Sunday, unless you have a good couple of hours to spare."

Chaloner showed him the charm. "I don't suppose you know anyone who might recognize this? It was around the stranger's neck. It's a black bird, perhaps a crow."

Leybourn's jaw dropped. "No, my friend, that's a raven. And Raven is the name of the man who wore it – Henry Raven. He was in your line of work – a tall, crook-backed fellow with a beaky nose."

"A spy?" asked Chaloner. "Working for whom?"

"For the government, of course. He often came to chat to me, pick my brains – just as you do. But then he stopped, and I assumed something like this had happened. You don't need me to tell you it's dangerous work. Poor Raven!"

"Could he have been one of Margaret's past lovers?"

"Never. He wasn't interested in women – or men, for that matter. Rather, he was consumed by a passionate interest in Barbadan sugar, of all odd things."

Chaloner watched the flames in the hearth, his thoughts whirling. If Raven was a government spy, then perhaps it was not the first time the Lord Chancellor had sent an agent to investigate Pargiter and Warren – and he recalled that Warren's lost fortune had been in the sugar trade. Chaloner supposed he would have to watch *he* did not suffer a fate similar to Raven's.

The notion that it was a colleague in someone else's coffin was enough to drive Chaloner back into his gravedigger costume. The nature of their work meant spies had few friends, and it was tacitly agreed that they could rely on each other to investigate any untimely ends. First, Chaloner went to see Pargiter at his mansion on Thames Street. The coat of arms over the door was picked out with gold, and there were fine woollen rugs on the floor of the hall. Chaloner, wearing clothes that still stank of death, was not permitted inside.

"I told you: I've no idea who the stranger was," snapped Pargiter, standing in a position that kept him dry and Chaloner under the dripping eaves. It was a clever way to ensure an unwanted conversation remained short.

"His name was Henry Raven," said Chaloner, watching for any sign of recognition. He saw none. "And he may have been involved in government business."

Pargiter's eyes narrowed. "How have you learned this so quickly?"

"Archbishop Juxon introduced me to a lot of people."

Pargiter stared at him, and Chaloner wished Bretton had not saddled him with quite such a prominent master. "Well, my answer remains the same. I didn't know him."

"When you hid your gold in Margaret's coffin, *where* did you put it, precisely?"

Pargiter looked angry. "Under her head, where it wouldn't be seen by anyone paying his last respects. Look, I know hiding it with her was an odd thing to do, but I was desperate and I didn't think she would object. God knows, she spent enough of my money when she was alive."

Next, Chaloner went to visit Eleanor at an address in Cheapside. She lived with Francis and his wife in a house with a roof that leaked. When he was shown into the main room, buckets littered the floor to catch the drips, and he was told to watch where he put his feet. It was a stark contrast to Pargiter's luxurious mansion, and he commented on it.

"We would never demean ourselves by accepting our father's charity," said Francis, watching his wife rock a fretful baby. "He might be rich, but his money is dirty."

"There are better things in life than gold," agreed Eleanor, smiling at Chaloner while she played with another brat next to the fire. Chaloner heard Francis's wife snort in disgust.

"We're happier here – with our leaking roof and smoking chimney – than we would be living with *him*," said Francis, glaring at her.

"But the children have no toys," snapped his wife. "They use your carpentry tools instead – a chisel is a soldier and a hammer is a dragon. And the reason these items are available for games is because *you* can't find work. Pride is all very well, but yours is affecting the welfare of your sons."

"You can always leave us and find something better, Alice," said Eleanor coolly. She turned back to Chaloner. "Our father is a selfish man, and Francis and I are better off here. It was his wicked behaviour that led our mother to seek solace in the arms of other men. He made her miserable."

"So did her lovers," said Alice tartly. "Except perhaps Bretton."

"You make it sound as though there were dozens of them," snapped Francis, turning on her. "There were not. But if that stranger was one of them, then he received his just deserts."

Chaloner raised his eyebrows. "You sound as though you're glad he died."

Francis gave an impatient sigh. "I didn't know him, but if he defiled my mother, then, yes, I am."

Eleanor came to stand next to him, resting her hand on his arm to calm him, as she had done earlier that day. "It was a long time ago, and she's at rest now. What else do you want to know, Fossor? Bretton ordered us to cooperate, and we have nothing to hide."

"Where did your mother die? Here or in your father's house?"

"The latter," replied Eleanor. "We all lived there, until she died."

"The stranger's name was Henry Raven," said Chaloner. "Someone recognized his neck-charm."

Eleanor was startled by the speed of his discovery. "Then you've succeeded, and we owe you a shilling. Do you know any more about this Raven?"

"He wasn't your mother's lover. I have it on good authority that he wasn't interested in women."

Francis gaped at him. "Are you sure?"

Chaloner nodded. "Why? Do you believe every man was a willing candidate for her affections?"

Francis was furious, and Eleanor stepped forward to prevent him from grabbing the spy by the throat. "Of course not. But you've exceeded our expectations – learning who he was *and* finding a 'good authority' who says he wasn't one of our mother's follies. You've cleared her name."

"You haven't said why he was in Margaret's coffin, though," Alice pointed out.

"We didn't ask him to do that," said Eleanor, searching in a pot for a shilling. "We only wanted to know the stranger's identity, so he can be buried in his own grave."

Francis grunted agreement. "We should let matters rest now. I don't want an ex-agent of Archbishop Juxon poking around in my family's affairs. Juxon is a creature of the Court, and—"

Suddenly, there was a piercing howl from the child by the hearth. Eleanor bent quickly to pick him up, soothing a cut finger with kisses and croons.

A petty expression crossed Alice's face. "I've warned him before about playing with that particular chisel – it's sharp – but he's just like everyone else around here. No one ever listens."

Warren's house was shabby, although it had once been fine, indicating that its owner had recently fallen on hard times. He answered his door himself, and explained sheepishly that he had no servants.

"I invested in Barbadan sugar, but there were several bad harvests in succession. Still, if I can weather this year, I may yet survive. The crops can't fail for ever."

"Did Henry Raven tell you that?" asked Chaloner. "He had an interest in sugar from Barbados."

Warren regarded him sharply. "Who?"

"The man in Margaret's coffin – as you know perfectly well. The others didn't recognize his neck-charm, but you did. I saw it in your face."

Warren closed his eyes. "Yes, that bauble belonged to Raven, although God alone knows how he got into Margaret's casket. It was nothing to do with me."

"You argued – probably about sugar investments. Did the disagreement end in violence?"

"No! There *was* no argument! He was very knowledgeable about Barbados, so I took him to Cousin Pargiter's house – not here, because I didn't want him to see the full extent of my losses – and asked his advice. He said mine was a bad venture, and recommended I withdraw while I could. I wish to God I'd listened! But I didn't kill him and I didn't put him in the coffin."

"How did you get into Pargiter's house? Does he not keep it locked?"

Warren looked furtive. "I have a key. Margaret gave it to me, a few years ago."

A short while later, Chaloner went to see the last of his witnesses. Rector Bretton was more welcoming than the others, and offered him wine and a seat by the fire. He was clearly under the impression that the liaison forced on them by the Lord Chancellor meant he was exempt from suspicion, and was surprised when Chaloner started to ask questions.

"You can refuse to answer," said Chaloner. "But the Lord Chancellor will want to know why. Everyone else has cooperated, although not always with good grace – people don't like Archbishop Juxon very much, and you should have chosen me a more popular master."

"He is a saint," said Bretton in surprise. "Who doesn't like him?"

"Margaret," prompted Chaloner, deciding he had better change the subject before he landed himself in trouble. Francis was right: Juxon *was* a creature of the Court. "Tell me about her."

Bretton stared unhappily into the flames. "All right. Yes, I was Margaret's lover. I think I was more important to her than the others, but perhaps I flatter myself. I was with her when she died."

"When was she put in her coffin?"

"The morning after her death. Francis had ordered a lead-lined box, and we put her in it together. We left it open for another day, then Pargiter and I sealed it before taking it to the charnel house. I know the others said someone could have put the stranger in at that point, but it isn't true. I stood vigil until her funeral – although I never told *them* that – and I'd have noticed anything untoward."

"The stranger was named Henry Raven," said Chaloner.

Bretton stared at him. "The tall man with the stoop? He came to see Warren around the time of Margaret's last illness, although I have no idea why. During one visit, he told us he disliked close contact with women, because he was afraid of catching the plague. He was an odd man."

"Who was the last person to visit Margaret, before the casket was closed?"

"Pargiter. He asked for a moment alone, and when I returned, he'd placed the lid across her and we nailed it down together. But this happened in Margaret's bedchamber, and unless Raven's body was hidden under the bed . . ."

Chaloner stood. "Will you summon the others? I think I know what happened now."

It was an uneasy company that gathered in Bretton's home. Warren and Pargiter claimed they were too busy for nonsense they never wanted started in the first place, and Eleanor and Francis said the investigation should have finished when Chaloner learned Raven's name. Only Bretton said nothing. The spy began his analysis.

"At first, I assumed Warren was the culprit. He recognized Raven's charm, and it was obvious they'd known each other. They discussed sugar investments, and the debate might have ended in violence. But it was Warren who asked for Margaret's grave to be opened, and he isn't so desperate for funds that he'd risk hanging for murder to claim them."

"But he was deeply unhappy about the exhumation," Bretton pointed out. "His reaction wasn't that of an innocent man."

"That's because he was one of Margaret's past lovers, too," explained Chaloner. "He said she gave him a key to the Pargiter house a few years ago – she would not have done that without good reason. And he still harbours an affection for her. He was torn between a selfish need for money and leaving her undisturbed."

Warren hung his head. "It's true – I did love Margaret. But I didn't kill Raven. Why would I? He gave me some good advice."

"Who *is* the culprit, then?" demanded Eleanor. She turned to the rector, who was regarding Warren with open-mouthed horror at the confession. "Bretton? Perhaps he was afraid Raven would take his place in my mother's heart – that he didn't come to discuss sugar with Warren, but to court *her*."

"Bretton didn't kill Raven, either," said Chaloner, cutting across the rector's spluttering denial. "He knew – from Raven himself – that the man spurned any kind of physical contact, because he was afraid of catching the plague. Thus there was no need for jealousy, and Bretton was more concerned with tending Margaret on her deathbed than in dispatching imaginary rivals."

"Well, *I* didn't do it," said Pargiter, when the others regarded him accusingly. "I didn't even know him. You say he was in my house, but I never saw him there."

"Warren invited him when you were away, hoping Raven would think the mansion was his," said Chaloner. "But Raven was killed in your house – and he was certainly stuffed in the coffin there."

"How can you know that?" demanded Pargiter in disbelief.

"Because Bretton was in constant attendance once Margaret's casket was in the charnel house. Therefore, Raven was hidden *before* you and Bretton closed the lid. At the same time, the killer removed the lead lining, to disguise the additional weight. I suppose he concealed it under the bed, or spirited it out of the house when everyone was asleep – we may never know. But although you lied about the coins, it proves you didn't kill Raven."

"I don't see how –" began Francis, while Pargiter gaped in astonishment.

"Pargiter claimed he put his bag of gold under Margaret's head," explained Chaloner. "But if that were true, he would have noticed Raven, who was already there – and he certainly would have said something. Instead of placing the coins *beneath* her, he tossed them *over* her in an act of defiance."

"I didn't –" began the goldsmith indignantly.

"You resented the amount of money Margaret spent; you said so yourself," Chaloner continued. "You hurled the gold at her, no doubt adding a taunt about her not being able to fritter it away now."

Pargiter regarded him with dislike. "I didn't anticipate that we'd have to reclaim it in the pouring rain *or* that there'd be another corpse to consider while we did so."

"And that leaves you two," said Bretton, looking at Francis and Eleanor. "Did you kill Raven and defile your mother's grave?"

Chaloner addressed Francis. "You disliked your mother's liaisons, and you loathed the men who took advantage of her. But you loved her, and you're the only one who stalwartly defends her reputation – everyone else acknowledges her indiscretions."

"Indiscretions is putting it mildly," muttered Pargiter. "She was flagrant."

Chaloner's attention was still fixed on Francis. "You said you'd never met Raven, and that's probably true. But you were so hostile to your mother's men that you were more than willing to dispose of the corpse of one of them – especially when it was to help someone else you love."

Francis licked dry lips. "This is pure fabrication. You have no proof."

"You're a man of fierce passions, who either loves or hates – there's no middle way for you. When someone told you Raven was one of your mother's beaux, you were only too happy to get rid of his body. At first, I thought you were the killer – you objected to the opening of the coffin, and you didn't agree to my investigation until Eleanor said it was a good idea. But you're a follower, not a leader, and you hid the body because you were obeying instructions."

Eleanor gazed at him, then started to laugh. "I hope you're not implying that *I* killed Raven!"

Chaloner nodded. "I *know* you did. You see, you jumped to the wrong conclusion about Raven – you *assumed* he'd come to tarnish your mother's reputation because he visited when your father was out. But poor Raven had come to discuss sugar with Warren. You killed him because *you* misjudged Margaret. By this time, she was in love with Bretton, and had forsaken all the others."

Francis rounded on Eleanor. "You said he was—" He faltered when she glowered at him.

"Eleanor told you the man she had killed was another of your mother's conquests," surmised Chaloner. "And you believed her – which is why you were startled when I mentioned that Raven wasn't interested in women. You realized then that Eleanor had stabbed an innocent man."

"But it was Francis and I who offered to pay you if you discovered Raven's identity," said Eleanor with a bemused smile. "Why would we do that, if we were the ones who'd killed him?"

"For two reasons. First, you were confident that you'd left no clues – especially ones that could be unearthed by a mere digger of graves. And second, you knew everyone would think you were innocent *because* you'd financed the investigation."

"And how did I kill Raven, exactly?" demanded Eleanor with a sneer. "A small woman against a tall, powerful man?"

"If you never met him, how do you know he was tall?" pounced Chaloner. Eleanor did not reply. "You killed him with one of Francis's carpentry tools, which he leaves lying around for his children to play with. Raven's wound was oddly shaped, and will almost certainly match the chisel – and the chisel is sharp, because his son cut himself on it today."

Rector Bretton regarded Eleanor with cold, unfriendly eyes. "Don't you remember the Latin I taught you? *Fossor* means a digger, or a man who delves. And that's what this Fossor has done – delved until he found the truth."

"I loved my mother," said Eleanor quietly. "And she was dying. I didn't want the gossips saying that she'd entertained lovers in her last hours on Earth – and Raven came to our house when Father was out, so who can blame me for thinking what I did?"

"You admit it?" cried Bretton in horror.

"No," said Pargiter sharply. "She doesn't. Fossor has no real evidence, only supposition. But if she confesses to the crime, she'll hang. Conversely, if she keeps her mouth shut, no one can prove anything. We may have had our arguments in the past, but I'll not see my daughter on a gibbet."

He went to stand next to her, gazing defiantly at Chaloner. Francis hurried to her other side, and Warren was quick to join them.

"You won't repeat what you've heard today, Bretton," said Pargiter softly. "You won't want Margaret's name dragged through the courts – nor her beloved daughter swinging on a rope. And who'll take Fossor's word over a family of wealthy goldsmiths and the King's chaplain?"

Bretton hung his head, and Chaloner knew Raven's murder would never be avenged. Pargiter was right: without a confession, there was not a jury in the country that would convict Eleanor.

The rain had abated by the following morning, and the sun glimmered faintly through thin clouds. Eleanor and her father stood side by side at the empty chasm that had been Margaret's tomb.

"Fossor came very close to discovering the real reason why I killed Raven," she said softly. "That Raven only visited Cousin Warren because he wanted to spy on our family; that his real objective was to confiscate our gold and give it to the government. Do you think Fossor will try to do the same – for whichever churchman he is working for now?"

"If he does, I'll call on your services again," replied Pargiter. "Only this time, don't ask Francis to help. He's too stupid for games of deceit, and almost gave you away."

Eleanor smiled. "But Warren played his role well. He was very convincing as the desperate debtor, and is more than satisfied with what you paid him."

Pargiter was less complacent. "What about Bretton? Do you think he was convinced by what Fossor deduced?"

Eleanor shrugged. "He seemed to be. And why not? He loved Mother very deeply, and Fossor's erroneous conclusions made it look as though I was desperate to protect her reputation as she lay dying. As far as Bretton is concerned, I'm a dutiful daughter, prepared to kill a man and hide his body to save his Margaret from ridicule and gossip."

"Well, now the spectre of a murdered government spy is truly dead and buried, you can come to live with me again," said Pargiter, placing an arm around her shoulders. "I've missed you these last three years. Francis can live in self-imposed poverty – he'll never love me as you do – but there's no longer any reason for you to endure leaking roofs and smoking chimneys."

Both jumped when someone emerged from the shelter of the churchyard yews.

"I heard you," said Bretton in a strangled voice. "You didn't murder Raven to protect Margaret's name, but to defraud the government. That's treason!"

"Rubbish," said Pargiter scornfully. "It's business. And if anyone ever claims otherwise, we shall blame the whole affair on Margaret – say she *demanded* to be buried with the gold as a way to stop the Royalists from getting at it."

"I've been such a fool," Bretton went on brokenly. "Three years ago, you paid for my roof to be mended – not out of kindness, but to pretend to your Goldsmith's company that you were a reformed man after they fined you for coin-clipping. The repairs included fine new lead drainpipes – *lead* drainpipes. You used the lining from Margaret's coffin, didn't you?"

"It seemed a pity to waste it – lead is expensive," replied Pargiter with a careless shrug. "And we could hardly sell it as it was! People have admired those drainpipes, so don't pretend you haven't enjoyed showing them off . . ."

The rector suddenly shoved Pargiter towards the grave. With a sharp cry, the goldsmith toppled inside the hole, where his head hit the remains of the coffin. He lay still. Eleanor tried to run, but Bretton grabbed her and hurled her after her father. She spat dirt from her mouth and tried to stand. Bretton struck her with a spade, and she dropped to all fours, dazed.

"I don't want Margaret associated with any more scandal – or her liaisons discussed in a way that make her sound like a whore," said Bretton brokenly. "I still love her, and I shall protect what remains of her good name. If you're dead, you can't harm her, can you?"

He gripped the shovel and began to fill in the hole.

Note

Robert Bretton was chaplain to Charles II and rector of St Martin's Ludgate. John Pargiter was a goldsmith, whom the diarist Samuel Pepys considered a "cheating rogue". Pargiter was fined several times by the Goldsmith's Company for persistently shoddy workmanship and coin clipping, and his name was removed from the list of aldermen in 1668, presumably because of his fondness for dubious practices. A merchant called Francis Pargiter also lived in London in the 1660s, although it is not known whether he and John were kin. Thomas Warren was a merchant who traded overseas.

Shortly after the Restoration of the monarchy in 1660, there were many tales of exiled Royalists returning home to retrieve hoards they had secreted years before – some found them undisturbed, others did not. One man was alleged to have chosen his wife's coffin as his hiding place, and was reputedly delighted when he excavated her and found his money just as he had left it.

THE SIXTH MAN

Bill James

The thing about Assistant Chief Constable Desmond Iles, as many knew by now, was that at funerals he could get really a bit out of proportion. This one coming up today after the crossfire killing: dicey, dicey, dicey, Harpur thought. It had big overtones and Iles loved overtones, danced and dreamed to them. Consider: a middle-aged, born-again factory worker, out ardently slipping salvation gospel tracts through people's letter boxes on his afternoon off, gets somehow in the way of a motorized turf battle between drugs firms and picks up two .38 bullets in the back. And a spread of spent bullets around, as well as those that hit him. Iles would scent chaos: this victim, born-again but dead. Did it *look* like salvation? Harpur himself scented chaos. Iles would love to sound off to folk in funeral pews a bit about chaos, and more than a bit.

As an additional element, sure to disturb the Assistant Chief, this shooting took place very close to the spot where a young, cheery, ethnic girl, rather favoured by him, had her beat, and he would fret in a very Iles style of fretting about the danger she, also, might have been in. Iles used to meet her down there on waste ground now and then, in change-every-time, by-the-hour hire cars, for anonymity. Part of Harpur's job was to know about anonymities.

At certain funerals following criminal violence, a police presence might be necessary as a public relations duty. It indicated concern and sympathy. Harpur always hated going with the ACC, whether the service happened at a church or chapel or the crematorium direct, but felt he must be handy in case some kind of restraint were needed against Iles so as to preserve reasonable calm. After all, Harpur considered it more or less obvious that funerals should have dignity, decorum. They could be ticklish events for him. Although only a Detective Chief Superintendent, he might be required to curb and lull a superior officer while eyed aghast by the congregation and minister, possibly in parts of a church that would reasonably be considered special, such as the pulpit.

Actually, "such as the pulpit" would not really do in describing these crises. If Harpur had to reach him, and apply a degree of quietening, repressive force, it would nearly *always* be because Iles had decided to bulk out the proceedings with a personal, extra sermon, and had somehow taken over the pulpit – or its equivalent in fundamentalist meeting halls. Then, at least until Harpur's intervention with muscle and/or pleas for sense, the Assistant Chief could not be persuaded out and/or silenced. Now and then at tragic funerals he would weep thoroughly; weep blatantly and noisily before he gave an address. Today's was unquestionably a tragic funeral. There'd been bloodied tracts on the pavement. Sometimes during these episodes, Iles would slander the Home Secretary for the national state of things leading to the death, or the Prime Minister, or the Trinity, or his mother and aunts, or school attendance officers, or all of the above, or permutations. Often he slandered himself and, of course, Harpur. Generally, these onslaughts came over impressively via a pulpit microphone and amplifying system. Failing these, Iles bayed.

Naturally, he would try to fight off Harpur, or anyone else who turned physical in an attempt to suppress him: say, a vicar, if he/she thought Iles's behaviour had become too wild. The ACC was not big, but possessed craftiness and knew head-butting well from way back in his career. Always, it had seemed especially unkempt to Harpur for someone to head-butt in a place of worship, whether he, Harpur, was on the end of it, or somebody else. Against anyone who opposed or attacked him,

Iles could summon an abnormal weight of momentary but true loathing, especially against Harpur, on account not just of immediate irritation, but that past chapter with the ACC's wife. These reserves of hatred seemed to help increase Iles's hideous strength and, more often than not, gave his lips true froth during tussles. He usually went to funerals in full dress uniform, and that made him additionally ferocious, unhinged and malevolent, as though convinced he should live up to the high-grade cloth, Queen's Police Medal ribbon, superb black lace-ups and insignia of his rank.

This funeral, then, Harpur considered could be one of the worst: one of the worst, that is, from the Iles aspect. Harpur guessed that, to describe the death, Iles would have been rehearsing some of his favourite terms, such as "symbolic", "ironic" and "encapsulates", for any pastoral chat he might choose to offer. If he turned to abuse of one or several or all of his targets, the words might be "slimy", "smug", "somnolent", "supine". Yesterday, Harpur suggested to him – hopelessly – that it would be wise, in view of the extraordinary tensions, to send someone of lower rank to represent them – for instance, Chief Inspector Francis Garland. "How about thinking of it for once from *my* angle, sir," Harpur had said.

"Which angle would that be, then, Col?"

"Well, it could be stressful. If you become – I mean, I might have to do another grapple, and—"

"My soul's involved here, Harpur," Iles replied.

"That's what I'm getting at, sir."

"What?"

"The buzz will be around."

"Which buzz is that, then, Col?"

"Re your soul, sir," Harpur said. "People will tell one another: 'This funeral: another Mr Iles soul session.'"

"I do try not to make too much of it – my soul. Showiness one abhors. Performances one detests."

"But people already know you can be very souly, sir. You're famed for it. Probably it's on your Personnel dossier. 'Deeply souly.' People will realise you're likely to become uncontrollably moved . . . well . . . even berserked by the funeral, so we'll get an enormous crowd there, sightseers, not just mourners, gawking in case you put on one of your perf . . . in case your soul takes over again in that tremendous way it has. The shouting, the arc of armpit sweat, the alliteration."

"I must go," Iles replied. "*We* must go." They had talked in the ACC's suite at headquarters. Harpur occupied a leather armchair. Iles paced. He liked to concentrate on nimbleness. There was a long wall-mirror near the door for him to check his appearance in civvies or uniform before going out. Harpur noticed Iles kept his eyes away from that now, though, which must signal he had bad feelings again about how his Adam's apple looked. The ACC regarded his Adam's apple as part of a skilfully focused, foul genetic joke against him. He had on one of his navy blazers, plus narrow-cut, dark grey flannel trousers to do his legs justice, and what might be a rugby club tie. He said: "This funeral demands me, Col. My presence. Well, our."

"I—"

"Unignorable, Col. This death, this pyre – unignorable."

"I—"

"Oh, you'll reply, 'It was merely someone accidentally peppered in a gang spat.'"

"Well, no, I don't think I would ever . . . I see nothing 'merely' about any death, sir. It's just that, perhaps as far as the funeral goes, we—"

"People, Col. You mentioned *people*."

"Is that OK?"

"People in relation to my soul."

"Very much so."

"They're an interesting entity, Harpur."

"Who?"

"People."

"Absolutely sir, but—"

"Yes, it's a fact, Col. Out there, where they immemorially are, people do seem fascinated by me."

"Patent, sir."

"Many would like an, as it were, glance *into* my soul."

"I've heard more than one express this longing," Harpur said.

"How many more?"

"Or a desire to know you in what they call 'the round'. They wonder what you're like 'in the round'."

"It's something I by no means understand."

"What, sir?" Harpur replied.

"This . . . well, yes, I don't think this exaggerates . . . this fascination."

"That's because of your astonishing flair for self-effacement and—"

"Much less do I actually *seek* their fascination, Col."

"Few would accuse you of that, sir."

"Which fucking few, Harpur?" The ACC stared from this third-floor window down on to passers-by in the street, as though some of that disgusting few might be there, conspiring. In a while he turned back: "Let me ask: what was that poor sod doing when wiped out, Col?"

"This has been thoroughly covered in the reports, sir."

"I know, I know. You see it's symbolic, do you, Harpur?"

"Symbolic?"

"You spot the irony?"

"Irony, sir?"

"These are terms that always confuse your struggling little mind, don't they? But I certainly absolve you of blame for this. I think of that bloody nothing school you went to."

"Someone was shot," Harpur replied.

"Let me ask again: what was this poor sod doing when wiped out?"

"Religious tract deliveries on Valencia Esplanade and in the side streets."

"Exactly, Col. And that is surely why we must be at the funeral. This death – I have described it as symbolic. Yes, I think so. This death – I have described it as ironic, painfully ironic. Yes, I think so. Doesn't it tell of our times, Harpur? Yes, tell of our dismal, sickening times. A man, Walter Rainsford Lonton, devotedly, pro-actively taking religion to house-holders, blasted suddenly by thugs. Anarchy? Hellishness? Barbarism triumphant? Forgive me, do, Col, but here's another one you may have heard me use before and been baffled by – 'encapsulates?' It's a word. You'll find it in the dictionary. For me, this shooting *encapsulates* appalling social decline, moral decline. It's happening everywhere, Harpur, accelerating."

Symbolic. Ironic. Encapsulates. Yes, Harpur feared these perennial insights would almost certainly pop up if Iles went into his standard mode at the funeral and splurged some bounteous, thudding, possibly actionable, bum oratory. Iles liked fixing a worldwide significance to limited local incidents and crises. It could be a tic taken from the former Chief Constable, Mark Lane, who'd always feared universal disintegration might begin on his patch from some seemingly limited local incident and crisis. A doorstepping, part-time missionary holed by two .38 bullets in the back would constitute such a seemingly limited local incident and crisis. Iles saw endless ramifications. Perhaps all officers who made it to Staff College had this habit of bumper-size thinking banged into them. Iles used to mock Mark Lane for his dreads. Now, though, the ACC seemed to echo them.

"But then again, I don't suppose you suffer much anxiety about social decline, moral decline, Harpur," Iles said. His voice shifted upwards towards an agony scream or screech-owl cry. Harpur took a few steps across the room and checked the door had been properly closed. This was routine when Iles seemed on his way to a reminiscence interlude. Headquarters staff would hang about the corridor outside Iles's suite if they knew he was talking privately to Harpur, in case they could eavesdrop one of the Assistant Chief's fits. Iles said: "Social decline, moral decline – they couldn't have mattered much to you when giving one to my wife in bed-bug hotels, vehicles – including possibly even official police vehicles – and, I wouldn't be surprised, on industrial canal tow-paths."

"How's your nice leggy friend down Valencia Esplanade, sir?" Harpur replied.

"Honorée? Troubled. A kind of superstition has crept in. Fears the Esplanade area's jinxed. She likes to work other sites since the shooting."

"We think we've got several decent leads on the people involved, sir," Harpur replied. "Some locals, some not."

"My faith in you is total, Col." the Assistant Chief said.

"Thank you, sir."

"As to the job, I mean, Harpur."

In fact, Iles behaved with great and sustained sweetness at the funeral. For Harpur, the proceedings turned out significant, not on account of any outbursts by the ACC, but because suddenly, from behind, someone, a male, muttered, very close to Harpur's ear, "I guessed you and Ilesy would be here, so took a chance. Number Three. Ten tonight."

This was at the very end. The coffin had left for the crem and a general shifting about among the congregation began as people edged from their seats towards the aisles, making for the door. The place was as crowded as Harpur had expected, so this dispersal took a while. Harpur did not turn to see the man who'd whispered. Unnecessary. And it might have been unwise. Of course, he recognized the voice. Although it stayed low, and had to compete with an organ finale, Harpur knew who'd spoken to him in the throng. And, of course, he understood the message.

Iles had, indeed, given an address, but by invitation, and he made it short and heartfelt. Today, in Harpur's opinion, the Assistant Chief could be regarded by almost anyone fair-minded as virtually decent and stable, even an asset, regardless of previous form at such functions. Iles referred to the "terrible symbolic impact" and "grim, searing irony" of Lonton's death. But he ditched "encapsulates". This, after all, was a Gospel Hall service, and the congregation mainly ordinary people whose education might have been as ramshackle as Harpur's. Iles, gazing out upon them, taking their tone, probably realized that "encapsulates" would sound fruity here. Iles could be surprisingly sensitive if you had time to wait.

Gospel Halls ran without clergy or ministers, and the funeral was conducted by a gruff, middle-aged man in a black jacket and silver pinstriped trousers. After he had preached from the platform about Lonton and his certainty of heaven, he asked if anyone else wished to say something. Iles hesitated. It astonished Harpur, but he detected a definite, as if modest, reluctance: perhaps Iles recognized the salt-of-the-earth qualities in this congregation and would not impose on it any of his mad monkeying and egomaniac slobber: witness, later, that editing out of "encapsulates". The simplicity, plainness, unpretentiousness of Gospel Halls might be new to him. Not to Harpur: he'd been sent to Sunday School at one as a child. He remembered emulsion-painted walls similar to these, adorned only with large-letter Bible verses.

The ACC went forward eventually and climbed on to the platform. He'd brought with him a couple of Lonton's tracts, mud-stained from the pavement and blood-flecked. Iles held them up for a time, and then read aloud the text from their front page: "It is appointed unto men once to die and after this the judgement." Iles nodded. "Harpur will do what he can about the judgement." Afterwards, the Assistant Chief remained up near the top end of the Hall until everything finished, and then talked there for a while with some of the family.

Back home, Harpur found his two daughters had watched television news coverage of the cortège. "Some of them at school say police can't keep the streets safe any longer," Hazel told him.

"Who at school?" Harpur replied.

"You want names? You want me to fink?"

"I mean, pupils or staff?" Harpur said.

"Which would worry you more?" Hazel replied.

"Neither. They'd both be wrong," he said.

"My friends say it," Hazel replied.

"Staff as well, I expect," Harpur said.

"I hate it when people say rotten things about you, Dad," Jill told him.

"I've heard worse," Harpur replied.

"Dad, listen, I think you ought to pack something," Jill said.

"We don't talk like that," Harpur said.

"Like what?" Jill asked.

" 'Pack something', of course," Hazel said. "Do you know how dim you sound, a thirteen-year-old, with words pinched from cop dramas – corny, ancient, reshown TV cop dramas?"

"I think Dad should have a gun," Jill said. "OK? What do the all-wise and wonderful fifteen-year-old and her all-wise and wonderful friends feel about that, then?"

"*Have* you lost control of the streets, Dad? Valencia Esplanade is 'No Go?' " Hazel asked.

"Of course he hasn't lost control of the streets,' Jill bellowed at her, half about to cry. "Or he wouldn't if he packed something. It's obvious. I think he should look after himself. You should look after yourself, Dad. People blasting from cars. What could you do? What could this poor Holy Joe do? He'd got some bits of paper. What's the use of them?"

"You sound like the US gun lobby: bang-bangs for everyone," Hazel said.

"Not for everybody. For Dad."

"I have to go out later," Harpur replied. "I might be late. Lock up properly and turn in." He single-parented since Megan's terrible death, and found it a strain sometimes.

"Go out where?" Hazel said.

"Work," Harpur replied.

"Is it?" Hazel asked.

"Yes," Harpur said.

"Of course it is," Jill said.

"What work?" Hazel asked.

She liked to keep track of his morals. "Routine," Harpur said.

"Is this a one-to-one with a grass, for example?" Jill said.

"Routine," Harpur replied.

"You ought to pack something," Jill said.

"And we don't call them grasses," Harpur said. Of course, everyone *did* call them grasses, but the term seemed wrong from a child. "Informants, Jill."

"What's the difference?" she asked. "Informants grass, don't they, the same as grasses grass? Wasn't there a song – 'Why Do You Whisper Green Grass?'"

"No police force could run without informants," Harpur said. "They are valuable and often brave people."

"I didn't say they weren't, did I? I only said they grass."

"'Grass' makes them sound contemptible," Harpur said.

"So?" Jill replied.

And, yes, it *was* for a one-to-one with an informant that Harpur left them at about 9.30 p.m., perhaps the greatest grass Harpur had ever met. Perhaps the greatest grass any detective had ever met. When Harpur did meet him, it had to be in reliable secrecy. Grasses could lose limbs for grassing, could get killed for grassing. Among villains, grassing rated as easily the greatest villainy, maybe the *only* villainy. Harpur made for an old concrete block house on the foreshore, built during the war to help throw the Germans back into the sea if they ever tried it on, and still standing. Harpur reached it just before ten o'clock. Jack Lamb was already there. Lamb seemed to like this spot best of their carefully varied rendezvous points, their Number Three, as he'd called it at the funeral.

It was dark, and darker inside the windowless block house. An occasional flash of moon poked through a loophole when the clouds cleared for a few minutes. Jack had on what might be a cavalry officer's "bum-freezer" greatcoat, designed for when cavalry meant horses, not tanks, and cut deliberately short, like a riding jacket. Jack stood six foot five and weighed over two hundred and fifty pounds, so there was a lot of bum to freeze. He also wore a green Commando beret, with some large badge on it, which Harpur could not identify in the darkness. Whenever they came to Three, Lamb liked to wear army surplus clobber, in keeping. In each hand tonight he carried a brown briefcase, perhaps also once military. These cases looked well-filled, as if he would soon be off to brief Eisenhower for D-Day. Jack put both on the filthy concrete floor, opened them and brought out six automatic pistols, which he laid alongside one another on the leather. Harpur thought they might be 9 mm Walthers.

"As to the Walter Rainsford Lonton aftermath, you'll need these, Col," he said. "You've got to pack something."

"I keep getting told that."

"Because it's right. Who by?"

"It's well intentioned," Harpur replied.

"Of course it's well intentioned. Tooling up – vital at this stage."

"That right, Jack? Which stage?"

"You've got to recruit a little private army – you and if poss five others."

"That right, Jack?"

"I don't want a big mob of police."

"Where don't you want a big mob of police?" Harpur said.

"Just you and a nice, capable, small team. And in such clandestine circumstances, you won't be able to draw official police weapons, will you?"

"Hardly."

"So, I supply. They're all loaded, of course."

"Of course."

"Fifteen-round magazine," Lamb said. "Good firepower."

"Yes, I know."

"At one time, the police used Walthers, I think."

"Some are still around," Harpur replied.

"Reliable. Stoppers."

Lamb, like some other informants, *most* other informants, went in for an amount of mystification when they presented their stuff. They let the material out slowly, perhaps to make it seem more, and so qualify for bigger cash; perhaps just as a playful, theatrical exercise by creating suspense and curiosity. With Jack, it would be the second. He did not have to worry about money. But he did enjoy acknowledgement and admiration. By puzzling Harpur and then gradually making things clear for him, Jack must feel he'd come over as abnormally bright and kindly. And it was true, he *was* abnormally bright, despite the beret. Even kindly.

Jack Lamb now did as he usually did and crouched for a while at one of the rifle apertures, gazing at what he could see of the sea, ready to take on anything Mr Hitler could chuck at him.

"What Lonton aftermath?" Harpur said.

"You know what happened there, do you?" Jack said. He abandoned his sentinel stint and came and stood over the pistols.

"He took two stray bullets," Harpur said. "Walter Rainsford Lonton had God on his side, most likely, but not luck."

"Somebody in one of the cars mistook him and panicked."

"Mistook him for what?"

"There were two cars," Lamb replied.

"That we know. Four people."

"It was to be a simple but ample deal. One car brought packets of substance – a lot of packets. The other brought cash, a lot of cash. There should have been a swap. Yes, simple, but also, as you'd expect, very nervy, very excitable. These are people who live with two-timing and rough tricks."

Ritualistically and uselessly, Harpur would always ask Jack where his information came from. Ritualistically Jack, like any other purposeful whisperer, always ignored this. Sources stayed secret, or next time there would be no sources. There might be no Jack, either, if he ever disclosed too much, or anything, about those who disclosed to him. When Jack told you something you'd better believe it, and you'd better be content with that. "Who've you been in touch with, Jack?"

"On the day, one of them in one of the cars, or perhaps more than one and in both cars, sees Lonton flitting between houses and assumes he's some sort of look-out and is alerting hit squads standing by behind a couple of front doors to dash out at the crux moment and hijack everything – substance and cash. Anyway, somebody opens fire on Lonton . . ."

"So *not* accidental, not just trapped in crossfire?" Harpur said.

"They open fire deliberately on him, and would have on anyone else who appeared from the houses, if anyone had, which, as we know, nobody did, because Lonton was a total innocent. The noise of firing convinces some of the others they're being attacked – that an attempted snatch of the substances or cash is under way – so, of course, they retaliate. But as far as I've discovered, neither car has injuries."

"I don't know," Harpur said.

"Both cars finally pull away. Only Lonton is left."

"So who, Jack? In the cars."

"No names, or you'll go and pick them up now and charges might not stick. I want them done as they are doing what they do. They'll come back. They won't let a botch muck up their trade, not trade of this scale."

"I—"

"Look, Col, I only give tip-offs when I think people have acted with real vileness and disregard. I'm not a mouth for mouthing's sake."

"Absolutely." Harpur had listened often to Jack's gospel of grassing. It was important for Lamb to feel all right about what he did. No money went to him for his help, but neither did Harpur ever ask too much about the rich art business Jack ran. That's how the arrangement worked, and overall it worked well.

"I consider it monstrous to knock over an amateur apostle on his divine rounds," Jack said. "All right, an error, but people so jumpy shouldn't be out with guns. So jumpy they can't even hit one other."

"They hit Lonton."

"I wonder how many shots it took. Did you recover other bullets?

"A quantity," Harpur said.

"A ton?"

"We're still searching."

"This kind of cruel, blast-off craziness – I see it as a symptom of something rotten nationally, Col. And it deteriorates."

"Mr Iles says that."

"There you are, then."

"He can get things right sometimes," Harpur replied.

"Yes, they'll come back," Jack said.

"The buyers and sellers?"

"That's part of their brazenness, part of the general rotten-ness. This is commerce, Col. This is gorgeous livelihoods, Col. A bit of a shoot-out, a mistaken shoot-out, can't be allowed to stop the free flow of merchandise – dirty merchandise, but merchandise. Yes, they'll come back, not to that particular bit of ground, obviously. But I can point you the right way."

"How the hell do you know this, Jack?"

"You, plus trusted pals – pals able to handle a Walther – will be waiting. Not a full-scale swarm operation, please. Now, *please*. Leaks can happen when too many are in the know. The business would be called off. And they'd guess how police came to find out about the new plans, the new site. How? Me. Too perilous, Col. You and your picked group can certainly manage them."

"How many?"

"Probably four again, two in each car. You'll outnumber. You'll have surprise."

"I hope."

"A big BMW. A big Volvo. These are a switch from pre-viously. They're not going to risk the same transport, are they, especially as their previous cars might be damaged? But I've got registration numbers for you. Can you call on some good, discreet boys?" He put an encouraging, huge palm on Harpur's shoulder: "But of course you can, Col."

"Francis Garland as a start. Yes, I'll be all right."

"And as long as you scoop them all up—"

"—it won't matter if they work out who sold them," Harpur said.

"I don't like 'sold'."

"Sorry. Let's amend: It won't matter if they work out who *scuppered* them," Harpur replied.

"Because they won't be around to do anything about it."

"You want the Walthers back afterwards?" Harpur asked.

"Not if they've been used. Police can prove all sorts from a used gun. But you probably know that already."

As it would turn out, only one of the Walthers was eventually used, and, a little later than eventually, Harpur committed that

to the river. He returned the rest to Jack at a subsequent short
and joyful debriefing session at Number Three.

Harpur had found he could recruit four helpers, including
Garland, not five. The pool to draw on was small. He wanted
good marksmen ready to believe they'd be passably safe, regardless: passably safe, regardless, from the crews they had to
stalk; and passably safe, regardless, from superior ranks after
running an uncleared shooting romp. Harpur considered that to
convince four in the circumstances might be good going.
Luckily, so luckily, one of them was Garland's sergeant, Vic
Callinicos, an esteemed marvel with handguns. In the swoop,
when it came he fired ahead twice from out of the passenger
window of a Citroën moving fast over uneven ground after shots
aimed at them from the Volvo and the BMW. Their shots
missed. Vic's didn't.

Harpur's interception platoon were in the Citroën and a
Ford, both unmarked. They'd waited and watched in the dark,
unnoticeable among a string of parked cars on the road bordering a public open sports field. This had been specified by Lamb
at the block house as the new transaction site. A Vauxhall and a
Peugeot already stood at one end of the field, probably im-
material. Harpur thought they could be love buggies: a soccer
ground in the day, nooky at night. Jack had said to expect the
target cars between ten thirty p.m. and eleven. At ten fifty, the
Volvo, its registration spot-on, arrived and waited. It was at a
distance, but near enough for them to hear that the driver kept
its engine running. At two minutes to eleven the BMW came to
a stop by the Volvo.

In the Citroën, Harpur said, "We go now." He drove, with
Vic Callinicos alongside him. Harpur took the car up over the
kerb and pavement and on to the grass. The Ford with Garland
in charge followed. They had fix-on blue lamps and got them
going at once. Garland also carried a loudspeaker in the Ford
and began yelling: "Armed Police, Armed Police, get out with
your hands up." Despite this din and the cars' engine roar,
Harpur heard shots from the BMW and Volvo, and heard Vic
Callinicos's reply. He saw the driver of the BMW pitch forward
against the windscreen and the man in the Volvo passenger seat
lurch to his right. In a minute the Citroën had reached the
BMW and Harpur braked and jumped out. He had a Walther in

of ambush, you need to have a girl with you, don't you, Harpur? She's like a theatrical prop, isn't she? It's called verisimilitude. You'll find that one in the dictionary, too."

"I hadn't thought of cover as an explanation for her, sir."

"Don't get despondent. I can think for both of us, Col. It's a habit."

"I haven't had time to congratulate you on the funeral, sir. You were very measured, if I may say."

"I think you may. I appreciated the setting. I loved that wall text."

"Which?"

"The main one," Iles replied.

" 'Without shedding of blood is no remission,' " Harpur said.

PROVENANCE

Robert Barnard

Leonid noticed the man when he was on his way to put a new label on a Manet picture on the third floor. The picture was due to be packed and taken away for exhibition in Lyons. The Hermitage, since the collapse of Communism, was readier to lend its treasures for special events such as the Lyons Manet show: sometimes they accepted loans in return, in lieu of payment, but mostly they insisted on payment, preferably in dollars. After all, they had more than enough pictures of their own.

The man Leonid noticed was dressed in a T-shirt and sneakers and was walking up the Grand Staircase, looking neither to left or right. The gilded curlicues decorating the walls, the gods on cloud nine on the ceiling, the sturdy grey pillars with thickly encrusted gilt at their feet went unregarded by him. Leonid had never seen, or never noticed, him before, but as he gained the second floor he showed no hesitation in setting off in the direction of the Large Hermitage. The Grand Staircase could rarely have had so summary a dismissal. The man acted as if he knew the palace too well to notice it, but Leonid felt sure he did not. He knew where he was going because he was well prepared. Leonid shook his head and went about his business.

A quarter of an hour later he descended from the French Impressionists and found himself among the Dutch paintings in the Large Hermitage. Perhaps curiosity about the man had something to do with his destination. Certainly he walked around without apparent goal until he spotted him in front of one of the Rembrandts which were the pride of the Hermitage collection, a jewel even among the palace's three million items. Leonid stood back and watched. The man put his face close to the bilingual label under the picture, then moved on. It could have been a picture by a teenage art student for all he cared. The next picture he stopped at, by a lesser figure, was considered, evaluated, taken in. Then the man put his head down again close to the label. A second or two later he straightened, a satisfied expression on his face.

He took out a little notebook, then wrote something in it, checking what he wrote against the label under the picture.

When the man had moved out of sight, Leonid went over to the picture, though he knew the description by heart. It was "Spring Landscape" by Cuyp, and it had been acquired by the Hermitage from the Yusupov Collection in 1922.

Leonid was more than intrigued. He was professionally interested. When a Spanish touring group swarmed into the gallery, surrounding a harsh-voiced woman holding a little banner aloft, he joined them as they went to one of the great Rembrandts. Leonid's quarry had been standing in front of it, but now he moved smartly aside to one of the small pictures hung beside it. Leonid became part of the Spanish group and managed to get the place beside the man with the notebook. In that little book there was a list, ending with the landscape by Cuyp, but headed by two intriguing entries. Leonid saw:

Renoir: Portrait of Mme. Bercy. Acquired from the Spaskov Collection, 1921.

Picasso: Young Girl With Parasol. Acquired from the Berisov-Vernet Collection, 1924.

So he had already done the twenty or thirty rooms on the top floor devoted to the French Impressionists and the moderns. Why had they provided him with so few entries for his notebook?

A possible answer floated into Leonid's mind, and his heart sank.

He turned his attention to the Rembrandt now being described by the Spanish-speaking guide. It was a painting im-

printed on his heart and brain down to the last casual brush-
stroke. He tried to estimate the guide's expertise by the number
of words he recognised: Amsterdam, Franz Hals, Saskia, National Gallery. Leonid had no foreign language beyond a rather
halting English. When the Spanish group moved on to the next
preselected high spot the man he was interested in was gone.
Leonid went down the central aisle of the Dutch galleries,
looking in every alcove, but the man was nowhere to be seen.

Leonid was troubled. Life had been so easy in the later years
of Communist rule, when he had first come to work at the
Hermitage. Then he had had a clearly defined specialist area
(preservation) in which he worked. He was not thanked if he let
his interest stray to any other area, where he would only be
trespassing on someone else's special preserve.

Now it was all so different. True, his salary was now once again
(Putin be praised!) paid regularly, but so much more was now
expected of him. He was *required* to have an interest in the whole
spectrum of the gallery's possessions and activities–conservation, display, inter-gallery loans, the education programme, the
shop and other commercial enterprises, PR . . . It was all very
bewildering. They even had staff meetings, which ranged over
these and myriad other topics. It was possible to make an awful
fool of oneself at these meetings, and though Leonid was not
aware that he had done that, he did feel he had not shone. How
could he shine? He was the product of a different age. How could
he talk confidently about the commercial exploitability of a Cuyp
landscape or Gauguin's South Sea Island girls?

On his way back to his office on the ground floor he struck
lucky. He was just passing the main cafeteria when he heard an
American voice and, turning, he saw the object of his interest.
He was standing at the coffee counter expostulating with the
woman behind it.

"Chocolate! CHOCOLATE! I always have chocolate with a
cappuccino."

The woman, one of Leonid's own generation, shrugged.
Then, an idea striking her, she grabbed a small bar of chocolate
from the display case, slapped it down on the counter, and held
out her hand for the money.

Leonid slipped ahead of the tourists, nodded to the woman,
and was given his usual minute but powerful coffee.

"You mind if I sit here?" he asked his prey, sitting alone at a table, his red T-shirt, Leonid now saw, bearing the legend KANSAS – WHAT A STATE WE'RE IN! The slogan puzzled Leonid. It seemed to have two meanings. Was it a Western-style joke? The man grunted at him and looked disgustedly at his cup.

"Freakin' natives," he muttered. "Wouldn't know a cappuccino from a milkshake."

"We like our coffee very strong, and just a little," said Leonid apologetically. The man seemed surprised to encounter a Russian in Russia. Then an idea seemed to strike him.

"Waterworks problem?" he asked.

"No. Is just how we like it," said Leonid. The man grunted again. Leonid looked around the cafeteria.

"It's getting crowded already," he said in English. "With the tourist season starting. I don't mean to offend. We in St Petersburg are very glad to see you."

The man's face twisted into something that was a sort of amusement.

"I'm no tourist. I'm here on business."

"Oh really? Something in the art world?"

"No way. All that crap just passes me by. I'm a lawyer."

Leonid's heart sank.

"Oh really? I noticed you as I passed through the Rembrandt Gallery. You're very thorough. That must be legal training."

"I like to double-check everything. That's not easy when half the labels on the pictures are in Russian."

"That's for the Russian visitors."

"Well, it doesn't help. How can I be sure that the English is a true translation?"

"The Russian is likely to be more accurate. It is a very subtle and precise language." With a faint idea of directing the visitor to other attractions he went on: "We have a church in St Petersburg dedicated to St Cyril, who gave us the Cyrillic alphabet."

"You should have thrown it back in his face," said the man, biting into an iced bun. "You're loaded down with a language no one but Balkan people can understand. I don't get it at all. Some of the letters are the same as ours. Some of them seem the same but turn out to be something different. Some of them are printed backwards. And some of them are way off the beaten track, never known as letters elsewhere. St Cyril did you no favours."

"Are you a linguist, then?"

"A linguist? What's he when he's at home? I told you, I'm a lawyer."

"I thought in your spare time."

"I don't have spare time. I'm interested in the background of this collection, where the things came from, who owned them before."

Leonid began to sweat.

"Why should you be interested in that?"

"Well, after 'Where did it come from?' I ask myself '*Should* it have come from there?' Was it legally acquired, and legally lodged in the museum that holds it? Or was it a five-dime government seizing what it had no right to?"

Leonid said in a flat voice: "So you are interested in provenance?"

"Providence? No way. Never give it a thought. I'm interested in seeing justice done. Financial justice."

"*Provenance*," said Leonid, his voice still emotionless. "The history of the piece, who has owned it in the past, how it has passed from one person to another. As one hears the history of a house or a palace."

"Right. Spot on. You're on the ball. One of the few people in this godforsaken country who is."

Fearing he was going to be the object of further attempts to spread international goodwill. Leonid downed his potent brew and – feeling rather daring – said, "Have a good day" and left the café.

But though he had left behind the brash American, the man stayed with him for the rest of the morning. He was interested in provenance, even if he didn't understand the word. Interested in whence the Hermitage had acquired the pictures it displayed. Mostly that question was quite easily answered. They had been bought by Catherine the Great or her predecessors or successors on the Imperial throne. Or indeed by her Communist successors in the 'twenties, who had acquired many of the Impressionists or twentieth-century paintings in a straightforward manner, buying them in the international market.

Which was why there were few entries from that massive collection on the third floor. They had been disapproved of and hidden away in the decades of Soviet realism, but they had been bought in the early years of the Revolution, when experiment was respectable, and now they were hung in all their glory with their provenance neatly detailed on the label.

In fact, *all* the pictures had their provenances neatly detailed. Had that been a bad mistake? Because though the upper galleries had yielded meagre results for the American lawyer, he was getting much more food for thought from the Dutch rooms. The Russian aristocrats of the nineteenth and twentieth centuries had not been in the vanguard of artistic progress: They had not bought the French Impressionists or Picasso – by and large they had probably thought them artistic frauds and impostors. Some Russians had collected them, though – specialists – and their pictures had been acquired, probably at knockdown prices, in the normal way.

The aristocrats, though, had preferred Dutch landscapes, Flemish portraits, church scenes, domestic vignettes. Also Spanish street scenes, English ladies in silks, Italian classical episodes. When the Yank (Leonid had lots of other words for Americans, and political correctness was a concept quite unknown in the new Russia) had finished with the Low Countries, fertile fields still lay ahead of him.

What had the foreign gangster said?

"A five-dime government seizing what it had no right to."

And what he had been looking for, Leonid felt quite certain, was pictures acquired during the twenties from the estates of aristocrats – probably all in exile. People whose descendants were still around, most often in the U.S.A., and anxious to reclaim what they still regarded as theirs.

Leonid was a product of the Age of Brezhnev, whose first name had been given him. He was not sorry that Communism had collapsed, but he was quite pleased it had existed. Many good things had happened in those seventy years, he felt: some because of the system, some by circumventing or questioning the system. Since its fall, Leonid had noted all over Eastern Europe the old families coming back, claiming their ancestral homes and acres, their royal status. The King of Bulgaria had been given back his palaces, and then had magnanimously given one of them back to the Bulgarian people. And then had graciously consented to become their Prime Minister. It was a better world, the larger part of Leonid's brain told him. But there was still a tiny part of it that told him that the world – *his* world – had gone mad.

What the imperialist gangster was doing, Leonid was quite sure, was identifying pictures that had been confiscated from the old aristocratic families in the early years of Bolshevik rule, so that they could claim them back in a court of law or receive their value today. Millions and millions of dollars! Billions of roubles! The idea was fantastic, repulsive! These pictures belonged to the Russian people.

He began once again prowling around *his* art gallery. He had no doubt it was the greatest in the world. He looked at his favourites, and at many pictures he had hardly noticed before but now felt he loved, because they were threatened.

What was to be done? Change the labels, for a start. There was no reason why a gallery should trumpet how its treasures had been acquired. But his heart sank. Even in brave new Russia everything took time.

Decisions were made, then passed up the hierarchy before they could be acted upon. Relabelling the collection was no more than a cosmetic change, but it would take months. No, years.

"Not now, I'm busy," he said when, his office attained, his secretary had thrust letters, requisitions, permits to sign into his hands.

But she noticed before five minutes were out that "busy" meant that he was thinking. He sat, slumped forward, his head in his hands.

He had had no impression from their talk that this man was part of a team, or a larger enterprise. On the contrary, aside from his knowledge of the layout of the Hermitage, he seemed to have come poorly prepared. A familiarity with the Cyrillic alphabet would surely have been a sensible piece of preparation, and so would a broad conspectus as to how the collection had been amassed over the centuries. This man seemed to be learning on his feet, coming from a zero position.

A maverick, then. Getting together a file of pictures that could have been confiscated in the early days of the Revolution from the estates of prominent noblemen no longer resident in their native country. Possibly his preparation had been to discover which of the main important families who escaped had descendants living in the States – men and women who could be approached with a view to representing them in a lawsuit. Leonid had heard of the expression "ambulance chaser" for rapacious lawyers eager to profit from accidents. The only stretchers involved in this kind of profiteering were the ones on which the canvases were once prepared. This was a piece of speculative moneymaking of the most blatant kind, and it threatened the collections of all the most important galleries in Eastern Europe.

Time. That was what was needed. Time. Time to prepare for the threat. To prepare in minor ways, like labels which said nothing about the provenance of the paintings. But, more important, preparing government for the threat, perhaps so it could pass special legislation, retrospective legislation, legalising the state's takeover of the property of émigré nobles decades before, and giving it democratic respectability.

He thought of how he would make these suggestions at next week's staff meeting, and what a furore his revelations about the threat to the collection would make.

Time . . . A maverick speculator working on his own.

He got up from his desk and, brushing aside his secretary, again went back into the body of the museum.

So many people. Crowds milling to and fro, almost like a revolution in the making. A people's uprising, an assertion of ownership in the great artworks of all countries and centuries that had found their home in the Hermitage. He wandered around the ground floor – the shops, the cafeteria, the children's assembly area, the cloakrooms. A city in itself.

And there he was again.

Walking purposefully towards the cafe again, but five minutes away from it, potbelly thrust forward, the legend KANSAS – WHAT A STATE WE'RE IN blazoned across the chest of his red T-shirt. His eyes were staring from left to right. Looking for somebody? An accomplice?

No, looking for a lavatory. Suddenly he swerved aside and went into the Gentleman's just outside Room 99.

Leonid waited, loosening his belt – the only weapon he had. Then he went into the small convenience and bolted the door, as the cleaner always did when she was at work inside. Then he disappeared into one of the cubicles.

The Yank was into serious business. Eventually, after sounds that made Leonid feel quite queasy, paper was torn, a flush was pulled, a door unlocked, and The Threat was out into the main part of the lavatory and running water into the basin. Leonid went out.

"Hi! You're the guy I was talking to in the cafe, aren't you?"

"That's right."

"Hey, I got an idea after you left. You're one of the gang – guys, I mean, who run this place, aren't you?"

His hands were all soapy, and he put his head down towards the water – Leonid noticed for the first time how nasty he found the little moustache, reminiscent of the last great threat to the Hermitage collection in 1941 – and washed his fat cheeks.

"Er – yes, I am."

"Seems to me we could be useful to each other. What I need is information, background, maybe classified stuff. I could pay well – in dollars, of course. Always in dollars."

He'd at least learnt *some*thing about the new Russia, Leonid thought.

"So what do you say? Mutually advantageous, that's what it would be. Is it a deal?"

He was tugging down the paper towel. Leonid slipped his belt from round his waist, quickly slipped it around the man's neck, and tightened it around his throat.

"No," he said. "No, I won't. No."

So much time it took! And so much strength. The capitalist pirate at least made a struggle of it, his face going first red and then purple, his eyes popping, his wet soapy hands flailing. At last, when Leonid's own face was red with the struggle, the man started to fail, the movements became feebler, and finally his body slumped down onto the tiled floor. For a minute or two Leonid held the belt tight around his neck, resisting the temptation to pull up his trousers, which were around his ankles. At last he straightened up, and secured them with his belt.

He looked around him. The Threat's cubicle, smelly and dirty, was the place to put him. He picked him up by his shoulders, dragged him in, and shut the door. He couldn't lock it, but he pushed the feet well inside. Then he went and looked at himself in the mirror. Quite presentable, really. Quite normal. He slipped back the bolt on the door and went out into the thronged, pulsating gallery.

He was too excited to go straight back to the office. He must go around the great artistic domain that he had saved. He walked with his head high, his heart throbbing with pride. He was on cloud nine with the gods on the Grand Staircase, and he knew it. Never had he been so prompt in decision, so effective in action. He felt like God himself, almost like the Museum Director.

So taken up was he with his new status as the man who saved the Hermitage that he did not notice in the Spanish Gallery the man with the off-white T-shirt with the barely legible slogan which read KERRY TO WIN. Or the man in the French seventeenth-century gallery in the green T-shirt with the slogan which read HANG NELSON MANDELA. Both were peering closely at the labels under the pictures, and both were clutching small notebooks and ballpoint pens. Both were purposeful, efficient, and smiling.

JADE SKIRT

Simon Levack

My mistress was concerned about her water supply.

This may seem an odd preoccupation for an Aztec. After all, our city, Mexico, was built on an island in a freshwater lake and was riddled with canals, one of which ran past my mistress's house. However you had only to think of all the rubbish and other things that were tipped into them by the city's thousands of households to know why the water we drank always came from springs. Some of these were within the city itself; but the city had long since outgrown them, and now the most important source was on the hill of Chapultepec, across the water on the western shore of the lake.

Years ago – before I was born – the rulers of Mexico had built a great aqueduct whose two stone channels linked Chapultepec to the city. Most households got their fresh water from men who filled their jars from the aqueduct near the point where it entered the city and carried them by canoe through the city's network of canals direct to our doors. They were paid in bags of cocoa beans and most Aztecs scarcely reckoned the cost, being happy to be spared the daily chore of fetching their own water. Merchants, however, took worldly wealth more seriously than most of us. My mistress – Tiger Lily, the lady to whom I was bound technically as a slave, although in reality our relationship was a good deal more complex than that – was a merchant. This all had something to do with why I was standing in one of the aqueduct's channels – the southern one, currently empty and closed for cleaning – with evil-smelling muck oozing between my toes and a fetid stench filling my nostrils.

"It's free water for two years, Yaotl," Lily had explained. "Just for standing around and watching a ceremony, and you can't claim you haven't done worse before. Not to mention the fact that you drink the water too."

"I know," I admitted. "It still seems like an odd request, though. What can I tell a water seller that he can't see for himself?"

Blue Feather, whose canoe brought a full jar to Lily's house every day, had asked her for my services for a day. The newly cleaned and reopened northern channel of the aqueduct was to be rededicated to the water-goddess, Lady Jade Skirt, and I was to watch the ceremony. I was to take careful note of every aspect of the proceedings, even down to precisely where the priest stood while he made his sacrifices – Blue Feather had been most particular about this.

My mistress's face, framed in a mass of dark, silver-streaked hair, wore a frown whose meaning I could catch better than anyone. She obviously thought my assignment strange too. "Does it matter?" she asked eventually. "He can't be there because he's got to make a sacrifice at Jade Skirt's temple, but he wants to be sure every detail of the ceremony at the aqueduct is right. And you have to admit you're a better person to observe something like this than most – after all, you used to be a priest."

That much was true although, as I stood in the slime watching Jade Skirt's devotee going through the ritual, I was still puzzled. This ceremony was not much like the bloody sacrifices of men and quails I had been used to when I had served in the temples.

The goddess's priest balanced precariously at the edge of the full channel. "Oh, Lady of the Jade Skirt!" he cawed in a harsh, deep voice, "Oh, Goddess of the rivers and springs, accept this, our unworthy gift!" And so saying he tossed the object in his hands into the water at his feet.

It made a soft "plop" and vanished from sight.

The Goddess had received many gifts that morning, each of them accompanied by the same self-abasing formula. Some had been humble enough: tortillas, ears of maize, drinking vessels, a ladle full of burning incense; but the priest had saved the best till last, and the offering he had just made had been splendid: a small gold statuette of the goddess with glittering emeralds for eyes. It had been paid for by the water-sellers. A small crowd of them stood around, some with the priest on the edge of the water-channel, others looking up from the empty conduit next to it. Their canoes jammed the canal running beneath us under the aqueduct. Others, including Blue Feather, were at the goddess's temple, where more offerings would be made.

It was the southern channel's turn in the regular maintenance schedule, which is why it was empty of water. I stood in it among the rest of the water-sellers and the other spectators, waiting silently for the ceremony to end and fervently wishing I were somewhere else. A fine drizzle had begun to fall. It plastered the priest's already long, lank hair to his pitch-stained temples and made his black cloak hang limply around him, and made me feel more miserable than ever.

"It always seems like a terrible waste to me," someone nearby remarked.

"A waste of time, certainly," I muttered. Then I peered around at the speaker. He had a plain, undyed cloak and the tonsured hair of a man who had never captured an enemy warrior in battle: the lowliest of commoners. I wondered whether he was one of the water sellers, but when he caught my eye he told me otherwise.

"I know what you mean." He spoke quietly, for fear of upsetting our neighbours, although they were all huddled and shivering in their cloaks and probably longing to be elsewhere too. "But we have to do it, don't we? My parish provided the work detail that cleaned out that half of the aqueduct, you see, so we have to be here."

"Cleaning these channels must be a nasty job," I remarked sympathetically. One of the quirks of slavery among Aztecs was that it freed a man from many of the onerous duties that ordinary commoners were subject to, such as taking part in public works whenever the Emperor or his officials demanded it. The only person I had to obey was my mistress. So I had no first-hand knowledge of the kind of labour that cleaning the aqueduct or shoring up the sides of a canal or whitewashing a palace might involve.

"Oh, it's all right, unless you have a problem with filth, stink and a back that feels like you'll never be able to straighten it again." The other man grinned. "Of course with this particular job we always live in hopes – if you see what I mean. Never comes to anything, mind you. Like I said, it's a terrible waste."

I frowned. "I don't follow."

"Stuff like that gold statue," he explained patiently. "And all the other jewels and things that get thrown in the water as offerings to the goddess. You'd think, wouldn't you, that some of that would come up when we're scooping all the muck out of the bottom? Never happens, though." He sighed regretfully. "A man could live for years on just one find like that, but I suppose the goddess can't spare it! All we ever get is the rubbish. She doesn't seem so interested in the clay bowls and tobacco tubes. Funny, that, isn't it?"

Eventually, the priest gabbled his way to the end of the ritual. It concluded with a sacrifice of his own blood, drawn from his earlobe with an obsidian razor and sprinkled on the water's surface.

By the time I had returned home, Blue Feather was already there, passing the time of day in Lily's courtyard and clearly itching to be told exactly what I had seen. He was all polite attention as I gave my account, but he might as well have been asleep, since he immediately asked me to repeat it.

After he had left Lily and I agreed that we still could not understand what he was about. Still, as Lily pointed out, that was up to him, provided she still got her water.

She was less sanguine the next morning, when she found out that her water-seller had vanished. And naturally it became my job to find him.

"I was looking for him in the marketplace," she explained, "to get our agreement witnessed. But he wasn't at his usual place, by the canal, and no one could tell me where he was. Go and see if he's ill, or something."

This was the start of a frustrating morning. Lily told me where he lived, and that part was easy enough. It was a typical Aztec house, two rooms opening onto a small square of courtyard, fronting a canal just broad enough for a two-man canoe.

I had to skirt a small pile of trash piled against one side of the house. It looked like the usual rubbish – ash from the hearth, broken shells of turkey eggs, maize husks, and so on – and I would normally not have spared it a glance, but I was surprised to see a hollow cane, the sort used as a smoking tube. This puzzled me because tobacco was expensive, imported from the hot lowlands for priests and lords; I could not understand what it would be doing in a humble water-seller's house.

The water-seller's wife was home: a weary-looking woman, fine boned and grey haired, whose patched and frayed blouse and skirt made the idea of her husband taking his ease with a pipe even more incongruous.

She received me politely, inviting me to squat in her courtyard and offering me food, as good manners required. It was a piece of a slightly stale tortilla which I had no hesitation in declining.

She had little to tell me. "He went out last night and didn't come back."

I waited for her to add something to that, but the silence merely dragged on. Eventually I said: "He didn't say why?"

"No."

"Was he in the habit of going out at night?" Few Aztecs were. The night was widely feared: it was ruled by spirits, creatures out of dreams and fateful beasts such as owls and weasels whose appearance could foretell a man's death. Only those trained to overcome such things, such as priests and sorcerers, usually went out after dark, unless there were some very good reason.

"No, he wasn't. That's why I'm worried." The woman did not sound especially worried to me. In fact she was downright curt, considering I was trying to find her missing husband. It was almost as if she resented my questions.

"Is there anyone else at home?" I asked. "Anyone who might know where he went?"

She hesitated for long time, her eyes in her lap. I suspected she was trying to think of a reason not to answer me, but at last she said: "My son. I don't think he'll help you, though. He's probably down by the aqueduct, filling his jars."

⋆   ⋆   ⋆

Blue Feather's son was called Cloud Eagle. He was a tall, burly young man of about twenty, his muscles developed by years of hauling heavy jars about. I found him at one of the water-sellers' favourite places for filling up, close to where the previous day's ceremony had taken place. Cloud Eagle was in a canoe on a broad waterway at the point where it ran beneath the aqueduct's twin channels. He was standing upright and trying to keep his craft steady using a long wooden pole jammed into the canal's bottom, while an older man poured water down towards him using a large clay jug. Unfortunately the boat kept moving, and while some of the water went where it was supposed to, tumbling into open jars with a hollow rattle, much of it ended up in the bottom of the boat, over the younger man's head, or in the canal.

"Hold that thing still, can't you?" cried the man on the edge of the aqueduct.

"I'm doing my best!" his colleague protested. He was sweating, his muscles straining with the effort of keeping the canoe where it was supposed to be. He was clearly not accustomed to this particular task and, from where I stood, it looked as though he was making a mess of it.

"Cloud Eagle?" I called out from the bank.

"Yes," snapped the youngster. "What do you want?"

"Sorry to distract you, but . . ."

The man on the aqueduct threw his jug down in disgust: it dropped straight into the canal, missing the canoe by a hand's breadth. The young man in the boat sat down heavily.

"Sorry," I said again, "but it's about your father . . ."

With a sigh he got up and took up his pole again, using it to push the boat towards me. "All right. I'm coming. Don't think I can help you, though."

From above my head a voice snarled: "Keep it short. We've still got a living to make!"

Cloud Eagle did not get out of the boat. He was taller than I so, although the bank was raised a little above the water's surface, we were almost eye-to-eye.

"My cousin lent me this boat," he explained, indicating with a glance over his shoulder that his cousin was the elder man still glowering down at us. "He said he'd help me until Father comes back . . . or at least until we find his canoe."

I felt my eyebrows lift. "Your father took his boat with him?" That was curious. His wife had not mentioned this. It was odd enough for a man to wander off by night for no apparent reason, but where could he possibly want to go that would mean he needed his canoe? It suggested he had not merely felt the urge to go behind the wicker screen hiding the nearest public latrine, and maybe fallen in a canal on the way. He had had some purpose in mind, one that meant travelling farther than he could easily walk.

"Yes, he seems to have done. I hope the boat comes back . . . I mean, I hope he comes back, of course, but there's no way we could afford to replace the canoe. In the meantime, Flint Knife up there has let us use his, and he agreed to help me fill the jars, just for today." The lad grimaced. "I should have suggested we do it the other way around. I'm usually the one scooping water out of the aqueduct and pouring it out, while Father holds the boat steady. I hadn't realized his part of the job was so difficult!"

I looked at the jars surrounding him in the boat. None was more than half full. "I expect you're right and you can't help, but have you any idea at all where your father might have gone? Or if he was, well, up to anything – well, you know what I mean . . ."

"I know," said the young man sadly. "Anything he wouldn't want my mother to know about, you mean? No, I don't think so. If there was anything like that he didn't share the secret with me."

I sighed. I was going to have to go back to Lily with nothing to report, but I could think of nothing more to ask. "All right, thanks. If he does appear, let him know that Tiger Lily wants to see him, won't you?"

As I turned away, and Cloud Eagle picked up his pole again, a thought struck me. "How are you going to carry on now that jug's gone in the water?" I asked curiously.

"Oh, that happens all the time." He laughed. "I'll just dive down and get it again. We've lost it in deeper water than this before! It's only waist-high here; that's one of the reasons we use this spot."

Lily was, as I had anticipated, not particularly pleased at my failure, and the prospect of her two years' free deliveries vanished somewhere beyond the city limits, but she was even less pleased the next morning.

"I don't believe it!" The words, uttered in her shrillest voice echoed around the courtyard of her house. "Both of them gone, now?"

The bearer of the news was none other than Flint Knife: Cloud Eagle's cousin.

"That man owes me a good deal," Lily was saying, "and if you're telling me his son's gone missing as well . . ."

"What happened?" I asked Flint Knife. "And why are you here?"

The man was almost as angry as Lily. His face was a peculiar purple colour. "How should I know what happened? All I know is, when I went to fetch my boat this morning, it wasn't there. I though my cousin might have borrowed it so I went to his house. But his mother told me he'd vanished in the night – just like his father before him! I came here because I knew you'd been looking for Blue Feather and you spoke to his son yester-day – I thought you might have some idea where he might have gone." The man breathed heavily, and added: "I need that boat, you understand? It's all very well helping out a relative in trouble, but I have to have it back, or else how am I supposed to live?"

The pitiful note in his voice did not impress Lily. "I don't understand what made you think we could help. I've got enough troubles of my own – what?"

Her last word was snarled at me, because I had just cleared my throat. "I don't know," I said. "Maybe we can help, after all." I turned to the water seller. "Just one question, though. When you spoke to Blue Feather's wife this morning, did she seem upset at all?"

He stared at me incredulously. "What, a woman who's just had both her husband and her son vanish into thin air?" He paused, frowning. "Actually, now you come to think of it, she didn't seem all that concerned. She didn't look as if she'd been up all night crying, anyway."

"What are you thinking, Yaotl?" my mistress demanded.

I glanced up at the sky. It was cloudy, but I sensed that the sun had not yet climbed very high. "It may not be too late," I muttered to myself. "If he waited until dawn . . . And he would, he might not find the place in the dark . . ." I looked at my mistress. "We'll have to go now, though," I said. "In fact if we can run, so much the better!"

I was to regret my suggestion four hundred times over before we had come to the water-seller's house. As a former priest I had been trained to endure pain and exhaustion, by the endless round of fasts, ritual self-mortifications and vigils that our rites demanded, but that had been many years before. By the time we reached our objective my lungs felt as though they had been seared by hot smoke and my legs were twitching and threatening to double up under me. Flint Knife looked and sounded worse than I was. Lily, who had kept pace with us with her skirts gathered about her knees, seemed, surprisingly, a little better, although in truth for the last part of the journey we had all more or less slowed to a brisk walk. All the same, as soon as the little house hove into sight I realized we had got there in time.

We all paused for a moment, panting. It was Cloud Eagle's uncle who was the first to utter words, staggering two further, exhausting steps towards the canoe moored by the house. "That's . . . my . . . boat!" he gasped incredulously.

"Yes," I muttered, starting forward myself. "And there's your nephew, and look what he's holding under his arm! Stop!"

The young man wasted only a moment staring at me and my exhausted and desperate-looking companions. Then he leapt straight into his canoe, the object still cradled under his arm, and seized a paddle with his free hand. At the same time his mother appeared from the house, screeched once and ran along the bank towards us.

Cloud Eagle managed one-handed to get the boat to move. It did not get very far. Flint Knife let out an angry howl and jumped into the waist-deep water in front of it, waving his arms wildly. The canal was too narrow for the vessel to pass, and Cloud Eagle could not get enough speed up to run his cousin down. He bellowed in frustration, lashing the water with his paddle. Then he raised it to strike at Flint Knife, which was when I drew level with the canoe, jumped in and wrested the trophy from the crook of his arm.

At the same time Lily raced past me to confront Cloud Eagle's mother. Recalling the words they used to each other still makes me blush. It took Cloud Eagle's despairing voice to call an end to the brawl. "It's all right, Mother," he moaned, tossing the paddle into the canal. "It's no good. They're on to us. They've got it now."

There was barely room for all of us to squat or kneel in the courtyard of Blue Feather's house. The water-seller's wife – widow, I reminded myself – did not offer us anything to eat. She stood in the corner and glared at us.

I set the thing I had taken from her son on the hard earth in front of me. The goddess Jade Skirt's emerald eyes gleamed into mine, sparkling as if with mirth. Well, I thought, nobody ever claimed the gods had no sense of humour.

"Well, now I've got my boat back, I'll be off," Flint Knife said.

"Not so fast!" snapped Lily. "I still want to know what happened, and where's Blue Feather?" When no one else answered she turned to me. "Yaotl?"

"In the lake, near where the aqueduct enters the city, I should think." I looked at his son. "But I don't think he'll be coming back from there, will he?"

The lad said nothing.

"You'd better explain," Lily said.

"It's easy enough. You remember how the water-seller wanted me to describe the ceremony at the aqueduct in detail – even down to things like exactly where the priest was standing when he threw the idol in the water? He claimed it was because he wanted to make sure it was all done right, but of course that was nonsense. Why should it matter to him? He's just an ordinary trader, and not a very successful one at that, judging by the state of this place." The grey-haired woman hissed reproachfully. "Which reminds me – I noticed tobacco tubes in the trash heap outside, and couldn't think what they were doing in such a poor household.

"I didn't work out what was happening when the old man vanished, but when we heard his son had disappeared too, it was suddenly obvious. They were after this statue – or at least the gold and jewels in it. This is what I think happened. Both Blue Feather and Cloud Eagle went out the other night, in Blue Feather's canoe. They knew where the statue was, thanks to my description. However they were a bit wary of just going straight to the place to fish it out, because it was inside the city and someone might see what they were up to. So instead, they took their boat to the point near the shore of the island, where the aqueduct first enters the city. Cloud Eagle here climbed up to the aqueduct and made his way along it. I'm not sure how deep it is when it's full, but I suppose he used one of those tobacco tubes to breathe through.

"He would have had to grope around under the water for a while, but he obviously found what he was looking for. Then he made his way back and threw the statue down to his father in the boat."

A groan from the young man told me I had got it right. "That's where it went wrong, isn't it?" I said. "Because Blue Feather didn't catch it – and being solid gold, it went through the bottom of the boat, straight into the lake. And by the time Cloud Eagle here realized what had happened, the boat and his father had both vanished."

Lily gasped. Even Flint Knife muttered something under his breath that may have been an expression of shock. Cloud Eagle looked at the ground. Only his mother was impassive.

"And that's it, really. The young man had to go home and tell his mother what had happened. She knew about the plot all along, of course – she could hardly fail too, with both of them out overnight – and they agreed that he should go back the next night and try to retrieve the statue from where it had sunk. He's a good diver – unlike his father, alas! Blue Feather and the boat will still be there, of course." Even if Cloud Eagle could have retrieved the body, I knew he would not: the drowned were sacred to the Rain God and only priests could touch them. "They must be in the lake – someone would have noticed them in a canal."

There was a long silence, which Lily eventually broke. "So, I'm not going to get my free water." She sounded philosophical enough about it. "What do we do with these, though?" she asked, indicating our unwilling hosts. Aztecs rarely went out at night, except with good reason; but Lily and I had a good reason. Besides, I had been a priest, and knew how to fight any demons we might encounter. And we had the gods on our side, I thought, as I extended a hand to help my mistress up to the edge of the aqueduct; one of the gods, at least.

"Amazing, the risks some people will take," I mused, as I gazed for the last time into Lady Jade Skirt's glittering green eyes.

"What, us perching here, you mean?"

"No, I mean fooling around with the gods, the way that water seller was prepared to do, and for what? For something he could sell in the marketplace."

We had not reported Cloud Eagle and his mother to the authorities. Losing Blue Feather and the boat had seemed punishment enough.

I smiled, and after a brief glance at my mistress, tossed the gold statue back into the water, where it belonged.

I watched it sink with a twinge of fear. What if it were looted a second time? What about all the other precious things that were tossed into the water and, as the workman had told me, never seen again? What if, in the end, the goddess never got anything but the kind of rubbish the labourers found when they dredged the aqueduct?

If that were the case, I thought, then we had better get used to drinking lake water, after all.

THE FERRYMAN'S
BEAUTIFUL DAUGHTER

Peter Robinson

The strangers came to live on the island at the beginning of summer, 1969, and by the end of August my best friend Mary Jane was dead. The townsfolk blamed the Newcomers and their heathen ways, but I was certain it was something else. Not something new, but something old and powerful that had festered in the town for years, or perhaps had always been there.

I remember the morning they arrived. We were all in chapel. It was stifling hot because the windows were closed and there was no air-conditioning. "Stop fidgeting and listen to the Preacher," hissed Mother. I tried my best, but his words made no sense to me. Flecks of spittle flew from his mouth like when water touches hot oil in a frying pan. Something about Judgment Day, when the dead would rise incorruptible.

Next to me, Mary Jane was looking down at her shoes trying to hold back her laughter. I could see the muscles tightening around her lips and jaw. If we started giggling now we were done for. The Preacher didn't like laughter. It made him angry. He finally gave her one of his laser-like looks, and that seemed to settle her down. He'd never liked Mary Jane since she refused to attend his special instruction evening classes. She told me that when he had asked her, he had put his face so close to hers that she had been able to smell the bourbon on his breath, and she was sure she had seen the outline of his thing pushing hard against his pants. She also said she had seen him touching Betsy Goodall where he shouldn't have been touching her, but when we asked Betsy she blushed and denied everything. What else could she have done? Who would have believed her? In those days, as perhaps even now, small, isolated communities like ours kept their nasty little secrets to themselves.

Across the aisle, Riley McCorkindale kept glancing sideways at Mary Jane when he thought she couldn't see him. Riley was sweet on her, but she gave him a terrible run-around. I thought he was quite nice, but he *was* very shy and he seemed too young for us, no matter how tall and burly he was. Besides, he was always chewing gum and we thought that looked common. We were very sophisticated young ladies. And you have to understand that Mary Jane was very beautiful, not gawky and plain like me, with golden hair, delicate soft skin and the biggest, bluest eyes you have ever seen.

At last the service ended and we ran out into the summer sunshine. Our parents lingered to shake hands with neighbors and talk to the Preacher, of course. They were old enough to know that you weren't supposed to seem in too much of a hurry to leave God's house. But Mary Jane and I were only fifteen, sophisticated as we were, and everybody knew that meant trouble. Especially when they said we were too old for our own good. "Precocious" was the word they used most often to describe us. I looked it up.

And that was when we saw the Newcomers. I think Mary Jane noticed them first because I remember seeing her expression change from laughter to wonder as I followed her gaze to the old school bus pulling into the parking lot. It wasn't yellow, but was painted all colors, great swirls and blobs and sunbursts of green, red, purple, orange, black and blue, like nothing we'd ever seen before. And the people! We didn't own a television set in our house, but I'd seen pictures in magazines tourists left on the ferry sometimes, and I'd even read in Father's newspaper about how they took drugs, listened to strange, distorted loud music and held large gatherings outside the cities, where they indulged in unspeakable practices. But I had never seen any of them in the flesh before.

They certainly did look odd, the girls in loose dresses of pretty, flowered patterns, the men with their long hair over their shoulders or tied back in ponytails, wearing Mexican-style ponchos and bell-bottom jeans and cowboy boots, the children scruffy, dirty and long-haired, running wild. They looked at us without much curiosity as they boarded the ferryboat carrying their few belongings. I suppose they'd seen plenty of people who looked like us before, and who looked at them the way we must have done. Even Riley, who had clearly been plucking up the courage to come over and say hello to Mary Jane before his ferry left, had stopped dead in his tracks, mouth gaping open. I could see the piece of gum lying there on his tongue like a misplaced tonsil.

Once the Newcomers had all boarded the ferry, the regulars got on. There was no chapel on the island. Only about thirty people lived there, and not all of them were religious. The Preacher said that was because most of them were intellectuals and thought they knew better than the SCRIPTURES. Anyway, the ones who weren't businessmen, like Riley's father, taught at the university in the city, about forty miles away, and commuted. They left their cars in the big parking lot next to the harbor because there were no roads on the island.

Just because we had the ferry, it didn't make our little town an important place; it was simply the best natural harbor closest to Pine Island. We had a general store, a rundown hotel with a Chinese restaurant attached, the chapel, and an old one-room schoolhouse for the children. The high school was fifteen miles away in Logan, the nearest large town, and Mary Jane and I had to take the bus. The sign read "Jasmine Cove, Pop. 2,321" and I'd guess that was close enough to the truth, though I don't think they could have counted Mary Jessop's new baby because she only gave birth the day before the Newcomers arrived.

Over the next few days, we found out a little more about the Newcomers. They were from inland, a thousand miles away, according to Lenny, who ran the general store. There were about nine of them in all, including the children, and they'd bought the land fair and square from the government and had all the right papers and permissions. They kept to themselves and didn't like outsiders. They shunned the rest of society – that's the word Lenny used, "shunned", I looked it up – and planned to live off the land, growing vegetables. They didn't eat meat or fish.

According to Lenny, they didn't go to chapel. He said they worshipped the devil and danced naked and sacrificed children and animals, but Mary Jane and I didn't believe him. Lenny had a habit of getting carried away with himself when it came to new ideas. Like the Preacher, he thought the world was going to hell in a hand basket and almost everything he saw and heard proved him right, especially if it had anything to do with young people.

That day, as we wandered out of the general store onto Main Street, Mary Jane turned to me, smiled sweetly and said, "Grace, why don't we take a little ferry ride tomorrow and find out about the Newcomers for ourselves?"

Mary Jane's father, Mr Kiernan, was the ferryman, and in summer, when we were on holiday from school, he let us ride for free whenever we wanted. Sometimes I even went by myself. Pine Island wasn't very big – about two miles long and maybe half a mile wide – but it had some very beautiful areas. I loved the western beach best of all, a lonely stretch of golden sand at the bottom of steep, forbidding cliffs. Mary Jane and I knew a secret path down, and we spent many hours exploring the caves and rock pools, or lounging about on the beach talking about life and things. Sometimes I went there alone when I felt blue, and it always made me feel better.

Most of the inhabitants of Pine Island lived in a small community of wood-structure houses nestled around the harbor on the east coast, but the Newcomers had bought property at the southern tip, where two abandoned log cabins had been falling to ruin there as long as anyone could remember. Some-one said they'd once been used by hunters, but there was nothing left to hunt on Pine Island any more.

We saw the Newcomers in town from time to time, when they came to buy provisions at Lenny's store. Sometimes one or two of them would drive the school bus to Logan for things they couldn't find here. They were buying drugs there, and seeds to grow marijuana, which made folk crazy, so Lenny said. Perhaps they were.

Certainly the Preacher found many new subjects for his long sermons after the arrival of the Newcomers – including, to the dismay of some members of his congregation, the evils of tobacco and alcohol – but whether word of his rantings ever got back to them, and whether they cared if it did, we never knew.

The Preacher was in his element. He told us the Newcomers were nothing other than demons escaped from hell. He even told Mr Kiernan that he should have nothing to do with them and that he shouldn't use God's ferryboat to transport demons. Mr Kiernan explained that he worked for the ferry company, which was based in the city, not for the Preacher, and that it was his job to transport anyone who paid the fare to or from Pine Island. The Preacher argued that the money didn't matter, that there was a "higher authority", and the ferry company was as bad as the Newcomers; they were all servants of Beelzebub and Mammon and any other horrible demon names he could think of. In the end, Mr Kiernan gave up arguing and simply carried on doing his job.

One bright and beautiful day in July around the time when men first set foot on the moon, Mary Jane and I set off on our own exploratory mission. Mr Kiernan stood at the wheel, for all the world looking as proud and stiff as if he were piloting *Apollo 11* itself. We weren't going to the moon, of course, but we might as well have been. It was only later, in university, that I read *The Tempest*, but had I known it then, Miranda's words would surely have echoed in my mind's ear: "O brave new world that hath such people in it!"

The little ferry didn't have any fancy restaurants or shops or anything, just a canvas-covered area with hard wooden benches and dirty plastic windows, where you could shelter from the rain – which we got a lot of in our part of the world – and get a cup of hot coffee from the machine, if it was working. Through fair and foul Mr Kiernan stood at the wheel, cap at a jaunty angle, pipe clamped in his mouth. Some of the locals made fun of him behind his back and called him Popeye. They thought we hadn't heard them, but we had. I thought it was cruel, but Mary Jane didn't seem to care. Our town was full of little cruelties, like the way the Youlden kids made fun of Gary Mapplin

THE FERRYMAN'S BEAUTIFUL DAUGHTER   215

because there was something wrong with his spine and he had to go around in a wheelchair, his head lolling on his shoulders as if it were on a spring. Sometimes it seemed to me that everywhere Mary Jane and I went in Jasmine Cove, people gave us dirty looks, and we knew that if we spoke back or anything, they'd report us to our parents. Mr Kiernan was all right – he went very easy on Mary Jane – but my father was a bit of tyrant, and I had to watch what I said around him.

Riley McCorkindale was hanging around the ferry dock, as usual, fishing off the small rickety pier with some friends. I don't think they ever caught anything. He blushed when Mary Jane and I walked by giggling, and said hello. I could feel his eyes following us as we headed for the path south through the woods. He must have known where we were going; it didn't lead anywhere else.

Soon we'd left the harbor and its small community behind us and were deep in the woods. It was cooler there, and the sunlight filtered pale green through the shimmering leaves. Little animals skittered through the dry underbrush, and once a large bird exploded out of a tree and startled us both so much our hearts began to pound. We could hear the waves crashing on the shore in the distance, to the west, but all around us it was peaceful and quiet.

Finally, from a short distance ahead, we heard music. It was like nothing I'd ever heard before, and there was an ethereal beauty about it, drifting on the sweet summer air as if it belonged there.

Then we reached a clearing and could see the log cabins. Three children were playing horseshoes, and someone was taking a shower in a ramshackle wooden box rigged up with some sort of overhead sieve. The music was coming from inside one of the cabins. You can imagine the absolute shock and surprise on our faces when the shower door opened and out walked a young man naked as the day he was born.

We gawped, I'm sure. I had certainly never seen a naked man before, not even a photograph of one, but Mary Jane said she once saw her brother playing with himself when he thought she was out. We looked at one another and swallowed. "Let's wait," Mary Jane whispered. "We don't want them to think we've been spying."

And we waited. Five, ten minutes went by. Nothing much happened. The children continued their game and no-one else entered the shower. Finally, Mary Jane and I took deep breaths, left the cover of the woods and walked into the clearing.

"Hello," I called, aware of the tremor in my voice. "Hello. Is anybody home?"

The children stopped their game and stared at us. One of them, a little girl, I think, with long dark curls, ran inside the nearest cabin. A few moments later a young man stepped out. Probably only three or four years older than us, he had a slight, wispy blonde beard and beautiful silky long hair, still damp, falling over his shoulders. It was the same man we had seen getting out of the shower, and I'm sure we both blushed. He looked a little puzzled and suspicious. And why not? After all, I don't think anyone else from Jasmine Cove had been out to welcome them.

Mary Jane seemed suddenly struck dumb, whether by the man's good looks or the memory of his nakedness I don't know, and it was left to me to speak. "Hello," I said. "I'm Grace Vincent, and this is my friend Mary Jane Kiernan. We're from the town, from Jasmine Cove. We've come to say hello."

He stared for a moment, then smiled and looked at Mary Jane. His eyes were bright green, like the sea just beyond the sands. "Mary Jane," he said. "Well, how strange. This must be a song about you. The Mad Hatters."

"What?" I said.

"The name of the band. The Mad Hatters. They're English."

We listened to the music for a moment, and I thought I caught the words, "Mary Jane is dreaming of an ocean dark and gleaming." I didn't recognize the song, or the name of the group, but that didn't mean much. My parents didn't let me listen to pop music. Mary Jane seemed to find her voice and said something about that being nice.

"Look, would you like to come in?" the young man said. "Have a cold drink or something. It's a hot day."

I looked at Mary Jane. I could tell from her expression that she was as uncertain as I was. Now that we were here, the reality was starting to dawn on us. These were the people the Preacher had called the Spawn of Satan. As far as the townsfolk were concerned, they drugged young girls and had their evil way. But the young man looked harmless and it *was* a hot day. We were thirsty. Finally, we sort of nodded and followed him inside the cabin.

The shade was pleasant and a gentle cross-breeze blew through the open shutters. Sunlight picked out shining strands of silver and gold in the materials that draped the furnishings. The Newcomers didn't have much, and most of it was make-shift, but we made ourselves comfortable on cushions on the floor and the young man brought us some lemonade. "Home-made," he said. "I'm sorry it's not as cold as you're probably used to, but we don't have a refrigerator yet," He laughed. "As a matter of fact, we've only just got the old generator working, or we wouldn't even have any music." He nodded towards the drinks. "We keep some chilled in the stream out back."

By this time the others had wandered in to get a look at us, most of them older than the young man, and several of them lovely women in bright dresses with flowers twined in their long hair.

"I'm Jared," said the young man, then he introduced the others – Star, Leo, Gandalf, Dylan – names we were unfamiliar with. They sat cross-legged on the floor and smiled. Jared asked us some questions about the town, and we explained how the people there were suspicious of strangers but were decent folks underneath it all. I wasn't certain that was true, but we weren't there to say bad things about our kin. We didn't tell them what lies the Preacher had been spreading.

Jared told us they had come here to get away from the suspicion, corruption and greed they had found in the cities, and they were going to live close to nature and meditate. Some of them were artists and musicians – they had guitars and flutes – but they didn't want to be famous or anything. They didn't even want money from anyone. One of them – Rigel, I think his name was – said mysteriously that the world was going to end soon and that this was the best place to be when it happened.

Someone rolled a funny cigarette, lit it and offered it to us, but I said no. I'd never smoked any kind of cigarette, and the thought of marijuana, which I assumed it was, terrified me. To my horror, Mary Jane took it and inhaled. She told me later that it made her feel a bit light-headed, but that was all. I must admit, she didn't act any differently from normal. At least not that day. We left shortly after, promising to drop by again, and it was only over the next few weeks that I noticed Mary Jane's behavior and appearance gradually start to change.

It was just little things at first, like a string of beads she bought at a junk shop in Logan. It was nothing much, really, just cheap colored glass, but it was something she would have turned her nose up at a short while ago. Now, it replaced the lovely gold chain and heart pendant that her parents had given her for her fifteenth birthday. Next came the red cheesecloth top with the silver sequins and fancy Indian embroidery, and the first Mad Hatters LP, the one with "her song" on it.

We went often to the island to see Jared and the others, and I soon began to sense something, some deeper connection, between Mary Jane and Jared and, quite frankly, it worried me. They started wandering off together for hours, and sometimes she told me to go back home without her, that she'd catch a later ferry. It wasn't that Mary Jane was naïve or anything, or that I didn't trust Jared. I also knew that Mary Jane's father was liberal, and she said he trusted her, but I still worried. The townsfolk were already getting a bit suspicious because of the odd way she was dressing. Even Riley McCorkindale gave her strange looks in chapel. It didn't take a genius to put two and two together. At the very least, if she wasn't careful, she could end up grounded for the rest of the summer.

Things came to a head after chapel one Sunday in August. The Preacher had delivered one of his most blistering sermons about what happens to those who turn away from the path of righteousness and embrace evil, complete with a graphic description of the torments of hell. Afterwards, people were standing talking, as they do, all a little nervous, and Mary Jane actually said to the Preacher that she didn't believe there was a hell, that if God was good, he wouldn't do such horrible things to people. The Preacher turned scarlet, and it was only the fact that Mary Jane ran off and jumped on the ferry that stopped him taking her by the ear and dragging her back inside the chapel for special instruction whether she liked it or not. But he wouldn't forget. One way or another, there'd be hell to pay.

Or there would have been, except that was the evening they found Mary Jane's body on the western beach of Pine Island.

*   *   *

The fisherman who found her said he first thought it was a bundle of clothes on the sand. Then, when he went to investigate, he realized that it was a young girl and sailed back to Jasmine Cove as fast as he could. Soon, the police launch was heading out there, the parking lot was full of police cars and the sheriff had commandeered the ferry. Mr Kiernan was beside himself, blaming himself for not keeping a closer eye on her. But it wasn't his fault. He wasn't as mean-spirited as the rest, and how could he know what would happen, anyway? By the time it started to get dark, word was spreading around town that a girl's body had been found, that it was the body of Mary Jane Kiernan and that she had been strangled.

I can't really describe the shock I felt when I first heard the news. It was if my whole being went numb. I didn't believe it at first, of course, but in a way I did. So many people said it had happened that in the end I just had to believe it. Mary Jane was gone.

The next few days passed as in a dream. I remember only that the newspapers were full of stories about some huge gathering out east for folks like the Newcomers, at a place called Woodstock, where it rained cats and dogs and everyone played in the mud. The police came around and questioned everybody, and I was among the first, being Mary Jane's closest friend. The young detective, Lonnegan was his name, seemed nice enough, and Mother offered him a glass of iced tea, which he accepted. His forehead and upper lip were covered by a thin film of sweat.

"Now then, little lady," he began.

"My name's Grace," I corrected him. "I am not a little lady."

I'll give him his due, he took it in his stride. "Very well, Grace," he said. "Mary Jane was your best friend. Is that right?"

"Yes," I answered.

"Were you with her when she went to Pine Island last Wednesday?"

"No," I said.

"Didn't you usually go there together?"

"Sometimes. Not always."

"Why did she go there? There's not exactly a lot to see or do."

I shrugged. "It's peaceful. There's a nice beach . . ." I couldn't help myself, but as soon as I thought of the beach –

it had been *our* beach – the tears started to flow. Lonnegan paused while I reached for a tissue, dried my eyes and composed myself. "I'm sorry," I went on. "It's just a very beautiful place. And there are all kinds of interesting sea birds."

"Yes, but that's not why Mary Jane went there, is it, for the sea birds?"

"Isn't it? I don't know."

"Come on, Grace," said Lonnegan, "we already know she was seeing a young man called David Garwell."

David Garwell. So that was Jared's real name. "Why ask me, then?"

"Do you know if she had arranged to meet him that day? Last Wednesday?"

"I'm sure I don't know," I said. "Mary Jane didn't confide in me about everything." Maybe he did know that Mary Jane was "seeing" Jared, but I wasn't going to tell him that she had told me just two days before she died that she was in love with him, and that as soon as she turned sixteen she planned to go and live with him and the others on Pine Island. That wouldn't have gone down well at all with Detective Lonnegan. Besides, it was our secret.

Lonnegan looked uncomfortable and shuffled in his seat, then he dropped his bombshell. "Maybe she didn't tell you that she was having a baby, Grace, huh? And we think it was his. Did Mary Jane tell you she was having David Garwell's baby?"

In the end, it didn't matter what I thought or said. While the bedraggled crowds were heading home from Woodstock in the east, the police arrested Jared – David Garwell – for the murder of Mary Jane Kiernan. They weren't giving out a whole lot of details, but rumor had it that they had found Mary Jane's gold pendant in a drawer in his room.

"He did it, Grace, you know he did," said Cathy Baker outside the drug store a few days later. "People like that . . . they're . . . ugh!" She pulled a face and made a gesture with her hands as if to sweep spiders off her chest. "They're not like us."

"But why would he hurt her?" I asked. "He loved her."

"*Love*?" echoed Cathy. "They don't know the meaning of the word."

"They call it *free* love, you know," Lynne Everett chirped in. "And that means they do it with anyone."

"And everyone," added Cathy.

I gave up. What was the point? They weren't going to listen. I walked down Main Street with my head hung low and the sun beating on the back of my neck. It just didn't make sense. Mary Jane stopped wearing the pendant when she bought the cheap colored beads. Jared couldn't have stolen it from her, even if he was capable of such a thing, unless he had broken into her house on the mainland, which seemed very unlikely to me. And she hadn't been wearing it on the day she died, I was certain of that. It made far more sense to assume that she had given it to him as a token of her love.

The problem was that I hadn't seen Jared or any of the others since the arrest, so I hadn't been able to ask them what happened. The police had searched the cabins, of course, and they said they found drugs, so they hauled everybody into the county jail and put the children in care.

I was so lost in thought that I didn't even notice Detective Lonnegan walking beside me until he spoke my name and asked me if I wanted to go into Slater's with him for a coffee.

"I'm not allowed to drink coffee," told him, "but I'll have a soda, if that's all right."

He said that was fine and we went inside and took a table. He waited a while before speaking, then he said, "Look, Grace, I know that this is all a terrible shock to you, that Mary Jane was your best friend. I respect that, but if you know anything else that will help us in court against the man who killed her, I'd really be grateful if you'd tell me."

"Why do you need me?" I asked. "I thought you knew everything. You've already put him in jail."

"I know," Lonnegan agreed. "And we've probably got enough to convict him, but every little helps. Did she say anything? Did you see anything?"

I told him how Jared couldn't possibly have stolen the locket unless he went to the mainland.

Lonnegan smiled. "I don't know how you know about that," he said. "I suppose I shouldn't underestimate small town gossip. We know she wasn't wearing the locket on the day she died, but we don't know when he stole it."

"He didn't steal it! Jared's not a thief."

Lonnegan coughed. "I beg to differ, Grace," he said. "David Garwell has a record that includes larceny and possession of dangerous drugs. He should have been in jail to start with, but he skipped bail."

"I don't believe you."

"That's up to you. I could show you the evidence if you want to come to headquarters."

"No, thank you."

"It's your choice."

"But *why* would he hurt Mary Jane? He told her he loved her."

Lonnegan's ears pricked up. "He did?" He toyed with his coffee cup on the saucer. It still had an old lipstick stain around the rim. "We think they had an argument," he said. "Maybe Mary Jane discovered the theft of the pendant. Or perhaps she told Garwell that she was pregnant, and he wanted nothing further to do with her. Either way, she ran off down to that cozy little beach the two of you liked so much. He followed her, maybe worried that she'd tell her parents, or the police. They fought, and he strangled her."

"But then he'd *know* for certain that the police would suspect him!"

"People ain't always thinking straight when they're mad, Grace."

I shook my head. I know what he said made sense, but it *didn't* make sense, if you see what I mean. I didn't know what else to say.

"You're going to have to accept it sooner or later, Grace," Lonnegan said. "This Jared, as you call him, murdered your friend, and you're probably the only one who can help us make sure he pays for his crime."

"But I can't help you. Don't you see? I still don't believe Jared did it."

Lonnegan sighed. "They had an argument. She walked off. He admits that much. He won't tell us what it was about, but like I said, I think she confronted him over the gold pendant or the pregnancy. He followed her."

I squirmed in my seat, took a long sip of soda and asked, "Who else was on the island that day? Have you checked?"

"What do you mean?"

"You must have asked Mr Kiernan, Mary Jane's father, who he took over and brought back that day. Was there anyone else who shouldn't have been there? Have you questioned them all, asked them for alibis?"

"No, but . . ."

"Don't you think you ought to? Why can't it be one of those people?"

"Like who?"

"The Preacher!" I blurted it out.

Lonnegan shook his head, looking puzzled. "The Preacher? Why?"

"Was he there? Was he on the ferry?"

"You know I can't tell you that."

"Well, you just ask him," I said, standing up, "because Mary Jane told me she saw him touching Betsy Goodall somewhere he shouldn't have been touching her."

The Preacher was waiting for me after chapel the following Sunday. "Grace, a word in your ear," he said, leading me by the arm. He was smiling and looked friendly enough, in that well-scrubbed way of his, to fool anyone watching, including my parents, but his grip hurt. He took me back inside the dark chapel and sat me down in a corner, crowding me, his face close to mine. I couldn't smell bourbon on his breath – not that I would have known what it smelled like – but I could smell peppermint. "I had a visit from the police the other day," he said, "a most unwelcome visit, and I've been trying to figure out ever since who's been telling tales out of school. I think it was you, Grace. You were her friend. Thick as thieves, the two of you, always unnaturally close."

"There was nothing unnatural about it," I said, my heart beating fast. "And yes, we were friends. So what?"

His upper lip curled. "Don't you give me any of your smart-talk, young lady. You caused me a lot of trouble, you did, a lot of grief."

"You've got nothing to worry about if you're pure in heart and true in the eyes of the Lord. Isn't that what you're always telling us?"

"Don't take the Lord's word in vain. I swear, one day . . ." He shook his head. "Grace, I do believe you're headed for a life of sin, and you know what the wages of sin are, don't you?"

"Did you go to Pine Island that day, Preacher? The day Mary Jane died. Were you on the ferry? You were, weren't you?"

The Preacher looked away. "As a matter of fact, I had some important business there," he said. "Real estate business." We all knew about the Preacher and his real estate. He seemed to think the best way of carrying out God's plan on earth was to take ownership of as much of it as he could afford.

"Why haven't they arrested you?" I asked.

"Because I haven't done anything wrong. The police believe me. So should you. There's no evidence against me. I didn't strangle that girl."

"Mary Jane told me about Betsy Goodall, about what she saw."

"And just what did she see? I'll tell you what she saw. Nothing. Ask Betsy Goodall. The police did. Your friend Mary Jane was a wayward child," the Preacher said, his voice a sort of drone. "She had a vile imagination. Evil. She made up stories. The police know that now. They talked to me and they talked to Betsy. I just want to warn you, Grace. Don't you go around making any more grief for me, or you'll have more trouble than you can imagine. Do you understand me?"

"Betsy was too scared to say anything, wasn't she? She was frightened of what you might do to her. What did you do to Mary Jane?"

There. It was out before I realized it. That's the problem with me sometimes: I speak before thinking. I felt his fingers squeeze into my arm and I cried out. "Do you understand me?" he asked again, his voice a reptilian whisper.

"Yes!" I said. "You're hurting me! Yes, I understand. Leave me alone." And I wrenched my arm free and ran out of the chapel over to the ferry dock. I wanted to be by myself, and I wanted to walk where Mary Jane and I had walked. There was really only one place I could go, and I was lucky, I had only ten minutes to wait.

The day had turned hazy, warm and sticky. There'd be a storm after dark, everyone said. Mr Kiernan seemed worried about me and told me if I wasn't on the next ferry home he'd send someone looking for me. I said that was sweet but I would be all right. Then he said he'd keep an eye on the weather to make sure I didn't get stuck out there when the storm came.

I walked past the houses and through the woods to the southern tip of the island, where the Newcomers used to live. They had been taken away so fast they hadn't even had time to grab what few belongings they had. Nobody seemed to know what would happen to their things now, whether anyone would come for them. I stood behind the cover of the trees looking into the clearing, the way Mary Jane and I had done that first time, when we saw Jared come out of the shower. And there it was again, faint, drifting, as if it belonged to the air it traveled on: Mary Jane's song. "And Mary Jane is dreaming/Of oceans dark and gleaming."

But who was playing it?

Heart in my mouth, I ducked low and waited. I wanted to know, but I didn't want to go in there, the way people went into basements and rooms in movies when they knew evil lurked there. So I hid.

As it turned out, I didn't have long to wait. As soon as the song ended, a furtive head peeped out of the doorway and, gauging that all was clear, the young man stepped out into the open. My jaw dropped. It was Riley McCorkindale.

Some instinct still held me back from announcing my presence, so I stayed where I was. Riley stood, ears pricked, glancing around furtively, then he headed away from the cabins – not back towards his parents' house, but west, towards the cliffs. Now I was really puzzled.

When I calculated that Riley had got a safe distance ahead of me, I followed through the trees. I couldn't see him, but there weren't many paths on the island, and not many places to go if you were heading in that direction. Once in a while I would stop and listen, and I could hear him way ahead, snapping a twig, rustling a bush as he walked. I hoped he didn't stop and listen the same way and hear me following him.

As I walked, I wondered what on earth Riley had been doing at the Newcomers' cabin. Playing the record with the Mary Jane song on it, obviously. But why? I knew he had been sweet on her, of course, but he had always been too shy to say hello. Had he made friends with the Newcomers? After all, they were practically neighbours. But Riley went to chapel, and he seemed the type to take notice of the Preacher. His father was a property developer in Logan, so they were a wealthy and respected family in the community, too, which made it even more unlikely that Riley would have anything to do with Jared and the others.

When I reached the cliffs, there was no one in sight. I glanced over the edge, down towards the beach but saw no one there, either. I wasn't sure whether Riley knew about the hidden path Mary Jane and I used to take. He lived on the island, so perhaps he did. I stood still for a moment and felt the wind whipping my hair in my eyes and tugging at my clothes, bringing the dark clouds from far out at seas, heard the raucous cries of gulls over a shoal of fish just off the coast, smelled the salt air. Then, just as I started to move towards the path, I heard a voice behind me.

"You."

I turned. Riley stepped out from the edge of the woods.

"Riley," I said, smiling, trying to sound relaxed, and holding my hair from my eyes. "You startled me. What are you doing here?"

"You were following me."

"Me? No. Why would I do that?" I felt vulnerable at the edge of the cliff, aware of the golden sand so far below, and as I spoke I tried edging slowly forwards. But Riley stood his ground, and right now he didn't seem shy at all.

"I don't know," he said. "But I saw you. Maybe it's something to do with Mary Jane?"

"Mary Jane?"

"You know I loved her. Until that . . . that freak came and took her away from me. Still, he's got what he deserves. Let him rot in jail."

"Now, listen Riley. You don't have to say anything to me." The last thing I wanted was to be Riley's confessor with a hundred foot drop behind me. "Let's just go back, huh? I don't want to miss my ferry."

"I used to watch them, you know," Riley said. "Watch them doing it."

I didn't know what to say to that. I swallowed.

"They'd do it anywhere. They didn't care who was watching."

"That's not true, Riley," I said. "You know that can't be true. You were spying on them. You said so."

"Maybe so. But they did it down there." He pointed. "On the beach."

"It's a very secluded spot." I don't know what I meant by that, whether I was defending Mary Jane's honor, deflecting the shock I felt, or what. I just wanted to keep Riley talking until I could get around him and . . . well, getting back to the ferry was my main thought. But if Riley had other ideas there wasn't much I could do. He was bigger and stronger than me. Drops of rain dampened my cheek. The sky was becoming darker. "Look, Riley," I said. "There's going to be a storm. Move out of the way and let me go back to the ferry dock. I'll miss my ferry. Mr Kiernan will be looking for me."

"I didn't mean to do it, you know," Riley said.

I had been trying to skirt around him, but I froze. "Didn't mean to do what?" There I was again, speaking without thinking. I didn't want to know, but it was too late now.

"Kill her. It just happened. One minute she was . . ."

Now he'd told me I just had to know the full story. Unless I could make a break into the woods when he wasn't expecting it, I was done for anyway. I didn't think I could outrun him, but with the cover of the trees, and the coming dark, perhaps I had a chance of staying ahead of him as far as the ferry dock. "How did it happen?" I asked, still moving slowly.

"They had a fight. I was watching the cabin and they had a fight and Mary Jane ran out crying."

The baby, I thought. She told him about the baby. But why would that matter? The Newcomers loved children. They would have welcomed Mary Jane and her child. It must have been something else. Perhaps she wanted to get married? That would have been far too conventional for Jared but just like Mary Jane. Whatever it was, they had argued. Couples do argue. "What happened?" I asked.

"I followed her like you followed me. She went down to the beach. Down that path you both thought was your little secret. I went after her. I thought I could comfort her. You know, I thought she'd dumped him and maybe she would turn to me if I was nice to her."

"How did it go wrong?"

"She did it with him, didn't she?" Riley said, his voice raising to a shout against the coming storm. "Why wouldn't she do it with me? Why did she have to laugh?"

"She laughed at you?"

He nodded. "That's when I grabbed her. The next thing I . . . I guess I don't know my own strength. She was like a rag doll."

There was a slim chance that I could slip into the woods to the left of him and make a run for it. That was when he said, "I'm glad I told you. I've been wanting to tell somebody, just to get it off my chest. I feel better now."

I paused. "But Riley, you have to go to the authorities. You have to tell them there's an innocent man in jail."

"No! I ain't going to jail. I won't. Only you and me know the truth."

"Riley, if you hurt me they'll know," I said, my voice shaking, judging the distance between his reach and the gap in the trees. "They'll know it was you. I told Mr Kiernan I came here to talk to you." It was a lie, of course, but I hoped it was an inspired one.

"Why would you do that?" Riley seemed genuinely puzzled. "You didn't know anything about it until just now. You didn't even know I existed. You didn't want to know. None of you did."

"I mean it, Riley. If you hurt me, they'll find out. You can't get away with murder twice. You'll go to jail then for sure."

"They say killing's easier the second time. I read that in a book."

"Riley, don't."

"It's all right, Grace," he said, leaning back against the tree. "I ain't going to hurt you. Don't think I don't regret what I did. Don't think I enjoyed it. I'm just not going to jail for it. Go. Catch your ferry. See if I care."

"B-but . . ."

"Who'd believe you? The police have got the man they want. There sure as hell's no evidence against me. My daddy doesn't know where I was, but he already told them I was home all day. Last thing he wants to know is that his son killed some girl. That would surely upset the applecart. Nobody saw me. The Preacher's with us, too. He was at the house talking real estate with daddy. I don't know if he knows I did it or not, but he don't care. He was the one told me about Mary Jane and that freak, what they were doing and how it was a sin. That's why I went to spy on them. He told me he knew she was really my girl, but she'd been seduced by the devil. He told me what that long-haired pervert was doing to her and asked me what I was going to do about it. The Preacher won't be saying nothing to no police. So go on. Go."

"But why did you tell me?"

Riley paused. "Like I said, I knew I'd feel better if I told someone. I'm truly sorry for what I did, but going to jail ain't going to bring her back."

"But what about Jared? He's innocent?"

"He's the Spawn of Satan. Now go ahead, Grace. Catch the ferry before the storm comes. It's going to be a bad one."

"You won't . . .?"

He shook his head. "Nope. Don't matter what you say. Go ahead. See if I'm not right."

And I did. I caught the ferry. Mr Kiernan smiled and said I was lucky I just made it. The storm broke that night, flooded a few roads, broke a few windows. The next day I took the bus into the city to see Detective Lonnegan and told him about what Riley had said to me on the beach. He laughed, said the boy was having me on, giving me a scare. I told him it was true, that Riley was in love with Mary Jane and that he tried to . . . I couldn't get the words out in front of him, but even so he was shaking his head before I'd finished.

So Riley McCorkindale turned out to be right. The police didn't believe me. I didn't see any point running all over town telling Mr Kiernan, father, the Preacher or anyone else, so that was the end of it. Riley McCorkindale strangled Mary Jane Kiernan and got away with it. Jared – David Garwood – went to jail for a crime he didn't commit. He didn't stay there long, though. Word made it back to town about a year or two later that he got stabbed in a prison brawl, and even then everyone said he had it coming, that it was divine justice.

None of the Newcomers ever returned to Jasmine Cove. The cabins fell into disrepair again, and their property reverted to the township in one of those roundabout ways that these things often happen in small communities like ours. I thought of Mary Jane often over the years, remembered her smile, her childlike enthusiasms. The Mad Hatters became famous and once in a while I heard "her" song on the radio. It always made me cry.

After I had finished college and started teaching high school in Logan, the property boom began. The downtown areas of many major cities became uninhabitable, people moved out to the suburbs and the rich wanted country, or island, retreats. One day I heard that McCorkindale Developments had knocked down the cabins on Pine Island and cleared the land for a strip of low-rise, ocean-front luxury condominiums.

I suppose it's what you might call ironic, depending on the way you look at it, but by that time the Preacher and Riley's father had managed to buy up most of the island for themselves.

TELL ME

Zoë Sharp

"So, where is she?"

Crime Scene Investigator Grace McColl ducked under the taped cordon at the edge of the crime scene and showed her ID to the uniformed constable stationed there.

The policeman jerked his head in the direction of the band shelter as she signed the log. "You'll have your work cut out with this one, though," he said.

Grace frowned and moved on. She was already dressed from head to foot in her disposable white suit and she made sure she followed the designated pathway, picking her way carefully to avoid undue contamination.

The girl was on the stone steps in front of the band shelter, no more than sixteen years old but still a child, with dirty blonde hair. As Grace approached she could see the girl had her thin arms folded, as though hugging herself against the cold. And she must have been cold, to be out in the park in this weather in just a mini skirt and a skimpy top. Unless, of course, he'd taken her coat with him when he'd left her . . .

Over to the right, the rhododendron bushes grew thick and concealing. It might have been Grace's imagination, but she thought the girl's eyes turned constantly in their direction, as though something might still lurk amongst the glossy foliage.

She squatted down on her haunches next to the girl and waited until she seemed to have her full attention.

"Hello," she said quietly. "I'm Grace. I'm going to be taking care of you now. Can you tell me who you are?"

There was a long pause, then: "Does it matter?"

Grace eyed her for a moment. The girl might have been pretty if she'd taken a little time, a little care. Or if someone had taken a little care over her. Her hair was badly cut and her fingernails were bitten short and painted purple, the varnish long since chipped and peeling.

"Of course it matters," Grace said, keeping her tone light. "Finding out about you will help us find out who did this to you. Help us to catch him. You want that, don't you?"

"'Spose." The girl shrugged, darting a little glance from under her ragged fringe to see if her attitude achieved the desired level of sullen cool. The action revealed the livid bruise, like spilt ink on tissue, that had formed around her left eye.

Grace tilted her head, considering. "He caught you a belter, didn't he?" she murmured.

"I bruise easy," the girl said, suddenly defensive now. "And I'm clumsy."

"Don't tell me," Grace said, setting her bag down and opening it. "You were always walking into doors at home, falling down the stairs." She shook her head. "Did no one stop to wonder?"

The girl's face darkened. "They knew, all right," she said. "They just didn't give a—"

"No," Grace said dryly. "I can see that." She pulled out evidence bags and swabs, and paused. "Is that why you ran away – ended up on the streets?"

The girl's head jerked up and she looked at Grace fully for the first time, scowling. "Who said I'm living rough?"

Grace regarded her calmly. "Your clothes are dirty enough," she said.

"What do you expect?" the girl snapped. She gestured angrily towards the rhododendrons. "Being dragged through the mud, having him –" She broke off, bit her lip, looked away.

"Your clothes were dirty before that," Grace said, no censure in her quiet voice. 'And you're a pretty girl. Your nails are painted – or they were. You wouldn't have done that if you hadn't wanted to look nice, once upon a time."

The girl's lip curled. "That's for fairy stories."

"Mm," Grace said. "Let me see your hands."

Reluctantly, the girl put both hands up, backs towards Grace, fingers splayed rigidly. Grace almost smiled at the defiance she read there, taking hold of one carefully in her gloved fingers, scraping out minute debris from under the receded nails.

"Ah-ha," she said, under her breath. "You got a shot in, I see. Marked him. Oh, well done, you."

The girl looked unaccountably pleased at this praise and it occurred to Grace that she must have received very little by way of approval in her short life. She thought of her own mother, who lavished praise and nurtured self-confidence in her only child. Ironic, then, that the pre-adolescent Grace had always been so desperate to win the approbation of her more distant father.

"*Your* father wasn't around much, was he?" she said absently, noting the time and date and case number on the evidence bag as she sealed it.

The girl scowled at her again. "You're guessing," she accused. "No way can you tell that from looking at my hands." Her mouth twisted into a sneer. "Read tea-leaves as well, do you?"

"No," Grace said levelly, "but I've been doing this job long enough to recognize the other signs."

The girl took her hand back and folded her arms, a challenge in her voice. "So, go on," she goaded. "If you're so clever, *you* tell *me*. Who am I?"

"All right." Grace sat back on her heels, oblivious to the activity going on around her. She focused inwards, closing her eyes for a moment.

"You can't do it, can you?" the girl jeered.

Grace's eyes opened. "Your father left when you were young," she began. "Your mother blamed you and lost herself in the bottle – pills or booze, or possibly both."

The girl rolled her eyes, gave a derisive laugh. "Oh, big deal," she said. "You could be talking about half the kids round here." She jerked her head towards the nearby high-rise. "Not good enough."

"OK," Grace conceded. "Then you're going to tell me it's also obvious that your mother brought home a procession of one-night stands to pay the rent. How old were you when the first of them asked if *you* were for sale, too?"

The girl wouldn't meet her eyes. "None of your business," she muttered.

"Mm, I thought so." She paused again but the girl wouldn't respond. "But you didn't leave then, did you? You clung in there. For a while. Until it got too much and you attempted self-harm."

"Who says I did?"

Grace nodded towards the old scars on the girl's wrists. "You cut yourself," she said, picking her words with care. "Not a serious attempt, I don't think. A cry for help. But nobody answered, did they?"

The girl twisted the cheap ring round on her finger and didn't speak, staring across the grass to where the row of uniforms swept the parkland.

"He listened," she said at last, so quietly Grace hardly caught the words.

"Ah," she said softly. "Of course he did."

The girl's head jerked up at the tone in her voice, eyes flashing. "Don't say it like that," she snapped, harsh. "You don't know how it was. He loved me!"

"I'm sure he told you he did," Grace said, bland. "Gave you that ring, didn't he? Told you that you were his girl now. Just like all the others."

"I was. I *am*."

"So how long was it before he told you about the man he owed money to? About how it would all be all right if only you'd just have sex with this man. Did you refuse? Is that why he hit you?"

"I made him angry. He was sorry – after."

"But he still made you do it, didn't he?"

"I wanted to help him. He didn't force me or nothing."

"Not that first time, no," Grace said. "But that was just the beginning, wasn't it? When did you realize he wasn't your boyfriend any more, but your pimp? Or did you ever realize it?"

"If I'd had someone looking out for me," the girl said, her voice bitter now, "do you think something like this would've happened?"

"It might have done. If it was him – your boyfriend – who did this to you."

The girl shrugged. "Might have been," she said, dismissive. Her glance was defiant. "Might not."

"So, was he a client?"

"Client?" the girl spat. "Would that make it better for you if he was? Would that make it not so shocking, not so bad, if I was on the game? Oh well, just another hooker picked the wrong john. Had it coming."

"No," Grace said evenly. "It would just give us a better place to start looking."

"Yeah, right," the girl snorted, still surly. "You're thinking it, though. I can tell."

"I try to keep an open mind but you're not making it easy for me. You shouldn't have been here at that time of night, you see. It's where the working girls come with the men they pick up when the clubs turn out. And you could have just been trying to make the money for your next fix."

The girl opened her mouth, saw Grace's gaze on the evidence of her addiction that tattooed the crook of both arms, and shut her mouth again with a glower.

"You see too much," was all she said.

"It's my job," Grace agreed. "Just as it's my job to find out who you are, and who did this to you. To stand for you, when no-one else would."

The girl looked at her with doubt and speculation in her eyes for the first time. "And you'll do that, will you?"

"I will."

"Just for me?"

"Yes."

The girl sighed. "You'll be the first, if you do."

"Well, better late than never, then."

The girl was silent again. The sky had darkened overhead and she looked up into the gathering clouds. "It's going to rain," she said.

"I know," Grace said. She stood. "I'd better get back to work. The rain will destroy the evidence if we don't protect the scene quickly."

The girl nodded. "You'll be back, though, won't you?" she said. "You won't leave me?"

"Of course," Grace said. "They'll take you in, but you'll certainly see me again. I'll need more from you, if we're to catch him."

"That's good," the girl said and gave a small smile, rusty from lack of use.

"How are you getting on, Grace?" asked a brisk voice from behind her. Grace turned to see one of the Detective Constables who'd just arrived on scene. She bent and snapped her bag closed, then straightened.

"I'm about done," she said.

"Will you get anything useful from her, do you think?"

Grace glanced back.

The girl lay on the damp steps, arms wrapped across her body, in the position they'd first found her. Her eyes were open and glassy, her lips tinged with blue. The marks of the stranglehold that had killed her showed dark and ugly around her throat.

"I think so," Grace murmured. "The dead always talk to me in the end."

COLOUR ME BLOOD

Jerry Sykes

The side of the building had been painted in a thin coat of white emulsion, but the solid colours of more than a decade's worth of graffiti still showed through the paint like blood vessels under pale Irish skin. In front of the wall, a tall scruff of a man with thick knots of dark hair was making shapes in the emulsion with a piece of charcoal. His name was Rob Blake, a local artist, and he had been commissioned by the local residents' association to create a mural on the side of the Community Centre.

Surrounding him in a loose arc, all ADD head jerks and hot feet, was a group of around ten children aged between twelve and fourteen holding in their hands face masks and cans of spray paint in a rainbow of colours. The idea was that once the artist had laid out the basic outline of the mural on the wall, the kids would then fill in the larger shapes to create the solid cast of the image, leaving the artist to add the final details later.

Across the street from the Community Centre, Detective Sergeant Marnie Stone sat and watched from the open window of her old blue Saab. In the centre of the group surrounding the artist, little more than a short head taller than the children, she could see Kate Phillips, one of the hardier members of Camden's Social Services department and an old friend. After a couple of minutes, Marnie called out her name and stuck her hand in the air, but, like the children, Kate seemed fascinated with the workings of the artist, the fluid motion of his hand, the beats of creation, and appeared not to have heard. Marnie could not see much of what was happening through the forest of shuffling limbs, just the occasional glimpse of the hand leaking sinuous lines of soft carbon, and so she had no choice but to sit back and wait.

Marnie had read about the project in the local paper and was curious to see if it would lead to a reduction in crime on the estate, as had been promised in the tenants' association's pitch to the police and the council. There were a couple of faces that she knew for a fact were responsible for a string of robberies and muggings in the area – she had just not been able to gather sufficient evidence, and so at least a couple of old people would be able to walk home in peace tonight. But she would be fooling herself if she thought it would go further than that.

A few minutes later, the artist stood up to stretch his back and the spell he held over his audience was broken. Kate glanced around and saw Marnie watching them. She stooped and said something to one of the kids nearest her, and then walked over to the Saab. The closer she came, Marnie noticed, the deeper the lines that bracketed her mouth became. But then it had never surprised Marnie that social workers appeared to age faster than the rest of the world, including police officers.

"Hello, Marnie, what are you doing out here?" asked Kate, smiling. "You're not going to arrest Rob, are you?"

"You mean that vandal trying to make the estate a better place to live?" replied Marnie, reflecting the smile. "Sure, I just wanted to see who his accomplices were first . . ."

"Ooh, don't be cruel," replied Kate, resting her hand on the lip of the door.

"What's it going to be, anyway?" asked Marnie, pointing towards the Community Centre.

"A warning about the perils of drink and drugs," said Kate. "There's going to be the usual logo, Keep it Clean, and then a street scene with kids and families and stuff like that. I don't know, I think I also heard Rob say something about a large bin with needles and guns sticking out of it or something . . ."

"And here's me thinking Walt Disney was dead," said Marnie.

"Hey, don't knock it," Kate chastised her. "If it gives these kids some stake in the estate then it'll be worth it."

"Yeah, I know," agreed Marnie, glancing away. She still had her doubts, but she also knew that she would never be able to win an argument with Kate. She started the engine and put the car in gear. "Anyway, I better be getting back to the station. I just thought I'd drop by and see how you were getting on . . ."

"Much better than I thought," said Kate, nodding. "There are far more kids here than I thought there would be . . . Including one or two I never expected to see in a million years."

"Yeah, I know who you mean," said Marnie. "So just remember to count all the paint cans at the end of the night . . ."

Kate gave her a look of mock admonishment, and then broke into a smile. "Go and chase some real villains," she said.

The children had been filling in shapes for a little more than ten minutes when the first argument started. Calum Breen, a short kid with dark hair and a pronounced lower lip that made him look like he was sulking all the time, a mask that suited his character to the ground, had been assigned a couple of letters at the end of the slogan, but what he wanted to do was something a bit more artistic, or something a bit more real, as he put it.

"Why can't I do one of the people, or even some of the background?" he asked, a sneer pushing his lip out further.

"Because that's just the way it worked out," replied Blake, wishing that Kate was still there with him. Five minutes earlier she had told him that she had to go and see a client on the estate but would be back in an hour. He was not used to dealing with a bunch of kids on his own and, although he was loath to admit it to himself, having her there made him feel safer.

"But I don't want to do the letters," replied Calum.

"Well, how about you just do one of the letters and then we move everyone around," said Blake. "That way everyone'll get to do a figure and a letter, or a bit of background, or whatever . . ."

"He's just scared of getting it wrong because he can't read," called out a kid in the centre of the group.

"There's no need for that," said Blake.

"Yeah, piss off," said Calum.

"Come on, let's not fight about it," said Blake. He could feel the group starting to slip out of his grasp, but he wasn't quite sure what to do about it.

The two kids shuffled around in the pack for a brief moment, alternating between hiding behind their colleagues and stepping out into makeshift clearings, before squaring up to one another. Blake waited until the last moment, fearful of wounding their pride, perhaps, and then stepped between them with his palms raised. And just stood there, still and silent, waiting for them to return to the growing spread of colour on the wall. Long minutes later, egos satisfied, the pair traded final insults and then broke up and returned to the task at hand. Blake folded his arms and waited to make certain that it was indeed all over, and then stepped over to watch Calum work. It did not take him long to realize that behind the brash tongue the kid had a natural talent and that perhaps he should give him a break and let him have a bit more input to the project. Trouble was he would have to do it without looking like he was cutting out the other kids.

But fifteen minutes later, two minutes after the kids had traded shapes, Calum had another complaint.

"How come we're just doing a picture of the estate, anyway? It's pretty boring, don't you think? I mean, we live here all the time. Why can't we do something a bit more interesting?"

Blake sighed. "I thought we talked about this."

"What about a beach with horses running through the surf?" suggested Calum. "I don't know, just something different . . ."

"I thought we agreed to do a mural of what we wanted the estate to look like," said Blake.

"Calum wants it to look like a building site with sand and shit," piped up a small kid from the centre of the group.

"I never said that," replied Calum, looking for the source.

"Clubbers sleeping off their highs from the night before," said another kid, his idea of a beach.

"No, that's not the kind of beach I mean," protested Calum, still looking for the source of the first voice.

"Grannies pumping coins into slot machines," suggested another, stretching the beach connection to breaking point.

"What the hell is wrong with you people?" squealed Calum. "You've got the chance to bring a bit of colour into your lives and what do you do? Paint a cartoon version of what you've already got. Jesus, give it some imagination, won't you?"

"Imagine this," said one of the kids, giving him a finger.

"This is for all of us, not just for you," said another.

"Yeah, piss off and find your own wall," said yet another.

With faceless jibes coming at him from all directions, Calum felt a sickness rise in his throat. He took a deep breath and tried to shake it loose, dampen the tension, but it just seemed to make things worse. Seconds later, past frustration, he turned and pointed his can at the wall, pressed down on the button and held it there, as if that could relieve the pressure within himself. Dark blue paint bubbled and frothed on the wall and a thin trail soon snaked down through the white emulsion.

"Oh, for Christ's sake, Calum," said Blake.

"I knew he'd turn it all to shit," said one of the kids.

Calum continued to press down on the button.

"Give me the can," said Blake, his long fingers beckoning. But Calum just ignored him, and after one more polite request, Blake stepped forward and slammed the can out of his hand.

Calum snarled at him and watched the can as it bounced and rattled on the ground, and then stormed off across the estate.

Blake watched him go, and then ran forward a couple of steps and kicked the can into the wall as hard as he could.

Calum was still feeling a little out of sorts a few hours later. Sitting on the back of a bench in the centre of the estate with a couple of his friends who had not been part of the mural project: Match, like the name suggested – kids are nothing if not literal – tall and thin and with a shock of red hair, and Tusk, a regular-looking kid with a left canine tooth that poked out from between his lips even when his mouth was closed. The pair had been messing with his head ever since he had joined them on the bench after supper. Word had travelled fast, and he was starting to get dark and pissed off, to believe that there was nowhere left to run. At one point, Match had accused him of losing his balls, and as the night had progressed and the more he had brooded on it, the more he had started to believe that Match might in fact be right. A couple of solutions had passed through his head – for an instant he had considered damaging the mural, but then he knew that he would be the main suspect – but nothing had made itself clear. Approaching midnight, he knew that he had to act soon to distance himself from the project and therefore restore his ego.

Taking a final drag on his cigarette, Calum flicked it out into the air and climbed down from the bench. He set off across the estate, breathing hard through his nose like a minotaur.

"Yo, what's happenin', man?" Match called out, standing up and following him. "What's going on, Calum?"

"Yo, wait up," cried Tusk, setting off after them.

Match and Tusk fell into step beside Calum, and the three of them headed up through Kentish Town before cutting a right into Dartmouth Park. Here the streets were quieter, darker, and there were less people about, less traffic. Calum led them through a labyrinth of backstreets and alleys, streetlights sending shadows to track them, making no attempt to hide themselves, confident in their solid presence. Fifteen minutes after leaving the comfort of the estate, he led them behind a dark parade of shops that represented another kind of comfort.

The off-licence sat in the middle of the parade between a vet's surgery and a greengrocer's, and was well known to all the kids in the area as a cheap target. Calum himself had broken into it at least three times – three that he could remember – and almost every other kid he knew had burgled it at least once. It was like a training ground for them, a rites of passage kind of place.

Match had been following Calum in glum silence, but as soon as he figured out where Calum was going, a broad grin had spread across his face as he knew his friend was coming back to them. It had been a bad time, with Calum either buried in paint and a social conscience or in despair. Match leaned into Tusk and told him the news, watched the other kid respond in the same manner.

"You going to hit the cashpoint," said Match, his nickname for the off-licence.

"Time I felt the muscle working again," replied Calum, clenching a fist in front of his heart.

"Yo, back in the world," said Tusk.

"Oh, right, let's get it on," said Calum. He led them down the back of the buildings, their feet creating scuffles and echoes in the trash that carpeted the ground. At the back of the off-licence, he held out his right hand and gestured to Match with his left. Match lifted his jacket aside, pulled out a short-bladed knife from the deep thigh pocket in his cargo pants, and handed it to Calum. As Calum lifted the knife to jam it into the gap between the door and the frame, he noticed the line of dried blood at the base of the blade and an icicle threaded his spine. The blood was from where Match had stabbed some kid in the hand the week before when he had been too slow in handing over his mobile phone. Calum had seen the attack and, although he had been witness to unprovoked violence before, the cold action of his friend had shaken him more than he cared to admit. It had been an insight too far into the mental state of their situation.

The uncomfortable thought stilled him, and when the door creaked and opened a fraction, he thought for a moment that he must have popped it open himself without realizing it and looked at the knife for a second in disbelief. And when it creaked again and opened a little further, a slice of light falling across the ground, he was still none the wiser, even when a look of keen surprise appeared on Match's face and his friend turned on his heel and fled. Understanding what was happening, Tusk too was soon up and off on his jaundiced feet into the darkness.

Stuck in that awkward space between thought and action, it was just when the manager's scared face appeared around the door that the truth of the situation hit Calum. Shaking the indecision from his limbs, he took off after his friends, but not before the manager had caught a clear glimpse of his startled face.

At nine o'clock the following morning, Rob Blake, the artist, and Kate Phillips, the social worker, were sitting on a threadbare sofa in the living room of the flat Calum Breen shared with his mother. DS Marnie Stone had been on the phone to Kate first thing: the owner of the off-licence had recognized Calum at once but because he had not committed an actual offence she was reluctant to speak to him. Could Kate go round there and have a quiet word? "Sounds like I don't have much choice," Kate had replied, but here she was with Rob at her side for moral support.

Calum's mother was sitting in a matching chair, a cup of hot coffee in one hand and a cigarette in the other. She looked like she had a hangover, bloodshot pupils and red skin.

"So who else was there last night, Calum?" asked Kate. "The manager said he saw two other kids running off."

Calum twisted in his seat and said nothing.

"It was almost midnight," continued Kate. "Somehow I just don't think that you'd have been out there on your own at that time of night. Do you want to tell me who you were with, Calum?"

Again Calum said nothing.

"Was it Match and Tusk?"

At the mention of the names Match and Tusk, Blake glanced at Kate, a little surprised, and then turned to Calum.

"I thought you said you'd left those two behind when you signed on for the mural," said Blake, feeling a little hurt.

"Yeah, well, maybe if I'd been allowed to put something of my own in it . . ."

"Is that what all this is about?" said Kate, pressing her hands between her knees. "A cry for attention?"

"You mean you jeopardized your freedom just because you didn't get your own way," interjected Blake, incredulous.

Kate rested her hand on his forearm and tried to ease him back, but he pushed on regardless.

"If it really means that much to you then I'm sure we could work something out," said Blake, feeling the soft touch of the hand on his arm fade. "It's one thing being a tortured artist, but there's no need for you to go and get into trouble over it."

"You've torn yourself away from those bad influences before," said Kate. "It'll be easier the second time around."

"I'll think about it," muttered Calum, and Kate knew then that that was as much as they were going to get from him for now.

Kate touched Blake on the arm again, and this time he knew that it meant something different.

"It'll be good to see you again," he said, rising to leave.

Under normal circumstances, stubborn pride would have kept Calum from the mural for at least another afternoon, but knowing that it would take no more than three sessions to complete, he understood he had no choice but to swallow that pride and return to the site that afternoon if he wanted to be a real part of it.

And so four o'clock found him walking across the estate with the other kids, together but apart. Without having to ask, the other kids intuited what had happened. Most of them had been witness to his original strop, and also knew his street reputation, and so knew better than to irritate him further. When the group arrived in front of the mural, Blake also tuned into the common mood and just handed Calum a can of paint with a smile and motioned for him to do as he pleased.

For two hours Calum worked in silent concentration, the shadow of the other kids staining his back like perspiration. And the following night he was there again. Blake was impressed with his dedication and the sense of Calumness that he brought to the character of the mural, little touches that added a much-needed sense of humour – a man in an open window shaving the hair on the top of his ears, a woman in a tracksuit watching aerobics on TV with a cigarette in her mouth. At the completion, both Blake and the kids were pleased with how it had turned out. Not quite as it had been planned, but perhaps all the better for that.

As the kids were cleaning up, or rather sneaking off and leaving Blake to do the cleaning up, a tall black man in a crumpled suit named Johnson approached the scene. He stood and stared at the mural, smiling, tilting his head from side to side, and then after a couple of minutes looked across at Blake.

"That's some piece of work," he said.

"The kids did a great job," agreed Blake.

"I like the little comic touches the best."

"You mean the figures in the windows," said Blake, pointing.

"Yeah, those," said Johnson.

"Yeah, I like those too," agreed Blake, stuffing tins of paint into a canvas holdall. "A touch of original thinking."

"It wasn't part of the plan, then," said Johnson.

"That was one of the kids," admitted Blake, not too proud to give credit where due. "Nothing to do with me, I'm afraid."

"I think it was the kid with the fat lip," said Johnson, smiling and pointing at his own mouth.

"You mean Calum," replied Blake, reflecting the smile.

"And he lives here on the estate," said Johnson.

"In one of the blocks near Castle Street," said Blake.

"You think he'd be interested in a solo project – that's if it's all right with you, I mean," said Johnson.

"Depends what you have in mind, I suppose."

"You know Carlo's, the café on Kentish Town Road?

"I've been there a few times," said Blake. "Nice homemade fish-cakes if I remember right."

"The wife makes them," said Johnson, and then fell silent, regarding the mural once more. "It could be a nice place, a better place, but the trouble is I have a metal shutter that's forever covered in graffiti. If I clean it, then it's covered again the following night. I think the people who walk past at night and see the graffiti must think it's a bad place and decide never to go and eat there. You must understand what I mean. I've been thinking about what to do about it . . . You think . . . You think Calum would be interested in helping me out?"

Blake thought about Calum and what he had brought to the project. "He's got some strong ideas of his own."

"But that's what I'm looking for," said Johnson. "I wouldn't know where to start if we had to do it ourselves. As long as I have some idea of what he's going to do beforehand. Perhaps if he had one or two ideas I could choose from . . ."

"And he'd be paid for the work, of course," said Blake.

"Whatever's the going rate," replied Johnson.

"All right, I'll ask him," said Blake.

For his shutter on Kentish Town Road, Johnson chose a cartoon version of his café with cartoon customers looking out at the real people passing on the street outside. At the rear of the cartoon café were caricatures of Posh and Becks tucking into large plates of pie and mash, fat bellies pushing at their cheap clothing and raw cigarettes burning in a saucer in the centre of the table. Most of the café's trade was during the week and so Johnson shut the café for the weekend to allow Calum to complete the mural in time for opening the following week.

Just like he had learned from Blake, Calum started with painting the shutter in a coat of white emulsion and then sketching the basic shapes of the characters and the furniture with a piece of charcoal. Working hard, he had the outline of the design laid out in full ten minutes short of noon and so decided to have some lunch before starting with the paint. He walked to the newsagent's on the corner and bought a can of Coke and a cheese bagel in cling-film, but the woman behind the counter rebuffed his offer of coins, telling him that she was pleased that Johnson was at last doing something to brighten up the area and that she was thinking of following his lead. She just wanted to see how it turned out first. Calum thanked her and told her to keep him in mind. Popping the top of the Coke he stepped out onto the street and bumped straight into Match and Tusk.

"We've been wondering where you'd got to," said Match.

"Thought you might be avoiding us, like," added Tusk.

Calum ignored them and strolled back to the café. He sat on the step and unwrapped his bagel, started to eat. The other two followed him and stood on the edge of the kerb facing him, holding onto a lamp post and swinging their feet in the gutter.

"You coming out with us tonight?" asked Tusk. "Finish off what we started the other night."

Calum presumed he was referring to the humiliating episode at the rear of the off-licence in Dartmouth Park, but he had no desire for a repeat performance and, besides, he had something else to keep him occupied now. He took another bite and continued to ignore them, looking off down the street towards Camden Town.

"What's the matter, can't you hear us or something?" asked Tusk.

"He must think he's too good for us now," said Match, his head poking out of his dark hood like a poison tortoise.

Still Calum ignored them, drinking from the Coke.

"I reckon the police must've put the frighteners on him or something," said Tusk.

"Turned him back into a child," agreed Match.

"Won't be the first time. Still, it's like riding a bike. He wants to get back in the saddle, it shouldn't be too hard . . ."

"If he leaves it much longer he's going to need those whatch-amacallits, those little wheels on the back . . ."

"Stabilizers," said Tusk. "Kiddie wheels."

"If he leaves it much longer he's going to need stabilizers . . ."

Calum listened to the barrage of jibes in silence. On the one hand it hurt him, his friends attacking him like that, but on the other he just wanted them to leave so that he could get on with the mural. He finished the bagel, drained the Coke, and then put the scrunched-up cling-film into the open mouth of the can.

He stood and walked across to the kerb, and stuffed the can into one of the bulging black bin liners piled there like boulders.

"You coming with us, then?" asked Match. "Finish what we started the other night . . . You can hold the knife . . ."

"I have to finish the mural," said Calum, uncomfortable.

"That's all right, we can wait," said Tusk.

"It might be a while . . ."

"We have to wait until it gets dark, anyway," said Tusk.

"I don't know . . . Perhaps some other time," said Calum.

"Come on," said Tusk, a note of pleading in his voice.

"Oh, forget him," snapped Match, stamping his foot. "He's not going to come with us. He's just pissing us about. He's gone over to the other side. Painting, for Christ's sake . . . I bet he's not even getting paid for it . . ."

"That's not the point . . ." started Calum, frowning.

"Child," Match shouted him down, rattling his fist at the shutter. "Pissing about with a big fat colouring book . . ."

A smirk creased Tusk's face.

"What do we care?" said Match. "You know if we get caught we're going to say that you were with us anyway."

This time DS Marnie Stone came to the flat herself. She said hello to Calum and his mother, accepted the offer of coffee, and then asked Calum where he had been the night before.

"I was here," muttered Calum, looking at the floor.

"You were here all night?"

"I finished working on the mural when it started to get dark and then I came straight back here."

"And what time would that have been?"

"I don't know," replied Calum, shrugging. "I suppose it must've been about nine or so. Quarter past . . . I don't know."

"You're sure about that?"

"Half past, then," said Calum. "I don't have a watch but I'm sure it was no later than about half past nine . . ."

"You stop and talk to anyone on the way home . . ."

Calum shook his head.

". . . or call in at any of the shops?"

Calum shook his head again.

"All right, let's come at it from another direction," said Marnie, looking out across the estate for a moment. "You know the old ironmonger's on Kentish Town Road? It's about two or three doors down from the café you've been working on . . ."

"Yeah, I know it," said Calum.

"You ever been in there?"

"I suppose I must've been at some point. Getting new locks and stuff after we've been broken into . . ."

"So you'll be familiar with the layout of the place?"

"I suppose so," shrugged Calum.

"Does that include the office in the back?"

"I don't know what you mean."

"The place was broken into last night, Calum," said Marnie, leaning forward in her chair. "A large amount of cash was stolen from the office. Cash and a lot of other stuff."

Calum kept quiet, averted his eyes.

"You know anything about that?"

Calum shook his head. "No."

"You're positive about that?"

"Sure I'm positive," muttered Calum.

"All right, then, what about Match and Tusk?"

"What about them?"

"They're your friends, Calum, your comrades in arms. You must know if they had anything to do with it . . ."

"I haven't seen them in a couple of days," said Calum.

"You didn't talk to them last night?"

Calum shook his head again, glanced hard at Marnie in confirmation.

"All right," said Marnie, sighing. "Let's look at what we've got, shall we: A known thief starts working on a mural in a café down on Kentish Town Road and just a few hours later an ironmonger's shop a couple of doors down from there gets broken into – so that's just a coincidence, is it, Calum?"

"Suppose it must be," said Calum, shrugging.

"We like Match and Tusk for this one," said Marnie. "You case the place for them, Calum? You tell them how to get in?"

Calum kept silent, his attention focused on the floor.

Marnie shook her head and looked out of the window across the estate. "All right, I'll leave it there for now," she said after a short time, getting up to leave. "But just so you know . . . I don't think you were there last night, Calum, but I do think that your two friends were, and it's just a matter of time before I find

the proof. If you don't want to help me then that's your
decision. But when we do nail them, don't kid yourself that
they'll think we figured it all out by ourselves . . ."

Although he was at first pleased with himself for not telling the
police that Match and Tusk had been around earlier the afternoon before, the following morning Calum awoke to find it
troubling him like a burgeoning toothache. On the one hand he
still felt a little proud that he had not offered up Match and
Tusk to DS Stone – a solid feature of his culture, he knew – but
on the other he knew that it was just a matter of time before she
arrested them and that when she did so it was almost inevitable
that he would be lumped into the gang as the third man. And
although he did not like to think about what that might mean, at
best he knew that he would not be allowed to continue with the
murals.

The dilemma continued to trouble him long after he returned
to school, but a couple of weeks later he saw his chance to get
out of the situation on what he saw as his own terms.

On the strength of his work at the café, word spread and he
was soon offered another commission, this time to paint a large
mural on the side of a car wash at the foot of Camden Road. The
wall faced the traffic coming down the hill, a huge area, and
after agreeing the design he set to work on it one weekend.

But just as Calum might have predicted, Match and Tusk
turned up late on the third night that he was there. He had just
completed the background and was about to start on the figures
in the cars he had painted – the mural was on a side wall of the
car wash and Calum had created a full-scale cartoon version of it
as if the wall were made of glass: in the centre of the wall he had
drawn a giant foam and rain machine with a grime-streaked car
going in one end and a bright clean car coming out of the other –
and the sight of his friends made his heart sink in his chest. But
Match and Tusk seemed to have lost some of their fire, poking
Calum with sullen and blunt jibes as if taunting him had
become a bore, and it did not take him long to get rid of them.
Watching them walk across Camden Road, Calum felt a smile
touch his face.

But it was a brief success: the following morning Detective
Sergeant Stone was on his doorstep once more, the electrical

store two doors down from the car wash having been burgled the night before. She went at him harder this time, refusing to believe that he had had nothing to do with it. And the harder she went at him, the more Calum dug in his heels. But even as he did so he felt something stirring deep inside, something far deeper than a cultural mistrust of the police and a refusal to grass. This time he knew that it was nothing less than fight or flight.

Ten minutes after Stone left the flat, Calum returned to the car wash to complete the details in the mural.

A little before two o'clock the following morning, chasing up on a call that had come into the station, DS Marnie Stone pulled up in front of the mural with anger and sadness in her heart. Someone had made a good attempt at defacing it, scratching and rubbing different colours of paint across the artwork, but from what she could still make out, the mural looked to be of a police car chasing another car through the car wash. And after taking in some of the finer details the message was made clear to her: Calum was giving her the people she was looking for. In the front car were two clear characters, their features a little smudged but still recognizable: a match with human features and another face with one huge tusk curling out of its mouth. But Calum had not been clever enough, and after his old friends had seen his latest artistic efforts they had meted out their own retribution. Calum had been nailed to the wall where he had painted the chasing police car. His feet were hanging in the air about three feet from the ground and his head rested on his chest in a thick splash of blood. For a moment Marnie had the horrific thought that perhaps his tongue had been cut out, but when she climbed out of the car for a closer look she was relieved to see that he was still breathing and that he had in fact been silenced with a cork rammed in between his bloodied and swollen lips.

PROS AND CONS

Donna Moore

Barry Sheehan looked at the sparkling diamonds around the wrinkled throat of the woman in front of him and surreptitiously adjusted his Y-fronts. Wealth always gave him a hard-on and these two auld bitches were dripping with it. It wasn't so much the wealth itself, as the idea of separating it from its rightful owners. In this case La Contessa Letitzia di Ponzo and her sister Signora Teodora Grisiola.

Sheehan smiled at the two frail old dears in front of him and thought how easy this was going to be. He considered his smile to be the deal-clincher. He'd practised it in front of the bathroom mirror, and convinced himself he looked like Cary Grant, when in reality he looked more like a constipated ferret.

"Well, Mr Sheehan," the Contessa adjusted the diamond necklace with a liver-spotted hand, "I think you will do very well as our chauffeur." Her Italian accent was light and soft. It reminded Sheehan of some actress in an old black and white film he'd seen on video when he was last in Mountjoy Prison. "If you would like to come back tomorrow in the morning, we will have ready a uniform for you and you can drive us out to Fairyhouse Racecourse to meet some of our potential clients."

Sheehan's interest was piqued. "You ladies are interested in horseracing?" He patted the crumpled *Racing Post* in his pocket. Things were looking better and better. The chance to drive a Daimler, a shot at stealing some rather fine diamonds, and a day at the track.

"Gambling? No." The Contessa made a moue of distaste and her silent sister looked shocked at the thought, raising a jeweled hand to her throat as if to cross herself. "But we have an interest in fine thoroughbreds, yes. Now, Mr Sheehan. I will see you out. I apologize for the lack of etiquette, but we haven't yet got around to hiring a butler." She picked an almost invisible speck of dust off her suit – Hardy Amies, dress designer to the Queen – and Sheehan stood up. He'd been dismissed. Fighting the dual temptations of bowing to them and nutting them, he allowed the Contessa to usher him to the door of the Georgian townhouse that she and her sister were currently calling *casa*.

Back in the Drawing Room, the Contessa stood at the window and watched Sheehan strolling up Lower Leeson Street towards St Stephens Green. Her sister looked at her curiously. "Well, Letty, will he do?"

"He's a dodgy, rat-faced, little wanker who wouldn't know the word 'honesty' if it gave him a lap dance and bit him on the arse. He's perfect." Her accent was now more Isle of Dogs than Island of Venice. "Didn't he remind you of that punter you had in the 60s, Dora? The politician who liked you to dress up as a milkmaid and squeeze his udders? Assistant to the Assistant of the Minister of Agriculture, Fisheries and Foods wasn't he?"

Dora giggled. "Old Marigold? Yes, but I do hope Mr Sheehan doesn't want me to slap him on the buttocks and hit him with a fly switch. I'm getting too old for that sort of thing."

Letty removed the diamond necklace and threw it down on the table, rubbing her neck. "That cheap tat is giving me a rash. Did you see Sheehan fixing his beadies on it?" She pulled a packet of Rizlas and a pouch of tobacco out of her fake Chanel handbag and expertly rolled a cigarette one-handed, lighting it with a Zippo displaying a Hell's Angels emblem and the motto "Live Fast, Die Young." She groped under the chintz cushion of the settee for the bottle of tequila she had planked there earlier, and opened the *Racing Post* which, just a couple of minutes ago, had been in Sheehan's pocket. She still had all the old skills.

Just plain Lettice and Dora Huggins – ex-high class hookers,
ex-brothel madams, ex-pickpockets, -drunk rollers and -petty
criminals – had moved up in the world.

Sheehan leaned against the Daimler in the private enclosure at
Fairyhouse and watched Ireland's rich and famous swarm
around his new employers like bluebottles around diamond-
encrusted shit. Gobshites. He had to admire the Italian pair
though. Their scam was a good one. From what he'd observed
today they were selling certificates of part ownership in thoroughbred horses. 50,000 euros a share. The women had the
right patter, references from top names in the horseracing
world, the backing of Lord This and Duke That. Most of all
they were fluently talking the language of the greedy bastards
drooling all over them. The language of cold, hard cash.

"A 25 percent to 30 percent return in 3 months," the
Countess was saying in her clipped, lightly accented tones, as
she tapped out strings of numbers on the slim laptop computer
on the table in front of her. "Guaranteed. The stud fees on their
own are worth a fortune in income. Why, the Duke of Chalfont
was able to restore the family seat in a year from his returns.
200,000 euros, Mr Kavanagh? Certainly. Just give me your
bank account details and we'll effect the transaction immediately."

These rich tossers might not be able to recognize a hoor with
the clap when they saw one, but Sheehan certainly did. He'd
made a fair packet from this sort of scam himself until he'd gone
to jail for it. His was on a smaller scale of course, but Sheehan
recognized the signs. He'd sold dodgy TV advertising (he'd
even got a film student friend to film a couple of fake adverts –
and they'd made a porno while they were at it; Sheehan was
rather proud of his starring role – OK, it was a short fuckin'
fillum and it was all wobbly cameras and badly dubbed sound,
but they'd got the money shot and that was the main thing).
He'd guaranteed his investors a 30 percent return every 60 days.
And, of course, he'd made sure to deliver to the first few
investors. They spread the word and all the other suckers
signed up. Needless to say, the other suckers never got their
promised returns. Or their capital back as it happened. It was
risky, and you had to have balls to pull it off. For a while

Sheehan had managed to juggle those balls in the air as he robbed Peter to pay Paul, but eventually the whole thing had collapsed like a drunken sailor, and Sheehan hadn't managed to disappear before the Gardai came a-calling.

Sheehan narrowed his eyes and ground out his cigarette under the heel of his boot. He was decked out in his new green and gold uniform – knife-edge creases in the trousers, gold buttons shining, black boots polished to within an inch of their life. He was hot, uncomfortable and he'd nearly lamped the auld bitch one when she gave him the uniform. Green and gold? He was a Unionist all the way. Green and feckin' gold? If it hadn't been for that insult he might have stuck with his original plan of heisting the diamonds. Now he was going to make this job really worth his while. Sheehan had a grudging admiration for the auld wans. But it wasn't going to stop him relieving them of some of the cash. It would be like taking candy from a baby.

"Well, Dora, how much have we made?" Letty put her feet up on the rented Georgian table in the drawing room, popped the cork of a magnum of Dom Perignon and opened a packet of pork scratchings.

Dora entered the final few numbers into the laptop. "Just short of 4 million euros. Not too shabby." She opened one of the miniature bottles of Tia Maria that she'd stolen off the trolley on the EasyJet flight over from Luton the week before, clinked it against the bottle of champagne in Letty's hand and knocked it back.

"Piece of piss, Dora. Piece of piss." Two enormous trunks were open at Letty's feet, each of them half full of clothes. "I checked the flight to Rio. We need to be at the airport in an hour or so. Sheehan should be back in a few minutes to drive us."

"And here I am, *ladies*." Sheehan lounged in the doorway, a smile on his thin lips.

Letty dragged herself back into Countess mode, removed her feet from the table and gently placed the half empty champagne bottle down, burping in a ladylike manner as she did so. "Ah, Sheehan, please could you take these trunks to the car."

"Oh, I don't think so. I think you and I and Dora here need to have a nice wee chat, about an equitable sharing of the proceeds of your day at the races. It's only fair after all."

He moved to where Dora had been sitting and turned the laptop round to face him. "4 million euros, eh? And what are two auld bitches like yerselves going to do with 4 million euros? A nice old peoples' home should set you back a couple of thousand at the most. I might let you have 10,000 or so, just so you can keep yourselves in Rich Tea Biscuits."

Letty jumped up from the sofa and took a couple of tottering steps towards him. Sheehan picked up the plane tickets lying next to the laptop and laughed, as Letty and Dora stared at him wide-eyed and open-mouthed, dewlaps quivering in unison.

"And yez think yez are heading off to Argentina with your ill-gotten gains?"

"Brazil," muttered Letty, as she regained her composure, hefted the half empty magnum of champagne, and swung it at the back of his head with as much vigour as she'd once used to whip politicians and High Court judges into submission in her previous career. "Rio de Janeiro is in Brazil, you stupid fucking little twat." She dropped the champagne bottle onto Sheehan's rat-like face as he lay on the floor staring blankly upwards. As the bottle smashed his nose Letty said "That'll teach you, you little wanker," and wiped her hands on her skirt.

Colm O'Neil knocked on the door of the Georgian Townhouse, his home-made collecting tin in hand. If he'd chosen to use his IT degree wisely he could have had a future. But he didn't like to get up in the morning so, instead, he'd printed out some imposing looking business cards and brochures for a charity proclaiming itself "The Holy Sisters of Perpetual Misery" and spent his afternoons fleecing Dublin's tourists and residents alike of the odd 20 euros. Just enough to get himself a wee carry-out from the offy and a couple of ounces of the finest cannabis from his dealer in Gardiner Street.

An elderly lady opened the door and looked at him calmly, a smaller woman fluttering behind her like a stressed-out moth. Quickly sizing them up – the well-cut suits, the jewels adorning their necks and fingers, the general aura of wealth, Colm decided to go for broke. "Howya ladies. I'm collecting for The Holy Sisters, and wondered if you'd be after sparing 50 euros for a good cause?" He rattled his tin to tempt them.

"Certainly young man, do come in." The non-fluttering woman opened the door wider and he stepped into the hall. Two huge old-fashioned trunks and several smaller bags were in the hallway, coats draped over them. "You've just caught us on our way out. We're waiting for a taxi to take us to the airport." The woman looked at him appraisingly for a long moment and then rummaged in her handbag. Pulling out a large wallet she gave him a hundred euros. "A fine strapping young chap like you – I wonder if you'd do us a small favor. Would you take these two trunks here to the dump? We just . . . don't have the time. And although they're on wheels they're terribly heavy and my sister and I are not as young as we used to be. It's just some old papers and old clothes that we don't want."

Colm practically snatched off her hand to get to the 100 euro note. "Sure, and whyever not."

"I just need to put a couple more things in." The woman disappeared into a room to the left, came out a couple of minutes later and slid a fat envelope into a compartment at the side of one of the trunks.

Colm lifted the handle of the brown trunk. She was right. It was heavy. Maybe he should ask for 200 euros. Still, there might be something inside worth having – he didn't want to appear too greedy. "Have a lovely trip ladies. And thank you. The Sisters of Perpetual Misery will bless you."

Letty and Dora sat in Business Class with their feet up, watching *Ocean's Eleven* on the screen in front of them as they sipped their champagne on the flight to Rio.

Dora smiled happily. "Letty, that nice young man is going to open the trunks, isn't he, dear?"

"Of course he is Dora. He won't be able to resist."

"What do you think he'll do when he finds those nicely packaged portions of Mr Sheehan?"

"I have absolutely no idea. But hopefully the 10,000 euros I also put in the trunk will offset the horrible shock." Letty studied George Clooney on the screen as he scammed the Las Vegas casino out of a fortune. "Dora, do you know if they have casinos in Rio?"

SHERLOCK HOLMES
AND THE *TITANIC* SWINDLE

Len Deighton

It was handwritten in a bold, attractive and well-formed writing style, on a cream-coloured heavy paper. There was a small crease on the corner but there was no sign of fading and the colour was the same on both front and back. Held to the light, this single sheet revealed a watermark of a floral design that I did not recognize. The upper edge of the sheet was slightly rough as if it might have been torn from a writing pad, but it may have been because the paper was handmade. Most significantly, the writing varied in ink density. The sentences started in a strong dark greyish-blue and then faded slightly as happens when writing with an old-fashioned pen frequently dipped into a bottle of ink.

Sherlock Holmes and the *Titanic* Swindle

It was a raw and foggy night in early December when Holmes and I sat either side of a blazing fire in our sitting room in Baker Street. Inspector Lestrade of Scotland Yard was there. He was likely to call in on us of an evening, and Sherlock Holmes always welcomed him, as he liked to hear the latest news from police headquarters. On this particular evening Lestrade puffed at his cigar and was uncustomarily quiet. "It's this terrible disaster," said Lestrade, shaking his head sadly.

"Some fine old families will be mourning still," I said.

"There are fears abroad that this failure of an unsinkable vessel could deliver a crippling blow to our whole shipbuilding industry," said Holmes. "I can reveal that I have already been in contact with the captain, the helmsman and several others who were on watch at the time. I am presenting my spiritual research to the directors of the White Star Line. There remain many unanswered questions."

"Surely not?" said Lestrade. "The Titanic *struck an iceberg, was ripped open and sank. How can there be a mystery concerning it?"*

"The Titanic, *was it?" said Holmes. He waited a long time before continuing. "There is not one article; not one piece of flotsam or jetsam bearing the name* Titanic." *He watched our faces and then answered the tacit question. "'White Star Line' yes, but not one item with the word* Titanic."

He held up his hand to still our questions. "To other matters," he said.

"And where's the rest of it?" I asked.

"In his father's bank or in a private Swiss vault or in a tower of his auntie's Bavarian castle," said Percy.

"Is that what's he's like?"

"Strong London accent; almost like an Aussie, carefully trimmed black beard; brown corduroy suit; pompous, assertive; aggressive almost."

"Could be any one of our authors," I said.

"My authors are respectful," said Percy.

"Because you send the aggressive ones to me."

"And they are the ones that make the money," said Percy. "Ever since that piece in *The Bookseller*, they all want you to be their editor, you know that. Fiction writers do anyway."

I read the sheet of paper again and said nothing.

"So what do you think?" said Percy after looking around the room. "Bloody untidy; your office." He had removed a pile of books in order to sit in the soft leather chair I put authors into when I have bad news for them. One leg was resting across the other to display a red cashmere sock and handmade Oxford shoe. Percy always looked like a page from a fashion magazine even on days like today, when the rain was thrashing against the windows, and the sky was so dark that all the office lights were turned on.

"Is it a parody or what?" I said. "It has the same plodding style that I remember from all Conan Doyle's Sherlock Holmes yarns."

"Is that a recommendation? Do you mean it's genuine?"

"We have quite a big list, and it will be too late for the new catalogue, no matter how fast we move. I think we should stay out of this. Send him one of your sad rejection letters."

"Send him where? To HarperCollins? To Random House?"

"Why did he pick us?" I asked.

"He wanted to bring it to the last independent publisher in London, he said."

"You didn't tell me he was a philanthropist."

"Now, now, Carl. Don't let your nasty Teutonic streak show."

"It's been a long day," I said. Percy's Teutonic joke, a reference to my Christian name, had worn thin.

"And you've had your regular kick-boxing lesson from Princess Diana all afternoon."

"Her agent told her our contract will have to be renegotiated."

"More money. She can go to Hell and take *Footsteps to Heaven* with her."

"We did rather well with her last Sharon du Parr," I reminded him. "And she has a new agent now: Freckles. Her other agent was not commercial enough for her. New agents, Percy, always want to flex their muscles."

"Her last agent was a man," said Percy who was high enough in the command structure to be in on the deals. "Sensible enough to keep her feet on the ground."

"Was he? I never met him."

"Blonde lady bomber pilots and female secret agents toting machine guns. The artwork on her last dust-jacket haunts me. I don't know why we publish that crap."

"You don't?" I enjoyed winding him up. "She loved the dust-jacket. She wanted us to make it into a poster."

"That wretched Freckles? Has she really started her own agency? Good grief."

"I think we might be dealing with her for more of our lady writers before long. She wrote an amusing article in *The*

Author. She said men authors always got paid twice as much as women authors and she was going to fight for them. And you'd better not call her Freckles to her face, Percy."

"Let's get back to this Sherlock Holmes story," said Percy. He put a finger on to his starched shirt cuff to sneak a look at his gold Rolex. "You want me to tell him to get stuffed? He's demanding some 'token' money down before we see the rest of it."

"That's just to keep us on the hook," I told him.

"So I'll tell him we're not interested?"

"Not in as many words, Percy. You don't want to make headlines as the publisher who turned down a Sherlock Holmes story that has been locked away undiscovered for a hundred years."

He wetted his lips and then sighed. "Make up your mind, Carl."

"Everyone loves Sherlock Holmes," I said. "If it's the real thing this will make news. Not trade news; big international headline news and TV."

"The paper looks old," he picked it up and looked at it and smelled it. "But is it Conan Doyle's writing?"

"Well, I don't imagine he would bring us an autograph edition; he may have copied it out."

"You'd think he'd put it on a computer or something."

"Not very secure, computers, Percy. Put something like that on the hard drive and it's only a couple of keystrokes away from going on to the Internet. And into the Public Domain, as you lawyers say. Your – what did you say his name was? – seems to be a careful chap."

"He says he wants a definite answer, and cash on the table, by the fifteenth of the month."

"The fifteenth? Next week?"

"He's out of the country till then; a business trip he said."

"Writers all say that; they have a guilt complex about holidays."

I was very busy over the next few days. One of our best line-editors had gone sick with what they suspected was chickenpox. Her daughter phoned us to say her mother might need hospital treatment. She was having blood tests. I knew that would mean a week or more out of action. The worst of it was that she lived in deepest, darkest Cornwall and there was a tall pile of typescripts sitting on her shelf. I couldn't find time to go down there, and Percy was frightened he might catch chickenpox. Finally we decided to wait and see what the medical tests showed. And Percy found an urgent need to visit one of our writers in Ireland. As usual, this meant a diligent exploration of the local pubs and Percy running at half speed for several following days.

Once back in action, Percy took his single sheet of hand-written Sherlock Holmes all around the building, swearing them all to secrecy, as he had before showing it to me. By Thursday he must have run out of people to consult for he came back to talk to me again.

"That young fellow who does the computer stuff in accounts had a good suggestion."

"About Sherlock Holmes?"

"He said we must insist on having a sheet from the original, and then have the paper examined and tested in a laboratory to see how old it was."

"No great problem getting your hands on sheets of old paper, Percy. We could probably find some in the store room, or the slush pile, if we rooted around long enough."

"And I thought of that too, Carl. I'm not a complete fool. It might be better to get one of these computer people to compare the syntax against other stories." I suppose I did not light up in the expected fashion. "Verbs, adjectives, the length of the sentences and so on. That 'customarily', for instance. Was that a word Doyle ever used?"

"It wouldn't be conclusive. We shouldn't assume that this fellow, What's-his-name, is an untutored oaf. If he's a forger he will have looked at the stories: verbs, adjectives and the length of sentences."

"You don't have to be so bloody sarcastic, Carl. I'm trying to see some way out of this situation."

"Way out?"

"Yes, I didn't tell you but I've had the newspapers sniffing around, asking if we'd found some long-lost manuscript."

"Sherlock Holmes?"

"One of them said H. G. Wells – he'd heard it was a sequel to *Things to Come* and the other didn't have a clue about who wrote anything."

"That must have been a senior literary editor. Let me guess which paper."

"No, that's just the point. These queries are coming from the news desks. The H. G. Wells loony had heard that it was going to be a major film."

"Why doesn't your punter just put it up for auction? One of the big boys might be willing to put it into their New York auctions."

"Perhaps he's frightened of it being turned down as a fake," said Percy. "That could be a crippling setback for anyone selling it."

"Will an auction house care too much whether it's a fake? They'll get their money; then it's *cave canem* for the bidders. I sometimes think half the junk put up for auction is bogus in one way or another."

"*Caveat emptor*," Percy solemnly corrected me.

"Same goes for the film," I said. "If some sharp film man grabs it, he could ride along on the publicity generated by a controversy about whether it's genuine. And if it turns out fake that will hardly dent the takings at the box office."

"So you think we should publish it?"

"I didn't say that, Percy."

"It's all right for you. You can just move on if the firm hits a rock. I'm stuck here." Percy was determined not to be deprived of his crisis.

"I don't see why."

"Because my uncle is the chairman, Carl. Be your age. You've made enough jokes at my expense."

"Have I, Percy? I hope I have never been offensive."

"I don't mind your jokes. You can be very humorous sometimes. It's the crap I get when people have to be sacked."

"People say things they don't mean."

"They mean it all right," said Percy and I almost felt sorry for him. It was, after all, Percy who had got me the job. The ad agency let me go after they lost the breakfast food account I was working on. Percy got to his feet. "Well, I must leave you now. I have an important lunch appointment."

When I saw Percy later that afternoon he was roseate and ebullient. And it wasn't all due to the unspecified number of bottles of Chevalier-Montrachet he and his luncheon guest had consumed. "There it is," he said. He put a brown packet on my desk. His aim erred to the extent that it sideswiped my keyboard and put about three hundred z's across a letter I was concocting for the "Princess" about the bewildering way her characters were apt to change names and/or appearance and then some-times change back again. "That's it." He pointed. "That's the Sherlock Holmes story. That's your Christmas bonus and my seat on the board."

"He gave it to you?"

"It wasn't easy but lunch at the Ritz can have a magical effect upon authors. I've noticed that before."

"And this is the only copy? No photocopies in your desk?"

He hesitated. "He made me promise on my honour. I signed a piece of paper for him. It wouldn't have much effect in a court of law but he knows I wouldn't want him brandishing it if there was evidence that I'd cheated on him. So look after it. Don't leave it on the train or something. You remember how you went past your station and had to get a minicab home that night after the Christmas party?"

"Yes," I said. I wished I'd never mentioned that journey home to him. At the time I was hoping he'd offer to reimburse the cab fare but instead of that he kept using it to beat me over the head with implications that I got everything wrong. "So how much did you have to pay him?"

"Nothing. Not a penny."

"He just handed it over?"

"I said the directors would have a meeting on Monday and have an offer and a contract ready for Tuesday morning. I thought that would give you a chance to read it."

"What about you reading it?"

"I have read it," said Percy. "I read it as soon as I got back from lunch."

I noticed that the packet had been torn open and then sealed up again, so perhaps he had.

"And?" Percy was not an avid reader.

"It's damned clever; almost too clever for a Sherlock Holmes yarn. *Corpus delicti*, it all turns on that. You know what I mean?"

"You don't plough your way through a thousand whodunits without discovering what *corpus delicti* means," I told him.

Percy was not to be denied a chance to display his legal qualifications. "Body; but not necessarily a human body. It's the facts, money, physical substance, evidence of any kind that a crime has been committed."

"How does the story read?"

"You'll have to read it for yourself but at the conclusion of the story, Holmes finds there is no written evidence, no substance, no witnesses, not even this gigantic ship, to prove that any crime was ever committed. Holmes ends up baffled . . . but anyway you must read it."

"Doyle was ingenious," I admitted

"It's good," said Percy. "A page-turner. But you are the senior editor, senior fiction editor, anyway."

"Ummm," I said. I could see into Percy's mind. If it turned out well, the firm would make umpteen thousands, Percy would get his seat on the board – there was going to be a vacancy in January anyway – and I would get a small Christmas bonus. If it became the sort of fiasco that Percy feared, it would all be my fault.

"Take it home. Read it over the weekend and let me know on Monday."

"Monday is a difficult day for me, Percy."

"Your day at home, I know."

"It's the only way I can get through the backlog. Here in the office there is always something cropping up."

"Like me."

"It's not only that, Percy. I have to see Sergeant McGregor in the morning and so I asked him to come to my flat for a sandwich and a beer. I want to switch a couple of his chapters and I've drafted out a new beginning. It's not as much work as it sounds but getting an author to understand the need for revisions is always a delicate job."

"Who the devil is Sergeant McGregor?"

"Peter Cardiff. He writes the 'Copper's Diary' series. We've done six of them now. They have all been trade paperbacks but marketing think he's ready to go mass-market."

"Why do these fellows have to have nom de plumes? Isn't Cardiff a good enough name? Better, in my humble opinion."

"Not for a police series about Glasgow criminals. And when he first started he was still on the Glasgow force. He had to have an assumed name."

"Move him to Tuesday, Carl. This Sherlock Holmes decision is important."

"He's coming all the way down from the other side of Aberdeen. And he is a widower; with a school-age child. He has to arrange for someone to collect her and look after her. I really wouldn't like to throw a spanner into his arrangements. And he's one of our best authors, Percy."

"What is best about him?"

"He can spell; he puts a capital letter at the beginning of each sentence and a full-stop at the end. He knows an adjective from a verb and doesn't use flashbacks or dream sequences or try to write sexy scenes that he can't handle."

"He's old fashioned, is that what you mean?"

"Yes, exactly."

"And now I've annoyed you."

"A few more old-fashioned writers like Cardiff and I would have a weekend to myself now and again."

"A palpable hit, Carl."

"Yes, well, he's not old-fashioned, Percy. He's a fine writer who stays within his capabilities, and understands instinctively the taste and intelligence of the reading public in a way that not many people in this building do."

"I say, Carl. A streak of passion! You are always able to surprise me. Very well then; 10 a. m. Tuesday morning. And don't leave it on the train tonight." He rummaged around in the cupboard where unpublished books grow dusty before going into the bin and found a green plastic bag with a Harrods motif. He put the manuscript into it, and hung it on the bentwood stand with my raincoat.

"Red sealing wax and string." I observed.

"I wanted it to be secure. On this floor, any wrapped parcel of A4 size gets thrown into the slush pile without being opened."

"Is that your signet ring you used on the wax?"

"It looks good doesn't it? I'm going to start using it on letters too. What about on the contracts?" I gave him a wintry smile. "We worked hard at college didn't we Carl? Not many parties; not very often drunk; work, work, work." I nodded. "Well I was going through the numbers with Uncle John last week, and I noticed that only one of our top earners even got into college, and she didn't graduate."

" 'There are only three things needed for writing a best-seller; but no one knows what they are.' Somerset Maugham."

"Yes it's all very well for an old buzzard like that to be sardonic but he was sitting on a barrel of cash in his villa in the south of France and lunching with the likes of Winston Churchill."

"Maugham was a doctor at St Thomas's Hospital. Doesn't that rather undermine your theory about illiterate best-selling authors?"

"And Conan Doyle was a doctor, too. So were a lot of bestselling authors but that was all long ago. Now we all know what is needed for a best-seller. Not three things, only one damned thing: TV. It doesn't matter what illiterate rubbish you write, if it becomes a TV series you'll be feted and feasted and rich, and people will say you are a famous writer."

"Not always, Percy."

"Yes, always. Good grief, Carl, who would have guessed, in Maugham's day, that any silly little cookery book could be made into a best-seller? Or a book about exercising, wriggling your *derrière*, like that one we did with that frightful athlete woman who insisted on having her photo on every page?"

"We did well with it, as I remember."

"That was because the photographer did such wonders. Or his retoucher or someone at the printer. He made her look like Jane Fonda, that's why it sold."

"For whatever reason. She asked for twice as much for her second book."

"She didn't get it from us," said Percy with some force. "She didn't get another TV series. I could see that it was going to be the end of her. Her end, perhaps I should say." He didn't need to remind me that she'd made a loud and angry scene in Percy's office before taking her book to another publisher. And they had advertised it in the Sunday papers and lost a great deal of money on it. He laughed. It was good to see him happy and there is nothing that makes a publisher happier than to have a rival company steal authors, and then lose money with them.

Peter Cardiff arrived at my flat on the dot. A result of twenty-five years on the force, I suppose. His books had the series title "A Copper's Diary" and everyone in the trade, including me, admired them as fast-moving, well-written stories. Judging by his mail, the police service liked them too. But the joke was that Cardiff had actually kept a diary right from the first day he joined up as a constable recruit. He retired with dozens of notebooks and was unhurriedly making them into a literary career.

He hadn't been to my flat before. After I took his coat, he moved around the room. There wasn't much furniture. He went to the built-in shelves and started looking at all my books in a systematic way. "Reference mostly," I said. "Specialist dictionaries and encyclopaedias, maps and so on. I do most of my editing work here, away from the telephones and interruptions."

"I thought my stuff went off to someone in the country for corrections of that sort."

"For line editing; yes it does, but if I can pick something up in the early readings I can call the author with a query. It's quicker like that." I opened two cans of beer and poured them out. Then I opened the packets of smoked salmon sandwiches and arranged them on the plates. He bent to look at one of the photos on the fireplace. "My wife," I said. "She's a wonderful woman."

"I thought you were getting divorced," he said. "I'm sorry, it's the policeman in me."

I had no doubt referred to my wife in one of my letters or emails; it was sharp of him to remember so well. "We've had our ups and downs," I explained. "She went to see her family in Brisbane. My teenage son is with her. She wants me to join her there. It's not something I want to rush into. On the other hand, if I decide to go, her fare back here and return would be money wasted."

"Looks like you were there when you were getting married," he said, pointing to our wedding photo in a silver frame on the hi-fi. "The eucalyptus trees, the coastline and the man in the bush shirt – just a guess, of course."

"Ten years back. It can get very hot in summer and I'm very fond of hot weather."

He smiled and we both listened to the wind howling in the chimney. Despite the heat turned fully on, it was cold in the flat and it had been raining on and off for almost a week. "And my son wants to go to college there."

"What will he study?"

"He'll try for a Ph D in surfing and sunning."

"I'd miss you if you moved," he said. "You are painstaking and understand what I would like to be able to do. The editor they gave me at first scribbled all over my typing, scribbled in red ballpoint. That was before I got the word processor. It all had to be typed again. It used to make me livid."

He was still looking around when I said: "I like the new one very much. You are really exploring McGregor's character now. The indecision and the anger . . . and that chapter with the kid who can't speak English. You've come a long way from your first book with the motorcycle cops." It was enough to bring him to the table where I had my notes.

"So you went back and read my first one?" he said. He sipped some beer and bit into a sandwich.

"I try to see how writers develop. And I must keep you to the continuity. We don't want you slipping up about past references; things like the new inspector going to the staff college."

"No, that was stupid. So you picked that one up? I wondered who had spotted it. I should have sent a proper thank you letter. I'm not in touch as closely as I should be."

"You need a London agent," I told him.

"That doesn't sound like a publisher speaking." He was much more relaxed now and I could hear his soft Glasgow accent; the only Scots accent that I could recognize.

"Someone who knows the way around town could get you some radio plays and maybe TV too. It would get you known to a larger public and that's what publishing is all about nowadays."

"Yes, I know but I'm a slow worker. You wouldn't believe how many hours I spend in front of that damned screen. And I've always liked to be outdoors." He tucked into the sandwiches. He probably hadn't eaten since getting off the train. I should have offered him something more substantial.

"Peter, old pal," I said. He looked up sharply. I usually kept to more distant forms of address. It made it easier to criticize if I made it a bit formal. 'I have a safe here. I was broken into over the weekend."

He looked at me as if I had gone mad. "How much did you lose?"

"There was no money there; just my lease and bank statements and passport and so on. Other than that: six silver spoons that were my mother's, and a packet."

"Packet?"

"With a small manuscript inside. Keep it to yourself. I haven't told anyone at the office about it. I didn't go to the police either."

"No, I understand. It's more or less useless reporting robberies to your local coppers. Can I look at the front door?" He got up. He was a policeman now.

We went and looked at the door and the surround. "The door shows no sign of being forced," I said. "And all the windows look OK too."

"What sort of safe?"

"Not very wonderful." I went and opened the closet in the hall to show him where the safe was hidden behind the coats. "Guaranteed fireproof; that was important to me. Four figure combination lock. No sign of it being forced either."

He ran his hands round the back of it to see if he could detect damage of any kind. "Only four digits. That's useless."

"The salesman said it meant almost ten thousand variations."

"Who else has the key to this place?"

"No one. At least, there is an extra one I keep in the main safe at the office – in case I locked myself out – and the cleaning lady has one."

"Look at it like this," he said as he sat down and swallowed the rest of his beer, "most of these combination safes have locks that are quick to operate. User friendly. That means it's quick to swing through the numbers. Try and you'll see."

"Ten thousand numbers."

"Five hundred wouldn't be too daunting, would it?"

"No, it wouldn't."

"Five hundred a day. Try it; click click click. You'd be through it in twenty visits. And your winning combination is unlikely to be at the very end. On average, a thief would find the number halfway through his search. That may not be in line with the science of probability but you see what I mean."

"Yes, I see what you mean. But I don't know what I should do."

"If it's insured you'd better report it as soon as possible. Insurance companies are always looking for an excuse not to pay out."

"I'll speak to the cleaning lady. She's Estonian. She only comes in twice a week: She's a nice young woman. She's been doing the flat for almost a year." I realised how stupid it all sounded but I suppose Cardiff knew that crime victims are likely to become a little disoriented.

"She probably met some tearaway. It's a familiar story, I'm afraid. They meet in a pub and he gets the key and makes a copy. She may not be in on it but I doubt if you will see her again. It's a nasty old world. That's why I was happy to retire to my little hovel in the highlands."

We went quickly though some literals and questions that I'd sent him in advance. Then I got to my feet. "Thanks, Peter. Your new book is very good. It will have to be finally decided by the money men and the marketing people but I would be amazed if there was any hitch about your next one going mass market. We will have the same artist. You said you were happy with the previous covers."

"I leave all that to you London laddies," he said. "That's what a publisher does, isn't it?"

"That's what a publisher does if he's lucky enough to have a sensible author," I said. "Another beer?"

He shook his head but he didn't leave. He didn't even put his coat on, he picked it up and held it awkwardly and said. "You'd better tell me about it. I might be able to help. The parcel. Why would anyone crack open a safe to get a manuscript? Is it valuable? Why?"

I didn't answer.

"Come along, man. I won't be telling any of your secrets to the sheep."

"I didn't open it," I admitted. "I thought it was a photocopy of a manuscript but perhaps it's an autograph manuscript. If it's written by a famous writer from the past, it could be valuable."

"How valuable?"

"I've no idea. Anything up to a hundred thousand pounds."

"Glasgow's full of gentry who would slit their mother's throat for a crate of scotch. London's worse. You'd better tell your local law, or someone might start thinking it's an inside job."

"That I've stolen it?"

"There's no evidence of a break-in, is there?" he reasoned.

I shivered. "I'll give it another day or so. You'll keep all this to yourself, won't you?"

He nodded but he didn't say yes. Peter Cardiff was a decent chap but once a policeman always a policeman. I had a feeling he was wondering about me. Wondering if I was trying to use him to cover some ingenious theft. All the other times I'd seen him it was in the office; so why ask him to come here today? I could see that question written in his face as he shook hands and said goodbye.

"I don't have my cleaning lady's address or phone number," I said.

He smiled and nodded and I went down to the street and said goodbye. By that time I believe he thought I was the same sort of accident-prone schlemiel that Percy thought I was.

Percy's office was almost directly below mine, so on the Tuesday morning I arrived early and then went down to tell him I was ready for the meeting. I was still wondering how I was going to tackle him and his uncle. I would have indulged myself in a stiff drink before leaving home but I didn't want to make things worse by arriving with booze on my breath. "Percy not here yet?" I asked his secretary.

"Has no one told you? He never arrived yesterday." She was flustered.

"What?"

"Poor Percy. He was waiting for a bus yesterday morning and a little car came out of nowhere." She seemed to welcome the chance to relate the story again. "The ambulance took ages apparently and you know how dreadful the rain was. They took him to the little cottage hospital near where he lives. It's not life threatening or anything. But his leg is broken. And he has what they call 'superficial injuries' – bruises and grazes. It didn't stop; the car didn't stop. What brutes people are. They're doing tests, of course, in case he has anything internal. But he sounded quite cheerful on the telephone this morning. I'll give you the number. He has a private line. You can visit him any time they say. It's only a little hospital. I sent him some nice things to eat. He's not on any special diet or anything." Finally she ran out of steam.

"So, no meeting this morning?"

"It could be days," she said. "Next week perhaps. He's got his laptop and a dozen books he wanted from the London Library."

The phone rang. When she answered it I could tell it was an author complaining about a late arriving royalty cheque. I waved goodbye and left.

At first I thought, hooray, reprieved. But then I thought of Percy in the hospital and I put aside the bundle of sentimental scribble that Princess bloody Diana expected me to transform into her next best-seller. Percy lived in a rather verdant neighbourhood on the edge of the green belt. The hospital was just half a mile away, a private one, situated in many acres of countryside. It was almost possible to forget the thunder and filth of the heavy traffic grinding along the nearby North Circular.

"I see our client is a publisher by the cruel look in his eyes. His well-nourished countenance reveals a convivial lifestyle, and the faint remains of a tan suggest either an army man lately returned from service in the orient, or a playboy who takes extended holidays in Provence. As for the casing on the lower leg, this reveals a propensity to cross the road without looking both ways."

"Hello, Carl," He was sitting up in bed with a cast on his leg and extensive dressings on one arm. I'd always thought of Percy as somewhat effete. He was continuously getting colds and was likely to be found pausing breathless on the landing when the lift was out of order. He was only slightly younger, but I'd been in the army while he was getting his law degree and somehow that made a difference to our relationship.

But today I saw a new side to Percy. Despite having had surgery, he was energetically researching the world of Sherlock Holmes. On the bedside table he had his shiny new Sony laptop open and lit up. Beside it there was a tower of books from which grew a torrent of yellow sticky markers.

I decided that the best line of defence was attack. "Look, Percy, the *Titanic* sank in April 1912 – I looked it up – and Doyle didn't become interested in spiritualism until long after that. Long after Sherlock Holmes was dead and buried."

"If the old man offers you non-fiction editing, old lad, be sure to say no."

"Then what?"

"First of all, Doyle joined the Psychical Research Society in 1893. That was the same year the *Strand* magazine ran 'The Final Problem' with Holmes tipping over into the waterfall. Doyle didn't stop writing about Holmes just because his hero had died. He wrote 'The Hound of the Baskervilles', perhaps his best and most famous, in 1902, and predated the events. He simply said that this story was something that had happened to Holmes before he wrestled with Professor Moriarty above the lethal torrent of the Reichenbach Falls."

"I see." I put a bottle of Johnny Walker on the bed and Percy grabbed it and hid it under his pillow. "You've been working hard, Percy. What are you going to be like when the anaesthetic wears off?"

He beamed. Percy was enjoying it all. Sherlock Holmes had got to him as it has done to many thousands of readers over the years. And, from my point of view this was splendid. Anything that kept Percy explaining the manuscript to me, instead of the other way around, was a relief. "Tell me what else you found out?"

"This is the interesting stuff, Carl." He tapped one of the books. "Can you believe it? A new Sherlock Holmes story was published in the August 1948 issue of *Cosmopolitan* magazine. August 1948. Doyle died in 1930, didn't he?"

"Maybe they got it from a Ouija board."

"Very good, Carl. A very good joke," he said solemnly. I think he hated jokes. He once told me that jokes diverted and diluted serious thought and conversation. He was right and that's what I liked about them. "And I went on the Internet and found some *Titanic* nutters. It seems that Holmes got that one right too. None of the remains: flotsam, jetsam, anything-elsesam, had the name *Titanic* on it. Nothing! Nothing so far retrieved can be positively identified as from the *Titanic*."

"What are they saying then? That some other ship struck the iceberg?"

"Yes. The *Olympic*. But let's not get into that just yet, Carl. *Corpus delicti*, remember what I told you? Our concern is the story we are offered. Let me tell you about another situation that might – at law – be comparable with the one we find ourselves in." Percy was really enjoying himself. "This one surfaced in 1948. This was a Sherlock Holmes story called 'The Man Who was Wanted'. It wasn't written by Sir Arthur Conan Doyle; it was the work of another Arthur; a hard-up English architect named Arthur Whitaker. He sent it to Doyle. Feeling sorry for him, Doyle sent Whitaker a check for ten pounds and a sarcastic note telling him to invent his own characters rather than using Sherlock Holmes and co. Doyle tossed the story into the waste paper basket and forgot it. But someone – Lady Conan Doyle probably, or perhaps Doyle's secretary – rescued it and filed it away with Doyle's other papers."

A woman in a white starched overall came in, bringing a tray bearing two cups of tea and four chocolate biscuits. She wanted to adjust his pillows but Percy waved her away so he could get on with his story.

"Ten years after both Doyles are dead, someone finds 'The Man Who was Wanted' tucked away in the Doyle archives. It's unpublished and the law says that trustees are obliged to maximize the income of the estate. In good faith, they sell it to Hearst Newspapers. In England the *Sunday Dispatch* published this 'new unpublished story'. January 2nd, January 9th and January 16th, 1949. It's a big circulation booster for all concerned."

"But your story hasn't come from the Doyle estate," I pointed out to him.

"I wish you would stop being such a damned wet blanket."

"I'm trying to stop you setting yourself ablaze."

"In fact, Carl, old bean, you are the one who struck the match. What you said about controversy, about a lot of people who will care less about authenticity than about wallowing in the financial benefits that widespread controversy will bring . . . well, that's it."

I held up my finger in tacit protest. "It's all very well to say that to me, Percy. But you must be very careful in expressing such ideas to other people. You're a lawyer; I don't have to tell you the implications. Conspiracy and so on."

He vigorously waved away my objections with his bandaged arm. "Just tell me one thing, Carl. Did you like the story?"

"It's all right," I said cautiously.

"It's not just all right; it's marvellous, isn't it? It would make an exciting film with all the exteriors that film people call production values. It's not just two old Victorian dinosaurs chatting by the fireplace in a Baker Street sitting room. You have the shipyards, the squalid Liverpool back streets and signing the contract in the fabulous Belgravia home of the White Star chairman. New York, too. It has enough to expand the American end of the story."

"Well, that would need a lot of extra writing and dialogue. A lot."

"Film people don't mind that, Carl. They love extra writing. It gives them a chance to make the sort of film they prefer to make. Is that tea all right?"

"Yes, the tea is fine," I took a biscuit and bit into it. "The film end is a long shot," I cautioned him.

"Ah. That's what you think. One advantage to having this private room is I can talk to New York and Hollywood while they are still awake out there."

"Hollywood?"

"Yes, Hollywood, you damned Jeremiah. A film production company has been phoning everyone they can think of to ask about the new Sherlock Holmes story."

"A big company? How did they find out?"

"Big enough to be talking about half a million dollars. And a share of the profits. What do I care about how they found out?"

"But why?"

"They need to schedule it. They need time to get the stars they want. They don't want to wait around while we stage some prolonged kind of auction. Cash: up front."

"You talked to them?"

"It's better than that, Carl. These film company idiots in California have made enough phone calls to stir up our cousins in New York. I now have two publishers – one quite small, I admit – who want to do a deal. The word will soon get out. World volume rights; film and TV rights. There are all these disks and things nowadays. It could add up to a fortune."

"I've never been a party to that sort of thing, Percy. I just edit the books."

"And if the manuscript is in Doyle's hand, it could bring an immense price at auction. It's only in the last few hours, on the Internet, that I have learned how many rich collectors of Sherlock Holmes material are still active. There's money in every aspect of this deal."

"Really?"

"Yes, really, you old misery. And don't tell me that the whole manuscript is a forgery, because I think it's kosher."

"Well, I don't know."

"Let me put it another way. Is there anything at all to suggest it's a fake?"

I pulled a face, not knowing how to proceed. "I'm not an expert."

"It's real, isn't it? It's exactly like Doyle's handwriting even to the sloping words on the title page . . . I was able to compare the writing with pages and pages of Doyle's. I went carefully through every line of that facsimile edition of a Doyle manuscript that was published in Santa Barbara in 1985."

I nodded.

"Yes, you know the one I mean: 'The Adventure of the Priory School'." Percy gave a triumphal grin. "You remember, do you? I've got it here now. My secretary found it. And do you know where my secretary found it? On the floor in your office."

"I was sorting through my books to throw some out. I need shelf space."

"On the floor in your office, Carl. On the top of a pile near the door. That's where she found it." He laughed indulgently. "You need shelf space, do you? You probably didn't even look at it."

"I was working at home yesterday."

"With that policeman, Peter Cardiff. Yes, I know. Well, now you can drop everything like that until we get this story contract in the bag. I'll want you with me when we face the board."

"You'll buy it?"

"We don't want the Americans to share the purchase. If we can get it for half a million sterling, perhaps even more, we can't lose. It's better that we have it to ourselves, and then sell it piecemeal according to the best offers. The film people are in contact with New York and desperate to conclude. We have to move fast, Carl. And, let's face it, you are not renowned as a fast mover."

"I've always been a cautious animal."

"That's why you are still an editor. I do believe that if it was up to you, you wouldn't buy this story."

"It's a lot of money, Percy."

"Uncle agrees with me. It's a business opportunity. You don't have to have a degree in English Literature to see that."

"What about provenance?"

"You are not to be swayed, are you? Personally I think this is a genuine story written, and hand-written too, by the master himself. But let's suppose it's not. You don't imagine that this fellow Whitaker was the only one ever to have sent Doyle a Sherlock Holmes story, do you?"

"I see what you mean."

"Yes, now at last, you are getting to see what I am driving at. I contend that, at the worst, this is a story that Doyle read and grudgingly approved. A story that perhaps Lady Doyle rescued and that people in his office filed away in his archive."

"Umm."

"And that's at the worst."

"We'd better keep this conversation to ourselves, Percy."

"Everyone will make money."

"And the Doyle Estate?"

"I will provoke them into denying that it's genuine, or that they have ever seen it, or handled it."

"I'm glad I'm not a lawyer, Percy."

"That's not nice. That's the sort of joke I resent."

"I'm sorry," I said. "Having a wife in Australia is not very good for the morale."

"A bonus and a long weekend will restore your morale. That new advertising girl is rather sweet on you, Carl. The one with the long blonde hair who wears those white sweaters. Did you notice that?"

"I hadn't even noticed there were girls in the advertising department."

"Exactly," he said with the triumph of a diagnosis proved correct. "It's no good sitting at home moping, Carl."

"I might go to Australia, Percy."

"That would be a blow, Carl."

"It's my marriage, Percy. She has her family there and her parents are getting old. And my son doesn't want to come back here."

"What work will you do?"

"There's an ad agency there. They would probably like the idea that I'd worked for a big London agency."

"You haven't been negotiating all this on the sly, have you?"

I shook my head and he smiled. I think he would have thought more of me if I'd said yes, I had.

When I phoned my wife, I did it on a public phone from a railway terminal. It was better done that way. It was evening in London but noon in Los Angeles where she had a temporary secretarial job in a big movie production company. At noon Irene's boss was always at lunch.

"I sold our lovely Volvo. I didn't have many offers. It went for a song but I'm using it for another few days and we did rather well on the lease of the flat. The new tenant moves in next week."

"Are you managing all right, darling?"

"It's not much fun without a cleaning lady – the dishes pile up – but it was better to let her go well in advance. She's gone home for a few weeks. I gave her half towards her plane ticket and told her it was time she visited her mother."

"Well, in that case I shall give notice this afternoon."

"You should have seen Percy," I said. "He was like a small child."

"We are going to ask for six. My brother is sure they'll pay another hundred grand. They are very keen indeed. You are so clever, darling. A regular Sherlock."

I was silent for a minute or so.

"Are you there, darling?" she asked.

"It was just a goodbye joke," I said. "You remember what we agreed."

"Why are you always such a wimp, darling? This is six hundred thousand pounds. This is a new life of high-living in a new land. We start again."

"Just a goodbye joke," I said. "Taking the money would be . . ." I trailed to a halt.

"Would be wonderful," she completed her version of the sentence. "Your son could go to Harvard the way you said you would have liked to have done." She took a deep breath and became charming. "We will live a life of ease. Be sensible."

"No, Irene. It was just an idea for a story. Then it became a joke to play on Percy."

"No *corpus delicti*, darling. It's foolproof. No manuscript as evidence. No witness to the negotiations. All concerned disappear to the other side of the globe with no forwarding addresses." There was a sudden note of concern: "Your policeman swallowed the robbery story?"

"Everything went OK," I said. "But the answer is still no. No, Irene. Do you hear me?"

"Don't 'no Irene' me, Carl. My brother and I have worked damned hard on this one. And spent good money on airline tickets. All you did is scribble a silly story and sit on your ass in London. It's going ahead no matter what you think about it. So have an aspirin and go to bed. Tell the office you have a virus and by the weekend you will have vanished."

"Very well, Irene. But I don't like it."

"You have your airline ticket. Don't forget your passport. See you on the beach, darling."

"Poor Percy," I said.

And when, six months or so later, the letters started arriving, Percy's letter was one of the first. No hard feelings, he said. No crowing. I read the letter several times; I had the feeling that he was half inclined to offer me some money towards my legal costs. But he could afford to be generous. He'd got the greater part of the money back, and the world rights on my "silly story" was eventually added to that. And there is to be a movie, too, they say. Nature follows art, I suppose.

There was no point in putting more money into my lawyer's pocket. When Irene's brother, Gordon McPhail, confessed, I had no alternative but to fill in the gaps. Most of the people who heard about it got it wrong and the newspapers did too. Even Percy, who should have known everything about it, thought that the Bali bomb in October had destroyed our "lovely restaurant". Some latecomers to the bad news thought we were victims of the tsunami, which came two years later. In fact we never did buy the restaurant we were negotiating for in Bali. We found a place we liked better, in Surabaja – Irene always said that I went for it only because of the Brecht song lyrics – and we were doing quite good business when the blow fell. "We got it for a song," she used to say before telling everyone that we had paid almost double the real value.

It was the terrorist bomb in Bali that did for us, of course. The Indonesian cops opened up the bank records to the Australian security service and they noticed the big money transfer. They became really excited. Sydney told London and Washington, and before I knew what was happening I was locked up in a prison in Jakarta with dozens of cops giving me hell on a shift for shift basis. Either they were convinced that I was the moneyman for the terrorists or they put on a wonderful act. They were rough and kept saying they'd hold me for ever and they didn't care about giving me a lawyer or bringing me to trial. They put Gordon through the wringer too. He was treated worse than me.

But ours had been a good plan. Even when they had Percy identify photos of Gordon and got their tame experts to agree about Gordon's signatures it still made a flimsy case to bring before a jury.

But my mind was changed by an avuncular old Aussie detective: "I'll tell you this much, Mohammed, old son, the only way you can avoid serving fifty years in an Indonesian clink as a terrorist is to convince me you are a thief."

I shook my head.

He gave a mirthless grin and said: "The locals tell me there are 365 islands out there. That's bullshit, of course, but there are plenty of them, fever ridden and overgrown, some of them no bigger than a football field. Ideal in fact to use as high security prisons. I went to one of them once. The local coppers were showing us how they handled local law-breakers. It was a stinking hole: dense jungle, everyone as skinny as a rake, even the guards. One of the jokers there said that either the prisoners ate the snakes and rats, or the snakes and rats ate them. It was a good joke but it didn't get much of a laugh from any of our boys. The cons never come back. The guards only do six months at a time. Any questions asked and the pen-pushers at headquarters say the paperwork got eaten by termites." He sat down and mopped his brow. "You wouldn't think it was still winter, would you?"

Perhaps it was a contrivance. No doubt the same cop did the same fatherly routine with Gordon, and they were all determined not to let us discover who cracked first. I could see it might all be a bluff at the time but I didn't feel like betting my life on it.

And all through this, Percy was decent. He told the police he'd known me all his life, and that I couldn't be a terrorist. But he wouldn't lift a finger to help Irene's brother. It was understandable really; Gordon was the one who had duped him. He didn't have the same animosity towards me. He told the cops I was a weak character who had been drawn into crime by a shrewish domineering wife and criminal brother-in-law.

So I have no resentment concerning Gordon's confession. It was just bad luck and he managed to get Irene totally exonerated. They treat me quite decently now that I've got the transfer back to the UK, but I'll never eat rice, boiled fish or any of those damned fiery sambals for as long as I live. The governor here is a Sherlock Holmes devotee, so he likes to talk and display his knowledge to me, and I think I've persuaded him to try his hand at a pastiche of a Sherlock Homes story. I'll help. We are going to invent "The Adventure of the Tired Captain", a case that Doyle mentions in passing at the beginning of "The Naval Treaty" but never used. We won't be the first to have a go at it but no matter. There is no pressure of time and Percy says if it's good enough he'll publish it. And why not? He published my previous Sherlock Holmes story, didn't he?

Mind you, that's not going to be the end of the story. Next week I have a lawyer coming in to see me and that kind of visit doesn't have some big-eared warder sitting in to hear what we say. The court found me guilty of a whole string of offences, and writing that damned *Titanic* story is only one of them. So what are Percy and his uncle going to do when I claim copyright and my share of all the money they have put away? I'll get legal aid, so I won't have to find the money for the lawyers.

It's only now that I can understand why writers were always complaining to me about the way publishers treat them. Why should we writers be exploited?

LOVE

Martyn Waites

Love it. Fuckin love it. No other feelin in the world like it.

Better than sex. Better than anythin.

There we was, right an there they was. Just before the Dagenham local elections. Outside the community centre. Community centre, you're avina laugh. Asylum seeker central, more like. Somali centre.

June, a warm night, if you're interested.

Anyway, we'd had our meetin, makin our plan for the comin election, mobilisin the locals off the estate, we come outside, an there they was. The Pakis. The Anti Nazis. Shoutin, chantin – Nazi Scum, BNP Cunts. So we joined in gave it back with Wogs Out an that, Seig Heillin all over the place. Pakis in their casual leathers, Anti Nazis in their sloppy uni denims, us lookin sharp in bombers an eighteen holers. Muscles like taut metal rope under skin tight T-shirts an jeans, heads hard an shiny. Tattoos: dark ink makin white skin whiter.

Just waitin.

Our eyes; burnin with hate.

Their eyes; burnin with hate. Directed at us like laser death beams.

Anticipation like a big hard python coiled in me guts, waitin to get released an spread terror. A big hard on waitin to come.

Buildin, gettin higher:

Nazi Scum BNP Cunts
Wogs Out Seig Heil
Buildin, gettin higher –
Then it came. No more verbals, no more posin. Adrenalin
pumped right up, bell ringin, red light on. The charge.
The python's out, the hard on spurts.
Both sides together, two wallsa sound clashin intaya. A big,
sonic tidal wave ready to engulf you in violence, carry you under
with fists an boots an sticks.
Engage. An in.
Fists an boots an sticks. I take. I give back double. I twist an
thrash. Like swimmin in anger. I come up for air an dive back in
again, lungs full. I scream the screams, chant the chants.
Wogs out seig heil
Then I'm not swimmin. Liquid solidifies round me. An I'm
part of a huge machine. A muscle an bone an blood machine. A
shoutin, chantin cog in a huge hurtin machine. Arms wind-
millin. Boots kickin. Fuelled on violence. Driven by rage.
Lost to it. No me. Just the machine. An I've never felt more
alive.
Love it. Fuckin love it.
I see their eyes. See the fear an hate an blood in their eyes.
I feed on it.
Hate matches hate. Hate gives as good as hate gets.
Gives better. The machine's too good for them.
The machine wins. Cogs an clangs an fists an hammers. The
machine always wins.
Or would, if the pigs hadn't arrived.
Up they come, sticks out. Right lads, you've had your fun.
Time for us to have a bit. Waitin till both sides had tired, pickin
easy targets.
The machine falls apart; I become meself again. I think an
feel for meself. I think it's time to run.
I run.
We all do; laughin an limpin, knowin we'd won.
Knowin our hate was stronger than theirs. Knowin they were
thinkin the same thing.
Run. Back where we came from, back to our lives. Our selves.
Rememberin that moment when we became somethin more.
Cherishin it.

I smiled.
LOVED IT.

D'you wanna name? Call me Jez. I've been called worse.

You want me life story? You sound like a copper. Or a fuckin social worker. Fuckin borin, but here it is. I live on the Chatsworth Estate in Dagenham. The borders of East London/Essex. You'll have heard of it. It's a dump. Or rather a dumpin ground. For problem families at first, but now for Somalis an Kosovans that have just got off the lorry. It never used to be like that. It used to be a good place where you could be proud to live. But then so did Dagenham. So did this country.

There's my dad sittin on the settee watchin Tricia in his vest, rollin a fag. I suppose you could say he was typical of this estate (an of Dagenham an the country). He used to have a job, a good one. At the Ford plant. Knew the place, knew the system, knew how to work it. But his job went when they changed the plant. His job an thousands of others. Now it's a centre of excellence for diesel engines. An he can't get a job there. He says the Pakis took it from him. They got HNDs an degrees. He had an apprenticeship for a job that don't exist no more. No one wants that now. No one wants him now. He's tried. Hard. Honest. So he sits in his vest, rollin fags, watchin Tricia.

There's Tom, me brother, too. He's probably still in bed. He's got the monkey on his back. All sorts, really, but mostly heroin. He used to be a good lad, did well at school an that, but when our fat slag bitch of a mother walked out all that had to stop. We had to get jobs. Or try. I got a job doin tarmacin an roofin. He got a heroin habit. Sad. Fuckin sad. Makes you really angry.

Tarmacin an roofin. Off the books, cash in hand. With Barry the Roofer. Baz. Only when I'm needed, though, or seasonal, when the weather's good, but it's somethin. Just don't tell the dole. I'd lose me Jobseeker's Allowance.

It's not seasonal at the moment. But it's June. So it will be soon. So that's me. It's not who I am. But it's not WHAT I AM.

I'm a Knight of St George. An proud of it. A True Believer. A soldier for truth.

This used to be a land fit for heroes, when Englishmen were kings an their houses castles. A land where me dad had a job, me brother was doin well at school an me fat slag bitch of a mother hadn't run off to Gillingham in Kent with a Paki postman. Well, he's Greek, actually, but you know what I mean. They're all Pakis, really.

An that's the problem. Derek (I'll come to him in a minute) said the Chatsworth Estate is like this country in miniature. It used to be a good place where families could live in harmony and everyone knew everyone else. But now it's a run down shithole full of undesirables an people who've given up tryin to get out. No pride anymore. No self respect. Our heritage sold to Pakis who've just pissed on us. Love your country like it used to be, says Derek, but hate it like it is now.

And I do. Both. With all my heart.

Because it's comin back, he says. One day, sooner rather than later, we'll reclaim it. Make this land a proud place to be again. A land fit for heroes once more. And you, my lovely boys, will be the ones to do it. The footsoldiers of the revolution. Remember it word for word. Makes me all over again when I think of it.

An I think of it a lot. Whenever some Paki's got in me face, whenever some stuck up cunt's had a go at the way I've done his drive or roof, whenever I look in me dad's eyes an see that all his hope belongs to yesterday, I think of those words. I think of my place in the great scheme, at the forefront of the revolution. An I smile. I don't get angry. Because I know what they don't.

That's me. That's WHAT I AM.

But I can't tell you about me without tellin you about Derek Midgely. Great, great man. The man who showed me the way an the truth. The man who's been more of a father to me than me real dad. He's been described as the demigog of Dagenham. I don't know what a demigog is, but if it means someone who KNOWS THE TRUTH an TELLS IT LIKE IT IS, then that's him.

But I'm gettin ahead. First I have to tell you about Ian.

Ian. He recruited me. Showed me that way.

I met him the shopping centre. I was sittin around one day wonderin what to, when he came up to me.

I know what you need, he said.

I looked up. An there was a god. Shaved head, eighteen holers, jeans an T-shirt so tight I could make out the curves an contours of his muscled body. An he looked so relaxed, so in control. He had his jacket off an I could see the tats over his forearms an biceps. Some pro ones like the flag of St George, some done himself like Skins Foreva. He looked perfect.

An I knew there an then, I wanted what he had. He was right. He did know what I needed.

He got talkin to me. Asked me questions. Gave me answers. Told me who was to blame for my dad not havin a job. Who was to blame for my brother's habit. For my fat slag bitch mother runnin off to Gillingham. Put it all in context with the global Zionist conspiracy. Put it closer to home with pictures I could understand: the Pakis. The niggers. The asylum seekers.

I looked round Dagenham. Saw crumbling concrete, depressed whites, smug Pakis. The indiginous population overrun. Then back at Ian. An with him lookin down at me an the sun behind his head lookin like some kind of halo, it made perfect sense.

I feel your anger, he said, understand your hate.

The way he said hate. Sounded just right.

He knew some others that felt the same. Why didn't I come along later an meet them?

I did.

An never looked back.

Ian's gone now. After what happened.

For a time it got nasty. I mean REALLY nasty. Body in the concrete foundations of the London Gateway nasty.

I blamed Ian. All the way. I had to.

Luckily, Derek agreed.

Derek Midgely. A great man, like I said. He's made the St George pub on the estate his base. It's where we have our meetins. He sits there in his suit with his gin an tonic in front of him hair slicked back, an we gather round, waitin for him to give us some pearls of wisdom, or tell us the latest installment of his masterplan. It's brilliant, just to be near him. Like I said, a great, great man.

I went there along with everyone else the night after the community centre ruck. I mean meetin. There was the usuals. Derek, of course, holdin court, the footsoldiers of which I can proudly number myself, people off the estate (what Derek calls the concerned populace), some girls, Adrian an Steve. They need a bit of explainin. Adrian is what you'd call an intellectual. He wears glasses an a duffelcoat all year round. Always carryin a canvas bag over his shoulder. Greasy black hair. Expression like he's somewhere else. Laughin at a joke only he can hear. Don't know what he does. Know he surfs the internet, gets things off that. Shows them to Derek. Derek nods, makes sure none of us have seen them. Steve is the local councillor. Our great white hope. Our great fat whale, as he's known out of Derek's earshot. Used to be Labour until, as he says, saw the light. Or until they found all the fiddled expenses sheets an Nazi flags up in his living room an Labour threw him out. Still, he's a tru man of the people.

Derek was talkin. What you did last night, he says, was a great and glorious thing. And I'm proud of each and every one of you.

We all smiled.

However, Derek went on, I want you to keep a low profile between now and Thursday. Voting day. Let's see some of the other members of our party do their bit. We all have a part to play.

He told us that the concerned populace would go leafletin and canvassin in their suits an best clothes, Steve walkin round an all. He could spin a good yarn, Steve. How he'd left Labour in disgust because they were the Pakis friend, the asylum seeker's safe haven. How they invited them over to use our National Health Service, run drugs an prostitution rings. He would tell that to everyone he met, try an make them vote for him. Derek said it was playin on their legitimate fears but to me it just sounded so RIGHT. Let him play on whatever he wanted.

He went on. We listened. I felt like I belonged. Like I was wanted, VALUED. Meetins always felt the same.

LIKE I'D COME HOME.

The meetin broke up. Everyone started drinkin.

Courtney, one of the girls, came up to me, asked if I was stayin on. She's short with a soft barrel body an hard eyes. She's fucked nearly all the footsoldiers. Sometimes more than once, sometimes a few at a time. Calls it her patriotic duty. Hard eyes, but a good heart. I went along with them once. I had to. All the lads did. But I didn't do much. Just sat there, watched most of the time. Looked at them. Didn't really go near her.

Anyway, she gave me that look. Rubbed up against me. Let me see the tops of her tits down the front of her low cut T-shirt. Made me blush. Then made me angry cos I blushed. I told her I had to go, that I couldn't afford a drink. My Jobseeker's Allowance was gone an Baz hadn't come up with any work for me.

She said that she was gettin together with a few of the lads after the pub. Was I interested?

I said no. And went home.

Well not straight home. There was somethin I had to do first. Somethin I couldn't tell the rest of them about.

There's a part of the estate you just DON'T GO. At least not by yourself. Not after dark. Unless you were tooled up. Unless you want somethin. An I wanted somethin.

It was dark there. Shadows on shadows. Hip hop an reggae came from open windows. The square was deserted. I walked, crunched on gravel, broken glass. I felt eyes watchin me. Unseen ones. Wished I'd brought my blade. Still, I had my muscles. I'd worked on my body since I joined the party, got good an strong. I was never like that at school. Always the weak one. Not any more.

I was kind of safe, I knew that. As long as I did what I was here to do I wouldn't get attacked. Because this was where the niggers lived.

I went to the usual corner an waited. I heard him before I saw him. Comin out of the dark, along the alleyway, takin his time, baggy jeans lung low on his hips, Calvins showin at the top. Vest hangin loose. Body ripped an buff.

Aaron. The Ebony Warrior.

Aaron. Drug dealer.

I swallowed hard.

He came up close, looked at me. The usual look, smilin, like he knows somethin I don't. Eye to eye. I could smell his warm breath on my cheek. I felt uneasy. The way I always do with him.

Jez, he said slowly, an held his arms out. See anythin you want?

I swallowed hard again. My throat was really dry.

You know what I want. My voice sounded ragged.

He laughed his private laugh. I know exactly, he said, an waited.

His breath was all sweet with spliff an alcohol. He kept starin at me. I dug my hand into my jacket pocket. Brought out money. Nearly the last I had, but he didn't know that.

He shook his head, brought out a clingfilm wrap from his back pocket.

Enjoy, he said.

It's not for me an you know it.

He smiled again. Wanna try some? Some skunk, maybe? Now? With me?

I don't do drugs. I hardly drink. An he knows it. He was tauntin me. He knew what my answer would be.

Whatever, he said. Off you go then, back to your little Hitler world.

I said nothing. I never could when he talked to me.

Then he did somethin he'd never done before. He touched my arm.

You shouldn't hate, he said. Life too short for that, y'get me?

I looked down at his fingers. The first black fingers I'd ever had on my body. I should have thrown them off. Told him not to touch me, called him a filthy nigger. Hit him.

But I didn't. His fingers felt warm. And strong.

What should I do, then? I could hardly hear my own voice.

Love, he said.

I turned round, walked away.

I heard his laugh behind me.

At home, dad was asleep on the sofa. Snorin an fartin. I went into Tom's room. Empty. I left the bundle by his bedside an went out.

I hadn't been lyin to Courtney. It was nearly the last of me money. I didn't like buyin stuff for Tom, but what could I do? It was either that or he went out on the street to sell somethin, himself even, to get money for stuff. I had no choice.

I went to bed but couldn't sleep. Things on me mind but I didn't know what. Must be the elections. That was it. I lay starin a the ceilin, then realized me cock was hard. I took it in me hand. This'll get me to sleep, I thought. I thought hard about Courtney. An all those lads.

That did the trick.

The next few days were a bit blurry. Nothin much happened. It was all waitin. For the election. For Baz to find me some more work. For Tom to run out of heroin again an need another hit.

Eventually Thursday rolled round and it was election day. I went proudly off to the pollin station at the school I used to go to. Looked at the kids' names on the walls. Hardly one of them fuckin English. Made me do that cross all the more harder.

I stayed up all night watchin the election. Tom was out, me dad fell asleep.

Steve got in.

I went fuckin mental.

I'd been savin some cans for a celebration an I went at them. I wished I could have been in the St George with the rest but I knew us footsoldiers couldn't. But, God, how I WANTED TO. That was where I should have been. Who I should have been with. That was where I BELONGED.

But I waited. My time would come.

I stayed in all the next day. Lost track of time.

Put the telly on. Local news. They reported what had happened. Interviewed some Paki. Called himself a community leader. Said he couldn't be held responsible if members of his community armed themselves and roamed the streets in gangs looking for BNP members. His people had a right to protect themselves.

They switched to the studio. An there was Derek. Arguin with some cunt from Cambridge. Least that's what he looked like. Funny, I thought people were supposed to look bigger on TV. Derek just looked smaller. Greasy hair. Fat face. Big nose. Almost like a Jew, I thought. Then felt guilty for thinkin it.

It's what the people want, he said, the people have spoken. They're sick an tired of a government that is ignorin the views of the common man and woman. An the common man an woman have spoken. We are not extremists. We are representin what the average, decent person in this country thinks but doesn't dare say because of political correctness. Because of what they fear will happen to them.

I felt better hearin him say that. Then they turned to the Cambridge cunt. He was a psychologist or psychiatrist or sociologist or somethin. I thought here it comes. He's gonna start arguin back an then Derek's gonna go for him. But he didn't. This sociologist just looked calm. Smiled, almost.

It's sad, he said. It's sad so few people realize. As a society it seems we base our responses on either love or hate, thinking they're opposites. But they're not. They're the same. The opposite of love is not hate. It's indifference.

They looked at him.

People only hate what they fear within themselves. What they fear themselves becoming. What they secretly love. A fascist – he gestured to Derek – will hate democracy. Plurality. Anything else – he shrugged – is indifference.

I would have laughed out loud if there had been anyone else there with me.

But there wasn't. So I said nothing.

A weekend of lyin low. Difficult, but had to be done. Don't give them a target, Derek had said. Don't give them an excuse.

By Monday I was rarin to get out the flat. I was even lookin forward to goin to work.

First I went down the shoppin centre. Wearin me best skinhead gear. Don't know what I expected, the whole world to have changed or somethin, but it was the same as it had been. I walked round proudly, an I could feel people lookin at me. I smiled. They knew. Who I was. What I stood for. They were the people who'd voted.

There was love in their eyes. I was sure of it.

At least, that's what it felt like.

Still in a good mood, I went to see Baz. Ready to start work.

An he dropped a bombshell.

Sorry mate, I can't use you no more.

Why not?

He just looked at me like the answer was obvious. When I looked like I didn't understand, he had to explain it to me.

Cos of what's happened. Cos of what you believe in. No don't get me wrong, he said, you know me. I agree, there's too many Pakis an asylum seekers over here. But a lot of those Pakis are my customers. An, well, look at you. I can hardly bring you along to some Paki's house an let you work for him, could I?

So sorry, mate, that's that.

I was gutted. I walked out of there knowin I had no money. Knowin that, once again, the Pakis had taken it from me.

I looked around the shoppin centre. I didn't see love any more. I saw headlines on the papers:

RACIST COUNCILLOR
VOTED IN TO DAGENHAM

Then underneath:

KICK THIS SCUM OUT

I couldn't believe it. They should be welcomin us with open arms. This was supposed to be the start of the revolution. Instead it was the usual shit. I just knew the Pakis were behind it. An the Jews. They own all the newspapers.

I had nowhere to go. I went to the St George but this was early mornin an there was no one in. None of my people.

So I just walked round all day. Thinkin. Not gettin anythin straight. Gettin everythin more twisted.

I thought of goin to the St George. They'd be there. Celebratin. Then there was goin to be a late night march round the streets. Let the residents, the concerned populace, know they were safe in their houses. Let everyone know who ruled the streets.

But I didn't feel like it.

So I went home.

An wished I hadn't.

Tom was there. He looked like shit. Curled up on his bed. He'd been sick. Shit himself.

Whassamatter? I said. D'you wanna doctor?

He managed to shake his head. No.

What then?

Gear. Cold turkey. Cramps.

An he was sick again.

I stood back, not wantin it to go on me.

Please, he gasped, you've got to get us some gear . . . please . . .

I've got no money, I said.

Please . . .

An his eyes, pleadin with me. What could I do? He was my brother. My flesh an blood. An you look after your own.

I'll not be long, I said.

I left the house.

Down to the part of the estate where you don't go. I walked quickly, went to the usual spot. Waited.

Eventually he came. Stood before me.

Back so soon? Aaron said. Then smiled. Can't keep away, can you?

I need some gear, I said.

Aaron waited.

But I've got no money.

Aaron chuckled. Then no sale.

Please. It's for . . . it's urgent.

Aaron looked around. There was that smile again.

How much d'you want it? he said.

I looked at him.

How much? he said again. An put his hand on my arm.

He moved in closer to me. His mouth right by my ear. He whispered, tickling me. My heart was beatin fit to burst. My legs felt shaky.

You're like me, he said.

I tried to speak. It took me two attempts. No I'm not, I said.

Oh yes you are. We do what our society says we have to do. Behave like we're supposed to. Hide our true feelings. What we really are.

I tried to shake my head. But I couldn't.

You know you are. He got closer. You know I am.

An kissed me. Full on the mouth.

I didn't throw him off. Didn't call him a filthy nigger. Didn't hit him. I kissed him back.

Then it was hands all over each other. I wanted to touch him, feel his body, his beautiful, black body. Feel his cock. He did the same to me. That python was inside me, ready to come out. I loved the feeling.

I thought of school. How I was made to feel different. Hated them for it. Thought of Ian. What we had got up to. I had loved him. With all my heart. An he loved me. But we got found out. An that kind of thing is frowned upon, to say the least. So I had to save my life. Pretend it was all his doing. I gave him up. I never saw him again. I never stopped loving him.

I loved what Aaron was doing to me now. It felt wrong. But it felt so right.

I had him in my hand, wanted him in my body. Was ready to take him.

When there was a noise.

We had been so into each other we hadn't heard them approach.

So this is where you are, they said. Fuckin a filthy nigger when you should be with us.

The footsoldiers. On patrol. An tooled up.

I looked at Aaron. He looked terrified.

Look, I said, it was his fault. I had to get some gear for my brother . . .

They weren't listening. They were starin at us. Hate in their eyes. As far as they were concerned I was no longer one of them. I was the enemy now.

You wanna run nigger lover? Or you wanna stay here an take your beatin with your boyfriend? The words spat out.

I zipped up my jeans. Looked at Aaron.

They caught the look.

Now run, the machine said, hate in its eyes. But from now on, you're no better than a nigger or a Paki.

I ran.

Behind me, heard them layin into Aaron.

I kept running.

I couldn't go home. I had no gear for Tom. I couldn't stay where I was. I might not be so lucky next time.

So I ran.

I don't know where.

After a while I couldn't run any more. I slowed down, tried to get me breath back. Too tired to run anymore. To fight back.

I knew who I was. Finally. I knew WHAT I WAS.

An it was a painful truth. It hurt.

Then from the end of the street I saw them. Pakis. A gang of them. Out protecting their own community. They saw me. Started running.

I was too tired. I couldn't outrun them. I stood up, waited for them. I wanted to tell them I wasn't a threat, that I didn't hate them.

But they were screaming, shouting, hate in their eyes.

A machine. Cogs an clangs an fists an hammers.

I waited, smiled.

Love shining in my own eyes.

JUST FRIENDS

John Harvey

These things I remember about Diane Adams: the way a lock of her hair would fall down across her face and she would brush it back with a quick tilt of her head and a flick of her hand; the sliver of green, like a shard of glass, high in her left eye; the look of surprise, pleasure and surprise, when she spoke to me that first time – "And you must be, Jimmy, right?": the way she lied.

It was November, late in the month and the night air bright with cold that numbed your fingers even as it brought a flush of color to your cheeks. London, the winter of fifty-six, and we were little more than kids then, Patrick, Val and myself, though if anyone had called us that we'd have likely punched him out, Patrick or myself at least, Val in the background, careful, watching.

Friday night it would have been, a toss-up between the Flamingo and Studio 51, and on this occasion Patrick had decreed the Flamingo: this on account of a girl he'd started seeing, on account of Diane. The Flamingo a little more cool, a little more style; more likely to impress. Hip, I suppose, the word we would have used.

All three of us had first got interested in jazz at school, the trad thing first, British guys doing a earnest imitation of New Orleans; then, for a spell, it was the Alex Welsh band we followed around, a hard-driving crew with echoes of Chicago, brittle and fast, Tuesday nights the Lyttelton place in Oxford Street, Sundays a club out at Wood Green. It was Val who got us listening to the more modern stuff, Parker 78s on Savoy, Paul Desmond, the Gerry Mulligan Quartet.

From somewhere, Patrick got himself a trumpet and began practicing scales, and I kicked off playing brushes on an old suitcase while saving for the down payment on a set of drums. Val, we eventually discovered, already had a saxophone – an old Selmer with a dented bell and a third of the keys held on by rubber bands: it had once belonged to his old man. Not only did he have a horn, but he knew how to play. Nothing fancy, not yet, not enough to go steaming through the changes of *Cherokee* or *I Got Rhythm* the way he would later, in his pomp, but tunes you could recognize, modulations you could follow.

The first time we heard him, really heard him, the cellar room below a greasy spoon by the Archway, somewhere the owner let us hang out for the price of a few coffees, the occasional pie and chips, we wanted to punch him hard. For holding out on us the way he had. For being so damned good.

Next day, Patrick took the trumpet back to the place he'd bought it, Boosey and Hawkes, and sold it back to them, got the best price he could. "Sod that for a game of soldiers," he said, "too much like hard bloody work. What we need's a bass player, someone half-decent on piano, get Val fronting his own band." And he pushed a bundle of fivers into my hand. "Here," he said, "go and get those sodding drums."

"What about you?" Val asked, though he probably knew the answer even then. "What you gonna be doin'?"

"Me?" Patrick said. "I'm going to be the manager. What else?"

And, for a time, that was how it was.

Private parties, weddings, bar mitzvahs, support slots at little clubs out in Ealing or Totteridge that couldn't afford anything better. From somewhere Patrick found a pianist who could do a passable Bud Powell, and, together with Val, that kept us afloat. For a while, a year or so at least. By then even Patrick could see Val was too good for the rest of us and we were just holding him back; he spelled it out to me when I was packing my kit away after an all-nighter in Dorking, a brace of tenners eased down into the top pocket of my second hand Cecil Gee jacket.

"What's this?" I said.

"Severance pay," said Patrick, and laughed.

Not the first time he paid me off, nor the last.

But I'm getting ahead of myself.

That November evening, we'd been hanging round the Bar Italia on Frith Street pretty much as usual, the best coffee in Soho then and now; Patrick was off to one side, deep in conversation with a dark-skinned guy in a Crombie overcoat, the kind who has to shave twice a day and wore a scar down his cheek like a badge. A conversation I was never meant to hear.

"Jimmy," Patrick said suddenly, over his shoulder. "A favour. Diane, I'm supposed to meet her. Leicester Square tube." He looked at his watch. "Any time now. Go down there for me, okay? Bring her to the club; we'll see you there."

All I'd seen of Diane up to that point had been a photograph, a snapshot barely focused, dark hair worn long, high cheek bones, a slender face. Her eyes – what colour were her eyes?

"The tube," I said. "Which exit?"

Patrick grinned. "You'll get it figured."

She came up the steps leading on to Cranbourne Street and I recognized her immediately; tall, taller than I'd imagined, and in that moment – Jesus! – so much more beautiful.

"Diane?" Hands in my pockets, trying and failing to look cool, blushing already. "Patrick got stuck in some kind of meeting. Business, you know? He asked me to meet you."

She nodded, looking me over appraisingly. "And you must be Jimmy, right?" Aside from that slight flaw, her eyes were brown, a soft chocolatey brown, I could see that now.

Is it possible to smile ironically? That's what she was doing. "All right, Jimmy," she said. "Where are we going?"

When we got to the Flamingo, Patrick and Val had still not arrived. The Tony Kinsey Quintet were on the stand, two saxes and rhythm. I pushed my way through to the bar for a couple of drinks and we stood on the edge of the crowd, close but not touching. Diane was wearing a silky kind of dress that clung to her hips, two shades of blue. The band cut the tempo for *Sweet and Lovely*, Don Rendell soloing on tenor.

Diane rested her fingers on my arm. "Did Patrick tell you to dance with me, too?"

I shook my head.

"Well, let's pretend that he did."

Six months I suppose they went out together, Diane and Patrick, that first time around, and for much of that six months, I rarely saw them one without the other. Towards the end, Patrick took her off for a few days to Paris, a big deal in those days, and managed to secure a gig for Val while he was there, guesting at the *Chat Qui Pêche* with René Thomas and Pierre Michelot.

After they came back I didn't see either of them for quite a while: Patrick was in one of his mysterious phases, doing deals, ducking and weaving, and Diane – well, I didn't know about Diane. And then, one evening in Soho, hurrying, late for an appointment, I did see her, sitting alone by the window of this trattoria, the Amalfi it would have been, on Old Compton Street, a plate of pasta in front of her, barely touched. I stopped close to the glass, raised my hand and mouthed "Hi!" before scuttling on, but if she saw me I couldn't be sure. One thing I couldn't miss though, the swelling, shaded purple, around her left eye.

A week after this Patrick rang me and we arranged to meet for a drink at the Bald Faced Stag; when I asked about Diane he looked through me and then carried on as if he'd never heard her name. At this time I was living in two crummy rooms in East Finchley – more a bed-sitter with a tiny kitchen attached, the bathroom down the hall – and Patrick gave me a lift home, dropped me at the door. I asked him if he wanted to come in but wasn't surprised when he declined.

Two nights later I was sitting reading some crime novel or other, wearing two sweaters to save putting on the second bar of the electric fire, when there was a short ring on the downstairs bell. For some reason, I thought it might be Patrick, but instead it was Diane. Her hair was pulled back off her face in a way I hadn't seen before, and, a faint finger of yellow aside, all trace of the bruise around her eye had disappeared.

"Well, Jimmy," she said, "aren't you going to invite me in?"

She was wearing a cream sweater, a coffee-coloured skirt with a slight flare, high heels which she kicked off the moment she sat on the end of the bed. My drums were out at the other side of the room, not the full kit, just the bass drum, ride cymbal, hi-hat and snare; clothes I'd been intending to iron were folded over the back of a chair.

"I didn't know," I said, "you knew where I lived."

"I didn't. Patrick told me."

"You're still seeing him then?"

The question hung in the air.

"I don't suppose you've got anything to drink?" Diane said.

There was a half bottle of Bell's out in the kitchen and I poured what was left into two tumblers and we touched glasses and said, "Cheers." Diane sipped hers, made a face, then drank down most of the rest in a single swallow.

"Patrick . . ." I began.

"I don't want to talk about Patrick," she said.

Her hand touched the buckle of my belt. "Sit here," she said. The mattress shifted with the awkwardness of my weight.

"I didn't know," she said afterwards, "it could be so good."

You see what I mean about the way she lied.

Patrick and Diane got married in the French church off Leicester Square and their reception was held in the dance hall conveniently close by; it was one of the last occasions I played drums with any degree of seriousness, one of the last times I played at all. My application to join the Metropolitan Police had already been accepted and within weeks I would be starting off in uniform, a different kind of beat altogether. Val, of course, had put the band together and an all-star affair it was – Art Ellefson, Bill LeSage, Harry Klein. Val himself was near his mercurial best, just ahead of the flirtations with heroin and free form jazz that would sideline him in the years ahead.

At the night's end we stood outside, the three of us, ties unfastened, staring up at the sky. Diane was somewhere inside, getting changed.

"Christ!" Patrick said. "Who'd've fuckin' thought it?"

He took a silver flask from inside his coat and passed it round. We shook hands solemnly and then hugged each other close. When Diane came out, she and Patrick went off in a waiting car to spend the night at a hotel on Park Lane.

"Start off," Patrick had said with a wink, "like you mean to continue."

We drifted apart: met briefly, glimpsed one another across smoky rooms, exchanged phone numbers that were rarely if ever called. Nine years later I was a detective sergeant working out of West End Central and Patrick had not long since opened his third night club in a glitter of flash bulbs and champagne; Joan Collins was there with her sister, Jackie. There were ways of skirting round the edges of the law and, so far, Patrick had found most of them: favors doled out and favours returned; backhanders in brown envelopes; girls who didn't care what you did as long as you didn't kiss them on the mouth. Diane, I heard, had walked out on Patrick; reconciled, Patrick had walked out on her. Now they were back together again, but for how long?

When I came off duty, she was parked across the street, smoking a cigarette, window wound down.

"Give you a lift?"

I'd moved up market but not by much, an upper floor flat in an already ageing mansion block between Chalk Farm and Belsize Park. A photograph of the great drummer, Max Roach, was on the wall; Sillitoe's *Saturday Night and Sunday Morning* next to the Eric Amblers and a few Graham Greenes on the shelf; an Alex Welsh album on the record player, ready to remind me of better times.

"So, how are things?" Diane asked, doing her best to look as if she cared.

"Could be worse," I said. In the kitchen, I set the kettle to boil and she stood too close while I spooned Nescafé into a pair of china mugs. There was something beneath the scent of her perfume that I remembered too well.

"What does he want?" I asked.

"Who?"

"Patrick, who else?"

She paused from stirring sugar into her coffee. "Is that what it has to be?"

"Probably."

"What if I just wanted to see you for myself?"

The green in her eye was bright under the unshaded kitchen light. "I wouldn't let myself believe it," I said.

She stepped into my arms and my arms moved around her as if they had a mind of their own. She kissed me and I kissed her back. I'd like to say I pushed her away after that and we sat and drank our coffee like two adults, talked about old times and what she was going to do with her life after the divorce. She was divorcing him, she said: she didn't know why she hadn't done it before.

"He'll let you go?"

"He'll let me go."

For a moment, she couldn't hold my gaze. "There's just one thing," she said, "one thing that he wants. This new club of his, someone's trying to have his licence cancelled."

"Someone?"

"Serving drinks after hours, an allegation, nothing more."

"He can't make it go away?"

Diane shook her head. "He's tried."

I looked at her. "And that's all?"

"One of the officers, he's accused Patrick of offering him a bribe. It was all a misunderstanding, of course."

"Of course."

"Patrick wonders if you'd talk to him, the officer concerned."

"Straighten things out."

"Yes."

"Make him see the error of his ways."

"Look, Jimmy," she said, touching the back of her hand to my cheek, "you know I hate doing this, don't you?"

No, I thought. No, I don't.

"Everything has a price," I said. "Even friendship. Friendship, especially. And tell Patrick, next time he wants something, to come and ask me himself."

"He's afraid you'd turn him down."

"He's right."

When she lifted her face to mine I turned my head aside. "Don't let your coffee get cold," I said.

Five minutes later she was gone. I sorted out Patrick's little problem for him and found a way of letting him know if he stepped out of line again, I'd personally do my best to close him down. Whether either of us believed it, I was never sure. With or without my help, he went from rich to richer; Diane slipped off my radar and when she re-emerged, she was somewhere in Europe, nursing Val after his most recent spell in hospital, encouraging him to get back into playing. Later they got married, or at least that's what I heard. Some lives took unexpected turns. Not mine.

*   *   *

I stayed on in the Met for three years after my thirty and then retired; tried working for a couple of security firms, but somehow it never felt right. With my pension and the little I'd squirreled away, I found I could manage pretty well without having to look for anything too regular. There was an investigation agency I did a little work for once in a while, nothing too serious, nothing heavy, and that was enough.

Patrick I bumped into occasionally if I went up west, greyer, more distinguished, handsomer than ever; in Soho once, close to the little Italian place where I'd spotted Diane with her bruised eye, he slid a hand into my pocket and when I felt where it had been there were two fifties, crisp and new.

"What's this for?" I asked.

"You look as though you need it," he said.

I threw the money back in his face and punched him in the mouth. Two of his minders had me spread-eagled on the pavement before he'd wiped the mean line of blood from his chin.

At Val's funeral we barely spoke; acknowledged each other but little more. Diane looked gaunt and beautiful in black, a face like alabaster, tears I liked to think were real. A band played *Just Friends*, with a break of thirty-two bars in the middle where Val's solo would have been. There was a wake at one of Patrick's clubs afterwards, a free bar, and most of mourners went on there, but I just went home and sat in my chair and thought about the three of us, Val, Patrick and myself, what forty years had brought us to, what we'd wanted then, what we'd done.

I scarcely thought about Diane at all.

Jack Kiley, that's the investigator I was working for, kept throwing bits and pieces my way, nothing strenuous like I say, the occasional tail job, little more. I went into his office one day, a couple of rooms above a bookstore in Belsize Park, and there she sat, Diane, in the easy chair alongside his desk.

"I believe you two know each other," Jack said.

Once I'd got over the raw surprise of seeing her, what took some adjusting to was how much she'd changed. I suppose I'd never imagined her growing old. But she had. Under her grey wool suit her body was noticeably thicker; her face was fuller, puffed and cross-hatched around the eyes, lined around the mouth. No Botox; no nip and tuck.

"Hello, Jimmy," she said.

"Diane's got a little problem," Jack said. "She thinks you can make it go away." He pushed back from his desk. "I'll leave you two to talk about it."

The problem was a shipment of cocaine that should have made its way seamlessly from the Netherlands to Dublin via the UK. A street value of a quarter of a million pounds. Customs and Excise, working on a tip-off, had seized the drug on arrival, a clean bust marred only by the fact the coke had been doctored down to a mockery of its original strength; a double shot espresso from Caffè Nero would deliver as much of a charge to the system.

"How in God's name," I asked, "did you get involved in this?"

Diane lit a cigarette and wafted the smoke away from her face. "After Val died I went back to Amsterdam, it's where we'd been living before he died. There was this guy – he'd been Val's supplier . . ."

"I thought Val had gone straight," I said.

"There was this guy," Diane said again, "we – well, we got sort of close. It was a bad time for me. I needed . . ." She glanced across and shook her head. "A girl's got to live, Jimmy. All Val had left behind was debts. This guy, he offered me a roof over my head. But there was a price."

"I'll bet." Even I was surprised how bitter that sounded.

"People he did business with, he wanted me to speak for him, take meetings. I used to fly to Belfast, then, after a while, it was Dublin."

"You were a courier." I said. "A mule."

"No. I never carried the stuff myself. Once the deal was set up, I'd arrange shipments, make sure things ran smoothly."

"Patrick would be proud of you," I said.

"Leave Patrick out of this," she said. "This has nothing to do with him."

I levered myself up out of the seat; it wasn't as easy as it used to be. "Nor me." I got as far as the door.

"They think I double-crossed them," Diane said. "They think it was me tipped off Customs; they think I cut the coke and kept back the rest so I could sell it myself."

"And did you?"

She didn't blink. "These people, Jimmy, they'll kill me. To make an example. I have to convince them it wasn't me; let them have back what they think's their due."

"A little difficult if you didn't take it in the first place."

"Will you help me, Jimmy, yes or no?"

"Your pal in Amsterdam, what's wrong with him?"

"He says it's my mess and I have to get myself out of it."

"Nice guy."

She leaned towards me, trying for a look that once would have held me transfixed. "Jimmy, I'm asking. For old time's sake."

"Which old time is that, Diane?"

She smiled. "The first time you met me, Jimmy, you remember that? Leicester Square?"

Like yesterday, I thought.

"You ever think about that? You ever think what I would have been like if we'd been together? Really together?"

I shook my head.

"We don't always make the right choices," she said.

"Get somebody else to help you," I said.

"I don't want somebody else."

"Diane, look at me for fuck's sake. What can I do? I'm an old man."

"You're not old. What are you? Sixty-odd? These days sixty's not old. Seventy-five. Eighty. That's old."

"Tell that to my body, Diane. I'm carrying at least a stone more than I ought to; the tendon at the back of my left ankle gives me gyp if ever I run for a bus and my right hip hurts like hell whenever I climb a flight of stairs. Find someone else, anyone."

"There's nobody else I can trust."

I talked to Jack Kiley about it later; we were sitting in the Starbucks across the street, sunshine doing its wan best to shine through the clouds.

"What do you know about these types?" Jack asked. "This new bunch of cocaine cowboys from over the old Irish Sea?"

"Sod all," I said.

"Well, let me give you a bit of background. Ireland has the third highest cocaine use in Europe and there's fifteen or twenty gangs and upwards beating the bollocks off one another to supply it. Some of them, the more established, have got links with the IRA, or did have, but it's the newer boys that take the pippin. Use the stuff themselves, jack up an Uzi or two and go shooting; a dozen murders in Dublin so far this year and most of the leaves still on the fucking trees."

"That's Dublin," I said.

Jack cracked a smile. "And you think this old flame of yours'll be safe here in Belsize Park or back home in Amsterdam?"

I shrugged. I didn't know what to bloody think.

He leaned closer. "Just a few months back, a drug smuggler from Cork got into a thing with one of the Dublin gangs – a disagreement about some shipment bought and paid for. He thought he'd lay low till it blew over. Took a false name and passport and holed up in an apartment in the Algarve. They found his body in the freezer. Minus the head. Rumour is whoever carried out the contract on him had it shipped back as proof."

Something was burning deep in my gut and I didn't think a couple of antacid tablets was going to set it right.

"You want my advice, Jimmy?" he said, and gave it anyway. "Steer clear. Either that or get in touch with some of your old pals in the Met. Let them handle it."

Do that, I thought, and there's no way of keeping Diane out of it; somehow I didn't fancy seeing her next when she was locked away on remand.

"I don't suppose you fancy giving a hand?" I said.

Jack was still laughing as he crossed the street back towards his office.

At least I didn't have to travel far, just a couple of stops on the Northern Line. Diane had told me where to find them and given me their names. There was some kind of ceilidh band playing in the main bar, the sound of the bodhran tracing my footsteps up the stairs. And, yes, my hip did ache.

The McMahon brothers were sitting at either end of a leather sofa that had seen better days, and Chris Boyle was standing with his back to a barred window facing down on to the street. Hip-hop was playing from a portable stereo at one side of the room, almost drowning out the traditional music from below.

No one could accuse these boys of not keeping up with the times.

There was an almost full bottle of Bushmills and some glasses on the desk, but I didn't think anyone was about to ask me if I wanted a drink.

One of the McMahon brothers giggled when I stepped into the room and I could see the chemical glow in his eyes. "What the fuck you doin' here, old man?" the other one said. "You should be tucked up in the old folks' home with your fuckin' Ovaltine."

"Two minutes," Chris Boyle said. "Say what you have to fuckin' say then get out."

"Supposin' we let you," one of the brothers said and giggled some more. Neither of them looked a whole lot more than nineteen, twenty tops. Boyle was closer to thirty, nearing pensionable age where that crew was concerned. According to Jack, there was a rumour he wore a colostomy bag on account of getting shot in the kidneys coming out from the rugby at Lansdown Road.

"First," I said, "Diane knew nothing about either the doctoring of the shipment, nor the fact it was intercepted. You have to believe that."

Boyle stared back at me, hard-faced.

One of the McMahons laughed.

"Second, though she was in no way responsible, as a gesture of good faith, she's willing to hand over a quantity of cocaine, guaranteed at least eighty percent pure, the amount equal to the original shipment. After that it's all quits, an even playing field, business as before."

Boyle glanced across at the sofa then nodded agreement.

"We pick the point and time of delivery," I said. "Two days time. I'll need a number on which I can reach you."

Boyle wrote his mobile number on a scrap of paper and passed it across. "Now get the fuck out," he said.

Down below, someone was playing a penny whistle, high-pitched and shrill. I could feel my pulse racing haphazardly and when I managed to get myself across the street, I had to take a grip on a railing and hold fast until my legs had stopped shaking.

★   ★   ★

When Jack learned I was going through with it, he offered to
lend me a gun, a Smith & Wesson .38, but I declined. There was
more chance of shooting myself in the foot than anything else.

I met Diane in the parking area behind Jack's office, barely
light enough to make out the color of her eyes. The cocaine was
bubble-wrapped inside a blue canvas bag.

"You always were good to me, Jimmy," she said, and reaching up, she kissed me on the mouth. "Will I see you afterwards?"

"No," I said. "No, you won't."

The shadows swallowed her as she walked towards the taxi
waiting out on the street. I dropped the bag down beside the
rear seat of the car, waited several minutes, then slipped the
engine into gear.

The place I'd chosen was on Hampstead Heath, a makeshift
soccer pitch shielded by lines of trees, a ramshackle wooden
building off to one side, open to the weather; sometimes pickup
teams used it to get changed, or kids huddled there to feel one
another up, smoke spliffs or sniff glue.

When Patrick, Val and I had been kids ourselves there was a
murdered body found close by and the place took on a kind of
awe for us, murder in those days being something more rare.

I'd left my car by a mansion block on Heath Road and walked
in along a partly overgrown track. The moon was playing fast
and loose with the clouds and the stars seemed almost as distant
as they were. An earlier shower of rain had made the surface a
little slippy and mud clung to the soles of my shoes. There was
movement, low in the undergrowth to my right hand side, and,
for a moment, my heart stopped as an owl broke, with a fell
swoop, through the trees above my head.

A dog barked and then was still.

I stepped off the path and into the clearing, the weight of the
bag real in my left hand. I was perhaps a third of the way across
the pitch before I saw them, three or four shapes massed near
the hut at the far side and separating as I drew closer, fanning
out. Four of them, faces unclear, but Boyle, I thought, at the
centre, the McMahons to one side of him, another I didn't
recognize hanging back. Behind them, behind the hut, the trees
were broad and tall and close together, beeches I seemed to
remember Val telling me once when I'd claimed them as oaks.

"Beeches, for God's sake," he'd said, laughing in that soft way of his. "You, Jimmy, you don't know your arse from your elbow, it's a fact."

I stopped fifteen feet away and Boyle took a step forward. "You came alone," he said.

"That was the deal."

"He's stupider than I fuckin' thought," said one or other of the McMahons and laughed a girlish little laugh.

"The stuff's all there?" Boyle said, nodding towards the bag.

I walked a few more paces towards him, set the bag on the ground, and stepped back.

Boyle angled his head towards the McMahons and one of them went to the bag and pulled it open, slipping a knife from his pocket as he did so; he slit open the package, and, standing straight again, tasted the drug from the blade.

"Well?" Boyle said.

McMahon finished running his tongue around his teeth. "It's good," he said.

"Then we're set," I said to Boyle.

"Set?"

"We're done here."

"Oh, yes, we're done."

The man to Boyle's left, the one I didn't know, moved forward almost to his shoulder, letting his long coat fall open as he did so, and what light there was glinted dully off the barrels of the shotgun as he brought it to bear. It was almost level when a shot from the trees behind struck him high in the shoulder and spun him round so that the second shot tore through his neck and he fell to the ground as good as dead.

One of the McMahons cursed and started to run, while the other dropped to one knee and fumbled for the revolver inside his zip-up jacket.

With all the gunfire and the shouting I couldn't hear the words from Boyle's mouth, but I could lip read well enough. "You're dead," he said, and drew a pistol not much bigger than a child's hand from his side pocket and raised it towards my head. It was either bravery or stupidity or maybe fear that made me charge at him, unarmed, hands outstretched as if in some way to ward off the bullet; it was the muddied turf that made my feet slide away under me and sent me sprawling headlong, the two shots Boyle got off sailing over my head before one of the men I'd last seen minding Patrick in Soho stepped up neatly behind Boyle, put the muzzle of a 9mm Beretta hard behind his ear and squeezed the trigger.

Both the McMahons had gone down without me noticing; one was already dead and the other had blood gurgling out of his airway and was not long for this world.

Patrick was standing back on the path, scraping flecks of mud from the edges of his soft leather shoes with a piece of stick. "Look at the state of you," he said. "You look a fucking state. If I were you I should burn that lot when you get home, start again."

I wiped the worst of the mess from the front of my coat and that was when I realized my hands were still shaking. "Thanks, Pat," I said.

"What are friends for?" he said.

Behind us his men were tidying up the scene a little, not too much. The later editions of the papers would be full of stories of how the Irish drug wars had come to London, the Celtic Tigers fighting it out on foreign soil.

"You need a lift?" Patrick asked, as we made our way back towards the road.

"No, thanks. I'm fine."

"Thank Christ for that. Last thing I need, mud all over the inside of the fucking car."

When I got back to the flat I put one of Val's last recordings on the stereo, a session he'd made in Stockholm a few months before he died. Once or twice his fingers didn't match his imagination, and his breathing seemed to be giving him trouble, but his mind was clear. Beeches, I'll always remember that now, that part of the Heath. Beeches, not oaks.

SAY THAT AGAIN

Peter Lovesey

We called him the Brigadier with the buggered ear. Just looking at it made you wince. Really he should have had the bits surgically removed. He claimed it was an old war wound. However, Sadie the Lady, another of our residents, told us it wasn't true. She said she'd talked to the Brig's son Arnold, who reckoned his old man got blind drunk in Aldershot one night and tripped over a police dog and paid for it with his shell-like.

Because of his handicap, the Brigadier tended to shout. His "good" ear wasn't up to much, even with the aid stuck in it. We got used to the shouting, we old farts in the Never-Say-Die Retirement Home. After all, most of us are hard of hearing as well. No doubt we were guilty of letting him bluster and bellow without interruption. We never dreamed at the time that our compliance would get us into the High Court on a murder rap.

It was set in motion by She-Who-Must-Be-Replaced, our so-called matron, pinning a new leaflet on the notice board in the hall.

"Infernal cheek!" the Brig boomed. "They're parasites, these people, living off the frail and weak-minded."

"Who are you calling weak-minded?" Sadie the Lady piped up. "There's nothing wrong with my brain."

The Brig didn't hear. Sometimes it can be a blessing.

"Listen to this," he bellowed, as if we had any choice. "'Are you dissatisfied with your hearing? Struggling with a faulty instrument? Picking up unwanted background noise? Marcus Haliburton, a renowned expert on the amazing new digital hearing aids, will be in attendance all day at the Bay Tree Hotel on Thursday, 8 April for free consultations. Call this number now for an appointment. No obligation.' No obligation, my arse – forgive me, ladies. You know what happens? They get you in there and tell you to take out your National Health aid so they can poke one of those little torches in your ear and of course you're stuffed. You can't hear a thing they're saying from that moment on. The next thing is they shove a form in front of you and you find you've signed an order for a thousand-pound replacement. If you object they drop your NHS aid on the floor and tread on it."

"That can't be correct," Miss Martindale said.

"Completely wrecked, yes," the Brigadier said. "Are you speaking from personal experience, my dear? Because I am."

Someone put up a hand. He wanted to be helped to the toilet, but the Brigadier took it as support. "Good man. What we should do is teach these blighters a lesson. We could, you know, with my officer training and George's underworld experience."

I smiled faintly. My underworld links were nil, another of the Brig's misunderstandings. One afternoon I'd been talking to Sadie about cats and happened to mention that we once adopted a stray. I thought the Brig was dozing in his armchair, but he came to life and said, "Which of the Krays was that – Reggie or Ronnie? I had no idea of your criminal past, George. We'll have to watch you in future."

It was hopeless trying to disillusion him, so I settled for my gangster reputation and some of the old ladies began to believe it, too, and found me more interesting than ever they'd supposed.

By the next tea break, the Brigadier had turned puce with excitement. "I've mapped it out," he told us. "I'm calling it Operation Syringe, because we're going to clean these ruffians out. Basically, the object of the plan is to get a new super-digital hearing aid for everyone in this home free of charge."

"How the heck will you do that?" Sadie asked.

"What?"

She stepped closer and spoke into his ear. "They're a private company. Those aids cost a fortune."

The Brig grinned. "Simple. We intercept their supplies. I happen to know the Bay Tree Hotel quite well."

Sadie said to the rest of us, "That's a fact. The Legion has its meetings there. He's round there every Friday night for his g&t."

"G&T or two or three," another old lady said.

I said, "Wait a minute, Brigadier. We can't steal a bunch of hearing aids." I have a carrying voice when necessary and he heard every word.

"'Steal' is not a term in the military lexicon, dear boy," he said. "We requisition them." He leaned forward. "Now, the operation has three phases. Number One: Observation. I'll take care of that. Number Two: Liaison. This means getting in touch with an inside man, Cormac, the barman. I can do that also. Number Three: Action. And that depends on what we learn from Phases One and Two. That's where the rest of you come in. Are you with me?"

"I don't know what he's on about," Sadie said to me.

"Don't worry," I said. "He's playing soldiers, that's all. He'll find out it's a non-starter."

"No muttering in the ranks," the Brigadier said. "Any dissenters? Fall out, the dissenters."

No one moved. Some of us needed help to move anywhere and nobody left the room when tea and biscuits were on offer. And that was how we were recruited into the snatch squad.

On Saturday, the Brigadier reported on Phases One and Two of his battle plan. He marched into the tea room looking as chipper as Montgomery on the eve of El Alamein.

"Well, the obbo phase is over and so is the liaison and I'm able to report some fascinating results. The gentleman who wants us all to troop along to the Bay Tree Hotel and buy his miraculous hearing aids is clearly doing rather well out of it. He drives a vintage Bentley and wears a different suit each visit and by the cut of them they're not off the peg."

"There's money in ripping off old people," Sadie said.

"It ought to be stopped," her friend Briony said.

The Brig went on, "I talked to my contact last night and I'm pleased to tell you that the enemy – that is to say Marcus

Haliburton – works to a predictable routine. He puts in a fortnightly appearance at the Bay Tree. If you go along and see him you'll find Session One is devoted to the consultation and the placing of the order. Session Two is the fitting and payment. Between Sessions One and Two a box is delivered to the hotel and it contains up to fifty new hearing aids – more than enough for our needs." He paused and looked around the room. "So what do you think is the plan?"

No one was willing to say. Some might have thought speaking up would incriminate them. Others weren't capable of being heard by the Brigadier. Finally I said, "We, em, requisition the box?"

"Ha!" He lifted a finger. "I thought you'd say that. We can do better. What we do is requisition the box."

There were smiles all round at my expense.

"And then," the Brigadier said, "we replace the box with one just like it."

"That's neat," Sadie said. She was beginning to warm to the Brigadier's criminal scheme.

He'd misheard her again. "It may sound like deceit to you, madam, but to some of us it's common justice. They called Robin Hood a thief."

"Are we going to be issued with bows and arrows?" Sadie said.

"I wouldn't mind meeting some merry men," Briony said.

The Brigadier's next move took us all by surprise. "Check the corridor, George. Make sure no staff are about."

I did as I was told and gave the thumb-up sign, whereupon the old boy bent down behind the sideboard and dragged out a flattened cardboard box that he rapidly restored to its normal shape.

"Thanks to my contacts at the hotel I've managed to retrieve the box that was used to deliver this week's aids." No question: he intended to go through with this crazy adventure. In the best officer tradition he started to delegate duties. "George, your job will be to get this packed and sealed and looking as if it just arrived by courier."

"No problem," I said to indulge him. I was sure the plan would break down before I had to do anything.

"That isn't so simple as it sounds," he said. "Take a close look. The aids are made in South Africa, so there are various customs forms attached to the box. They stuff them in a kind of envelope and stick them to the outside. What you do is update this week's documents."

"I'll see what I can manage."

"Then you must consider the contents. The instruments don't weigh much, and they're wrapped in bubblewrap, so the whole thing is almost as light as air. Whatever you put inside must not arouse suspicion."

"Crumpled-up newspaper," Sadie said.

"What did she say?"

I repeated it for his benefit.

Sadie said, "Briony has a stack of *Daily Mails* this high in her room. She hoards everything."

I knew that to be true. Briony kept every postcard, every letter, every magazine. Her room was a treasure house of things other people discarded. She even collected the tiny jars our breakfast marmalade came in. The only question was whether she would donate her newspaper collection to Operation Syringe. She could be fiercely possessive at times.

"I might be able to spare you some of the leaflets that come with my post," she said.

Sadie said, "Junk mail. That'll do."

"It doesn't incriminate me, does it?" she said. "I want no part of this silly escapade."

"Excellent," the Brigadier said, oblivious. "When the parcel is up to inspection standard, I'll tell you about the next phase."

The heat was now on me. I had to smuggle the box back to my room and start work. I was once employed as a graphic designer, so the forging of the forms wasn't a big problem. Getting Briony to part with her junk mail was far more demanding. You'd think it was bank notes. She checked everything and allowed me about one sheet in five. But in the end I had enough to stuff the box. I sealed it with packing tape I found in Matron's office and showed it to the Brigadier.

"Capital," he said. "We can proceed to phase four: distracting the enemy."

"How do we do that?"

"We inundate Marcus Haliburton with requests for appointments under bogus names."

"That's fun. I'll tell the others."

Even at this stage, it was still a game, as I tried to explain later to the police. Some of us had mobiles and others used the payphone by the front door. I think a couple of bold souls used the phone in Matron's office. I don't know if we succeeded in distracting Haliburton. He must have been surprised by the number of Smiths, Browns, Jones and Robinsons who had seen his publicity. The greedy beggar didn't turn any away.

And so the day of the heist arrived. Almost everyone from the Never-Say-Die had been talked into joining in and clambered onto the bus the Brigadier had laid on. Half of them were so confused most of the time that you could have talked them into running the London Marathon. The notable exception was Briony. She wanted no part of it. She stayed put, guarding her hoard of newspapers and marmalade jars. The Brigadier called her a ruddy conchie when he found out.

In their defence, few of them knew the finer points of the battle plan. But they still amounted to a formidable squad as they alighted from the bus and listened to the Brigadier's Agincourt-style speech.

"There are senior citizens all over Britain who will think themselves accursed they were not here with us. We few, we happy few, deaf but not downtrodden, stand on the brink of victory. Onward, then."

So began the main assault, as the Brigadier called it. Four old ladies crossed the hotel foyer Zimmer to Zimmer, a vanguard forging a route for the main party, twelve more on sticks and crutches, with two motorised chairs like tanks in the rear. Inexorably they headed for the suite used by Marcus Haliburton for his consultations. Their task: to block all movement in the corridor.

Because of my supposed underworld connections I had been selected for a kind of SAS role, along with the Brigadier himself. At some time in the first hour, while all the new patients were being documented, tested and examined, a security firm would deliver the latest box of hearing aids to the hotel. One of the staff was then supposed to bring it to the suite for Haliburton to begin handing out the aids to people who had placed orders on his previous visit. Thanks to the congestion in the corridor this would not be possible.

The next part was clever, I must admit. The Brigadier had booked the room two doors up and he and I were waiting in there with our own box filled with crumpled-up junk mail. The porter was bound to come past with the box containing the expensive digital aids.

We waited three-quarters of an hour and it was a nervous time. I had my doubts whether two elderly gents were capable of intercepting a burly hotel porter, but the Brigadier was confident.

"We're not using brute strength. This is our strength." He tapped his head.

"But if it doesn't work?"

To my horror he took a gun from his pocket and gave a crocodile grin. "My old service revolver."

"That would be armed robbery," I said, aghast. "Don't even think of it."

He misheard me, of course. From another pocket he produced a flask of brandy. "You need to drink a bit? Take a swig, old boy. It stops the shakes, I find."

Before I could get through to him I heard the squeak of a trolley wheel in the corridor outside. The moment of decision. Should I abort the whole operation? Unwisely, disastrously as it turned out, I decided to go on with it. I stepped into the corridor, right in the path of the trolley, and said to the porter pushing it, "Mr Haliburton said to lock the parcel in here for the time being. He'll collect it when the people waiting have been dealt with."

He said, "I can't do that. I'm under firm instructions to hand it to Mr Haliburton in person."

I winked and said, "I work with him. It's as good as done." I pressed a five-pound note into his sweaty palm.

Persuaded, he wheeled the parcel into the room and left it just inside the door. The Brigadier meanwhile had stepped out of sight into the bathroom. The porter had the impression he was locking the parcel in an empty room. The idea was that the Brigadier would then emerge from the bathroom with our box of junk mail and make the switch, returning to the bathroom with the box containing the aids, where he would lock himself in for an hour.

My job was to shepherd the Never-Say-Die residents as quickly as possible out of the corridor and back to the bus. I was starting to do so when a man in a grey pinstripe suit came marching up and said, "What's the trouble here? I'm Buckfield, the hotel manager."

"No trouble, Mr Buckfield," I said. "The system can't cope, that's all. Some of these old people have been waiting an hour for an appointment with the ear specialist. I'm suggesting they come back next time. We've got transport outside."

He looked at me with some uncertainty. "Are you their warden?"

"Something like that."

"One of the bellboys tells me he delivered a box of valuable hearing aids to Room 104. Was that at your bidding?"

I said, "Yes. I think you'll find it's still there."

He had a pass key and opened the door and picked up the parcel that was waiting there. I gave all my attention to ushering the old ladies towards the foyer and the waiting bus. Most of them were pleased to leave and didn't understand what we had achieved. A few genuine customers for the hearing aids were just as confused, and when we got to the bus I had difficulty persuading two of them that they weren't in the Never-Say-Die party.

Finally everyone except the Brigadier was on board. It was my job to see that all was clear and help him out of Room 104 with the parcel we had requisitioned, the most dangerous part of Operation Syringe.

Trying to look like any other guest, I crossed the foyer and stepped along the corridor. It was now empty of people. I tapped on the door of 104 and immediately realized that there was a fatal flaw in our plan. How would the Brigadier hear my knocking? I tried a second time.

No response.

Along the corridor, the door of Haliburton's suite opened and an old man came out. I tried to ignore him, but he said, "Are you waiting for a consultation? It's that room I just came out of."

I thanked him, but I don't think he heard. I took off a shoe and tried hammering on 104 with it.

At last the door opened and there was the Brigadier with the parcel in his arms. For the first time since I'd known him he looked concerned. "Take this to the bus and tell the driver to put his foot down."

"Aren't you coming?" I said.

"Cunning? Far from it," he said. "I'm a silly arse. Left my service revolver on the bed and some beggar in a pinstripe picked it up."

"Leave it," I shouted into his ear. "Come with me."

"Can't do that," he said and made a little speech straight out of one of those war films when the doomed Brit showed his stiff upper lip. "That revolver is my baby. Been with me all over the world. I'm not surrendering, old boy. I'll get back to base. See if I don't."

I said, "I'm leaving with a heavy heart."

He said, "Don't be so vulgar."

No use trying to talk sense into him. He really had need of a decent hearing aid.

I carried the parcel to the bus. Everyone cheered when they saw it. Then Sadie said, "Where's the Brigadier?"

I didn't want them to know he'd brought a gun with him, so I said he was hiding up until it was safer to leave.

The bus took us back to the home and we tottered off to our rooms for a nap after all the excitement. We'd agreed not to open the box before the Brig returned.

All evening we waited, asking each other if anyone had heard anything. I was up until ten-thirty, long past bedtime. In the end I turned in and tried to sleep.

Some time after midnight there was a noise like a stone being thrown at my window. I got out of bed and looked down. There in the grounds was the Brigadier blowing on his fingers. He shouted up to me, "Be a good fellow and unbolt the front door will you? I just met a brass monkey on his way to the welder's."

In twenty minutes every inhabitant of the house except the Matron and her two night staff assembled in the tea room. The nightwear on display is another story.

"Open it, George," the Brig ordered.

They watched in eager anticipation. Even Briony had turned out. "Ooh, bubblewrap," she said. "May I have that?"

"You might as well, because you're not getting a hearing aid, you conchie," the Brigadier said.

I unwrapped the first aid. It was a BTE (behind the ear), but elegance itself. I offered it to the Brigadier. He slotted it into his ear. "God Lord!" he said. "I can hear the clock ticking."

Everyone in the room who wanted a replacement aid was given one, and we still had a few over. The morale of the troops couldn't have been higher. Even Briony was happy with her stack of bubblewrap. We all slept well.

At breakfast, the results were amazing. People who hadn't conversed for years were chatting animatedly.

Then the doorbell chimed. The chime of doom. A policeman with a megaphone stood in the doorway and announced, "Police. We're coming in. Put your hands above your heads and stay where you are."

Sadie said, "You don't have to shout, young man. We can all hear you."

We were taken in barred vans to the police station and kept in cells. Because there was a shortage of cells some of us had to double up and I found myself locked up with the Brigadier.

"This is overkill," I said. "We're harmless old people."

"They don't think so, George," he said in a sombre tone. "Marcus Haliburton was shot dead in the course of the raid."

"Shot? I didn't hear any shots."

"After you left, it got nasty. They'll have me for murder and the rest of you for conspiracy to murder. We can't expect all our troops to hold out under questioning. They'll put up their hands, and we're all done."

He was right. Several old ladies confessed straight away. What can you expect? The trial that followed was swift and savage. The Brigadier asked to be tried by a court martial and refused to plead. He went down for life, with a recommendation that he serve at least ten years. They proved that the fatal shots had been fired from his gun.

I got three years for conspiracy to murder – in spite of claiming I didn't know about the gun. Sadie was given six months. The Crown Prosecution Service didn't press charges against some of the really frail ones. Oddly, nobody seemed interested in the hearing aid heist and we were allowed to keep our stolen property.

The Never-Say-Die Retirement Home had to carry on without us. But there was to be one last squirt from Operation Syringe.

One morning three weeks after the trial Briony decided to sort out her marmalade jars and store them better, using the bubblewrap the aids had been kept in. She was surrounding one of the jars with the stuff when there was a sudden popping sound. One of the little bubbles had burst under pressure. She pressed another and it made a satisfying sound. Highly amused, she started popping every one. She continued at this harmless pastime for over an hour. After tea break she went back and popped some more. It was all enormous fun until she damaged her fingernail and had to ask She-Who-Must-Be-Replaced to trim it.

"How did you do that?" Matron asked.

Briony showed her.

"Well, no wonder. There's something hard inside the bubble. I do believe it's glass. How wicked."

But it didn't turn out to be glass. It was an uncut diamond, and there were others secreted in the bubblewrap. A second police investigation was mounted into Operation Syringe. As a result, Buckfield, the manager of the Bay Tree Hotel, was arrested.

It seemed he had been working a racket with Marcus Haliburton, importing uncut diamonds stolen by workers in a South African diamond mine. The little rocks had been smuggled to Britain in the packing used for the hearing aids. Interpol took over the investigation on two continents.

It turned out that on the day of our heist Buckfield the manager suspected something was afoot, and decided Haliburton might be double-crossing him. When he checked Room 104 he found the Brigadier's revolver on the bed and he was certain he was right. He took it straight to the suite. Haliburton denied everything and said he was only a go-between and offered to open the new box of aids in the manager's presence. We know what it contained. Incensed, Buckfield pointed the gun and shot Haliburton dead.

After our release, we had a meeting to decide if we would sue the police for wrongful imprisonment. The Brigadier was all for it, but Sadie said we might be pushing our luck. We had a vote and decided she was right.

The good thing is that every one of us heard each word of the debate. I can recommend these new digital aids to anyone.

CONTINUITY ERROR

Nicholas Royle

Christine rang Maddox on his mobile. A little accident, she said. A bump.

"Was anyone hurt?"

"No, no one was hurt."

He made his way to the side street in Shepherd's Bush where it had happened. A one-way street temporarily blocked off by roadworks at the junction with Goldhawk Road. Estate agent's on the corner. Christine had reversed away from the roadworks and at five miles an hour hit a silver Toyota coming out of the concealed exit from the sunken car park behind the estate agent's.

By the time Maddox arrived, the driver of the silver Toyota was in full magnanimous third-party mode, confident the insurance companies would find in his favour. Maddox hated him on sight. Too reasonable, too forthcoming. Like providing his address and insurance details was some kind of favour.

Maddox's son Jack had got out of the car and stood staring at the small pile of shattered glass on the road, seemingly transfixed by it. Christine was visibly upset, despite the unctuous affability of the Toyota driver and Maddox's own efforts to downplay the situation.

"It's only a couple of lights and a new wing. No one was hurt, that's the main thing."

Two days later, Maddox and Jack were walking past the top of the side street. The roadworks had been removed and a car was exiting into Goldhawk Road without any difficulty.

"Is that where the accident happened, Daddy?" asked the little boy.

"Yes."

Jack stopped, his big eyes taking in the details. The fresh asphalt by the junction, the concealed exit from the sunken car park behind the estate agent's.

"Is it still there?" the little boy asked.

"What? Is what still there?"

"The accident. Is the accident still there?"

Maddox didn't know what to say.

They were getting ready to go out. Christine was ready and Maddox was nearly ready, a too-familiar scenario. She waited by the front door, smart, made-up, tall in new boots and long coat, enveloped in a haze of expensive perfume.

"Are you nearly ready, Brian?"

That she added his name to the harmless query was a bad sign. It meant her patience was stretched too thin. But he'd lost his car key. He'd looked everywhere. Twice. And couldn't find it.

"Where did you last have it?" she shouted up the stairs.

The unhelpfulness of the question grated against his nerves.

"I don't know. That's the whole point."

He started again. Bedroom (bedside drawer, dressing gown). Jacket pockets. Kitchen.

"Have you looked in your box?"

"Yes, I've looked in my box."

They each had a box, like an in-tray, in the kitchen. Christine never used hers, but always knew where everything was. Maddox used his, but still managed to lose at least one important item every day. Wallet, phone, keys. Chequebook, bank card. Everything always turned up, sooner or later, but in this case, not soon enough.

"I can't find it. I've looked everywhere."

Heavy sigh.

If the atmosphere hadn't become tense he would jokingly accuse her of having hidden it, of trying to make him think he was losing his mind. But that wouldn't play now. They were beyond that.

"It's probably at the *flat*," she said, loading the word with her customary judgmental emphasis.

"How could it be at the flat when my car's outside?" he snapped before realizing that *she* must have been joking.

"It's a pity you don't have a spare key," she said.

"It's a pity your car's in the garage," he retorted, "about to be declared uneconomical to repair. Look, Christine, it's very late. I can't find it and I certainly won't find it with you hovering, getting all wound up, so I suggest you get a cab and I'll follow."

"But what if you don't find it?"

"I'll find it. I'll be there, just a little late, that's all. You go. You'll easily pick up a black cab on the Green. You're only going to Ladbroke Grove."

Sweating, he listened as the front door was opened and shut – slammed. Gate clanged. Fading echo of footsteps receding. He felt the tension flow out of him and collapsed on to the nearest chair. He loosened his tie and reached for a glass.

In their bedroom he pressed the power button on his laptop. While waiting, he stared blankly at the framed poster on the wall. A production he'd been in more than twenty years ago. *Colossus*. Clive Barker's play about Goya. He allowed the faces of cast members to run through his mind, particularly those who'd gone on to other things. Lennie James – you saw him on television all the time now. A part in *Cold Feet*. A one-off drama, something he'd written himself. That prison series. *Buried*. Right. Buried in the schedules.

Aslie Pitter, the most naturally talented actor in the cast. He'd done one or two things – a Channel Four sitcom, guest appearance in *The Bill* – then disappeared. Maddox had last seen him working for a high-street chain. Security, demonstrating product – he couldn't remember which.

Elinore Vickery had turned up in something at the Waterman's. Maddox had liked her, tried to keep in touch, but there was an invisible barrier, as if she'd known him better than he knew himself.

Missing out on a couple of good parts because of his size (five foot five in stocking feet, eight stone dead), Maddox had quit the theatre and concentrated on writing. Barker had helped with one or two contacts and Maddox sold a couple of horror stories. Over the years he'd moved away from fiction into journalism and book-length non-fiction. The current project, *New Maps of Hell*, hadn't found a home. The publishers he'd offered it to hadn't been able to reject it quickly enough. They didn't want it on their desks. It made them uncomfortable. That was fine by Maddox. He'd worry if it didn't. They'd want it on their lists, though, when it was too late. He'd finish it first, then pick one editor and let the others write their letters of resignation.

He read through the afternoon's work, then closed the laptop. He opened his bedside drawer and there was his car key. He looked at it. Had it been there before? Of course it had. How could it not have been? But he'd not seen it, so it might as well not have been. It had effectively disappeared. Hysterical blindness? Negative hallucination?

He pocketed the key and went downstairs. The door closed behind him and the car started first time. He sneaked past White City – the exhibition halls were gone, torn down for a future shopping centre – and slipped on to the Westway. He didn't think of Christine as he approached Ladbroke Grove, but of Christie, John Reginald Halliday. The former relief projectionist at the Electric, who had murdered at least six women, had lived at 10 Rillington Place, later renamed Ruston Close before being demolished to make way for the elevated motorway on which Maddox was now driving. The film, starring Dickie Attenborough as the killer and John Hurt as his poor dupe of an upstairs neighbour, who swung for at least one of Christie's crimes, had been filmed in Rillington Place itself. Maddox understood, from comments posted on ghoulish message boards on the internet, that the interiors had been shot in No.8 and the exteriors outside No.10. But when the police, acting on a tip-off from Timothy Evans, yanked open a manhole cover outside No.10, Attenborough could be seen peering out through the ground-floor window of the end house in the terrace, No.10, where three of Christie's victims had been walled up in the pantry, his wife Ethel being found under the floorboards in the front room. For Maddox it was the key shot in the film, the only clear evidence that they'd gained access to the charnel house itself. The only other explanation being that they'd mocked up the entire street in the studio, which he didn't buy.

The case accounted for five pages in Maddox's book. He concentrated mainly on the interweaving of fact and fiction, the merging of film and reality. Attenborough as Christie. No.8 standing in for No.10, if indeed it did. The internet also yielded a piece of Pathé film footage of the demolition of Ruston Close. Two men with pickaxes. A third man speaking to camera. A burning house. Shots of the house at the end of the street with the white (replacement) door. Clearly the same house as that in the film. But there was no sound, the reporter mouthing inaudible commentary. Maddox lured a lip-reader to the flat, a junior editor from one of the publishers that had turned down his book. She reminded him of Linzi with her green eyes and shoulder-length streaked hair. Even in heels she didn't reach Maddox's height, but she had a confident, relaxed smile, She held his gaze when he spoke to her and appeared to be looking into his eyes, but must have been watching his lips, as she relied heavily on lip-reading.

Maddox was careful to make sure she was looking in his direction before speaking to her, probably over-careful. She must have spent a lifetime compensating for situations in which people wouldn't have made such allowances. Working backwards from the first words she managed to lip-read and then having to catch up. So much information assumed rather than known for certain, but Maddox could relate to that. In some areas of life he, too, knew nothing for certain. The deaf woman's name was Karen. He assumed the proposal for his book had been rejected by someone senior who had given Karen the unpleasant job of telling the author, but he didn't know *that* for certain. Possibly she'd read it and rejected it herself and only agreed to provide lip-reading services because she felt bad about it.

When she entered the flat, Maddox felt at ease. In control. He apologised for the loud, bass-heavy music coming from the downstairs flat, but she said she couldn't hear it.

"I thought you might be able to feel it," he said.

"It's a new building," she said. "Concrete floors. Otherwise . . ."

He showed her the footage. She said it wasn't straightforward. The quality was poor and the picture kept pixellating, plus the reporter unhelpfully turned his head to the side on several occasions.

Maddox asked her if she would come back and have another go if he was able to tidy the picture up a bit.

"I don't think I'll be able to get much off it for you," she said.

"If you wouldn't mind just trying one more time, perhaps when you're less tired," he said. "It's very important to me, for my book, you know."

Maddox pulled into one of the reserved spaces outside a block of purpose-built flats in the depressed residential trapezium bordered by Green Lanes and the roads of West Green, Seven Sisters and St Ann's. He listened to the ticking of the cooling engine for a few moments as he watched the darkened windows of the second-floor flat. The top flat.

The street door had been left open by one of his neighbours. He walked up.

Inside the flat, he left the light switched off, poured himself a drink and sat in the single armchair. He pulled out his phone and sent a short text message. Orange street-lighting cast a deathly glow over the cheap bookshelves stacked with pulp novels, true crime, horror anthologies and dystopian science fiction. His phone chimed. He opened it, read the return message and replied to it. When he'd lived here, the room had been dominated by a double bed. Moving into Christine's house had allowed him to turn the tiny flat into the dedicated office he'd always wanted by burning the bed on the waste ground out the back. He'd considered giving it away, since selling it had struck him as tiresome: placing an ad, answering calls, opening the door to strangers. Easier to burn the damn thing and all the memories associated with it. So then he'd moved his desk from the east end of the room, under the Velux window, to the west-facing windows overlooking the street.

Another text arrived. He read it and closed the phone without replying.

As usual, loud music was playing in the downstairs flat.

He drained his glass and let his head fall back against the soft cushion. The Artex ceiling had attracted cobwebs and grime, but he doubted he would ever feel the need to repaint or clean it. Very few people ever came here. Linzi had spent a lot of time in the flat, of course. He laughed bitterly, then chewed his lip and stared at the ceiling, sensitive to the slightest noise in spite of the thump of the bass from the downstairs flat. Christine had hardly stepped over the threshold. She'd been once or twice soon after they'd met, but not since. There was no reason to. It was clear from the odd comment that she resented his keeping the flat, since it was a drain on resources, but as he'd argued, there was no room in the house for all these books and tapes. Not to mention the stuff stored in the loft. He chewed his lip again.

He switched on the stereo and the ordered chaos of Paul Schütze's *New Maps of Hell* clattered into battle with the beat from below. Schütze's 1992 release was the constant soundtrack to any work he did on the book in the flat. (On the rare occasions that he worked on it at the house, he played the follow-up, *New Maps of Hell II: The Rapture of Metals*.) He believed it helped. *It started out as an aid to getting the mindset right,* he sometimes imagined telling Kirsty Wark or Verity Sharp in a television interview, *and soon became a habit, a routine. I simply couldn't work on the book without having the music playing in the background. It was about the creation of a hermetically sealed world. Which, I suppose you have to admit, Hell is. Although one that's expanding at an alarming rate, erupting in little pockets. North Kensington, Muswell Hill. London is going to Hell, Kirsty.*

He opened a file and did some work, tidied up some troublesome text. He saved it and opened another file, "Dollis Hill". Notes, a few stabs at an address, gaps, big gaps. He was going to have to go back.

He replayed the mental rushes. Autumn 1986. A fine day. Gusty, but dry, bright. Walking in an unfamiliar district of London. A long road, tree-lined. High up. View down over the city between detached houses and semis. Victorian, Edwardian.

The entry-phone buzzed, bringing him back to the present with a start. He closed the file. He got to his feet, crossed to the hall and picked up the phone.

"The door's open. Come up," he said, before realising she couldn't hear him.

He remained standing in the hall, listening to footsteps climbing the interior staircase. When the footsteps stopped outside his door there was a pause before the knock came.

He imagined her composing herself, perhaps straightening her clothes, removing a hair from her collar. Or looking at her watch and thinking of bolting. He opened the door as she knocked, which startled her.

"Come in," he said. "Thanks for coming."

All Maddox had done to improve the image on the video was change the size of the Media Player window so that the reporter's mouth, while slightly smaller, was less affected by picture break-up.

While Karen studied the footage, Maddox crossed to the far side of the room. He returned with a glass of red wine, which he placed beside the laptop. Karen raised a hand to decline, but Maddox simply pushed the glass slightly closer to her and left it there. Finally, while she was watching the footage for a third time, her hand reached out, perhaps involuntarily, to pick up the glass. She took a sip, then held the glass aloft while studying the image of the jaunty reporter: Michael Caine glasses, buttoned-up jacket, button-down shirt, hand alighting on hip like a butterfly.

Maddox watched as she replayed the footage again. Each time the reporter started speaking, she moved a little closer to the screen and seemed to angle her head slightly to the left in order to favour her right ear, in which she had a trace of hearing, despite the fact there was no sound at all on the film. Habit, Maddox decided.

Karen leaned back and looked at Maddox before speaking.

"He's saying something like *newspaper reports . . . of the investigation . . . into the discovery of the burned-out bodies of two women . . . Fifteen – or fifty – years ago . . . Something of the century.* I'm sorry, it's really hard."

Her speech was that of a person who had learned to talk the hard way, without being able to hear the sound of her own voice.

'That's great. That's very helpful, Karen. It would be fifteen, not fifty. I didn't even know for certain that he was talking about Christie's house. *Burned-out,* though, are you sure? That's strange."

"No, I'm not sure, but that's what it sounds like."

Karen's choice of expression – *sounds like* – reminded him of a blind man who had asked Maddox for help crossing the road as he was going to *see* the doctor.

Maddox went to fill up her glass, but she placed her hand over it.

"I've got to go," she said. "I said I could only stop by for a minute."

Maddox stood his ground with the wine bottle, then stepped back.

"Another time," he said.

"Have you got something else you want me to look at?"

"I might have. If it's not too much of an imposition."

"Just let me know."

He showed her out, then switched the light off again and watched from the window as she regained the street. She stopped, looked one way, then went the other, as if deciding there and then which way to go. Hardly the action of a woman with an appointment. He watched as she walked south towards St Ann's Road and disappeared around the corner, then he sat down in the armchair and emptied her wine glass. His gaze roved across the bookshelves and climbed the walls before reaching the ceiling. He then sat without moving for half an hour, his eyes not leaving the ceiling, listening to the building's creaks and sighs, the music downstairs having been turned off.

He took a different route back, climbing the Harringay Ladder and going west past the top of Priory Park. He floored the pedal through the Cranley Gardens S-bend and allowed the gradient to slow the car so that he rolled to a stop outside No. 23. There he killed the engine and looked up at the second-floor flat where Dennis Nilsen had lived from October 1981 to February 1983. One of Nilsen's mistakes, which had led to his being caught, was to have left the window in the gable dormer wide open for long periods, attracting the attention of neighbours.

Maddox looked at his watch and started the engine. He got on to the North Circular, coming off at Staples Corner, heading south down Edgware Road and turning right into Dollis Hill Lane. He slowed to a crawl, leaning forward over the wheel, craning his neck at the houses on the south side. He was sure it would be on the south side. He definitely remembered a wide tree-lined avenue with views over central London. Land falling away behind the house. Long walk from the tube. Which tube? He didn't know.

He turned right, cruised the next street. He wasn't even sure of the street. Dollis Hill Lane sounded right, but as soon as he'd got the idea of Cricklewood Lane off the internet that had sounded right too. He'd gone there, to 108/110 Cricklewood Lane, after reading on the net that that was where they'd shot *Hellraiser*. When he got there and found it was a branch of Holmes Place Health Clubs, he worked out it must have been the former location of Cricklewood Production Village, where they'd done the studio work.

Some time in the autumn of 1986, Maddox had come here, to a house in Dollis Hill. A movie was being made. Clive Barker was directing his first film. *Hellraiser*. They were shooting in a rented house and Maddox had been invited to go on the set as an associate of Barker's. He was going to do a little interview, place it wherever possible. Could be his big break. It was good of Clive to have agreed to it. Maddox remembered the big white vans in the street outside the house, a surprising number of people hanging around doing nothing, a catering truck, a long table covered with polystyrene cups, a tea urn. He asked for Steve Jones, unit publicist. Jones talked to him about what was going on. They were filming a dinner party scene with Andrew Robinson and Clare Higgins and two young actors, the boy and the girl, and a bunch of extras. Maddox got to watch from behind the camera, trying to catch Barker's eye as he talked to the actors, telling them what he wanted them to do. Controlling everybody and everything. Maddox envied him, but admired him as well. A make-up girl applied powder to Robinson's forehead. A hair-dresser fixed Ashley Laurence's hair. They did the scene and the air was filled with electricity. Everyone behind the camera held their breath, faces still and taut. The tension was palpable. The moment Barker called "Cut", it melted away. Smiles, laughter, everyone suddenly moving around. Maddox noticed the hairdresser, who looked lost for a moment, diminutive and vulnerable, but Steve Jones caught Maddox's arm in a light grip and cornered Barker. The director looked at Maddox and there was a fraction of a second's pause, no more, before he said, "Brian," in such a warm, sincere way that Maddox might have thought Clive had been looking forward to seeing him all morning.

They did a short interview over lunch, which they ate on the floor of a room at the back of the house.

"We're surrounded by images which are momentarily potent and carry no resonance whatsoever," Barker was saying in transatlantic Scouse. "Advertising, the pop video, a thing which seems to mean an awful lot and is in fact absolutely negligible."

Maddox noticed the hairdresser carrying a paper plate and a cup. She sat cross-legged on the floor next to another crew member and they talked as they ate.

"What frightens you?" he asked Barker.

"Unlit streets, flying, being stuck in the tube at rush hour. Places where you have to relinquish control."

Once they'd finished, Maddox hung around awkwardly, waiting for a chance to talk to the hairdresser. When it came – her companion rising to go – he seized it. She was getting up too and Maddox contrived to step in front of her, blocking her way. He apologised and introduced himself. "I was just interviewing Clive. We've known each other a couple of years. I was in one of his plays."

"Linzi," she said, offering her hand. "I'm only here for one day. The regular girl called in sick."

"Then I'm lucky I came today," he said, smiling shyly.

She was wearing a dark green top of soft cotton that was exactly the same shade as her eyes. Her hair, light brown with natural blonde streaks, was tied back in a knot pierced by a pencil.

"Are you going to stick around?" she asked.

"I've done my interview, but if no one kicks me out . . ."

"It's a pretty relaxed set."

He did stick around and most of the time he watched Linzi, promising himself he wouldn't leave until he'd got her number. It took him the rest of the afternoon, but he got it. She scribbled it on a blank page in her Filofax, then tore out the page and said, "Call me."

The chances of finding the house in darkness were even less than in daylight. He'd been up to Dollis Hill a couple of times in the last few weeks, once in the car and once on foot. Lately, he'd been thinking more about Linzi, and specifically about the early days, before it started to go wrong. He'd spent enough time going over the bad times and wanted to revisit the good. He wanted to see the house again, but couldn't. He needed to locate it for his book. He'd rewatched the film, which contained enough shots of the house's exterior that it should have been easy to locate it, but it didn't seem to matter how many times he trailed these suburban avenues, the house wasn't there. Or if it was, he couldn't see it. He'd begun to think it might have been knocked down, possibly even straight after the shoot. It could have been why the house had been available. In the film there was a No.55 on the porch, but that would be set dressing, like the renumbering of 25 Powis Square, in *Performance*, as No.81.

He looked at his watch and calculated that if he was quick he could get to Ladbroke Grove in time for coffee and to drive Christine home, thereby reducing the amount of grief she would give him. Negligibly, he realized, but still.

In the morning, he feigned sleep while she dressed. Her movements were businesslike, crisp. The night before had been a riot, as expected. When he had turned up at the dinner, two and a half hours late, she had contented herself with merely shooting him a look, but as soon as they left she started. And as soon as she started, he switched off.

It didn't let up even when they got home, but he wasn't listening. He marvelled at how closely he was able to mimic the condition with which Karen, his lip-reader, had been born. Thinking of Karen, moreover, relaxed him inside, while Christine kept on, even once they'd got into bed. Elective deafness – it beat hysterical blindness.

When he was sure Christine had left the house – the slammed door, the gate that clanged – he got up and showered. Within half an hour, having spent ten minutes pointing the DVD remote at the television, he was behind the wheel of the car with his son in the back seat. South Tottenham in twenty minutes was a bigger ask by day than by night, but he gave it his best shot. Rush hour was over (Christine, in common with everyone who worked on weekly magazines, finished earlier than she started), but skirting the congestion charge zone was still a challenge.

He parked where he had the night before and turned to see that Jack was asleep. He left him there, locked the car and walked up. He had decided, while lying in bed with his back to

Christine, that it would be worth going up into the loft. Some-where in the loft was a box containing old diaries, including one for 1986. He had never been a consistent diarist, but some years had seen him make more notes than others. It was worth a rummage among the spider's webs and desiccated wasps' nests. His size meant he didn't bang his head on the latticework of pine beams.

The loft still smelled faintly of formalin. He suspected it always would until he got rid of the suitcase at the far end. He shone the torch in its direction. Big old-fashioned brown leather case, rescued from a skip and cleaned up. Solid, sturdy, two catches and a strap with a buckle. Could take a fair weight.

He redirected the torch at the line of dusty boxes closer to the trap door. The first box contained T-shirts that he never wore any more but couldn't bear to throw away. The second was full of old typescripts stiff with Tipp-Ex. The diaries were in the third box along. He bent down and sorted through: 1974, a shiny black Pocket Diary filled mainly with notes on the history of the Crusades; 1976, the summer of the heatwave, *Angling Times* diary, roach and perch that should have been returned to the water left under stones to die; 1980, the deaths of his three remaining grandparents, three funerals in one year, coffins in the front room, all burials; 1982, his first term at university, meeting Martin, his best friend for a while. Martin was a year older, which had impressed Maddox. The age difference hadn't mattered. Everything was changing. Leaving school, leaving home. Living in halls. Martin was a medical student. They would stay up late drinking coffee and Martin would smoke cigarettes and tell Maddox about medicine, about anatomy and about the bodies he was learning to dissect.

Maddox could listen to Martin for hours. The later they stayed up, the more profound their discussions seemed to become. Maddox watched as Martin dragged on his cigarette and held the smoke in his lungs for an eternity, stretching the moment, before blowing it out in perfect rings. When Martin talked about the bodies in the anatomy lab, Maddox became entranced. He imagined Martin alone in the lab with a dozen flayed corpses. Bending over them, examining them, carefully removing a strip of muscle, severing a tendon. Getting up close to the secrets, the mysteries, of death. Martin said it didn't matter how long he spent washing his hands, they still smelled of formalin. He held them under Maddox's nose, then moved to cup his cheeks in an affectionate, stroking gesture.

"You don't mind, do you?" he said, as his hand landed on Maddox's knee.

"Could you get me in there? Into the lab?" Maddox asked, shaking his head, picturing himself among the bodies, as Martin's hand moved up his thigh.

"No. But I could bring you something out. Something you could keep."

Martin's hand had reached Maddox's lap and Maddox was mildly surprised to discover that far from objecting, he was aroused. If this was to be the downpayment on whatever Martin might fetch him back from the dissection table, so be it.

"I've got something for you," Martin said a couple of days later, "in my room."

Maddox followed Martin to his room.

"So where is it?" Maddox asked.

"Can't just leave that sort of thing lying about. But what's the rush?"

Martin lay down on the bed and unbuckled his belt.

Maddox hesitated, considered walking out, but he felt certain he'd always regret it if he left empty-handed. Instead, he knelt beside the bed and spat into his palm.

Afterwards, Martin pulled open his desk drawer.

"There you go," he said.

Maddox withdrew a strong-smelling package. He started to work at the knot in the outermost plastic bag, but it wouldn't come easily. He asked Martin what it contained.

"A piece of subcutaneous fat from the body of a middle-aged man. If anyone ever asks, you didn't get it from me."

Maddox returned to his own room on the seventh floor, washing his hands on the way. He cut open the bag and unwrapped his spoils. The gobbet of fat, four inches by two, looked like a piece of tripe, white and bloodless, and the stench of formalin made him feel sick and excited at the same time. Maddox was careful not to touch the fat as he wrapped it up again and secured the package with tape. He opened his wardrobe and pulled out the brown suitcase he'd liberated from a skip in Judd Street.

He saw less of Martin after that. At first he contrived subtly to avoid him and then started going out with Valerie, a girl with fat arms and wide hips he picked up in the union bar on cocktails night. He wasn't convinced they were a good match, but the opportunity was convenient, given the Martin situation.

The piece of fat remained wrapped up in its suitcase, which smelled so strongly that Maddox only had to open the case and take a sniff to re-experience how he had felt when Martin had given him the body part. As he lay in bed trying to get to sleep (alone. Valerie didn't last more than a few weeks) he sometimes thought about the man who had knowingly willed his cadaver to science. He wondered what his name might have been and what kind of man he was. What he might have been in life. He would hardly have been able to foresee what would happen to the small part of him that was now nestled inside Maddox's wardrobe.

When Maddox left the hall of residence for a flat in Holloway, the case went with him, still empty but for its human remains. He kept it on top of a cupboard. It stayed there for two years. When he moved into the flat in N15, he put the suitcase in the loft, where it had remained ever since. The piece of fat was no longer in Maddox's possession, but the suitcase was not free of the smell of formalin.

Maddox's 1986 diary was at the bottom of the box. It took only a couple of minutes to find what he was looking for. "*Hellraiser*, 11:00 a.m." he'd written in the space reserved for Friday 10 October. A little further down was an address: 187 Dollis Hill Lane.

He drove to Dollis Hill via Cranley Gardens, but on this occasion didn't stop.

"Why didn't I think of checking my old diaries before, eh, Jack?" he said, looking in the rear-view mirror.

His son was silent, staring out of the window.

Turning into Dollis Hill Lane from Edgware Road, he slowed to a crawl, oblivious to the noisy rebuke of the driver immediately behind him, who pulled out and swerved to overtake, engine racing, finger given. Maddox brought the car to a halt on a slight incline outside No.187. He looked at the house and felt an unsettling combination of familiarity and non-recognition. Attraction and repulsion. He had to stare at the house for two or three minutes before he realised why he had driven past it so many times and failed to recognise it.

Like most things recalled from the past, it was smaller than the version in his memory. But the main difference was the apparent age of the building. He remembered a Victorian villa, possibly Edwardian. The house in front of him was new. The rendering on the front gable end had gone up in the last few years. The wood-framed bay windows on the first floor were of recent construction. The casement window in the top flat, second floor, was obviously new. The mansard roof was a familiar shape, but the clay Rosemarys were all fresh from the tile shop. The materials were new, but the style was not. The basic design was unchanged, from what he could remember of the exterior shots in the film, which he'd looked at again before coming out, but in spite of that the house looked new. As if a skeleton had grown new muscle and flesh.

"Just like Frank," he said out loud.

"What, Daddy?"

"Just like Frank in the film."

"What film?"

"They made a film in this house and I came to see them make it. You're too young to see it yet. One day, maybe."

"What's it about?"

"It's about a man who disappears and then comes back to life with the help of his girlfriend. It happened in that room up there." He pointed to the top flat. "Although, the windows are wrong," he said, trying to remember the second-floor window in the film. "I need to check it again."

The only part of the exterior that looked as if they'd taken care to try to match the original was the front door.

As he'd walked from the *Hellraiser* set back to the tube two decades earlier, he'd read and re-read Linzi's number on the tornout piece of Filofax paper. He called her the next day and they arranged to meet for a drink.

"Why are you so interested in this house, Daddy?" Jack asked from the back seat.

"Because of what happened here. Because of the film. And because I met somebody here. Somebody I knew before I met your mother."

★ ★ ★

Linzi lived in East Finchley. They went to see films at the Phoenix or met for drinks in Muswell Hill. Malaysian meals in Crouch End. He showed her the house in Hillfield Avenue where he had visited Clive Barker.

"Peter Straub used to live on the same road, just further up the hill," he told her.

"Who's Peter Straub?"

"Have you heard of Stephen King?"

"Of course."

"Straub and King wrote a book together. *The Talisman*. They wrote it here. Or part of it, anyway. King also wrote a story called 'Crouch End', which was interesting, not one of his best."

Maddox and Linzi started meeting during the day at the Wisteria Tea Rooms on Middle Lane and it was there, among the pot plants and mismatched crockery, that Maddox realised with a kind of slow, swooning surprise that he was happy. The realisation was so slow because the feeling was so unfamiliar. They took long walks through Highgate Cemetery and across Hampstead Heath.

Weeks became months. The cherry blossom came out in long straight lines down Cecile Park, and fell to the pavements, and came out again. Linzi often stayed at Maddox's flat in South Tottenham, but frowned distastefully at his true-crime books. One morning while she was still asleep, Maddox was dressing, looking for a particular T-shirt. Unable to find it, he climbed up the ladder into the loft. Searching through a box of old clothes, he didn't hear Linzi climbing the ladder or see her head and shoulders suddenly intrude into the loft space.

"What are you doing?" she said.

"Shit." He jumped, hitting his head. "Ow. That hurt. Shit. Nothing. Looking for something."

"What's that smell?"

"Nothing."

He urged her back down the ladder and made sure the trap door was fastened before pulling on the *Eraserhead* T-shirt he'd been looking for.

Whenever he went into the loft from then on, whether Linzi was around or not, he would pull the ladder up after him and close the trap door. The loft was private.

When he got back to the flat that evening, he went up into the loft again – duly covering his tracks, although he was alone – and took the small wrapped parcel from the suitcase. The lid fell shut, the old-fashioned clasps sliding home without his needing to fasten them. Quality craftsmanship.

When it was dark, he buried the slice of tissue in the waste ground behind the flats.

As the decade approached its end, the directionless lifestyle that Maddox and Linzi had drifted into seemed to become more expensive. The bills turned red. Maddox started working regular shifts on the subs' desk at the *Independent*. He hated it but it paid well. Linzi applied for a full-time job at a ladies' salon in Finsbury Park. They took a day trip to Brighton. They went to an art show in the Unitarian Church where Maddox bought Linzi a small watercolour and she picked out a booklet of poems by the artist's husband as a return gift. They had lunch in a vegetarian café. Maddox talked about the frustrations of cutting reviews to fit and coming up with snappy headlines, when what he'd rather be doing was writing the copy himself. Linzi had no complaints about the salon. "Gerry – he's the boss – he's a really lovely guy," she said. "Nicest boss I've ever had."

They spent the afternoon in the pubs and secondhand book-shops of the North Laines. Maddox found a Ramsey Campbell anthology, an M. John Harrison collection and *The New Murderers' Who's Who*. On the train waiting to leave Brighton station to return to London, with the sun throwing long dark shapes across the platforms, Linzi read to Maddox from the pamphlet of verse.

" 'This is all I ever wanted / to meet you in the fast decaying shadows / on the outskirts of this or any city / alone and in exile.' "

As the train rattled through Sussex, Maddox pored over the photographs in his true-crime book.

"Look," he said, pointing to a caption: "Brighton Trunk Crime No.2: The trunk's contents."

"Very romantic," Linzi said as she turned to the window, but Maddox couldn't look away from the crumpled stockings on the legs of the victim, Violette Kaye. Her broken neck. The pinched scowl on her decomposed face. To Maddox the picture was as beautiful as it was terrible.

Over the next few days, Maddox read up on the Brighton Trunk Murders of 1934. He discovered that Tony Mancini, who had confessed to putting Violette Kay's body in the trunk but claimed she had died accidentally (only to retract that claim and accept responsibility for her murder more than forty years later), had lodged at 52 Kemp Street. He rooted around for the poetry pamphlet Linzi had bought him. He found it under a pile of magazines. The poet's name was Michael Kemp. He wanted to share his discovery of this coincidence with Linzi when she arrived at his flat with scissors and hairdressing cape.

"Why not save a bit of money?" she said, moving the chair from Maddox's desk into the middle of the room. As she worked on his hair, she talked about Gerry from the salon. "He's so funny," she said. "The customers love him. He certainly keeps me and the other girls entertained."

"Male hairdressers in women's salons are all puffs, surely?"

Linzi stopped cutting and looked at him.

"So?" she said. "So what if they are? And anyway, Gerry's not gay. No way."

"Really? How can you be so sure?"

"A girl knows. Okay?"

"Have you fucked him then or what?"

She took a step back. "What's the matter with you?"

"How else would you know? Gerry seems to be all you can talk about."

"Fuck you."

Maddox shot to his feet, tearing off the cape.

"You know what," he said, seizing the scissors, "I'll cut my own fucking hair and do a better job of it. At least I won't have to listen to you going on about *Gerry*."

He started to hack at his own hair, grabbing handfuls and cutting away. Linzi recoiled in horror, unable to look away, as if she were watching a road accident.

"Maybe I should tell you about all the women at the *Independent*?" he suggested. "Sheila Johnston, Sabine Durrant, Christine Healey . . . I don't know where to start."

It wasn't until he jabbed the scissors threateningly in her direction that she snatched up her bag and ran out.

The next day he sent flowers. He didn't call, didn't push it. Just flowers and a note: "Sorry."

Then he called. Told her he didn't know what had come over him. It wouldn't happen again. He knew he'd be lucky if she forgave him, but he hoped he'd be lucky. He hadn't felt like this about anyone before and he didn't want to lose her. The irony was, he told her, he'd been thinking his flat was getting a bit small and maybe they should look for a place together. He'd understand if she wanted to kick it into touch, but hoped she'd give him another chance.

She said to give her some time.

He shaved his head.

He drove down to Finsbury Park and watched from across the street as she worked on clients. Bobbing left and right. Holding their hair in her hands. Eye contact in the mirror. Gerry fussing around, sharing a joke, trailing an arm. As she'd implied, though, he was distributing his attentions equally among Linzi and the two other girls.

Mornings and evenings, he kept a watch on her flat in Finchley. She left and returned on her own. He chose a route between his flat and hers that took in Cranley Gardens in Muswell Hill. He parked outside No.23 and watched the darkened windows of the top flat. He wondered if any of the neighbours had been Nilsen's contemporaries. If this man passing by now with a tartan shopping trolley had ever nodded good morning to the mass murderer. If that woman leaving her house across the street had ever smiled at him. Maddox got out of the car and touched the low wall outside the property with the tips of his fingers.

Linzi agreed to meet up. Maddox suggested the Wisteria Tea Rooms. It was almost like starting over. Cautious steps. Shy smiles. His hair had grown back.

"What got into you?"

"I don't know. I thought we'd agreed to draw a line under it."

"Yes, you're right."

At the next table a woman was feeding a baby.

"Do you ever think about having children?" Linzi asked, out of the blue.

"A boy," Maddox said straightaway. "I'd call him Jack."

Maddox didn't mention Gerry. He took on extra shifts. Slowly, they built up trust again. One day, driving back to

his place after dropping Linzi off at hers, he saw that a board
had gone up outside 23 Cranley Gardens. For sale. He rang the
agents. Yes, it was the top flat, second floor. It was on at
£64,950, but when Maddox dropped by to pick up a copy of
the details (DELIGHTFUL TOP FLOOR ONE BEDROOM
CONVERSION FLAT), they'd reduced it to £59,950. He
made an appointment, told Linzi he'd arranged a surprise.
Picked her up early, drove to Cranley Gardens. He'd never
brought her this way. She didn't know whose flat it had been.

A young lad met them outside. Loosely knotted tie, shiny
shoes. Bright, eager.

Linzi turned to Maddox. "Are you thinking of moving?"

"It's bigger and it's cheap."

Linzi smiled stiffly. They followed the agent up the stairs. He
unlocked the interior door and launched into his routine.
Maddox nodded without listening as his eyes greedily took
everything in, trying to make sense of the flat, to match what he
saw to the published photographs. It didn't fit.

"The bathroom's gone," he said, interrupting the agent.

"There's a shower room," the boy said. "And a washbasin
across the hall. An unusual arrangement."

Nilsen had dissected two bodies in the bathroom.

"This is a lovely room," the agent said, moving to the front of
the flat.

Maddox entered the room at the back and checked the view
from the window.

"At least this is unchanged," he said to Linzi, who had
appeared alongside.

"What do you mean?"

He looked at her and realized what he'd said.

"This flat's all different. I've seen pictures of it."

The story came out later, back at Maddox's place.

"You took me round Dennis Nilsen's flat?"

He turned away.

"You didn't think to mention it first? You thought we might
live there together? In the former home of a serial killer? What
the fuck is wrong with you?"

"It's cheap," he said, to the closing door.

He watched from the window as she ran off towards West
Green Road. He stayed at the window for a time and then pulled

down the ladder and went up into the loft. He pulled up the ladder and closed the trap door. He opened the big brown suitcase. It was like getting a fix. He studied the dimensions of the suitcase. It was not much smaller than Tony Mancini's trunk.

Christine was at work. Maddox read a note she'd left in the kitchen: "We need milk and bread."

He went into the living room and took down the *Hellraiser* DVD from the shelf. Sitting in the car with Jack outside the house on Dollis Hill Lane, Maddox had noticed something not quite right about the windows on the second floor. They were new windows and set in two pairs with a gap between them, but that wasn't it. There was something else and he didn't know what. He fast-forwarded until the exterior shot of Julia leaving the house to go to the bar where she picks up the first victim. The second-floor window comprised six lights in a row. For some reason, when rebuilding the house, they'd left out two of the lights and gone with just four, in two pairs. But that wasn't what was bothering him.

He skipped forward. He kept watching.

Frank and Julia in the second-floor room, top of the house. She's just killed the guy from the bar and Frank has drained his body. Julia re-enters the room after cleaning herself up and as she walks towards the window we see it comprises four lights in a row. Four windows. Four windows in a row. Not six. Four.

Maddox wielded the remote.

Looking up at the house as Julia leaves it to go to the bar. Second floor, six windows. Inside the same room on the second floor, looking towards the windows. Four, not six.

So what? The transformation scenes, which take place in that second-floor room at the front of the house, weren't shot on Dollis Hill Lane. Big deal. That kind of stuff would have to be done in the studio. The arrival of the Cenobites, the transformation of Frank, his being torn apart. It wasn't the kind of stuff you could shoot on location. But how could they make such a glaring continuity error as the number of lights in a window? Six from outside, four from within. It couldn't be a mistake. It was supposed to mean something. But what?

"Daddy?"

Maddox jumped.

"What is it, Jack?"

"What are you watching?"

Maddox looked at the screen as he thought about his response.

"This film, the one shot in that house."

"The house with the windows?"

"Yes."

"Why is it important?"

"I don't know. No, I do know." His shoulders slumped. "I don't know. Maybe it's not."

He drove to the supermarket. Jack was quiet in the back. They got a trolley. Maddox stopped in front of the newspapers. He looked at the *Independent*. Although he'd first met Christine on the *Independent* arts desk, it wasn't until they bumped into each other some years later, when they were both freelancing on TV listings magazines at IPC, that they started going out. Although they were equals at IPC, Christine had routinely rewritten his headlines at the *Independent* and while he pretended it didn't still rankle, it did. Not the best basis for a relationship, perhaps. Then a permanent position came up on *TV Times*, and they both went for it, but Christine's experience counted. They decided it wouldn't affect things, but agreed that maybe Maddox should free himself of his commitments at IPC. He said he had a book he wanted to write. Together they negotiated an increasingly obstacle-strewn path towards making a life together. If they stopped and thought about it, it didn't seem like a very good idea, but neither of them had a better one.

Maddox looked around to check that Jack was still in tow, then moved on.

He stood silently in cold meats, swaying very gently.

"Gone," he said quietly. "All gone. Disappeared."

"What, Daddy? What's gone?"

"Wait there, Jack. I'll be back. Don't move."

He walked to the end of the aisle and turned the corner. He walked to the end of the next aisle and then the next, looking at the items on the shelves, familiar brands, labels he'd seen a thousand times. All meaningless. He recognised nothing. What was he looking for? Bread and milk? Where were they? He couldn't remember. He went back to where he'd left the trolley. It was there, but Jack wasn't.

He looked up and down the aisle. The brand names that had meant nothing to him a moment ago now leapt out at him, shouting, screaming for attention. It was as if the two sides of the aisle had suddenly shifted inward. Jack was nowhere to be seen.

"Jack!"

Maddox ran to the end of the aisle and looked both ways. He looked up the next aisle, then up the next and the one after. He kept calling Jack's name. Shoppers stopped and stared, but Maddox moved faster and shouted louder. He looked at the line of tills and wondered if Jack had gone that way. He could already be out of the store, wandering around the car park, about to be run over or abducted. He told himself to calm down, that he would find him, but at the same time another voice suggested that sometimes the worst thing imaginable did happen. It had before, after all. Would this be the next case heard about on the news? A half-page in the paper. London man loses child in supermarket. Brian Maddox, 42, took his eyes off his son for one moment and he was gone. But he hadn't taken his eyes off him for just one moment. He'd gone to the next aisle, or the one after. He'd gone away. He could have been gone five minutes. Ten, fifteen.

"Jack!"

"Sir?"

A young lad, a shelf stacker, was standing in front of him. Maddox told him his son had disappeared. The shelf stacker asked for a description. Maddox gave him one and the lad said he would start from the far end of the store and advised Maddox to start from the other. They would meet in the middle and most likely one of them would have found Jack. Maddox did as he was told and neither of them found Jack. Maddox was short of breath, dry in the mouth, his chest rising and falling, unbearable pressure being exerted on his temples. He could no longer call out Jack's name without his voice breaking. More staff were on hand now. They took Maddox's arms and led him to an office where he was sat down and given a drink of water.

"Maybe the boy's with his mother?" someone suggested.

Maddox shook his head.

"Do you have a number for her?"

Maddox produced Christine's number. He was dimly aware of a phone call being made. The office was full of people. Managers, security, cashiers. They swopped remarks, observations. Some expressions hardened. "What did she say?" a voice asked. "There is no son," another one answered. "No kids at all, apparently." A security guard replayed videotape on a monitor. Grainy, vivid. Maddox entering the store on his own with a trolley. Standing in front of the newspapers, on his own. Leaving the trolley in cold meats. No unattached children.

They gave Maddox another glass of water while waiting for the police to arrive. The store didn't want to press charges. "What would be the point?" Maddox was free to go. "Has this happened before?" Shake of the head. "If it were to happen again, the store would have to consider taking action . . . Very upsetting for other shoppers . . . You *will* see someone?"

Maddox sat in the car park, behind the wheel of the car. He hadn't got what he'd come for. The milk and the bread. Maybe it didn't matter any more. He sat in the car for a long time and only turned the key in the ignition when he realized the sky over central London was beginning to get dark.

He didn't go to the house. He didn't imagine Christine would be there, but it was kind of irrelevant either way. Instead, he drove to South Tottenham. He drove through the top of the congestion charge zone. It didn't matter any more. It was rush hour. It took an hour and a half to get to N15. The street door was open. He walked up, entered the flat. Thump-thump-thump from downstairs. He took out his phone and sent a text message, then stood by the window for a while watching the street. He left the phone on the window ledge and pulled down the ladder and climbed into the loft, retrieving the ladder and closing the trap door behind him. Stooping, he walked over to the suitcase, which smelled strongly of formalin. He knelt in front of it for several minutes, resting his hands on the lid, then touching the clasps.

He released the clasps and opened the case.

It was empty.

He frowned, then sat and stared at the empty case for some time, listening to the creaks of the beams and the muffled basslines from the downstairs flat. He wondered if Karen would come, how long she might be. He wasn't sure what he would do when she arrived.

Slowly, he rose, then lowered the upper half of his body into the case, folding his legs in afterwards. Inside the case, the smell of formalin was very strong. He stared at the pine beams, the cobwebs, the shadows clinging to the insulating material. He could still faintly hear his neighbour's loud music, which Karen had been unable to hear, and then, rising above it, the clear and unmistakeable chime of his phone, down in the flat, announcing the arrival of a text message. He started to uncurl his body and the lid of the case fell forward.

He had twisted his body far enough that the hump of his shoulder caught the closing lid.

He climbed out and lay down next to the suitcase.

A minute later his phone chimed a reminder.

He thought about Linzi. Linzi had been good for him, until things went bad. He wondered where she was. He looked at the empty suitcase again and plucked a long fine strand of fair hair from the lining. He thought about Karen and her need, unacknowledged, to be looked after. He remembered how vulnerable Linzi had seemed when he saw her for the first time.

Karen would be along soon. Probably. She hadn't let him down yet.

He still had options.

THE LAST KAYFABE

Ray Banks

Don't matter what city you're in, what town. Three hundred days a year on the road, you could be in Shitsville, Ohio or New York fuckin' city. All it looks to you is another hotel room charging ten dollars for a stubby bottle of beer. Outside, you got the same old shit too: drizzle throwing a mist over the streets and their barred-up liquor stores. And you know if there's a place with Martin Luther King's name on it, that's where you're gonna score.

"That time you fucked up New Jack," says Monty. "That for real?"

They don't always recognize me. This one can't believe a white boy pinned a former bounty hunter with four justifiables. I stare at him, wish he'd move his ass and hand over the fuckin' dimes.

"No," I say. "Wasn't for real."

"*Any* of that shit for real?"

Shake my head. Apart from the blood. The blood was real. The *pain*. Shit, you wanna talk pain, we can talk pain. I got a constant steel-band ache across the back of my neck thanks to a guitar broke over my head by an Elvis-looking motherfucker called himself The Honky Tonk Man. Then Hardcore, list it out: second-degree burns on my hands and arms; been spiked so many times with barb wire I lost count; broke all my ribs, individual and all at once; broke my sternum; eight concussions and I got a total of over six hundred stitches holding me together like a beefed-up rag doll with bad dreams.

Might've been sports *entertainment*. Might've been rehearsed. Bret Hart saying he never hurt anyone – fuck Bret Hart. But just 'cause you *planned* that three-hundred-pound grizzly dropping on your ass from fifty feet in the air, didn't mean your damn bones didn't shake and break.

"What about that time – shit, musta been ten years ago – you was on RAW—"

"Your name's Monty, right?"

"Yeah."

"Just making sure, 'cause your man up the way there, he told me I should come down here and get the shit from Monty. Now I gave him the money, but you ain't given me shit but an interview. So how about we turn off the fuckin' Biography Channel and do some business?"

Run the numbers: work twenty-seven days out the month, twice daily on the weekends. Nine airplane connections a week. Adds up to a couple dimes a day. In the way-back, I didn't know a jobber who didn't pop, snort, guzzle or spike. Pills for the pain, drink or tie off to sleep, snort to wake and grapple. Better living through chemistry, and mine came boulder-shaped.

Beat those old memories like dust from a rug. No good for me in the here and now.

"You give the money to Leon?" says Monty.

I point at a stringy guy who looks like he's trying to shit his pants slowly. "That Leon? 'Cause that's the motherfucker got my money."

Monty nods. "That's Leon."

"Then we're all acquainted."

"How much you give him?"

I squint at him. He's stalling. "What's the problem, Monty?"

"Ain't no problem at all, man."

Except he's looking over my fuckin' shoulder.

I turn, get the picture in Hi-Def.

Leon's quit shifting his weight, coming down on me full-bore. Got this crazy-ass chimp face on him, grin to grimace, like he's playing heel in his own private smackdown. Hands outstretched, but I knock the lunge out of him. Grab his head, bring it to mine solid – stamp the sidewalk as I do, force of habit. Another collision, Leon totters back. Reach for his skull, grab what I can of his hair. Adjust the tape on my fingers, sneak the razor out.

In the trade, they call it a blade-job. You need to sell a pillowstrike, you cut yourself. One time I caught a gash so bad, I made a 0.7 on the Muta Scale.

Leon tries to jerk, makes me dig an artery. I let him go as he squeals and bleeds like a chiselled pig.

He ain't the only one bleeding. I spin at a spike in my leg, see something drop to the ground as I turn and grab Monty. Motherfucker's heavy, but I reckoned he'd carry it slow. No more bullshit: sometimes you got to close the fist and fuck somebody up. I tear into Monty, drop him to the concrete. The sidewalk opens his head at the scalp. I put my foot in his ribs, then pull back when the pain in my stuck leg is too much.

Hearing screams melt into hoarse breath now. Monty rolls onto his back. A blood bubble appears in his open mouth, pops when his lungs are empty. Look over at Leon, he can't see through the blood in his eyes. Curled up like a fuckin' baby on the ground. Sounds like he's crying.

I look at the ground: Monty's weapon, the one he stuck me with. It's a boxcutter.

Another word we use in the trade: *kayfabe*. Means fake. Some jobber threw for real, tried to hurt you, that was breaking kayfabe. You didn't do it unless you wanted your fuckin' papers.

These two: kayfabe fuckin' dealers, no stones to back 'em up. Broke roles 'cause they reckoned me another crackhead cracker.

Thinking now, picturing these two hanging out with their pipe-hitting pals: "That whiteboy wrestler, Babyface – you remember that motherfucker? He came round my shit wanting *rocks*, man. Me an' Leon, we fucked that boy *up*."

"This fun to you?" I say. "You having fun, boys? 'Cause you want some more, I'll stretch both you motherfuckers blue."

Leon whines.

"That's what I thought."

Look at me now, you think I'm FUBAR. Lean and old, holding my fuckin' leg like it's gonna drop off. It's why they don't recognize me. Been a long time since I was the ultimate face in the Federation. But then, I was Babyface. The crowd *popped* at me, man. I put so many heels to the mat, I was a fuckin' hero. Spin out a running DDT as a finish, hear twenty thousand people calling my name.

The ladies shouting: "Nobody puts Babyface in the corner!"

Got the men: "That Babyface ain't for crying!"

Hear it now, the applause like a fuckin' rainstorm.

And then wait for the lightning to strike. The Attitude years, hearing the cheers turn to jeers, the crowd turned vicious. They need a hero like they need a bag on their collective hip. I go up against Stone Cold, I do my gimmick – rip my T and throw it to the crowd – but they ain't having it. They throw my T back. Faces are victims, there to be stomped. Some turn heel, some leave the business to sell used cars. I take flop on flop, pin on pin. Do whatever the bosses tell me 'cause I'm a good worker and I believe that people'll want their heroes back some day.

They don't.

Clean that from my mind as I limp over to Monty and see if he's legit. Sure enough, the guy's been holding. I pull two baggies of vials out of his pockets. He whistles as he breathes, tries to speak, but he don't put up a fight. Go to Leon, get my money back and more besides. Leon's hand clamps over mine.

I bend two fingers till they snap. Leon finds the breath to scream again.

"Hush up, Leon. Listen. You know Vince?"

Leon shakes his head.

Course he don't know Vince. That's what I call him. Reminds me of my old boss. It don't matter what he's called, though, 'cause the point's the same:

"Vince says you deal on this corner, you gonna get fucked up. You feel me?"

Leon's eyes get to slits.

"You know me," I say. "I'm a *good* guy. That's why I didn't fuckin' kill you. When you get yourself stitched, you remember that. And pass it on to Monty."

I turn my back, go to the rental.

Every time playing out the same shit in my head.

I go to the car, there's gonna be a gun. These guys, if they're real dealers, they'll have a fuckin' piece between 'em.

Welcoming the gun, *hoping* for it. Some fuck wants to put this Old Yeller out his misery, they can go right ahead. I seen that movie a million times and I know. Don't matter what a good dog Yeller was. Once you get bit by the fuckin' wolf, you're a short time dying.

Ain't gonna happen with these kayfabe motherfuckers. Small time. Stick me with a boxcutter instead of shooting me. I check the leg situation as I get in the car: if I was still fighting, I'd be fucked. 'Cause the damage don't matter – you have to do what your bosses tell you to do. Vince is the same. He wants me to fuck somebody up in Detroit, Baltimore, Cleveland, fuckin' *Anchorage*, I do it. He got some wide-ranging business interests and a lot of ants trying to make off with his sugar.

Start the engine. The rental coughs. I check the count on the cash. Couple thou, should be good for gas.

And enough rocks in these bags to last me a while.

Vince wants me to hit a corner in Atlanta tomorrow night. Don't know if I can do that with my leg, but I'll see how I feel after I hit the stem.

'Cause right now I need something. All us jobbers do.

TO HAVE AND TO HOLD

Ken Bruen

"I should have married Johnny Cash."

The cop was taken aback. Of all the things he expected her to say, this was never on the table.

He looked at her, the dishwater-blonde hair, the hard mouth, the slight, jagged scar along her cheek and the air of exhaustion she exuded. The coffee he'd sent out for was before her and she moved her manacled hands to take a sip, the Styrofoam cup tilted back, and he glimpsed very white teeth. He had her statement before him and if he could just get her to sign the goddamn thing, he might beat the gridlock, get home to supper before eight. His partner had gone for a leak and the tape recorder had been shut off.

She raised her hands, asked,

"Y'all could maybe take these off for a time?"

He could see where the metal had cut into her wrists and angry welts ran along the bone. He said,

"Now, Charlene, you know I gotta keep you cuffed 'til booking is done."

She sighed, then asked,

"Got a smoke?"

He had a pack of Kools in his suit pocket, for his wife, shook his head, said,

"No smoking in a Federal building, you know that."

She gave him a smile and it lit up her whole face, took twenty
years right off her. She said,

"I won't tell if you don't."

And what the hell, he took out the pack and a battered Zippo.
It had the logo, "First Airborne." He slid them across the table
and she grabbed them, got one in her mouth, cranked the
lighter, the smell of gasoline emanating like scarce comfort.
She peered at the pack, Menthol, asked,

"What's with that, you're not a pillow-biter are you? Not that
I have anything against Gays but I can read folk. I'd have you
down for a ladies' man."

He nearly smiled, thinking,

"Yeah, right."

In his crumpled suit, gray skin, sagging belly, he was a Don
Juan. What was it his daughter would answer . . . *Not.*

She wasn't expecting an answer, said,

"Years back, I was working one of those fancy hotels, still
living high on the hog, and I ran the bar. Guess who walked in,
with his band?"

Her eyes shining at the memory, she continued,

"The Man in Black, he'd done a concert and they dropped in
for a few quiet brews and some chicken wings."

Foley was impressed. He liked Cash, except for that prison
crap he did, and in spite of himself, asked,

"No shit, the Man himself?"

She was nodding, the smoke like a halo around her head,
said,

"I couldn't believe it, I never seen anyone famous, not, like,
in real life. I gave 'em my best service, and in those days, I was
hot, had some moves."

Foley nearly said,

"You still do."

But bit down and wondered where the hell his partner had got
to. Probably gone for a bourbon, Shiner back. He'd return,
smelling of mints, like that was a disguise. He asked,

"You talk to him, to Mr Cash?"

"Not at first. I was getting them vittles, drinks, making sure
they were comfortable and after, I dunno, an hour, Johnny said,

'Take a pew little lady, get a load off.' "

She rubbed her eyes, then.

"He had these amazing boots, all scuffed but, like, real expensive, snakeskin or something, and he used his boot to hook a chair, pull it up beside him."

She touched her face, self conscious, said,

"I didn't have the scar then, still had some dreams. Jesus."

Foley was a cop for fifteen years, eight with Homicide and he was, in his own cliché, *hard bitten*. There wasn't a story, a scam, an excuse, a smoke screen he hadn't heard and his view of human nature veered from cynical to incredulity. But something about this broad . . . a sense of, what . . .? He didn't want to concede it, but was it . . . dignity? A few months later, a Saturday night, his wedding anniversary, he'd taken his Lottie for clams and that white wine she loved. Had a few too many glasses himself – that shit crept up on you – and told Lottie about the feeling and Lottie had gotten that ice look. He wouldn't be having any lovemaking that night; she hissed,

"You had a shine for that . . . that trailer trash?"

His night had gone south.

And c'mon, he hadn't got a thing for Charlene, but something, her face now, in the middle of the Cash story, it got to him, she was saying,

"I sat down and Mr Cash, he asked me my name, I done told him and he repeated it but with an S . . . like . . . *Shur . . . leen*. He had that voice, the gravel. Luckies and corn whiskey melt, give a girl the shivers, and then he said,

"That's a real *purty* name . . . how he said 'pretty'."

She massaged her right wrist, the welt coming in red and inflamed. She said,

"I had me a leather thong on my wrist. My Mamma done give it to me, real fancy, little symbols of El Paso interwoven on there, and I dunno, I saw him look at it and maybe it was the heat, it was way up in them there 90s, even that time of the evening, and I took it off, said,

"Can I give you this?"

"His boys went quiet for a moment, the long-necks left untouched and them fellers could drink. He took it, tied it on his wrist, gave me that smile, sent goose bumps all down my spine, said,

"*Muchas gracias, señorita.*"

"Then I noticed one of the guys give a start and I turned and June Carter came in, that bitch, full of wrath. Dame had a hard on so I got my ass in gear, got back behind the bar. They didn't stay long after, and Johnny never came to say goodbye, that cow had him bundled out of there like real urgent business. The manager, he come over to the bar, paid the tab and gave me one hundred dollars for my own self. What do you think of that, one hundred bucks, for like, real little service?"

Foley knew hookers. For fifteen minutes, they'd be lucky to get thirty and change. Charlene's face got ugly, a coldness from her eyes, mixed with . . . grief? She said,

"I was on a high, floating, my face burning, like I was some goddamn teenager, and not even that Carter cunt . . ."

The word was so unexpected and especially from a woman, that Foley physically moved back, reconsidered the handcuffs. Charlene finished with,

"I was cleaning the table, them good ol' boys sure done a mess of wings and long-necks and there . . . in the middle of the table, sliced neatly in half, was my Mama's wrist band."

A silence took over the room, she fired up another Kool, taking long inhales like she was stabbing her body, her eyes like slits in her face and she said,

"When I'd be clearing up, I'd been humming, *I Walk the Line.*"

Years after, Johnny came on the juke, the radio, that tune, Foley would have to turn it off.

Go figure.

When Foley's partner got back, minted almighty, his face with that bourbon glow, he brought some sodas and if he noticed the cuffs were off, he let it slide, turned on the tape recorder, asked,

"You grew up in El Paso, am I right?"

Charlene gave him a look, a blend of amusement and malice, said,

"Cinco de Mayo."

He looked at Foley, shrugged, and Charlene took a slug of the soda, grimaced, asked,

"No Dr Pepper?"

Then,

"Damn straight, between Stanton and Kansas, you get to the bus station? . . . Turn right on Franklin, walk, like maybe a

block-and-a-half? . . . Little side street there, we had us our
place, me and my Mom, near the Gardner Hotel. That building
is, like, eighty years old?"

Foley's partner gave a whistle, said,

"No shit?"

Like he could give a fuck.

Foley was pissed at him, felt the interview had gone downhill
since he had joined them. Something like intimacy had been
soiled, and he had to shake himself, get rid of those damn foolish
notions. Charlene stared at him, asked,

"I know he's Foley. Who are you?"

"Darlin', I'm either your worst nightmare or your only hope,
comprende, chiquita?"

She tasted the insult, the loaded use of the Spanish, then said,

"*No me besas mas, por favor!*"

He didn't get it, said,

"I don't get it."

She laughed, said,

"The next whore sits on your face, ask her."

He leaned fast across the table, slapped her mouth, hard, and
Foley went,

"Jesus, Al."

His fingers left an outline on her cheek and she smiled. The
week after, when Al asked his regular hooker for a translation,
she told him,

"Please don't kiss me."

Foley wound back the tape, couldn't have the slap on there,
then asked,

"So what brought you back to Houston?"

She shrugged, said,

"A guy, what else."

Foley looked at his notes, double-checked, then,

"That'd be the deceased, one Charles Newton?"

She lit up the cigarette she'd been toying with, blew a cloud of
smoke at Al, said,

"Charlie, yeah, he promised me he'd marry me, and he was
into me for Five Gs."

Al gave a nasty chuckle, more a cackle, asked,

"The matter with you broads, you give your dollars to any
lowlife that says he'll marry you?"

She looked away, near whispered,

"He had a voice like Johnny Cash."

Al spread his hands in the universal gesture of *the fuck does that mean?* Charlene was thinking of her third day in Houston: one of those sudden rainstorms hit and she ducked into a building. Turned out it was a library and she looked to see if maybe they had a book on Johnny. Passing a Literature section, she saw a title . . . *To Have and Have Not.*

For some reason, she read it as *To Have and To Hold* and was about to open it when the librarian approached, a spinster in her severe fifties, demanded,

"Are you a member, Miss?"

A hiss riding point on the *Miss.* Charlene knew the type – the dried-up bitter fruit of TV dinners and vicious cats. Charlene dropped the book, said,

"If you have anything to do with it, I'm so fucking out of here."

And was gone.

She'd have asked Foley about the book if Al wasn't there, but she shut it down. Charlie was the usual loser she'd always attracted, but he had an apartment near Rice University and she was running out of time, looks and patience. When she caught him going through her purse, she'd finally figured,

"What the hell?"

And knifed the bastard, in the neck. Then it felt so good, she stuck him a few more times . . . twenty five in all, or so they said. What, they counted? She was still holding the blade when the cops showed up and it was, as they say, a slam-dunk.

Foley said,

"You turned down the offer to have an attorney present."

She gave him what amounted to a tender smile, said,

"They'd assign some guy, and you know what? I'm sick to my gut of men."

Al was unrolling a stick of Juicy Fruit, popped it in his mouth, made some loud sucking noises, said,

"You're a lesbian, that it? Hate all men?"

She let out a breath, said,

"If I sign this, can I get some sleep, some chow?"

Foley passed over a pen, said,

"Have you some ribs, right away."

She signed and Al said,

"Now the bad news darlin'. Ol' Charles, he was the son of a real prominent shaker right here in Houston. Bet he didn't tell you that. You're going away for a long time."

She stretched, asked,

"And what makes you think I give a fuck?"

She got fifteen years. As she was being led down, Al leaned over, said,

"Come sundown, a bull dyke's gonna make you think of Johnny Cash in a whole new light."

She spat in his face.

Six months later, Foley went to see her. He didn't tell Al. When they brought her into the interview room, he was shocked by her appearance. Her frame had shrunk into itself and her eyes were hollow, but she managed a weak smile, said,

"Detective, what brings you out to see the gals?"

He was nervous, his hands awash with sweat, and he blamed the humidity, asked,

"They treating you okay?"

She laughed, said,

"Like one of their own."

He produced a pack of Kools and a book of matches. She looked at him, said,

"I quit."

He felt foolish, tried,

"You can use them for barter, maybe?"

She had a far away expression in her eyes, near whispered,

"They got nothing I want."

He had a hundred questions he wanted to ask, but couldn't think how to frame them and stared at the table. She reached over, touched his hand, said,

"Johnny was on TV last week, did a song called *Hurt*, he sang that for me."

Then she changed tack, said,

"You ever get to El Paso and want to cross the border, take the number 10 green trolley to the Santa Fe Bridge. Don't take the Border Jumper Trolley – it's, like, real expensive. Walk to the right side of the Stanton Bridge and it's twenty-five cents to cross and in El Paso, you want some action, go to the Far West

Rodeo, on Airways Boulevard. They sometimes got live rodeo, and hey, get a few brews in, you might even try the mechanical bull, that's a riot."

Relieved to have something to talk about, he asked,

"You went there a lot?"

"Never, not one time. But I heard, you know?"

He looked at his watch and she said,

"Y'all better be getting on, I got to write me a letter to Johnny, let him know where I'm at."

Foley was standing and said,

"Charlene, he's dead. He died last week."

For a moment, she was stock still, then she emitted a howl of anguish that brought the guards running. She wailed,

"You fucking liar – he's not dead. He'll never be dead to me – how do you think I get through this hell?"

As he hurried down the cellblock, he could still hear her screams, his sweat rolling in rivulets, creasing his cheap suit even further.

As he got his car in "drive," he reached in his jacket, took out the packaged CD of Johnny's Greatest Hits . . . slung it out the window, the disc rolling along the desert for a brief second, then coming to a stop near some sagebrush.

A rodent tearing at the paper exposed Cash's craggy face, and, viewed in a certain light, you'd think he was looking towards the prison.

Impossible to read his expression.

THE 45 STEPS

Peter Crowther

Luddersedge's Regal Hotel lived up to its grand name in only one way.

The building was forbidding rather than imposing, a towering grey edifice of soot-ingrained stone and stained, greasy windows that squatted alongside the traffic lights on the corner of Smithfield Road and Albert Street. The somewhat less-than-impressive facade looked more like an old mill building – examples of which could still be seen dotted around the Calder Valley landscape, all the way from Halifax to Burnley and points even further west – than like a supposedly luxurious establishment catering for visiting gentry. But then, it was highly unlikely that any gentry taking advantage of the Regal's dubious hospitality would actually be visiting Luddersedge itself. Rather, such occasional tenants would more realistically be those whose misfortune was so dire that their mode of transportation between departure and arrival points had chosen Luddersedge to give up the vehicular ghost . . . and at a time to render impossible any solution other than booking into the Regal.

On the top of the five-storey building, amongst the aerials and the blackened windows, pigeons and starlings roosted noisily beside the quieter permanent residents, a troupe of bizarre gargoyles intermittently positioned amidst the stone balustrades and fashioned by Cecil Blenkinsop at the turn of the century. These monolithic decorations – whose artistic merit was questionable at the very least – were presented by Blenkinsop to the hotel in a rare demonstration of generosity.

However, the smart money around the older citizens of the town had it that the "gift" was actually a means to eradicate the excessive gambling debts run up by the gruff mill-owner's son-cum-sculptor in the hotel's extensive gambling casino, a huge two floor area in the belly of the hotel that had since been refashioned and refurbished after the Great War into a ballroom.

To say that hotels in Luddersedge were thin on the ground was an understatement of gargantuan proportions. Although there were countless guest houses, particularly along Honeydew Lane beside the notorious Bentley's Tannery – whose ever-present noxious fumes seemed to be unnoticed by the guests – usually truck drivers, who stayed there as a mid-way point on the long haul from Glasgow to the South Coast, parking their rigs on the spare ground between Carholme Place and Carholme Drive – the Regal was the only full-blown hotel, and the only building other than the old town hall to stretch above the slate roofs of Luddersedge and scratch a sky oblivious to, and entirely disinterested in, its or even the town's existence.

The corridors of the Regal were lined with threadbare carpets, hemmed in by walls bearing a testimonial trinity of mildew, graffiti and spilled alcohol, and topped by ceilings whose anaglypta was peeling at the corners and whose streaky paint-covering had been long ago dimmed by cigarette smoke.

The rooms themselves boasted little in the way of the creature comforts offered by the Regal's big-town contemporaries in Halifax and Burnley.

Only the Albert, Calder and Bickerdyke suites on the fourth floor featured tea- and coffee-making facilities, not to mention sufficient room to swing a cat . . . should such an activity be desired (though deplorable TV reception and the absence of satellite or cable-fed hotel movies imbued even the most unusual in-room entertainment with dizzily heightened credibility and attraction).

The truth, however, was that the Regal's guests brought their own entertainment in the form of a partner whose intimate attentions they might enjoy amidst the carbolic soap-smelling bed linen rather than propped against the building walls surrounding the club district of the metropolis of Halifax or parked up in one of the pull-ins overlooking Todmorden, testing the suspension and upholstery of old cars whose MOTs had been just a little too readily granted by Pete Dickinson or Tony Manderson at Tony's garage over on Eldershot Road.

Such activities were entirely safe inasmuch that, while the Regal's facilities were often found lacking, the discretion of the staff was legendary . . . and with room rates being so modest, even with breakfast added on, an additional gratuity in the form of a folded fiver jammed into the hand of the appropriately named manager Sidney Poke or one of his team was a small price to pay for uninterrupted passion in the relative comfort and complete anonymity accorded by the Regal.

For most of the year, the Regal's register – if such a thing were ever to be filled in, which it rarely was . . . at least accurately – boasted only couples by the name of Smith or Jones, and the catering staff had little to prepare in the form of sustenance other than the fabled Full English Breakfast, truly the most obscenely mountainous start-of-the-day plate of food outside of Dublin. Indeed, questions were frequently asked in bread shop or bus stop queues and around the beer-slopped pub tables at the Working Men's Club as to exactly how the Regal kept going.

But there were far too many other things to occupy the attention and interest of Luddersedge's townsfolk and, anyway, most of them recognized the important social part played by the Regal in the lives of their not-so-distant cousins living in the towns a few miles down the road in either direction . . . just as they recognized the equally important part played for themselves by similar establishments in those same towns. There were far too many scarf-bedecked Juliets and blue-collar Romeos – some young and some not so young – who had taken advantage of such no-questions-asked solitude . . . some long ago, when their flesh seemed more artistically arranged, and some only a day or two earlier, when they had supposedly been visiting relatives in far-off Leeds or Manchester or delivering a van-load of unpronounceable grommet-type things down to Birmingham or up to Newcastle: after all, it didn't do to defecate on one's own doorstep, and the status quo could only ever be maintained by not asking awkward questions.

Not that awkward questions were not asked about other situations in which the Regal played a key role, one of which came to pass on a Saturday night in early December on the occasion of the Conservative Club's Christmas Party . . . and which involved the one hotel feature that was truly magnificent – the Gentlemen's toilet situated in the basement beneath the ballroom.

To call such a sprawling display of elegance and creative indulgence a loo or a bog – or even a john or a head, to use the slang vernacular popular with the occasional Americans who visited the Calder Valley in the 1950s, the heyday of Ludders-edge's long-forgotten twinning with the mid west town of Forest Plains – was tantamount to heresy.

Listen to this:

A row of shoulder-height marble urinals – complete with side panels that effectively rendered invisible anyone of modest height who happened to be availing themselves of their facility – was completed by a series of carefully angled glass panel splashguards set in aluminium side grips and a standing area inlaid with a mosaic of tiny slate and Yorkshire stone squares and rectangles of a multitude of colours. It was an area worn smooth by generations of men temporarily intent on emptying bladders filled with an excess of John Smith's, Old Peculiar and Black Sheep bitter ales served in the bars above.

Two wide steps down from the urinals, set back and mounted on ornate embellishments of curlicued brass fashioned to re-semble a confusion of vines interlinked with snakes, a row of generously sized washbasins nested beneath individual facing panels split one half mirror and the other reinforced glass. The glass halves looked through onto an identical set of basins on the other side of the partition and behind them stood the WCs.

It was these wood-panelled floor-to-ceiling enclosed retreats – with their individual light switches, oak toilet seats and covers and matching tissue dispensers, and stained glass backings behind the pipe leading from the overhead cistern – that were, perhaps, the room's crowning glory, being even more impress-ive than the worn leather sofas and wing-backed chairs situated on their own dais at the far end of the toilet, bookended by towering aspidistras and serviced by standing silver ashtrays and glass-topped tables bearing the latest issues of popular men's magazines.

But while these extravagant rooms – albeit small rooms, designed for but one purpose – had rightly gained some considerable fame (particularly as the town was not noted for anything even approaching artistic or historical significance) they had also achieved a certain notoriety that was not always welcome.

Such notoriety came not from merely from the time, in the late 1940s, when an exceptionally inebriated Jack Walker (father of the unfortunate Stanley, who was to meet his tragic end at the hands of his wife when she administered a lethal dose of EXTERMINATE! into his bottle of beer) pitched forward rather unexpectedly – after failing to register the aforementioned double step leading to the urinals – and smashed his head into one of the glass-panelled splashguards. The accident resulted in the loss of Jack's left eye which, Jack being reluctant to wear a patch covering the now vacant socket ("Makes me look like a bloody pirate," Jack remarked to his friend Alan, down at the steel mill one morning soon after the incident), was replaced by a strangely coloured (and shaped, for that matter) orb that more resembled the marbles his then six-year-old son Stan delighted in firing across the living room carpet than an eye.

Nor did it come only from the legendary night when Pete Dickinson was ceremoniously divested of all of his clothes on his stag night and reduced to escaping the Regal, staggering drunkenly through Luddersedge's cold spring streets, wearing only one of the toilet's continuous hand towels (those being the days before automatic hand dryers, of course), a 50-foot ribbon of linen that gave the quickly sobering Dickinson the appearance of a cross between Julius Caesar and Boris Karloff's mummy.

Rather, the toilet's somewhat dubious reputation stemmed solely from the fact that, over the years, its lavish cubicles had seen a stream of Luddersedge's finest and most virile young men venturing into their narrow enclosures with their latest female conquests for a little session of hi-jinks where, their minds (and, all too often, their prowess and sexual longevity) clouded by the effects of ale, a surfeit of testosterone, the threat of being discovered, they would perform loveless couplings to the muted strains of whatever music drifted down from the floor above.

The practice was known, in the less salubrious circles of Calder Valley drinking establishments, as "The Forty Five Steps Club". The name referred, in a version of the similar "honorary" appellation afforded those who carried out the same act on an in-flight aeroplane ("The Mile High Club"), to the toilet's distance below ground – three perilously steep banks of fifteen steps leading down from the ballroom's west entrance.

And so it was that, at precisely 10 o'clock on the fateful night of the Conservative Club's Christmas Party, it was to this bastion room of opulence and renown that Arthur Clark retired midway through a plate of turkey, new potatoes, broccoli and carrots (having already seen off several pints of John Smith's, an entire bowl of dry roasted peanuts – Planters, Arthur's favourite – and the Regal's obligatory prawn cocktail first course) to evacuate both bladder and bowel. It was a clockwork thing with Arthur and, no matter where he was nor whom he was with, he would leave whatever was going on to void himself – on this occasion, all the better to concentrate his full attention and gastric juices on the promised (though some might say "threatened") Christmas Pudding and rum sauce plus a couple of coffees, and a few glasses of Bells whisky. Arthur's slightly weaving departure from the ballroom, its back end filled with a series of long dining tables leaving the area immediately in front of the stage free for the inevitable dancing that would follow coffee and liqueurs, was to be the last time that his fellow guests saw him alive.

"Edna. *Edna!*" Betty Thorndike was leaning across the table trying to get Edna Clark's attention, while one of the Merkinson twins – Betty thought it was Hilda but she couldn't be sure, they both looked so alike – returned to her seat and dropped her handbag onto the floor beside her. Hilda – if it was Hilda – had been to the toilet more than fifteen minutes ago, while everyone else was still eating, her having bolted her food down in record time, and had spent the time since her return talking to Agnes Olroyd, as though she didn't want to come back and join them: they were a funny pair, the Merkinsons.

When Edna turned around, from listening – disinterestedly – to John and Mary Tullen's conversation about conservatories with Barbara Ashley and her husband, whose name she could never remember (it was Kenneth), she was frowning.

"What?"

"He's been a long time, hasn't he?" she said across the table, nodding to the watch on her wrist. "Your Arthur."

"He's had a lot," Edna said with a shrug. The disc jockey on the stage put on Glen Campbell's "Wichita Lineman".

"Oh, I love this me," Mary Tullen announced to the table, droopy-eyed, and promptly began trying to join in with the words, cigarette smoke drifting out of her partially open mouth. She took a long drink of wine and frowned. "Who is it again? Name's on the tip of my tongue."

Edna shook her head.

"What was it like?" the Merkinson twin who had been to the toilet said to the one who had not.

A shrug was the reply. "You've been a long time, Hilda," she said, pushing her plate forward. Hilda noted that the food had been shuffled around on the plate but not much had been eaten.

"Been talking to Agnes Olroyd."

"So I saw."

"She was asking me about the robbery," Hilda said.

"Robbery? I thought you said nothing had been taken."

Hilda shrugged. "Robbery, break-in – it's all the same thing."

Hilda worked at the animal testing facility out on Aldershot Road where, two days earlier, she had come into work to discover someone had broken in during the night – animal rights protesters, her boss Ian Arbutt had told the police – and trashed the place.

Not wanting to talk about the break-in again – it having been a source of conversation everywhere in the town the past 36 hours, particularly in the Merkinson twins' small two-up, two-down in Belmont Drive – Hilda's sister said, "How's her Eric?"

Hilda made a face. "His prostate's not so good," she said.

"Oh." Harriet's attention seemed more concentrated on Edna Clark.

As Mary elbowed her husband in the stomach, prising his attention away from a young woman returning to a nearby table with breasts that looked like they had been inflated, Betty Thorndike said to Edna, "D'you think he's all right?"

John Tullen spun around, glaring at his wife. "What?"

"Who, my Arthur?" Edna said.

"D'you know who's singing this song?" Mary asked her husband. "It's on the tip of my tongue."

"I'm surprised you can sense anything with that tongue," John said as he reached for his pint of Guinness. "You've near on pickled the bloody thing tonight. Whyn't you slow down a bit?"

Edna said, "He's fine. He always goes at this time. Regular as clockwork. Doesn't matter where he is." This last revelation was accompanied by a slight shake of her head that seemed to convey both amazement and despair.

"I know," Mary Tullen agreed, still wondering who it was that was singing. "It's common knowledge, your Arthur's regularity." She had trouble getting her mouth around the word "regularity", splitting it into three single-syllabled words with the following "ity" barely covering a watery burp. " 'Scuse me," Mary said.

"But he's been a long time." Betty nodded to Arthur's unfinished meal. "And he hasn't even finished his dinner."

"He'll finish it when he gets back," Edna said with assurance.

Behind her, somebody said, "There's no bloody paper down there."

Hilda Merkinson knocked her glass over and a thin veil of lager spilled across the table and onto her sister's lap. "Hilda! For goodness sake."

"Damn it," Hilda said.

Edna threw a spare serviette across the table and turned around. Billy Roberts was sliding into his seat on the next table.

Sitting across from Billy, Jack Hanlon burst into a loud laugh. "You didn't use your hands again, did you, Billy? You'll never sell any meat on Monday – smell'll be there for days."

Billy smiled broadly and held his hand out beneath his friend's nose. Jack pulled back so quickly he nearly upturned his chair. He took a drink of Old Peculiar, swallowed and shook a B&H out of a pack lying on the table. "If you must know," Billy said, lighting the cigarette and blowing a thick cloud up towards the ceiling, "I used my hanky." He made a play of reaching into his pocket. "But I washed it out, see—" And he pretended to throw something across the table to his friend. This time, gravity took its toll and Jack went over backwards into the aisle.

As Jack got to his feet and righted his chair, Billy said, "I flushed it, didn't I, daft bugger. But I was worried for a few minutes when I saw there wasn't any paper – course, by that time, I'd done the deed. When I got out, I checked all the WCs and there isn't a bit in any of them." He blew out more smoke.

"Aren't you going to tell somebody, Billy?" Helen Simpson asked, her eyes sparkling as they took in Billy Roberts's quiffed hair.

"Can't be arsed," Billy said. "There's some poor sod down there now – probably still down there: he'll have something to say about it when he gets out," he added as he did a quick glance at the entrance to see if he could see anybody returning who looked either a little sheepish or blazing with annoyance.

"That'll be Arthur." Edna looked over her shoulder at Betty. "I bet that's my Arthur," she said. She tapped Billy on the shoulder. "That'll be my Arthur," she said again.

"What's that, Mrs Clark?" Billy said, turning. "What's your Arthur gone and done now?"

"He went to the toilet ages ago."

Harriet Merkinson shuffled around in her handbag, produced a thick bundle of Kleenex and she held them out. "Here, why don't you take him these?"

Edna nodded. "Thanks, er—"

"Harriet," said Harriet.

"Thanks Harry – good idea." She passed the tissues back to Billy and gave a big smile. "Here, be an angel, Billy and go back down and push these under the door for me."

"You haven't been down to the gents . . . have you, Mrs Clark?" There was a snigger at the last part from Jack Hanlon. "You can't get sod all under them doors."

"Well, can't you knock on his door or something?" She nodded to the table behind her. "He hasn't even finished his meal."

Hilda looked across at Arthur's plate and noted that it didn't look much different to her sister's – the only difference was that one meal was finished with and the other wasn't.

*   *   *

When he got back to the toilet, Billy saw one of the waiters was already going into each cubicle to fasten a new roll of tissue into the dispenser. "Bugger me, you're already doing it," he said to the young man, whose face coloured immediately. "Somebody tell you, did they? Was it Arthur Clark?"

The boy shook his head and the colour on his cheeks darkened. "It was some bloke, don't know what he's called," the waiter said, shifting his weight from one foot to the other. "Said he'd come down and couldn't find a—" The boy paused, searching for the word.

"A trap?" Billy ventured.

The boy smiled. "Said he couldn't find a trap with any paper." He nodded to a closed door at the end of the line of cubicles. "He's all right now, though."

Outside the door to the toilet there was a sudden burst of high-pitched giggling. "There's a bloody waiter in there!" a girl's voice said. Billy chuckled. Presumably only the waiter's presence was preventing the girl from coming into the gents with her partner and not the fact that the toilet area was filled with men, young and old, either standing at the urinals or washing at the basins. Alcohol was a wonderful thing and no denying.

The chuckling continued and was complemented by the sound of feet hurriedly ascending the 45 steps back to the ballroom. A man Billy didn't know wafted through the doors unzipping his flies and grinning like a Cheshire cat.

Billy exchanged nods with the man and turned his attention back to the waiter. He was still smiling – until he saw that the door to the cubicle which had been occupied while he was down here was still firmly closed.

"Has somebody just gone in there? I mean, while you've been down here."

The boy glanced at the closed door and shook his head. "Not while I've been down here."

Billy walked across and tapped gently on the door. "Hello?" There was no response.

"He'll be sleeping it off, lad, whoever he is," a stocky bald man confided to Billy as he held his hands under the automatic drier. "You'll need to knock louder than that."

Billy nodded slowly. He rapped the door three times and said, "Mister Clark – are you in there? I've got some tissues for you."

No answer.

The bald man finished his hands off on the back of his trousers and moved across so that he was standing alongside Billy. Although he was short, a good six inches shorter than Billy and three or four beneath the lofty height of the young waiter, the bald man had a commanding air about him. The waiter shuffled to one side to give the man more room.

The bald man hit the door several times with a closed fist and shouted, "Come on, mate, time to get up. You'll be needing a hammer and chisel if you stay in there much longer, never mind bloody toilet paper."

Still no answer.

"He must be a bloody heavy sleeper," Billy said. "Either that or he's pissed as a newt."

The bald man turned to the waiter. "Is there any way into these things? I mean, some way of getting in when they're locked."

"I don't know," the boy said.

"Well, can you find somebody who does know? And can you do it bloody sharpish?"

The boy turned around and ran to the door and disappeared, his clumping feet echoing up the steps to the ballroom.

The man lifted his hands and felt around the door. "Do you know this bloke, whoever he is?"

Billy shook his head and jammed the toilet tissue into his jacket pocket. "No. Well, I do . . . I know his name and that but I don't really know him. His wife asked me to come down."

The man nodded. "Why was that, then?" he said, turning around.

"Well, there was no paper in any of the toilets."

"How did his wife know that?"

"She heard me telling them on my table. I'd just got back from . . . you know –"

"Having a crap. I know – get on with it, lad."

Billy straightened his shoulders. He would usually square up to anyone who spoke to him like that – after all, he wasn't a lad: he was almost 25 – but there was something about the bald man that made him shrink back from confrontation. "That trap was closed when I came down here and it was still closed when I went back up."

The bald man reached into his inside pocket and removed a packet of Marlboro. As he pulled a cigarette out, he said to Billy, "Do you smoke?"

Billy nodded. "Yeah," he said, lifting his hand towards the man's cigarettes. The man closed the pack and returned it to his pocket. "Well, give it up," he said as he flicked a lighter under the cigarette and drew in smoke. "It'll stunt your growth. Did you hear anything while you were down here?"

Billy shrugged. "Like what?"

The man blew smoke out. "Groans, plops, farts, throwing up . . . the usual."

"No. No, I didn't."

The man nodded. He hammered on the door again, louder this time. "What did you say his name was?"

"Arthur Clark."

"Not the bloke who wrote *2001*, I suppose? I loved that picture."

"I don't think so," Billy said with a chuckle.

"No, me neither." He hammered again. "Mister Clark . . . if you can hear me, open the door. It's the police."

Billy was watching the door but when he heard that he turned to the man. "Are you really the police? I mean, are you a . . . a copper?"

Before the man could answer, the waiter came back into the toilet. He was trailing behind a tall man with bushy eyebrows that met over his nose. His face, which was scowling, was a mask of excess, folds of skin lined with broken blood vessels. He said, "What's going on?"

"Who are you?" the bald man asked.

"Sidney Poke. I'm the manager of the Regal."

The bald man nodded. "Any way into these things when they're locked on the inside?"

Sidney Poke said, "Who are you?"

The bald man jammed his cigarette in the corner of his mouth, pulled a credit card holder from his inside pocket and shuffled through the little plastic flaps. He found what he was looking for and held it out for inspection. "Detective Inspector Malcolm Broadhurst, Leeds CID," he said.

"What's the problem, Inspector?" Sidney Poke said, his manner suddenly less aggressive.

"Somebody's in here and we can't get them to open the door. Been here a while, this lad says," Malcolm Broadhurst said, nodding at Billy Roberts.

"Who is it? Who's in there?" Sidney Poke asked Billy.

"Never mind who he is," the policeman said. "How do we bloody well get in to him?"

Sidney Poke shrugged. "I suppose we have to knock the door down."

Malcolm Broadhurst nodded. "Why did I know you were going to say that? Right—" He threw his cigarette on the floor and ground it with his foot. "One of you go upstairs and call for an ambulance – just to be on the safe side."

A blond-haired man said, "I'll do it," and disappeared at a run out of the toilet.

The policeman took hold of Billy's left arm and squeezed the biceps. "What do you do for a living, lad?"

"I'm a butcher."

"Just the job," he said, and he stepped back out of the way. "Right, break that bloody door down – and, daft as it sounds, try not to go mad: he could be on the floor at the other side."

As he squared up to the door, Billy said, "How the hell do I do that? Knock the door down but go steady, I mean."

"Just do your best. Now, you others stand back and give him room."

The door jamb splintered on the sixth try. It came away on the eighth, still fastened but only loosely.

"Brilliant job, lad," Broadhurst said taking Billy's arm. He pulled him back and stepped close to the door, squinting through the small gap that had appeared. "It's still fastened, but only just."

He stepped back and frowned. "No time to bugger about looking for something to prise it open. If the fella couldn't hear all that din then he's in a bad way." He stepped back and nodded to Billy. "Break it down, lad."

Billy pulled himself back onto his left foot and hit the door with all his strength. The lock snapped and they heard something – a screw, maybe, or part of the actual lock – clatter inside the cubicle. The door stopped against something on the floor.

Malcolm Broadhurst pushed Billy out of the way and, holding the door, squeezed his way into the cubicle. When he was inside, the policeman closed the door again.

They heard shuffling.

"Is he all right?" Sidney Poke asked. Billy thought it was a pretty stupid question.

For a few seconds there was no answer and then the policeman said, "He's dead." Then, after a few seconds more of shuffling sounds and sounds of exertion, he said, "Bloody hell fire."

Billy said, "What is it?"

When the door opened again the policeman was rubbing his face, looking down at the floor.

Billy and Sidney Poke and the young waiter – whose name was Chris and for whom this was his first night working at the Regal – followed Malcolm Broadhurst's stare.

Arthur Clark was now sitting up against the side wall of the cubicle, the toilet paper dispenser – containing almost a full roll of paper – just above and to the side of his left ear. He was fully clothed but his shirt had been ripped apart at the stomach. Worse than that, the man's flesh looked to have been flayed . . . with thick red welts and deep gashes covering the skin, and the top of his light grey trousers seemed to have been dyed black around the waistband: but they knew the original colour had been a deep red.

Chris the waiter gagged and turned away, his hand clamped over his mouth as he made for the washbasins. He made it just in time. When he was through, he leaned his head on his hand to one side of the basin and, in a surprised voice, said, "Hey, that's where they were."

The boy crouched down and reached his hands to the deep metal basket on the floor between his basin and the one next to it. When he stood up he was holding an armful of toilet rolls, some full and still thick and some partly used.

"Bloody idiots," said Sidney Poke. "Do anything for a laugh but they wouldn't think it was so damned fun—"

"Get everyone out, Mister Poke," the policeman said. His voice sounded tired. "Get everyone back upstairs. But not you, butcher boy," he said, turning to Billy. "You can give me a hand getting him out of here."

The toilet was completely empty when they finally struggled out with Arthur Clark and laid him on the floor beside the washbasins.

"He looks like he's been got at by a wild animal," Billy said. "And scared to death, by the look on his face."

The policeman shook two Marlboros from his pack and handed one to Billy. "Give it up tomorrow," he said as he held his lighter under Billy's cigarette.

Billy drew in the smoke and watched the bald man crouch down by the body. He turned over Arthur Clark's hands one by one and said, "He was the wild animal. He did it to himself. See—" He held one of the hands up for Billy to see. The nails were caked with blood and skin – they looked like the hands of a butcher.

"Why? What did he think he was doing, do you think?"

"Looks to me like he was trying to get into his own stomach."

"Arthur?" a woman's voice shouted from outside the toilet door.

Then a man's voice said, "You can't go in there, madam."

"Arthur!" the woman's voice screamed.

There was a crash outside the door that sounded unquestionably like someone falling over.

"Shit," said Detective Inspector Malcolm Broadhurst.

The ambulance arrived with siren wailing but it left silently.

Malcolm Broadhurst sat with Edna Clark for a long time, initially with Betty Thorndike, Joan Cardew and Miriam Barrett by her side, offering consolation in the undoubtedly heartfelt but seemingly sycophantic way that people have when they feel *There but for the grace of God.* To the policeman from Leeds CID the trio was doing more harm than good and he sent them packing. "Like the bloody witches from 'Hamlet'," he said to Billy Roberts over at the bar, ordering a couple of stiff Jamesons from Sidney Poke, who had assumed bar duties for the duration.

The rest of the guests and all the staff had given their names to a couple of uniformed officers from Halifax and had gone home.

"Macbeth," Sidney Poke said quietly.

Billy looked up from his Irish frowning. He would have been happier with a pint but the policeman had ordered. "What?"

"The three witches. It was 'Macbeth', not 'Hamlet'."

"Oh."

"And what about Bill and Ben? That was a turn-up for the books."

"Who's Bill and Ben?"

"Oh, the Merkinsons. The two old women."

"Oh, the one who collapsed."

Billy nodded. "And her sister."

"Was it Bill or was it Ben?" Broadhurst mumbled.

"Huh?"

The policeman shook his head. "Which one of them was it who collapsed?"

Billy shrugged. "You can never tell. They both always look the same – dress the same, talk the same . . . it's really weird."

The two "old" women, as Billy Roberts had called them, were 53 years old. Malcolm Broadhurst wouldn't have been far out with his own estimate of 50–51. The same age, give or take a year – he always forgot his own age but he knew he'd had his fiftieth because of the stripper they'd bought for him down at the station – and he didn't consider himself as old. But then again, maybe he was. "Twins, are they?" he said.

Billy nodded.

Broadhurst had noticed them, standing by while he was talking to Edna Clark, because they were identically dressed, right down to the two-string necklace of fake pearls hanging over the first half-inch of their maroon dresses. One of them was looking after the other, the one who had collapsed, feeding her sips of brandy brought over by Sidney Poke.

"Like a couple of weirdos," Billy Roberts said, remembering the scene in vivid detail. "Funny though, her keeling over like that."

Now it was the policeman's turn to nod. "She the Hilda Merkinson who works at the animal rights centre? The one that was done in this week?"

Billy frowned. "Don't know. But she's the only Hilda Merkinson in Luddersedge."

"Cheers!" said Malcolm Broadhurst. He lifted his glass and drained it, then set it back on the bar top. "How much do I owe you?" he said to the Regal's manager.

Poke shook his head. "On the house. Think I'll have one myself."

It was one o'clock.

"What was it, d'you think?" Billy asked. He lit a B&H from the packet he'd retrieved from the table and offered it to the other two. Poke waved a hand and the policeman simply produced his Marlboros and took one out.

"We'll know when the autopsy boys know," Broadhurst said around a cloud of smoke. "His missus says he didn't have a bad heart or anything, but it's either that or something he ate."

"I thought that," Billy offered, and then wished he hadn't when he caught the glare from the Regal's manager.

"Or drunk," Broadhurst said. "I've had his meal wrapped up for tests, along with the pint he was working his way through."

"Fancy," Billy said, more to himself than to the others, "getting up for a crap halfway through your meal."

"His missus says he does it regular as clockwork," Broadhurst said.

"That's right," Billy said. "Doesn't matter where he is or who he's with. Come ten o'clock he has to disappear to do the deed. It's legendary around town – everybody knows."

"Another?" Poke said, holding the bottle of Jamesons over the policeman's glass.

Broadhurst frowned over the answer to that and other questions that were already forming in his mind.

It was almost two o'clock when Broadhurst made his way from the ballroom and along the corridor towards reception. At the steps leading down to the Gentlemen's toilet he paused. The steps were well lit but only in stages, the main house lights of the hotel having been dimmed an hour earlier. Now only single bulbs, secured behind half shells equally spaced down the flights, lit the steps leaving a well of darkness at the bottom.

The darkness seemed inviting and off-putting, both at the same time.

The policeman shook a cigarette from his packet, lit it and breathed smoke around him. It felt good . . . felt normal somehow. For there was a lot about what had happened that was not normal.

Before he even realized he was moving, Broadhurst had reached the landing at the foot of the first flight, his hand on the rail and his eyes squinting into the gloom. He took the next two flights two steps at a time but when he reached the bottom, with the ornate doors leading into the toilet right in front of him, he stopped and listened.

What was he listening for, he wondered. Was he listening for the sounds of Arthur Clark, screaming in agony? For didn't some folks say that no sound ever died but only grew faint, waiting to be heard once more by those with the most finely tuned sense of hearing? No, it was something more than that . . . something more than the late-night campfire thoughts of ghoulies and ghosties and things that went *phrrrp!* in the night.

He threw his cigarette stub to the floor and stepped on it hard, pushing open the doors and stepping inside.

The toilet was silent. There was no sound save for the distant chuckle of water moving through ancient pipes, turning over in radiators and cisterns, and *dlup dlupping* down drain holes.

He looked around.

Someone else had been in here, someone who knew more about Arthur's tragic death than he did. A lot more. Broadhurst felt it – felt it in his water, he thought, cringing at the unintentional pun. The death was neither natural nor unintentional. But he couldn't understand how it could be anything else.

He walked along the row of cubicles, their doors either fully open or ajar, and felt a sense of threat . . . as though someone was going to step out of them . . . perhaps someone recently dead come to exact his revenge . . . or someone who knew more about the death, come to prevent being caught. Broadhurst stepped away from the line of cubicles and stopped, staring at the open doors.

What was he thinking of? How could the death be anything other than natural? The cubicle walls went from floor to ceiling, the door the same . . . save for barely an inch of space top and bottom – certainly far less than would be required to get into the cubicle if the door were locked from the inside. And, of course, the same went for getting out again when the deed was done.

"What deed?" Broadhurst said softly. There was no answer, just a giggle of water over by the sofa at the far end of the room.

He leaned on one of the basins and continued to look around. He moved from the basin, reluctantly turning his back on the cubicles until he was reassured by their reflection in the mirror over the basin in front of him, and looked some more. *What are you looking for, Kojak?* a small voice whispered in the back of his head, using the name granted to him by those colleagues in Halifax CID who could remember the TV show. *It's an open and shit case, seems to me*, it added with what might have been a wry chuckle.

"Funny!" Broadhurst snapped, and he looked along the basin-tops, down to the floor and then along beneath them. There was a basket beside each one.

Hey, that's where they were.

The young waiter's voice sounded clear as a bell in his head. Broadhurst could half see him, stooping down to lift an armful of toilet rolls.

Then Sidney Poke's voice chimed in. *Bloody idiots . . . Do anything for a laugh.*

Broadhurst frowned.

The ghost of Billy's voice said, *That's right, doesn't matter where he is or who he's with. Come ten o'clock he has to disappear to do the deed. It's legendary around town – everybody knows.*

Broadhurst turned around to face the cubicles

everybody knows

and walked slowly towards them, his back straightening as they came nearer. He started at one end and walked slowly, pushing open each door and staring at the empty tissue holder

Hey, that's where they were

attached to the wall of each cubicle, right next to where an arm would be resting on a straining knee . . . where so many arms had rested on so many straining knees

It's legendary around town

until he reached

everybody knows

a cubicle with toilet paper. *The* cubicle.

He stared down at the now empty floor and closed his eyes. He saw Arthur Clark writhing in agony, crying out for help . . . so much pain that he could not simply unlock the cubicle door and crawl for help.

Broadhurst removed his handkerchief from his pocket and, stepping into the cubicle, wrapped it around the toilet roll.

Seconds later he was going up the steps away from the Regal's Gentlemen's toilet, two steps at a time . . . and wishing he could move faster.

★　　★　　★

Sundays in Luddersedge are traditionally quiet affairs but the events of the previous evening at the Conservative Club's Christmas Party had permeated the town the same way smoke from an overcooked meal fills a kitchen.

In the tiny houses that lined the old cobbled streets of the town, over cereals and toast and bacon butties, and around tables festooned with open newspapers – primarily copies of the *News of the World*, the *Sunday Mirror* and the *Sunday Sport* – voices were discussing Arthur Clark's unexpected demise in hushed almost reverent tones.

Conversations such as this one:

"I'll bet it was his heart," Miriam Barrett said from her position at the gas stove in the small kitchen in 14 Montgomery Street.

Her husband, Leonard, grunted over the *Mirror*'s sports pages. "Edna said not," he mumbled. "Said he hadn't had no heart problems."

Miriam was unconvinced. She turned the sausages over in the frying pan and shuffled the ones that looked sufficiently cooked across to the side with the bacon and a few pieces of tomato that looked like sizzling blood-clots. "All that business with his . . . *toilet*," she said, imbuing the word with a strange Calder Valley mysticism that might be more at home whispered in the *gris gris* atmosphere of a New Orleans speakeasy. "Can't have been right."

Leonard said, "He was just regular, that's all."

"Yes, well, there's regular and there's *regular*," Miriam pointed out sagely. "But having to go in the middle of your meal like that, just cos it's ten o'clock, well, that's not regular."

Leonard frowned. He wondered just what it was if it wasn't regular, but decided against pursuing the point.

But not everyone in Luddersedge was talking.

In his bedroom over his father's butcher's shop at the corner of Lemon Road and Coronation Drive, Billy Roberts opened his eyes and stared at the watery sun glowing behind his closed curtains. His mouth was a mixture of kettle fur and sandpaper and using it to speak was the very last thing on his mind. It was all he could do to groan, and even then the sound of it sounded strange to him, like it wasn't coming from him at all but maybe drifting from beneath the bed where something crouched, something big and unpleasant, waiting to see his foot appear in front of it.

Billy turned to his side and breathed deeply into his cupped hand. Then he stuck his nose into the opening in his hand and sniffed. The smell was sour and vaguely alcoholic, almost perfumed. He slumped back onto the pillows. It was those bloody whiskies that did it. He should have stuck to the beer, the way he usually did. It didn't do to go mixing drinks.

Billy had had a bad night, even after all the booze. He supposed there was nothing like messing around with a dead body – particularly one that had smelt the way Arthur Clark's had done, Arthur having so recently dumped into his trousers – to sober a person up. It had taken Billy more than an hour to drop off after getting in – despite the fact that it was three in the morning – and even then his dreams had been peppered with Arthur's face . . . and the man's ravaged stomach.

Work had been underway in the ballroom of the less than palatial Regal Hotel for several hours when Billy Roberts was beginning to contemplate getting out of bed.

The wreckage was far worse than usual somehow, even though the festivities had been cut short by the tragic events in the gentlemen's toilet. But at least most of the explosive streamers were still intact and there were fewer stains than usual on the cloths and the chairs. The most surprising thing was the number of personal possessions that had been left in the cloakroom, particularly considering the very careful population of the town. But then the unceremonious way the guests had been dispatched for home after been questioned made a lot of things understandable.

Chris Hackett had arrived after the clear-up had begun, clocking into the ancient machine mounted on the green tiled wall leading to the Regal's back door at 7.13. He didn't think anyone would object to the fact that he was almost a quarter of an hour late, not after last night.

He set to straight away, throwing his yellow and blue bubble jacket onto one of the chest freezers in the kitchen and emerging through the swing doors into the ballroom. It was a hive of activity.

Jeff Wilkinson was busy dismantling one of the trestle tables over near the stage. Several of the tables had already been folded up and were standing propped against the ornate pillar beside the steps leading up to the stage, and chairs were stacked in towering piles against the side wall.

In the centre of the floor, Mervyn Frith was adding to a huge mound of tablecloths lay jumbled up – the cloths were waiting for somebody to fold them, an unpleasant job given their size and the amount of spilled food that still clung to them.

Elsewhere, various young men and women were loading glasses and bottles and plates and cutlery onto rickety wooden trolleys, the sound of their labours dwarfed by the sound of similar items being loaded into the huge dishwashers in the kitchens.

Wondering where he should start, Chris Hackett saw a table that had been untouched, over by the far wall. He went across to it, moving around to the wall side to begin stacking the plates. Halfway along the wall he caught his foot on something and went sprawling onto the floor, knocking over two chairs on the way.

Somebody laughed and their was a faint burst of applause as Chris got to his feet and looked around for the culprit of his embarrassment.

It was a ladies' handbag.

Malcolm Broadhurst sat smoking a cigarette. He had been up since before dawn, having snatched a couple of hours' fitful nap lying fully clothed on the eiderdown.

He had watched the sun pull itself languidly over the rooftops of Luddersedge and had then spent the next 40, 45 minutes trying to get something resembling decent reception from his TV. In the end, faced with either the Tellytubbies or an Open University programme on quantum physics, he gave it up and sat waiting for the day outside to catch up with him. That and thinking about the previous evening.

The call came through at a little after ten o'clock.

A man's voice said, "You up?"

"Yeah."

"Been to bed?"

Broadhurst grunted. "Didn't sleep, though."

"Well, you were right not to," the voice said. "We've been on this all night – well, all morning would be more accurate."

"And?"

"We've not finished yet but we've got a pretty good idea."

The voice with the pretty good idea belonged to Jim Garnett, the doctor in charge of forensic science at Halifax Infirmary and who doubled as the medical guru for Halifax CID. He chuckled. "It's a goodie. You were right to be suspicious."

The policeman shook another cigarette from his packet and settled himself against the bed headboard. "Go on."

"Okay. Two hours ago, I'd've been calling you to tell you he'd had a heart attack."

"And he didn't."

"Well, that's not exactly true: he did have a cardiac arrest . . . but it wasn't brought on by natural causes." Garnett paused and Broadhurst could hear the doctor shifting papers around. "What made me a little more cautious than usual – apart from your telephone call last night . . . for which Yvonne sends her thanks, by the way – was the list of symptoms, all classical."

Broadhurst didn't speak but it was as though the doctor had read the question in his mind.

"There were too many. Profuse salivation—"

"Profuse – is that like, there was a lot of it?"

"You could say that," came the reply. "The poor chap's shirt was soaked and he'd bitten through the back left side of his tongue; he'd vomited, messed his pants – diarrhoea: most unpleasant – and there were numerous contusions to the head, arms and legs."

"Suggesting what?"

"The contusions?" Garnett smacked his lips. "Dizziness, auditory and visual disturbances, blurred vision . . . that kind of thing – and not the kind of thing you want to experience when you're stuck in a WC. It's my bet he shambled about in there like a ping pong ball, bouncing off every wall. And, of course, the pain would have been nothing to what he was having from his stomach – that's why he'd clawed at himself so much. By then, he'd be having seizures – hence the tongue – and he'd be faint."

"Why didn't he just come out, shout for help?"

"Disorientation would be my guess. And panic. He'd be in a terrible state at this point, Mal."

Broadhurst waited. "And?"

"And then he'd die. I've seen cases before – cardiac arrests – with two or three of the same symptoms, but never so many together . . . and never so intense. This chap suffered hell in his final minutes."

Garnett sighed before continuing. "So, we checked him out for all the usual bacteria – saliva, urine, stool samples . . . and there were plenty of those, right down to his ankles – and—"

"So he hadn't even been to the toilet?"

"No, he *had* been. His large bowel was empty. This stuff came as the result of a sudden stimulation to the gut and that would release contents further up the bowel passage. Anyway, like I said, we checked everything but it was no go. Then I checked the meal – bland but harmless – and the beer . . . nothing there either."

Garnett moved away from the phone to cough. "God, and now I think I'm coming down with a cold."

"Take the rest of the day off."

"Thanks!" He cleared his throat and went on. "So, in absolute desperation, we started checking him for needle marks . . . thought he might be using something and that was why he always went to the toilet so regularly. But there was nothing, skin completely unbroken. And then . . ."

"Ah, is this the good bit?"

"Yes, indeedy – and this is the good bit."

Broadhurst could sense the doctor leaning further into the phone, preparing to deliver the *coup de grâce*.

"Then we turned him over and we found the rash."

"The *rash?* All that and a rash too?"

"On his backside, across his cheeks and up into the anus . . . nasty little bastard, blotches turning to pustules even five hours after he died. At first I thought maybe it was thrush but it was too extreme for that. So we took a swab and tested it."

The pause was theatrical in its duration. "*And* . . . go on, Jim, for God's sake," Broadhurst snapped around a cloud of smoke.

"Nicotine poisoning."

The policeman's heart sank. For this he had allowed himself to get excited? "*Nicotine* poisoning?" he said in exasperation.

"Nicotine as in *cigarettes*?" He glanced down at the chaos of crumpled brown stubs in the ashtray next to him on the bed.

Garnett grunted proudly. "Nicotine as in around eight million cigarettes smoked in the space of one drag."

"What?"

"That was what killed him – not the heart attack, though that delivered the final blow – nicotine . . . one of the most lethal poisons known to man."

"And how did he get it . . . if it wasn't in the drink or in the meal, and it wasn't injected? And assuming he didn't smoke eight million cigarettes while he was sitting contemplating."

Garnett cleared his throat. "He got it in the arse, Mal . . . though God only knows how."

Broadhurst glanced across at the solitary toilet roll sitting on his chest of drawers. "I know, too," he said. "But the 'why' . . . that's the puzzler."

"And the 'who'?"

"Yeah, that too."

Edna Clark sat at her kitchen table, her hands wrapped around a mug of steaming tea. Sitting across from her was Betty Thorndike.

When the knock came on the front door, Betty said, "You stay put, love – I'll get it."

Hilda Merkinson had been in every room in the house but her sister was nowhere to be found.

Worse still, she couldn't find her handbag.

"Harry?" She had already shouted her sister's name a dozen times but, in the absence of a more useful course of action, she shouted it again. The silence seemed to mock her.

Hilda knew why Harriet had gone out. She had gone out to clear her head, maybe to have a weep by herself. No problem. She would get over it. It might take a bit of time, but she would get over it – of that, Hilda was convinced.

They had lived together, Hilda and Harriet Merkinson, in the same house for all of their 53 years . . . just the two of them since their mother, Hannah, had died in 1992.

They had a routine, a routine that Hilda did not want to see altered in any way. It was a safe routine, a routine of eating together, cleaning together, watching the TV together, and occasionally slipping along to the Three Pennies public house over on Pennypot Drive for a couple of life-affirming medicinal glasses of Guinness stout. It was a routine of going to bed and kissing each other goodnight on the upstairs landing and of waking each morning and kissing each other hello, again in the same spot; a routine broken only by Harriet's job in Jack Wilson's General Store – a sop to his love of America – and Hilda's work at the animal testing facility on Aldershot Road, where she'd been for almost seven years. The same length of time that Harriet had worked. Since their mother had slipped finally into a coma in a small side ward in Halifax General, her six-stone body reduced to wattled skin and brittle bone.

During that time, the routine had persevered.

It had been all and its disappearance was unthinkable.

Not that there hadn't been times when things looked a little shaky . . . namely the times when Ian Arbutt had cornered Hilda in the small back room against the photocopier and sworn his affection – despite Ian's wife, Judith, and his two children. But basically, Ian's affection had been for Hilda's body and Hilda had recognized this pretty quickly into the relationship – if you could call the clumsy gropes and speedy ejaculations performed by her boss on the back room carpet a relationship.

Hilda had had to think of how to put an end to it – thus maintaining her and Harriet's beloved routine – while not having it affect her position at the testing centre.

The solution had been simple, if a little Machiavellian. She had sent an anonymous letter to Judith Arbutt saying she should keep a tighter rein on her husband. "I'm not mentioning any names," the carefully worded – and written – letter had continued, "but there are some folks around town who think your Ian's affections might be being misplaced." Hilda had liked that last bit.

A very anxious and contrite Ian had suggested to Hilda, on the next occasion that they were both alone in the centre, that he felt he wasn't being fair to her. "Trifling with her affections" is what Hilda imagined he was wanting to say but Ian's pharmacological expertise did not extend to the poetic. "I hope you're not leading up to suggesting I look for other work," Hilda had said, feigning annoyance, brow furrowed, "because that would mean something along the lines of sexual harassment, wouldn't it?"

The answer had been emphatic and positive. "A job for life", is how he worded it. "You're here for as long as you want to be here, Hilda," he said. And he had been true to his word, at least Hilda could give him that.

No, Hilda would have nothing come between her and her sister. They were all either of them had and their separation was something she could not contemplate. She had thought that Harriet felt the same way.

And then came the fateful day, almost a week ago – was it really only a week? It seemed so much longer – that had threatened to change all that.

Every Thursday, without fail, Harriet always walked along to the fish and chip shop on the green – Thursday being Jack Wilson's early closing day – and had the tea all ready for Hilda when she got in. But on this particular Thursday, following four days of solid rain, when Hilda – a little earlier than usual because Ian also had flooding and wanted to get off – had gone past the General Store, she had seen Harriet helping Jack with moving boxes around due to the leakage through the front windows. He had asked her to stay back and give him a hand, and Harriet couldn't refuse . . . despite her other "commitments".

"We'll just have some sandwiches," Harriet had shouted through the locked door of Jack's shop, looking terribly flustered. "You just put your feet up and I'll make them when I get in," she added.

Hilda had nodded. Then she had gone home, put the kettle on and, at the usual time Harriet always left the house en route for the fish and chips, Hilda had embarked into the darkness on the very same journey. Imagine her surprise when, from behind the big oak tree on the green, a shadowy figure leapt out, grabbed her by the shoulders and planted a big kiss on her mouth.

It was Arthur Clark.

"Thought you weren't coming," Arthur had announced to a bewildered Hilda. "Been here bloody ages," he had added. "Edna'll be getting ideas – mind you," Arthur had confided, "it won't matter soon. Must dash." Then he had given her another kiss and had scurried across the green bound for home, calling over his shoulder, "See you on Saturday anyway, at the Christmas do."

Hilda had stood and watched the figure disappear into the darkness, and she was so flabbergasted that she almost forgot all about the fish and chips and went home empty-handed. But already she was thinking that that would not do. That would not do at all.

The "meeting" had given her advance knowledge of a potential threat to the beloved routine. And by the time she was leaving the fat-smelling warmth of the shop, Hilda had hatched a plan.

She knew all about poisons from Ian's explanations, long drawn-out monologues that, despite their monotony, had registered in Hilda's mind. Which was fortunate. She knew about nicotine, and about the way it was lethal and produced symptoms not unlike heart failure.

Getting a small supply would not be a problem. There were constant threats against the centre – notably from animal rights groups based out in the wilderness of Hebden Bridge and Todmorden – so a small break-in, during which most of the contents of the centre could be strewn around and trashed, was an easy thing to arrange . . . particularly after administering a small dose of sleeping tablets to her sister, who obligingly nodded off in front of the TV during "Inspector Morse" (Hilda didn't mind missing it because it was a repeat).

Hilda scooted along Luddersedge's late night streets, let herself in with her own key – thanking God that he had seen fit to make Ian make her a joint key-holder with him . . . undoubtedly a result of Ian's keenness to make her feel important after his calling off their "affair" – did what she considered to be an appropriate amount of damage, and removed a small amount of nicotine from the glass jar in Ian's office cabinet, to which, again, she had a key. She left the cabinet untouched by "the vandals" who had destroyed the office. Then, after resetting the alarm, she had smashed in the windows with a large stick and returned home.

It wasn't until she was almost back at the house that she heard the siren. She had smiled then – it had been long enough for whoever had broken in to do all the damage and escape without challenge. The night air had smelled good then, good and alive with . . . not so much possibilities but with continuance. Back in the warmth, she had settled herself down in front of the TV and, after about half an hour, had dropped off herself. The icing on the cake had been the fact that it was Hilda's sister who woke Hilda up. A wonderful alibi, even though none would be needed.

Two days later, on the night of the Conservative Club's Christmas Party, Hilda had bolted her meal and – though she knew she was risking things – had gone to the toilet at ten minutes to ten (Arthur Clark's toilet habits being legendary in Luddersedge). Once out of the ballroom, she had run down to the gentlemen's toilet, removed the tissue rolls from all but one WC, and had treated the first few sheets of the remaining roll with the special bottle in her handbag. It was four minutes to ten when she had finished.

She had arrived back in the ballroom at 9:58 just in time to see Arthur get up from the table and set off for his date with his maker. She had not been able to go straight back and was grateful for Agnes Olroyd catching her to talk about the break-in – there was nothing that the people of Luddersedge liked more than a bit of intrigue – and about her Eric's prostate (in the absence of intrigue, family ailments being the order of the day).

By the time she had finished talking with Agnes, Hilda's composure was fully restored and she was able to rejoin the table.

And now Harriet was nowhere to be seen. But that could wait.

The main thing as far as Hilda was concerned was to find her bag.

And she had a good idea as to where it was.

Harriet's revelations had hit Edna Clark harder even than her husband's death less than twelve hours earlier.

In Edna's kitchen, with the sun washing through the window that looked out onto the back garden and with steam gently wafting from the freshly boiled kettle, Edna sat at the table feeling she had suddenly lost far more than her life partner: now she had lost her life itself. Everything she had believed in had been quickly and surely trounced by the blubbering Harriet Merkinson when she burst through the front door, ran along the hall – pursued by a confused Betty Thorndike – and emerged in the kitchen, tears streaming down her face. And now Edna's 27 years with Arthur lay before her in tatters . . . every conversation, every endearment whispered to her in the private darkness of their bedroom, every meal she had prepared (if not always lovingly – for how can one "lovingly" make egg, chips and beans three times a week for 27 years? – at least with profound affection) and every holiday snapshot they had taken in Dorset and Derbyshire (dressed in shorts, T-shirts and walking boots, their backpacks on the ground before them) and Cornwall (sitting on the beach amidst the inevitable clutter that always resulted from such seaside expeditions).

While Harriet continued sniffling and Betty simply stood leaning against the kitchen cabinets (installed by Arthur, Edna recalled, one laughter-filled weekend in the early 1980s), her eyes seemingly permanently raised in a mask of disbelief, Edna looked around at the once-familiar ephemera and bric-a-brac of a life that now seemed completely alien. The painting on the kitchen wall; the small collection of tea pots and milk jugs on the wide window sill; the stacked plates and cereal bowls stacked behind the glass door of the cupboard – all of them. It might just as well have been the priceless jewellery and artefacts unearthed in an ancient Egyptian tomb . . . so devoid now of meaning and familiarity and understanding. These were things from another life – another *person's* life – and nothing to do with Edna Clark, newly bereaved widow of one Arthur Clark, late of this parish.

The story had been a familiar one. Even as Harriet Merkinson had been burbling it out – the clandestine meetings, the whispered affections, the promise of a new life once Arthur had built up the nerve to leave his wife – Edna felt that she had heard it all before . . . or read it in a book someplace, maybe even watched it on television. The Arthur revealed by Harriet was not the Arthur she remembered . . . save for one thing: his toilet habits. At least something was constant in her husband's two lives.

And now, while Edna's mind raced and backtracked and questioned and attempted – in the strange and endearing way of minds – to rationalize and make palatable the revelations, the "other" woman continued to burble a litany of regret and sorrow and pleas for absolution and forgiveness.

"I can't forgive you," Edna said at last, her words cutting through the thick atmosphere like a knife through cheese. "Never," she added with grim finality. "I can understand, because I know these things do happen, but I can never forgive you. You haven't taken only my husband's memory, you've completely removed my entire life." It was the most articulate statement Edna had ever made, and the most articulate she would ever make in what remained of her life. Of course, she would come to terms with what had happened, but she would never get over it.

"Edna, Edna, Edna, Ed—"

"Now get out," Edna said, cutting Harriet's ramble off mid-word. Her voice was quieter now, more composed . . . gentle even. There was no animosity, no aggression, no threats of retribution: just a tiredness and, the still silent Betty was amazed to see, a new-found strength that was almost majesterial. "I never want to speak with you again."

Minutes later, Betty and Edna heard the distant click of the front door latch closing. It sounded for all the world like the closing of a tomb door or the first scattering of soil on a recently lowered coffin. Edna leaned forward and placed her face in her hands, and she began to sob, quietly and uncontrollably.

While Malcolm Broadhurst was greeting the two uniformed policemen on the steps of the Regal's ornate front door, two things were happening . . . both of them personally involving the Merkinson twins.

For Harriet, the routine so cherished by her sister had been a chore. More than that, it had been the bane of her life.

Harriet had long wanted to get out of the repetitive drudgery of the existence she shared with Hilda, and Arthur Clark – dear, sweet Arthur, with his strange toilet habits – had been her ticket to salvation. Love was a new experience to Harriet: for that matter, she did not know – not truly, down in those regions of the heart and the soul where such things reside, safe from the prying eyes of light and Society – whether she really loved Arthur, for she had never experienced such feelings, even as a teenager and a young woman, when such experiences and experimentation are commonplace. But she did see in him the means whereby she could attain a new life, a life of relative importance . . . "Harriet and Arthur", "Arthur and Harriet" – she couldn't decide which she preferred but she preferred either to "the Merkinson twins" or "Hilda and Harriet"!

As she fished out the old clothesline from the kitchen cupboard, taking care to replace the various bottles and cartons of disinfectant and packets of soap powder, she felt a calmness come over her. Arthur's death had effectively removed her last chance for salvation, and she had been destitute. But now, thanks to the clothesline, she saw a solution. It wasn't the one she would have preferred but it was now the only one available. The only game in town. She could neither face life with Hilda nor life without the constant frisson of excitement she got prior to meeting Arthur . . . and she certainly could not face the comments and whispers around town when she walked down the high street or around the green. No, this way was best for all concerned. It was best for Edna – who might at least derive a little satisfaction when she heard – and it was best for Hilda, who would have to put up with her own share of her sister's shame.

She climbed the stairs wearily and attached one end of the clothesline to the upstairs banister rail. Then, after ensuring that the line's drop was sufficiently short to do the job, she fashioned a noose of sorts and slipped it over her head. With one final look around the landing she climbed over the rail and sat on the banister, staring down at the floor far below. As she jumped, in that fleeting but seemingly endless second or two before the line pulled taut without her feet ever touching the hall floor, she wondered where Hilda was . . . and what she would say when she came home.

"You've got something for forensics?"

Broadhurst nodded. "It's inside. I didn't want to be seen with it outside."

They started to walk.

"I came up last Wednesday," Malcolm Broadhurst explained to the two uniforms. "To check into the break-in down at the animal testing centre."

"Oh, yeah?" one of the policemen observed. His name was James Proctor and he had perfected that same aggressive and questioning response to even the most innocent facts or snippets of information, seeming to require confirmation or substantiation to anything said to him.

"Yeah," Broadhurst confirmed. They were now walking up the Regal's steps and approaching the wide, oak-panelled revolving door. "Your Inspector Mishkin asked me up because there were a few things he wasn't too happy about. I take it you two aren't working on that case?"

"We didn't know it was a case," the second policeman said as they emerged from the revolving door into the hotel's reception area. He said the word "case" with a heavy-handed touch of sarcasm. "Thought it was just a simple break-in."

"Yes, well," Broadhurst continued. "That's the way it looked, and Inspector Mishkin and I decided to keep it that way until things made a little more sense."

"And have they now?" the second policeman asked. His name was John Dearlove and he had recently transferred from Manchester when his wife got a job at the Halifax's head office. Janet Dearlove had a degree in computer science and she was working on a new IT project for the bank. John didn't know anything about IT but, while he appreciated the generous salary his wife had always managed to secure, his resentment at feeling like a "kept man" – as so many of his colleagues on the Manchester force had delighted in calling him – had blossomed first into a resentment of all women and latterly into a resentment of any kind of authority at all.

Broadhurst hit the bell on the reception desk.

"Look at it this way," the policeman said, turning from the desk and looking the two uniforms in the eye. "Whoever broke in through the window managed to trash the place and then place all the broken glass on top of the wrecked office." He nodded, smiling. "That's a pretty good trick, don't you think?"

"So—"

"So," Broadhurst continued, watching the main staircase as a young man appeared and started down, "the 'vandal' clearly had access to the centre and wanted to cover up the fact that they had been there. Now that reason could be simply a matter of their wanting to fight the animal testing . . . kind of like a fifth columnist, or it could be another reason. I think we now have that reason . . . although the reason itself must have a reason – and that's what I now bloody well intend to find out."

"Yes, sir?" the young man said as he reached the bottom of the stairs and approached the three men at the desk. "Sorry to keep you waiting."

"Is Mister Poke around?" Broadhurst asked. "I gave him something to look after for me."

The man nodded and moved around the desk. "I'll give him a call, sir," he said.

As Harriet Merkinson was swinging gently from side to side in the hallway of the house she shared with her sister, Hilda Merkinson slipped quietly into the back door of the Regal.

"Hello, Miss Merkinson," Sidney Poke said. His tone was quite reverential . . . a tone he would use when speaking with anyone who had been at the previous evening's party, and particularly those who had been closely involved with the tragic death of Arthur Clark.

Hilda nodded. "I wondered," she said, "if you had found anything this morning. When you were cleaning up, I mean."

Sidney frowned attentively. "Have you—" The ring of his mobile phone interrupted him. "Excuse me just a minute," he said, pulling his phone from his side pocket. He pressed a button and said, "Yes?"

Hilda looked around as Poke listened on the phone.

"Right," he said. "I'll get it and bring it through." He waited another few seconds and then said, "Very well, I'll meet them on the way."

"Now," Poke said as he returned the phone to his pocket. "Where we were? Ah yes . . . have you lost something?"

They started walking slowly through the ballroom which was now cleared.

Tables were folded and leaning against the far wall; chairs were stacked in towering piles in front of the stage; and an army of young men and woman were busy with vacuum cleaners, criss-crossing the floor, their attention fixed on the carpet.

"My handbag," Hilda shouted above the drone of the cleaners. "I think I must have left it last night." Poke nodded and looked around absently. "In all the excitement," Hilda added, suddenly wondering if "excitement" were the correct word to use under the circumstances.

"Ah!" Sidney Poke motioned Hilda towards a small occasional table set up by the door leading out to the toilets. "The table contained a few jackets plus an assortment of bags.

"All those were left last night?" Hilda said in astonishment.

Poke gave an approximation of a laugh which sounded more like a snort. "No, these belong to the cleaners," he said, "but your bag – if you did leave it, and if it has been found – is most likely here as anywhere."

As they reached the table, Hilda saw her bag. Her heart rose – or surfaced . . . or whatever it was that hearts did that was the opposite to sinking – and she reached out for it, careful not to appear too anxious. "That's it," she said triumphantly.

She picked up the bag and unfastened the sneck. She removed her purse, noting with grim satisfaction that the small bottle was still there, nestled in the bottom amongst Kleenex tissues, lipstick, comb and all the other rudiments of a woman's handbag, and flipped it open. "There," she announced, proudly displaying her library card, "just to show it's mine."

Hilda replaced the card and dropped the purse back into the depths of the handbag. Fastening the sneck, she said, "Well, I'll get off, then."

Sidney Poke nodded. He took her arm and gently led her towards the main door that went on to the toilets and out to the reception area.

"How are you today? I mean, how are you feeling?"

Hilda made a face. "Oh," she said, "you mean after—"

Poke nodded with the quietly attentive air of an undertaker.

"It was my sister. It was Harriet who collapsed. Not me."

"Ah." He pushed open the door and ushered her through ahead of him. "Well, I'll leave you here, if that's okay, Miss Merkinson." Poke stopped at a desk in a small recess and shuffled in his pocket. He produced a set of keys and set about opening the desk's deep drawer. "We're running a little behind, what with . . . you know."

Hilda nodded, watching Poke reach around into the drawer.

Somewhere far off, but coming closer, she could hear footsteps.

"Ah, here it is," Poke grunted. "Must have pushed it further back than I thought." His back to Hilda, Poke pulled out a small bundle and closed the drawer.

The footsteps were getting closer. Hilda tried to ignore the yawning staircase on her right, the fabled 45 steps that led down to the Gentlemen's toilets. Deep in her mind, the footsteps belonged to Arthur Clark as he descended less than 12 hours earlier to empty his bowel and meet his end . . . except they seemed to be coming towards her rather than away from her. She shook her head and turned back to see the Hotel manager holding a toilet roll enclosed in a polythene bag.

"Right then," Poke was saying, though his words sounded like rushing water in Hilda's ears. Rushing water and footsteps, now getting very close . . . echoing . . . as though there were more than just Arthur coming back.

Poke moved the bag from one hand to the other as he returned the keys to his pocket.

Hilda frowned at the bag, looked at Poke, smiled awkwardly, and turned around to face the toilet steps, half expecting to see Arthur climbing up to see her . . . to ask her why she had done what she had done, and bringing other people with him, friends of his . . . friends who

wanted toilet paper.

wanted to talk to her and smooth her troubled brow with grave-cold hands. She turned sharply, took a couple of steps in the direction of the reception area and then stopped. There were figures approaching, figures making footstep-sounds. Her initial relief at discovering that the footsteps didn't belong to her sister's fancy man quickly evaporated when Malcolm Broadhurst called out to her.

"Ah, one of the Misses Merkinson." Broadhurst's tone was cheery. There were two policemen with him. "Now, which one are you?"

Hilda started to speak and then, clutching her bag tightly, she spun around. Behind her, Sidney Poke was still standing by the doors leading into the ballroom, the toilet roll in his hand.

"Miss Merkinson?"

Hilda looked all around, clutching the bag even tighter, willing it to disappear . . . willing it to be a week earlier . . . willing there to have been no rain so that Jack Wilson's General Store had not been flooded and Harriet had not had to stay and so Hilda had not gone for the fish and chips and so met Arthur who believed that she was her own sister . . . willing herself, back seven years ago, not to take the job at the animal testing centre . . . so many things. So many opportunities for her to have avoided this single instant.

But it was too late.

The footsteps were growing louder and slightly faster, moving towards her along the polished floor.

"Miss Merkinson?"

Then it all became clear.

She could escape through the toilets somehow. Escape and find Harriet and they could run off together, start a new routine . . . just the two of them.

She turned and almost leapt forward.

The piece of slanted ceiling that descended with the steps stayed straight for a second or two and then tilted.

Just as she was wondering why that was, Hilda hit her head on the side railing. She felt something warm on her cheek, spun around, and smashed her shin on one of the steps. For a second, amidst the confusion and the pain, she thought she could see a figure standing at the foot of the 45 steps, a figure patiently waiting for her to come down. She heard a crack.

Hilda slipped backwards and to the side somehow, hitting the back of her head on another step before turning over fully and ramming her face into one of the rail supports. More warmth . . .

And then blackness.

Another step broke her nose and her pelvis, another her third and fourth ribs – sending a splinter of bone into her left lung and scraping a sliver of tissue away from the second and third ventricles of her heart.

Two more steps fractured her skull, broke her left collarbone and smashed the base of her spine. The final step on the first flight sent another piece of rib through her heart.

She rolled onto the first landing and then proceeded down the second flight. And then onto the third.

It was Betty Thorndike who found Harriet.

She had called around on her way back from Edna Clark's house, just to see if Harriet was all right. Of course, she wasn't.

By Monday afternoon, it was all over bar the shouting. And as far as Malcolm Broadhurst was concerned, there would be little of that.

He had been to see Edna Clark on the Sunday afternoon, with both of the Merkinson sisters lying on metal trays in the cold and strangely smelling basement of Halifax General.

In the silent loneliness of Edna's kitchen, the widow had told him everything that Harriet had told her. Broadhurst put the rest of it together himself.

He had spoken with his boss at Halifax CID and they had agreed between the two of them that there was little to be achieved by releasing all of the gory details. They decided that Hilda had been a keen promoter of animal rights, using her position at the centre to obtain vital information of the testing Ian Arbutt was carrying out – hence the break-in.

Harriet, meanwhile, had been unable to come to terms with her sister's death and had hanged herself. Only a slight discrepancy in timing suggested that such might not be the case and nobody would hear about that discrepancy. Now the two of them were united again . . . in whatever routine they could arrange.

Edna Clark cried when the policeman explained what he had organised. It meant that her life had been partially restored. To all intents and purposes, she was still the grieving widow of a fine and upstanding member of the Luddersedge community. Betty Thorndike, who had not said anything to anyone about Harriet Merkinson's revelations – and had had no intention of doing so – consoled Edna and assured her that everything was all right.

"He was a good man," Edna whispered into her friend's shoulder. "Deep down," she added.

"I know he was, love," Betty agreed. "They all are . . . deep down."

Driving back to Halifax late afternoon on Monday, there was just one thing that niggled Malcolm Broadhurst. He could not understand why Ian Arbutt had seemed somehow relieved – albeit momentarily – when he was told of Hilda's unfortunate accident.

But the policeman did not believe Arbutt was in any way involved in either the break-in or Arthur Clark's murder. There was another story there, somewhere . . . as, of course, there always is.

STEPPING UP

Mark Billingham

I was never cut out to be the centre of attention. I never asked for it. I never enjoyed it.

Some people love all that though, don't they? They need to be the ones having their heads swelled and their arses licked; pawed at and fawned over. Some people are idiots, to be fair, and don't know what to do with themselves if they aren't smack in the middle of the fucking action.

Of course, there were times when I *did* get the attention, whether I wanted it or not. When things were going well and I won a title or two. I got it from men *and* women then, and you won't hear me say there was anything wrong with that. Blokes wanting to shake your hand and tarts queuing up to shake your other bits and pieces, well nobody's complaining about that kind of carry on, are they?

But *this*, though . . .?

The doctor had been banging on about exercise, especially as I was having such a hard time giving up the fags. It would help to get the old ticker pumping a bit, he said. Get your cholesterol down and shift some of that weight which isn't exactly helping matters, let's face it. You used to box a bit, didn't you, he said, so you shouldn't find it too difficult to get back in the swing of it. To shape up a little.

Piece of piss, I told him, then corrected myself when he smiled and straightened his tie.

"Cake, I meant. Sorry, Doc. Piece of cake."

I don't know which one of us I was kidding more.

I got Maggie's husband, Phil, to give me a hand and fetch some of my old gear out of the loft. We scraped the muck off the skipping rope and hung the heavy bag up in the garage. I thought I would be able to ease myself back into it, you know? Stop when it hurt and build things up slowly. Trouble was it hurt all the time, and the more I tried, the more angry I got that I'd let myself go to shit so badly; that I'd smoked so many fags and eaten so much crap and put so much booze away down the years.

"It was mum's fault for spoiling you," Maggie said. "If she hadn't laid on meat and two veg for you every day of her life, you *might* have learned to do a bit more than boil a bleeding egg. You wouldn't have had to eat so many take-aways after she'd gone . . ."

Once my eldest gets a bee in her bonnet, that's it for everyone. It was her that had nagged me into going to the doctor's in the first place, getting some exercise or what have you. So, even though the boxing training hadn't worked out, the silly mare had no intention of letting the subject drop.

One day, in the pub with Phil, I found out that I wasn't the only one getting it in the neck.

"Help me out, for Christ's sake," he said. "She won't shut up about it, how she thinks you're going to drop dead any bloody second. Just do *something*."

"Snooker?"

"Funny."

"Fucked if I know, Phil. There's nothing I fancy."

I'd told Mags I wouldn't go jogging and that was all there was to it. I've been there, so I know how that game works; shift a few pounds and fuck up your knee joints at the same time. Tennis wasn't for the likes of me and the same went double for golf, even though a couple of blokes in the pub had the odd game now and again. The truth is, I know you have to stick at these kind of things, and that's never been my strong suit. I had a talent in the ring, so I didn't mind putting the hours in, and besides, I had more . . . drive back then, you know? Day after day on a golf course or a sodding tennis court, just so I wouldn't look like a twat every time I turned out, didn't sound much fun.

Plus, there weren't that many people I could think of to play with, tell you the truth . . .

"There's a class," Phil said. "Down our local leisure centre. One night a week, that's all."

"Class?"

"Just general fitness, you know. Look it's only an hour and there's a bit of a drink afterwards. You'll be doing me a favour."

"Hmmm." I swallowed what was left of a pint and rolled my eyes, and that was it. That's how easily a misunderstanding happens and you get yourself shafted.

I should have twigged a couple of weeks later when Maggie came by to pick me up. On the way there I asked her where Phil was, was he coming along later and all that, and she looked at me like I'd lost the plot. See, I thought it was *his* class, didn't I? A few lads jumping about, maybe a quick game of five-a-side and then a couple of beers afterwards. When I walked out of that changing room in my baggy shorts and an old West Ham shirt, I felt like I'd been majorly stitched up. There was Maggie, beaming at me, and a dozen or so other women, and all of them limbering up in front of these little plastic steps.

A fucking *step* class. Jesus H . . .

And not just women, either, which didn't help a great deal. There were a couple of men there to witness the humiliation, which always makes it worse, right? You know what I'm talking about. There were three other fellas standing about, looking like each of them had gone through what I was going through right then. An old boy, a few years on me, who looked like he'd have trouble *carrying* his step. A skinny young bloke in a tight top, who I figured was queer straight away, and a fit-looking sort who I guessed was there to pull something a bit older and desperate.

Looking around, trying my hardest to manage a smile, I could see that most of the women were definitely in that category. Buses, back-ends, you see what I'm getting at? I swear to God, you wouldn't have looked twice at any of them.

Except for Zoe.

I met her forty-odd years back, when I was twenty-something and I'd won a few fights; one night when I was introduced to some people at a nightclub in Tottenham. Frank Sparks was doing pretty well himself at that time, and there were all sorts of faces hanging about. I wasn't stupid. I knew full well what was paying for Frank's Savile Row suit and what have you, and to tell you the truth, it never bothered me.

There weren't many saints knocking around anywhere back then.

Frank was friendly enough, and for the five or ten minutes I sat at his table, it was like we were best friends. He was one of those blokes with a knack for that, you know? Told me he was following my career, how he'd won a few quid betting on me, that kind of thing. He said there were always jobs going with him. All sorts of bits and pieces, you know, if things didn't work out or I jacked the fight game in or whatever.

I can still remember how shiny his hair was that night. And his teeth, and the stink of Aramis on him.

She was the sister of this bloke I used to spar with, and I'd seen her waiting for him at the back of the gym a few times, but it wasn't until that night in Tottenham that I started to pay attention. She was all dressed up, with different hair, and I thought she was an actress or a stripper. Then we got talking by the bar and she laughed and told me she was just Billy's sister. I said she was better looking than any of the actresses or strippers that were there guzzling Frank's champagne, and she went redder than the frock she was wearing, but I knew she liked it.

I saw her quite a bit after that in various places. She started going out with one of Frank Sparks' boys and wearing a lot of fancy dresses. I remember once, I'd just knocked this black lad over in the fourth round at Harringay. I glanced down, sweating like a pig, and she was sitting a few rows back smiling up at me, and the referee's count seemed to take forever.

You just get on the thing, then off again; up and down, up and down, one foot or both of them, in time to the fucking music. Simple as that. You can get back down the same way you went up, or sometimes you turn and come down on the other side, and now and again there's a bit of dancing around the thing, but basically . . . you climb on and off a plastic step.

I swear to God, that's it.

Maybe, that first time, I should have just turned and gone straight back in that changing room. Caught a bus home. Maggie had that look on her face though, and I thought walking out would be even more embarrassing than staying.

So, I decided to do it just the once, for Mags, and actually, it didn't turn out to be as bad as I expected. It was a laugh as it goes, and at least I could do it without feeling like it was going to kill me. It was a damn sight harder than it looked, mind you, make no fucking mistake about *that*. I was knackered after ten minutes, but what with there being so many women in the class, I didn't feel like I had to compete with anyone, you know what I mean?

Ruth, the woman in charge, seemed genuinely pleased to see me when I showed up again the second week and the week after that. She teased me a bit, and I took the piss because she had one of those microphone things on her ear like that singer with the pointy tits. They were *all* quite nice, to be honest. A pretty decent bunch. I'd pretend to flirt a bit with one or two of the women, and I'd have a laugh with Anthony, who didn't bang on about being gay like a lot of them do, you know?

Even Craig seemed all right, to begin with.

The pair of us ended up next to each other more often than not, on the end of the line behind Zoe. Him barely out of breath after half an hour; me, puffing and blowing like I was about to keel over. The pair of us looking one way and one way only, while she moved, easy and sweet, in front of us.

One time, he took his eyes off her arse and glanced across at me. I did likewise, and while Ruth was shouting encouragement to one of the older ladies, the cheeky fucker winked, and I felt the blood rising to my neck.

I remember an evening in the pub with Maggie and Phil, a few weeks in, and me telling Maggie not to be late picking me up for the class. To take the traffic into account. She plastered on a smart-arse smile, like she thought she'd cottoned on to something, but just said she was pleased I was enjoying myself.

It only took one lucky punch from a jammy Spaniard for everything to go tits up as far as the fighting was concerned. I had a few more bouts, but once the jaw's been broken, you're never quite as fearless. Never quite as stupid as you need to be.

Stupid as I had been, spending every penny I'd ever made, quick as I'd earned it.

With the place I was renting in Archway, the payments on a brand new Cortina, and sweet FA put by, it wasn't like I had a lot of choice when it came to doing door work for Frank Sparks. Besides, it was easy money, as it went. A damn sight less stressful than the ring anyway, and I certainly didn't miss the training. Your average Friday-night drunk goes down a lot easier than a journeyman light-heavyweight, but the fact is, I couldn't have thrown more than half a dozen punches in nearly a year of it. I was there to look as if I was useful, see, and that was fine. Like I said before, I was happier in the background and I think Frank was pretty pleased with the way I was handling things, because he asked me if I fancied doing a spot of driving.

And that's when I started seeing a lot more of her.

She wasn't married yet, but I'd heard it was on the cards. Her boyfriend had moved up through the ranks smartish, and was in charge of a lot of Frank's gambling clubs. Classy places in Knightsbridge and Victoria with cigarette girls and what have you. She used to go along and just sit in the corner drinking and looking tasty, but some of these sessions went on all night, and she'd always leave before her old man did.

So, I started to drive her.

I started to ask to drive her; volunteering quietly, you know? There were a couple of motors on call and we took it in turns at first. Then, after a few weeks, she asked for me, and it sort of became an arrangement.

In the image I still have of her, she's standing on a pavement, putting on a scarf as I indicate and drift across towards the curb. She's clutching a handbag. She waves as I pull up, then all but falls into the back of the Jag; tired, but happy as Larry to be on the way home.

In reality of course she was thinner, and drunker. Her eyes got flatter and the bleach made her hair brittle, and she was always popping some pill or other. That crocodile handbag rattled with them. The smile was still there though; lighting up what was left of her. The same as it was when I looked down through the ropes that time and saw her clapping.

When I felt as though I was the one who'd had the breath punched out of me.

How bloody old am I?

It's a fair question, but I don't suppose it really matters. *Too* old, that's the point, isn't it? Too old to smoke and not worry

about it; to put on a pair of socks without sitting down; to think
about running for a bus.

Too old to feel immortal . . .

Like you'd expect, it was mostly Diet Coke and fizzy water in
the pub afterwards. I had orange juice and lemonade myself, for
the first week anyway, but Zoe drank beer from the off.

Ruth didn't give a monkey's what anyone did once the class
was over, but there was one woman who didn't approve; who
clearly enjoyed having another reason to dislike Zoe. She was
glaring across at her from an adjoining table, one night a few
weeks in, and I was giving it the old cow back with bells on.

"Maybe she's jealous because she secretly fancies you," Zoe
whispered.

I pulled a face. "Christ, don't put me off me pint!"

She really enjoyed that one. Her laugh was low and dirty, and
it still amazes me really, to think of it coming out of a mouth like
hers. A face like that.

"She's just dried-up and bitter," I said. "Hates it that she's
doing this to try and change how she looks, or what have you,
while others don't really have to."

Zoe smiled, leaned a shoulder against mine. "Some people
just don't know how to have fun, you know? Think their bodies
are temples and all that."

"My body's more of a slaughterhouse these days," I said.

She enjoyed that one too. It felt fantastic to make her laugh.
We shared a big packet of crisps, which really wound up the old
bag on the next table. She left early, while Zoe and me and a few
of the others stayed until they rang the bell, same as always.
Ruth and Anthony were giggling by the jukebox, and Maggie
kept an eye on me from a table near the door, where she sat
clutching her mobile phone, waiting for Phil to come and pick
the pair of us up.

"Why *do* you come?" I asked her. "It's not like you need to
lose weight or anything. You seem pretty fit . . ."

She leaned a shoulder into mine. "You're sweet."

"I'm just saying."

She took another swig from her bottle. "I'm lazy," she said. "I
need to make myself do things, get out and do something a bit off
the wall, you know? Anyway, it's a laugh, don't you reckon?"

I did reckon, and I told her.

"I work in a stupid office," she said. "The people there are all right I suppose, but I don't want to see them after work or whatever. I think it's good to meet people who aren't anything like you are. People with different lives, you know? I tried a French class, but it was too hard, and the teacher was a bit stuck-up. This is much better. Much."

She had a voice it was easy to listen to. She certainly wasn't posh, but there wasn't really an accent either. Just soft and simple, you know?

"What about you?" she asked.

I said I was basically there to keep Maggie happy, and to try and get at least some of the old fitness back. I mentioned that I used to box a bit and she said that she could see it. That it was in the way I carried myself.

I had to hide my face in my glass, and I'd all but downed the rest of the pint by the time the blush had gone away.

"Someone needed a drink," she said.

There was a burst of high-pitched laughter from Ruth and Anthony, and when I looked across, I could see that Maggie had gone from a smartarse smile to something that looked like concern.

I went up to get the two of us refills, and exchanged nods with Craig who was deep in conversation with the woman behind the bar. He was smoking which made me deeply fucking envious. If Maggie hadn't been sitting by the door, I might well have ponced one.

"Enjoying yourself?" he said.

When the barmaid went to fetch the drinks, Craig span slowly round and leaned back against the bar. He looked across at Zoe for a minute, more maybe, then turned to me. His face said "I *know*, I couldn't agree more, mate. But look at *me* and look at *you*."

Or he might just have been asking me to pass the ashtray.

Oh fuck it, who knows?

Her old man had a place in Battersea, on the edge of the park. There was a night I was driving her back from one of Frank's casinos, down through Chelsea towards Albert Bridge, when she started asking me all manner of funny questions.

"Do you actually like any of them, though? Are any of them really your mates if you think about it?"

The gin had slowed her up a little. Thickened her voice, you know?

"Any of who?" I said.

She jerked a thumb back towards where we'd come from. "That lot. The boys. They're just people you work with, aren't they? Just blokes you knock around with, right, and I don't suppose any of them give a toss about you, either. Wouldn't you say?"

I shrugged and watched the road. It wasn't like I'd never heard her talking bollocks before. Next time she spoke, her voice had more breath in it, and she kept saying my name, but that's something else people do when they've had a couple, isn't it?

"It's just London, right?" she said. "Frank doesn't own stuff anywhere else, does he?"

"I don't know. I don't think so."

"I don't think so either."

"He's been up north on business, definitely. Manchester . . ."

"It was only a few times," she said. "Just to meet people."

"Birmingham as well. I drove him to the station."

"He was just looking, though, that's what I heard. Nothing came of it. It's all here really, don't you reckon?" She said my name again, slow with a question in it. Wanting me to agree with her. "Everyone's here, aren't they?"

I heard a song I knew she liked come on the radio and I turned it up for her. That girl who did Eurovision without any shoes on. I was waiting for her to start singing along, but when I looked in the rear-view I could see that her eyes were closed.

Her head was tipped back and her mascara was starting to run.

Things really started to go pear-shaped the time Zoe turned up looking like she did and Craig didn't turn up at all.

I hadn't admitted it to myself, not really, that the two of them were seeing each other outside the class, but I had to stop being stupid and face facts when I saw her walk in like that. It was like I suddenly knew all sorts of things at once. I knew that they'd got together, that everyone else had probably sussed it a damn sight faster than me, and I knew exactly what had happened to her face.

In class, I stepped that bit faster than usual. I stamped on and off that bastard thing, and it was automatic, like I could do it all day and I wasn't even thinking. Ruth said how well I was doing and when Zoe smiled at me, encouraging, I had to look away.

Afterwards, she didn't turn towards the pub with the rest of us, and when I saw that she was heading for the car-park, I moved to go after her. Maggie took hold of my arm and said something about getting a table. I told her I'd be there in a minute, to get one in for me, but she didn't look very happy.

I tried to get a laugh out of Zoe when I caught her up; made out like I was knackered, you know, from chasing after her, but she didn't seem to really go for it. "Do you not fancy it tonight then?" I said. "Not even a swift half?"

She was fetching her car-keys from her bag. Digging around for them and keeping her head down. "I've got an early start in the morning," she said. "New boss, you know?"

I nodded, told her that one wasn't going to hurt.

She caught me looking, not that I was trying particularly hard not to. It was like a plum that someone had stepped on around her cheek, and the ragged edges of it were the color of a tea-stain. There was a half-moon of blood in her eye.

"I didn't know there was a cupboard open and I turned round into it," she said. "Clumsy bitch . . ."

"Shush . . ."

"I actually knocked myself out for a few seconds."

"Listen, it's all right," I said.

"What is?"

"Come and have one quick drink," I said. "Who am I going to share my salt and vinegar crisps with if you don't?"

It was as though she suddenly noticed that my hand was on her wrist, and she looked down and took half a step back. "I'll see you next week."

"Look after yourself." It came out as a whisper. I didn't really know what else to say.

She pressed the button on her car-keys and when the lights flashed and the alarm squawked, I saw her jump slightly.

In the pub, I couldn't blame Maggie for being off with me. I sat there with a face like a smacked arse, and I couldn't have said more than three words to anyone. After half an hour I'd had enough, and I asked her to call Phil, get him to fetch us early. That didn't go down too well either because she was having a laugh with Anthony, but I just wasn't in the mood for it.

As we were leaving, Ruth raised her glass and said something about me being her star pupil.

Zoe didn't turn up at all the following week.

We were driving, same as always. Seemed like, when it came to being close or what have you, that was the only time we ever really saw each other. Me in the front, her in the back.

"Go slowly, will you?" she'd said when she got in.

Obviously I was going to do what she wanted, right, and it was raining like a bastard anyway, so it wasn't like I could have put my foot down. Still, I wanted to get back to her place as quickly as I could. Don't get me wrong, I hated it when she got out of the car, hated it, but lately I'd taken to stopping some-where after I'd dropped her off; soon as I'd got round the corner sometimes.

I'd pull over in the dark and sit quiet for a minute. Reach for a handkerchief. Throw one off the wrist, while I could still smell her in the car.

Sounds disgusting, I know, but it didn't feel like it back then.

I drove, slow like she wanted, along the Brompton Road and down Sydney Street. Staring at the jaguar leaping from the end of the bonnet; the road slick, sucked up beneath it.

When I turned up the radio to drown out the squeak of the wipers, she leaned forward and asked me to switch it off.

Pissing down now. Clattering on the roof like tacks.

"There's people been talking to me," she said.

"What people?"

"They've been going over my options, you know?"

"What options?"

"The choices I've got."

I looked in the mirror. Watched her take a deep breath when she saw that I didn't understand.

"Billy's fucked up," she said. "Silly bugger's really gone and dropped himself in it."

Her brother. My ex-sparring partner. Always had been a bit of a tearaway.

"What's he done?" I asked. Prickles on my neck.

"He went for some flash Maltese fucker with a knife . . ."

"Jesus."

"Didn't really do him too much harm, but they'll happily bump it up to attempted murder. Put him away for a few years unless I decide to help."

I knew who she was talking about now. Coppers were the same as anyone else at the end of the day. There were plenty of stupid ones, but enough of them with brains to make life interesting.

"There's only Billy and me," she said. "The bastards know how close we are."

She started to cry just a little bit then. I went inside my jacket for the handkerchief I'd be using later on, but she'd already pulled one out from her handbag. I'd heard the pills rattling as she rummaged for it.

I was taking us over the bridge by now. Gliding across it. The lights swung like a necklace up ahead and the rain was churning up the water on either side of me.

"It's not like I know a fat lot."

"Fat lot about what?" I said, but it was obvious what she was banging on about.

"Frank. Frank's business. All that."

All that.

"Obviously they think I know something." She raised her hands, let them drop down with a slap on to the leather seat. "Maybe I know enough."

Course she did; she wasn't stupid, was she? Enough to get her little brother out of the shit and herself slap bang in it.

I wanted to slam on the anchors and stop the car right there on the bridge. To reach into the back and shake her until her fillings came loose. I wanted to tell her that her brother was a pissy little waster, and that she shouldn't be such a daft bitch, and to say absolutely fuck all to anyone about fuck all.

I was the one that kept my mouth shut, though, wasn't I? The one who just gripped the wheel that little bit tighter and manoeuvered the car like I was on my driving test. Checking the wing mirrors, hands at ten to two, watching my speed.

"I need to go away," she said.

Ten to two. Both eyes on the road . . .

"Somewhere abroad might be best. Somewhere hot, near the sea if I get a choice, but it might not have to be that far. Maybe Scotland or somewhere. I've tucked a bit away and I'm sure I can make a few bob later on. I can type for a kick-off."

Slowing for lights. No more than a mile away from the flat on the edge of the park. Checking the mirror and feathering the brake; moving down through the gears.

"I just don't feel like I can do it on my own, you know? That's the only bit I'm scared of, if I'm honest. It's pathetic I know, relying on someone like that, but the thought of nobody being there with me makes me feel sick, like I'm looking over the edge of something. I don't mean sex or whatever, but that's not out of the question either. It's mostly about having someone around who gives a toss, do you know what I mean?"

Waiting for the amber, willing that fucker to change.

"Someone who worries . . ."

She said my name, and it felt like I had something thick and bitter in my gullet.

Neither of us said anything else after that, but we were only five minutes away from the flat by then. The silence was horrible, make no mistake about that, but it just lay there until it sort of flattened out into something we were both willing to live with. Until she asked me to turn the radio back up.

When we pulled up, I got out to open her door, then climbed back in again quick without saying much of anything. When I looked up she was standing there by my door. She had an umbrella, but she never even bothered getting it out; just stood there getting pissed on, with the rain bringing her hair down, until thick strands of it were dead and dark against her face.

She was saying something. I couldn't hear, but I was looking at her mouth, same as always.

I thought she said: "It doesn't matter, Jimmy."

Then she put the tips of two fingers to her lips and pressed them against my window. They went white where she pressed, and I could still see the mark for a few minutes after I drove away.

I didn't stop the car where I normally did. Just kept going for a bit, trying to swallow and think straight. I drove up through Nine Elms and pulled in a mile or so past the power station.

Sat there and stared out across the shitty black river until it started to get light.

Craig looked confused as much as anything when I walked round the corner. Grinned at him. It was half way through the morning, and him and a couple of older women in blouses and grey skirts had come out the back entrance of the bank for a crafty smoke.

"All right, mate?"

"Ticking along," I said. "You?"

It must have been there in my face or the way I spoke, because I saw the women stubbing out pretty long fag-ends, making themselves scarce. Neither of them so much as looked at him before they buggered off.

Craig watched his colleagues go, seemed to find something about it quite funny. He turned back to me, taking a drag. Shook his head.

"Sorry, mate. It's just a bit strange you turning up here, that's all. How d'you know where I worked?"

"Zoe must have said, last time she came to the class, you know?"

Something in his face that I couldn't read, but I didn't much care.

"How's she doing, anyway?" I said.

"Er, she's good, yeah."

"It was a shame she stopped coming, really. We were all saying how she made the rest of us work a bit harder, trying to keep up."

"She just lost interest I think. Me an' all, to be honest." Then a look that seemed to say they were getting their exercise in other ways, and one back from me that tried and failed to wipe it off his face.

It was warm and he was in shirt-sleeves. I was sweating underneath my jacket so I slipped it off, threw it across my arm.

"Are you feeling OK?"

"I'm fine," I said.

"You've gone a bit red."

I nodded, looked at the sweat patches under his arm and the pattern on his poxy tie.

He flicked his fag-end away. "Listen, I've got to get back to work . . ."

"Right."

"I'll say hello to Zoe, shall I?"

"How's her face?"

That took the smile off the fucker quick enough. Put that confused look back again, like he didn't know his arse from his elbow.

"It's fine now," he said. "She's all gorgeous again."

"Nasty, that was. Not seen many shiners worse than that one. Door wasn't it?"

"Cupboard door."

"Yeah, that's what's she said."

"She forgot it was open and turned round fast, you know? Listen—"

I was just looking at him by now.

"What?"

I knew I still had *that*. You never lose the look.

"What's your problem?"

Breathing heavily, a wheeze in it. For real some of it, like the red face, but I'd bunged a bit extra on top, you know. Laid it on thick just to get his guard down.

"I think maybe you ought to piss off now," he said.

I bent over, suddenly; dropped the jacket like I might be in some trouble. He stepped across to pick it up, like I wanted him to, which was when I swung a good hard right at his fat, flappy mouth.

I never had her in the car again after that night. Only saw her a couple of times as it goes, and even then, when she looked over, I always found something fascinating in the pattern on the carpet or counted the bits of chewing gum squashed onto the pavement.

Spineless cunt.

She went away some time after. I suppose I should say I was told she went away. It's an important distinction, right? Told like there was actually nothing to tell, but also like there wasn't much point me asking about it again or wasting any money on postcards.

A few years ago we were having a meal, me and one of the lads I used to knock about with back then. You have a curry and a few pints and you talk about the old days, don't you? You have a laugh.

Until her name came up.

He was talking about what he thought had happened and why. Wanted to know what I thought had gone on; fancied getting my take on it. You used to know her pretty well, didn't you, he said. That's what I heard, anyway. You used to be quite close to her is what somebody told me.

I had a mouthful of ulcers at that time. It was when my old girl was suffering, you know, and the doctor reckoned it was the stress of her illness that was causing it. Ulcers and boils, I had.

When he mentioned her name the first time, I started to chew on a couple of those ulcers. Gnawing into those bastards so hard it was making my eyes water, though my mate probably thought it was the vindaloo.

You used to be quite close to her, he said.

I bit the fuckers clean out then, two or three of them. I remember the noise I made, people in the restaurant turning round. I bent down over the table, coughing, and I spat them out into a serviette.

That more or less put the tin lid on our conversation, which was all right by me. My mate didn't say too much of anything after that. Well, we'd been talking about what was happening with me and my old lady before, and when he saw the blood in the napkin, maybe he was confused, you know, thought I was the one with the lung cancer.

It wasn't the best punch I ever threw, but it made contact and I concentrated on the blood that was running down his shirt-front as he swung me round and pushed me against the wall.

"What the fuck's your game, you silly old bastard?"

I tried to nut him and he leaned back, his arms out straight, holding me hard against the bricks.

"Take it easy."

I thought I felt something crack in his shin when I kicked out at him. I tried to bring my leg up fast towards his bollocks, but the pain in his leg must have fired him right up and his fists were flying at me.

It was no more than a few seconds. Just flailing really like kids, but Christ, I'd forgotten how much it hurts.

Every blow rang and tore and made the sick rise up. I felt something catch me and rip behind the ear; a ring maybe. Stung like fuck.

I swore, and kept kicking. I shut my eyes.

My fists were up, but it was all I could do to protect my face, so I can't have been doing him a lot of damage.

But I was trying.

When the gaps between the punches got a bit longer, I tried to get a dig or two in, just to keep my fucking end up, you know? That was when the background went blurry, and his face started to swim in front of me, but as far as I'm concerned that was down to the pain in my arm. It had bugger all to do with any punishment I might have taken.

The fucker hit me one more time, when I dropped my fists to clutch at my arm. It was all over then, more or less. But it was the pain in my chest that put me down, and not that punch.

Not the punch.

There's always a *something* that gets you from one place to the next, right? That you're chasing after in some way, shape or form. Granted, some people are happy enough to let themselves get pissed along like a fag-end in a urinal, and yes, I know that some poor bastards are plain unlucky, but still . . .

OK, then, to be fair there's *usually* a something. For me, anyway, is all I'm saying. If I'm centre of attention right now, for all the wrong reasons, it isn't really down to anyone else, and I'm not going to feel sorry for myself.

That's more or less what I tried to say to Maggie and Phil when they came in, but they were in no fit state to listen, and I don't think I made myself very clear.

Fuck, they're *at* me again . . .

Loads of them, and I thought there was supposed to be a shortage. Poking and prodding. Talking over me like I'm deaf as well as everything else.

It's not pain exactly.

It's warm and wet and spreading through my arms and legs like I'm sinking into a bath or something. They've got those things you see on the TV out again, like a pair of irons on my chest. Like they're going to iron out my wrinkles.

Now they're going blurry either side of me, same as that fucker did when I was punching him. The sound's gone funny too.

And clear as you like, I can see her face. The stain around her eye and the purple bruise. The hair lying dead against her cheek in the rain.

Music as I step up and step up. Some tuneless disco rubbish while I'm sneaking looks at her in that tight leotard thing and Ruth bawls at me through her stupid microphone.

As I step up off the beach. With the sea coming up on to the sand behind me. Noisy, like the sigh of someone who's sick of waiting for something.

Stepping up on to the hot pavement, where she's stood waiting with a drink. That mouth, and her hair darker now and she looks magnificent. And we lean against each other and drink sangria at one of them places where you can sit outside.

The music's still getting louder, so I ask them to turn it up.

That song she likes on the radio.

The bird with the bare feet.

"I wonder if one day that, you'll say that you care.

If you say you love me madly, I'll gladly be there . . ."

TOM OF TEN THOUSAND

Edward Marston

12 February 1682

The crime occurred in broad daylight. When the coach reached the main street, it slowed down and rumbled around the corner, its iron-rimmed wheels slipping on the frosted cobbles. Before it could pick up speed again, it was ambushed. Coming out of nowhere, three men rode alongside the coach so that they could discharge their weapons at its occupant. Two of the attackers had pistols but it was the blunderbuss held by the third that proved fatal. It went off with a deafening bang and split the victim's stomach wide open. Blood gushed out over his velvet breeches and dripped on to the floor. Confident that the man had been killed, the villains kicked their horses into a gallop and disappeared at once from the scene.

Christopher Redmayne saw it all from a distance. He had just entered the other end of the street when the murder took place. He heard the sounds of shooting clearly and the horrified screams from passers-by. He watched the coachman pull the horses to a sudden halt and caught a glimpse of the attackers, escaping in the confusion. Christopher did not hesitate. Riding at a canter, he made straight for the coach around which a small crowd was now gathering. There was an uneasy feeling in the pit of his stomach. An aspiring young architect, he was on his way to meet a wealthy potential client at a tavern in that street.

The closer he got to the coach, the more convinced he became that it belonged to the very man with whom he had arranged to dine that day.

Having leapt down from his seat, the coachman opened the door to find his employer doubled up on the floor. He was still alive but he was fading with each second. Christopher's horse skidded to a halt and the architect dismounted at speed. He looked over the coachman's shoulder.

"Is that Mr Thynne?" he asked.

"Yes, sir," replied the other.

"Is he injured?"

Without waiting for an answer, Christopher eased the man aside so that he could see for himself. Thomas Thynne was beyond help. Face contorted in agony, he made a futile attempt to speak then his eyes rolled and he collapsed in a heap. The coachman gasped. Christopher leaned in close to examine the body. When he was certain that Thynne was dead, he offered up a silent prayer before taking control of the situation. Having sent a bystander to fetch an officer, he turned to the coachman, a stout man of middle years, deeply shocked at the murder of his employer.

"Do you know who those men were?" asked Christopher.

"No, sir."

"Have you seen any of them before?"

"Never."

"Were they lying in wait for you?"

"Yes, sir," said the coachman, wiping away a tear with the back of his hand. "As soon as we turned the corner, they were there."

"Can you think of any reason why they should do this?"

"None, sir."

"Did Mr Thynne have any enemies?"

"No, sir. He was the kindest man in the world."

Prompted by loyalty, and annoyed by people staring at the corpse with ghoulish interest, the coachman took off his coat and used to it to cover Thomas Thynne's face. Then he waved his arms to force the onlookers back.

Christopher asked for any witnesses and half-a-dozen came forward to tell the same gabbled tale. None of them, however, had been able to identify the men. It was only when a constable came running to take charge of the incident that Christopher spotted a short, thin, ragged individual, lurking in a doorway on the other side of the street. He beckoned the architect across to him.

"I might know who one of them is, sir," said the man, slyly.

"You *might* know?"

"If my memory was jogged, sir."

Christopher understood. "Who was the fellow?" he said, reaching into his purse for a coin. "Give me his name."

"I could give you his address as well," promised the other, eyeing the purse meaningfully. Christopher took out a second coin and pressed both into the man's grubby palm. "Thank you, sir." He snapped his hand shut. "The person you want is Ned Bagwell. He stays at the Feathers, not two hundred yards from here."

Christopher knew the inn by reputation. After thanking the man, he mounted his horse and urged it forward. He was soon trotting briskly in the direction of the Feathers, situated in one of the less salubrious areas of Westminster. London was a dangerous city and Christopher was always armed when he went abroad. In addition to his sword, he wore a dagger and was adept with both. He was not deterred by the fact that there had been three men in the ambush. They had not only robbed a respectable gentleman of his life. They had deprived the architect of a handsome commission to build a house for Thomas Thynne. It served to harden Christopher's resolve to find the killers.

When he got to the Feathers, he tethered his horse and went into the taproom. Filled with smoke from the fire in the grate, it was a dark, dingy, unappealing place. Customers looked up in surprise. The inn was not used to welcoming someone as wholesome and well-dressed as the young architect. Christopher went across to the man behind the counter.

"Does one Ned Bagwell lodge here?" he asked.

"Aye," came the surly reply. "What do you want with Ned?"

"I need to speak to him."

"And supposing he doesn't want to speak to you?"

"Then my sword will give him some encouragement," warned Christopher, meeting the landlord's hostile stare. "Is he here now?"

"Aye – Ned is always here."

"I fancy that he went out a little earlier."

"Then you must think again."

"He had two friends with him. Are they here as well?"

The man folded his arms. "Ned's not stirred from here all day."

"I've only your word for that," said Christopher, whipping out his dagger and holding it to the man's throat, "and I wouldn't trust you for a second. Take me to him."

"No need," said the other, unperturbed. "I'll call him for you." He cupped his hands to his mouth. "Ned! Ned Bagwell, you've a visitor!"

A string of ripe obscenities issued from the next room then Christopher heard the thump of crutches on the wooden floor. When he appeared in the doorway, Ned Bagwell was a one-legged old man who let loose another stream of abuse. Christopher had been tricked. The man to whom he had given the money was already spending it in another tavern.

"Tom Thynne shot down in the street by ruffians!" cried Henry Redmayne in dismay. "It's a devilish crime."

"I mean to solve it," vowed his brother.

"I was at Court when the news came. His Majesty was greatly upset. Tom Thynne was a leading member of the Duke of Monmouth's party. It was his money that has been helping the King's bastard to win support around the country. There's your motive, Christopher," he went on, wagging a finger. "Some scurvy Roman Catholic has set these men on to kill poor Tom."

"I make no assumptions, Henry."

"But it's as plain as the nose on your face."

"Not to me," said Christopher.

They were in the parlour of Henry's house in Bedford Street. It was he who had recommended Christopher to Thomas Thynne. The contrast between the two brothers was startling. Christopher was tall, slim and well favoured while Henry's features showed clear signs of dissipation. As one led a decent, healthy, conscientious life, the other pursued vice in every corner of the city. Though he did not approve of Henry's passion for drink, gambling and lechery, Christopher was grateful for the many introductions his brother had given him to people in search of a talented architect. Henry Redmayne knew everyone of consequence in London society.

"Tell me about Mr Thynne," said Christopher. "All that I know is that he was very rich and recently married."

"Yes," replied Henry. "We called him Tom of Ten Thousand. How I envied him! Think what *I* could do with an annual income of that size."

"You'd drink yourself to death in a fortnight."

"That was not what Tom Thynne did. He was a sober gentleman but not without an eye for the ladies. The beautiful widow, Lady Ogle, was half his age yet he wooed and won her. There was only one problem."

"Was there?"

"Yes, Christopher. She let him wed her but not bed her. Repenting of the marriage, she fled abroad to Holland and is rumoured to be staying with Lady Temple. One of the ways her husband hoped to lure his wife back was to have a new house built for her. That's why I whispered your name into Tom's ear."

"We were supposed to dine at the Golden Fleece today so that we could discuss the project. Mr Thynne was murdered on his way there."

"The blackguards must be punished."

"They will be," said Christopher, gritting his teeth, "but I may need your help to catch them."

"What can I possibly do?"

"Find out who else knew about the arrangements for dinner. Those men were waiting for him, Henry. Someone told them when and where he would be at a certain time."

"So?"

"The most likely person is employed in Mr Thynne's household. You were a guest there in the past. See what you can learn at the house. The body was taken there. You'll be able to pay your respects."

"But I'm expected at the card table within the hour."

Christopher was decisive. "Solving a murder is more important than gambling away money that you can ill afford," he argued. "Get over there at once."

"I take no orders from you."

"Then take them from His Majesty. You told me how alarmed he was by the turn of events. This news will inflame those who hate the Court and its political friends. What better way to curry the King's favour than by helping to track down the culprits? He would be eternally grateful to you. Now ride across to Mr Thynne's house."

"Very well," said Henry, peevishly. He adjusted his periwig in the mirror then preened himself. "What will you be doing in the meantime?"

"Seeing what Jonathan has managed to find out."

"Jonathan?"

"Jonathan Bale."

"That gloomy constable? A sour-faced rogue, if ever there was one. He has far too many Puritan principles to be allowed in respectable company." Henry snorted. "A hue and cry will have been granted. Westminster will be crawling with officers. Why bother to involve Bale?"

"Because he is so tenacious."

"Too damned tenacious!"

"He once helped to save your life, Henry."

"Yes," wailed the other, "then he read me a lecture on the need to abandon my evil ways. The brazen audacity of the man!"

"Jonathan Bale is a godsend," insisted Christopher. "He's not without his faults, I grant you, but he has a gift for finding out things that other men would never even sniff."

"When was this, Reuben?" asked Jonathan Bale.

"Soon after I heard the shots being fired."

"And you *saw* the men?"

"I did," confirmed Reuben Hopkiss. "The three galloped straight past me and all but knocked over our chair."

"Did you recognize them?"

"I recognized one of them, Mr Bale. We carried him from his lodging here in Westminster only yesterday."

"And where did you take him?"

"To the Black Bull."

Hopkiss was a brawny man in his fifties with the strength and stamina needed to carry heavy passengers in a sedan chair. He knew Jonathan Bale of old but was surprised to see him so far from his own parish of Baynard's Castle. Bale seemed to read his mind.

"A certain gentleman has taken an interest in this case," he explained, "and he sent me a note. I was asked to search for anyone who could put a name to the face of any of the killers."

"Lieutenant Stern – that's what he was called."

"Lieutenant?"

"A naval man."

"And a foreigner to boot, then?"

"A Swede."

"That will make him easier to find. Describe the fellow, Reuben."

"Gladly."

As the chairman gave a description of the man, Jonathan Bale memorised every detail. The constable was a big, solid, serious man in his late thirties with an ugly face that was puckered in concentration. He and Christopher Redmayne had been thrown together in an unlikely friendship, and they had solved a number of crimes together. When the request from Christopher came, Bale had responded at once. Other constables had combed the scene of the crime for witnesses. Bale was the only one to wander off into the side streets. His encounter with Reuben Hopkiss had been productive. He now had a clear description of one of the attackers. He also knew where the man lodged and in which tavern he preferred to drink.

Jonathan Bale walked swiftly off to the Black Bull, hoping to catch the Swede – if not his two confederates – at the place. He was out of luck. Stern was not there and neither were any friends of his. Bale therefore retraced his steps and made for the man's lodging. Once again, he was thwarted. The landlord told him that Stern had left early that morning and not been seen since. That worried the constable. He feared that the Swede might have quit London altogether after the crime.

The booming of a bell reminded him that he had been asked to meet Christopher Redmayne at two o'clock. Hastening to Tuthill Street, he found his friend waiting impatiently at the corner. After an exchange of greetings, Bale told him what had been gleaned so far. Christopher was impressed with his diligence.

"I've just come from my brother," he said, noting the look of disapproval in Bale's eye at the mention of his sibling. "Henry spoke to the steward at Mr Thynne's house. It appears that his master used to dine at the Golden Fleece at least four times a week. Those who lurked in ambush must have known that he would come that way sooner or later."

"Can you tell me *why* Mr Thynne was killed?" asked Bale.

"Henry believes that it may be linked to his support of the Duke of Monmouth's cause."

Bale frowned. "Yet another of the King's many bastard sons."

"The duke is claiming to be the legitimate heir to His Majesty, insisting that he has written proof that the King was legally married to his mother, Lucy Walter, at the time of his birth." Bale said nothing. Having fought against the Royalists at the Battle of Worcester, he remained an unrepentant Roundhead. "It provoked the Exclusion crisis," Christopher went on. "Monmouth is resolved to exclude the King's brother, James, Duke of York, from the succession because he is an ardent Roman Catholic."

"Then you believe this murder to be a Catholic conspiracy?"

"Henry does, certainly."

"What of you, Mr Redmayne?"

"I think that we should look to the lady."

"What lady?"

"Mr Thynne's wife," said Christopher. "No sooner did she marry him than she took to her heels and fled to Holland. Now, why should any wife do such a thing?"

Bale shook his head. "It's beyond my comprehension."

"I can't imagine your wife behaving so recklessly."

"Sarah would never let me down – nor I, her."

"Yours is a real marriage. Mr Thynne's, alas, was a sham. I think that it behoves us to find out why."

"How can we do that?"

"We begin with the Swedish gentleman, Lieutenant Stern."

"But we have no idea where he is, Mr Redmayne."

"Oh, I think I can hazard a guess," said Christopher. "Let's go to the Black Bull. He may not be there but I'll wager that someone will know where to find him. A few coins will soon loosen a tongue. If he is a hired killer, he'll have collected his payment by now."

"That was my reasoning," said Bale. "I thought that he would be spending his blood money with his accomplices."

"Perhaps he sought choicer company."

"What do you mean?"

Christopher smiled grimly. "Look to the lady," he repeated, "though this particular one may not merit that title."

Her name was Jenny Teale and she picked up most of her trade at the Black Bull. The majority of her clients were eager sailors who took their pleasure quickly in a dark alley before moving on. Lieutenant Stern was different. He bought her favours for a whole night. In this instance, he had come to her at midday and adjourned to her lodging. They had spent frantic hours in bed before falling asleep in a drunken stupor. Jenny Teale lay naked across his body. When someone pounded on her door, she did not even hear the noise at first. It was only when Christopher Redmayne's shoulder was put to the timber that she was hauled unceremoniously out of her slumber.

There was a loud crash, the lock burst apart and the door was flung wide open. Christopher stood framed in the doorway. Jumping off the bed, Jenny Teale confronted him.

"You'll have to wait your turn, young sir," she said, angrily.

"I'm here for Lieutenant Stern," declared Christopher, averting his gaze from her naked body. His eye fell on the rapier lying beside the bed and he snatched it up at once, using it to prod the sleeping foreigner. "Wake up!" he demanded. "You're coming with me."

The Swede let out a yelp of pain then swore volubly in his own language. Sitting up in bed, he saw Christopher standing over him and tried to retrieve his sword from the floor.

"I have your weapon, lieutenant," said Christopher, "and I daresay that I'll find your pistol in here somewhere as well. I'm arresting you for your part in the murder of Thomas Thynne."

"Ze devil you are!" roared Stern.

"Get dressed and come with me."

"No!"

Grabbing a pillow, Stern leapt out of bed and used it to beat back Christopher. The Swede then hurled the pillow in his face and, clad only in his shirt, opened the window and dropped to the ground below. Christopher had no need to pursue him. He had taken the precaution of stationing Jonathan Bale in the garden. When he glanced through the window, he saw that the constable had easily overpowered the suspect. Christopher gathered up the rest of the man's clothing together with the pistol that had been used in the shooting. He turned to leave but found that Jenny Teale was blocking his way.

Naked and unashamed, she gave him a bewitching smile.

"Do you have to leave so soon?" she asked.

"I fear so."

She spread her arms. "Don't you like what you see?"

"The only person I'm interested in is the man we just apprehended. He's a vicious killer," Christopher told her. "Try to choose your clients with more care in future."

Moving her politely aside, he went out of the room.

Henry Redmayne had repaired to a coffee-house near Temple Bar. He was deep in conversation with his friends when he saw his brother enter the room. Excusing himself from the table, he took Christopher aside.

"Really, sir!" he complained. "Must you always come between me and my pleasures?"

"Count yourself lucky that you are not Lieutenant Stern."

"Who?"

"One of the men who attacked Thomas Thynne," said Christopher. "I caught him in bed with his whore. He is now in safe custody. You might pass on that intelligence to His Majesty, and you can assure him that this crime did not arise from political intrigue."

"It must have done."

"No, Henry."

"The Duke of Monmouth has grown bold. The King exiled him yet he insists on returning to this country to press his absurd claims to the throne. Tom Thynne endorsed those claims to the hilt. He paid for his folly with his life."

"I think not."

Henry was petulant. "That's only because you are so ignorant about affairs of state. I move among the great and the good, and know how corrupt their greatness and goodness really is. What prompts them in the main," he said, airily, "is envy, malice and perverse ambition. There are hundreds of people who seek to pull Monmouth down. What better way to do it than by having his chief paymaster assassinated?"

"Lieutenant Stern has never heard of the Duke of Monmouth."

"Has he confessed who suborned him?"

"No," said Christopher. "He admits that he was one of the three men who shot at Mr Thynne but it's all he will tell us. That's why I must turn to you again."

"But I'm enjoying a coffee with my friends."

"Thomas Thynne was a friend of yours once."

"Yes," said Henry, blithely, "and I mourn his death."

"By carousing in here?"

"I gave you help. You can't ask any more of me than that."

"I can," returned Christopher. "Your aid is crucial. You can provide information that is way beyond the reach of Jonathan and myself. We must learn more about Mr Thynne's wife."

"Elizabeth, the former Lady Ogle? A pretty little thing."

"Why did she betray her marriage vows and flee the country? Had her husband been unkind to her? Was any violence involved?"

"Tom Thynne would not harm a fly."

"Then what made his wife desert him?"

"Covetousness," said Henry, knowledgeably. "The fault that mars all women. She left one man because another one must have offered her more than he could. Tom of Ten Thousand was outbid by someone with even more money and, most probably, with a title to dangle before her."

"We need his name."

Henry tried to move away. "I need my cup of coffee."

"No," said Christopher, restraining him. "It will have to wait, Henry. You are part of a murder hunt. Something is missing and only you can track it down."

"Am I to be allowed no leisure?"

"Not until this case is solved. We have one villain behind bars but two others remain at liberty. Additional people may yet be involved but the person who interests me most is the wife."

"Any man with red blood in his veins would be interested in *her*," said Henry with a lewd grin. "A most bed-worthy lady in every sense. Tom Thynne was by no means her only suitor."

"She must have preferred someone else."

"I told you – she covets wealth and position."

"Then give us the name of the man who offered it to her."

★   ★   ★

The second arrest was made early that evening. Bribed by Christopher Redmayne, the landlord of the Black Bull had not merely supplied the name and whereabouts of Lieutenant's Stern's favourite prostitute. He had told them that the Swede's closest friend was a Polish sailor called Borosky. Jonathan Bale went in search of him but not in the guise of a constable. He first returned to his house on Addle Hill to change into the clothing he had worn in his former life as a shipwright. Bale then worked his way through the various taverns frequented by sailors.

He was at ease in their company. Bale talked their language and shared their interest in a seafaring life. He met more than one man who had sailed with Stern and Borosky, but it was not until he called at the Blue Anchor, the fifth tavern on his list, that he actually came face to face with the Pole. Borosky was a sturdy man of middle height with a flat face and high cheekbones. He had clearly been drinking heavily and was off guard. Bale had no difficulty getting into conversation with him.

"Where do you sail next, my friend?" he asked.

"To the Baltic," replied Borosky.

"Under which captain?"

"Captain Vrats of the *Adventure*."

"I helped to build a ship of that name once," confided Bale. "She was a frigate of thirty-two guns with a crew of a hundred and twenty. But your *Adventure* is just a merchant ship, I daresay. What do you carry?"

Borosky talked freely about the vessel and mentioned that it would be sailing in a few days. Bale acted promptly. He enticed his new acquaintance out of the Blue Anchor with the promise of a meal at another tavern. As soon as they stepped into the fresh air, however, Bale arrested him. There was a brief scuffle but Borosky was too drunk to offer much resistance. He was marched off to join Lieutenant Stern in a dank cell.

Buoyed up by his success, Bale went immediately to Christopher Redmayne's house in Fetter Lane to tell him what had transpired. The architect was delighted to hear of the second arrest and, like Bale, guessed the name of the third suspect.

"Captain Vrats of the *Adventure*," he said.

"The Polander talked of him with affection."

"Did he say that the captain instigated the crime?"

"No," admitted Bale, shaking his head, "he swore that the man had nothing to do with it. He told me over and over again that Captain Vrats was innocent."

"What conclusion did you reach?"

"He was hiding something."

"I think we should pay Captain Vrats a visit."

"But he's aboard his ship in the Thames."

"So? You know how to row a boat, don't you?"

"Of course, Mr Redmayne."

"Then let's go out to the *Adventure*," said Christopher, reaching for his sword. "My instinct tells me that we're getting closer to solving this crime. We are entitled to congratulate ourselves – all three of us."

Bale was mystified. "All *three*?"

"Do not forget my brother."

"What has he done to help us?"

"Henry discovered that Mr Thynne was a regular visitor to the Golden Fleece in Westminster. All that the villains had to do was to lie in wait nearby, knowing that he would eventually turn up there."

"Reuben Hopkiss was far more use to us than that," contended Bale. "He guided us towards Lieutenant Stern. With respect to your brother, sir, he has not pointed us towards any of the suspects."

"But he has," said Christopher, holding up a letter.

"What's that?"

"A message from Henry. It arrived minutes before you did."

"What does the letter contain?"

"The one thing that I wanted above all else."

"And what was that, Mr Redmayne?"

"A name."

The *Adventure* was anchored in the middle of the river, its masts pointing up into the clear night sky like giant fingers. Two watchmen had been left aboard but they were too busy playing dice by the light of a lantern to see the boat that was being rowed out to them. A call from below alerted them to the fact that their ship had visitors.

"Ahoy, there!" yelled a voice.

"Who's below?" asked one of the men, leaning over the bulwark to peer at the boat. "Give me your name."

"Christopher Redmayne."

"What's your business?"

"I wish to see Captain Vrats," said Christopher. "I have news for him about a member of your crew – Lieutenant Stern."

"Has something happened to him?"

"He's been badly injured and cannot be moved. But he's calling for your captain. We promised him that we'd convey the message."

The watchman pondered. "You'd best come aboard," he said at length. "The captain is in his cabin."

Jonathan Bale secured the rowing boat then, in spite of his bulk, shinned up the rope ladder with consummate ease. Christopher found the ascent much more difficult and he was grateful that the ship was so stable. He clambered over the bulwark and stood on the deck. One of the watchmen held up a lantern so that he could study them carefully. Satisfied that they presented no danger, he led them to the captain's cabin and introduced them. The watchman returned to his post.

Two lanterns burned in the cabin, illumining a room that was small, cluttered and filled with curling tobacco smoke. Captain Vrats took one more puff on his pipe before setting it aside. He appraised the visitors shrewdly.

"What's this about Lieutenant Stern?" he asked.

"He was stabbed in a fight at the Black Bull," replied Christopher. "It seems that he was drinking with a young woman named Jenny Teale when another man tried to take her away from him. There was a brawl and the lieutenant came off worst."

"You don't look like the sort of man who'd deign to enter the Black Bull," said Vrats, suspiciously, looking at Christopher's fine apparel. "It's not for the likes of you, Mr Redmayne."

"Too true, captain," Bale put in, "but I drink there from time to time. And I saw the fight with my own eyes. I helped to carry the wounded man to Mr Redmayne's house nearby and he sent for a surgeon. There was not much that could be done, sir."

"Stern is dying?"

"He'll not live through the night."

"And he's calling for me?"

"He has something important to tell you," said Christopher. "He begged me to fetch you so I asked Mr Bale to row me out to your ship."

"I see."

Captain Vrats sat down behind a table that was littered with documents and maps. He watched them through narrowed lids. He was a handsome man with dark hair and a neatly trimmed beard. His command of English was good though he spoke with a strong German accent. He pretended to search for something on the table.

"Lieutenant Stern and I are old shipmates," he observed.

"That's what he told us," said Christopher.

"And he's no stranger to tavern brawls."

"He fought well," claimed Bale. "Then a knife was pulled on him. He was stabbed in the stomach. He's lost a lot of blood."

"You'll lose some of your own if you tell me any more lies," said Vrats, seizing a pistol from beneath a pile of papers. "I don't believe that Stern is injured at all. This story is just a device to get me ashore."

"Is there any reason why you shouldn't come with us?"

"I'm holding it in my hand."

Captain Vrats stood up and pointed the pistol at each of them in turn. Their ruse had failed. Bale bided his time, hoping for the opportunity to disable the man. Christopher took over.

"That weapon is a confession of guilt," he decided.

"I confess nothing."

"You ambushed Thomas Thynne with the aid of two others."

"I spent the whole day aboard," asserted Vrats, "and I have members of my crew who will vouch for me."

"Then they'll be committing perjury," said Christopher. "You are right about one thing. Lieutenant Stern was not injured in a brawl. He and Borosky have been arrested. They will hang for their crime and you will take your place on the gallows beside them."

Captain Vrats laughed. "Nobody will catch me."

"You can only kill one of us with that pistol," noted Bale. "Whoever survives will arrest you on the spot."

"What chance would one man have against three? As soon as they hear the sound of gunfire, the watchmen will come running."

"Then we must be ready for them," said Christopher.

He had been edging slowly towards the table and now made his move. Diving suddenly at the captain, he grabbed the barrel of the pistol and turned it upwards. The gun went off with a loud report. Bale reacted quickly. As Christopher grappled with the captain, Bale stepped forward to fell Vrats with a powerful punch to the ear. He then indicated that Christopher should stand behind the door. After blowing out both lanterns, Bale took up his position on the other side of the door. It was a matter of seconds before the two watchmen came hurrying down the steps to see what had happened. Bale knocked the first one senseless and Christopher held his dagger at the other's throat.

"Find some rope," ordered Christopher.

"No shortage of that aboard a ship," said Bale.

The constable left the cabin but came back with some rope almost immediately. He trussed up both of the watchmen then hauled Vrats off the floor. The captain was still dazed. Christopher lit one of the lanterns before holding it a few inches from the captain's face.

"Tell me where we can find him," he demanded.

"Who?" asked Vrats, clearly in pain.

"The man who set you on to kill Thomas Thynne."

"Nobody set me on."

"His name is Count Konigsmark."

Captain Vrats was astounded. "How ever did you find that out?"

"My brother, Henry, kindly provided the name," said Christopher, cheerfully. "He has a gift for smelling out scandal."

Gravesend was rimed with frost. The passengers who waited at the harbour that morning shivered in the cold. A rowing boat arrived to take them out to the ship. Before they could climb aboard, however, they heard the clatter of hooves and half-a-dozen horsemen came galloping out of the gloom towards them. Reining in his mount, Christopher Redmayne leapt from the saddle and surveyed the passengers. He was disappointed. The man he sought did not appear to be among them.

"Count Konigsmark?" he asked.

Nobody answered. Some of the passengers shrugged, others shook their heads. Christopher's gaze shifted to the man on the fringe of the group. Tall and lean, he had long, fair hair that spilled out beneath his hat to reach his waist. He was shabbily dressed but, when Christopher took a closer look at him, he saw how impeccably well-groomed he was. The man had poise and striking good looks. There was an aristocratic disdain in his eye. Christopher gave a signal and two of the riders dismounted to stand either side of the passenger.

"You must come with us, Count Konigsmark," said Christopher.

"But my name is Lindegren," argued the other, reaching into his pocket. "You may see my passport, if you wish. I am sailing back to Stockholm."

"No, you are fleeing the country to avoid arrest. The passport is a forgery. This, however," Christopher went on, producing a letter to wave in front of him, "is not. Do you recognize your own hand?"

"I told you. I am Oscar Lindegren."

"Then we will arrest you in that name, though we know full well that you are Count Konigsmark. Your countrymen will be shocked to learn that one of the leading figures in their kingdom is party to a brutal murder." He snapped his fingers. "Take him."

The two officers grabbed hold of the man. He was outraged.

"Is this the way you treat innocent people in England?" he protested. "You have made a terrible mistake."

"It was you who made the mistake," said Christopher, indicating the letter. "You should not have sent word to Captain Vrats that you were leaving Gravesend on a Swedish ship this morning. We found this in his cabin when we arrested him. I've ridden through the night to catch up with you, Count Konigsmark."

"I committed no crime."

"You paid others to do it for you and that is just as bad. And if you are as innocent as you pretend, why are you sneaking away in disguise with a false passport?"

Konigsmark was trapped. He was hopelessly outnumbered and was, in any case, unarmed. There was no point in further denial.

"Tell these men to unhand me," he said, peremptorily, "I demand the right to be treated with respect."

"You did not treat Thomas Thynne with respect."

"Mr Thynne was a fool."

"Yet it was he whom Lady Ogle married and not you." Christopher saw the flash of anger in the other man's eyes. "I know that you courted her as well for a time. Was that why you had Mr Thynne ambushed in Westminster? Were you racked with envy?"

"I would never envy such a man. He was beneath contempt."

"From what I hear, he did not have too high a regard for you either." Konigsmark scowled. "Is that what provoked your ire? Were you upset by slighting remarks that Mr Thynne made about you?"

"He should have remembered who I am," growled the other.

"Save your breath for the trial," advised Christopher, slipping the letter back into his pocket. "Captain Vrats is languishing in prison with two other villains. You will soon join them."

The officers tried to move him away. Konigsmark held his ground.

"I am a member of the Swedish aristocracy," he said with dignity, "and I insist on the privileges due to my rank."

"Of course," said Christopher with a deferential smile. "I'll make absolutely sure that you are hanged first."

In fact, Count Konigsmark did not hang at all. Captain Vrats, Lieutenant Stern and Borosky were found guilty of murder and were hanged in the street where the crime occurred. At the Old Bailey trial, Konigsmark was charged with being an accessory but he was acquitted. Captain Vrats went to his death with remarkable equanimity. His body was then embalmed by a new method devised by William Russell, an undertaker. When he was shipped back to Germany fifteen days after execution, the body of Captain Vrats was in an exceptional state of preservation.

A CASE OF ASYLUM

Michael Jecks

It had cost him a fortune, that passport. Not because it was illegal, but because his need was so obvious. Someone in his position couldn't afford to stay, not even when his wife and daughter remained. When the authorities were after you there was only limited time to escape; and the desperate have to pay.

He'd known he'd have to bolt when he realized he was being watched.

The farm had long been the centre of attention, and the dogs had patrolled his fences enthusiastically all through the hotter weather, their ridged backs terrifying his workers when they materialized from the bushes, heads lowered in truculent demonstration, brows wrinkled and glowering. Alan had loved those two, the dog and the bitch. When he found their corpses out by the boundary fence, even as he wept over them, he was reviewing his options. The two were proof that an attack would come soon.

The government didn't want his family. Others might – it was possible that they could be held and ransomed – but even here women and children tended to be safe. No, it was him they'd try to "arrest"; *him* whom they would shoot and leave in a dirt track far from anyone. Not the dignity of a grave for someone who worked against this government.

He'd escape and go to England. Where people were free.

*   *   *

Paul Jeffries yawned and glanced across the Arrivals hall to Jeannie.

She was wearing her "invisible" clothes today: grey trouser suit; a small briefcase of ballistic material holding her laptop hanging from her shoulder; dark hair bobbed in a vaguely professional cut; her face partly concealed behind small, rectangular glasses. But it couldn't hide her delicate bone structure. Like Michelle Pfeiffer, Paul reckoned. Really good looking, but with a sort of healthiness about her. Pfeiffer was almost unwell looking, with those big pale eyes and all. Jeannie was plain gorgeous once you noticed her – not that many did. She just blended into the background, the best of their intake.

He lifted a finger to his right eye and scratched at the eyebrow three times – "I need a pee" – saw her acknowledge tersely, and moved away from Arrivals to the toilets.

She was often short with him. Probably she'd guessed he was crap. She'd been with him almost from day one, and perhaps because she was so much older and more confident in herself, she resented his laziness and stupidity. That was his impression, anyway. Meanwhile, all he wanted to do was rip her clothes off and get sweaty with her.

It could just be the shift. Most hated this – first thing in the morning, keeping an eye on tourists, holidaymakers, businessmen, and Christ knew who else, but Paul liked it. He'd always wanted to make use of his degree, and although this wasn't the way he'd anticipated things panning out, with his good second in Anthropology and Psychology, he was happy enough. Standing about here, simply watching the folks walking back into the country was itself an education.

Sometimes the best part was watching the others who worked here. Especially cops. Jesus, he'd almost jumped a crew last month. He'd seen them shoving packets into pockets before walking to customs, and it was only when the first in the line had held up his warrant card at the gate that he'd realized they'd come over from Holland. There were enough who'd go there for a smoke, and these had brought back a small stash. Bleeding idiots, if you asked Paul. He'd never smoked, and didn't see why others should.

Jeannie smoked sometimes. It had been useful, when she'd been watching someone who was a smoker. There was a sort of fraternity among the morons. They'd stand and exchange side-long, self-effacing grins; rapport established without words. She'd been able to get closer to them by bringing out her own pack and apologetically nodding towards their lighter. Fluent in Arabic and Swahili, she'd been able to stand nearby and listen without their having the faintest idea. Not that many would look twice at her anyway. No one thought that a coloured woman would work for a disgraced government like this British one.

Yeah, she was a diamond among the watchers.

He washed his hands, fastidious to the last, left the toilets and strolled over to the concessions. Buying good filter coffee, he moved over to the farther side of the hall, from where he still had an unimpeded view of Jeannie.

"Hi, Pete! How's it hanging?"

"Dave. Nothing so far today."

David was the massively ineffectual section head of the team. More proof of the rash of urgent recruiting and promotions in recent years, and the perfect example of the *Peter Principle* – once a moderately competent operative, as manager of the team he had reached his own level of incompetence. Soon it would be noticed, and another effective watcher would be removed from the field. Daft.

After 9/11, the British government had reversed decades of under-investment in immigration and customs controls, and started making changes. The disaster of 7/7 in London added urgency to the new policy. Where politicians had floundered ineffectually, the big guns of business took their opportunity.

Weapons and surveillance companies had suffered with the peace dividend after the cold war, and turned their best sales teams onto the police and politicians. Police commanders keen to exercise more authority demanded better guns, more cameras, identity cards, new laws to ban everything from airguns to congregations larger than two people with a child; and a callow, incompetent government swallowed every worst-case scenario presented to them. The power to arrest and hold men and women, uncharged, returned for the first time in four hundred years.

With these came the need for accurate surveillance on the ground.

The Watchers had been all but disbanded under previous administrations, but suddenly they were needed. Once-redundant officers were offered new packages, tempted with golden hellos, but few wanted to return. Burned once, they were less eager to return. So Human Resources had to seek new blood, returning to the usual fertile grounds: the universities. Not only Oxbridge, either. The new government couldn't swallow that sort of injustice. The new world order demanded equality in controlling the public.

Yes, the services were taking on people from the smaller universities. The main thing was, bodies on the streets and at ports. Which was how Paul had slipped in, really. And how David had been put in charge of his own team when he was scarcely able to use a phone, let alone the radios.

"We have a new one," Dave was saying.

Paul took the file with surprise. It was not usual for his leader to present him with a file so conspicuously. Just as Paul was not allowed to have his earpiece plugged in, because the little clear plastic coil gave away his profession, all briefings were supposed to be given in the room out at the back, behind the Special Branch area. He glanced at it, and felt a little worm of anxiety moving in his belly. "What is it?"

"FARC. Watch the BA flight from Bogotà. Twenty minutes."

Andy Campbell was in the armoury already. His vest was itching, the heavy weight of the ceramic plates pulling at his shoulders as he pulled out the magazine from his H&K submachinegun, then drew back the cocking lever to empty the breech. The cartridge flew out, and he caught it with a practised snatch of his hand. He racked the breech a couple of times, from habit, pulled the trigger to ease the springs, and put the gun down on the table.

He wouldn't be here many more times. He'd been a specialist shooter here at the airport for some months, but he couldn't carry on. Not once he'd admitted what had happened.

It was last night. He'd knocked off bloody late after doing a favour and working a shift at Heathrow because they'd had a minor flu epidemic. Jack, his partner, and he'd taken overtime and given them a hand, but he'd known he had to be up at four to get to Gatwick airport for the first shift. He'd been dog tired, though. Knackered. So when he got home, he'd started undressing in his hallway, before going up to bed. He had three hours to kip before the alarm was going to go off, and the last thing he wanted was a row with the missus about his hours again. So he'd left his clothes downstairs, his handgun on the belt. The sub-machinegun he took upstairs, of course. But the Glock stayed there in the hall.

He knew he shouldn't have brought it home, but shit, when the hours were this daft, what the fuck were you supposed to do? If he'd driven to the airport armoury last night to dump his guns before going home, he'd have had no time to sleep. All the lads took risks sometimes – it was the old rule: don't get found out.

Well, he would be found out this time. Some fucker had broken into his house, gone through the stuff in the hall, and his Glock had been nicked. Bloody gone, just like that. Today he'd been able to get away without it, saying he'd left it behind, and he had the H&K, so there was little enough to be said, but when he got home tonight, he'd have to have a good hunt, just in case. Maybe it had fallen down behind the umbrellas, or got kicked along the hall . . . Andy just prayed – Jesus, please don't let it be – yes, that either the thing hadn't been taken by some crook who was going to use it to hold up a bank or something, or that it hadn't been thrown away in the road outside his house.

He'd looked, of course, he'd looked everywhere, and just now all he could feel was a cold sweat breaking out at the mere thought that he'd be discovered at any moment. He had to get back home and make sure that the thing wasn't just lying there.

God, but any moment he could be called to be asked what the fuck his gun was doing in the hands of some drugged up shite who'd been holding a hostage or . . .

"Andy? Stop that. We've got a shout on. Some wanker with bombs or something. Get tooled up again."

He had to stop thinking of his real name. Now he was Ramón, not Jean-Jacques. Ramón Escobar. The lightness in his belly was unbearable as he peered down through the window at Britain.

It was surprisingly green. He wasn't used to that. In Bogotà the city lay almost dead on the equator, although at that height it was hard to believe sometimes. The weather was not too hot. Not like Africa. The temperature in Colombia remained constant, and there was little in the way of seasonal variation. No summer and winter, just a slight change, a little cooler or a little warmer.

Like this, it was very green. You took off from Bogotà airport, and all you could see for miles around was greenhouses. The hothouses spread all over the plain, and even when the plane lifted and the ground fell away from that high plateau up in the mountains, the glass reflected the light all about the area. They said that Colombia's biggest legal export was cut flowers to America, and . . . *Ramón* could believe it. Easily.

Here, though, the plane was slowly descending through wisps of pale cloud, and beneath the greenness was . . . darker. Not so rich and blooming as the plant life of Bogotà. It looked harsher, as though the trees and shrubs were struggling more to survive, and it was easy to see why as the aircraft drew nearer to the ground. Here the greyness of concrete and tarmac was all about, but without the bright colours of jacaranda and bougainvillea to ease the sight. No, here, all was unrelenting, grey, miserable, and he felt the tears welling again to think that this place was his refuge.

His sanctuary in his exile. His new motherland.

The system was well worked out, and they swung into action as soon as the papers had been digested.

Paul walked casually away from the main hall as soon as he had checked the details in the print out and glanced up at the arrivals display. The plane was close, but not here yet. He had time.

Jeannie had seen the discussion, and now was play-acting as only she could. She looked up at the boards, and frowned at her watch, looking about her with a discontented expression, before wandering off in the direction of the women's toilets. Paul made his own way through a security barrier with a palmed card shown discreetly to the man at the gate, and into the Special Branch section. She was waiting for him.

"What's going on?"

He passed her the papers. "Terrorist, they reckon. Bloke from Colombia. He's used this ID before – it was noted when the IRA three were over there. It's fake. Why the hell he didn't get something new before taking off . . ."

"Perhaps no time?" She frowned as she absorbed the description of the man.

"He was with FARC, the terrorists who control the country out towards Venezuela," Paul said. He shivered. This was the kind of incident he had feared. "They were trained by the IRA in new bombs and mortars. This Escobar was a cousin of one of the cartel leaders from Medellin, and he escaped the crack down when his cousin was killed. He made it to Panama originally, then turned up back in Colombia with FARC. Now he's coming here."

"Why?"

"Jesus! I don't know, all right?" he snapped. "All we have to do is find him and watch, just like we always do. And when we see him, we go live on radio in case we have to call in the shooters."

Jeannie nodded, and he saw a small smile of satisfaction on her face – she liked to needle him. There was a reasonably fresh brew of coffee in the jug. She poured, added a good slug of milk, and sipped it easily, walking from the room out to the main hall again, leaving him alone with his fears.

He should have been honest about his education, but when he was interviewed, he assumed that they'd never want him for active duties. He'd said he was good with languages, because that was what his mate said they wanted, but it never occurred to him that he'd be needed. God – the nearest he'd got to languages was a smattering of Bantu and Ndebelele when he took a gap year to study anthropology in Botswana.

Anyway, when he wrote out his CV, no one had seemed remotely interested. There'd been no time for checks. Perhaps someone would spot his lying later, when they went back through the CVs they'd collected in the last years since 9/11. Probably not, though. Human Resources had been reduced as they increased the Watchers – if you spend in one area you have to cut a budget elsewhere – and now there weren't the HR people to check all the new staff, let alone trawl through existing ones.

At his interview they were more keen on his post as a prefect at school. Responsible character, they'd said. No one had guessed he'd lied about that as well.

His eyes were drawn back to the sheet of paper, to the words that were highlighted: *Paul Jeffries to keep close. Spanish essential.*

Shit!

The H&K was soon made ready again. The mag slammed into the gun and smacked with the palm of his hand to seat it. He pulled the cocking lever back and let it drive forward, stripping the first round from the magazine and leaving the gun cocked and ready. He switched on the safety, keeping his finger well away from the trigger. In the last few years more police officers had been wounded because of negligent discharges than by criminals. He had enough on his plate without that, sod it.

Jack was waiting at the door. "Shit of a day to leave the Glock behind, eh?"

"Fuck it!" Andy hissed. They both walked out together, their guns across their chests, fingers clear, and they turned their radios on as they entered the thronging main hall.

The man who called himself Ramón knew a fair amount about Bogotà, but only from reading. Not many people went to the city unless they had to. The bombs, the bullets, the murdering, the kidnapping and ransoming all dissuaded tourists, not only foreign ones. Locals were as unlikely to travel there. Anyone could be stopped and kidnapped, and a man like him, with a price on his head, would be best served keeping off the roads. Travel was very dangerous. Just like home. Except here the terrorists and guerillas were better armed than the police, whereas back home only the police and army had guns. And the President's friends.

Bogotà was beautiful. Ringed by the high, dark peaks, the place had an atmosphere all of its own. He had thought that, sitting in the *Parc de Periodistas*, waiting for the man to arrive with the new passport. There was a smell of thick smog in the air, and he could see the coal smoke rising from several chimneys in the tower blocks nearby. A sulphurous odour that caught in his throat, and yet the buildings were typical Spanish colonial in so many areas of the city, especially the older parts where the emeralds were sold for so little. Spanish, American, there were so many influences. It was a lovely country.

His contact was a scrawny man, with a sallow, pock-marked complexion and a thatch of filthy brown hair. He spoke English only haltingly, and that suited Ramón. Neither wanted to know much about the other, and Ramón had been assured he was safe. He'd paid well for the advice.

Their business was soon completed, an envelope with much of Ramón's remaining cash, all in US dollars, was passed over, and in exchange a fake passport, driving licence, and some local identification cards. With these Ramón was safe. With these he could fly from the country and not be turned away at British immigration. It was too easy for asylum-seekers to be refused now, unless they had applied before leaving their homes, but he couldn't apply back home, and no one would help in Colombia. They had other things to worry about: terrorists and drug-dealers.

The jerk of the wheels hitting tarmac brought him back to the present. In his bag in the hold there was the explosive material, and soon he would be in a position to light the touch-paper, he told himself.

Paul's first warning was the nod from immigration. There was no need for a buzzer or pager to call when a watcher was present. Only if there was an immediate danger did they "hit the tit" for the armed fuzz. Otherwise everything had to be managed silently, with a minimum of fuss to alert the bad guys that they were being followed.

At the carousel Paul stood back, watching his mark. Not tall, but well muscled, and a face that spoke of a warmer climate than Britain in November. Yes, he was the one, all right. There were plenty of Spaniard types on the place, but this one definitely fitted the photo and profile best. Jeannie was down in the carousel hall, and they had a dummy bag for her to collect. She stood near the mark, and grabbed her bag as it came round.

Paul took a deep breath, shivering with expectation. Then he walked out through the customs tunnel, walking through the red channel and waiting with his own small luggage bag in case the target came this way. Jeannie would wait until he had left, then go through green no matter what.

The customs officer was a slim blonde girl, and she waited with Paul patiently until he had the signal from another officer. Then Paul hurried through the channel and out into the main hall.

Jack and Andy were waiting idly when the call came through.

"He's in the main hall now. Following him out."

Andy beckoned with his head and wandered over to the main arrivals corridor. There was a family, then a couple of teens with backpacks, long fair hair straggling. A gap, a long gap. Andy felt his palms begin to sweat. He took his pistol hand away from the H&K and wiped it down his trousers, willing himself to look a little away from the corridor, but unable to obey. The bright fluorescent glow of the arrival tunnel transfixed him. He saw the tall figure appear.

Ramòn. Ramòn. Not Jean-Jacques Bressonard. He had to remember his new name until he could get his package delivered, but the officials on all sides petrified him. There was a young brunette watching him, and he forced himself to blink slowly, smiling through his exhaustion, looking away innocently and striding on determinedly, through the wide corridor, turning right at the end, passing through the crowds. He was safe.

There were two policemen in armour ahead of him, and he hardly glanced at them. He was thinking about his ancestors. They had fled from the terror in France, first arriving here in England, then making the long and dangerous journey to Africa. There they had thrived until the independence, until the new regime.

Over the centuries, England had remained their homeland. They owed their existence to the British who welcomed his Huguenot forebears. His grandfather volunteered and died in the trenches of the first war, his father nearly died in the Battle of Britain as a Hurricane pilot. Yes, Ramón was coming home.

In his own land he had ceased to exist. When his ID card was confiscated, he became a non-person. A man with no ID was nothing. He had no rights.

He smiled and nodded to the police, but then a chill entered his blood as he took in their faces: dead; cold, inhuman. Just like at home.

Walking more swiftly, he went right, avoiding them. Ahead of him was a beautiful woman, just like his lovely Miranda, and he felt a pang in his breast at the thought. He missed his family so much . . . but hopefully he could have them rescued too. They could come here to this cold, grey country.

For a moment he thought he could hear Miranda calling to him: "Good morning!" just one instant before he saw the gun, realized it was flashing, felt the slugs hit his breast, and collapsed slowly, sinking to his knees even as the police emptied their H&Ks into him.

"Fuck, fuck, fuck!"

Andy shivered, his finger still tight on the trigger as he stood over the body.

"Cease firing! Cease firing! Cease firing!"

The terrorist was down, bullet wounds weeping all over his torso. An eye was punctured, and wept jelly, and Andy could only stare, too shocked even to feel sick yet. That would come later.

"Andy. ANDY! Get a fucking grip. Secure the place! Come on!"

"Why'd he do that? Why'd he fire?"

Paul had been hit twice that he knew of. He had been behind the target when he saw the man's body jerk and collapse, saw the bullets strike from the police guns, saw the body suddenly lifeless like a dummy, arms flailing as he was thrown to the side.

"No need for Spanish after all!" he said, almost giggling with reaction.

At his side a young girl was weeping, sprawled, a bloody mess on her back to show the exit wound. Near her a man was still and silent, an elderly woman was slumped by the wall, staring with surprise at a bloody hole in her belly, while her husband stood beside her with an expression of spaniel-like hurt and confusion. Paul gazed about him at them all, and tried to stand, but couldn't. All he could do was sit and watch as the police bellowed at the people in the area to get clear. Dazed, he looked up at the policeman with the sub-machinegun when he approached, and began to wonder what he might do. He'd just seen the man empty his magazine into a crowd.

"There's an ambulance on its way," Jack said. He stood behind Andy. "You all right?"

"I'm hit."

"I can see that."

Paul shook his head, tasted bile. "Why did she say that? Why did she call to him and shoot him?"

Jack sighed and walked off. Andy frowned. "Who did?"

"Jeannie," Paul said. He choked a little on the phlegm that had materialised in his throat. "My partner. Where is she?"

It was late when Andy returned to the gun room. He sat on the bench, exhausted. Jack walked in a few minutes later to unload his weapon.

"You all right?"

"I'm fine."

"Unload, then. Come on, Andy! Unload."

Andy stood and fumbled with the cocking lever, but there was nothing to do. His magazine was empty. Instead he pulled the mag free and stared at it dumbly.

Jack eyed him, then unloaded his own weapon. It was unfired. He set it in the safe, and as he did so, his foot kicked something under the bench. "Shit, Andy – is that your gun? You didn't lock it in the safe, you prick!"

Andy jerked awake from his nightmare and gazed at Jack dumbly. Seeing the direction of his pointing finger, he reached down and took up the Glock in its holster. He hefted it in his hand, pulled it free. It had been fired. He could smell the powder in the barrel. And when he looked closer, the serial number on the side was one he knew all too well.

His hand began to tremble.

Paul took the advice from the ambulance driver, still shivering slightly as the needle went in and he watched the clear liquid pushed into his arm. The wounds were small: one bullet had winged his shoulder, which was already as sore as hell, and a second had caught his rib, running around the outside of it, and ending up in his back after running around underneath his skin. The medic had offered to cut it loose, but he refused the offer.

"You'll need it taken out soon," the medic said. He didn't bother to add that Paul would have to have the entire bullet's track opened and cleaned to remove all the bits of material and burned powder, or risk septicaemia.

"Davie? Where is she?"

"Who? Jeannie? I told her to go home. She was in shock."

Paul shivered. Davie looked at him sympathetically. "Look, Paul, you need to rest, mate. Get on home."

"She murdered the guy."

"What?"

"She had a handgun. I saw her. She shouted something and opened fire. The cops started shooting as soon as she started. She started it, though. I saw her."

"What did she shout? Spanish?"

"*Lotjhani* – in Ndebele it means 'Hello'."

"Are you sure?"

The files in the bags were exhaustive. Details of murders, of officially sanctioned brutality. Paul shivered as he took in pictures of bodies in streets, strewn in fields, punctured with gunshots, or slashed with pangas, and he felt the sickness in his belly.

"Who is he?" Dave muttered.

"An asylum seeker. We killed an asylum seeker from Zimbabwe," Paul spat. The pain was washing through him now as he stared at the sheet of paper, and he could feel a cold sweat run over his spine. Nausea roiled in his belly. "And Jeannie murdered him."

Perhaps, he wondered, the HR team hadn't only cocked up with *his* application?

The woman he had known as Jeannie climbed out of the car with the diplomatic plates, and walked in through the guarded doors into the High Commission as the car purred round to the parking space. The lift took her up, and soon she was seated, waiting for the debriefing, running the events through her mind once more.

It had been perfect. The theft of the policeman's firearm was a calculated risk, but when she had seen the changed rotas, it seemed a good bet. All the police took their guns home occasionally, even though it was officially disapproved of, and when a man had to travel far to his next shift, it made sense for him to keep his gun nearby. And the gamble paid off.

She had waited for the man this morning, and he had passed her the Glock at the airport entrance. The theft had gone without a hitch. The fool was too exhausted to hear the two as they rifled his clothing and bags. After that all she had to do was wait until she saw Bressonard while the policeman was present. Shoot, and run. They'd said that the police expected a terrorist, so they'd shoot as soon as they heard shots, and they'd been right. They always saw what they expected, or what they feared. No one would suspect her, a "spook".

So the enemy of the country was dead. He had been led carefully down a route preplanned for him. A contact with FARC had agreed to provide obvious ID for him, and then they had known which aircraft he would take to Britain, and now he was dead. Well, now the world would see what a safe country Britain was for asylum seekers. Like the Brazilian, a white farmer had been removed, and the police were guilty of his homicide. Either the machine gun or the pistol had killed him, and both were one officer's weapons.

The woman who had been called Jeannie removed her ID and placed it carefully before her on a glass-topped table. She wouldn't need these again. No. She was looking forward to returning to her own name. Her real one.

And returning to the glorious Zimbabwe sun, of course. Perhaps she could buy a small farm. Maybe even take Bressonard's?

Life was good.

THE DEATH OF JEFFERS

Kevin Wignall

Heg the Peg was the end of it. Marty had known from the start which creek he was up; this was just the confirmation on the whereabouts of the paddle. If it had won, he'd have been in the clear, or as near as made any difference.

True to its name though, the first race had finished five minutes ago and Heg the Peg was still running. So much for Bob and his cast-iron tips, straight from the stable, the whole crowd of them laying money on it like it was the only horse in the race. If there was any cast-iron, it was in Heg the Peg's saddle.

So now Marty had two choices. First was finding some other way of raising two thousand euros by the end of the month – and frankly, that was looking about as likely as the stewards disqualifying every other horse in the last race. Second was borrowing the money off Hennessey and paying back the interest for the rest of his life.

Three choices – he could tell McKeon to sing for the money, leave Dublin, leave Ireland, and find a monastery in Bhutan that was recruiting. Four choices – his next fare could be some crazy American on his first trip to Dublin, wanting to hire him for the whole week, money no object. You never knew with the airport.

The door opened and Marty turned off the radio.

"Wynn's Hotel, please." English, in a suit, overnight bag; no big tip here. The fare leaned over and handed him a piece of paper with an address on it. "Could you stop here on the way? I'll give you a good tip."

Marty glanced at the address. It wasn't far out of the way.

"No problem. First time in Dublin?"

"Yes, it is."

Marty pulled away. He could probably take the guy around the houses and he wouldn't be any the wiser. He found himself taking the direct route though; that was why he ended up in positions like this in the first place, because he was too honest for his own good.

He looked in the rear-view. The fare looked like a civil servant, or someone who worked in life insurance, nondescript, late thirties, the kind of guy who was born to make up the numbers and get lost in the crowd. But he'd still offer him the same old patter.

"I suppose you'll be wanting to sample some of the good stuff while you're here?"

"Sorry?"

"Guinness."

"Oh." The fare smiled like it was something he wasn't used to. "Actually, I don't drink. Very rarely, anyway."

Marty nodded and said, "So what brings you here, then?"

"Business." He smiled again, but he wasn't getting any better at it. "But I've been wanting to come to Ireland for a long time. I'm of Irish stock."

Jesus, who wasn't? The day he picked up a fare at that airport who *didn't* claim to have Irish blood, that was the day he'd win the lottery. Still, he put on his best "that's amazing" smile and said, "Really? What's your name?"

"Jeffers. Patrick Jeffers."

Well, sure, anyone could call their kid Patrick, but he wasn't so sure about the Jeffers bit. Didn't sound particularly Irish to him.

"Don't know any Jeffers. Must be a name from out West."

"I think it is." End of conversation.

Jeffers kept him waiting no more than two minutes. He went into the house empty-handed and came out with a briefcase. Now that was suspicious – no other way of looking at it, particularly some guy who'd never been to Dublin having business in a regular suburban street.

By the time he got him to the Wynn's, though, there was no doubt it was his first time here – he'd been looking out of the window like a tourist for the last ten minutes.

"That'll be twenty-two euros."

"Keep the change," said Jeffers, handing him thirty.

"That's kind of you, Mr Jeffers. Enjoy your stay in Dublin."

One thousand, nine hundred and ninety-two to go.

Bryan was a charmer, all right, and there was no doubt about what he thought he'd be getting when they went out later. First day on the job, all the girls had told Kate not to fall for any of his talk, and here she was, second day behind the reception desk, going out with him tonight.

She was smiling at him now as he leaned across the desk. And he thought she was smiling at the silver words coming from his mouth, but it was how much he looked like Danny that was really tickling her. If it weren't for Bryan's blue eyes, the two of them could meet and think they were long-lost brothers.

Of course, Bryan would be the good brother. They all thought she was some naïve young slip of a thing, but twenty-four hours had been enough to tell her that Bryan was decent to the core. He was one for the girls, sure, but a good family lad at heart, working his way through college, a bright future ahead of him.

Danny, on the other hand, he was sexy and dangerous and the biggest mistake she'd made in her eighteen years. He'd come to a nasty end sooner or later and probably take a good few with him. The important thing was knowing that Danny wouldn't stick around, and that she wouldn't want him to.

Suddenly, Bryan pushed himself up and stepped away, making himself busy, and she saw one of the guests heading toward the desk, a businessman, boring-looking. She put on her best smile.

"Yes, sir, what can I do for you?"

"I checked in a short while ago?"

He sounded like he was asking a question, and she felt like telling him straight, Mister, if you don't remember, I'm sure as hell, I don't. He certainly didn't look familiar.

"That's right. Is your room satisfactory, Mr . . .?"

"Jeffers."

"Mr Jeffries, that's it."

"It's fine. But it's Mr Jeffers. Actually, it's an Irish name."

"It is so. From up north, I think, Donegal, that way."

"Yes, I think you're right." He smiled, wonky somehow, like he'd had botox and was still getting used to his face again. "How do I get to Trinity College?"

"Ah, you have to work really hard at school." His smile stayed fixed – no sense of humour. "Just a little joke there. It's just around the corner. Bryan here will point the way."

Bryan had been straightening leaflets but snapped to attention now and ushered the Englishman out onto the street. He was cute, Bryan, a tight little backside on him, and he was going to get exactly what he wanted tonight, and the dates would be close enough that he'd never think to question whether the kid was his. How could he? In all probability, it was even going to look like him.

Jeffers had listened attentively as Bryan gave him directions for the short walk across to Trinity, but he seemed in no mood to move anywhere once he'd finished. So Bryan stood in silence with him, the two of them surveying the street like they were looking out over their ranch at sunset.

Then, absentmindedly, Jeffers said, "Have *you* heard of the name? Jeffers?"

"I haven't. Sorry." Jeffers nodded but still looked straight ahead, feet planted firmly, and so Bryan tried to fill the pause by saying, "I'm a student at Trinity myself. History."

Jeffers turned and looked at him as if he'd revealed something vital. He stared at him for a few seconds, a look intense enough to be unnerving, and Bryan couldn't help but see that Jeffers looked troubled. Finally, he said, "Let me tell you something, don't ever fall into the trap of believing you don't have choices. You always have a choice, in everything."

He seemed to consider that for a moment, then nodded to himself and handed Bryan five euros before walking off along the street with Bryan's thanks lost in the noise behind him. Bryan stood there looking at the five euros, wondering what might have induced such a bizarre fit of profundity.

He was close to laughing it off as he walked back into the hotel, ready to get another smile out of Kate by telling her, and then for some reason, it made him think of Lucy and it was no longer funny. You always have a choice, in everything. Lucy – if ever a girl could have turned him into a poet.

It was strange, though – two minutes with an English businessman who didn't know how to smile, and suddenly he felt that if he didn't get in touch with Lucy right now, see her this very evening, he'd regret it for the rest of his life. What was that all about?

Kate was smiling at him as he walked toward the desk. She was a pretty girl, and Danny had said she was easy, but he wasn't sure he wanted it any more – not with her, not with any of these other girls.

"I've just got to make a call." She smiled back at him, coquettishly, he thought, but girl, it wouldn't be tonight.

"Mr Parker, you do not have to write essays on Joyce, and when we're discussing him, I will not mark you down for opting out of the conversation, but if you insist on writing essays and speaking your mind, please be so kind as to read something other than *Dubliners*."

The others laughed but Parker was smiling, too. She only teased him because she knew he could take it and because he was probably smarter than all the rest put together.

"You know, Dr Burns, I have skim-read *Ulysses*."

"Would that be the jogging tour of Dublin, Mr Parker?" That earned another laugh, but the hour was upon them and they were already putting their things together. Parker was first out the door. Clare was the last, waiting till everyone had left before shyly handing in an essay.

She started to read through it once she was on her own again, but was only a page or two in – impressive, if lacking a little in flair – when there was a knock at the door and it opened a fraction.

"Come in."

The man who stepped into the room was about thirty-five, six foot, the average kind of build that couldn't easily be read under a suit. Facially, he looked innocuous, which immediately put her on her guard.

"Dr Elizabeth Burns?" She nodded, smiling, and he closed the door behind him.

"Call me Liz, Mr . . .?"

She'd gestured at the seat across from her desk and as he sat down and placed his briefcase in front of him, he said, "Patrick Jeffers. The office sent me."

The office. It was about twenty years since she'd heard anyone call it that.

"And what office would that be?"

He didn't answer, just smiled awkwardly and relaxed into his seat.

He seemed to relax then, confident and in control as he said, "I've got a lot of admiration for people like you." She offered him a quizzical expression. No one had ever contacted her like this so, whoever he was, she wanted to draw him out a little more. "People in 14. And no, I don't expect you to admit it but, being buried deep the way you were for, what was it, four years, that really takes something."

Her expression unnerved him a little, and with no wonder, for she was wearing a look of utter astonishment. "Mr Jeffers, I have absolutely no idea what you're talking about. People in fourteen, what?"

He nodded knowingly, uncomfortable, as if he'd spoken out of turn and made himself look unprofessional, which he had. At the same time, she was unnerved herself, wondering what this Jeffers was doing here, wondering why she'd had no word that he was coming. He knew she'd been in 14, so somebody must have sent him.

"You don't sound Irish." He tilted his head questioningly. "Jeffers is an Irish name, but you don't sound Irish. Irish grandparents, perhaps?"

"Yes, I think so." He hesitated before saying, "So you've heard of the name? I think you're the first person since I arrived who recognizes it."

"There's actually a folk song, somewhere down in the Southwest, though the exact location escapes me at the moment, about the death of a Jeffers."

"Oh, I didn't know that."

"Of course, there's also the American poet, Robinson Jeffers."

"Yes." She could tell he didn't like being sidetracked. He was here on business and wanted to get on with it.

"What do you want here, Mr Jeffers? Why has your office sent you?"

"Yes, I'm really just here to deliver a message." He bent down and picked up his briefcase, but started to cover himself, saying, "Just some paperwork you need to read and sign."

Amateur! He was opening the briefcase on his lap and she had absolutely no doubt what kind of message he was about to produce from it. There were all kinds of thoughts running through her head, questions of whether she'd been double-crossed, and if so, by whom, questions of who he was working for and whether she'd have to move on, but there was something more immediate, an instinctive reflex that would never leave her.

She picked the phone up off the desk and threw it hard. It cracked him on the head with a clatter, and then a further clatter as the briefcase and the gun inside it fell onto the floor. He was dazed for only a second, but she was around the desk before he came up for air and she was pulling the telephone cord tight around his neck.

"Who sent you?"

His arms flailed, trying to strike her a body blow but unable to find her where she stood directly behind him.

"Who sent you?"

He tried another approach, trying to pull her own hands off, then trying to get his fingers under the cord, desperately tearing at his neck, drawing blood with his fingernails. He wouldn't talk; he was at least that professional. She yanked up the tension an extra notch, and the flailing of the arms gave way to a more convulsive movement through his entire body. She had to use all her strength to keep him in the seat, but she couldn't resist leaning down, whispering breathlessly into his ear.

"You know that song about Jeffers? It's a celebration. See, Jeffers was a diamond trader, and he was English!"

She couldn't get the phone working again, even after she'd disentangled it from his body. She took her cell phone and dialled. When Lambert picked up she said, "Someone came after me. I'll need removals."

"Someone from the North?"

"No, he claimed to be one of us."

"Name?"

"Patrick Jeffers. Passport backs that up." She looked at the passport she'd retrieved from his jacket. He certainly had the right look.

"Jeffers? There has to be a mistake. Let me just check something." She could hear Lambert tapping away on his computer keyboard. He was as much an old timer as she was and always hit the keys like they belonged on a manual typewriter. 'Liz, Patrick Jeffers is on his first assignment, but he's in Damascus; he's a Middle East specialist."

She looked at the throttled body, slumped in the chair like a drunk, and now that she thought of it, he hadn't seemed to recognize the name of Robinson Jeffers, and surely he would have done, as surely as she knew who Robbie Burns was.

"Well, I hope he's doing better than the Jeffers in front of me now."

Lambert laughed. She liked Lambert; he had a good sense of humour. People didn't need to look much in this game, but a sense of humour was an absolute must.

DISTILLING THE TRUTH

Marilyn Todd

The instant Marie-Claude's husband told her that he'd compiled a dossier detailing the Chief Inspector's corruption complete with dates, names and times, then placed the file personally in the hands of the Commissioner, she knew it was all over. No wonder he waited until he'd finished his *tartiflette* to tell her what he'd done. She'd have thrown the damned dish on the floor and to hell with dinner, and he could have whistled for his *île flottante* as well. As it was, she didn't hear him out. What on earth was the point of lengthy explanations?

"You're a fool, Luc. No one likes a whistle blower."

"I didn't join the police to be popular."

"It's the end of your career, you know that? They won't keep you on in Paris after this!"

"Blackmail, extortion, what was I supposed to do, Marie-Claude?" He laid down *Le Figaro* and turned his gaze to her. "For years, Picard has been preying on the very people he was meant to protect. I couldn't simply turn aside."

"And I'm sure the Commissioner shook your hand and thanked you warmly for your efforts."

One side of Luc's face twisted uncomfortably. "Not exactly, no."

"You see? No one likes a whistle-blower. They'd rather close ranks and have a bastard in their midst than admit to one bad apple, and you already know my feelings about the Commissioner."

Like when they were invited over to dinner and she overheard him talking to her husband in his study when she went to find the bathroom.

"Your wife is truculent, selfish and a pain in the *cul*, Luc—"

The rest was drowned by children's laughter upstairs, but who cared? That's the last time she'd eat at that pig's house, she told Luc, and if her husband felt bad about making excuses when future invitations arrived, then so much the better. She wanted nothing to do with a man who insulted her, and it wouldn't have hurt Luc to have stuck up for her, either.

"– couldn't agree more, sir—"

Truculent and selfish, her *cul*. She pushed her thick curls back from her face. She had married too young, that was the trouble, and to a man ten years older than herself at that. Admittedly, after six years Luc was no less handsome and his back was as strong, but that type of love can't sustain a marriage indefinitely. And when he wasn't working all the hours *le bon Dieu* sent, he had his head stuck in a file or wanted to talk politics, and not even French politics, either. Honestly! Who cared whether rich diamond deposits had been found in Siberia or how many communists this Senator Mc-Whatever-His-Name accused in the American State Department? What was going to actually change people's lives were things like the new television transmissions that were now coming out in colour, not some piece of paper signed by Egypt and Britain over a canal in Suez that Luc insisted was going to have far-reaching consequences. But however exasperated Marie-Claude got with her husband, she'd never once known him to lose his temper.

Not even when, a mere fortnight after delivering his sanctimonious dossier, the Commissioner transferred him to Cognac.

"You'll like the South," Luc said confidently, as their train pulled away. "Twice as much sunshine, warmer summers, better winters—"

"Better theatres, Luc? Will they have better street cafés and shops? Will they get subtitled versions of 'On the Waterfront', do you think?" By all accounts, it was set to scoop an Oscar. "Will they have better parks? Better gardens? Women in *peignoirs* leaning over the balconies, calling obscenities to men in the street?"

He looked at her beneath lowered lids as the train chugged through the forests of Rambouillet. "You never liked Montmartre."

"It had life," she retorted. "It had character and substance, it was always noisy, colourful, constantly changing—"

Marie-Claude broke off. Why was she referring to these things in the past tense? For heaven's sake, it wasn't as though she wasn't going back! No, no, once she'd seen Luc settled in (she owed him that) she would start a new life. A new life with a man who appreciated art, the cinema, fashion and fun. Someone who liked dancing, for sure!

"I'll bet they've never heard of Perry Como in Cognac."

"You can probably count yourself lucky if they've heard of Bing Crosby," he murmured behind his guide book. "But this is promotion, Marie-Claude. We're lucky to get it. Do you want to look through this, by the way?"

Marie-Claude shook her head. She'd seen enough of those military vines and flat-bottomed boats from upside down, thank you.

"We'll be able to afford a house of our own, instead of a poky apartment on the fifth floor where you can hear everything that happens next door. We're close to the seaside, and I'll bet the air's better, too."

There was nothing wrong with the air in the Rue de Roc, she wanted to say, but his nose was back in the pamphlet and, as Orléans rumbled past, she stroked the hat in her lap. Such a jaunty little number, as well. *Très* Audrey Hepburn with just a dash of Ava Gardner. She sighed and closed her eyes. By the time she got the chance to wear it again, it would either have too many feathers or too few, and who would be seen dead wearing green for next season? At Tours, the only other couple in the carriage got off and an old woman with a runny nose got in.

"Amazing," Luc said, turning the page of his paper to avoid creasing. "It says here construction's underway on the St Lawrence Seaway that'll allow deep-draught ships direct access to the rich industrials of the Great Lakes. Direct access. Can you imagine?"

Marie-Claude switched off. Her husband was clever, conscientious, honourable, but dull. Handsome, rugged, muscular
and tall, yet he lacked passion where it really counted. And now,
it seemed, he was a failure into the bargain.

At Angoulême they changed trains.

She blamed herself for marrying him.

A week later, the vineyards around Cognac sprang into leaf and
an Englishman called Bannister ran a mile in under four
minutes. Less than two months down the line, once the vines
had been pruned and tied back, an Australian beat the Englishman's record, but by the time the summer sun was swelling the
grapes on the hillsides, the Englishman had once again reclaimed his crown in Vancouver, Little Mo's tennis career
was cut short by a riding accident and a pair of Italians were
the first climbers to reach the peak of K2. These things seemed
to excite everyone except Marie-Claude, but it didn't matter,
because she kept herself busy making the house nice for Luc.

It was pleasantly located in the old quarter, halfway between
the chateau and the covered market, where the streets were
narrow, hilly, twisting and cobbled, and the houses built of
thick stone to keep them cool in summer, retain heat in the
winter, and with fireplaces large enough to secrete a small army.
But an old man had lived alone here for the past twenty years
and she was damned if she'd be accused of leaving her husband
to a place which looked (and smelled) like a pig-sty.

A week's scrub with carbolic transformed it no end, but the
shutters could use a coat or three of paint and although she'd
considered returning to Paris in August, the weather was
perfect for strolls along the tow-path, and whilst Marie-Claude
knew of lots of people who didn't bother with curtains and just
used the shutters, Luc worked so hard that the very least he
deserved, if he wasn't to have a decent dinner waiting on the
table, was to be able to pore over his paperwork in a house that
was cosy. One or two rooms, that was all. Bedroom. *Salon.*
Enough to lend a bit of warmth and character where it mattered
the most.

By the time workers had been drafted in for the harvest and
Pope Pius X had been canonized, the Algerians had started a
guerrilla war against their French protectors, "This Ole

House" was on everyone's lips and Marie-Claude had run up another pair of drapes, this time for the kitchen, and accepted the offer of part-time work in an upmarket dress shop.

"I'll be late tonight," Luc announced one lunchtime, as he washed his hands in the sink. Close by, the bells of St Léger pealed merrily. "The proprietor of one of the smaller Cognac houses has been murdered."

Marie-Claude laid the *cassoulet* on the table and lifted the lid. "Good."

"Good?" He chuckled as he sniffed appreciatively through the steam. "Some poor woman has been battered over the head and all you can say is good?"

"Not good that she's dead." She heaped his plate. "Good that you've got some proper detective work to do at last."

All he'd been called upon to investigate over the past five months had been robbery, the inevitable smuggling and once, right at the beginning, an art theft that turned out to be a simple insurance fraud. Luc was a first-rate detective and at last this would give him something to sink his teeth into. In fact, with such a high-profile case demanding his attention, Marie-Claude doubted he'd notice she'd left, although she might as well wait until the warm weather ended. Paris was desperately wet in October.

"Marie-Claude, this duck is delicious."

It was the market, she explained, scraping out the dish for him. So close it made shopping each day easy, and you could buy the freshest produce without it having been hanging around in a vans for several days as it made its way slowly up country. Luc shot a covetous glance at the second pot on the stove.

"Tomorrow?"

"Certainly not!" Tomorrow she was planning *coq au vin*. "I made that for Suzette next door. Her husband died last year from an accident in the boiler room in one of the distilleries down on the quay, so with three small children and no work, I thought it might help."

"That's very generous."

"Nonsense. We can easily afford one extra duck. My job, your pay rise—"

"No hat bills, no theatre tickets." He wiped both *cassoulet* and smile from his mouth with a serviette. "Do you miss them, Marie-Claude? Honestly?"

"If you've finished, I need to get back to the shop," she said briskly. "Madame Garreau's visiting her mother and I'm all on my own this afternoon." She scraped the bones into the bin while he brewed the coffee. "So who died, then?"

"A woman by the name of Martine Montaud—"

"Madame Montaud?" She wiped her hands on the dishcloth and set out a plate of *palmiers* still warm from the oven. "Handsome, late forties, with dark hair?"

"You know her?"

"As one would expect of the owner of a cognac house, she was one of Madame Garreau's best customers." Marie-Claude sat on the table and began swinging her legs. "Very elegant lady," she said. "Exquisitely made up, hands neatly manicured and I wouldn't like *her* hairdresser's bill, I can tell you." She sighed. "I shall miss her coming in, though," she added. "She never took offence when I told her what didn't suit her—"

"Marie-Claude, that's the reason Madame Garreau adores you. You give her clientele an honest appraisal and you don't hold back. People respect that."

She wondered how he could possibly know her employer's opinion. As far as she knew, Luc had never met Madame Garreau, but that was beside the point. No woman wants to be told lilac suits her when it makes her look bland, any more than being sold the concept that wide stripes will flatter her hips. Especially Madame Montaud, who invariably left the shop hundreds of francs lighter, but every inch looking the successful businesswoman she was.

"She never struck me the type to get herself murdered," Marie-Claude said, sipping her coffee. "Well, not bashed on the head, anyway. It seems so . . . vulgar."

"You'd have preferred she was strangled?"

She shot him a look to say that wasn't funny. "Who killed her, do you have any idea?"

"Everything points to the cellar master," he said sadly. "Like that art theft back in May, there's very little detective work involved in this case, – oh, and talking of art, I suppose you know Matisse is dead?"

"Cellar master? Luc, the cellar master of a cognac house is just one step below God. He's not just responsible for the blend, he oversees the whole process of distillation from beginning to end, he even chooses the oak trees from which the barrels are made that will store his precious cognac, for heaven's sake!"

"And you know this because . . .?"

"Suzette. I told you. Her husband died in a boiler room fire." She brushed a curl out of her eyes with the back of her hand. "We spend a lot of time talking when she picks up the kids."

"You *babysit?*"

"Don't sound so surprised. It gives her chance to do a typing course and – *hein*. The point is, you're looking at the wrong person, Luc. The cellar master couldn't possibly have clonked Madame Montaud on the head. That wouldn't have been *his* style, either."

"Ah. You'd have preferred he strangled her?"

"That wasn't funny the first time, and besides! What motive would he have for killing his employer?"

"Something sexual probably, it usually is." Luc shrugged as he reached for the last pastry. "Money or sex lies at the root of most murders, plus his were the only fingerprints that we lifted and I found one of her ear-rings in his bed—"

"It was so obvious, you searched his house?"

"Not exactly." He leaned his weight against the back of the chair and folded his arms over his chest. "But because her body was found in the cellars, I conducted a thorough search of the entire factory, including the distillery, which happens to have a small room sectioned off that serves as the cellar master's bedroom."

"Only from November until March, when distillation takes place around the clock and he needs to be on hand night and day."

"Suzette?"

"Suzette."

"Hmm." He scratched his chin. "Well, if you know so much about the cognac process and you don't believe my suspect is the killer, why don't you go up there and tell me who is?"

Marie-Claude jumped down from the table. "I'll need a cardigan."

"What about the shop?" he called up the stairs, and look! it proved the acoustics in this house were rubbish. It sounded for all the world as though he was laughing.

"What about the shop?" she called back, reaching for her green hat with the feathers. "They're rich, these women. They can afford to wait a while longer."

Poor Madame Montaud could not.

The Domaine de Montaud lay on the north side of Cognac, protected by woodlands and snug inside a bend in the river. For almost two thousand years, its sun-kissed slopes had gazed over the valley of the Charente and the hills that unfolded beyond, but the acidic soil and low alcohol content played havoc with the wine's conservation and so, in the seventeenth century, foreign merchants hit upon the idea of importing it in spirit form and diluting it on arrival. Because of the double distillation process involved, the Dutch named this spirit *brandwijn* – burnt wine – which had the added advantage of being cheaper to ship. But no matter how economical the costs of transport, when recession hits, luxury goods are the first to suffer. Huge stocks of brandy piled up in the cellars. Things were not looking good.

Until local producers noticed that their spirit not only improved with age, it tasted even better drunk neat . . .

But as cognac was born, so evolved a world of secrets and magic. In each dark saturated cellar, the cellar master became sorcerer, blending smooth with mellow, amber with gold, elegance with subtlety, to produce a unique and individual range of cognacs, from the youngest, at under five years, to prestigious *réserves* that had been maturing in oak casks for decades.

Marie-Claude had imagined such sorcerers to be sober, unsmiling, aloof and dull. Undertakers in different suits. If they were, Alexandre Baret broke the mould.

"*Enchanté, madame.*"

Any other time and the eyes behind the spectacles would be twinkling flirtatiously. The crows' feet either side said so. But today they only viewed the inspector's assistant with mistrust, and were clouded with something else, too. Guilt? Grief? Fear? Marie-Claude couldn't say but, following him through the shadowy barrel-lined chambers, their walls black from evaporation, she felt prickles rise on her scalp. With its rigorously controlled temperature, light rationed to brief and rare visits, the okay tang to the air, it was like walking through a cathedral.

That same air of reverence. Humility. Silence. Tranquillity. The taking of life here seemed sacrilegious.

"I have informed the workforce that this area is out of bounds until further notice," Monsieur Baret said, studiously avoiding the outline of a body chalked on the flagstone floor. "But in any case, only a handful of employees have access, and I assure you it is quite impossible to enter without the necessary keys. Indeed," he added dryly, "one would stand a better chance breaking into the *Banque de France*."

"You don't think this could be a robbery turned sour, then?" Marie-Claude's voice echoed softly. "After all, there are hundreds of migrants in the vineyards right now, breaking their backs to bring in the harvest."

Alexandre Baret watched dust motes dance in the air over the spot where every trace of his employer's blood had been scrubbed clean. "No, *madame*, I do not think that."

"You're not exactly helping your case," she said, and behind her heard Luc grind his teeth.

"Why?" The cellar master swung round sharply to face him. "Am I under suspicion, inspector?"

Marie-Claude was acutely conscious that her husband didn't look at her when he replied. "Madame Montaud was found with just one emerald cluster in her left ear," he said mildly. "An identical cluster was found in your bed next to the still."

Monsieur Baret said nothing, but his eyes flickered, she noticed, as he opened the door from the cellars. Perhaps it was nothing more than passing from darkness into the light.

"I cannot explain that," he said at length. "But if you are suggesting—" he indicated the cramped sleeping quarters partitioned off with nothing more than wood and glass "—I'm sorry, inspector, you are mistaken."

Marie-Claude opened the door and peered in. There was just about enough room for the bed and a small chest of drawers. The blankets did not look very clean.

"The night watchman confirms that you have been leaving very late. Past midnight on several occasions."

"I did not conduct an affair down here with Madame Montaud," Baret insisted, "that's simply too sordid to contemplate, I am a married man. And the notion that I killed her – pff! What possible motive would I have?"

Luc drew a carbon copy from his breast pocket. Reading upside down, Marie-Claude saw that the letter bore yesterday's date, was addressed to the cellar master and had been type-written.

"This was on top of the paperwork in Madame Montaud's desk," Luc said. "The desk, incidentally, that we were only able to open with the key that was found in her pocket."

Baret took the proffered letter and, as he read, the colour drained from his face. His jaw tightened. "I–I have never seen this before."

Marie-Claude didn't get the chance to read every last word before it disappeared back inside Luc's pocket, but the gist was enough. In the most civil of terms, Martine Montaud was dismissing her cellar master.

"Is it, do you think, too sordid to contemplate?" Luc asked, once they were alone in the distillery. "Tall, fifty, and with that thick thatch of dark hair, it seems perfectly reasonable to me that the earring of the widowed and lonely Martine would end up in his bed."

"Not this bed," Marie-Claude said, sending clouds of dust into the air as she tried to pull the curtains and found the hooks had rusted solid.

"Wouldn't the risk of discovery have been the spice, though? Two educated, articulate, respected people fired by the danger of being caught in the act?"

"If there's any danger, it comes from fleas, not ruined reputations," she said, prodding the unsheeted mattress. "And anyway, who said she was lonely?"

When Madame Montaud tried on clothes in the shop, those were not sensible foundations garments she'd been wearing underneath!

"Who else has a key to the distillery and cellars?" she asked.

"No one who doesn't have a cast iron alibi."

"While Monsieur Baret . . .?"

"Claims he went for a walk, and if you believe that, you believe anything." Luc ran his hand over the ticking on the bolster. "You know, Marie-Claude, just because they're both polite, refined individuals, it doesn't mean they don't enjoy the occasional foray into degeneracy."

She considered the new baby doll pyjamas that were all the rage at the moment. Both she and Luc agreed that these were the most depraved and decadent garments that had ever been invented, and indeed they'd considered them so depraved and decadent that they ripped them off no less than three times last Saturday night.

"So you're saying Alexandre met with Martine last night, as usual. They came down here, as usual, made love in his seedy little camp bed, as usual, where she lost an earring in the heat of their passion . . . then fired him?"

"No," he said, leaning his hip against the chest of drawers. "That's what the evidence is saying. Not me."

Marie-Claude threw her hands in the air. "Luc Brosset, you are the most impossible man on God's earth! If you suspected all along that this was a set-up, for heaven's sake why didn't you just come straight out with it and tell me you wanted my help?"

"That's funny," he said. "I thought that was exactly what I had done."

Centuries had come and gone, but the method of distilling cognac hadn't changed. The still itself, the *alambic*, was made of gleaming red copper and, with its swan neck, long pipes and balloon shape resembled more a giant oriental hookah than a boiler. For nearly four months of the year, once the grapes had been pressed and their precious juice extracted, these three pieces of apparatus would be working night and day to produce the first distillation, the *brouillis*, before undergoing its distinctive second boiling. Only after that could the "heads" and "tails" be separated from the clear "heart" of the spirit that would eventually mature into cognac.

During these four months, though, the cellar master would virtually live next to his *alambic* while, outside, the town would grow warm from so many boilers pumping round the clock, the air would become impregnated with the sweet smell of brandy, and the characteristic black on the buildings would deepen, a symbol of status and pride. Incredibly, a tenth of the cognac was lost to evaporation, a contribution known as the angels' share. Marie-Claude wondered whether Madame Montaud would be able to distinguish her own cognac from where she sat on her cloud. And how silly to get misty-eyed over someone she hardly knew!

"The way she was killed," Luc said, "hit on the back of the head with a marble bust of the founder that took pride of place next to the *alambic*, that suggests the crime wasn't premeditated."

Marie-Claude thought about the key in her pocket. The fact that Alexandre's were the only fingerprints. The way nobody else here had access.

"It suggests an earring coming off when she fell," he continued, "and the killer taking the opportunity to implicate someone else."

She wondered what the gem-smith who made Madame Montaud's jewellery would have to say about such odds.

"Or," she said, "it's a double-bluff designed to look that way."

Luc spiked his hands through his hair. "You mean Baret planned it from the outset, then left clumsy clues that pointed directly to him, leading us to think they had been planted?"

"If it was a spur-of-the-moment act, why didn't he plead *crime passionel* straight away? Cellar masters are respected all over France, Luc, and think about it. Sex, rejection, dismissal? Any one of these things are enough to make a man feel emasculated and strike out in the heat of anger, yet here we have three stacked on top of each other. Alexandre Baret could have thrown up his hands and admitted his crime, and even the worst advocate in the country would have had him walking away a free man."

She stared up at the shining copper works and saw Madame Montaud holding up two evening dresses, the navy blue and the green. *What discount will you give me, Madame Garreau, if I take both? I see. Well, thank you for your time, but I think I'll drive into Angoulême and see — Why, yes, Madame Garreau. Ten percent would be perfectly acceptable. But shall we say twelve?*

"Madame Montaud was elegant, successful, she drove a hard bargain, but by all accounts she was fair. While a man who blends cognac that not only his successor won't see sold but *his* successor either, is a man who is patient, clever and selfless."

Luc scratched his head. "Are you saying he did or he didn't?"

Marie-Claude straightened her hat in the boiler's reflection. "It's late," she said. "I have to get back to the shop."

*   *   *

"Some joint," she murmured as they snubbed the workforce's entrance in favour of the broad sweep of the drive.

"Twelve bedrooms, five wings and ceilings so high you can house a giraffe in each room, should you so desire," Luc said. "And to prove how handsomely this business pays, the house is surrounded by seventeen hectares of beautiful but totally unproductive parkland."

"If you think I'd live there, you're mistaken," Marie-Claude said. "Look at the number of windows for a start. And the height of them! I'd spend all my day washing them."

"You'd have people to do that for you."

"I would not," she protested.

What? Strangers trooping all over her house, snooping all over her business?

"Some people might envy the rich for their lifestyle," she said firmly. "Not me. Madame Montaud may have been successful, but the poor woman was a martyr to the business, she barely took a day off, and look at that sister of hers. Dresses like Grace Kelly, but never gets a chance to breathe, much less be her own person. No privacy, not even a house to call her own, and when her husband leaves the shop, it stinks of stale wine and cigars for simply hours."

"Oh? And what do I stink of?"

"Nutmeg and citron and cool, mountain forests," she said, and his eyes weren't just green, they crinkled at the corners and were flecked with red, grey and brown, and his mouth twisted sideways when he smiled. With his thick mop of dark hair and square practical hands, she was glad Luc would have no trouble finding a new wife once she'd gone.

"Hmm."

He stuffed his square practical hands in his pockets and whistled *Mambo Italiano* under his breath as they sauntered past the bustling vineyards down the hill towards the river. Since the Domaine was only a fifteen-minute walk from the house, they hadn't bothered with the car, and Marie-Claude was wrong about the cardigan. She hadn't needed it at all.

"I don't suppose this sudden obligation to duty has anything to do with the sister?" he asked after working his way through *Three Coins in the Fountain*, *Smile* and *Hernando's Hideaway*.

"Madame Montaud wasn't having an affair with her cellar master," Marie-Claude said, wondering at what point her arm had become linked with his. "She ordered far too many evening gowns for an illicit liaison."

More likely she was being courted discreetly, preferring to wait and see how things developed before going public with the relationship.

"Loose women aren't taken seriously in business," she pronounced. "But the sister, Madame Delaville, now that's a different story."

Husband reeking of stale booze and smoke, choosing all her clothes? She'd lost count of the number of times she'd seen him sitting in Madame Garreau's plush armchair, squat and pot-bellied like a cocky little toad, while his wife paraded in unflattering suits with slow and mechanical precision.

"Natalie Delaville is a woman of loose moral standards?"

"Exactly the opposite," Marie-Claude said, turning the key in the shop. "Her husband has the word bully all but etched on his forehead, but the more I think about it, the more I remember that her chin hasn't drooped quite so much lately, there's been colour in her pale cheeks, and miracle of miracles, Madame Delaville actually called in half a dozen times on her own over the past month. I want to look up what she – *voilà!*"

"Well?" Luc held out his hands in exasperation. "Are you going to tell me what the little mouse bought?"

"Certainly not." Such matters were private! "But I can tell you that the dresses were feminine and flattering, and I can tell you whose account they were charged to, as well." She shot her husband a sideways glance. "Alexandre Baret."

"All right . . ." Luc rubbed his jaw in thought. "But is this actually getting us anywhere?"

"It explains his unease and reluctance to provide an alibi."

"Because he was protecting Natalie Delaville."

"Absolutely." She locked the door and tested the catch. "Now all we have to do is prove how that bitch killed Martine."

"Metamorphosis is a wonderful thing," Luc observed, stretching his pace to match hers. "One minute she's a mouse, the next she's a bitch – what? What have I said?"

"Honestly!" Marie-Claude stopped outside the baker's and shook her head in disbelief. "I don't know where you get your ideas, sometimes! Not Madame Delaville, Luc. She didn't kill Madame Montaud."

It was Madame Baret, of course. Alexandre's wife.

"*And* she killed the wrong woman."

As the hills slowly turned to russet and gold and the French populace finally came to terms with defeat in Indochina, the Empire State Building had been eclipsed as the world's tallest structure, civilization was facing extinction from something called Rock and Roll, and Luc had been proved right about Suez, especially in light of that botched attempt earlier on the Egyptian president's life.

"By the way, Marie-Claude, I received a letter from the Commissioner this morning."

More and more these days Luc had taken to joining her on walks along the tow-path, although sometimes their route took them through the town hall park or onto the islands, where they would take a picnic providing they wrapped up warm.

"He writes that he has finally rounded up everyone involved in the blackmail and extortion ring. Some seven police officers are awaiting trial, he says, and commends me for a job well done."

"That the letter?" Marie-Claude tossed it into the Charente, where a squadron of ducks came steaming in, mistaking it for a bread roll. "You know my opinion of the Commissioner."

"For the life of me, I can't imagine why."

"He said I was truculent, selfish and a pain in the *cul*."

Luc laughed. "Well, if you overheard that much, you'd have also heard him qualify his statement by adding that you were spirited, funny, and I was lucky to have you."

Couldn't agree more, sir, Luc had replied, and damn those horrid children upstairs for drowning out the Commissioner's words.

"He congratulated me on the Montaud murder, as well." Luc stuffed his hands in his pockets. "Being a high-profile case, I suppose word found its way back to his desk, but what I'm getting to is that he ended by saying that, now the corruption ring's been wrapped up and my life is no longer in danger, there's a job for me in Paris, should we want it."

"You never told me your life was threatened!"

"Hell hath no fury like a Chief Inspector jailed. So, then. Do we? Want that job, I mean."

"It might have been high-profile, but it wasn't exactly brain surgery, Luc."

All those late nights in the distillery, indeed! *I did not conduct an affair down here with Madame Montaud*, the cellar master had insisted, *that's simply too sordid to contemplate.* Quite right. It may have been his employer's sister he'd been carrying on with, not his employer, but he wouldn't have dreamt of taking the delicate, browbeaten Natalie to the distillery had it not been the only place where they could meet and not be either seen or overhead. His office was too close to the main works. They dared not be seen in public. So they either sat down there, talking long into the night, or they sneaked off in his car to plan their new life together, and what a lot of planning there was. For all that cellar masters are handsomely paid and live in grand houses, they still don't live like the Montauds! There would be no majestic mansion for Natalie once she left Delaville. No parklands, no servants, no prestigious balls. Alexandre had wanted her to be one hundred percent sure before making the leap. He knew there would be no going back.

For her part, of course, Madame Baret hadn't believed for a second that her husband had been required to work late.

In the way of deceived wives everywhere, she followed him, saw the lights in the distillery, knew about the bed, heard him whispering on the telephone in the hall. She'd had no trouble tracing the number to the Domaine and knew immediately who he was carrying on with. (Who else was there, for goodness sake? Hardly that pale, downtrodden sister!) So, again in the way of deceived wives everywhere, she hoped and then prayed the affair would blow over. Until the day she overheard him talking about their new life together . . .

From that moment on, revenge was all that consumed her. Revenge on the woman who had destroyed her life. Revenge on the man who discarded her.

"The marble bust might look like the instrument of a crime of passion, a spur-of-the-moment decision, grabbing the first object to hand," Marie-Claude said, as they paused to watch the churning waters of the millrush merge with the stately river.

"But equally it smacked of a squeamish reluctance to be facing the victim."

A uniquely feminine approach to murder. As was the cold-blooded planning.

"It was easy enough to get a set of her husband's keys cut."

"One of the locksmiths confirmed it straight away, but as evidence it was still far from conclusive."

"No, but it all mounted up." She kicked the fallen leaves as she walked. Alder, willow and poplar. "Madame Baret's mistake was planting the desk key in Martine's pocket."

Good heavens, women as elegant as Madame Montaud don't use pockets! They tuck them away tidily in their *Chanel* handbags, which meant someone had used that key to get into her desk and replaced it in a hurry. And if it wasn't to take something out, then it must be to put something in.

A quick check of the keys proved that the letter had been typed on the Barets' private typewriter, not in the office at the Domaine, but it had been a clever move on Madame Baret's part. If the head of a cognac house wanted rid of their cellar master, this would not be made public knowledge. A gentleman's agreement between the two parties, however bitter underneath, would not show on the surface. Both had too much invested in the business to jeopardize their reputations.

"She was smart about fingerprints, too."

Taking care the only ones lifted were her husband's, and who would think anything odd about seeing a lady of quality going round in evening gloves? Exactly. And whatever excuse she'd used to lure Madame Montaud down to the cellars, she must have thought it was her lucky day when Martine agreed so easily. But then, of course, she didn't know she was setting a trap for the wrong woman.

"Too smart about the fingerprints," Luc said. They had stopped to watch one of the wooden, flat-bottomed *gabarres* pass through the lock, laden with casks lashed with ropes. "That was one of the things that bothered me from the outset. That if Martine Montaud was exerting so much passion in the cellar master's quarters, why weren't hers there, too?"

"She misjudged the calibre of Madame Montaud's jewellery, as well."

How cold must her heart have been, as she stood over the corpse, unscrewing the emerald cluster? Extracting the key from Martine's handbag, placing the letter of dismissal in her desk, then walking out as if nothing had happened and secure in the knowledge that her husband would not plead *crime passionel*. Why should he, after all? The man was innocent.

"Never mind Madame Baret," Luc said. "Just tell me whether we want that job in Paris."

Marie-Claude watched the *gabarre* sail round the bend and disappear from sight. Above, the sun shone through the falling leaves and blackbirds foraged in the litter. Next week "Dial M for Murder" would be running back to back with "Rear Window" and in subtitles, plus she still hadn't finished those curtains for the bathroom, the cellar really needed a new blind, the old one was a disgrace, the bedroom could use fresh wallpaper, ditto the *salon* now she came to think about it, and she'd promised Madame Garreau two more days a week with the winter collection.

"Maybe when the rains come," Marie-Claude said slowly.

Besides. She wasn't sure Luc was quite ready to live alone yet.

WISH

John Rickards

Four days since I called in sick. I think.

I've been awake for three of them straight. I think.

My fellow *gardai* would piss themselves if they could see me, no doubt. Then they'd have me committed.

But they don't know. They haven't seen. They're all out getting drunk, or off fucking their wives, or fucking their mistresses and lying about it to their wives, or passed out in front of their TVs in their nice safe homes while I'm

fucking

dead.

And I don't know if even I believe it.

It started with Michael. A mental case, low-grade nut. We have quite a few. A handful of paedophiles, stalkers, minor assaults. Care in the community jobs, not criminal enough to be locked up for good, criminal enough to be in and out of the cells on a regular basis. Since jail seems to do fuck all by way of curing them – worse, many come out of it even more damaged than they went in – my own policy is not to arrest. Talk, threaten, watch, but don't arrest if possible. Jail only makes them more of a risk to everyone in the long run.

Some of these guys are homeless, but not Michael. It's a shithole of a flat, though, overlooking the railway tracks not far from where they cross the Tolka, north of Dublin's city centre. Building that smells of boiled vegetables and cat piss. Walls the colour of boiled vegetables and cat piss.

"That woman hasn't been poisoning your kitten, Michael. She doesn't even know who you are. She wouldn't know how to poison a kitten, even if she wanted to."

"Could swear I've seen her . . ."

"No, you haven't. She hasn't done a thing. Trust me on this, OK? Jesus, they train me for this sort of thing and, believe me, if she was guilty, I'd know and I'd have dealt with her. You've got to stop yelling at the woman and threatening her, Michael."

Sullen look. A child being unfairly chided. A flash of malice. I wish for something to shut him up. I wish for something to stop this kind of shit.

So I do it. I drop the threat. Let the genie out of the bottle. Make the wish.

"And you listen good to me, Michael. You leave that woman alone from now on, or else I'll send your name, address and photo to Iron Kurt's Gay Nazi website."

Let me explain. I have a friend, Curt, who's funny, erudite, can hold his drink remarkably well, and who happens to be gay. One night in Fallon's, the conversation turns to gay rights and marriage, a subject which he understandably feels strongly about. He speaks his piece, and someone else makes some comment about him being a "fascist homo" or something. Funny in its stupidity. And so the remark resurfaces and transforms, blossoming into something so much more.

It helps that there's been trouble with a couple of Neo-Nazi crackpots in the city on TV recently, even with the NSRUS pulling out of Ireland. Nazis make the best bad guys. Ask Indiana Jones. And I see a twitch of fear or homophobia in Michael's eyes.

"I'll do it," I tell him. "And you know what'll happen then . . ."

Of course, his mind fills in the blank with its own worst fears. He promises to be good.

And over the next few weeks, he is. And I trot out the same threat to other lunatics I have to deal with. And they don't see me as a punisher. Iron Kurt is the punisher. I'm just the messenger. So they don't even resent me for it.

My fellow *gardai* find the whole thing fucking funny. Some of them start using Kurt themselves. And Dublin sleeps safer at night. Kurt's out there, watching over the city. A spectre in the fog blowing in off the harbour, creeping upriver. A paper tiger keeping evil at bay.

One afternoon, I see William, one of our deranged, sitting in the doorway of a boarded-up shop with an Iron Cross badge pinned proudly to his battered old blue Leinster rugby top. Next to him is a scratched metal strongbox.

"Hey, William."

"It's . . . you're gonna beat me."

"Leave it alone, William. What's in the box?"

"They're mine, see."

"Fine. But show me what you've got."

"It's private. Mine."

"Last time we had this conversation, you had a petrol bomb on you. I just want to make sure you don't have another one. Anything else, you can keep."

He thinks, pops open the box. Inside, an untidy pile of black fur.

"Why are you carrying a bunch of dead rats around?" I ask.

"They pay me. It's my deal. Not yours."

"I've got no ambitions of being a ratcatcher. Who pays?"

"The big red building down Castleforbes Road. Food warehouse. To set traps. Ten cents a rat."

"And you get them from somewhere else, and they pay for them."

"Yeah. It's a good job."

"Good for you. What's with the Iron Cross?" I point at his chest.

"It's protection, is what. Keith saw Iron Kurt."

I try not to smile. "Yeah?"

"And he said, you wear stuff like this and you'll be OK."

"Unless you've been posted on his website."

"Well, yeah."

"While we're on the subject, you're keeping away from that playground, right?"

He nods vigorously. "Yeah. Never meant to do anything."

"Did Keith say what Iron Kurt looked like?"

"Yeah. A big guy, tall, built like a brick shithouse. Bald. With a beard. Tattoos all over."

The real Curt is 5′5″ and built for comfort, not speed. Again, I stifle a smile. "Yeah, that sounds right. You'd better stay out of trouble, huh?"

Not long after, I see Keith himself. The shopping trolley that holds his worldly possessions has a bunch of plastic German soldiers on string looped all the way around it like fairy lights. Now I'm looking for it, I start to notice similar items on most of the other nutcases in my patch.

A belt buckle like an Iron Cross around the neck. A pencil-drawn swastika. An SS-style shoulder patch. In one house in Clontarf, a guy named Terry has a toy soldier shrine in a foil-lined cardboard box.

Votive offerings. Symbols of fear, not worship, not support. Warding off Kurt and his unholy wrath.

I shouldn't be surprised. They all gather together in Duff Alley off East Wall Road to drink Tennant's Super until someone passes out or pisses themselves. And they talk, and share stories. Chinese whispers. Some believe them, some don't. But they all listen.

They say Kurt's the son of an SS officer. They say he's raped and killed more than two hundred men. They say his website has more than a thousand followers, all over the world, who take perverse delight in making each victim last as long as possible. They say – and when I tell Curt this he practically wets himself laughing – that he has a fourteen-inch dick and that most of his victims die from blood poisoning caused by massive anal tearing.

Iron Kurt.

My creation. My Frankenstein. My cartoon monster.

And then Keith disappears. One day, gone. No one knows where. No one's seen him. They find his trolley round the corner from a soup kitchen on North Quay, but he never comes back for it. Shit happens, these people move on.

William stops picking up pay for his rats and vanishes from the hostel he's been staying at. Someone tells me he'd been beaten up and his badge taken a couple of days before.

I stop seeing Terry. When I go to his house, his toy soldier shrine is still there, but he's gone. The neighbour says the last they saw of him, he was going to get a pint of milk. A couple of the others disappear too.

Duff Alley gets very empty, and the conversation there becomes very muted. They get drunk, huddle together, and after dark they whisper that Iron Kurt has come for them. And now I'm

shit

scared.

Another trip to the piss-stained steps outside Michael's flat. He's almost the only one left, and I need to know what he knows. To find out if he can reassure me. Keith left for Cork. William found a winning lottery ticket in the street and moved to the Caribbean. Some other *gardai* told the Duff Alley crazies to get out, so they're meeting somewhere else now.

When I knock on the door, I hear a wet thudding noise from inside. When I try the handle, it's unlocked. When I should turn and run away, I push it open and walk in.

The sickly-sweet smell of blood on the air. The acrid spike of human waste. The cloying taste of someone else's sweat. Michael lies in a crimson-splashed, naked tangle in the middle of his living room floor. The carpet around him soaked black with blood. Legs splayed at an unnatural angle, and pink-yellow ribbons of intestines running from the torn and tattered gash that yawns between them.

He twitches, and I realize he's still alive.

"Michael? Can you hear me?"

Whimper. Twitch. One eye creaks open and fixes me with a stare of utter agony and shock.

"Who did this? What the fuck's going on?"

"*It . . . Kurt . . . didn't . . .*"

"Kurt? You're sure? Christ."

"*Said . . . name . . . site . . . to punish . . . I didn't . . .*"

I should be calling an ambulance. I should be calling my colleagues. "Where is he now?"

Michael's eye looks down. Pleading. Betrayed. "*You said . . . wouldn't . . . website . . . I . . . good . . .*"

He thinks I did it. "I didn't tell him," I say. "Jesus, Michael, I wouldn't even know how. I swear to you."

"*He . . . told . . .*" Michael smacks his lips. Dry mouth. Lost too much fluid already. Bleeding out. Dying.

"What did he tell you?"

"*No . . . he asked . . . who . . . gave my name . . .*" Smack. Smack. "*I . . . told him . . . you . . .*"

As Michael's head drops to the carpet, something thumps out in the stairwell and my heart jumps into my mouth. Again I think about running, but I don't. Again I think about calling the station, but to tell them what? That some kind of phantom is stalking lunatics on my beat?

I step outside, check the stairs with shaky steps and trembling hands. And there's nothing there.

When I come back down to Michael's flat, the body is gone. So is the blood that soaked the carpet a moment ago. Is the smell gone as well? I can't tell. But there's no sign that Michael was ever here. And was he – could I be imagining it? Could all this be in my head, a product of my own fear?

Fuck. Fuck.

When I search the flat, I can't see any of the protective trinkets the others had. He was an unbeliever.

I'm not. Not now.

When I walk away from Michael's, I see the tall figure of a bald man watching me from the trees on the far side of the park across the street. He's massive, and bare-chested. The dark outlines of tattoos that litter his skin flicker and swirl like flames. He points at me, long and hard, then slides back into the undergrowth.

So now it's been four days since then, since I called in sick. Since I barricaded myself into my flat to wait for the end. In the yellow glare of the 40-watt bulb, in the air that reeks of stale sweat and fear, I'm protected by a butcher's knife and an Iron Cross. A spray paint swastika on every wall. A replica of one of those Nazi imperial eagles they'd carry everywhere in those films. Terry's foil-lined box with his tableau of half a dozen toy German WWII soldiers.

Maybe they'll help me. I certainly won't step beyond their protective radius.

Because Kurt is coming to kill me. His creator. To close the circle. I'm the last one he's looking for here. And he won't let me go. I know it.

Soon I'll hear his footsteps on the stairs. Slow, heavy, deliberate.

Thump.

Thump.

Thump.

Be careful what you wish for, you just might get it.

THE BRICK

Natasha Cooper

It all started with the broken window. That was what was so infuriating. If those wretched children hadn't found the brick next door's cowboy builders had left in the front garden and thought it would be fun to smash a big bit of clean glass, none of it would have happened. We'd still have been OK; not in seventh heaven or anything extravagant like that, but OK.

The randomness of it still makes me swear. It needn't have happened; none of it. That's what gets to me when I let myself think about it.

There I was peacefully sitting on a beanbag on the floor (we'd sanded the boards by then but not varnished them and they looked a bit splintery; but they were clean, which was something after the state we'd found them in when we tore up the old lino) reading short stories for a prize. They were all about spouses killing each other, of course: short stories for prizes nearly always are. And I'd been congratulating myself rather because however livid I'd been with John, I'd never, even in my wildest, most secret fantasies, wanted to kill him. Stiffen him, maybe; tell him not to be such a baby and to get on out there and do his bit of the bargain, like I'd always done mine. I mean, I'd given up my job when it was clear that he needed more input than I'd been able to give him while I was working so hard.

It wasn't only the comfort and the listening and the putting-up with stress-induced sulks, you see; he'd needed a lot more practical help with all sorts of things, and meals suddenly became important to him in a way they'd never been before. We'd always just picked for supper whenever we both got back from work, but suddenly he wanted three courses with both of us sitting down at the table, whenever he got back. And my publishing salary just wasn't up to paying a housekeeper, not after tax and all the things I'd had to pay for, you know, decent clothes and that sort of thing. So I'd given up. I'd always done a bit of freelance, luckily as it turned out. So when John cracked up, I still had all my contacts in place.

Anyway, where was I? Being on my own all day means that I do get very short of chat, which is why I can't stop talking when there's any opportunity. Sorry about that. I've lost my drift. Oh, yes, the brick. Well, you see, there I was, sitting by the window, thinking that at least this titchy little South London cottage was a bit lighter than our Kensington house, when this bloody brick crashed through the window and landed by my feet. It must have been in next door's garden for a while because it was coated with mud and had woodlice clinging to it. You know, those prehistoric-looking horrid little black things.

They were all over the house when we bought it, but once we'd sorted the damp we got rid of most of them. They crunch under your bare feet. In a way that was nearly the worst thing, getting out of bed that first morning in the new house and hearing the crunch under my feet. I could have hit John then. I wouldn't have, honestly, and I never told him that's how I felt, but it was the last straw.

He was lying there with most of the pillow over his head, not getting up, hating the potty little job that was all he'd managed to get. I know he was feeling awful. And I did sympathize. I really did. You couldn't not if you loved him, and I did. But I wished he'd just pull himself together a bit. I mean, the rest of us had to.

Anyway, the brick. Well, it wasn't so much the brick as the bits of glass. One of the bigger splinters sliced through my forearm, you know, the one bit of one that stays looking reasonably firm even when the rest begins to go scraggy. It was such a shock. I was still reeling from the noise. You can't imagine how much noise one of those plate-glass windows makes when it's broken. And then there was a kind of stinging down my arm; that's all it seemed to be at the beginning, a sting. And I looked down and there was this great long red line, getting redder and wider all the time. Spreading. It was about six inches long, I think, and the lips of it opened as I looked, like a cut in a bit of steak.

Anyway, for a while I just sat and looked at it. Then when the blood started dripping down onto the beanbag – it was natural canvas, so it showed – and the planks we'd spent so long sanding, I knew I'd have to do something. It was hurting by then, too. And I felt like a child. Perhaps that was why I let her in. I felt wobbly and pathetic, nothing like Penny-who's-such-a-brick, Penny who's always kept everything going even when her husband cracked up like that and both the children went so peculiar.

She rang the bell just as I'd got to the hall, gripping the sides of the cut with my other hand. Well, it would have to be the other hand, wouldn't it? Honestly, sometimes I forget I've ever been a copy-editor. Where was I? I know, trying not to think too much about her. She'd have said I was in denial and she'd have been right. I sort of thought it must be whoever'd chucked the brick through the window who was ringing the bell and I wasn't going to answer. I was leaning against the hall wall – we hadn't painted that yet, just stripped off the awful old spriggy paper we'd found when we came – and feeling faint, really. Anyone would have. And then she called out:

"Are you all right? I saw them throw it and tried to catch them, but I was just too far away."

She did sound breathless, as though she'd been running. And she had a nice voice, rich and deepish, and very warm. It sounded so safe and sure that I came over even more wobbly than before, which was barmy. Children always do it if you're too sympathetic when they've bumped themselves, but I was old enough to know better.

"Hello? Are you all right? My name's Sophie Allen. I live just round the corner. I'm perfectly respectable. Can I come in? Give you a hand? There's a very good glazier I know who does our windows whenever we're burgled. I can give him a ring for you, if you'd like. Are you there?"

So then I stammered out something idiotic and opened the door. And there she was, just about my age but much younger looking. She wasn't having to hold down all that fury, for one thing. Or not by then. I found out later that she'd been through the same sort of thing in a way, but she'd got over it. People do. Or so they say.

"You poor thing," was all she said. But she came right in, put an arm round my shoulders and nearly pushed me towards the kitchen. I'd hated that, too, being able to see into the kitchen from the front door. It really drove the down-shifting bit home.

She knew all about the house because hers was exactly the same. They all are in those little streets between the commons. She had my arm under the cold tap in seconds. The firmness of her was lovely then, just as safe-making as her voice. The brick and the malice of it were washed off just like the blood. They came back. But for a bit they'd gone. She kept on talking and I didn't really listen to the words, just the sureness of her voice.

It sounded as though she knew everything that mattered and would always help but never ask the sort of questions you didn't want to answer. She always did see a lot, and she knew what you could take and what you needed – and offered it straight off. Always.

When she'd got me bloodless and dried out and bandaged up, she called the glazier she knew and swept up the glass, found the Hoover and sucked up the splinters from the beanbag, too, and even Hoovered my jeans. I wouldn't have thought of that, but she was right; there were chips of glass caught in some of the seams. I saw them gleaming as she sucked. It was a weird sensation, that powerful pull all down my thighs and her lovely, warm matter-of-fact voice, telling me what she was doing and why and what the shock of it all was doing to me, and why I was feeling so awful, and who she thought the children were who'd thrown the brick and how it wasn't me they were throwing it at but the old bat who'd lived there before us. She'd been a bit of a witch apparently, always complaining about ordinary noise and making a great fuss about children playing in the street. They still do that, round here. I couldn't believe it at first: roller-blading in the middle of the road, chucking balls about. As though they weren't ten minutes' walk from two huge open spaces. And they always did make a bit of a row. I saw what she meant: the old bat, I mean, who in a way caused the trouble because if she hadn't upset them in the first place, they wouldn't have chucked the brick and none of the rest of it would've happened.

"But there's a SOLD sign outside," I said at the time. I remember that. It was nearly the first thing I'd said in the torrent of all the comfort she'd poured out. I'd meant to say something about how amazing it was to find a friendly neighbour in a place where I'd never expected to, but all that came out was that peevish little protest. "Can't they read?"

"Probably not. Lots of the more delinquent ones can't. I'm a woodentop, and I see a fair amount of children like them."

"A woodentop?" I thought I hadn't heard properly, but she smiled, a great huge smile that showed off her perfect, white teeth. Mine aren't like that: crossed over at the front and a nasty grubby colour like stale clotted cream. Ugh.

"Magistrate," she said, laughing. She had a lovely laugh, too, and none of us had laughed for ages, not happily like that. "No one calls us that these days, but in the old days they did and I like it. Now, you're glass-free. You'd better have something hot. Tea? Coffee? God! I sound like an air hostess, don't I? Shall I put the kettle on?"

And so she made herself at home. I liked it, which I'd never have let myself do if it hadn't been for the brick and the blood. I sat on the beanbag, looking at the jagged great hole in the window and thought about the violence of South London and how much I hated it and how scared I was even though I couldn't afford to be. They say it's changed now, but in those days it was pretty rough. So there I was, thinking how amazing it was that she was there, and perhaps even in South London there would be people to meet and like and talk to. Damn! I'm forgetting the copy-editing again. But I can't stop once I've started. Sorry. I don't often talk as much as this. Well, I do actually, but it feels new each time I do it and I always mean not to afterwards.

There was one little bit of glass she'd missed. Even she'd managed to miss one and it lay on the scrubbed board just near a stickying puddle of my blood, glinting. It was a sunny day. All the days that summer were sunny. It seemed unfair in a way.

She came back with the tea, very strong, tea-bag tea. It tasted like her, strong and warm and helping. Then we just talked. She was still there when the woman who was doing the school run to the local comprehensive dropped my two off and she stayed to tea and made them laugh and helped with their homework. Then she went, giving me her number and telling me she'd drop in again. She only lived round the corner.

It wasn't for weeks that I got round to asking her for supper so that John could share in it all. I suppose in a way I'd wanted to keep her as my treat. But then it seemed selfish, so I fixed it so that he could meet her too.

When he took one look at her and said, "Sophie?" in that surprised but blissful voice I suppose I knew what was going to happen. I was angry with her for not telling me she knew him, but when I looked at her I saw that she was just as surprised as he'd been. She knew my married name, of course, but I never talked about John because it would have been disloyal and so she'd never made the connection; she'd been married, too, for about ten years and so he hadn't recognized her name when I'd talked about her.

That was it, really. They tried not to, I think. They really did try, but she was just so much better at making him feel all right than I was. I understood that. She did it for me, too, when he could only make me feel miles worse. In a way it wasn't what they did that made me so angry. It was what he said when he'd made his decision, as though I'd be pleased to hear it, as though he was giving me something again after all.

"If it wasn't for everything you've taught me I'd never have been able to love Sophie as she deserves. I couldn't do it when I first knew her because I didn't know enough. It was you who taught me how to know people and let them know me. It's all your doing, Penny. You've shown me how to be all the things she wanted me to be then and I couldn't. We owe it all to you and we'll never forget it."

I won't either. Not ever. You see, that was when I *did* want to kill him. But even then, if I hadn't been jointing the chickens when he said it and had a sharp knife in my hands, we'd still have been all right. I know we would.

THE KILLER BESIDE ME

Allan Guthrie

"We're long past our sell-by date." Trevor switched his grip on his cane. He'd been clutching it hard for ages now and his hand was clammy. What were the bastards up to, taking so long to get here?

"Bollocks," Harry said. "We've got a good couple of years in us yet. We've defied the odds so far. I'm looking forward to old age. Has its perks. You can spit on the floor and beat nosey children with your cane."

"But after a while," Trevor said, "you'll get tired of lying in a pile of your own shite."

"Or somebody else's."

"What're you saying? If anything, you'll lose control of your bowels before me."

"At least I can still get it up."

"Fuck you. Anyway, that's not what I mean. Just making a point," Trevor said. "We shouldn't be here. Not at our age."

"Fuck, we're not in our seventies yet. Don't write us off. I can see the day when we'll need special adult undergarments. I long for that day."

Trevor didn't move. He couldn't, not without his brother's help. The settee was too deep. A faded old two-seater, that's the best the fuckers could come up with. Stuffed out of the way in a room that was some kind of cleaning room. A hoover, mop in a bucket, stink of furniture polish. The bank manager had had to move a cardboard box full of rubber gloves and dusters before they'd been able to sit down. When he left, he'd locked the door behind him.

Where the fuck were the police?

Trevor said, "I once gave a blind man a blow job, you know."

"You did not."

"Did."

"Not."

"You were asleep."

"Shite."

"You were."

"I'd have woken up."

"You were drunk. Paralytic."

"Then you must have been too."

"You can't hold your drink. Anyway, it's true. Back at Aggie's—"

"I don't want to hear about it."

"Well, I'm telling you."

"I'm not listening." Harry started singing. But he couldn't drown out Trevor's voice. Especially after Trevor started shouting. Harry gave in, asked, "What happened?"

"He wandered into the bedroom by mistake. I heard him scuffling around, banging into things. I put on the light." Trevor adopted a high-pitched voice. "I spoke like this," he said. "Made him think he'd walked into a lady's room. Completely fooled him."

"But why?"

"For fun."

"No, why did you blow him?"

"He asked. Completely up front about it. And I felt sorry for him."

"That's fucking disgusting."

"A selfless act," Trevor said. "Some might say it was noble."

"Wonder what he'd think if he knew you were male."

"He'll never find out."

"I could tell him."

"But you don't know who it is."

"Bet I can guess."

Trevor said, "How the fuck?"

"How many blind people stayed at Aggie's?"

"Three. At least."

"One was a woman, so it wasn't her. So there's a fifty-fifty chance of me getting it right."

"Well, I'm not going to tell you."

"But I know, anyway."

"No way."

"Do too."

"Ah, away and shite, you old fuck."

The two old men were silent for a while. The sound of traffic seeped through the walls behind them.

"Who was it, then?" Trevor asked.

"Not telling."

"You don't fucking know. You were asleep. You don't remember it. So how can you know? You can only guess."

Harry shrugged. Well, as much as he was able to. "This conversation is over."

"Fine."

"Yeah, fine."

"Good."

"Well, shut up."

"I will."

"How did you turn out gay, anyway?"

"I'm not fucking gay."

"You gave a blind man a blow job."

"So?"

"That's pretty gay."

"You think so? How do you explain Edna, then?"

"Okay, so you're bisexual."

"At least I'm sexual."

"What's with you today? You've done nothing but pick on me from the minute we woke up."

Silence.

"The surgeon's in town."

"Huh?"

"The surgeon." Trevor stared at Harry's annoying blank face. "*The* surgeon. *Our* surgeon."

Harry looked away. "Shut up about that. It's not happening. You want to end up like Carslaw, back in '98?"

"Don't remember him."

"Yeah, you do. Big guy. Talked about cars all the time?"

"Vaguely."

"Went into hospital for a hip replacement," Harry said. "Never saw him again."

"Died?"

"Escaped. Outran the bastards, him and his dodgy hip."

"Yeah?"

"Course not, you thick twat. He went under the knife. Didn't have the heart for it. Went to sleep and never woke up. You don't remember?"

"Nope."

"Jesus. Maybe you're senile already."

"Fuck off."

"Can't speak to you. Don't know why I bother."

Trevor said, "Leave me alone then."

"I will."

"Give your pecker a tug."

"You sure you don't want to?"

"Fuck off, you dirty bastard."

"Well," Trevor said, after a while, "I expect an apology at the very least."

"For?"

Trevor crossed his arm over his chest. Said nothing.

"Huh?" Harry said. Shook his head. "Okay, I'm sorry I said you were gay."

"Not that. I don't care about that."

"Thought you wanted an apology."

"I do. But not for the gay remark."

"Well, what, then?"

"What do you think?"

"Fuck's sake, how am I supposed to know?"

"Take a wild guess."

"No," Harry said. Thought for a minute. "Nope. Nothing." Trevor looked him in the eye.

"Well, maybe," Harry said. He looked down at his hand. He was better with his hand than Trevor was. Maybe because Harry was right-handed.

"Say it."

Harry sighed. "The robbery? Us ending up here?"

"Great fucking guess. You're a fucking genius."

"Sarcasm's unbecoming."

"Oh, but robbing a fucking bank without telling me is okay?"

"Didn't think you'd mind."

"Like I had any choice."

"You knew about the gun."

"Yeah, but how was I supposed to know what it was for?"

"What'd you think if was for?"

"I dunno. Self-defence?"

"Oh, yeah. You really believed that."

"Lots of kids about, what're they called, hoodies. You know they'll fuck us over, pair of old codgers like us, joined at the hip. Anyway, that's what you said."

"I lied. You always know when I lie."

"Not this time."

Silence. "So, you're claiming you had no idea? Not even an inkling?"

"That's right."

"Up until what point?"

"What do you mean?"

"At what point did you realize what was going on?"

"Once you got the gun out and said, 'Everybody freeze. This is a robbery.'"

"Pretty fucking cool, that."

"No, it wasn't. You're not cool. You'll never be cool. It's not even a proper fucking gun. You're retarded."

"Speak for yourself."

"Thanks, I will."

"So what's going to happen now?"

"Dunno. They'll fetch the police. And they'll probably come and handcuff us. Lead us off to some pokey room somewhere in a police station and bombard us with questions." Trevor paused. "I'm going to tell them the truth."

"Which is?"

"I was coerced into it."

"Coerced? Co*fucking*erced? I hate it when you know words I don't. How do you do that? I've never seen you so much as pick up a dictionary."

"You *forced* me to do it. That better?"

"Suit yourself. Doesn't bother me what you say."

"You'll back me up."

"I will?"

"Sure. You know it's the truth."

"But why should I?"

"Because you don't want to go to prison."

"What's you getting off with it got to do with me going to prison?"

"Everything. Think about it."

Pause.

"Well?"

Harry said, "I'm thinking."

"Nothing clicked?"

"If I'm guilty, they'll send me to prison."

"Yeah. But if I'm innocent, they can't send *me* to prison. So how do they arrange that, short of an operation?"

"Ah, I'm with you. Fucking nice."

A key scraped in the lock. Harry and Trevor got to their feet. Took a well-timed joint effort. A difficult operation, but they'd had lots of practice. They waddled forwards a couple of steps as the door opened. A young guy in a suit walked in tucking his bleached blonde hair behind his ear.

"Hi," Harry said. "You're the manager, right? I'm Harry. This is Trevor. Nice bank you've got. Don't like this room much, though. Smells like a summer breeze."

The bank manager ignored Harry, looked at Trevor.

Trevor said, "I'm innocent."

He nodded. "It's clear you weren't a willing participant. I could see you trying to get your brother to put down . . . this." He held up the gun. "Whatever it is."

"I was coerced." Trevor looked sideways at Harry.

"Don't you mean co-*arsed*?" Harry said. "Fucking cockjockey."

"So can I go?"

The bank manager said, "That may be problematic."

"But I'm innocent."

"I dare say." He pulled a face. "You'll have to wait for the police to decide."

"I want to go home."

"That's too bad."

"Harry can stay."

"That's impossible. Even if I could let you, it's physically impossible."

"But you've no right to keep me here."

"You have to stay till the police get here." The manager tucked his hair behind his ear again. "I have every right to insist on that."

"You're fucked," Harry said. He started laughing. "I robbed your bank. I pulled out my gun and waved it around and threatened people with it and there's fuck all you can do because I'm a Siamese twin and my brother's innocent."

"I thought," the bank manager said, "that the correct expression was 'conjoined twin'."

"To you," Harry said, "it is."

Trevor lashed out with his cane, struck the bank manager on the temple.

"Oh," Harry said. "Nice fucking shot."

"Thanks," Trevor said. The bank manager was sprawled on the floor. He groaned. "After three," Trevor said.

Together the conjoined twins lurched out of their seat. They bent over and Trevor picked up the gun. "You okay?" he asked the bank manager.

The bank manager opened his eyes, saw the gun in Trevor's hands, flinched.

"Know what it is?" Trevor said. "Humane killer. Used for killing livestock. Place the weapon to the animal's forehead like this." He placed the gun to the bank manager's forehead. "And then when you pull the trigger, it fires a steel bolt into the animal's brain."

The bank manager said, "No. For God's sake."

Trevor shrugged, straightened up. He turned, smiled at Harry. Placed the gun to his brother's forehead and pulled the trigger.

Harry jolted. A red circle beauty-spotted his brow. Blood began a slow trickle downwards. His eyes closed.

Trevor dropped the gun. "Jesus," he said.

Harry slumped to the side, dragging Trevor sideways. They fell on the floor, landing on top of the bank manager.

The bank manager cried out. Trevor struggled to get his wind back, then said, "Sorry."

No point trying to get back to his feet. That was an impossibility now.

The bank manager struggled out from beneath them, sat with his back to the wall, hugging his knees. After a while, he relaxed, gently massaged his temple. He moved forward, slowly, eyes on Trevor. Then he examined Harry. "You've killed him," he said. He picked up the gun, stared at it.

"Yeah," Trevor said. "Can you call an ambulance? Tell them they'll need to perform an emergency separation on a pair of conjoined twins. And they'll need to do it now. There's a number in my back pocket. They'll need to phone it. It's the number of a surgeon who can perform the operation."

"You planned this?"

"Harry would never agree to the op. Too risky."

"So you did agree to the robbery? You weren't as innocent as you claimed?"

"I'm admitting to nothing. Just call for an ambulance. And get the surgeon. He's in Edinburgh at the moment. But he's on standby." Trevor paused. "Hurry. I think I'm going into shock."

"What if I refuse?"

"No matter." Trevor was short of breath. "The police'll bring an ambulance with them. Where are they?"

"Ah, Trevor," the bank manager said. "You really believe a couple of geriatric Siamese – forgive me – *conjoined* twins having a public argument constitutes a serious enough threat for us to call the police?"

"But my brother asked for your money."

"And you told him to be quiet."

"But he waved his gun around." Trevor glanced at the humane killer in the bank manager's hand.

"And you took it off him and gave it to a teller."

"So, what are you saying? You didn't call the police?"

"Nope. No police." He paused. "No ambulance." He walked towards the door.

"Fuck," Trevor said. "I won't survive longer than a couple of hours on my own. Harry's dead. Don't you understand what that means?"

The bank manager turned in the doorway, said, "I understand completely."

"Come on," Trevor said. "What kind of a sadistic fuck are you?"

"I'm a bank manager." The door closed.

UNCLE HARRY

Reginald Hill

"What I need to make clear and you need to get clear is, any resemblance between me and a real terrorist is purely coincidental.

"We've nothing in common, me and those guys. My thing was personal, not ideological. The only common ground was putting the thing together, which did teach me one thing about their line of business that I'd never realized before.

"The trouble with being a terrorist is that you experience a lot of terror!

"Not perhaps if you're one of those mad sods who reckon that blowing up a busload of people on their way to work is a first-class ticket to a world full of warm sunshine, sweet music, soft couches and doe-eyed virgins.

"But for a middle-aged, rationalist, atheist humanist who claims to believe that this life is all you get – *finito* – good night Vienna – this is the end, there is no more – then sitting in your flat trying to follow the instructions on your laptop that will turn the motley assembly of chemicals, wires, batteries and clock parts strewn across your kitchen table into a lethal weapon is fraught with terror, believe me.

"You will note I say *claims* to believe.

"It never really goes away, does it, all that religious stuff you get drummed into you when you're a kid? Mature logic and experience may seem to wash it all out of your mind, but scrub as hard as you like, if you look carefully under a bright light you can still find the faint outline of an indelible *what if*?

"And a laptop screen showing a DIY bomb recipe casts a very bright light indeed.

"Now this may not be so bad if your *what if*? tunes in images of all that sweet music and doe-eyed virgins stuff. The trouble is no matter how I cut it, the *what if*? my upbringing has left me with produces pictures of fires that burn but do not consume, grinning devils, souls in paroxysms of pain, eternities of agony.

"Killing people is wrong, my dad used to say. Doesn't matter who, how, why, when or where, take a life and your soul belongs to Satan.

"Of course being a preacher, he would say that, wouldn't he?

"Not necessarily, you may think. There are plenty of preachers able to trot out any number of exceptions to the sixth commandment. Where would politicians be without them? But my dad was a fundamentalist, which was surprising, seeing that he was C of E from a good old traditional Middle England background. When he got up in the pulpit you'd have looked for skeins of soporific platitude followed by a pre-lunch sherry at the vicarage. Instead he made most Welsh chapel sermons sound like Christopher Robin saying his prayers.

"'Ten commandments there are!' he'd thunder. 'Just ten. Not a lot to remember, not a number to over-tax even the mind of a poor stockbroker wending his weary way home on the five-fifty-five after a long hard day breaking stock. No! God reviewed his Creation and He thought, *these humans look all right, most of them, even the stockbrokers, but I've got to face it, I did skimp on the brain power. So best keep it simple. Ten fingers they've got, so surely they'll be able to count up to ten?* And that's how we got the Decalogue. Ten simple commandments. No riders, no sub-clauses. You do what they say, or else! There's no Fifth Amendment saying, *honour thy father and thy mother until you become a teenager, then anything goes*. There's no Six-and-a-halfth Commandment that says, *Thou shalt not kill except in the following circumstances*. NO! These are God's rules!! Break them, and, believe me, YOU WILL BURN!!!'

"I found that gem in a bundle of his old sermons which had turned up in the Bombay Mission. They'd been moving premises and Dad's papers would have been burned with all the other rubbish if Sister Angela, the Mission's chief administrator, hadn't spotted them. She always had a soft spot for me and we've kept in touch, even though she knows I've strayed a long way from my father's path since last we met. Possibly she thought that forwarding a small selection of the sermons might nudge me back. Sorry, Angela, no deal, though they certainly brought Dad back to me, and that early one at least gave me a laugh as I imagined how sentiments like these must have gone down in the rich Surrey parish where he started his ministry! No wonder it wasn't long before his bishop suggested his talents might be better employed in a more challenging environment (i.e. one a long way away from Surrey). He probably meant anywhere north of Watford, but Dad never did things by half and that was how he came to be pastor of the Ecumenical Mission settlement in Mumbai, or Bombay as it still was back in the Seventies.

"So if we look for first causes, it was the dear old bishop who was responsible for putting my father into the predatory path of Uncle Harry. He's dead too, the bishop, so in the unlikely event of their mythology proving true, Dad will have eternity to harangue the poor chap for not letting him continue his God-given task of bashing the brokers.

"I suppose by the same token we could say that ultimately it was the bishop's pusillanimity that led to me setting out on my long bus journey from Battersea this morning, gingerly clutching an eight by four by two brown paper package on my knee.

"Dad had got it wrong, you see. In my view there definitely is a Six-and-a-halfth Commandment, and what it says is: killing's OK when the target has enjoyed the rewards of his villainy for decades and looks like he's heading for the winning post so far ahead of the Law, he no longer even bothers to glance back over his shoulder.

"Religion, if you've got it, might be a comfort here. *Vengeance is mine; I will repay, saith the Lord*, Dad liked to thunder, meaning don't worry that there's no justice in this world, there'll be plenty in the next. Well, I'd like to believe that, Dad, but despite those residual *what-if*s I mentioned earlier, I really don't. Meaning, unless I take care of the bastard, no one else will.

"So there I was carrying a bomb through the streets of London to rid the world of the villain who'd destroyed my family.

"Does that make me a terrorist? In the eyes of the Law, I suppose it does. To me, what I was planning to do was an act of justice, but I suppose that's what all the doe-eyed virgin boys say too. Though I must confess it did occur to me as I sat on the bus that if I'd got something wrong – an ingredient too volatile, a connection too loose – and we bounced over a pothole a bit deeper than the norm even on this stretch of the Earls Court Road, none of these innocent people around me would be interested in making fine distinctions.

"I had learned to clasp my package a bit tighter as a stop approached. This driver must have missed the bit on his training course about gradually applying the brakes. By this time I only had one more stop to go. I was glad to see most of the other passengers had got out. Only a perspiring bald man and his glossily veneered companion remained, and they didn't look too innocent.

"I glanced down at my package. It looked good. I never throw anything away and when I decided it would be both convincing and appropriate if the instrument of Uncle Harry's death seemed to have come from the site of his infamy, I had dug out the brown paper Sister Angela had wrapped the sermons in. Of course I couldn't simply reuse it, not with my address all over it in the Sister's fine copperplate. But with infinite care I had been able to remove the stamps and enough of the Mumbai post mark to be convincing, and transfer them to my own parcel.

"An Indian fan, he would think, an admirer on the sub-continent who has remembered my birthday. How terribly kind! And full of anticipation he would rip the package open . . .

"Surprise!

"I hoped he'd have time to take in the writing on the inside lid of the box before the bang. I'd cut it from the title page of one of my father's sermons and pasted it there.

"It read: *On Divine Retribution* by DLP Lachrymate DD.

"Yes, he was a three initial man too. Perhaps that was why it was so easy for Uncle Harry to ensnare him. *Three forenames means a man comes from a family with a pride in their past*, Dad would say. *You can always trust a man with three initials. Never buy a used car from a one initial man. Hesitate to lend money to someone with only two. But give your hand and your trust when you see that third initial!*

"Four he felt a little ostentatious except in the case of royalty.

"I have three, of course. PDL. Same as my father's only the order is changed.

"That's me all over. All the same elements as my father only the order is changed.

"I too believe in retribution and hellfire, but I want them now!

"I wouldn't like you to think that I have spent my life obsessing about my poor father's fate. I was only six when he died. To me, one day he was there, the next he wasn't. Everyone talked about him being in a better place, but how a place could be better that didn't have me and Mum in it, I could never fathom. As to how he got there, throughout my youth I was well protected from any real knowledge of what had actually happened. Certainly without him the place we were in seemed a great deal worse. My mother continued to work at the Mission. I don't think she really had a wage, just the occasional subsistence level hand out. I expect it was the same for the rest of them. It was probably believed that any complaints about wage levels could be answered by pointing to the squalor and abject poverty around us and saying, 'How can you look at that and still complain?'

"Myself, I don't think Mother gave a toss about remuneration levels. I don't even think she had any real interest in the Mission's work. All she wanted was see me through to the age of independence then, with a sigh of relief, give up the ghost and go to join her lost husband, which is exactly what she did.

"It was after the funeral, in dribs and drabs, that Sister Angela told me the story. She had to support her own memory of events from a report she had written for the Mission Trustees at the time. It was couched in a curious mixture of Indian Civil Service jargon and King James Bible English. It went something like this.

"*The comprehensive recording procedures installed at the Mission by the present writer acting on the excellent advice of CK Bannerjee (Bachelor of Law-University of Bombay) by the grace*

of God our legal officer, enable us to trace precisely the first
appearance of the subtle serpent, Keating, on our premises. For
it is clearly written in the Book of Visitors that he was a guest in our
midst at tea-time on the fifteenth day of May in the year of our
Lord, 1974, as testified by his own signature, HRS Keating.

"As her narrative unfolded, it took me some time to realise
that this serpent she was talking about, the architect of all our
woes, was in fact Uncle Harry.

"Not really my uncle, of course. But within a very short
time of his first appearance at the Mission, that's what I was
calling him. I remembered him very well, and all my memories were pleasant ones. He was a merry, voluble man in his
late forties, always willing to spend time with me and treat me
to ices from one of the street vendors that my mother warned
me against but whose wares I adored. (In fact I never had any
stomach trouble all my life till I came to England and tried a
Shepherd's Pie out of a pub microwave.) I knew vaguely that
he was some kind of writer and Sister Angela now confirmed
that the fraud by which he gained access to the Mission was
that he was gathering material for a book about the disen-
franchised, destitute and often criminal classes that my father
worked amongst. Certainly he had real creative talent. Often
when his visits coincided with my bedtime, he would fill my
head with marvellous stories of high adventure and wild
excitement. These were a rare treat. Mother had no narrative
gift and for Father any story that did not come from the Bible
was so much factitious frippery.

"Curiously, it is Dad's tales of Samson pulling down the
temple, and the death of Jezebel, and the slaughter of the
Benjamites, that remain with me while Uncle Harry's marvellous stories have all faded. But at the time I waited like a drug
addict for the next instalment.

"But the real evidence of Uncle Harry's powers of invention
lies in the way he took in my father.

"I think the trouble was – and Sister Angela confirmed this –
that Dad believed his life was directed by God. When he asked a
question, God answered it with the result that in decision he
was incisive and in judgment, absolute. And for the twenty
years of his adult life, this had worked.

"So when he asked God about Uncle Harry and he thought

he heard God telling him *Harry's OK*, that was it. In my father's eyes, friends, and enemies, were forever.

"Thus when Uncle Harry came to him in a distracted state, he didn't hesitate. The pitch was that Harry's widowed mother who lived in the States was seriously ill and her only chance of survival lay in a new transplant procedure, which only one hospital in the country could offer. Harry was on his way to see her now. He had realized his assets and managed to raise most of what was needed to pay for the procedure. But he was still short, and though he would have the rest in a fortnight's time when an investment bond matured, by then it might be too late.

"I can remember Uncle Harry's distraction, though its alleged cause was of course unknown to me till Sister Angela filled me in. My reason for remembering was purely selfish. It was 19 May, my sixth birthday, and I felt I ought to be the centre of everyone's attention.

"Not that Harry's pretended agitation prevented him from bringing me a splendid present, a wooden locomotive big enough for me to straddle which made whooping noises just like the real thing when you pulled a cord.

"It might have been this generosity, plus of course the three initials, that made my father rise to the bait.

" 'How much do you need?' he asked.

" 'Fifteen hundred pounds,' said Harry.

"Now you should understand that the Mission finances were on a very hand-to-mouth basis. Only the big charities could afford to do national appeals in those days, and even they weren't yet the streamlined corporate machines for extracting money from the public they have since become. So the Mission relied very much on local charitable donations and there was rarely much in the kitty. But just the day before, a rather dodgy local businessman had decided to spring-clean his conscience by donating a couple of lakhs of rupees. He'd been on the brink for a week or so, and the proposed act of charity had almost turned into a bazaar haggle with my father as to how much, or rather how little, would see him right with the Christian God. My father had probably entertained Uncle Harry with a description of the man's hesitations. Finally the previous day, a threat of police investigation had made the vacillating villain decide he needed help from all the deities available and he'd turned up with the cash which was now in the Mission safe.

"How much cash?

"In sterling, about fifteen hundred pounds.

"Surprise.

"To my father this was evidence of God's handiwork.

"To Angela, with hindsight, it was evidence of Uncle Harry's brilliant opportunism.

"Dad, who had a key to the safe – why wouldn't he? – gave Harry the money on the promise that it would be paid within two weeks. Harry left that night with protestations of eternal gratitude and the cash. Probably his gratitude was genuine enough, or does a con man simply despise his mark? Whatever, Uncle Harry and the fifteen hundred pounds quickly vanished from Bombay and our lives, never to be seen again.

"It evidently took my father a whole month to admit that neither was about to reappear.

"So that was it. A sting. Not a particularly big one in the grand scale of stings, though fifteen hundred was worth a lot more back then. The trustees of the Mission took it, if not in their stride, at least with the resigned philosophy of men long accustomed to dealing with humanity at its worst. They read Sister Angela's report and, judging that chances of the police catching up with Uncle Harry were remote and of recovering the money non-existent, they decided it was better to hush the whole thing up rather than risk putting off other potential benefactors.

"So, all in all, an unpleasant experience which many men after the first shock might have treated as a rough but salutary lesson.

"Not Dad.

"You see it undermined that supremely confident belief in his own God-backed judgment which had been the mainstay of his being these many years. If he'd got this wrong, what else had he got wrong? It pulled away or at least seriously damaged one of the mainstays of his faith.

"Within a fortnight of recognizing he'd been conned, a fortnight during which by Angela's account he worked like a man possessed, he went out on some errand of mercy one night and that was all that anyone saw of him till his body was pulled out of the Mazagon Docks a fortnight later. The fish had worked at it so much that cause of death could never be established. Suicide? I don't like to think so. I want to believe he just took a risk too far and paid the price.

"All these memories rolled through my mind as I sat on that bus, and the violent jolt as the vehicle crashed to a halt at my stop took me by surprise and I almost dropped the package. As I stepped onto the pavement, despite the cool autumn air I was sweating.

"I had walked the route before while making my plans so I set off at a brisk pace towards my destination. Getting the package delivered without arousing suspicion was always going to be the hard part, but I'd worked out a method. It was not without risk, but apart from knocking at Uncle Harry's door and handing it over to whoever answered, I couldn't think of anything better.

"Now the end was near, I felt only relief. Like I say, at the time of Dad's death I'd been a child, and was devastated like a child, and then had adapted like a child. Mother's death had hit me harder. And when I learned from Angela that Uncle Harry's chicanery had ultimately been the cause of both of them, I got very angry.

"But I was only eighteen and at eighteen you're very angry at a lot of things. The main long term effect of learning the true facts was to finally make me dump the religious baggage I'd been dragging after me all my short life. I looked around and saw that the world was full of goodies and the only way to get your share was to go in hot pursuit. So that's what I did, mainly in the sub-continent where I'd grown up, with occasional forays to Malaysia and the Antipodes.

"Then with youth well behind me and my fortieth birthday lumbering ever closer, I got the chance to come and work in England.

"Why not? After all I was English, that's what my passport said. So back I came to this cold, damp, unwelcoming country. After six months I was beginning to think it was a mistake. I reached the dreaded fortieth in May and in this dreadful climate, it felt more like fifty. I had to get out, but my contract bound me here at least till Christmas. By the end of September I was feeling desperate. I looked back at my life and it seemed a wasted journey, and I looked forward and saw only a road to nowhere. Then one evening as I travelled back to my lonely apartment, I picked up a bookshop magazine that someone had left on the train.

"Now I'm not a reading man myself, and it was in a mood of cynical mockery that I glanced down a list of newsworthy forthcoming events in the literary calendar. Who the hell could really be interested in dinners to award prizes to novelists or the publication of a ghosted life of some idiot sportsman too thick to write his own biography?

"Then something leapt out at me.

"*Notable Anniversaries*

"*On 31 October, the distinguished crime writer and well known figure on the London literary scene, Mr Harry Keating, best known as the creator of the famous series of books featuring Inspector Ghote of the Bombay Police, will be celebrating his eightieth birthday, to general rejoicing.*

"Keating . . . Bombay . . . it couldn't be coincidence. This had to be Uncle Harry!

"When I arrived at my station I popped into the bookshop.

"Quite a lot of his books were on the shelves. I bought a couple and took them back to my flat.

"I raced through them. The detailed knowledge of Bombay life and topography could only have come from a man who knew the city inside out. And when I looked at the author photo on the back cover of the book, I knew I was right.

"He had attempted to change his appearance by growing a rather fine bushy beard, but there was no disguising that splendid hook nose.

"Uncle Harry. The subtle serpent who had destroyed my family's personal paradise.

"I thought of my dead parents. Then I thought of this man, approaching eighty, basking in the love of friends and family, acknowledging the applause of the world of literature. And suddenly it seemed to me that here was fate offering me a chance to do at least one meaningful act before I died! I told you that Dad used to believe God spoke directly to him. It must be in the genes. For the first time in my life I heard a voice speak in my head.

"*Let him get to eighty. But make sure he gets no further!*

"God? I didn't think so. After all, I don't believe in God. I refuse to believe in God!

"But as I approached Northumberland Place I found myself thinking, this is the real test, this is where things need to go absolutely smoothly or it's all in vain. If the Almighty really reckons this is a good idea, then the next few minutes will be a stroll in the park.

"And a few minutes later, I knew I had the divine seal of approval.

"The post van which I'd watched for five mornings on the trot the previous week showed up within the usual fifteen minute range. And about five minutes before it turned into Northumberland Place, it parked in its usual spot outside a block of flats. The driver got out with an armful of letters and packages and went into the building. On previous evidence he would be in there a good five minutes, sometimes longer. Perhaps someone gave him a cup of tea, or something. I moved forward, checked there was no one watching me, opened the van door and leaned inside. There were several bags filled with mail. I pulled a couple of envelopes out of the nearest one. I was really on a divine providence roll, for they both bore Uncle Harry's name and address! As I'd anticipated from all I'd read about him, the world was so overcome with joy at the great man's eightieth birthday that his numerous gifts and greetings merited a separate bag.

"I dropped my packet into it, closed the door and went on my way.

"I thought of hanging around to listen for the bang, but there was no way of foretelling how long it would be before he opened his last present, and I didn't want to be picked up on CCTV loitering in the area. So I came home and waited for the news to come over the airwaves. *Famous writer killed by bomb on 80th birthday.* That must make the headlines, surely?

"Instead after nearly three hours just as I was getting really impatient, the doorbell rang, I opened the door, and there you were holding up your ID, and I knew things had gone seriously wrong.

"But not so wrong, Detective Inspector Gospill, that you need to treat me as a terrorist! So why not get that out of the way, then perhaps you won't need to sit here any longer waiting for this Commander Grisewood who seems to be such a very bad time-keeper.

"You could start off by telling me exactly what's happened. And where did it all go wrong?"

After my arrest, I'd been brought to Scotland Yard and left sitting in an interview room for well over an hour with a blank faced constable for company.

Finally DI Gospill reappeared, the constable left, and I waited for the interview to start. When nothing happened, I asked him what the hold-up was. He said that we were waiting for his superior, Commander Grisewood, who was returning from a conference in the Midlands. I said surely there must be enough senior officers sitting around on their thumbs in Scotland Yard for one of them to deal with the matter. What was so special about this man Grisewood anyway?

And that was when he told me, in a tone of some irritation not totally aimed at me, that Commander Grisewood was in charge of the unit which dealt with terrorist acts by British nationals and that for reasons best known to himself he wanted to conduct my interview personally, to which end he had given strict orders that nothing was to be done until he arrived, which should have been half an hour ago.

I might have been amused by the thought that Gospill was clearly missing a very important date because of this, but one word had caught all my attention and there was nothing amusing about it.

Terrorist!

That's what had launched me into my long defence and justification.

Gospill tried to interrupt me a couple of times, presumably to point out that the tape wasn't on and I'd have to say it all again. But once I got started, out it all came, and finally he sat back and listened. He never switched the recorder on but after a while he did start making notes.

When I finished he made no attempt to answer my concluding question but sat with furrowed brow in complete silence.

Then his phone rang.

He listened, said, "Jesus H. Christ!" and switched off.

I said, "What?"

"Accident on the motorway," he said, not really in answer to me but in accusation against some malevolent fate. "Twenty-mile tailback. Jesus!"

Then he picked his notes and without another word rose and left the room, to be replaced by the silent constable.

Another hour went by. I tried to provoke the constable to speech by requesting a drink. He went to the door and bellowed, "Tea!" and that was all I got for my effort at social intercourse, except for a cup of tea so foul there'd have been a riot if it had been served in India. By the time Gospill returned I was feeling very irritated and ready to be extremely uncooperative.

"Now listen, inspector," I said. "Either you start answering my questions or you'll get no answers when you start asking yours."

To my surprise he smiled.

"Certainly, Mr Lachrymate," he said. "Now let me see. I seem to recall the last question you asked me was, where did it all go wrong? Where indeed? My problem is knowing where to begin. You made more mistakes than Tony bloody Blair! But let's start with the biggest one of all, shall we? You clearly didn't stop for a moment and consider who it was you were dealing with!"

I said weakly, "Sorry, I don't understand. . . ."

"Clearly! Well, listen and learn. Now, I like watching detective series on the box as much as the next man, and I've read quite a lot of crime novels too, and I can tell you, from a professional point of view, they're mainly very ripe farmyard manure. What most of them writers know about real detection you could write on the end of a gnat's cock without arousing it.

"But this Mr Keating, he's different. He's been at it so long, there's stuff he could teach us! So there he is, on his eightieth birthday, opening his prezzies, and he sees this package from India. Or at least it looks as if it's from India. Except that he can't see a Customs Declaration.

"Funny, he thinks. So he looks closer. Now he gets a lot of mail from India, does Mr Keating. He's big out there, it seems. And he's got lots of young relatives and friends who collect stamps so he takes note of the postage. So here's what his sharp detective mind gets puzzling over. He knows the Indian Post Office Speedpost rates to the UK are 675 rupees for the first 250 grams and 75 for each additional 250 grams. So why should a package which weighs about 1200 grams only have the basic 675 rupees postage on it?"

He paused. If his intention was to alleviate his own irritation by making me feel foolish, he was succeeding. Seeing this, he smiled malevolently and pressed home his advantage.

"But there was something else, something much more basic. The very first thing that attracted his keen detective eye was the fact that you got his name wrong."

"I don't believe that," I said indignantly. "I'm absolutely sure I didn't misspell Keating."

"No, you got that right," he admitted. "It was the initials you cocked up. It's HRF, not HRS."

I checked my memory bank which is usually pretty reliable. It definitely printed out Uncle Harry's initials as HRS.

"Are you quite sure?" I asked.

"Dead sure. Look for yourself."

From his pocket he produced one of the Keating paperbacks I'd bought and dropped it on the table.

He was quite right.

HRF Keating.

"I don't know how I got that wrong," I muttered disconsolately.

"I do," he said smugly. "As soon as we were alerted to this attempt on Mr Keating's life, we contacted our colleagues in Mumbai to check if the postmark was genuine and to ask if they might be able to throw any light on the outrage. They got back to us about forty minutes ago. And it was the thing about the wrong initial that put them on to it. Very efficient record keepers, those boys. It seems that about thirty years ago, in 1973 to be precise, they had their eye on a suspected con man who was using the name Keating. Our Mr Keating's name was already getting to be well known in literary circles over there, and this fellow was obviously trying to cash in on it by implying that he was the distinguished British crime writer, without actually saying it. By using the famous three initials he put the idea into people's minds, but by changing the last one from F to S (which sounds very much the same if you say it fast) he put himself just out of reach of a charge of personation. Clever that. Of course from what you say, in your parents' case it probably didn't matter as they don't sound the types to be interested in anything so worldly as detective novels."

"No, I'm pretty sure they thought Agatha Christie was a nun," I burbled as I tried to come to terms with what he'd just said. "I'm sorry, inspector, but are you telling me that HRF Keating the writer isn't the same man as HRS Keating, my Uncle Harry, the con man?"

"Of course he's not, you moron," snapped Gospill. "Do you think a man like Mr Keating would go around conning people out of money? In any case, what happened to your father happened in 1973, right? Well, it's on the record that our Mr Keating didn't make his first visit to India till a couple of years later!"

"No, that can't be true," I objected. "From the dates on those books of his, he'd been writing about Inspector Ghote for a whole decade by then. How could a man show such an intimate knowledge of a country without visiting it? Who's to say he didn't make an earlier trip before this official one he admits to?"

"You are," he cried triumphantly. "You mentioned it was your birthday, your sixth birthday, on the day that your father let Uncle Harry con him out of them rupees. And that would be the nineteenth of May, right?"

"Right."

"Well, by one of those quirks of fate which protect good innocent people and put toe-rags like you in jail, Mr Keating, who is a meticulous record keeper, was able to tell us exactly where he was on that date. He was at a Crime Writers' Conference in Harrogate on the weekend of Friday 18 to Sunday 20 May 1973, and he was able to give us the names of several other writers of unimpeachable character and unfaultable memory who were delighted to confirm what he said. So there it is. You picked on the wrong man, stupid!"

I was beginning to be seriously annoyed by his attitude. I mean, I might be a murder suspect, but there was no need to be rude!

And in any case, now I thought about it, I wasn't actually a murder suspect, was I? From the way he was talking, the attempt must certainly have failed.

For the sake of certainty, I continued to ignore his rudeness and asked, "So Mr Keating is all right, is he? I mean, from what you say, the bomb didn't go off?"

"Yes, I'm glad to say Mr Keating is alive and well and at this very moment no doubt entertaining his friends at his birthday party with the story of the idiot who tried to blow him up. Of course, what he doesn't know yet because the bomb squad only confirmed it an hour ago was that he never was in any real danger. Don't know where you got your recipe from, Mr Lachrymate, but the experts say there was as much chance of your bomb going off as there is of Mr Keating's birthday cake blowing up when they light the candles!"

I suppose I should have felt relieved, but all I felt at that moment was an utter incompetent fool.

"So," I said wretchedly, "I got the wrong man and I made a dud bomb."

Then cheering up a little because it's not in my nature to be down for long, I went on, "But if my bomb wasn't really a bomb and no one actually got hurt, I can't have committed a crime, can I? Certainly not a terrorist crime. In fact, nothing more than a slap on the wrist, ASBO, two weeks community service kind of crime!"

He laughed.

If Bloody Judge Jeffreys laughed as he was handing down sentences, it probably sounded like that.

"Never believe it, sunshine. We've got you bang to rights. That's another little error you made. A pro knows that you burn all the stuff that could be evidence against you as you go along. But with you we've got the lot. All them notes you made planning out the attack, the hard disk from your computer showing the terrorist sites you accessed, not forgetting the bomb itself. OK, it might be a Mickey Mouse device with as much chance of working as a chocolate teapot, but it's got your prints all over it. This government may not have done much but they did pass some legislation that makes the intention as culpable as the deed. As the very old bishop said to the actress at the third time of asking, 'it's intent that counts, darling'. Way people feel about terrorist threats these days, I'd say you're looking at ten years minimum."

The shock nearly made me faint. *It's intent that counts*. That's what my dad used to say about sin. I never knew it applied in law too.

Ten years . . . I'd be fifty by the time I got out . . . I'd be an old man!

Gospill's phone rang.

He growled, "Yeah?", then suddenly sat up to attention and said, "Yes, Commander! I'm with him now, Commander. No, I haven't started the interrogation. Definitely not. Yes, I've collected all the physical evidence, and I've put it on your desk so that you can take a look at it before you start. Yes, sir, it's confirmed the device is quite safe. Commander, can I suggest . . . yes . . . what I meant was . . . thank you, sir. See you soon. Look forward to it, sir. Goodbye."

I got the impression the Commander had cut him off short and the last few phrases were for my benefit.

He caught me looking at him and snarled, "That's happy hour over, Lachrymate. Commander Grisewood's just coming into the building and he'll be along here soon as he checks out the evidence bags on his desk. And that's when your troubles are really going to begin, believe me."

I believed him. So much so that for the first time since I was a child, I found myself saying a little prayer to God. To Dad's God. Something on the lines of, "OK, God, after the crap you heaped on my mum and dad, you owe the Lachrymate family. I'd really appreciate it if you could come through now."

My lips must have moved.

Gospill said, "What?"

I said for the want of anything else to say, "So how did you get on to me so quick?"

"Easy," he said. "That sermon title you pasted on the lid of the box. *Divine Retribution* by DLP Lachrymate DD. Not many Lachrymates in London, believe me. In fact, you're the only one. With the same initials in a different order. And as soon as you opened the door, I saw you were our boy."

He looked so smug and self satisfied, I offered another little prayer, this time for a thunderbolt to come down and destroy him.

At the same moment we both heard a distant bang, like a birthday balloon being punctured. Perhaps God had taken aim and missed.

For a moment nothing happened, then came the distant shrill of an alarm bell.

Gospill sat looking at me for a moment then he rose.

"Wait there," he commanded and went to the door.

He closed it firmly behind him but I didn't hear a lock click.

After a little while I stood up, went to the door and opened it a crack.

I could see Gospill at the end of the corridor. He was talking to a uniformed sergeant who had a phone to his ear.

I opened the door a little further so I could hear them.

"What's going on, sarge?" I heard Gospill ask.

"Not sure, sir. Just checking it out. Think there's been an explosion."

"I gathered that!" snapped the DI. "Where?"

"Hang about, sir, I'm getting something now . . . yes . . . yes . . . you're sure? So no evacuation . . . that's good . . . that's very good . . . OK, thanks."

He switched off his phone and said to Gospill, "It's OK, sir, Seems a device went off, and there's been a bit of a fire and quite a lot of damage, but it's all been confined to one room and no one's hurt. So no panic and we can stay put. Reckon someone's head's going to roll though. Doesn't look good, letting a bomber get right into the heart of the Yard!"

A pause, then Gospill asked too casually, "Whose room?"

Even at a distance I could here the tremolo in his voice.

"Not absolutely sure, sir, but they think it was Commander Grisewood's. Made a right mess from the sound of it. All those lovely water colours his missus did and he was so proud of, they'll have gone. Oh, someone's in real trouble, believe me!"

I closed the door quietly and went back to my seat.

Things were looking better. I'd been very stupid but there wasn't a commandment saying *Thou shalt not be stupid*. And now with nothing of what I'd said so far on tape, and all the physical evidence against me probably burning merrily away with the Commander's desk, all I needed to do was continue to look stupid and say nothing.

Thank you, Dad's God. You came through!

The Ghote novel Gospill had produced still lay on the table. I picked it up and looked at the author photo.

No longer could I see much resemblance to the plausible crook who all those years ago had touched on my family's life then gone on his way. Probably he'd been dead for years.

IN SOME COUNTRIES

Jerry Raine

The day's work was over and the sun was sinking on the horizon. Inside the kitchen Woody Granger was eating supper on his own. He usually ate with the Cutter family but he'd been late coming back from the field where he'd been fixing fences all day and the family were next door in the living room playing cards. Woody preferred eating on his own though. He wasn't much of a conversationalist. Never had been, never would be. He was a sixteen-year-old orphan drifting through Tennessee, getting work where he could.

He finished his cup of coffee and carried his dishes to the sink. The living room door opened and Harold Cutter came in. He was a large red-faced man with thick hairy arms and a belly that hung over the belt of his jeans. Woody was a bit scared of him because he could never tell what kind of mood his employer would be in. Sometimes they would joke together, and other times, when either the work was too hard or the sun too hot, they would nearly come to blows.

"Do you want to come with me tonight Woody?" Harold asked, as he made his way to the pantry.

Finishing his dishes, Woody said over his shoulder, "Okay," when he really wanted to be going back to his room.

Harold came out of the pantry carrying a bucket with a chopper and two large knives inside. Woody's heart dipped.

He dried his hands and Harold pointed to a lantern that was sitting on the table. "Carry please," he said, then they walked out into the yard.

At the sound of the screen-door slamming, six dogs sprang out from under bushes and chairs and came running towards their master with heads bowed low and tales wagging. Woody smiled at them and patted Mickey, the eldest.

"Are we taking the horses?" Woody asked.

"No, we'll walk," Harold said. "The sheep are only in the home paddock."

Woody was disappointed. He always liked riding, especially at night. He walked alongside Harold and threw sticks for the dogs. His favourite was Snowy, who was in fact black. He also had a soft spot for Skunk, a grey and white streaked dog who was permanently chained at the back of the house. Skunk was a sheep killer and was very rarely let off his leash.

Ten minutes later and they were at the home paddock. Harold unlocked the gate and they all went through, the dogs getting excited when they saw the hundred or so sheep in the distance.

They walked to a large tree in the centre of the field. The tree had no leaves and the branches were wrinkled and crooked like the fingers of an old man. Hanging from one of the branches was a large hook and the bottom of the trunk was stained with dried blood. Harold left his bucket by the tree and called out to the dogs.

"Get back! Get back! Fetch 'em up! Fetch 'em up!"

The dogs ran towards the herd, some going right and some going left. They got right behind the sheep and barked at them and nipped their legs. The herd moved slowly forward.

Harold and Woody waited by the tree. The sun was almost down and soon it would be dark. Woody lit the lantern and hung it from a branch.

"Just watch what I do this time," Harold said, "and next time you can have a go yourself. Just give me the knives when I tell you."

Woody had only been working on the farm for six months. He'd been down on his luck, sitting in a bar in town, wondering where to go to next, when he'd overheard a conversation about work. He'd walked the five miles to the Kerren Ranch and started work straight away. He was the only person the Cutters employed.

Woody watched as the sheep came nearer and soon they were surrounding the tree with no escape, the dogs keeping them in a neat circle.

Harold walked into the middle of them still calling to the dogs, but not so loudly now. He pushed and prodded, looking for the right sheep, then grabbed one round the neck and dragged it over to the tree.

"Okay, Woody," he said.

Woody took one of the large carving knives from the bucket and gave it to him. Harold had the sheep lying backwards between his legs with his strong hands around its neck. He took the knife and started cutting into its throat. It made a crunching noise as it cut through the main arteries and Woody winced as he saw the blood coming out. It ran dark red down the sheep's stomach and then as the knife went deeper it started to bubble in the deep cut and now and then a small fountain would squirt on to the ground. The sheep's eyes stayed open for what seemed like a long time and then they shut and Harold let the body fall. It lay on the ground with the blood spreading into the ground, and then its back legs twitched and then the animal was still.

Harold wiped his bloody hands on a tuft of grass and went back to find another sheep. He killed this one the same way and then he told the dogs to back away. The sheep slowly wandered back to where they had been before, minus their two friends that lay at the foot of the tree.

Woody watched Harold go to work on the sheep. His arms were now covered with blood as he chopped off the two heads. Then he skinned the two animals by slitting open their bellies. The dogs were sniffing and looking anxiously, eager for the innards that Harold would eventually give them.

"Give me a hand here, Woody," Harold said. Together they lifted the first sheep and hung it upside down from the hanging hook. Woody turned away from the smell as Harold cut out the stomach, bright green chewed grass falling from a split. He threw it to the dogs along with the intestines. The dogs gathered around hungrily and ripped the flesh to bits. Woody was disappointed to see Snowy joining in the fun.

Harold continued cleaning out the carcass and took it off the hook and laid it out on an old rug that was lying behind the tree. Then they hooked up the second sheep and Harold went to work again.

"It's pretty easy," he said, "once you get used to the smell. The smell's the worst bit."

"Yeah, it doesn't smell too good," Woody said.

They took down the second sheep when the carcass was clean and placed it alongside the other one on the rug. They also placed the two skins on there. Although they were bloody and dirty they would be put on the shed roof and later on when they were dried out and stiff, they would be sold.

They each took a corner of the rug and started pulling it and the sheep back towards the farm. It was slow going and Harold kept shouting at the dogs to move away as they were now getting interested in the good meat.

"I usually just kill one sheep," Harold said, "but with you here I can pull an extra one back. When we've eaten this lot I'll let you kill the next two."

Great, Woody thought to himself. *I'll be looking forward to that*.

When they were back at the farm they lifted the carcasses on to one of the water tanks where they would be out of reach of the dogs. They would stay there until morning when Harold would cut them into smaller chunks and his wife Molly would then put them into storage.

From a tap in the garden the two of them washed their hands and shook them dry. They stood in the kitchen light that came across the veranda. The dogs had crept back to their bushes and chairs to sleep.

"You can knock off now, Woody," said Harold. "I'll see you in the morning."

Woody said okay, and tried to smile, but the dead sheep smell was still with him. Harold sensed how he was feeling and grinned.

"You'll get used to it," he said, and patted him on the back.

Woody went back to his room, but before he reached it, he doubled over and puked in the bushes outside.

The next day Woody was back in the field fixing fences again. He was wearing a hat to keep the sun off his face. Just last year, on one of the other farms he'd worked on, he'd been digging a ditch all day and telling the time by looking at the sun. When he'd returned to his lodgings he'd had a terrible pain in his eyes, like someone had thrown sand in them. Much to the amusement of the other workers he'd spent the whole of the next day lying in a darkened room. They'd told him he had sunstroke. Eventually the pain had disappeared, but he'd learnt his lesson.

At lunchtime, Woody saw a horse approaching, and as it came nearer, he was pleased to see the rider was Harold's daughter Jane. She was fifteen years old, pretty, with long blonde hair. She climbed down off her small horse, and carried over a bag of lunch for him.

"Hello," Woody said shyly. "How are you?"

"Fine, Woody," said Jane. "Have you recovered from last night?"

Woody decided to play it dumb. "Recovered from what?"

Jane handed him the bag of food. She was wearing a white dress with a flower pattern on it, a straw hat on her head. "The killing of the sheep. I heard you puking after."

Woody felt embarrassed. Jane's room was just behind his. He shrugged. "So I puked. So what?"

"You'll never be a farmer if you can't kill a sheep."

"Who says I want to be a farmer?"

"What are you doing here if you don't want to be a farmer?"

"I need the money. When I've saved a bit I'll do something else. Like maybe rustle cattle. Or rob trains."

Jane laughed. "Just keep dreaming, Woody. We all need our dreams. I have to get back. My dad said to come straight home."

Woody watched Jane walk back to her horse and climb on. He looked down at the lunch bag and started opening it.

"Woody?"

He looked up and Jane was still sitting on her horse. Only now she had her skirt pulled high up on her thigh and she was rubbing her leg. "Do you think I have nice legs?" she asked.

Woody was so shocked he didn't know what to say.

"If you kill a sheep for me, Woody, I'll let you see more," and then her dress fell back into place and she was riding away.

Woody was stunned. He looked at Jane until she was almost out of sight. Then he looked down at his lunch bag but he didn't feel so hungry any more.

Woody kept thinking about Jane's leg for the rest of the day. What did she mean exactly by saying she'd let him see more? Was she going to let him go the whole way? He was still a virgin and wasn't sure he knew exactly what to do. Maybe he should just forget the whole thing. Maybe she was just leading him on. And what did she mean by "kill a sheep for me"? Was this some kind of test of his manliness? Or was she trying to lead him into trouble?

Woody worked hard on the fence and then started walking home. At the dinner table that night he couldn't keep his eyes off Jane. She kept smiling at him and even winked one time. Her younger brother Billy did most of the talking, so Harold and Molly were easily distracted.

When the dishes were done Woody went back to his room. Evening times always passed slowly. His room was only big enough for a bed and a wardrobe and was right next to the back veranda. On the other side of the veranda was the washer room, and several times he had watched Jane in there, washing clothes in the sink.

He still thought of her words. "Kill a sheep for me." What was that meant to mean? Was he meant to bring the body back to her room and lay it out in front of her? What kind of a sick person was she? Or would just the head be enough? Bring me the head of a sheep and I'll let you see my body. He wished she'd been clearer in her intentions. He lay on his bed and looked at the ceiling.

After an hour of turmoil he could wait no longer. He left his room and edged round to the veranda. He crept on to it and looked into the kitchen. It was empty. He eased open the screen-door and crept into the pantry. He took a large knife and slid it under his shirt. Then he crept outside.

His heart was pounding with excitement as he made the short walk to the home paddock, the carving knife now stuck down the belt of his jeans. He had decided to kill a sheep and bring the head to Jane. Then she would show him her body. Then he would see what would happen next. He quickened up his pace.

He found the herd easily, a grey moving shape in the dark. He walked slowly up to them, but they heard him coming and moved away. He tried running at them but they ran away, faster than he'd thought they could be. He stopped to catch his breath. He tried again. They ran away.

It took him ten minutes to finally catch one, and he was so angry and frustrated he just plunged the knife straight into the sheep's chest. It seemed to have little effect, so he stabbed it in the neck and then stabbed it again. Eventually the bleating animal was still.

Woody sat on the grass next to it, catching his breath. Sweat was pouring off him and he was covered in blood. He looked at the sheep and immediately felt guilty. Why was he doing this? Taking away a life just so he could see Jane naked? He felt the same revulsion he'd felt last night. He felt his supper starting to come into his throat. He moved away from the sheep and sat down again. Then he lay on the grass and looked at the stars. He waited until he'd cooled down. There was no way he could cut off the sheep's head. He would just make his way home and forget the whole thing. He would have to throw his blood-stained clothes away.

He left the sheep where it lay. When Harold found it tomorrow maybe he would think a wolf had done it. Woody left the paddock and made the walk home, the knife stuck down into the belt of his jeans once again.

He approached his room from the privy side, where no one could see him. He walked on the path where Skunk was tied up, but as he approached Skunk began to growl.

"It's only me, Skunk," Woody said softly.

But then Skunk barked loudly and ran straight for him, his chain rattling as it took up the strain. Woody took a step backwards and then Skunk made another charge. This time, to Woody's horror, the chain broke and Skunk was on top of him. He wrestled with the dog as it went for his throat. Skunk was going berserk and Woody didn't know why. Then he thought that maybe it was the smell of the sheep's blood. Then he remembered the knife in his belt. He managed to get it free and he slammed it into Skunk's side. The dog whimpered and fell off him on to the dirt. Then Woody passed out.

When he came to, Woody didn't know where he was. He was lying on his back on something hard and he didn't recognize the ceiling. He turned his head and looked around. A sofa and some armchairs. A chest of drawers. A cabinet for plates and cutlery. He was in Harold's living room.

He was lying on a table. He had an incredible pain in his left arm. He looked down and wondered if he was imagining things.

He looked down again. His left arm was covered in a white bandage but it was much shorter than it used to be. He tried to wriggle his fingers but he didn't seem to have any. His hand just wasn't there any more.

Feeling a panic sweep over him he rolled off the table and put his feet on the floor. He held his two arms out in front of him but the left one was nearly a foot shorter.

"NO!" he screamed, and staggered out of the room.

He was in his own room now. Sedated.

He stayed there for a week while the pain in his arm lessened and his neck healed. But he wasn't too worried about his neck, he was worried about his missing hand. How was he going to get work now? No one would employ a one-armed man. Maybe Harold would be kind and keep him on. He would have to have a talk with him real soon.

Molly brought him his meals. He hadn't seen Jane at all. He tried talking to Molly as she fed him, but all she would say was that his hand had been mangled by Skunk. Skunk was dead, of course. She didn't mention the dead sheep.

Another week passed before Harold came to his room. Woody was sitting up in bed and Harold pulled up a chair and sat down.

"How's it going, Woody?" he asked.

"Not too good," Woody said. "What happened to my hand?"

Harold looked down at the floor and didn't meet his eyes. "Skunk got a hold of it. Chewed it all up. The doc said he couldn't save it."

"Are you sure?"

Harold looked up. "Sure about what?"

"Sure that he couldn't save it."

"Sure I'm sure. I saw it myself. It's just bad luck, that's all."

"Shit," Woody said. "I don't even remember Skunk attacking my hand. All I remember is him going for my throat."

"Well, it probably happened too quickly for you to remember. You probably passed out before he did it."

"Maybe," Woody said.

They were silent for a minute and then Harold cleared his throat. "I'm going to have to let you go, Woody."

Woody had suspected as much. He nodded.

"After all," Harold continued. "You won't be able to do much with one hand."

"I know," Woody said. "I'm no use to anybody now."

They were silent again.

"Sorry," Harold said, and then he stood up and reached for the door.

The day before he left Woody asked Harold for just one thing. He asked him for a pistol with just one bullet in it.

Harold said okay, but asked him why just one bullet?

Woody said, "Eventually I'll probably have to shoot myself because I won't be able to get any work. When I do it though, I want to be sure that I'm doing the right thing. If I have six bullets I'm likely to do it when I'm drunk. If I only have one bullet I won't know which chamber it's in when I'm drunk and the feeling will pass. If I kill myself I want to be sober, just so I'm sure that's really what I want to do."

Harold had looked at him with a little respect in his eyes. "That's a good idea Woody, a good idea."

Woody walked down the road away from the farm, his few belongings in a bag over his shoulder. From the front veranda Harold and Molly watched.

"Do you think he'll be okay?" Molly asked.

"I don't know," Harold said. "I really don't know."

"He was a nice boy," Molly said. "I wish you hadn't cut off his hand."

Harold didn't look at her. "He shouldn't have killed that sheep. I can't afford to have sheep killed for nothin'."

"Oh, I think you know very well it wasn't for nothin'."

Harold looked at her. "In some countries they cut off your hand if you steal something, you know. He killed a sheep. I don't see what the difference is."

Molly gave him a scornful look. "In some countries. But we're not in those countries. We don't have to do things those ways."

"The real problem," Harold said, "is that daughter of yours. That makes three we've had to get rid of because of her. This can't go on forever. We're gonna have to talk to her again."

And then he walked back inside the kitchen.

BRYANT AND MAY'S MYSTERY TOUR

Christopher Fowler

"Mr Bryant is so old that most of his lifetime subscriptions have run out." Leslie Faraday, the Home Office crime liaison officer, poked about on his biscuit tray looking for a Custard Cream. "He's far beyond the statutory working age limit, but no one has the heart to broach the matter with him."

"Sentimentality can't be allowed to stand in the way of modern policing procedures," replied Oskar Kasavian, peering from the window into the tiled Whitehall courtyard. Faraday took a quick peek to see if the new supervisor in charge of Internal Security cast a shadow, as his cadaverous pale form created office rumours of supernatural lineage. "We're not here to provide the inefficient with a living."

This last remark confused Faraday, who believed that this was precisely the purpose for which Whitehall had been created. "Quite," he replied, "but surely we must take into account his long and illustrious career working with the Peculiar Crimes Unit. He and his partner pioneered research in the field. One doesn't force admirals into retirement simply because they no longer go to sea. We benefit from their experience."

"Old generals are the cause of military disasters," said Kasavian, drumming long fingers on the window pane. "The elderly are weak precisely because they live in the past." He released a long, desperate sigh. "However, in this situation I see no other recourse than to put them on the case."

So it was that the Home Office called Arthur Bryant of the Peculiar Crimes Unit, and Bryant visited a crime scene in King's Cross, and then called his partner, John May, with instructions to meet him at 10:15 a.m. beside a bus stop in Marble Arch. It was a muggy wet morning, and May resented being summoned from his bed.

"Ah, there you are." The elderly detective hailed his partner with a wild whip of his walking stick, and nearly pruned a passing tourist. Bryant had misbuttoned his shapeless brown cardigan and dragged his moth-eaten Harris tweed coat over the top of it. He looked more like a tramp than a detective. "I got here early and had a potter through Hyde Park."

"You had your mobile with you?" asked May, surprised. Arthur was three years his senior, but two decades behind the rest of the world when it came to technology.

"I did have, yes," Bryant admitted, tugging his battered brown trilby further onto his head. "Here's our bus." He indicated the open-topped Routemaster that was just pulling up.

May was suspicious. "Then where is it now?"

"I think I dropped it in the Princess Diana Memorial Drain. Don't worry, it'll just keep going round. I'll get it when I come back. You're probably wondering what this is all about."

"And why we're boarding a sightseeing bus, yes," said May, helping his partner inside the idling vehicle. The portly driver stared at them through his windscreen.

"There was a rather sad little murder in King's Cross during the night. A 54-year-old cleaning lady named Joan March was strangled to death in her third floor flat in Hastings Street. The HO felt the case warranted our involvement."

"But this bus doesn't go anywhere near King's Cross." May checked the route, noting that it tacked through central London in a loop.

"Oh, we're not going to the murder site. I've already been there." Bryant seated himself on the arrow-patterned seat at the front of the bus, next to a gingery young man who was standing in the aisle with a microphone. His badge read; *Hi! I'm Martin!* "I wanted you here so that we could apprehend the murderer."

The Routemaster pulled away from the stop at Speaker's Corner, heading into Oxford Street. "My Uncle Jack used to get up on his soapbox over there, just after the war," said Bryant, tapping the rain-spattered window. "Less passion, less protein, ban licentious theatre, shoot the Welsh; he'd rant about anything so long as it involved getting rid of something. I suppose the preachers of Speaker's Corner still do."

"Now, does anyone know the name of the bi-i-i-g department store on our right?" Martin the tour guide was as wide-eyed as a first-time father, and as patronizing. There were no takers. "Anyone?"

Bryant raised his hand. "Selfridges, opened in 1909 by Harry Gordon Selfridge. He coined the phrase 'The customer is always right', and was the first salesman to put products out on display."

"Well, I don't know about that," said Martin.

"But I do," Bryant countered.

"We're catching a murderer on a bus?" asked May in disbelief.

"We are now heading toward Oxford Circus, which was once described by Noel Coward as the Hub of the Universe," announced the tour guide.

"This boy's a dunderhead." Bryant jerked a wrinkled thumb at Martin, who overheard him. "That was John Wyndham's reference to Piccadilly Circus." Bryant had recently given up working as a London guide in his spare time, after picking too many arguments with the tourists. He forgot most things, but never the facts he had painstakingly gathered about his city.

"I don't understand," May persisted. "Why did we get the case?" Bryant and May's division, the Peculiar Crimes Unit, only handled investigations the Home Office found detrimental to government policy. Arthur loved working with his partner John May, and revelled in the fact that they performed a service no one else in the city could offer. No one had their arcane depth of knowledge, or was able to use it in the cause of crime prevention. Across the decades they had closed the cases few could understand, let alone solve.

"There are three oddities." Bryant ticked his fingers. "One, after strangling Mrs March, the murderer ordered two pizzas, calmly eating both of them. B, he slept overnight in the apartment. And three, his victim killed someone after he left."

May considered the matter as the bus turned into Regent Street. "I'm sorry, Arthur, you've utterly lost me."

"Do try to pay attention. The murderer left the flat at 6:15 this morning, not realizing that his victim was still alive. Mrs March struggled to the window to raise the alarm, but the effort of opening it was too much for her. She lost consciousness and fell out into the street, landing on a gentleman called Sir Ian Lowry—"

"The MOD bigwig?"

"The very same, who was apparently just leaving a call-girl's flat, where he had presumably stayed the night. Mrs March broke her neck and his leg. And that's why the HO called us in. Obviously, it's a serious security breach, because Sir Ian is privy to all kinds of military secrets. The call-girl has already been brought in, and all that's left is the apprehension of her killer."

"So I'm here to help you identify him," said May, still a little confused.

"Oh, I know who the murderer is." Bryant cheerily flashed his oversized false teeth. "You were complaining about getting old the other day, so I thought this would be a chance for you to test your fading faculties."

The Routemaster stopped outside Hamley's toy store to allow a single Japanese tourist on board. There were eight passengers seated downstairs. The heavily falling rain prevented anyone from sitting on the open deck. It was now 10:44am.

"You already know the murderer's identity?"

"Better than that", said Bryant smugly. "I can tell you the precise time he'll be arrested." He checked his ancient Timex. "At 11:26 a.m."

"Are you saying we're looking for somebody on board this bus?"

"That's the general idea, yes."

The tour guide was attempting to deliver a potted history of the Haymarket, and was not happy about being distracted. "There are seats further back," he said pointedly.

"I'm quite happy here," Bryant insisted, withdrawing his pipe from his top pocket and absently striking a match to it. A middle-aged woman in a red baseball cap, a glittery tank-top and shorts reacted with horror behind him. "That's disgusting," she complained. "It's illegal to smoke in public in my country."

"But not to dress like an enormous toddler, Madam, which I find curious," Bryant turned back to his partner. "So take a look around you, and tell me who you suspect. Give me the benefit of your observational skills."

The ancient bus was now chuntering toward the rainswept plain of Trafalgar Square.

"On your left, Nelson's Column, finished in 1843, with four bronze panels at the base depicting his naval victories," said the guide.

"His left arm was struck by lightning in the 1880s, and he's only just getting it X-rayed this year," said Bryant. "That's the National Health Service for you."

"So you know exactly where the murderer will get on this bus, how long he'll stay on and where he'll get off?" asked May.

"Indeed I do." Bryant could be supremely annoying when he was holding privileged information.

At 11:02 a.m., the bus stopped near the corner of Craig's Court. "Pall Mall derives its name from a 17th-century mallet and ball game played here by, er, members of royalty," Martin the guide stated with a hint of uncertainty.

"Everyone knows that," said Bryant, fidgetting in his seat. "Tell them something new. Alleys of shops are called malls because they're shaped like the game's playing sites. Did you know that Pall Mall is only worth £140 on the Monopoly board?"

"I don't think he cares for your interruptions," whispered May. "You're unsettling him."

"Some people deserve to be unsettled," Bryant replied. "When a man is tired of London he should clear off. Oh dear, he's wearing a clip-on tie." Coming from a man as sartorially challenged as Bryant, this was a bit rich.

When the bus stopped halfway along Whitehall, May surveyed the new arrivals. One of them was a murderer, but which? There were now eleven passengers on the lower deck; four Americans, two Chinese, one Japanese and two couples of indeterminate origin. No singles. He decided that the murderer had yet to put in an appearance.

"Was this woman, Mrs March, in her own flat?" he asked.

"Correct."

May thought of the call-girl living on the ground floor. "Did she look after the other girls? Was her murderer a client?"

"No, she had nothing to do with them." Bryant sat back, pretending to listen to the tour guide's inaccurate description of the Cabinet War Rooms.

"But her killer left behind a clue to his identity."

"It was something he took with him that gave me the clue."

The bus continued along Whitehall, picking up three more passengers, and headed up toward Parliament Square. May eyed the newcomers with suspicion. A German couple – he overheard their conversation – and a fiftyish man with unmistakably Russian features and anxious, flitting eyes. May studied his shabby jacket, twisted T-shirt and unshaven chin. *A sad little murder*, Bryant had said. This man had dressed in a hurry, without stopping to shave, and looked around every time the bus came to a halt. But if he was a killer, why would he make his escape aboard a tour bus, on a trip that ended back where it began?

"Who can tell me the name of this building?" asked Martin the guide.

"Houses of Parliament," the assembly muttered faintly, as if being asked to recite a prayer in church.

"Now, many people think Big Ben is the name of the tower . . ."

"Dear God no," Bryant sighed loudly. "Can't he come up with anything more original than that?"

Martin shot him a filthy look. "But it is actually the name of the single bell housed inside . . ."

"Absolute rubbish." Bryant thumped the guide on the arm with his stick. "There are five bells in St Stephen's Tower, young man. The other four play the *Westminster Quarters*, variations of 'I know that my redeemer liveth' from Handel's *Messiah*."

"Look, who's giving this bloody tour?" The guide's cheeks were turning as red as his hair.

"It could be him," said May, pointing to the Russian. "The killer has to be alone, and he's the only one."

"I'll take over if you like," Bryant snapped back at the guide. "I'd do a better job."

"But Arthur, how could you know when he was due on the bus? That just leaves . . ."

"Listen, mate, I don't have to put up with this. My shift ends here, anyway." As the bus stopped on the corner of the square, Martin threw down his microphone and tapped on the glass, signalling to the driver.

As he made his way along the aisle, May said, "The guide, it's the guide, and he's getting away!"

Bryant did not move a muscle as a moon-faced young woman with a colourless ponytail took over from the departing Martin. "Hello, my name is Debbie, and I'll be your guide on the second half of this tour," she told them all. The bus pulled out into traffic and made its way around the square.

"Why didn't you stop him?" asked May with growing incredulity.

Bryant pulled back his sleeve and held up his watch so that his partner could read it. 11:19 a.m. There was still another seven minutes to go.

"Who can tell me the name of this building?" said Debbie, pointing to Westminster Abbey and cupping her hand around her ear.

"Is there some special nursery school where they're trained to speak in this fashion, I wonder?" said Bryant. The bus headed back onto Victoria Embankment.

"Where does the tour go from here?" asked May.

"Around Covent Garden, where Debbie will probably regale us with a re-enactment of *My Fair Lady*, then back toward Oxford Street," said Bryant.

"You said it was something he took with him that gave you a clue," May repeated.

Bryant rested his chin on his knuckle and regarded the distant stippled thread of the Thames. "She'll ask them to name the river next," he muttered.

"He was so unfazed by the thought of murdering Mrs March that he stayed all night . . ."

"I wonder if anyone knows where the lion on Westminster Bridge comes from," asked Debbie.

"Because he was used to her . . ." said May, following the thought.

"Good Lord, an intelligent question," Bryant beamed delightedly at the new guide.

"It stood on the parapet of the Lion Brewery until 1966, near Hungerford Bridge . . ." said Debbie.

"Because he was *married* to her . . ." said May.

"Yet we have come to regard it as a symbol of London . . ."

"And he stuck to his routine, getting up the next morning . . ."

"So when we photograph the lion beside Big Ben, we recreate the traditional link between members of Parliament – and alcohol." Debbie flourished a smile.

"Oh, bravo!" said Bryant. "I like her!"

"And he came to work just as he always did, driving a bus," said May as then truth dawned. "His jacket, cap and badge were missing from the flat."

Bryant rose unsteadily to his feet and pressed the stop bell. "I'm sorry, Debbie," he apologized, "but I'm afraid the tour terminates here."

May looked out of the window. The bus-stop faced New Scotland Yard. It was exactly 11:26 a.m.

"He won't run off," said Bryant. "He wants to be taken in for the murder of his wife. I imagine she never stopped nagging him about his weight."

The Japanese tourist took a very nice photograph of the detectives arresting their man.